Stefan's Promise

A NOVEL BY

SAM RENNICK

HUGO HOUSE PUBLISHERS, LTD.

Stefan's Promise

ISBN: 978-1-948261-20-3

Library of Congress Control Number: 2019911024

Cover Design & Interior Layout: Ronda Taylor, www.heartworkpublishing.com

Hugo House Publishers, Ltd.
Austin, TX • Englewood, CO
www.HugoHousePublishers.com

For my mother

CONTENTS

Main Characters

Book One

Alan Young, *college student*
Stefan Kopinski, *college student*
Kenneth "Bear" Hatcher, *college student*
Hon. Robert C. Young, *U.S. District Judge, Alan's father*
Dorothy Young, *Alan's mother*
Charles McCarran, *architect in Montreal, Jeanne's father*
Jeanne McCarran, *college student*
Margaret Page, *schoolteacher, Alan's friend*
John Walters, *expatriate, Alan's friend*
Hon. Daniel L. Bryant, *U.S. District Judge*

Book Two

Stefan Kopinski, *attorney-at-law in Pasadena, California*
Debra Kopinski, *Stefan's first wife and mother of Linda and Lisa*
Linda Kopinski, *elder daughter*
Sharon Kopinski, *Stefan's second wife*
Mike Huxtable, *insurance salesman in Pasadena, California*
Charlotte Huxtable, *Mike's wife and mother of Andrew and Todd*
Andrew Huxtable, *elder son*
Alan Young, *former federal prisoner now living in St. Louis*
Jeanne McCarran Young, *Alan's wife*
Abraham Holdermann, M.D., *Alan's physician*

Author's Preface

YOU ARE EMBARKING, MY DEAR READER, UPON A NOVEL INTO WHICH I have poured a lifetime. I've used everything, as authors do. I could not possibly identify the experiences I've had, what I've done, witnessed, embraced, wondered at, laughed over, endured, my triumphs, my mistakes, which have affected me and made me the writer I am. That said *Stefan's Promise* is a novel, not a memoir. It is not about me. It is fiction.

You will be introduced first to Alan, one of my heroes. The other, Stefan, comes along shortly. While there are many important characters, these two are always front and center. I could say more here, very much more, about them and my entire cast, but then why did I write the story?

The novel spans roughly thirty-five years, beginning in the tumultuous year of 1968. It is comprised of two books, the first focusing primarily on Alan, the second, on Stefan. While some years elapse between the close of the first book and the start of the second, what has transpired in those years becomes readily apparent. A step back across the years also figures in the narrative, but here, too, the groundwork is laid. The books read a little differently. This, you will find, is a good thing, and I wish I could say I planned it this way all along. The actual explanation is, a fair number of years separate the two writings. The latter was harder, because before I wrote the first, I didn't know I couldn't do it. That may sound like a witticism, but every experienced writer will know exactly what I mean.

As for my prose, be confident of purpose and clarity. I have little patience with writers who don't know an adjective from a noun, who never use ten words where one hundred will do, and who leave the reader in a constant state of befuddlement, like Faulkner, who, in his defense, cannot tell you where you are in his narrative, since he has no idea himself.

My objective at all times is to absorb you so completely in the tale, you can't put it down. What's more fun than that? Everyday life comes to a halt until one has finished the book he's reading. This has a way of irritating those around you, which can also be satisfying.

These days, there seems to be a tendency to stick books into pigeon-holes like "women's fiction," for instance, and "upmarket adult fiction," whatever that is, and "middle grade fiction." I suppose this is a marketing strategy, although I'm really not sure. In any event, I was taught novels are transcendent. They are not confined to a particular readership but are for everybody. That's the novel I wrote.

I mentioned experienced writers. May I insert a word here for the inexperienced writer? Acquire a vocation before you start filling pages with words. Writing is as demanding as any work, with the crucial difference a finished manuscript, unlike learning to build houses or fly airplanes or pull teeth, earns you no diploma, no license, no income, no recognition, no prospects. Rise to scribble at 4:30 only if you have a place to be at 8:30.

Before I conclude, I'd like to thank Patricia Ross, my publisher. Patricia thinks independently. She was solidly behind my novel before reading a word. Mary Walewski brings her expertise to sales and promotion. Veronica Yager produced my wonderful website. Ronda Taylor designed the superb book cover. My proofreader, "D.W.G.," told me she loved my story. Silvia Lorente-Murphy, a friend, expressed heartfelt praise of her own. Sal Cipolla had a key insight regarding the narrative. My thanks to you all.

I believe in books. You'd probably guessed that. The best among them are good stories, but not, of course, only good stories. There is a loftiness to great fiction. I do not mean by this it is unattainable. Certainly not. I mean the best books uplift us. Isabel's mistake wrecks her life, but Henry James' heroine in *The Portrait of a Lady* remains gallant and indomitable. So, too, with us. There is no escaping trouble, but we can choose how we deal with it. We can choose as Isabel chooses.

All the best.

S.R.

"… *all the words that describe them are false, and all attempts to organize them fail … they slip through the net and are gone.*"

— **E.M. Forster**

Book One

CHAPTER 1

Twenty-one twenty-thirds. Now what kind of fraction was that? Fold the box's sides. Which gear goes fastest?

In two efforts he had two bylines in the university's literary quarterly, but he was baffled by a mesh. "This mess is a mesh" he doodled on the exam sheet. He reflected he had not wanted to take the test anyway; the whole thing was Stef's fat idea. Still, there was no denying the Naval Reserve would be preferable to the Army, come summer. But that was a long way off, yet. The war could end. Alan wished the professor in the adjacent classroom would quit shouting. Impossible to concentrate. He couldn't get the boxes folded, and he couldn't see that it mattered. How to take things seriously?

"Five minutes left, Young," a friendly face in the door informed. Alan acknowledged. He thought it a nice gesture by the impeccably groomed officer of rank unknown. That he had not addressed him as "Mr. Young" amused Alan. "I'm not in the Navy, yet," he doodled. The face reappeared. "The first name is Alan? Alan Robert Young, is that correct?"

"Right."

The physical examination came next. Alan was led down a hall of the ancient ROTC building into a room that smelled of rubbing alcohol. The doctor, a fair-haired young man named Eberhart, greeted him, then got down to business, making small talk throughout a very complete physical. At its conclusion, he announced, almost apologetically, that Alan had not passed. Alan was stupefied to learn his old inner ear problem had disqualified him for the Naval Reserve. He had contracted an acute infection when he was eight and which, it was true, had stubbornly resisted treatment, but the only lasting effect was occasional, though sometimes severe, vertigo. Epilepsy had at one time been suspected, but conclusively ruled out. Alan

1

thought to ask the doctor whether the Army, allegedly less selective than the other services, would have him. Eberhart said he believed not.

What a fantastic surprise! Alan was euphoric. Never had the thought entered his mind he might fail the physical. Now, just like that, a burden was lifted. He made a beeline for the Student Union cafeteria, humming cheerfully all the way. His friend Stefan was already there, seated at their usual table, by the plants and the windows. Alan opted for a hamburger and iced tea, then joined him.

"Hi, Stef," he said, beaming from tip to top.

"How was it, sir?" Stefan quipped, realizing there was cause for joy.

"Oh, rugged. Really, really rugged."

"Rest and recreation, that's all you need, sir," Stefan said.

"And alliteration," Alan said, seeing he was going to be "sir" for the next few hours. "I just couldn't get the hang of it. Best of seven, it was. He took me four in a row."

"Yes, sir, I understand. What are you talking about?"

"Why the test, of course. We played battleships. Best of seven. He swept me. I never did get his submarine." Alan sighed deeply. "Blast that little sub!" he exclaimed, bringing his fist down on the table. "I just couldn't get it, you know?"

"You maniac," Stefan said, laughing. "How was the test, really? What gives?"

"I flunked it," Alan said gleefully. "I flat flunked it."

"You what? You flunked it? How?"

"My vertigo, of all things. Can you believe that? Unbelievable! But get this, the medic said the Army won't have me, either. So you can quit worrying, Stef."

"What vertigo?" Stefan blurted incredulously.

"What vertigo? You mean I've never mentioned it?"

"Never. Not once."

"I can't believe it." Alan was amazed. "I had a bad ear infection, when I was in grade school. All I remember is my folks taking me to a bunch of doctors before they finally figured out what it was. I got over it, but sometimes I'm dizzy. It's unpredictable." Alan sighed again in relief, but Stefan was absolutely astonished by the news, and aware, too, it disturbed him his best friend had never mentioned so serious an ailment. His friend, while not an athlete, certainly wasn't an invalid, either.

2

"Sometimes dizzy? When are you dizzy, Alan? You've never been dizzy. You've never said anything about being dizzy."

"Well, I think I probably have, and you just don't remember, Stef," Alan said. "Who cares, let's celebrate! I've got to be measured for my cap and gown at 4:30. After that, I'll pick up some beer. You game?"

"Sure," said Stefan, so amazed and perplexed by the news he had no idea what he had agreed to. Their conversation turned to other matters, but Stefan's mind was never far from the fantastic news the whole afternoon.

"Awake! For morning in the bowl of night has flung the stone that puts the stars to flight," Alan shouted from a pillow perspective, his head aching from too much beer. "Oh, my head." He pounded the side of his skull. "I should have turned down several glasses, Omar, old chap." He got up, shed his pajamas, located a towel and made his way to the showers, reciting other verses from "The Rubaiyat," at the top of his lungs, as he sauntered down the hall. It was deathly still in the dormitory, the usual for Sunday morning.

"Shut the f___ up, Young," a voice shouted as Alan went past one door.

"That you, Wexler?" Alan retorted, resuming the poem as before. There was no love lost between Roger Wexler and Alan. On reaching the showers, he announced, still as loudly as possible, "It's the showers for Omar."

"Hi there, Alan," Mark said, appearing with towel and large, plastic tumbler of ice-cold water, soon after Alan began showering.

"Well, if it isn't Beastly with his glass."

"Yeah, it's me. Hello, good morning and all that."

"Thirsty, Beastly?"

"Beasely, not Beastly. Yes, as a matter of fact, I am thirsty."

"Thirsting, you mean. To drench me."

"Now, that's not nice, to suggest that of a friend. Just for that ..." The water flew, striking its target, despite its swerve, squarely in the chest.

"A thousand curses upon you, you scoundrel," Alan shouted. "Ten thousand. May the God of Finding Lost Golf Balls ignore you today. May the rain fall upon your tiny, demented brain alone." Mark was beside himself with laughter.

"At it again, eh, Mark?" said a new entry, a half-asleep Stefan, stumbling beneath a second nozzle.

"Hi, Stef," Alan said.

"The trouble with you, Stefan, is that you don't have a sense of humor," said Mark. "Now take your best friend there."

3

"Oh, I have a sense of humor all right. It just doesn't happen to coincide with yours. Mine is normal."

"Now, that's not nice. I'll just have to get a refill."

"Oh, no you don't, Beastly. Not on me."

"I'll spare you this time," Mark said, remembering the one time he had tried it on Stefan, and the upshot. "I'll go wake up Bob."

"The most avid golfer, and he's always the last one up," said Alan.

"Have you seen what it looks like outside?"

"Yes."

"Well, it's obvious it's going to pour, so I'm not going," Stefan said. "One time is enough."

"You're going to make yourself unpopular, you know."

"Too bad. I'm staying."

"Oh, come on, Stef."

"No. Absolutely not. It's idiotic getting caught out there, hundreds of yards from shelter. Don't you remember the last time?"

"Of course, I do. It really wasn't all that bad."

"Do I hear voices?" someone else asked. "Good morning, fellow pros," Bob said cheerfully, taking the last shower.

"Right, Bob," said Stefan. "Right."

"What's with him?" Bob asked Alan.

"Those dark things floating across the sky, Bob. Haven't you seen them?"

"I saw them. It might not rain."

"And when the sun is shining, it might, is that it?" There was sarcasm in Stefan's voice.

"Look, it has only rained on us once."

"On a day that looked just like this one," Stefan interrupted.

"Well, does that mean you're not going?" Bob asked.

"Correct." Everyone was momentarily silent. "Look, Bob," Stefan continued, "don't you agree it's silly to walk five hundred yards, toting a golf bag, in a downpour? Surely you didn't enjoy it that time?"

"I did," said Mark. "Come on, Alan, you've been in long enough. My turn."

"I know you did," said Stefan, "but you're subnormal." Mark shrieked and leapt from beneath the streaming water, frantically turning the faucets.

"My God you like it hot, Alan."

"What did you expect, after that cold water?" Alan relished his revenge.

4

"I am not trying to start a controversy," Stefan said. "It's only that I don't see the sense in going out to play golf when it is sure to rain."

"No controversy, Stef," said Alan. "Had you said you weren't going to play, then, yes, I'd say we would have a controversy on our hands." Mark marveled at Alan's ability to say that with a straight face. Stefan merely smiled. Mark fell on his knees and began blessing the sun, and Stefan, thinking there were limits to inanity, started up again.

"I'm serious," he said, his tone a little harsh. "To look upon our Sunday game as such a sacrosanct thing is too ridiculous even to discuss. It's going to rain, and I'm staying in." Immediately he regretted having sounded so severe; why was that necessary with such close friends? Well, the truth was, Stefan was not half as close to Bob Shackleford or Mark Beasely as Alan was; it was Alan who was Stefan's friend. These two, in fact, were best friends, and had been for two and a half years. The strength of their bond was such, they were invariably linked, and jealousy was never completely absent among the satellites.

Stefan Kopinski was of Polish stock, stood at five six and weighed hardly 125 pounds. He had a sharp nose, small mouth with even teeth, was clean-shaven, and had large brown eyes draped with brown locks, an appearance Alan labeled as "urchin." He looked younger than he was, but those who knew Stefan felt his manner was that of one older than twenty. That was his nature; Stefan Kopinski was a sensible, prudent, solidly practical soul, always circumspect, never reckless. He wasn't dull, not by any means, but he thought before he spoke, and made his words count when he did. Stefan was an exceptional student, planning a career in law. He was, in addition, one of the world's worst athletes, worse, even, than Alan; Stefan never failed to finish last at golf and all other sports. This made not the least difference to him, as he refused to take sports seriously. People he did take seriously, and for those for whom he cared, he would do almost anything. Alan was among these.

"Look, Stefan, what makes you think we care what you do?" Mark said.

"Well, if that's the case, what's all the fuss?"

"I care, Stefan, even if Beastly doesn't," Bob said, maybe a little hurt. "You're coming, aren't you, Alan?"

"Sure, Robert. It may not rain." But Alan was going because, though it almost certainly would rain, that was what mattered less. He knew he was the center of the group. He knew neither Bob nor Mark would have fun, unless he went along. His friends, in truth, were all that kept college from being unbearable, nowadays. It wasn't that school was difficult, only that it had become insufferably boring. Alan was tired of the university where he had spent nearly four years of his life, sitting in the same classrooms, eating the same meals in the same cafeteria. He was weary of hearing various counselors and advisers and deans suggesting what he might do with himself, and he resented what frequently seemed implicit in their remarks, that they knew best, and he should take heed. In particular, he was angry with Irvin Whittier, Dean of Students, who only last week had quietly observed the incontestable, that Alan was unmotivated, apathetic, headed nowhere. The dean had inquired as to Alan's plans after graduation, correctly noting that only months previous, he had announced enthusiastically, in the dean's office, his intention to become a Shakespearean scholar, and teach. Somewhere since then, the glamour of Hamlet and Lear had faded, faded to the point Alan had forgotten his intention altogether. The Bard was but another infatuation, another in the long line of altered majors to accommodate a new, inevitably passing, interest. This endless drifting was all Alan had to show for college. He needed rejuvenation, a spark, a catalyst, a direction.

Golf was played, except by Stefan. Six holes of golf. Then it rained.

Not without some trepidation, Alan decided later in the week to call Jane Harsfield. A contractor's daughter, Jane was a tall, voluptuous redhead, with full breasts and freckles in her cleavage and red lips and sexy-white, fleshy thighs. Her eyes, in Alan's words, were "positively green." Her red hair Jane wore long. Its maintenance consumed many hours, but she kept it superbly, knowing its value. Well-versed in the feminine graces, and confident of her good looks, Jane could have the man she wanted. She had been close, not intimate, with Alan over the winter, but of late he had perceived an increasing coldness in her, manifested recently and unmistakably the evening they saw "La Dolce Vita" in the Union theatre. He could think of nothing he had said or done to upset her. That she had met his replacement Alan had only vaguely considered. He succeeded, after much cajolery, in persuading her into a cup of coffee; she, consenting, without a trace of interest in her voice.

"When did I last see you?" he asked over a cup of the Union's dishwater coffee, knowing full well when it had been. "The night we went to 'La Dolce Vita,' wasn't it?"

"Yes, I think so," she replied. "I lose track of time so easily, you know. Don't you?"

"No. I don't have to worry about that. I haven't a time schedule to lose track of."

"So, you don't," she said, and they fell silent.

"Well, how have you been?" he asked. Alan was experiencing the odd feeling they were not close, never had been. A distance never there before, inexplicably, was now.

"Fine, Alan," she said, smiling. Silence again.

"You were concerned about Hutchinson's exam," he thought to say. "How did it go?"

"I'd say I probably made a 'C.' It's my own fault for taking biology."

"Isn't Hutchinson about eighty?"

"Oh, at least."

"The poor old sedimentary goat. He ought to retire before he fossilizes."

"Oh, I think he'd make a fascinating specimen in that drab lab," Jane said. Alan laughed.

"Just what this school needs, something new. Latest from that great innovator, that Nobel Prize-studded leviathan, the University of California, a formaldehyde professor." Jane smiled but said nothing. "I'm tired of school," Alan said, for lack of anything else.

"That isn't exactly new," Jane said, sounding a trifle tired herself. "You're nearly through, though."

"Nearly through? With five years of grad school, or four, at least, ahead?" Alan sighed, but then abruptly brightened. "Which reminds me, my worries about the draft are over. I got the word from the Naval Reserve the other day. I'm physically unqualified, because of my vertigo. So, there's one problem solved."

"I'm very glad of that, Alan," she said, pooh-poohing it. She couldn't recall his having ever mentioned suffering from vertigo but said nothing. The manner of her response shocked him, and, as he could think of no further comment on the matter, he resorted to his coffee.

"God, that's abominable coffee!" he exclaimed, grimacing. "Ugh!" Jane remained silent, and, although she was there, arm's length from him, it no longer seemed to him she was present. "You know, I don't believe you said ten words the rest of the evening, after we saw 'La Dolce Vita'," he decided to say, shattering a silence that both discomforted and annoyed him. "Is something bothering you?"

"No, Alan, nothing is bothering me," she said, a bit sharply. He noticed and resented this.

"Look, what's going on, then?" he said. "Are you mad at me for something?"

"No, I'm not mad at you," she said calmly. "It does sound as though you're mad at me, though."

"What are you saying? I'm not mad at you. I'm just trying to figure out what's happened to our relationship." She did not respond. "Maybe it's all my imagination," he said, aware he meant not a word.

"Let's change the subject, Alan," she said. "I don't enjoy unpleasantness."

"Well, neither do I," he said hotly. "I'm not being unpleasant; I'm only trying to find out what has gone wrong."

"Please, Alan, let's discuss something else." Her tone made clear she would not remain, unless he complied. It was a bitter moment for him, the full acknowledgement she was no longer interested, but the need to know would not stop nagging. It wasn't right, wasn't fair, he thought, that she should act this way, considering how close they had been.

"Have you applied to those graduate schools yet, Alan?" she asked.

"Yes," he lied, thinking this an impossible time for small talk.

"Good! Which ones, besides Brown?"

"Wisconsin, Michigan, Berkeley and San Francisco," he said, sounding like a recording.

"I don't think I have heard of San Francisco," she said.

"It's a big city north of here," he shot back. "Or a saint from Assisi, if you prefer." The sarcasm failed.

"I thought you wanted to go to the East Coast," she said, passing over his remark.

"I never wanted to go anything," he exploded. "Anyway, what possible difference does it make to you?"

"I'd like to go back to my room now, Alan, if you don't mind," she said, keeping her composure. "Thanks for the coffee. Bye, bye." Just that quickly it was ended conclusively. Jane hastened to her residence hall, a little jittery, yet immensely relieved; Alan, considerably worse for wear, made his way to Creighton Dorm.

Arvino's was usually crowded, and tonight was no exception. There was not a vacant table at the popular pizzeria, much favored by students. Stefan and Alan decided to share a table, rather than wait for one of their own. They were escorted to a table where, over two enormous sausage pizzas, five long-haired students, four males, were locked in an intense political discussion. Conspicuous by his hair's average length—Stefan's was long enough to get him by—Alan immediately dreaded a scene.

"I'm Felicia, who are you?" the girl said to Stefan.

"Stefan, here. Glad to meet you." I think maybe not so glad, Stefan said to himself, for she was not attractive, and she had bad breath.

"What's the sergeant's name?"

"Who?"

"Your friend, there."

"You'll have to ask him that yourself," Stefan said reproachfully. Turning from her, he made an effort to get into the discussion, which concerned Eugene McCarthy and the recent announcement by Robert Kennedy that he, too, would enter the presidential campaign. Stefan was very interested in the race, and of late had even noticed a stirring or two in his conspicuous friend.

"Personally, I'm glad Kennedy's in the race," Stefan injected loudly.

"Who asked you?"

"Cool it, mole."

"You, too!" said another, a big fellow who needed no more pizza. He was dismayed by Stefan's position, but not too dismayed to decline additional argument.

"Kennedy," Stefan proceeded, matter-of-factly, "will be a stronger candidate than McCarthy, because he has a much broader constituency."

"No, he hasn't," Felicia said. "That's not so. Everybody's saying that, but it's not so."

"It is so. The Kennedy name is magic in this country. McCarthy is just another senator no one ever heard of before, except in Minnesota, and hardly even there, as far as I'm concerned. That's where I'm from."

"They've heard of him now," the big guy, Kenneth "Bear" Hatcher, addressed Stefan.

"So, what difference does it make if he was less known before?" said Felicia.

"Quite right," said Bear.

"It makes a difference," said the one at the far end of the table, Whitney by name. "Everything is relative, folks. McCarthy is better known now than, say, the junior senator from Montana, whoever he is, but he's still no Bobby Kennedy." Said with authority.

"That's it," said Stefan. "McCarthy can't hope to be, either. It's no contest, Kennedy is by far the stronger candidate."

"I just don't see how you can say that," said Bear. "Once you're known, you're known."

"You see, there is a Kennedy cult," said Stefan. "That's what I'm trying to say. Very few politicians have one, including McCarthy, but Kennedy has."

"What if he has?" Bear inquired. "How does that make him better?"

"Better, because he is the best bet to win. It isn't just the people, is it?"

"What do you mean?"

"It's the Democratic Party, too. Wouldn't you agree Kennedy will have much stronger backing from the party than McCarthy?"

"I agree, and that's what bothers me. Gene is the choice of the people, but the party is sure to go for Kennedy. So, you're right, Gene will probably lose at Chicago. Isn't that backwards? Isn't this the 'of, by and for' place?"

"Only on paper," Stefan said.

"I'm not so sure he'll lose at the convention," Bear went on. "Look"—and here he almost got the name— "look, Steven, I think you're underestimating McCarthy's constituency. He did great up in New Hampshire, much better than predicted. He's going to sweep Wisconsin, too. I'd put a small wager on it."

"He can't beat Kennedy, I guarantee you," Stefan said, wondering why the one called "Bear" would put only a small wager on it, if he was so sure. "What McCarthy should do is bow out and support Kennedy, who can win. Isn't that what we all want?"

"How can you say that, Stef?" Alan said emotionally. "McCarthy was first. You've got it all backwards. The indecency of this whole business is Kennedy's candidacy. He should support McCarthy." Alan's voice was filled with indignation, but Stefan, though caught off guard by Alan's outburst, understood it was directed at Robert Kennedy, not him.

"That's exactly how I feel," Bear said, thinking about how well that stranger had articulated his own view.

"Oh, that's fine," said Stefan, not giving up, "but it's the antithesis of pragmatism. Decency is not what makes this world go around."

"Gene just isn't that weak, Steven," Bear said anew. "I honestly believe you are underestimating him."

"I don't think so." Stefan would have said more, but their waiter appeared.

"You want a big pizza, or two little ones, Stef?" Alan said.

"Doesn't matter to me."

"Okay, one large pepperoni, please." The waiter left; Stefan turned back to the argument. "Go easy, Stef," Alan said, voice low. "It's obvious that poor guy feels strongly about this, but he can't debate worth a hoot. No use deflating him."

"He feels strongly!" Stefan said. "You're the one who brought the walls down a minute ago, and on me, too."

"Yeah, sorry about that," Alan said, laughing.

"I didn't know you cared," Stefan said.

"You knew I think Kennedy should support McCarthy."

"I did?"

"Amen," Bear said, having overheard.

"Who prayed?" Stefan said. The discussion resumed, as before. Much was repeated, and nothing was decided. However, by the time the pizza had run out, handshakes were sealing a new bond between Bear Hatcher and Alan, and Stefan, too.

Alan took Betty Kincaid to the intramural softball game Friday afternoon. Bob Shackleford, who played third base for Creighton Dorm, had said to come by and witness the league's worst representative in action. Evidently, it was no exaggeration. By the time they arrived, Creighton was already down by eight runs, with five innings to play. Alan and Betty stayed through the seventh, long enough to see the score sink to twelve to one; a crucial error by Bob accounted for two of those runs, but it hardly distinguished him from his teammates. Alan, after getting consent from Betty, asked Bob if he'd like to get a date and join them that evening. He declined.

The pair had hamburgers and went to a drive-in movie. He selected a triple bill of horror shows, and halfway through the credits of "Vampire Road" was unfastening the black brassiere which was in no way concealed by Betty's white blouse.

"That's why the dorm team kept messing up today," Alan said. "One black bra cost us the championship. What have you got to say for yourself, girl?"

"It wasn't the championship, because there was no crowd. That's what. Since you dislike my bra so much, I'll just keep it on."

"It was the championship. Nobody ever goes to dorm games. The only reason I went was that it was the big one, and Bob asked me to come."

"It wasn't the championship game, Alan," she insisted, playfully pushing him away. "You can't fool me all the time. That was just any old afternoon baseball game, and Creighton lost because Creighton has a lousy team. Your friend even missed one."

"Yes, because he was distracted by your black bra." Alan and Betty dropped the conversation. She would allow him almost all he wanted, but not quite all. Betty had to have a commitment from Alan for that, and if there was one thing Alan was not going to do, it was make a commitment. The night was warm, and as they clung together, the sweat flowed freely. In its mutuality it felt good.

"You're delicious, Miss Kincaid," he whispered.

"Why, thank you, Mr. Young," she said elegantly.

"Speaking of delicious, shall I get us Cokes and some popcorn?"

"Sure."

"Good drink, good meat, good God, let's eat," Alan said.

Bear was in a state of ecstasy over McCarthy's victory in Wisconsin, and Alan, himself pleased, found Bear's great happiness infectious. The foursome, engaged in a hand of bridge, were in Mark's room, where the television was, when the first bulletin interrupted the movie being televised. It was short: Martin Luther King, Jr., had been shot a few minutes ago in Memphis, Tennessee, where he was lending his support to a strike by the city's trash collectors; he had been rushed to the hospital, his condition was believed to be serious, the assailant was unknown, more news would be forthcoming as soon as more was known.

"Oh, no no no!" cried Bear, stunned, leaping to his feet. "I can't believe it! Not Martin Luther King. Anybody but him." Bear shook his head in anguished disbelief. "The most peace-loving guy in America, and they go after him."

"I knew it would happen someday," said Alan, who had seldom given much thought, one way or the other, to the civil rights leader, but figured any black man that outspoken would be shot sooner or later.

"Damn right," Mark said. "He's been courting it for a long time. Whites and blacks are never going to get along, so people like King are dreamers and nuisances and troublemakers." An intense idealist, for whom Martin Luther King was one among several heroes, Bear Hatcher was instantly furious.

"That's the stupidest thing I've ever heard!" he shouted. "One of the truly great men of our time, and you call him a troublemaker." Words failed; Bear was incensed.

"You think racial harmony is ever going to exist in this country? Forget about it. I happen to be from Dallas, and I know," Mark said. "So King is a troublemaker, it's as simple as that. Now don't get mad."

"Are you kidding? I'm already mad. King's given so much, maybe his life, now, for what he believed, and you're an idiot for what you said."

"Take that back or you've got a fight on your hands," Mark shouted, seemingly oblivious to Bear's superior size.

"Be quiet, you guys, would you?" Alan said firmly. "You sound like a couple of kids fighting in the sandbox. Mark may be dead wrong, Bear, but he has a right to his opinion. So, don't take it personally." Alan meant every word, although in truth it was Mark's comments that upset him. His intrusion succeeded in silencing the adversaries, whereupon Stefan spoke up.

"My turn, gentlemen," he said. "Martin Luther King is disingenuous. Now don't get me wrong, Bear. He's an extraordinary person, and I admire him. But King's just like Jesus. Just like him, he doesn't really believe what he says. Jesus stood for non-violence, too, but he knew he was a revolutionary, and that to achieve his ends would require violence. Same way exactly with King. Do you think whites are ever going to sit back and give in, without a fight? Of course not. King knows that." Bear, at best, was half-listening, and when Stefan was finished, he was ready.

"Incidentally, Mark, I was born in Pensacola, Florida and lived there quite a few years, and there's racial harmony in Pensacola, which is a Southern city. All I know about Dallas is that they killed a president there, so you're probably right when you say the place has no hope. That doesn't mean every place is that way. Okay?" Alan frowned at Bear, feeling he was rekindling the fire.

"No, not okay!" Mark shot back. "It's not okay, understand?" That was as far as Mark got.

"Determined to fight, fellows?" Stefan said sharply. "If you are, then I suggest you retire to that sandbox Alan mentioned. I've heard enough!" Both looked at Stefan.

"All right, Mark," Bear said, choosing to end it. "You're entitled to your opinion. I'm entitled to mine." He extended a hand and they shook, uneasily. Someone suggested a six-pack, Alan became the dummy, but Bear was overbid, the TV movie was a vintage Hollywood romance sealed with a kiss, and Martin Luther King, Jr., revered or vilified by his countrymen, perished from his wounds.

The rent-a-dog service was not located along university row by accident, for it was aimed at the dormitory resident who missed his Bernie the basset. The creator and owner was a bald, late middle-aged widower named Kahn, who, in truth, liked neither students nor canines; it was only that his wife had been—as she had often made clear—the backbone of a tidily profitable, now remorselessly defunct, jewelry store. One day Kahn's brainstorm had come, brought on, perhaps, by hunger. Dog-A-Day, Inc., was conceived, and, after a donnybrook with the Humane Society, an armistice was reached which, indeed, involved a working agreement between the two. Neither great dog lover nor authority, Kahn now was obliged to consider overhead; he hired two students and periodically watched them clean the mess, a ritual which invariably served to confirm his decision to hire them. Dog-A-Day, Inc., while not remotely as successful as the jewelry store, nonetheless was a living. The dogs were well cared for, and the customers gradually became steady. What had seemed to many a harebrained scheme turned out otherwise, and Kahn had the last laugh.

Alan picked up Rosie and headed for the park, where the pre-arranged Stefan was waiting. They had wanted a dog that could run, and in Rosie, a Dalmatian, they had all they could handle, and then some. Spotted, naturally, and swift as a cheetah, Rosie each week wore down her liberators, and then, eager for more, was set loose, never without misgiving. Exhausted today sooner than usual, Stefan quit trying to keep up with the dog and, unleashing her, shouted at Alan to toss him the Frisbee. Alan deliberately flung it far out of Stefan's reach, earning himself a string of fading epithets. It turned out to be too windy for the Frisbee, and to try to retrieve Rosie any time soon was even more futile, as much shouting established. While the Dalmatian knew both Alan and Stefan, she would not surrender her leash-less dashes for anyone. The only thing to do was sit and be patient.

"You know, I believe she enjoys ignoring us as much as the running," Alan said. "Such happy disobedience, to be that free. We should leave her. Kahn's cruel, using the dogs the way he does."

14

"Alan, he takes strays the Humane Society is going to destroy. There'd be no Rosie, but for him. That Dalmatian has a good life, I'll bet."

"Rosemarie," commanded a standing Alan, at the top of his lungs, "come here at once, or I will see that your spots are removed this very day!"

"Strange name for a dog," said Stefan. "I wonder who named Rosie."

"Probably some lovelorn fireman," said Alan. "There's a song called 'Rosemarie', come to think of it. Have you ever heard it?" Alan embarked on the one verse he knew, again at the top of his lungs, graciously acknowledging at the end the applause of his imaginary audience, and some disapproving looks from a nearby group.

His friend's spontaneity, a characteristic long since noted, amused Stefan. He had never known anyone like Alan Young, who had become a brother to him, and whom he indeed regarded with as much affection as his own brother. To Stefan, he was the true friend. The two had met the first week of Alan's sophomore year, when Stefan was an entering freshman, and immediately taken to one another. Since, they had lived two doors apart in Creighton Dorm nine months of each year; they were practically fixtures, and, while other friends came and went, Alan and Stefan remained.

Stefan could recall what he had first appreciated in Alan, his policy of minimizing the fact he had more money. Alan had a car; Stefan did not. He had more and finer clothes, superior stereophonic equipment, twice the budget. Alan easily had the means to purchase *a la carte* in the Union cafeteria, but always took the *plat du jour*, when they ate together. It was a small thing, and yet, it wasn't. From the very beginning, Alan had made a point of playing down his greater resources, and Stefan had noticed. There were other things, too. Alan, alone among Stefan's friends, was always prepared to lend an ear, regardless of what other matters were at hand. And his interest, Stefan knew, was never spurious; Alan Young, above all, was genuine. No one was more concerned about Alan's lack of motivation than Stefan. No one worried more about the draft. Alan's vertigo, after almost three years together, was news to him. Stefan wondered about its severity, considering Alan was not an invalid. He realized well enough his friend was no soldier, and he feared that whatever was wrong with Alan would not be more than the Army could accommodate.

Late afternoon the day of the Pennsylvania primary, Alan, Stefan and Bear spent the day at the beach. The latter two were off in search of a concessionaire when Jane Harsfield, in her green bikini, materialized.

15

"Hi, stranger," she said, sitting beside Alan and tucking her long white thighs together in a way she knew would be appreciated. "How are you?"

"Fine," Alan mumbled unenthusiastically. He had no wish to speak with her.

"Well, I saw you sitting alone over here," she said gently, "and I just thought I'd scamper over and say 'hello'."

"I'm with Stef and another guy," Alan said, pointing down the beach.

"How is Stef?"

"Like always. Stubborn and incorruptible as ever."

"I'd say that's more like you," Jane said, smiling. "By the way, I didn't tell you, I got into the Summer Scholars Program at the Sorbonne. I'll be there all summer. In Paris! I can hardly believe it."

"Think you'll pull a Henry?" Alan said. The thought made him smile.

"What's that?"

"A friend of mine last year, Henry Clark. He got into the Sorbonne program and stayed exactly one week. Then, he cut out and vagabonded around Europe for the rest of the summer." Alan laughed.

"What did the administration think of that?" she asked.

"Who knows? I suppose it made them unhappy. I got a card from him, in Switzerland, I think it was. He insisted nothing was premeditated. The lure of exotic places, he said."

"He broke an agreement, though."

"Yes, that's true, but I can understand it. I really don't think he planned it. Not Henry."

"I wouldn't do a thing like that," Jane said. "You wouldn't, either."

"I don't know," said Alan. "I guess I wouldn't. Can't say for sure." An uncomfortable silence ensued.

"Well," she finally said, "I just came over to say 'hi', and to tell you about my trip. I better get back to the others, now." She rose.

"Bon voyage," Alan said, "and remember, no fair leaving Paris."

"No danger of that," she winked. "Bye-bye, Alan."

That evening, the campus' McCarthy headquarters was again feverish. The candidate had done far better than expected in Pennsylvania, though his candidacy there was unopposed. It was a pleasant evening, the palm trees rustled quietly in the face of a cool breeze blowing in off the ocean, and the stars were bright in a cloudless sky. Pensive, Alan went walking. He meandered past the McCarthy office, plastered with stickers, paused to glimpse the goings-on inside and, finding himself envious of them, walked on.

Friday, he had another meeting with Dean Whittier. It proved as unproductive as Alan had anticipated. The dean was incredulous Alan still had not made application to graduate school. Alan said very little, and when he left, renewed his pledge never to become a university administrator. Somehow, the job brought on premature senility, he thought.

Tuesday was the Indiana primary. This was to be the first head-on confrontation between McCarthy and Kennedy, and for the first time, the new Kennedy organization on campus was as active as that of the other candidate. Kennedy was expected to win, and while Stefan and Alan were out with their occasional Dalmatian, he did just that: Robert Kennedy won going away, Eugene McCarthy finishing a poor third in a three-man race. The McCarthy office resembled a morgue that night, in marked contrast to Kennedy's. Stefan was elated, but he kept his feelings to himself, for Alan, it was apparent, was both angry and miserable. Angry at Robert Kennedy, and miserable over what he viewed as rank injustice. Thinking to offer Bear solace, Alan had his excuse to drop in at the McCarthy office, but, halfway there, he encountered his distraught friend. Alan did what he could, but it didn't help much, for he was too upset himself.

One week later, in the Nebraska primary, Kennedy defeated McCarthy again. Alan's anger was redoubled, and Bear's anguish knew no bounds. Near midnight, Bear stopped by Alan's room in Creighton Dorm. Finding nobody home, he slipped a note under the door, asking Alan to meet him for lunch the next day.

"I know what's on your mind, Bear," Alan said over a grilled cheese sandwich. "The poet for president, right? You're going to try to talk me into working for Gene, right?"

"That's what I call an educated guess," Bear said.

"I'm for him, Bear, you know I am, but he's finished. Kennedy's pulled the rug out from under him, and that's that. So, what's the use?"

"He hasn't pulled the rug out from under him," Bear said. "Pessimism like that doesn't help, of course, but he hasn't pulled the rug out from under him."

"The hell. First Indiana, now Nebraska. McCarthy hasn't even come close. It's all over for him." Bear only sighed at this, for he had come to know Alan well in the seven weeks since they met and believed Alan had made up his mind to work for McCarthy. He felt Alan was putting on an act at the moment, for some mysterious reason. "Look, Bear," Alan went on, "as far as I'm concerned, Bobby's a prima donna son-of-a-_____, but life is a dirty game. Gene's finished, Bear. He'll never make it against Kennedy. You might as well admit it."

"You may be right, Alan," Bear said quietly, after an interval, "but the guy's captured my imagination like no one else ever has, and I'm sticking with him until the last out. If we're striking out, we're striking out swinging." Bear stopped, and then, his voice even more subdued, said, "It looks like I figured you wrong. I thought you were bluffing. I guess you weren't."

"I am, Bear," Alan said, instantly sorry he had hurt his friend's feelings. "When I sat down here, I knew what you were up to, and I had already made up my mind to climb aboard this doomed bandwagon. Gene has a grip on me, too. I just realized it a few days ago." Bear grinned, then laughed, relieved and happy. Alan raised his iced tea in a toast. "Adieu to Rhett Butler," he said.

"I'll drink to that." Bear clinked his Seven-Up against Alan's tea. "Who's Rhett Butler?"

"Me. Who else?"

"You're a hard man, Alan," Bear said. "Nobody understands you half the time."

"Rhett Butler is the guy in 'Gone With The Wind'. Remember his famous line, 'Frankly my dear, I don't give a damn'?"

"I missed that one."

"Well, the guy didn't give a damn about much of anything, except himself. Understand now?"

"More or less."

"I didn't know anybody had missed 'Gone With The Wind'."

"Learn something every day."

"Yep. So, what's the next step? Oregon's the name of the game, right?"

"Absolutely!" Bear said.

"How are we going to pull it off there?"

"We're going." Bear became animated. "A bus trip is being organized. It isn't for sure yet, but I think it's going to come off. It won't cost much, about thirty bucks apiece. You're coming, right?"

"Yes, though this is the first I've heard," Alan said enthusiastically. "What about school?"

"You can afford to miss a few days, can't you? You're going to graduate, regardless."

"Bear, old boy, how long did it take you to figure all this out?"

"Oh, just a few minutes one day. That's all."

"Not very flattering," said Alan, laughing. Bear laughed, too.

"I've got to get to class," Bear said. "I'm glad McCarthy's grabbed you, Alan."

"Me, too."

Things began to go wrong almost immediately after the mission began. First, one of the buses broke down, which was, as one of the party said, "As inevitable as Kennedy's defeat, considering the rate we got." It rained almost all the way, particularly torrentially—it was the consensus—while the bus was under repair. Then, the expected rooms at Portland State College did not materialize, obliging the party to settle at the 'Y's. Which meant splitting up. Nor was Bear accurate in his per diem estimate.

These difficulties and inconveniences notwithstanding, enthusiasm was running high, for Portland and Oregon, it appeared, were there for the taking. Alan was gratified to discover that for each Kennedy sticker, for each Kennedy sign, for each Kennedy worker, there was one for his candidate as well. The city itself was vibrant with the excitement of the campaign; both candidates were present, this was the spotlight.

Alan canvassed at a furious pace, knocking on more than six hundred doors daily. One day, he kept a private tally, and, at day's end, was happy to find his figures at McCarthy 149, Kennedy 116 and the remainder either Republican or blank. Nothing peeved him more than uncooperative people who did little more than slam the door, something he thought happened astonishingly often.

Come Sunday, eager to see his candidate, Alan took some time off from canvassing to attend a rally at a downtown plaza. Tucked among the tall downtown office buildings, the plaza was a sea of signs and placards and banners, and the crowd itself was large and festive. Alan quickly found himself caught up in it. But, finally, it was Eugene McCarthy himself who worked the magic. Alan was electrified by the candidate's familiar, yet eloquent, criticism of the Johnson Administration and the Vietnam War. Even Bear found impossible keeping up with his friend's applause and cheers. A tremendous ovation arose with the speaker's last words, Alan clapping with aching hands and joining ineffectively in the chant, "We want Gene," for his voice had long since gone hoarse.

The next day, the last before the primary, Alan took in a speech by Kennedy, in the morning, and canvassed in the Reed College area during the afternoon. He was delighted to find Kennedy's crowd smaller and quieter, and he thought the candidate looked tired. At day's end, he returned to the YMCA, happy because his man had outpolled Kennedy by almost two-to-one in the neighborhood he had worked, happy because McCarthy seemed to him personally more dynamic than Kennedy, happy because he believed McCarthy would win, happiest just because Eugene McCarthy existed. He couldn't find Bear, but he did run across one of the 'Y' staff, to whom he gleefully said, "Tomorrow, it's bye-bye Bobby." The employee returned what Alan perceived to be a Republican frown. His exclamation had made him think of something else, however, and all the way down the corridor and up the stairs to his room Alan joyfully sang "bye-bye Bob" to the tune of "Bye-Bye Blues." When Bear finally did come in, an hour later, he, too, was buoyant with the prospect of a McCarthy victory. The two spent many happy minutes trying to convince each other that what so shortly ago had appeared impossible seemed likely to happen. They resolved on a great drunk the next night, if the impossible should indeed occur.

Late that night, as he lay restless in bed, Alan got the insight for which he had been groping. It was suddenly so awfully simple and clear; he was appalled at himself for having been unable to see it before. The war's issue was any war's issue: Could the killing of innocent people be justified? That was all there was. It was what Gene was saying, Alan thought. Everything became so clear; it was as though it were spelled out for him in bold letters on the wall. Vietnam was wrong because no argument could ever justify killing the innocent. Alan considered the rationale for the war. The "Domino Theory": Stop the Communists in Vietnam, lest their success there result in all Southeast Asia's capitulation. Give the South Vietnamese the freedom to choose their own government. Honor treaty commitments. Contain the Chinese. All horse dung, Alan said to himself. The truth was suddenly so unmistakable, Alan shuddered to think how long it had eluded him. Then, it struck him that the vast majority of Americans, far from weighing the real issue, never so much as saw it. Could there be a more terrible indictment of American morality? Alan thought not.

Gene McCarthy won Oregon. It was by no means a landslide, but he had won. His victory came as a surprise to most, for it seemed the Kennedy campaign had become the juggernaut many had forecast. Now, out of the blue, the senator from Massachusetts had been beaten. Neither Alan nor Bear, despite their feeling of the previous night, could yet fully grasp that their man was back in the race, that, face-to-face, he had defeated the invincible Robert Kennedy. Alan bought the beer, Bear being a year underage, and, after a stint at the pandemonium-racked McCarthy headquarters, the two, plus two other friends who had made the trip from Santa Barbara, began their own celebration. This was promptly ended by an irate YMCA official, who was correct in his observation they were violating a rule of which they had been advised. Such a reprimand was not nearly enough to stop this quartet this night, however; they stopped by a nearby store, bought more beer and returned to the joyous McCarthy party downtown, which was far from played out.

McCarthy's victory ignited a Santa Barbara campus which was still largely in his camp, despite the Kennedy successes. The one, head-on win erased in the minds of most memory of the impact and significance of the earlier setbacks. Against formidable odds, it was the feeling, McCarthy had won.

Though perhaps none relished the victory more than Alan himself, Oregon was, finally, a triumph for the likes of Bear, who had been with their candidate from the start, who had given themselves early to the man as well as to his platform, who had been hypnotized by the magic of New Hampshire and Wisconsin, only to be snapped gruesomely back to reality by Indiana and Nebraska. Oregon belonged to these. Oregon undid all the despair and resignation, and, because things had come to seem so hopeless, the elation now surpassed every precedent.

Among those not celebrating was Stefan, who, for two full days after his candidate's defeat, went about the halls of Creighton Dormitory, pretending to ask the senator, aloud, about his "Northwest No-No," a phrase coined by Alan. "Why, Robert," Stefan would ask, "why did you say you must carry Oregon to win? That was an unfortunate arrangement of words. I don't believe you did your geography homework. Oregon is a remote place bounded by four other states and a big body of water called an ocean, Robert. People have spent lifetimes in search of Oregon, and never found it (another Alan contribution). Oregon has more trees than people, Robert, which makes it important to beavers but not to us." Stefan's mock lecture made Alan laugh, in part because he found it funny, but chiefly because he knew his friend was not unduly upset. Stefan, he well knew, could be expected to dismiss the Oregon defeat. This he precisely did, noting it was but one defeat, and in an inconsequential state the Republicans would almost surely carry in November, anyway.

Nonetheless, Stefan was disturbed by what Alan, in infrequent objective moments, had to say about Kennedy in Oregon. He said McCarthy struck him as the more alert and vigorous and dedicated. He said, too, that Oregon was up for grabs at the campaign's inception, and that McCarthy had won because he had fought harder and come across better. This rather appalled Stefan, who regarded his candidate as infinitely more charismatic and capable than the dour Minnesota senator. But advice to change sides while this was still forgivable Stefan merely laughed at. Alan insisted he'd rue it when, after the California primary, it would be too late to make the switch gracefully.

California. The first prize. Alan expressed his "fervent hope Bobby has no concept of this." Stefan, privately, had no qualms about California, feeling that Kennedy, with much the broader constituency, would win handily in so mixed and varied a state. Final examinations were approaching fast, making it impossible for all except the very brightest to devote their every energy to the crucial campaign. While Alan was in no danger of not graduating, his grade point could suffer from a last-minute relaxation.

Study was not in his stars this night, however; Alan had scarcely finished the introductory paragraph of a course-completing comparison of Raskolnikov and the middle Karamazov when he was interrupted by a long-distance call. It was Los Angeles—his father. Alan's notice to report for the Army physical had come that day. Judge Young, though not caught unawares, was disconcerted. To think, his son would be a graduate of little more than three weeks! They were watching closely.

At 58, Robert C. Young was a federal district judge whose abundant brown hair, well-nigh wrinkle-free face and robust form made him appear many years younger. Privately opposed to the war, Robert Young, professionally, was not. He could see no sense whatever in destroying the real possibility of a Circuit Court appointment by succumbing to a personal bias, no matter how strongly felt. The judge long ago had learned when to keep his mouth shut. But this time a new ingredient was in the mix: Alan.

Alan was his only son, and now he might be faced with fighting in a war the judge thought a mistake. Somehow, he had to help Alan, without hurting himself. Father and son spoke about twenty minutes, father trying again and again to make son understand the value of expediency, son saying again and again what he, too, had said in previous conversation, that opportunism was out of the question, that his ear problem would certainly suffice. "The Navy wouldn't have me, so why would the Army?" In despair and frustration, the judge handed the phone to his wife, but Dorothy Dorsey Young could do no better than suggest Alan listen to his father; she having lost track of her son's development even before he went away to college. He *was* listening to his father, Alan insisted irately, and disagreeing—and was that all right? He would do things his own way—and why, after a thousand times, could they not understand this? He had learned to walk and even feed himself, Alan added. That broke the silence on the other end. An apology was demanded. Bear walked in; Alan apologized. The phone call ended, uneasily.

"Did he get the girl?" Bear inquired, ignoring what little he had heard of Alan's telephone conversation.

"Who?" Alan growled, and then, "Sorry, Bear. A small disagreement with the folks."

"What's-his-name, of course."

"Raskolnikov? Of course, he did. A regular Cinderella finish."

"And they lived happily ever after?"

"Happily, happily."

"I always thought Dostoevsky was morbid, but I haven't read any of his novels."

"Oh, no, he isn't morbid. He's been maligned by confused professors, that's all. He's the very best in the Cinderella tradition." Alan laughed at himself. "What if I were to write that on this paper?"

"Can the paper wait?" Bear asked.

"What have you in mind? Poker?"

"Pizza."

"Sounds good. Fyodor doesn't turn into a pumpkin till midnight." Alan and Bear departed, Alan saying "see you later" to Tom, his madly infatuated, rarely present roommate, with whom he did not get along.

"I asked Stefan to join us, but he said he was busy," Bear said.

"We'll see about that," said Alan. The pair barged into Stefan's room, Alan glad that Bear had suggested Stefan join them, for it was with these two friends he was happiest. "You are too coming along, because if you don't, you'll have selfishly spoiled our fun," Alan said. Stefan contorted his mouth into an expression of disgust and returned to his paperwork.

"Are you still working on that geometry?" Bear asked.

"I think so," Stefan said, not looking up.

"Bear," said Alan, laughing, "we're being had. Stef isn't even taking geometry. He doesn't even know the multiplication tables."

"No, but I'm learning them," Stefan quipped.

"Not even taking geometry, huh?" grunted Bear, twice the size of Stefan and half as ferocious. "This calls for a little investigation, I do believe." Bear took the paper Stefan had before him. It was covered with tic-tac-toe games.

"Howdy do, Bear," Stefan said sheepishly. "This is how they're teaching geometry these days."

"You fake," Bear said. "You can't even beat yourself at tic-tac-toe."

"Bet I could if I really tried," Stefan said, and Alan laughed joyfully.

"Enough of this," Bear said. "Are you coming with us peacefully, or not?"

They ordered two pizzas, one pepperoni, the other mushroom, and Alan, despite the usual commentaries, had his privileged beer. They spoke of Alan, mostly.

"Your dad said he'd help you?" Stefan said, greatly concerned over the arrival of Alan's Army notice.

"He said he might be able to help, if I'd be 'reasonable'," Alan said. The fact was, Robert Young had been so vague, Alan was not sure what to make of his conversation with his father.

"Then why not let him do it? You're no good for the Army, Alan, it's just not in you. Your dad's in a position to help. I'd say that makes you very lucky. So why not play it safe?"

"You can forget it, Stef. Whatever my dad has in mind, I don't need it, and if I did, I wouldn't do it."

"The heck you don't need it," Stefan shot back. "You told me the day of the Navy physical you were surprised your childhood ear infection flunked you. You've talked yourself into believing it's worse than it is."

"No, I haven't, Stef," Alan said quietly. "We've talked about this before. Who knows my condition, you or me?"

"What's that supposed to mean?"

"Just what it says." There was just the slightest edge in Alan's voice. Stefan said nothing for a moment, and Bear, too, fell silent, feeling somehow that to speak now would be to intrude.

"Good grief, Alan!" Stefan abruptly began in earnest. "You're staking your whole future on one thing. You're putting all your eggs in one basket. Don't you see you should avoid ever doing that, except when there is no other way? You've got another way, grab it, take it!" Stefan was beside himself, and so obviously sincere his outburst moved Alan and embarrassed Bear. Alan remained intransigent. No one spoke a word. Alan rose and went to the restroom. In his absence, Stefan went to work on Bear.

"You're a close friend, Bear," he said. "You know that." Stefan paused to catch the nod. "But Alan ..." he paused, unsure how to express it. "I've known Alan for three years. He's like a brother. I've never known anyone else like him, as a matter of fact. I know Alan, Bear. Better than anyone, I feel sure. He's no good for the Army. He's so straight. Like you, actually, in that way. I mean that as a compliment. Just this once, we've got to get him to be flexible. It could be the difference in being in the Army, and the war, or not. Everything depends on it." Bear sat pensive, seemingly reluctant to comment. Then, on seeing Alan emerge from the restroom, he spoke.

"We've got to stay out," he said quickly, but very deliberately. "What's right for Alan is right, and that's that. Quiet, here he comes." But this last was superfluous, for Bear's words struck Stefan dumb. Alan sat down, and, by their silence, his friends were betrayed.

"It won't work, fellows," he said. "Whatever the plan is, forget it."

"No plan," Stefan mumbled.

"Oh, I know," said Alan. "In the beer the poison placed, and the little prince fell fast asleep." Alan's effort at humor went nowhere.

"It's the mushrooms, actually," Stefan said, sarcastic in his frustration.

"Then why have you been eating them, too?" Alan fired back, sarcasm permeating his voice as well. Stefan glared at him, shot out of his seat and was gone.

McCarthy and Kennedy were both engaged in frantic barnstorming across the length and breadth of the state. Despite exams, Alan devoted enormous energy to the campaign and watched its progress avidly. He conceded to himself, ultimately, that his man was visibly lagging; the spark appeared to have shifted back to Kennedy. Though McCarthy, according to the polls, was doing well in the Bay Area, it was Kennedy who was clearly ahead in the far more populous southern part of the state.

Alan noted that Kennedy was indeed the choice of the minorities. Stefan was therefore right in claiming Kennedy's constituency was broader. What did that matter? Alan reflected. Was not the better man the most important consideration? Of course not. The only thing that counted was votes, and Kennedy—Alan daily became more apprehensive—had more of them than McCarthy.

Two days before the primary Alan's college days came to a close, and he went home. The farewells had been intolerably difficult, in particular with Stefan. How, it worried both, does one say goodbye, indefinitely, to his best friend? Neither could say when he would see the other again.

Home for Alan was not the idyllic place it had been in years past. This was not because love was spread thin. The problem lay in the linkage: Alan and his parents could not connect. For the better part of the last four years he had not been at home, and now, he was a stranger in his own house. In truth, however, college had severed the bond with his father alone; Dorothy Young, unable to accept her only child's maturity, had long ago ceased to relate realistically to him. A social lady, the quintessential Junior Leaguer, Dorothy Young gave prodigious quantities of her time to club activities and reaped every benefit her husband's status provided. Robert Young himself was listed in the Los Angeles Social Register. A hard-driving and ambitious man, considered humorless by many—although those close to him knew otherwise—Judge Young was wholly devoted to his profession and determined to continue advancing within it. Like any United States Judge, he owed his position to years of unswerving political loyalty: Robert Channing Young had stuck with his party through the lean Roosevelt and Truman eras, and, in 1957, had received his due. Now, as disenchantment with the Democrats increased, he stood a reasonably good chance of further advancement; a Republican in the White House might well have him on a Circuit Court bench. Although he had never been a Nixon enthusiast, he felt Nixon would get the nomination, and he could live with that. With the observation Sacramento had not improved Ronald Reagan's acting talent Robert Young heartily agreed, but this opinion he carefully kept within an intimate circle.

Alan would not be obliged to live at home this summer. He was looking forward to sharing an apartment with Jim Riley, a recurrently lost-and-found high school pal who attended a local college. Barbara Yancey was still single. Alan always called on her, and always she was eager to see him. Also, he expected to be hearing from the graduate schools, having finally submitted his applications. Alan was confident of acceptance somewhere, for his grades were good. His summer job alone loomed as an object of dread: A street crew! Alan would be spending hot summer days helping keep Los Angeles' streets in good repair. It was all he had been able to obtain, although he really had not made a bona fide effort to find something else. The main thing was, he wouldn't be idle. He'd make a little extra spending money, and the work wouldn't last long.

Meanwhile, Alan stumped furiously for McCarthy. The evening of the primary, he suggested that Jim join him at home—their apartment was secured, but they were not to move in for another week—for "pretzels and prayer." Jim, apathetic, declined. Alan's parents would not be home, this being the night of the Burns' annual extravaganza, so Alan was left alone with his hopes and his pretzels.

The evening was not a happy one for him. He had anticipated the outcome, yet its unfolding did not temper his misery. McCarthy was not badly beaten, but he had lost. Kennedy and McCarthy together had swept the state, the vote for the Johnson Administration coming to little. Alan's resentment of Kennedy reached new heights; he began cursing each time the candidate's name was mentioned and vehemently denounced one of the networks, persuaded its news team favored Kennedy. When, at last, the candidate appeared on the TV screen to make his victory speech, Alan vented his spleen and, switching off the set, retired, moments before Robert F. Kennedy was mortally shot.

The Burns' party, the usual marathon, complete with dance floor, hired musicians, lavish buffet, inexhaustible Scotch and consequent drunks, was far from done when somebody dashed down the stairs, shouted twice above the din, "Kennedy's been shot," then raced back up the stairs to the television room where he and a number of others were watching the election returns. Out in the spacious backyard, gathered around the bar there, were the Youngs and their crowd; the news reached them first as a rumor. Someone said Kennedy was shot, or something like that, no one was sure. These were the usual friends of the circuit, and thus, there was little danger in candor. Robert Young made no secret of his feelings, and his was a popular, much-echoed opinion. G -damn Catholic. Worse than his brother. Can't stand the way he talks. Can't stand that hair. Liberal jackass. Had he been shot? Certainly hope so. Somebody suggested they drink to it, and some did. But now William Burns, attorney, appeared. A Mexican in his employ, who was struggling with a hefty, portable television set and extension cord, trailed him. Burns held up his hands and asked for attention, an unnecessary act, for the television at once confirmed everything and hushed the group. Robert Kennedy had been shot just minutes ago, he said. Right after delivering his victory speech. Other people were hurt, too. They had the gunman. Nobody knew how badly Kennedy was hurt. The Mexican unscrewed one of the light bulbs from the outdoor string, inserted a convertor unit, placed the TV on the bar and plugged it in. Immediately, all who could gathered around the set. It was true, it was true!

"He's been asking for it for a long time, with those idiotic ideas of his," someone said. "Welfare for every Negro and Mexican in California. That's how he got their vote. Free money."

"I think he's pink around the edges."

"G -damn Catholic. Always got Rome on his mind."

"When he isn't having kids, that is."

"Why don't you shut up, Davis? The man's been shot."

"Yes, shut up. I can't hear what they're saying." A medical bulletin came on. The bullet had entered behind the right ear. There was massive fragmentation and hemorrhaging. Kennedy's condition was critical.

"He's a dead man," said a surgeon just ahead of the question. "If he lives, which is extremely unlikely, he'll be a vegetable. My bet is that he'll be gone by morning. He got it in the back of the brain, just like his brother."

"Too bad. I think I'd like him as a vegetable," said another.

"Congratulations on a brilliant diagnosis, doc. You turn my stomach. The man's been killed. The man's head has been blown off. I can't stand him either, but, by God, he's been assassinated! This country is killing everyone. Don't you give a damn about that?" Fred Cox, lawyer, had had his moment. Someone from behind placed a firm hand on his shoulder and pushed him into a seat.

"Please, Fred." Everyone was silent. Shame came and went, a few resumed talking, even as before. Most, including the Youngs, prepared to go.

One of the TV stations was still giving coverage to the shooting when the Youngs reached their door. They woke Alan, but the station had just signed off when he turned on the set. His parents told him about it as he tuned in the radio. Disbelief was his first response. Another assassination! They had just buried King. Yes, it was unbelievable. Yes, the country was in desperate condition. But now the man who could save the country was home free. Alan, in spite of himself, could not help rejoicing. McCarthy, he felt, had it now. Alan could not feel badly about Robert Kennedy; he hoped only that the senator would not suffer.

Robert Kennedy survived less than two days. During that period of frantic, hopeless medical activity, Alan did begin to feel more fully the magnitude of the event, yet, while he thought it a horrible crime, he could not bring himself to feel true sorrow for the victim. In his mind, there was no forgetting how Kennedy had stolen the campaign from McCarthy, and no forgiving it. Not even murder could change that. Alan's eyes remained dry.

Yet, the person in the best position to profit from Robert Kennedy's death, Eugene McCarthy, did not. Alan was puzzled. What circumstances, since the snowy New Hampshire triumph, had so affected him? One week, the candidate would strike his ardent admirer as forceful, impressive, determined, and the very next week, he was more nearly the "prosaic poet" an enemy had branded him. Nonetheless, Alan's enthusiasm for McCarthy did not flag. Much to the contrary, it grew steadily. McCarthy's inconsistency Alan wrote off to the strain of the campaign. Blame for his candidate's failure to gain ground Alan lay directly at the feet of the Kennedy people themselves, not a few among whom chose to stay with the name rather than switch to the McCarthy camp. This Alan viewed as incredible, and for these, his contempt was boundless.

And then, suddenly, just over two weeks into his return to L.A., and a mere six days before his Army physical, Alan opted to drop everything and go to Washington, to do there, with the national organization, whatever he could for McCarthy. This meant finding another roommate for Jim, who, although he would understand his friend's caprice, nevertheless could not afford the rent alone. It meant not seeing Barbara. Alan had six days to take care of matters, and then, with the physical out of the way, he would be off East. This became his plan.

At about this time, a note from Stefan to Alan's parents, whom he had met on three occasions, two Thanksgivings, one Easter, reached the judge's desk:

St. Paul
June 14, 1968

Dear Justice Young,

I hope you will not look upon this as an indiscretion, or worse. Alan has been my best friend for the past three years. Alan is my best friend, that is. It would be impossible for me to begin to recount the memorable times we have had together.

The night you called Alan about the arrival of his notice to report for the Army physical examination, he and I talked about it. He told me you might be able to help keep him from being drafted. (He wasn't specific.) He said he positively would not consent.

We argued, something we almost never did. I sided with you, strongly, and I still do. This is why I'm writing. Alan is no good for the military. It will wreck him. I know him well, maybe better, at this point, even than you, and I know he is not constituted to be soldier.

He refuses to discuss the issue. I do not know what can be done. I do not know if his inner ear problem, upon which he is relying entirely, is severe enough to defer him. Alan has never seemed in any way like an invalid to me. I believe he has talked himself into believing it is worse than it is. I have no idea what can be done, but I just had to write.

Maybe you can do something. I certainly hope so.

Sincerely,
Stefan M. Kopinski

Robert Young was aghast that Alan had been so indiscreet as to have mentioned their conversation to Stefan. He tore Stefan's letter into tiny pieces and dropped it into the trash can. It had unnerved him, but he found he appreciated it, too, for it forced him now to contemplate, without further procrastination, the step before him. Robert Young knew the chairman of the local draft board, knew him well, and had every confidence one quick phone call would bring a permanent end to Alan's predicament. Indeed, what so troubled the judge was the sure knowledge he could solve the problem. Around and around and around he went, wrestling with the issue, agonizing over it. He was deeply troubled, for it was many years since he had suffered this kind of profound emotional conflict. At arm's length on his big, judge's desk was the telephone, teasingly inviting him to grasp its handle. Robert Young stared at it blankly, and, as the minutes ticked by, he gradually discovered that the phone, at least for the purposes of this one, proposed call, was his enemy. The judge had a final, awful moment of irresolution, then rose very deliberately from his desk, crumpled the bit of paper on which the phone number was written, and calmly deposited it into the trash. The risk was just too great. He could be prosecuted. His meticulous career, nearing its zenith, would be shattered, his life—his very life—would be over. The scandal beyond imagination! It could happen! A thousand times he had sought to persuade himself there was no risk, a thousand times he had failed; for there was a risk, a small one, but a risk undeniably. A risk that would always be there, next week, next month, next year. He would never be free of it, could never again be completely at peace.

"Anyway, Alan doesn't care," the judge said to himself. He thought no more on the matter.

Chapter 2

Punctually at nine on the 23ʳᴰ, Alan checked in at Building 4 at the post, where, to his amazement and delight, he encountered a number of high school friends, unseen since those days. To a man, they, too, were recent college graduates.

Ralph Randolph was present. Ralph was one of those rare persons who possesses genius for one discipline and is pathetically inept at everything else. In ninth grade, Ralph's extraordinary quickness at math had been fully uncovered; he was enrolled in an integral calculus course at UCLA, and, as often as not, found himself playing professor to the professors. Overnight, he became a celebrity at West Los Angeles High. Someone coined "Einstein," and instantly "Ralph" was obsolete. He was a candidate, Ralph informed his former schoolmates, for his doctorate at Cal Tech. This surprised nobody. Ralph insisted—testily, Alan thought—they call him by his real name. Neither frail nor truly eccentric, and unhampered by physical limitation, Ralph, but for the letter his hopeful fingers clutched in his pocket, would surely be drafted, his peculiar intellect notwithstanding. The letter was a complete and shameless falsehood, and Ralph knew it would deceive none of these with whom he had grown up. Fearing exposure, he was barely amicable. Ralph did not know he would face an Army doctor who placed no stock in written excuses, which were often filled with mendacity. Indeed, it was curious how many draftees deluded themselves into believing a crafty lie could trump the long experience and common sense of the United States Army.

Broad-hipped, effeminate Bill Sharp was there, too. Now mustached, and more obese, he was as insouciant as ever. Long ago Bill's extroversion and sense of humor had proved his salvation. Everyone was glad to see him.

33

He informed he lived in Berkeley and worked with a small and "devotedly unambitious" repertory, which no one had heard of. Bill footnoted with "obscure." He said his sole professional desire was to give his interpretation to Hamlet, and everyone who knew Bill thought that was very funny.

Tom, too, was there, and the other Tom, and Mike, and Steve, and Andy and Cale. In addition, there were numerous other graduates Alan did not know, and there were a number who obviously had not gone to college. These lacked the community Alan's sort enjoyed; they were morose and silent. Alan pitied them, feeling it was they the draft would snare.

The first order of business was the mental test. The group, about forty in number, was led into a large classroom and instructed by a man in uniform named Atkinson to "sit down and maintain absolute silence." The graduates, united for the moment in the common cause, took the seats in the back of the room. Alan knew this test would be a waste of time, only a formality. A pair of aides passed around the tests, and Atkinson himself distributed scratch paper. This done, he returned to the front of the room.

"I want absolute quiet," he said sternly. "I want no wandering eyes. If I catch anyone doing this, he starts over, in a room by himself. Understand? Now open your tests to page one and read silently along with me as I read the instructions out loud." It was just like any other aptitude test he had ever taken, Alan reflected. Same format. Same booklet. Same little rectangles to blacken on the answer sheet. A verbal section, a mathematics section, a mechanical aptitude section. Atkinson read the first of the three sample questions, then went over the answer. He repeated the process with the second sample question, and then the third. He was brisk and businesslike. When there was a small commotion involving two individuals Alan didn't know, Atkinson resolved the matter with efficiency, but not discourteously.

The test began. Alan breezed through the first two sections, but, as usual, encountered trouble with the mechanical aptitude questions. No surprise there; he was not going to get those cursed boxes folded, now or ever.

The physical examination came next. It was methodical and very impersonal. Alan resented the way it was done. He thought they were treated like cattle. He found particularly demeaning standing naked in rows and, at the words "grab your ankles," bending over for that miserable test. It was over now, everything except the appearance before the doctor. They were lined up, all of them, for the nth time, and they were silent. Alan wondered what each guy's thoughts were. He was nervous and felt a certain apprehension, despite his confidence he had not passed the physical. Bill Sharp emerged from Cunningham's office, a big smile on his face. Bill alone knew that, on the record at least, it was his obesity which had been the deciding factor. Bill Sharp would not have been the first homosexual Capt. Raymond Cunningham, M.D., had found acceptable for service. Not an unfair man, Cunningham was a thorough one. Unlike some of his colleagues in the Army medical corps, he was not indifferent about sending young men to Vietnam, but he weighed each case carefully and drew an unforgiving line at dishonesty. Andy emerged, muttered a pair of "goodbyes" and departed. Cale came out, absolutely silent. Ralph emerged, obviously shaken, and Alan went inside.

"Alan Young," he announced to Cunningham, stammering slightly, and shaking the physician's hand.

"How are you today?" the doctor said, as though it were just any day. He re-sat.

"Fine," Alan said.

"Any reason you can't serve?" Cunningham said dryly, looking not at Alan but the wall.

"Well, yes, my vertigo," Alan stammered. A terrible dread, to which he could not quite give name, seized him. "It's here in these two letters—about my inner ear." Alan handed over both his official notification he had failed the Navy Reserve physical examination, and a letter from the physician he had seen during boyhood, explaining his ear malady; he had elected to bring the latter, despite having heard letters were sometimes faked and therefore inadvisable. Cunningham paid no attention to either document. He sniffed.

"I understand you play golf," the doctor said, now looking at Alan. "Is that right?"

"Yes, that's right," Alan said, wondering how Cunningham could know that.

"But you had swimming at school one year, too, didn't you?" Cunningham inquired.

Caught again by surprise, Alan was speechless. "You had swim …"

"Yes, sir, I did," Alan blurted, interrupting unintentionally. "But I can't swim much, because of my ear. I can't dive at all. Excruciating pain. I only took swimming because I enjoy being in the water."

"Uh-huh. But swinging a one-wood doesn't make you dizzy?" asked the doctor.

"No, otherwise I wouldn't."

"But diving and swimming are out?" Cunningham himself interrupted.

"Yes."

"That seems strange to me." Cunningham ran his tongue along his lower lip. "Tell me, how did you manage to pass the course?"

"Oh, they pass everyone in PE," Alan found himself saying.

"Uh-huh. Mr. Young, your vertigo can't be very serious, if you can play golf and half-swim, or whatever it is," the physician said, the sarcasm unmistakable in his voice. "You're acceptable." He checked in red ink the little box on Alan's form that read 'Acceptable', which was juxtaposed with one labeled 'Not Acceptable'. It was a matter of millimeters. Alan stared dumb at the checkmark. "I believe these are yours," Cunningham said, handing Alan his Naval Reserve notification and his doctor's letter. "You're holding up the line, Mr. Young."

"Dr. Cunningham, you've made a mistake." No, that wasn't what he wanted to say.

"I don't change my mind. Now, if you don't mind, there are others waiting."

"Appeal it, Alan," somebody remarked as he passed the queue outside the door, although Alan had not said a word.

Alan drove home in a state of shock. Trying to remember exactly how the conversation with Cunningham had gone, he could make no sense of it. Everything had happened so fast.

No one was home, a relief. Alan switched on the television, trying to get his mind off what had happened. Nothing but quiz shows and soap operas. He cooked himself a hamburger, succeeding in charring it. For more than an hour he wandered, abject, about the house, repeatedly telling himself what had happened hadn't. As the afternoon wore on, he began to get a grip on himself, and reason returned.

He could appeal the decision, as somebody had said. Better, he could apply for status as a conscientious objector. At this realization, Alan brightened. He was against all war, and he knew exactly why. This, surely, would guarantee his being granted C.O. By evening, when both parents arrived, Alan was actually cheerful. The news did not surprise Robert or Dorothy Young. It did greatly upset them. Of the three, Alan was the least agitated. He would file an appeal; he would apply for C.O. classification. Even if the appeal should fail, the C.O. application could not. Alan said the wonder of it was that he had never thought to seek classification as a conscientious objector. It rather amazed him, for it seemed an exceedingly obvious choice now. Alan's parents remained unconvinced. His father knew Alan's appeal, in particular, would be useless, but Alan could not be persuaded of this. The evening dragged along.

Late that night, Dorothy Young asked her husband why he hadn't simply taken the whole matter into his own hands. It was the question he dreaded.

"Because," he replied, grateful for the darkness of their bedroom, "that string I could have pulled could have turned into a rope with a noose at the end." Nothing further was said.

The next two days Alan devoted exclusively to his application for C.O. status. Once this was done to his satisfaction, he turned his attention to his candidate. Alan joined the local McCarthy organization, finding it a pitiful group for the nation's third-largest city. He was assigned to the mimeograph department, where he mimeographed and mimeographed. The work demanded only dedication, but of this he possessed his share and more. Too, the job was unsalaried, but neither did this matter to him.

On Friday evening, after an unusually long day at the McCarthy office, Alan rang Jim Riley, with whom the planned apartment had never come to pass, and suggested beer. Plain, medium tall, with dark black hair and an incipient paunch, Jim was studying to become an orthopedist. The family tradition was two generations old, and, since Alan or anyone else could remember, it had been Jim's plan to perpetuate it. At the core of their friendship was reminiscence, for the two in truth now shared little. There was a mutual interest in beer, however, and both knew the effect it could have on distance. They went to a bar Jim frequented in Westwood, popular with the UCLA crowd. It was fairly ritzy, not the usual college hangout. Jim made no secret of his penchant for high living, and Alan thought it a good thing he was studying medicine.

"First round's mine," Jim insisted. "A Schlitz for me, and for him, a Michelob," he said to the bartender.

"By the way, doctor, I happen to regard Schlitz as an abomination," Alan said.

"It made Milwaukee famous, didn't it?"

"Milwaukee who?"

"Milwaukee, Wisconsin. Didn't you say you might go to grad school in Wisconsin?"

"Did I? Wisconsin's at Madison, Jimbo. Marquette's at Milwaukee. Father, that is. Great sport but couldn't hold his booze."

"Is that a fact?" said Jim, noisily gulping his beer.

"Yes, and Mao drinks only Red tea."

"I agree," Jim said.

"So do I," Alan said. "No tickee, no shirtee. That's the rule."

"I lost you there." They drank, Jim rather like a horse at a trough, Alan thought. In another minute, he had drained it.

"Jimbo, you seem to be out of beer," Alan said. "Might I inquire as to whether you would be interested in another?"

"Does the sun shine, old standby?"

"On us, always." Alan drank his down. "Another round, please," he sputtered. "Things been okay with Gil?"

"Tolerable."

"Tolerable?"

"He's sloppy beyond belief. Not that I'm all that tidy, still, there's just no comparison. One thing really gets me: He never cleans the bath after using it, even though I've asked him to over and over. That's only an elementary consideration, don't you think?"

"Yes, I do," Alan said. "Is he a hairy son-of-a?"

"Why, of course. Ape-like, I'd say. Neanderthal at best." Alan laughed. They consumed three more rounds each, more slowly each time, and, between alternating trips to the toilet, they re-hashed high school days. By the sixth beer, they were prepared to ponder anything.

"You doctors. All filthy rich. Making money off sick people. You should be ashamed."

Alan was tipsy now.

"Oh, we are, most indubitably."

"You're just a bunch of shameless butchers."

"Orthopedists are not butchers. Surgeons, maybe. They're the ones who are filthy rich."

Alan stared in silence at the row of bottles behind the bar.

"Are you going to med school in L.A.?" he asked, having given up on the effort to remember whether he had asked that before.

"Not if I can help it. My first choice is Harvard. Boston is a great medical center, best in the U.S., except maybe for, I can't think. Chicago?" Jim burped loudly.

"How should I know?" Alan said. "Isn't Johns Hopkins supposed to be good?"

"Still respectable, but not what it was when Osler was there."

"Never heard of him."

"He was a pioneer at Johns Hopkins. Also a genius, I think. One terrific doctor and teacher." Jim sighed.

"Hello, I'm Dr. Osler, the well-known quack. Happy to know you, Dr. Quack. My name is Fitzgerald. F's Scott Fitzgerald. I wrote a book once. Silly boy said Dr. Quack."

"I assure you, Osler was not a quack," Jim said.

"Of course he was. Let's get something to eat. I'm starving."

"They have a restaurant here."

"They'd never be open this late."

"Is the restaurant still open?" Jim asked the bartender.

"Yes, sir, for another hour."

"Wait a sec," Alan said. "Have you a menu, by any chance?" The bartender disappeared, returned with a menu. "Seven dollars for a hamburger!" Alan exclaimed. "I'm not paying seven dollars for a hamburger, no way. Let's go somewhere else."

"Let's go to Santa Monica." They headed that way but elected to stop at a coffee shop next to the UCLA campus. "So what exactly are your plans, Alan?" Jim ventured over a sobering salad and black coffee. "When all else fails, I recommend orthopedics, strongly."

"I'd never have guessed," Alan said, not quite nicely. "I'll tell you, Jim, I wish I was as hot for something as you. Really. Going from one thing to another may look glamorous, but it isn't. It's horrible, to tell you the truth."

"You're not excited about grad school, then?" Jim said. "You talked like you were."

"I suppose I am," Alan hedged, "but the light just dawned. You've known for decades. That's what I meant." Jim nodded, understanding, but he could think of nothing to say. They sat in silence, relishing the food, neither able to conjure a topic.

"You're sure about the C.O.?" Jim finally initiated, embarrassed by the obvious difficulty. "What if it fails? There's always that chance. Then what?"

"It won't fail."

"How can you be so sure?"

"I spelled out my position to them, clearly and sincerely. I'm opposed to war, period. So no problem."

"Clarity and sincerity are not always enough," said Jim. "I know a guy who got into law school back East because his father made a gift at the proper moment. Brian's grades were barely average, he could never have been accepted by a prestigious law school with just them going for him."

"I know that sort of thing happens occasionally," Alan said disgustedly.

"More often than not, I should say," Jim said. "It's a dog-eat-dog world."

"I know it is," Alan said, just a bit angrily. That Jim should presume him so ingenuous he resented.

"Say your C.O. bid was to fail, Alan. Just a hypothetical. Then what?" Jim Riley withdrew from his pocket a crooked pipe, which to Alan looked like a doctor's pipe, and began preparing it.

"Canada, or jail. Or I can be on the run here. I'd get caught."

"That's it?"

"That's it. Or go into the Army. Almost forgot that."

"Some choice. You wouldn't survive jail five minutes." Jim didn't say he thought going to Canada would be cowardly, as he supposed Alan knew that.

"Be that as it may, it isn't my worry. I'm confident of the C.O."

"But what if … " Jim stopped himself there, realizing he had just asked that.

Alan secured an apartment, although he continued to be a daily presence at his home, if only to check his mail. The days passed quickly. Besides the occasional outings with Jim, Alan saw Barbara Yancey. The McCarthy campaign, weakening daily, was not so perceived by Alan, who remained optimistic and immensely dedicated; there was, however, less to do, as the campaign lost steam. Alan also found his interest in Shakespeare had revived, and he penned a short parody of his favorite play, *Antony and Cleopatra*, which he sent off to a local college's literary quarterly. Word came from the Graduate College at the University of Wisconsin, and it was favorable. Although he had never lived anywhere except California, Alan had developed a special fondness for Wisconsin, since that was the state where Gene McCarthy's campaign had first really taken hold. Brown University, in Rhode Island, said no, but for Alan this was a mild disappointment, and practically the only smudge on what had become carefree days indeed.

And then, on the 26th of July, Alan's summer ended. A letter came. Both his appeal and his bid for conscientious objector status were denied. Alan read it three times, but that was all it said. Denied. Alan was flabbergasted. He was shaken. Now, for the first time, the words of others began to ring in his ears. You're being unrealistic, you're kidding yourself, you've talked yourself into believing what may not be so, you're not being sensible.

Alan confronted the issue he had so tried to avoid and was amazed to discover he had already made up his mind about it. How odd, he told himself, to have known all along what I would do; why, then, have I agonized like this? Finding no answer, he concluded he had not really known all along what he would do, only entertained the idea, until the denial of the C.O. Yes, that had decided him, but now he was prompted to wonder if, even once, he had thought the matter through rigorously, start to finish. "Actually," he said to himself, "I think I've probably thought about it too much."

Three days later, the long envelope with "Department of the Army" printed in bold, black letters in the upper left-hand corner arrived. Prepared for the worst, Alan opened it without hesitation. It was his induction notice. Alan was to report for induction at Building 6, Fort Wilson, at 10:30 the morning of August 9.

He put the notice on the dining room table, walked to his bedroom closet, disappeared into its inner recesses, withdrew a dusty shoebox labeled "Grades One Through Five," knocked over two other boxes in the process, emerged from the closet and returned to the dining room. He opened the shoebox and, after some fishing about, withdrew a well-worn box of crayons. He selected the red crayon, and scrawled "After you, chum" across the length of his induction notice. He looked at it and smiled. He then replaced the crayon, placed the crayons back in the shoebox and returned it to its shelf in the closet. Then he went to the stationery drawer, took out a long envelope and a stamp, addressed the envelope and enclosed his induction notice. He then made a telephone call, reserving space to Minneapolis-St. Paul on the third, and space from the Twin Cities to Toronto, via Detroit, on the eighth. Finally, he wired Stefan:

> Stef. Headed for exile in Canada. Coming for brief visit.
> Arrive St. Paul Western Airlines flight 266 at 5:35 p.m.
> Aug. 3. See you then.
> Alan

The wire reached the Kopinski home early that evening.

"Of course he'll stay here," Stefan said, handing the telegram to his mother. At Western Union, Stefan sent Alan a succinct reply: "See you at the airport." Two hours after Stefan sent the wire, Alan held it in his hand. He had used the interval to tell his parents of his decision. To his amazement, his mother cried. Robert Young had to fight tears himself. Alan kept calm. He insisted it was not a cataclysm, that he would be but hours away by jet, that, after all, they could easily afford to visit whenever they pleased. They acknowledged he was right, but it seemed an utterly ruinous and unnecessary course, nonetheless. Alan wasn't exhibiting much courage, either, his parents felt with dismay, but Robert Young's own lack when it was demanded kept them silent. Although Alan consoled them as best he could, his words had no effect—for they were losing their only son.

At half-past four the afternoon of the third, Stefan left the white frame home in the Merriam Park neighborhood of St. Paul and headed for the airport. He was obliged to fight the growing congestion of the evening rush hour every mile, and, fearful he would be late meeting the plane, cursed his shortsightedness. He had resolved to make no mention of Alan's decision, to let Alan initiate everything. Stefan regarded his friend's folly as considerable, but he knew him as did no other, and he understood. The candor of a recent letter struck him now as the grossest insensitivity, and he made a mental note to apologize.

Never having seen Sioux Falls, at the announcement of that city's visibility, 22,000 feet below, from the left side of the plane, Alan strained his eyes. But, at that altitude, in the dazzling sunlight, he could make out nothing. His anticipation mounted. South Dakota was next to Minnesota; he couldn't be far now. Alan was not unhappy. He felt he had faced reality and found he could cope with it. Far from being sullen, he was optimistic, enthusiastic and confident.

The two friends shook hands warmly, exchanging names, and, for an instant, it occurred to each to embrace, but they did not.

"The allies have landed," Alan said. Stefan, finding his meticulously constructed fortitude had deserted him, could manage only a smile. "God bless St. Paul," Alan went on. "A pox on the one they always say first."

"It's good to see you, Alan," Stefan said. "I can't believe you're really here."

"I can't quite either," Alan said. He pinched himself. "Yep, I'm here."

"What do you say we celebrate with a quick beer?" Stefan suggested. "Your luggage can wait, and we'll just be hitting rush hour traffic if we drive home now, anyway."

"But you're . . . whoa, you have turned 21, Stef. I forgot all about it! How could I have done that?"

"Beats me," said Stefan, who had been 21 less than a month. It had surprised him that Alan had not mailed a card.

"What is more, you are a man now, my son," Alan intoned gravely, putting his hand on his friend's shoulder.

"What's that from? Shakespeare? I know I've heard it somewhere."

"A famous statement that inspired Michelangelo to Sistine ceilings," Alan said. They reached the bar, which was crowded and smoky, and took a pair of barstools. It was several minutes before the bartender came over.

"What'll it be?"

"Is this the land of sky-blue waters," said Alan, "or another redneck Louisiana parish?"

"Did you come here to drink or what?" said the bartender petulantly. "I don't have time for jokes."

"A Bud for me," Alan said, much taken aback by the man's sharpness.

"Same," said Stefan.

"How old are you?" the bartender inquired of Stefan.

"I've been 21 for three weeks," Stefan replied coolly. "Would you like to see some identification?" The bartender looked closely at Stefan, pursing his lips.

"No. Two Buds it is."

"What's going on here?" Alan said. "A convention?" He accomplished a 360 degree turn on his stool.

"These are big cities, remember? We're not out in the sticks."

"I think these people belong to the Women's Christian Temperance Union," Alan said. "They're all drinking with a missionary's zeal." Stefan shook his head. Same old irreverent Alan.

"Two Buds here," the bartender said upon reappearance, "and this is the land of sky-blue waters. You from the South?"

"Are you kidding?" said Alan.

"Well, you mentioned Louisiana, and something about you looks kind of Southern."

"You got it. Southern California," Alan said, finding the notion of a "Southern" look ridiculous. A number of his college friends had been from the South, and hadn't they looked like everybody else?

"Ah, well, that explains it," the bartender rejoined.

"Not a bad guy after all," Alan said, after the bartender had departed. Alan washed down a plate of belated peanuts, admiring the dark-hose adorned appendages of their provider. The two spoke of everything and nothing, slipping often into their private state of nonsense. Alan leaned over the shoulder of the man on his right to catch a glimpse of an illustration in the Cervantes novel with which he was absorbed. Just in time to pick up three huge suitcases and a trunk and make it home by seven, they left. Dinner was on, but Stefan's parents were out. Alan dug into the casserole with gusto.

They took drives, they went to shows, they went to the theatre, they saw a ball game.

Stefan's parents were both firm Humphrey people. Having met Alan only once, neither knew him. They did not regard Alan's conduct as exemplary, and both were disappointed in their son, for having so high a regard for Alan Young. But they said nothing about this, reasoning Alan would fall out of Stefan's life for good with his move to Canada. Mrs. Kopinski was the decision-maker. She was an intelligent, practical woman who, because her husband had frequently been away from home, had brought up their two sons practically on her own. Stefan's father, a salesman-turned-CPA, was neither a weak nor a shy man, but his will was no match for his wife's.

Stefan admired Alan's resolution, but found he could not quite persuade himself to call it courage. He had expected to find Alan morose and scared, but he happily judged he was neither. Quite the opposite, Alan's resolution bordered upon real enthusiasm, and where fear might have been, there was grit. Such was Stefan's appraisal. He did not rule out this might be only the calm before the storm, but he fervently hoped not, and, as their short time together became yesterdays, Stefan was gratified to conclude his misgiving was unfounded. Alan himself looked back as little as possible, for, as he said, it was useless, and only exacerbated his bitterness.

The days flew by, as was their way with these two, until suddenly the last evening was at hand. Stefan had insisted on something special and gotten it, dinner at the St. Paul Club, atop one of the downtown office buildings.

Before leaving for the club, Mrs. Kopinski asked Alan if he had spoken with his parents since coming to the Twin Cities.

"No, they haven't called," he replied.

"I think you should call them, then," Mrs. Kopinski said, betraying just the slightest irritation with Alan's answer.

"I could call them when we get back. L.A.'s two hours earlier than here."

"Why don't you call them now, dear," Mrs. Kopinski said insistently, "and then we can go."

"Well, okay," Alan said. He was not pleased that Stefan's mother had decided to play mother with him. He made the call and got no answer. "I can try again later," he suggested, and Mrs. Kopinski had no choice but to be satisfied with that.

They had Tanqueray tonics and New York steaks, and the Kopinskis danced, still occasionally betraying defensive expressions toward peers who only a few years ago had not been, yet nonetheless holding their own nicely. Alan and Stefan were taciturn. Alan stared blankly out the window that overlooked the great river, he reflected bitterly, that ran through the heart of the country, defining East and West. Did Canada have such a river? Did Canada have a river? Alan realized he could not name one. A barge, headed down river, passed, the light in the tugboat's cabin revealing the pilot's silhouette.

"Any freighters get up here this far, Stef?" Alan asked wistfully.

"No, course not. There's barges, though."

"I know that. There's one out there now. But a freighter, that would be class."

"Duluth has freighters."

"Let's ask Mark Twain over there," Alan said, indicating a man with a beard who did not resemble the author. Stefan made no response. "I wonder where that barge is headed," Alan said, giving up on the effort to conceal an encroaching misery. "St. Louis, you suppose?"

"Probably all the way to New Orleans. Why go only halfway?"

"From Minneapolis to Mardi Gras on a flatboat. Sounds like something Huck Finn would do." Alan was disconsolate. Stefan felt a lump in his throat. He searched for the right words.

"It's just plain silly," he said abruptly, characteristically using a word he used with particular efficacy, "to let yourself slip now." Stefan looked Alan straight in the eye. "Your outlook has been absolutely terrific, you've been cheerful, your old self, Alan, and now you're slipping. Alan, it would be so easy to be self-pitying. You aren't. You've shown determination and strength. Don't relinquish it!" Alan stared at Stefan intently and ground his teeth. His chest swelled, and he exhaled deeply.

"You're right, Stef," he said, almost inaudibly. Alan took a long drink of water. "God save the queen," he said, far from exuberantly, "since Old Glory is just that."

Refusal got Alan nowhere, when the time for departure arrived the next day; Mrs. Kopinski made him two ham and cheese sandwiches, for a late night snack. Thank yous and goodbyes were brief, Stefan drove Alan to the airport, the portmanteaus were removed as expeditiously as that much luggage could be, and Alan, before hearts could sink further, said only "until Windsor," and with a nod from Stefan in return, and a handshake, Alan was on his own.

He marched to the post office in the airport and now mailed his inscribed induction notice, which raised his spirits a bit. He then made his way to the departure gate, where it was announced boarding would be delayed fifteen minutes. He couldn't sit there listlessly that long. Alan found a newsstand and purchased a magazine that featured an article on the presidential race. Hubert Humphrey, it was forecast, would carry such-and-such states, Richard Nixon these others, George Wallace these. Wallace posed a serious threat, according to the article, to the Republicans in the South. Most of the "swing states" were not decided. Nixon had the edge at the moment. Alan finished the article, and, realizing Eugene McCarthy had not so much as been mentioned, angrily ripped the magazine in half, bringing some astonished looks from fellow passengers. Finally—it seemed an eternity to Alan—they boarded the plane. All the way to Detroit, he was miserable. At Detroit, he placed the 'Occupied' card on his seat and got off. He walked about briefly, wretched, and then, in a sudden change of heart, he hastily returned to his seat in the plane. What was Detroit, anyway? Alan reflected. Was it not the quintessential American city? Home of the automobile, America's gift to the twentieth century. Home of that magnificent pragmatist, Henry Ford. The City of Production, the American Creed. Produce, he thought. Be useful to your country. Stick a bolt on that Valiant, a bayonet into that Vietnamese. Do it for the country. Alan blurted a profanity, and the passenger across the aisle glared at him.

The plane sped down the runway, the navigator informing the pilot the point had been reached that committed them to flight.

CHAPTER 3

IT WAS POURING RAIN WHEN ALAN'S PLANE LANDED AT TORONTO. IT seemed to Alan that in the "north countries," there were only two seasons, rain and snow. Well, what of the climate? He was young and strong. Inclement weather was nothing. Alan, however, did readily accept the umbrella offered by the stewardess, and he managed a smile when she said, "Welcome to Canada."

Robert Young had had his way on one point: Alan would not burn his bridges on his meager savings alone. Alan had no source of income, outside summer work, no rich uncle, but he did have a wealthy father who, without excessive persuasion, had talked him into taking $3,000. Alan agreed to the sum, insisting vehemently he would take not a penny more, no matter what straits he might find himself in. He reminded his parents he had a nest egg of his own, amounting to $600, and he said there was no reason he could not find work, and go to school, too. He was intelligent and resourceful, he said. If they sent more money, he vowed to return it. His mother's lukewarm offer to make the trip with him to Toronto he had had even less difficulty in rejecting.

Alan had made up his mind to spend the first two or three nights in Toronto in a good hotel. From the list he had selected The Northumberland, liking the name because it sounded English. Maybe Canada was like England? The cab pulled up at the front door of what was an imposing building indeed. The Northumberland was an enormous hotel, at least thirty stories tall, with chandeliers, thick carpets, ponderous furniture, and a phalanx of shops and restaurants. Alan was dismayed, having figured on something far more modest; this place was doubtless astronomically expensive. But it was night now, and he had had a trying day, and didn't feel up to hunting blindly for another hotel, for the sake of a few dollars.

Alan stumbled momentarily on the address line of the register. None? No, that was impossible. How about The Northumberland Hotel, Toronto, Canada? That would set them to thinking, he chuckled. Better stick with home, just this once more. He'd take a room for two nights, please. Alan was handed the key to room 2123. Fine. Just the one bag, for he had had the foresight to pack the essential items in it and had left the rest of his luggage at the airport check, where all would be safe until he found housing. Alan insisted he could carry his one suitcase, but the bellhop, accustomed to this, simply wrenched it from his grasp. Alan was amazed by such impudence. When the pair reached his room, after a silent elevator ride, Alan merely thanked the man.

"That is not a tip, sir," said the bellhop, not unkindly. The remark made Alan laugh, but he stifled it as best he could.

"So it isn't," he said, struggling not to break out laughing. He found something likable in the wizened bellhop's manner, and, feeling oddly grateful to him, Alan fished into his pocket and gave the old gentleman a liberal tip.

"Thank you, sir. Just ring if you need anything."

It was a huge room, for one person, with a bath of dimensions equally intimidating. The tub had legs and old-fashioned faucets which matched those of the basin. There was a decanter of ice water, too, filled to the brim. The bed was large, the mirror large, the window large. Alan looked out at Toronto's lights. Tall buildings everywhere. Something familiar about them, he muttered to himself. Though comfortable, the room had a hollow atmosphere. Before long, it began to depress him. Alan turned on all the lights and the television, fully expecting to see John Wayne gallop right onto the new horizon. When this was precisely what it was, it struck him as so improbable, he laughed heartily. Alan disliked the outspoken actor's politics, but he conceded him credit here: This equestrian in chaps could rampage about for Canadians as well as anyone.

After watching the Western for an hour, during which he plowed grate-fully through Mrs. Kopinski's sandwiches, Alan elected to give Canadian beer a chance. The rooftop bar was closed, he discovered, but the one on the main floor was still open. It was dark, and very plush, and almost empty. Alan chose a stool and asked for a beer called Albertan Ale, which sounded intriguing but, disappointingly, proved to be only a lager, like any other. Of the four others in the lounge, the only person near him was a burly, middle-aged man also seated at the bar; a vacant barstool separated them. The man wore what appeared to be a green, satin-like suit that seemed to glow in the dark, and his tie, also green and which also seemed to glow, he had draped haphazardly on the bar. Stocky and broad-shouldered, with an iron profile whose strength lay in the jaw, the gentleman, but for the ubiquitous graying, might have passed for a young man. He looked inebriated, to Alan.

"I wonder if you could give me the time, sir?" Alan found himself asked. The man had an English accent, and there was no mistaking he wasn't sober; a lighted clock stared at him from behind the bar.

"Quarter past eleven," Alan said.

"Much obliged." The gentleman turned away, drank from his glass, then turned back toward Alan. "What's your business, in this dreary place?"

Alan had this worked out. To make up stories was pointless, and asinine, and, worst, an admission to a shame which had no basis.

"I've come from the States, to live here. The military draft, you know. Just arrived today, as a matter of fact." Alan took a swig of his beer; his listener, grinning strangely, eyed him with uncertain vision. The man's odd expression, and his silence, made him a little nervous.

"The draft, eh?" the man said, betraying no emotion whatever. "Sure you're not just a coward?" The last word he uttered so loudly, everybody in the bar heard. Alan froze, a pain in his chest, numb and dumb. "Know why you're not a Nazi today, sonny?" the man shouted angrily.

"Shut up or get out," warned the bartender, emerging quickly from behind the bar.

"Just a minute, I'm not finished," the man said, brusquely shoving him aside.

"Yes you are," Alan snapped, his eyes flashing. With that, he took his glass of beer and tossed its contents into the man's face.

"Why you dirty." Alan deftly dodged a wild backhand slap and leaped to his feet, fists clenched. His antagonist lunged desperately at him, but he was neither 29 nor sober, and, instead of landing a blow, he caught one, a right uppercut. He went straight down, landing between two barstools. Alan started in for more, but was restrained, with difficulty, by another patron. "Let go, please," Alan said coolly, and the stranger released his tenuous hold. "I'm through."

51

"Get off, would you?" Alan's adversary demanded of the bartender. The bartender got up, then helped the man to his feet. "You know how I feel," he told Alan, struggling with the words, but pointing menacingly. "There's millions of us all over Canada who hate you types."

"Get out of here, both of you," said the bartender. "You first," he directed Alan's antagonist. "You started it." The man wasn't listening; he was bristling at Alan. "I said to get out." Of a sudden, the man lunged again at Alan. Alan was quicker, however; he shoved the man hard, again knocking him off his feet. He landed with a dull thud. "Satisfied?" the bartender said, panic-stricken somebody would come. "Get out now."

"I'm leaving," Alan said huffily. "Real nice place you've got here."

"He didn't start it," noted the man who had restrained Alan. Alan looked at him, said nothing and departed. The young couple in the back, who had found the incident amusing, left, too. The bartender again helped the burly man to his feet.

Twenty-one floors above, Alan stared out the window at the lights of Toronto. Though not frightened, he was abject. It wasn't the viciousness of his foe that bothered him. After all, the man was drunk, and certainly he had provoked him; Alan smiled even now, recollecting the look on the man's face after being doused with beer. No, it wasn't the ferocity. It was the act itself, that it had happened. Was Canada no better than this? The words of Mrs. Kopinski came to him, that he should not expect too much from his new environment, that people everywhere were essentially the same, that there was no paradise. Had he, then, no place to go? Alan was very, very miserable.

Someone knocked on his door.

"Who is it?" Alan was cautious.

"Are you the American young man? I am the gentleman who helped you there in the lounge."

"The one who took my side?" Alan asked, knowing it could not be anyone else, and wondering how the man knew he was an American. And how he had found his room.

"Yes. May I come in for a moment, please?" Alan did not want to see him but opened the door. "Hello," said the stranger, extending his hand. "I came to tell you that we Canadians are not all against you. We are not all like that bum in the bar. You look tired, you've had a rough time. Very rough. I'll go now, and call again at eight in the morning, and will take you to the best breakfast house in the province." The man turned toward the door without waiting for an answer. Alan was dumbfounded and did not realize his failure to respond until the stranger said, "until eight," this time with a hint of doubt. "If you don't want to go, just say so."

"Eight in the morning, yes," Alan said. A smile crossed his face. "Excuse me, I was so surprised. I want to thank you for, uh, your help down there. But I don't even know your name?"

"Charles McCarran. I am an architect, from Montreal."

"Alan Young. I'm from Los Angeles. My former home. I've come here due to the, because of ... Vietnam, the war."

"Yes, so I gathered," McCarran said sympathetically. "Until tomorrow, then," he added, eager himself to end the day.

"Eight it is," Alan said, caught up in a sudden reversal in emotion, a whirlwind of good feeling.

At 7:55 the next morning, just as Alan was asking himself if the events of the previous evening had not, after all, been too preposterous really to have happened, there came a knock at the door. Alan opened it, and there stood Charles McCarran. For the first time, Alan took a good look at him. McCarran was of average height but slender, with prominent, high cheekbones and deep eye sockets that gave the impression of one never fully rested. Still, he did not appear unhealthy. His facial skin was robust and betrayed little sign of sagging. He had a fine, full forehead marked by a trio of nearly parallel creases, a full head of dark brown hair, and a strong, clean-shaven chin. He was blessed, too, with a set of even, healthy teeth, all his own. He wore a beret, and a well-tailored, bluish gray suit of French cut.

They drove to a smart, residential district that Alan thought had a somewhat bohemian character. There were few houses along here, mostly apartment buildings and small commercial establishments. Alan was faintly reminded of San Francisco, although, unlike San Francisco, this street was absolutely level. They turned onto a narrow, cobblestone street and drove its length, about six blocks. No place to park. Charles McCarran grunted his dissatisfaction. He turned onto a still narrower side street and found a place immediately.

"It's a short walk from here, but that will increase our appetites," he said. They reached the main commercial thoroughfare of the neighborhood, Leo Street, and encountered a plethora of swank shops, boutiques, cafes, taverns and pubs, including one with a sign reading 'Men Only', a bookstore, an artist's supply store, a bank, a beauty shop, a hotel. At last, they came to a simple door, sporting a swinging, wooden sign across the sidewalk, upon which was written 'Kipper & Kidney'.

The restaurant was animated. There were several tables, and they were occupied, but the modus operandi, in any case, was to eat standing at one of several large kiosks, where one found all the necessary condiments to make a plate of eggs or kipper just right. In the back, the kitchen was visible, being merely a continuation of the room rather than a separate one. Skylights provided ample light and gave a cheerful airiness to the place, which in fact was not large; every inch of space was used.

"All Ontario eats kipper here, as you can see," said Charles McCarran. Alan believed it. They weaved their way to the back, where they joined a number of patrons who were standing at the kitchen grill, avidly consuming kipper and kidneys and eggs and ham and potatoes. Alan was intrigued. This certainly was not an American coffee shop. People standing eating breakfast. "I recommend the kipper," McCarran said when their waiter arrived. "It's the house specialty, and I'm sure you'll find it very tasty." Alan knew only that kipper was some kind of fish but saw no point in betraying his ignorance; he'd have it and eat it, whether he liked it or not. "Run by an Englishman, name of Farnsworth, who left because the economy was so bad."

"Quite an unusual place," Alan said. "Well-to-do folks, aren't they?"

"Yes, this is one of Toronto's exclusive sections. All professional people, you know." That was apparent. Alan wondered what the reaction would be if he were to announce he was an exile from America.

"It never occurred to me to eat breakfast standing," Alan said. Charles McCarran laughed.

"We could try to get a table, if you prefer."

"No, this is just fine."

"I spotted a friend of mine, when we came in, if you will excuse me a moment."

McCarran went and grabbed by the arm a big man with an abrasive mustache and roaring manner and hauled him over.

"Stroud, I want you to meet a young friend, Mr. Alan Young. Alan, Bob Stroud. A local architect, and, unfortunately, a good one." Alan and Stroud exchanged greetings.

"Unfortunately a good one, did you say, McCarran? Or did my ears deceive me?'

"Of course not. Unfortunately, because you live in God-forsaken Ontario. Unfortunately, because I'm afraid Toronto is leaving Montreal behind. You have become far more innovative, whereas traditionally, the good city of Toronto has adopted Montreal's style. Toronto never had style, that's what made you distinctive throughout Canada."

"Nonsense," said Stroud, good-naturedly. "What about La Villette? We've nothing like that here. You're holding your own up in New France."

"That's what New York thought, while Chicago became the leading architectural city," McCarran said.

"Have it your way."

"Is everything measured against the States here?" Alan blurted, hardly aware of himself.

"McCarran said you were an American," Stroud said.

"What about Ontario Place, Stroud?" said McCarran, keeping the topic on architecture. "Even Chicago will be envious."

"Going to be special, all right, if they pull it off," Stroud replied skeptically. "Everybody knows the quote is ridiculously off. Aston's trademark, you know." McCarran nodded in agreement. Alan sipped his coffee in silence, thinking it was rude of the two men to carry on with their private conversation. "McCarran says you've come to stay," Stroud addressed Alan, as though reading his mind. "So permit me to welcome you to the best country in the world."

"Thanks," said Alan. "I hope you're right."

"Well, now, it's certainly better than its southern neighbor, don't you think?" Stroud declared.

"Oh, I don't know," Alan said. "America has its points."

"Of course. Racism, riots, crime, war."

"That's an interesting assessment," Alan said, a little warily.

"Do you know what Canada's greatest achievement is?" Stroud asked.

"Haven't the slightest," Alan said.

"Independence."

"Independence?"

"Precisely. Independence from your country. That you've never taken us over."

"When have we ever tried? They, they, ever tried." Alan thought Stroud's remark absurd.

"More than once, my dear young man, I can assure you. But we're tough, like Finland, you might say, which has an overbearing neighbor of its own."

"I see," Alan said, still thinking it a silly boast.

"He really doesn't hate America, Alan," McCarran introduced. "Just resents it, I think."

"No, I hate it," said Stroud. "Americans are arrogant, dishonest, condescending and prideful." The word, thought Alan, is 'proud,' and the speech, prepared. "Remember the meeting in Chicago, McCarran? Remember their reaction whenever they learned we were Canadians? Who? Where? Boy, that burned me." The Toronto architect was getting a bit worked up over it even now.

"Evidently still does," Alan said gently.

"Yes, I suppose it does," Stroud replied, taking it right, "but you can understand that, can't you?" He laughed. "Actually, I love being Canadian. I love this nation. I mean it, it's the best in the world. We live as well as anyone and have the fewest problems."

"Tell me," said Alan, "does Canada have an inferiority complex?"

"No," Stroud said firmly, although McCarran gave the opposite answer simultaneously.

The two architects looked at each other with surprise, and Alan chuckled.

"Now get your stories straight, then let me know," Alan said, ignoring age gaps and indeed suddenly treating these two strangers with the informality of long-time acquaintance.

"We do have an inferiority complex," McCarran said. "You're right, Alan, everything here is measured against the United States."

"I remember the taxi driver last night bragging about Toronto's skyline and asking me if it was as good as New York's," Alan said.

"Hold on," roared Bob Stroud. "That's hardly a fair match. New York is five times as big as Toronto. Let's make a fair comparison, say, St. Louis." It struck Alan as funny that this big Canadian might really be bothered by an inferiority complex.

"I've never been there," Alan said. "I do know they have an immense croquet wicket."

He left it there, figuring a pair of architects would understand, but neither did right away.

"You don't mean the Arch?" Stroud said.

"Yes, I do," Alan said, and both architects laughed.

"That's a good one," Stroud said. "Is that what they actually call it?"

"No, only what I just called it," said Alan, beaming with delight.

"Well, think what you like, McCarran," Stroud said, "but we Canadians don't feel inferior, not all of us, at least. We've got everything good that the U.S. has, and a fraction of the problems. Think about it. Are we involved in a war, the most important thing to this young man?" Stroud put his hand on Alan's shoulder, Alan resenting being treated like a child. "No! Do we have riots? No, except for a few idiots in Quebec yelling for a separate state. Racism? No! Mass murders, political assassinations? No! Canada is paradise, Alan. You've come to the right place."

"Golly," said Alan. "Aside from a bunch of loudmouths in Quebec, Shangri-La. And there went Jimmy Hilton, climbing hill and dale." Neither of the others understood this.

"What do you like?" asked Stroud. "Sports? Culture? The great outdoors? Architecture, maybe?"

"A cold beer, a good book and a fast woman," Alan said. "Not necessarily in that order."

"I'm sure we can accommodate you," Stroud laughed. "How about ice hockey? It's our national game."

"Don't know much about it."

"The Montreal Canadiens," Charles McCarran announced ex cathedra, "are the greatest hockey team the world has ever known." Stroud looked at McCarran as though he were a madman.

"Pay no attention to this gentleman," he told Alan. "He is from Quebec, and everyone knows they're a bit off. Otherwise wouldn't be living there, you see."

"Reminds me of the L.A.-San Francisco rivalry," Alan said. "Full of sound and fury and signifies nothing."

"The truth is, Stroud is right," McCarran said. "Canada, even Ontario, is a fine place. You're going to like it here."

"Must get back to my group," Stroud said. "We've a plot afoot against Aston. Going to send him to Quebec. Alan, after you get settled, call us and invite yourself to dinner. We'd love to have you. Here's my card." With that, Stroud returned to his party, Alan managing only a brief word of thanks.

"We must go," McCarran said. "I failed to mention why there are so many architects everywhere. The Canadian Architects Association is holding its annual convention here in Toronto this week. I have a meeting at eleven, so we must be going." Alan remembered now the sign in the hotel lobby about the convention. "What are your plans now, Alan?"

"I'm going to the bank, first, to open an account. Then, to the draft evader organization, to find out about housing. Also, I want to buy a car, not today, that is, but I'd like to shop around some, if there's time."

"I see." Charles McCarran sounded pensive. "May I make a suggestion? Forget Toronto, Alan, and come up to Quebec." McCarran paused. "We have been joking this morning, let me be serious. Montreal is our world city, although you'll hear different here. It has an Anglo air, yes, but it also has an even stronger Gallic air, lacking here. Montreal is less like an American city than Toronto which, I perceive, may be important to you. You mentioned about going to the university. We have the best English university in Canada, McGill University, and the best French university, the University of Montreal. You might learn French, in fact, I'm certain in time you would. Quebec is different. It is a mixture of two cultures. They get along fine except for the Parti Quebecois, the separatists, who are a pitiful minority. Come to Montreal, you are welcome to stay with us until you get established. I have a son who lives in Sherbrooke, his room is yours. My daughter Jeanne is a sophomore at McGill. You might enjoy meeting her. Oh, and one other thing. You will find less of the type you met in the hotel tavern last night in Quebec than in any other province. Quebec is the most cosmopolitan province and Montreal the most cosmopolitan city. That makes us more tolerant. Plus, allow me to add, we beat Toronto consistently in hockey." McCarran winked with his concluding remark. Alan said nothing momentarily. How much of this was fact and how much hyperbole, he had no notion, but what was the difference? One place was as good as another, as far as he was concerned. Charles McCarran was extending the hand of friendship with an extraordinary offer. Alan thought to refuse, just because he had originally planned on settling in Toronto, very stupid. Too, to stay with the McCarrans until he got his feet on the ground would save him some money. He accepted McCarran's offer enthusiastically.

"Oh, good," Charles McCarran said, smiling broadly and grasping Alan's hand. "Good, good." His pleasure seemed to Alan a trifle out of proportion.

The McCarran home had an appealing look, Alan thought when he arrived the following day. It in no way resembled his parents' hacienda-style home, common not only to southern California, but much of the Southwest. This was a frame house, white, two stories, with a pair of gables, a tall chimney of white brick, and a bay window jutting off the left side. There was a pathetic front yard, mostly devoted to a small garden. The house was anything but unique, for every other house on the street was much the same. Alan wondered how Charles McCarran, still at the convention in Toronto, had forewarned his family, wife Adele McCarran; son Charles, 22, who lived in another city; Jeanne, 20; and Rickie, 15. Had he said: This is an American exile I met in a barroom brawl? No, surely not.

Introductions were accomplished, Alan went in, only Adele McCarran was home, she offered coffee, they engaged in small talk, neither the least comfortable, for to both there was something ridiculous about a total stranger moving in, with the man of the house days, and hundreds of miles, away. Alan was exasperated with himself for having plunged so heedlessly into the difficult situation; he felt he was imposing, and worse, felt she thought so, too. Adele McCarran, for whom apathy was an art, was a middle-aged woman who looked a good ten years older than she was. Her hair was mostly gray, and the skin below her eyes was baggy. Her waistline, from neglect, was excessive, and her calves were thick and unshapely. The overall impression was one of haggardness. Adele McCarran appeared tired, and, in truth, was tired, of her husband, her children, her life as it was. Rather than take a single step to alter the status quo, she relied upon indifference, and, indeed, her husband's initiative with Alan was, as aggravation goes, not to be compared with burnt toast. She wouldn't be abusive; she would ignore him.

Alan came to appreciate her attitude almost immediately and, after briefly debating with himself not staying, decided he would remain pending Charles McCarran's return, but minimize the time he spent in the household. He went first to the American Expatriates Center. Its staff numbered five, occupying a drab office in an old building in downtown Montreal's most squalid quarter. The quintet looked about as reputable, Alan thought. The only one among them with credentials of any sort was the self-appointed leader, a Boston attorney named Paul Kelly. He introduced his "team": Bill Olson, Princeton '67; George James, Rhode Island

U. '66; John Walters, Baylor '67; and Frank Sprague of Seattle. They made a motley crew. Walters looked presentable, and Kelly was passable. Sprague and Olson weren't staff, only volunteers who showed up erratically. The one common denominator was a peace symbol locket around each neck. The wallpaper consisted of anti-war posters, some of them obscene, and a handsomely reproduced quotation from Mark Twain, on the wall behind Kelly's desk. Alan read it:

> I pray you to pause and consider. Against our traditions we are now entering upon an unjust and trivial war, a war against a helpless people, and for a base object—robbery. At first our citizens spoke out against this thing, by an impulse natural to their training. Today they have turned, and their voice is the other way. What caused the change? Merely a politician's trick—a high-sounding phrase, a blood-stirring phrase which turned their uncritical heads: Our Country, right or wrong! An empty phrase, a silly phrase. It was shouted by every newspaper, it was thundered from the pulpit, the Superintendent of Public Instruction placarded it in every schoolhouse in the land, the War Department inscribed it upon the flag. And every man who failed to shout it or who was silent, was proclaimed a traitor—none but those others were patriots. To be a patriot, one had to say, and keep on saying, "Our Country, right or wrong," and urge on the little war. Have you not perceived that that phrase is an insult to the nation?

> MARK TWAIN, on U.S. occupation of the Philippines

"Have you any money?" Kelly asked Alan, perfunctorily, after getting his name.

"Some," Alan replied, thinking that was none of his business.

"How much?"

"I can't see that that matters." Kelly smiled at Alan's evident irritation.

"It matters in this way. By knowing how much you have, I can advise you on your best bet in housing. Isn't that the main reason you came here?" Paul Kelly remained courteous.

"Yes," Alan answered remorsefully. "Sorry if I was rude. It just seemed an irrelevant question." Kelly nodded, smiling. "I have approximately $3,500."

"Three thousand five hundred!" John Walters exclaimed in disbelief. "Good God Almighty, you're a rich man."

"Hardly anyone comes here with resources like that," Kelly said. "Your own?"

"Some of it," Alan said, a bit sheepishly.

"My dad disowned me when I left," John said, and Alan reddened. "Disenfranchised, banished, good riddance. I got the message."

"You're fortunate," Kelly told Alan. "You have it made, comparatively speaking. I've seen plenty who have ended up in the gutter. It's rough for most of the guys who come to Canada."

"In what way?" Alan said.

"They have little or no money, and in many cases, like John's, they've alienated their family. Alone and scared, they just don't make it." Something in Kelly's manner struck Alan as affected, but he couldn't pin it down. Certainly, Alan mused, he was given to histrionics.

"What about jobs?" Alan asked.

"There are very few skilled jobs," Kelly said, "and there's considerable prejudice in hiring an exile. You can wash dishes, though that's not much of a life for a college grad. Yet, lots of guys who come up here have finished college and are using their BA's in a kitchen. The whole thing is a b_____."

"It wouldn't have to be a great job, just enough to keep me going for a while. My plan is to go to grad school at McGill University."

"You can forget that," said John Walters. "Every English-speaking Canadian in this part of the country wants to go to McGill. A better bet is Sir George Williams University, where, incidentally, I attend. I'm studying philosophy."

"Sir George Williams? That's the name of a school?"

"Yes."

"Do they offer doctorates?"

"I think a few, not sure, but once you've got your Master's, it's easier to get in elsewhere, like McGill."

"All I have is a BA."

"Well, Sir George is your best bet. Supposedly they're not as selective as McGill, although I'm very pleased with the level of instruction. It's a moot point anyway, since McGill is hopeless."

"What about housing?" Alan asked, disappointed, somehow, about McGill University, of which he really knew nothing.

"I live in the vicinity of Sir George," John said. "It's a student area, naturally. Lots of apartments. Very reasonable. That would be my suggestion." Alan appreciated John's helpfulness. Kelly gave Alan a one-page questionnaire, asking him to fill it out and return it, at his earliest convenience. Kelly said it was for an emergency.

"In the unlikely event something should happen, we'd have no other means of contacting your next of kin." That made sense to Alan. Like the sign said: This is your home away from home. Alan left in good spirits, feeling he had made at least one friend, in John Walters. Something indefinable about Kelly bothered him. Too, he now had an idea of where to start. The dinginess of the office and its occupants Alan dismissed with the cliché one cannot judge a book by its cover. That afternoon, he opened a savings account at the Bank of Montreal, and then reluctantly returned to his temporary residence. The next day, he devoted to shopping for a car, forfeiting a modest sum, come dusk, for a used Volkswagen. Again it was back to the McCarran's. It felt good to drive again, but Alan wondered en route why he had not used the day to find housing. Because, he remembered his reasoning, this would be facilitated with a car.

Remembering, however, did not make returning to the McCarran home easier. There was no respite for him there. Adele McCarran remained cold. Jeanne, the 20-year-old daughter, was taken by Alan from the first moment she saw him, and while they had had no true conversations, in their occasional exchanges she had made unmistakable overtures, and once had extended what he recognized was an invitation, simply. Alan thought her attractive, but puerile. He didn't like flirts. As for the 15-year-old, Rickie, he wished only to discuss Canadian and American football, in which Alan had only a mild interest, and, in the case of the former, no knowledge. On the day he found housing, Charles McCarran returned from Toronto, and Alan greeted him with alacrity. It was all very peculiar, for he had spent only hours with Charles, yet regarded him as less of a stranger than the family members with whom he had passed nearly three days. The older man chided Alan gently for having bought an automobile so hastily, and Alan, feeling it was one thing to be hospitable and another to get into his business, resented this. He perceived an incipient surrogate-father role and desired to shut it down before it developed. The morning of the day after Charles McCarran arrived back, Alan moved out.

He had found an efficiency apartment some eight blocks from Sir George Williams University. It consisted of a modest living room, a kitchen of approximately the same size, separated from the main room by a "bar" with two stools, and a bathroom. There was a kitchen table with a pair of chairs, functional if not fancy, a sofa which, when converted into the bed effectively used up the floor space, and a couple of plain lamps that gave off almost no light, so thick were their shades; these he would change. What displeased Alan most was the lack of a shower, as he was not one for tubs. He liked the dime store painting of a waterfall which hung over the sofa-bed, its obvious value notwithstanding, but he felt the smallness of the apartment would depress him, for it was abysmally small. Alan resolved to spend as little time as necessary alone there. John Walters was not far, and the street Alan lived on, La Forte, led directly to the university and was an unusually appealing one, with trees on each side that formed a canopy. Alan formulated his plan in his mind. He would try to find a decent job for autumn, and he would apply to Sir George Williams University, for admission to the Graduate School in January. He figured with application he could have his master's degree within a year, two at the outside, and then surely he could get a position as an instructor, while continuing work on his doctorate. With thrift and a half-decent job, he thought he could make it. Alan was optimistic.

But at once a kink in the plan presented itself: Alan could not find the sort of work he wanted. This was not due to the paucity of jobs, though in truth they were not plentiful. The problem lay in the fact a subtle discrimination existed against the American exile. Alan, at first, thought he imagined this, but after two instances of witnessing Canadians less qualified than he get the job, he felt he could draw no other conclusion. Warned of the obstacle, Alan was nevertheless rudely awakened. It more than merely frustrated him; it disillusioned. Alan felt destiny was piling insult upon injury. Seemingly, there was insufficient room in the world for one such as himself. Adamant in his refusal to accept himself as an outcast, Alan cried out at the injustice in the scheme of things, blaming his misfortune on the accident of birth at the wrong time. His was a bitter, self-destructive reflection, endured night after night in his small apartment, his radio his sole companion. In these straits Alan foundered, until, just when it seemed his resolve might crack, a visitor approached his door. His guest proved to be Jeanne McCarran, a surprise, for Alan had not had a word from Charles McCarran since leaving the household, and therefore had come to believe the contact was ended. Mrs. McCarran, Alan had surmised, had prevailed.

"Petite," Jeanne said after surveying the apartment with the glance this required, "but I like it, Alan. It's cozy." She sat sprightly on the sofa-bed and smiled. Twenty, a sophomore at McGill, Jeanne McCarran was a beauty, incontestably. She had sleek and shapely shoulders, framing a generous bosom. Her waist was slight, and she had fine, firm hips and superbly proportioned thighs and calves. She stood at five feet five. She was a brunette, she had turquoise eyes and a smattering of attractive freckles, and her cheeks had dimples whenever she smiled. Her mouth and teeth were impeccable. Her nose was somewhat flat and featureless, but if it was a blemish, it was the only one. Alan knew practically nothing of her, for her father had spoken sententiously about his family, while Jeanne, in their exchanges, had seemed to him a far cry from what her father described. Alan had not imagined her advances, nor mistaken for something else what he knew to be an invitation. His conclusion had been she was immature and flirtatious, and probably badly spoiled by her father. Nevertheless, he was glad for a visitor, and more than a little curious. "I came to see how you're doing," she said gaily. "An emissary from home, you might say. We've wondered, since you've not called."

"Didn't you get my note?" Alan asked, perplexed. Why should he have called?

"Yes, we received it. They liked it, but they don't understand why you haven't called, and neither do I."

"I've been busy," Alan said, unpersuaded he had owed the McCarrans a phone call.

"Yes, of course," Jeanne said sympathetically. "How are you faring?"

"Not very well, I'm afraid." A silence ensued. "Would you care for something to drink?"

"I don't believe so, thanks."

"The trouble is," said Alan, "they won't hire an exile. Not the good jobs. I have flatly seen another applicant hired over me, not once, but twice, and I had better credentials both times."

"That's a dirty trick. Are there many jobs available?"

"Are you kidding? There are hardly any, less for sure than in southern California, and the situation there isn't great."

"Dad has a job for you," Jeanne McCarran said, smiling. "Think I will have something to drink, after all."

"He what?"

"He has a job for you, and I'll tell you all about it, if you'll get me something to drink."

"My God," Alan said. "Well, look, what . . . what kind of job?"

"Oh, for goodness sake," Jeanne said, rising and retrieving for herself a ginger ale from his refrigerator. "Do you want one, Alan?"

"How did your dad know I needed work?"

"He didn't. He's had this waiting in the wings. He knew before you would have refused it, since you're obviously stubborn. So, he figured he'd let you try yourself, since you'd settle for nothing else, anyway. If you got something, fine. If not, then he could help"—she hesitated—"if you'll let him, that is. You really should, Alan," she added softly. Alan was suddenly moved, he was confused, he was vaguely aware that he had not the slightest idea of how to run his life and should simply turn it over to an older, wiser person, like Charles McCarran.

"He's a shrewd fellow, your dad," Alan said, shaking his head. Jeanne walked over to the window, and, admiring her from behind, Alan thought he must be wrong about her, maybe about many things. She looked out the window for half a minute, then in one motion wheeled around and slipped free of her blouse.

"Let's go to bed!" she said urgently. She flung herself beside him, and before he knew it, Alan found himself locked in a hard kiss. Amazed, Alan jumped to his feet. She sat quiet, hands behind her back. Alan was speechless, but now, her bra became added litter on the carpet. And now she was somehow in his arms, again, her breasts pressed tightly against his shirt, her lips against his, her genitals against his. Alan immediately had an erection, and, feeling this, Jeanne loosened her embrace, running one hand up his thigh; she would let him be the aggressor. But this undid her, for Alan, although clumsily returning kisses, abruptly broke free again.

"I can't, Jeanne, I just can't," he said, disbelieving her behavior.

"Can't what?" she replied, grinding her teeth, obviously about to be angry.

"Can't do this." Alan ran his hand through his hair, trying to make some sense of her conduct. "Don't you see what I mean?"

"No! I do not see what you mean!"

"I can't do this to your dad. That's what I mean."

"To my dad!" she shouted incredulously. "What are you talking about?"

"After all he's done, I can't do this to him."

"Dad, you id … dad will never know," Jeanne said in disbelief, her voice contemptuous.

To this Alan slapped his cheek in amazement.

"Don't you suppose I know that, Jeanne?" he said as calmly as possible. "Or do you really believe I believe you told him you were coming over here to climb in the sack with me?"

"Then what's the problem?" she said quietly, feeling a little foolish, although not quite sure why.

"The problem is, it makes no difference your dad would never know," Alan said, his thoughts clear. "I can't go to bed with you after all he's done."

"And what about embarrassing me?" she said acrimoniously. "Or is this standard procedure?" Alan took his eyes off her breasts and looked into her eyes. He hunted for the right words to alleviate the humiliation he saw beneath her anger.

"I'm sorry, Jeanne. It isn't that you aren't sexy, because you are. You're beautiful. It's only that"—how to say it just right?—"that I can't help but feel your dad would disapprove, and I can't go against him. It's as simple as that." This effort at amends produced a response: Jeanne McCarran deftly slipped free of her skirt, leaving herself only in panties, and teasingly threatened to remove them, too. "Forget it," he said with conviction. Embarrassment hell, he thought. She was shameless.

"All right, you win," she said with resignation. "I'll be a good sport. Won't shout or make a scene, won't hate you forever. Won't call on you again." Jeanne began dressing, huffily, but not with embarrassment.

"Nonsense," said Alan. "We're friends. Don't you see my position isn't a personal affront? God, I think you're ravishing." There was no mistaking he meant that.

"Well, dad did say he has something lined up for you," Jeanne said, "but he expects you to call him. I'm leaving now."

"I'll call him for sure," Alan said. "No hard feelings?" He opted for a quick kiss and planted one tenderly on her cheek.

"None." Now she laughed. "I've always wanted to know an eccentric. Now, I do." A moment of sore temptation rattled him as she fastened her bra, for he had never refused the kind of opportunity he had just been presented. He remained resolute, and they parted on good terms.

Alan saw Charles McCarran the very next morning. McCarran had found Alan a position, as a substitute teacher, in the Montreal Public Schools. The job apparently had no fixed requisites, other than a degree, so Alan, even without the smattering of undergraduate courses in education he had taken, was qualified. He was not, however, enthusiastic; what did he know of teaching adolescents? McCarran, as eager as Alan was not, insisted the job was the ideal temporary work. Alan equivocated until McCarran volunteered, proudly, that knowing a man "behind a big desk" had done the trick. This meant Alan was hedging in front of others on a waiting list. Now, he said he positively would not accept.

"Are you serious, Alan?" McCarran asked, obviously dismayed. "Don't you want the job?"

"Not this way," Alan responded. McCarran, not to be denied so easily, pointed out the advantages: If not at the level he was ultimately aiming for, Alan at least would be teaching. He would meet other teachers, academic people. He would begin building a reputation. Most important, he would be into something.

"You should not spurn a break, Alan," Charles McCarran said. Despite the older man's formidable salesmanship, Alan would concede no further than to say he'd think about it overnight. McCarran was bewildered, and not a little displeased, but he kept his feelings to himself, letting Alan have things entirely his way. Alan weighed it in his flat that evening. He saw he had far too much time on his hands, that daily he was breaking his first-day pledge to minimize time spent alone in his cubicle. The work would not be difficult, he felt, and he persuaded himself the environment might really be to his liking. He would meet other teachers, as Charles McCarran said, could make friends. It occurred to him he might enlighten Canadian youth on the matter of American rectitude; this brought a grim smile. Yet, the fact he would be robbing another of a post he had perhaps long-awaited, remained the sticking point. Finally, Alan realized he couldn't countenance that. But this was to be a fitful sleep, for the combatants here were locked in a mighty fight. He wanted the job desperately, and more, he knew how much he needed it, how crucial it was to escape the scourge of idleness. The job would get him going. In the morning, the clincher came. Whomever he was robbing, it would be only for the duration of autumn.

In the spring, he would be in graduate school. That settled it. Alan called Charles McCarran and told him of his decision. McCarran, delighted, said that "Adele and I" hope he would accept a standing invitation for dinner on Tuesdays. This, too, Alan accepted, knowing perfectly well Adele McCarran had had nothing to do with it. "I'm lucky," Alan said to himself, "to have met Charles McCarran." The circumstances of their meeting came to mind, and he chuckled.

It was at this time the Democratic National Convention took place in Chicago. The Canadian television networks were devoting some air time to the event, and Alan, particularly interested in seeing his candidate again, tuned in the proceedings. From the outset, he was furious; indeed, ere the convention's work was done, he was busy with a letter to Stefan, to whom he owed one anyway:

Dear Stef,

"We are members of the 'Lost Generation'" said a famous fellow who wrote books about Spain and found himself one day in Idaho. Hemingway must have been talking about us.

Not one single thing that has happened in Chicago has pleased me. In the first place, the mass skull-cracking by the Daley boys has been ignored by everyone except a few Democrats and an occasional intrepid reporter, who usually has paid for his courage. I saw one bleeding heavily from a head wound. He said they bashed his camera, and then him. One could see he was totally in shock that this could be happening in the United States.

I'll tell you this, I can count the number of Democrats I like on one hand: McCarthy, the guy from Iowa, who nominated Gene (can't remember his name), the delegate who was the speaker for the Wisconsin delegation (a hero!), and, Julian Bond. As for those I like least: Daley (a "boss"—and he's even proud of it) and the Texas delegation, who opposed, in toto, every good amendment and supported every bad one, and who looked every bit the horsesh__ their state is full of.

What's with the U.S., anyway? Gene does all the work, wins against huge odds, and for this he is regarded with apathy, or wrath, by almost everybody. He's been completely ignored at the convention. It's so unfair. I'm glad I'm clear of the whole shabby system.

Who is Susan, and what is "a pleasant interlude together?" (Come on, Stef, did you strap, or not?) "A pleasant interlude together" sounds like something McKuen would say. Speaking of girls, I got a letter from Betty (Kincaid). Remember her? The witless one who really liked me? Routine stuff. Was I going to school? Was I working? How do I like Canada? Etc. She spelled "drive-in" without the "e." I'm going to miss her.

I'm going to be a substitute teacher in the Montreal Public Schools. Better re-read it. Just for the fall, however, as I expect to be in grad school next spring. Looking forward to giving passes to go to the john.

Montreal is French at least as much as Anglo, maybe more. Kind of like an American city, though. Skyscrapers, etc. I think many Canadians have an inferiority complex, but, when you stop to think about it, California has about as many people as Canada, and more economic muscle. Maybe Canada will become the 51st state someday, but then where would I go? Me, and the other exiles. There aren't that many of us here, actually. (Toronto is the big place.) They have a small organization here, run by a lawyer from Boston. I met one of the guys in the group, who seemed like a good enough sort, but since that day I've not heard from him. I can't see that the organization does very much, yet, the truth is, there isn't much they can do. Bad job situation, discrimination against us. I had an incredible experience in Toronto that is too good a story for a letter, but when we get together, I'll relate it. When is that going to be? Write when you get the chance.

Alan

Alan posted the letter right away, not re-reading a line—a policy. In little more than a week, he had Stefan's reply:

St. Paul

Sept. 14, 1968

Dear Alan,

You're amazed, I'm sure, by the promptness of my reply. Your letter set many thinking gears into motion. First, in response to your comments on the convention. I up and went one day, but I made a point of not getting on TV. I stayed only one day, in fact. Chicago is never very safe, but a millionaire could not have bought life insurance there during that week. I didn't come close to getting hurt, but I saw what was going on. The fact is, the police were not entirely to blame. Some of those kids—no other word will do—were asking for it. I'll never believe that chant, "The whole world is watching," was spontaneous. Still, the cops did lose their cool, bad. Like you said, they were going after cameramen.

The worst thing was that the locals were siding unreservedly with the police. People are rather messed up these fine days. Those protesting the war may be loutish (not to mention ineffectual), but there is certainly nothing anti-American about them.

McCarthy's loss was of course the year's safest prediction. You know I can't stand Hubert. But Kennedy's assassination ended it all, as you know I feel. He was the only Democrat who offered a contrast to Nixon who could beat him. HHH may win, but, since he and Dick look alike to me, I can't see what difference it makes.

As for Susan, I met her at a U of M production of "The Importance of Being Earnest." Funniest play I have ever seen, without a doubt. If you're ever in a blue mood, this is the remedy. Infinitely better than his (Oscar Wilde's) "The Picture of Dorian Gray," which some idiot had us reading when I was a freshman, and which isn't funny at all. It was important to be Stefan that evening. I trust your curiosity is now satisfied.

You sound good. How did you get to be a high school substitute? Important work, giving passes to go to the bathroom. Otherwise, the old bladder bursts, and then "teach" is in trouble. I remember once in grade school I was ashamed to tell my teacher I had to go, so I didn't, and went anyway. In my pants, that is. Happened only once. I'm not a slow learner.

I don't know when we'll get the chance to meet in Windsor. Maybe over spring break. Long time off. Keep me posted on what you are doing.

Stef

Stefan's letter made Alan's day. Every time he read the penultimate paragraph, it made him laugh.

The teaching began, enabling Alan to establish a routine. On the days he was called to teach, averaging four per week, he found he had little time for anything else. He was surprised by the time preparation required. The work was not difficult, however, and he was grateful to be occupied. Much of his leisure time Alan devoted to an essay, in which he postulated that his was a lost generation. Thinking John Walters could be wrong about the difficulty of getting into McGill University, Alan made up his mind to make application to the graduate school there, as well as to Sir George Williams, aiming in each case for admission in the spring. Saturdays, he loafed determinedly, and Tuesday evenings he spent at the McCarran's.

The coldness of Adele McCarran he soon enough found a source of amusement, although Alan was mildly vexed that her behavior seemed not to scandalize her husband. Jeanne McCarran, absent as often as not, increasingly became an enigma. She could be charming and grown-up, Alan had found, if she so chose. Sometimes she was cordial, sometimes not. Frequently, the youngest McCarran also was away, and Alan, notwithstanding Charles' attempt to paint a contrary picture, gradually came to realize that his was not a happy household. Alan was resolved to stay out of what was neither his business, nor worry.

It developed he was invariably called to teach at the same school, Duval High, enabling him, before long, to make friends. Letters to and from home, mostly from, kept him in touch with his parents. Alan had insisted, and succeeded, in minimizing phone calls. A Christmas visit was already in the works; indeed, Alan's relationship with his parents, despite the upheaval in his life, was not much altered from what it had been for years. Among old school friends, Stefan alone wrote, excepting the one letter from Betty Kincaid. Alan was distressed by, and far from reconciled to, the silence of Bob Shackleford, Mark Beasely, and, in particular, Bear Hatcher. Neither had Jane Harsfield replied to the impetuous letter Alan dashed off during the despair of his first fortnight, although Alan only half-expected a response. But it was Stefan, as no one else, he wished to hear from, and often did:

Santa Barbara
Nov. 2, 1968

Dear Alan,

Election week. Ho-hum. That incomparable bastion of liberalism and free thinking, California, is going to put the biggest Philistine the GOP has in the White House. Nixon says he has a secret plan to end the war. Sure he has. Anyway, who cares? By now, probably even the Vietnamese don't.

Mark sends his greetings and says he liked your letter. That geology course has got him so infatuated he's even talking about changing his major. Bit late for that, seems to me. All he talks about is rocks. The other night, walking back from the Union, I kicked one, and he called it a sacrilege. Most of them are in his head. (Always have thought so.) We were coming back from "The Bank Dick." Fantastic. The great drunk at his best. I'll wager W.C. Fields could drink your friends Fitzgerald, Hemingway and Hart Crane (who's he, by the way?) under the table. Remember Fields' immortal comment, when he was in the hospital: "They found some urine in my alcohol?"

Took Rosie out. It's not the same. She knows, too. Kahn, believe it or not, is selling—or so I've heard. I don't know why Bear doesn't write. I don't see him that much, to tell you the truth. Some people just aren't letter writers.

I'd like to hear more about Jeanne McCarran, since you've described her as "beguiling though childish" and "heady, sensual and utterly shallow." What words! Also, what, or who, is "The Unabashed Schoolmarm?" And who are these other people whose names you dropped, and is the McCarran woman really made of stone? End questionnaire.

Mark just popped in and suggested Arvino's. Tipping one to you. Pizza just isn't as good with you up there, either. This is a humorless letter. I can recall telling you to keep your spirits up. Seems we've switched places. Something magical in Montreal's air?

Well, enough for now.

Stef

Alan appreciated his old college chum. But neither was his relatively good fortune lost on him.

He had made new friends, he could count among them a regular bed partner, he had Charles McCarran, mixed blessing though perhaps that was, he had a job and money in the bank. Come spring, he would be in graduate school, pursuing his goal. He wasn't lonely, he felt his time well spent, he was reasonably happy. Bitterness remained, for Alan's contempt for American values had not diminished, but he dwelt on the subject less.

The weekend preceding the American presidential election, Alan spent at the Mount Royale ski resort, with his friend Dave Hillsborough, and with another teacher at Duval High, Marcel Pirmont, whom Alan barely knew. Although Alan had skied on several occasions, in California, he was not a skillful skier, and had been spared addiction to the sport. His vertigo never interfered with his skiing.

Neither was Marcel Pirmont much of a skier. Twenty-eight, French-descended, he was slight and hirsute, with dark eyes and an aquiline nose. To Alan, who was eager to get to know him, he had a faintly sinister look. Marcel succeeded in spraining his ankle within a couple of hours, obliging him to retire. Alan remained on the slopes not a great deal longer. When he retreated to the lodge, he encountered Marcel, busy massaging a fast-swelling ankle.

"I do believe I hate skiing," Marcel announced.

"Does it hurt much?"

"At the moment, yes."

"At least you didn't break it."

"Yes, for that I am grateful."

"Do you suppose Dave will come in when they turn off the lights?"

"I would not put money on it," said Marcel. "He is too fond of skiing. Someday, he will break his neck out there." Alan considered that this was probable. Marcel, whose English was perfect, also spoke French fluently.

"Maybe a bourbon or two would help that ankle, you suppose?"

"Whiskey I never go near. Brandy, on the other hand, is not at all a bad idea." They made their way to the bar, Marcel hobbling. "How do you like Duval High?" Marcel inquired.

"I like it, although I wish they would call me the night before, when they need me, instead of six in the morning. I'm only a substitute, you know."

"Yes, I know that. Being aroused at six is no disadvantage. Dawn is by far the best time of day."

"Not to a somnolent soul like me, it isn't."

"Oh, but dawn is so beautiful," said Marcel. "I seldom miss the sunrise. One misses much who sleeps late."

"You sound like a Chinese Proverb," Alan said.

"A French Proverb, if you please." Alan laughed at that.

"I've heard you are a Separatist," Alan ventured. Marcel took a thoughtful drink, pondering whether he wanted to discuss the issue with a mere acquaintance.

"I am not a Separatist," he said abruptly. "They are idiots, this new Parti Quebecois. Idiot extremists. Besides, I would lose my job. This does not change my feeling that Quebec should be an autonomous state."

"Do you really believe that?" Alan asked, genuinely surprised to hear someone say what he knew a good many espoused.

"I would not have said it if I did not," Marcel said. "Quebec does not belong in Canada."

Alan looked puzzled.

"Quebec came before Canada. So the question is not whether Quebec belongs in Canada, but whether Canada belongs in Quebec. It does not." Alan thought Marcel's comment as silly a remark as he had ever heard. "Consider your country," Marcel continued. "What if Puerto …"

"I'm Canadian," Alan snapped, hardly realizing himself. Astonished by his outburst, he instantly apologized. "Sorry, Marcel. Don't know why I did that."

"My error," said Marcel, swallowing hard. "Of course, you are Canadian now." He faltered, swallowing again. "As I was saying, if Puerto Rico were to become an American state, as is sometimes suggested, it would be an anomaly. Puerto Rico's culture and language are Spanish. Quebec's are French. Do you see the analogy?" Alan did not, so he said nothing. "In fact," Marcel went on, "Quebec is much more out of place than Puerto Rico would be. Puerto Rico would be a very minor state. Quebec is the largest

74

province, has the main city and is second in population. Only Toronto in the rest of the entire country is of any importance."

"Well, that being the case," Alan said, "then just think what a blow it would be to Canada for Quebec to secede."

"Everyone would be happier and better off," said Marcel. "It is true the Canadian economy would suffer a setback, but Canada is on the move. It would be only a temporary setback. She would recover, and she would be rid of her biggest problem. It would be worth it."

"For Quebec to secede would split Canada, as India does Pakistan, would it not?" Alan asked, oddly irritated by the notion of a separate state.

"Yes, it would do that," Marcel admitted.

"Also," Alan pursued, "if as you say only Toronto in all the rest of Canada counts for anything, then for Quebec to secede would be a terrible blow for the country. Far more than a temporary setback, I should think." Marcel was silent, and Alan, sensing the power of his argument, pressed on. "In any event, while Quebec may be more French than any other province, it is hardly exclusively so. There are huge numbers of English Canadians here. So you have it backwards, haven't you, Marcel? Quebec is much less out of place in Canada than Puerto Rico would be in the United States." Alan concluded, proud of the case he'd made. Marcel was angry.

"Why do you use the verb 'secede'?" he inquired haughtily.

"Isn't that what it would be? Like the American South, in 1861."

"That is bad, is it? Splitting up a country?"

"Definitely." Alan fell flat into the trap.

"You are a fine one to talk, then," Marcel said with some malevolence. He resented Alan's attitude toward separatism, in truth, felt Alan had no right to an opinion. Marcel's harshness hurt Alan, who was unprepared, but he recovered himself quickly.

"Just what do you mean by that, Marcel?" Alan said, edginess apparent in his voice. Now it happened Marcel Pirmont was not opposed to the American exiles and had no wish to make an enemy of Alan Young. Feeling their conversation had taken an unfortunate turn, Marcel sought to make peace.

"I apologize, Alan," he said. "I did not mean that. I have nothing against you Americans who have come here. Nothing at all. I take off my hat to your defiance." Recognizing the sincerity of Marcel's apology, Alan accepted it immediately. Neither had he any desire to make an antagonist of a potential friend.

"It's a silly argument," Alan said. "I have been here a matter of months. I know practically nothing of Canada. I'm not really qualified to judge." That settled it, they dropped the subject. After a while, Dave Hillsborough trudged in.

"Worst skiing conditions I've ever seen," he announced. Alan and Marcel exchanged expressions of disbelief. Dave had been out there on the mountain since the moment they arrived, hadn't he?

"It took you all this time to figure that out?" Marcel said. "It took me five minutes. You are the one who is the expert, supposedly."

"Oh, I am, indubitably," Dave said. "One would have to be an expert, to ski amid all those rocks." The math teacher was never one to be modest about his skiing acumen. "How is your ankle, Marcel?"

"Painful, but I shall walk again," Marcel said, making Alan laugh.

The trio had a leisure dinner in a restaurant facing the ski run called Avalanche, which Dave allowed was the most treacherous at Mount Royale.

"Of course, Avalanche no longer offers me a true challenge," he said. He launched into a detailed description of all the ski runs, his chatter leaving the others bored. Alan had come to know Dave Hillsborough fairly well and was aware of his tendency to become wrapped up in himself. Often, Dave could be heard at school, relating, with no small self-congratulation, his latest triumph with his students. Alan was put off by this trait, initially, but had come to like Dave nonetheless, for Dave Hillsborough meant well. Indeed, this was the consensus; Dave had many friends. He was good-humored and sociable, and, while not witty himself, was one of those persons with a ready and infectious laughter, which made him fun to be around. Dave was loyal and dependable, fair with his students and his friends, and his dedication to teaching not only was inspirational, but had made him influential at Duval High. Yet, perhaps the best testimony to his appeal was a skiing trip with two pals who didn't much cotton to the sport.

The trio went their separate ways after dinner.

Dave visited a friend on the Ski Patrol, Marcel went to their room to doctor his ankle, and Alan tried some skirt-chasing, at which he had no success. Late that evening they re-grouped in their attic abode. It began to snow, and in thanks and celebration Dave opened a bottle of cognac he had brought along. Watching the snow out the single window, sipping brandy with friends in the warmth of their small but pleasant room, Alan again found himself thinking on his luck. The proximity of the Vermont line entered his mind, but he only shrugged.

"We have among us a new Canadian," Marcel said from the corner in which he was situated, or possibly stuck. He raised his glass. "Let us drink to him." They did, and Alan acknowledged the compliment. "How long does it take you to become a citizen?"

"It takes five years," Dave said.

"Right," Alan corroborated.

"Seems a long time," said Marcel.

"I agree," Alan said. "I don't know why it should take that long, and, considering how Canada wants for people; it doesn't seem very wise."

"He has Landed Immigrant status, now, Marcel," Dave said.

"What is that?"

"Just what it says, actually," Alan said. "I am an immigrant, and I have landed here. A kind of temporary citizenship, I suppose. They have something like this for Mexicans who live in the United States. I don't know what it's called."

"What did you have to do to get Landed Immigrant status?"

"There were some forms, but as far as I could see, it was all red tape. I had the status within a few days, as I recall. Week at the outside."

"It is a formality," Dave said. "For one such as yourself, that is. If you get my meaning."

"Oh, I get it," Alan said. "It's like an application for admission, say, to a private college in the South. They always ask for a photograph. I never knew why, and then one day someone told me. Then, it was so obvious, I couldn't see how I had failed to understand before."

"Odd, how often it is that that which is the most apparent is that which is most difficult to perceive," Marcel said.

"Man is a very strange creature," said Dave. "He obscures. Usually out of fear, I believe. Take religion. Every culture has had its god or gods. Religion and metaphysics have preoccupied philosophers and caused bloodshed in every age. Yet no human being who has ever lived or who will ever live can prove the existence of a single god. So, the greatest of all jokes may be on us. All that thinking, all that devotion, all that bloodshed, for nothing." Dave made a gesture heavenward, indicating futility. "Implicit in Darwin is that we should devote our energies to life here. The tangible. If there is a secret to the universe, the place to unlock it is here, not in the absurd fictions that mythology and religion are."

"You are what is known as an heretic, old chap," said Alan. "In Spain, they would have you at the cooking stake. Pun intended."

"Have you no thought of returning to America, if amnesty is granted?" Marcel inquired, wishing to change the subject.

"None," said Alan. "I am not of that land; I have no place there. Mine is a lost generation. I don't mind, really. After all, I'm not the first exile there ever was."

"Why did you come, exactly?" Marcel asked. "The specific complaint, I mean."

"It's painfully simple. I couldn't kill a Vietnamese."

"That is the only reason?" Marcel asked, surprised by Alan's answer.

"It has to be the only reason," Alan said. "No other reason exists."

"No other reason exists? Right offhand, I can think of several."

"Such as?"

"Not wanting to be in the Army, not being anti-Communist."

"That isn't very nice of you, Marcel," Alan said.

"You mistake me. I do not mean you, personally."

"You don't … oh, I see," Alan said, perceiving his error. "Sorry. What I was trying to say is that not being able to kill a Vietnamese is the only reason there is to oppose the war." But still Alan was not satisfied with his explanation.

"Tell me, then …"

"Excuse me, Marcel. I haven't made that clear. What I'm trying to say is, that Vietnam and any other war are categorically indefensible for the sole reason innocent people are dying. Period." Alan was satisfied he had it right.

"Tell me, then," said Marcel, "do you believe the end justifies the means?"

"No, never. That is just what I'm saying. Not if the world goes up in flames, which it won't, can Americans killing Vietnamese be justified."

"Vietnamese are killing Americans, too," Dave said.

"But Alan, that is what you have done, is it not?" Marcel said. "You have defied a law of your country in order to accomplish your end. Your end was to keep from having to kill a Vietnamese, and your means was to break the law."

"In the first place, Marcel, it is not my country," Alan said, wondering if Marcel was intent upon stirring anew their earlier trouble. "In the second place, my means was unlawful, insofar as it went against a highly questionable law. However, what I did hurt no one. In such a case, the end can be justified by the means. But how can you possibly justify the means when it involves hurting the innocent? Like killing millions of Vietnamese to make the world safe for democracy, or whatever?"

"Everything is connected, cause and effect," Marcel said. "Your leaving America hurt America."

"Not enough it didn't," Alan said, venting his bitterness.

"Okay, let me ask you this, then. What means might the Parti Quebecois employ, which you would defend, in order to achieve their ends?"

"Well, non-violence," Alan said after a brief interval. "Look, Marcel, I said before I don't know enough about it to talk about it."

"Yes," said Marcel. "So be it." Marcel didn't want to risk trouble any more than Alan, and, besides, he thought the subject exhausted.

"You know, Alan," said Dave, "you can be as critical as you want of the U.S., but what you're forgetting is that in any other country at almost any other time in history, if you had done what you have, you'd have been taken out back, stood up in front of the nearest wall, and shot. All right?"

"Your saying that doesn't make it so, Dave," Alan retorted.

"Fellows, enough," Marcel said, himself now playing peacemaker. "How about a game of chess, Hillsborough?"

"I pass."

"I don't play, sorry," Alan said. Even if he had, Alan felt chess, a game for two, would be thoughtless, and so did Dave. The conversation shifted to the snow, which was really coming down now, and before long they had drunk all the brandy and called it a night.

Alan spent election evening at the McCarran's. Believing Hubert Humphrey would win, Charles McCarran had staked Alan a nominal wager.

"Mark my words," said McCarran, "George Wallace will carry the South. That will finish Nixon."

"I doubt it," Alan said. "When I left, Wallace wasn't that strong. It's harder to tell from up here, but I don't believe he has picked up much more support. He'll carry Alabama, naturally, and Mississippi, and maybe Georgia and Louisiana. The Deep South, in other words. That won't be enough to derail Nixon."

"Well, you know far more than I, of such places," Charles McCarran said. Alan, in fact, thought McCarran unusually well-versed on the United States. "The Deep South is not the same as, say, Virginia?"

"Right. I don't know how great the difference is. I've never lived in the South. But there are differences. For example, take universities, of which I know something. Virginia has several with national reputations. North Carolina also. Mississippi hasn't any. Neither has Alabama. The Deep South is more reactionary politically and, I imagine, more racist, too."

"Wallace is of course a segregationist, is he not?"

"That would be understating it," Alan said.

"Have you taken any interest in Canadian politics, Alan?"

"Very little. I will sooner or later, I suppose, though the fact is, I can't even become a citizen for five years. I'm in a state of limbo. Also, I'm very averse to politics."

"The process should be expedited," Charles McCarran said. "Canada needs more people."

"Even so," Alan said, wishing to make his point, "I'll never feel the same about politics and politicians, again. They are by definition dishonest, I think. Infrequently, one comes along, like Gene McCarthy, who has integrity, and he gets nowhere. Absolutely nowhere. I had never heard of Gene until one day he, one lonely voice, arose to challenge President Johnson. That is unheard of, of course, a member of one's own party challenging the incumbent. Come to think of it, maybe that's why Gene got nowhere, for breaking one of their asinine rules." Alan paused, thinking. "That must be it. Hubert played the game, and therefore he got the nomination. Right? Anyhow, Gene undertook this hopeless task, because he was morally outraged by Johnson's war. It isn't good to be morally outraged in the States these days. People have no idea what it means. So Gene was ignored, or just plain despised. Nobody could find it within him to see his courage, much less listen to what he was saying." Alan was getting worked up. "Do you know why I am an expatriate, Charles? Because one man, Lyndon Johnson, decided to kill Vietnamese. That is the precise reason. There is no other. Do you think it has ever entered his head he is a murderer? Never. Johnson will retire to his ranch in the horsesh__ country and be honored until his death, then even more venerated." Alan was deeply frustrated. "Mustn't forget McNamara," he added.

"What experience has taught me," Charles McCarran began. He stopped to light himself a cigarette, and one for Alan, too. "What experience has taught me, Alan, is that you are right, in your appraisal of politicians. Most of them are crooked. Even your man McCarthy, I venture, if you don't mind my saying so. He must have pulled some strings to get as far as he did. Still, it seems to me our systems, with their faults, are the best around. You can't make a blanket condemnation. Somebody has to run for office. Somebody has to do the work."

"It's the man, not the system, I'm against."

"Well, perhaps so," Charles McCarran said, not wishing to argue the point. "You didn't let me finish what I was saying. The important thing is to put yourself first, always, always. That is the one great lesson of experience. This doesn't mean you must be selfish, necessarily, only prudent. The world is such a sham as it is, it is all one can do to manage it by looking out for himself, full-time. I believe I have told you about my experience as an apprentice architect, when I was nearly blacklisted."

"A couple of times," Alan said, not impolitely. "I can't go along with that, you know."

"Years of hard study would have gone for nothing," Charles McCarran said, even now feeling the catch at his throat in getting the words out. Realizing the uselessness of pursuing the matter with Alan, he changed the subject. Jeanne came in. She was in jeans at least one size too small, but she had the figure for this. Beneath her coat she wore a white blouse, which was tightly tucked in, and when she walked, she jiggled in such a way, Alan knew she was not wearing a brassiere.

"Hi, Alan," she said. "Who's winning the election?"

"What difference? You had just as well ask about the weather."

"Very well," she said, picking it up. "What's the forecast?"

"Dark clouds and the Republicans."

"You should be a poet, Alan."

"You're right."

"Nixon is winning at the moment," McCarran said, "but it is a long way from finished." Jeanne sat next to her father, across from Alan, and when she took a deep breath, he could see her nipples through her blouse.

"Well, Alan's convinced me McCarty was the only decent one in the bunch, so I don't care who wins," Jeanne said. The broadcaster informed that Nixon's lead had increased slightly.

81

"McCarthy, not McCarty," said Alan. "I wish I had had the chance to vote, just this once," he added wistfully. "I'd have voted for Gene. He made a big difference in my life."

"Another Coke, Alan?"

"Please." Charles McCarran exited to the kitchen, the thought that he had offered his daughter nothing not entering his head.

"McCarthy really meant a lot to you, didn't he, Alan?" Jeanne said, stressing the last syllable in the senator's name, so he would know this time she had it right.

"You know he did. I think I've talked about him nearly every time I've been here. You must be tired of listening, all of you."

"I never tire of listening to you," Jeanne said sweetly. Alan smiled, perhaps blushed slightly. She was inscrutable to him; he'd noted of late she was invariably present, when he was there, and she paid him elegant compliments. Alan no longer knew just what to make of her. "I have to go see Odette. Are you going to stay up late watching the returns, Alan?"

"Oh, I suppose. It is sort of interesting, in a perverse way."

"Then, if it's okay, I'll drop by your place, on my way home. Is it okay?" Alan wavered, caught off guard. She had not been with him there since that first incident, now sometime past. He wasn't sure he trusted her, or—it occurred to him—maybe now it was himself he wasn't so sure about. "See you later, then," she said in the void, scampering off before Alan could say a word.

Alan remained at the McCarran's two more hours, during which Richard Nixon's lead over Hubert Humphrey fluctuated, but never disappeared. It was sufficiently close, Alan did not insist on payment of his bet with Charles McCarran, only advised, facetiously, that remuneration must be made by not later than nine in the morning by special delivery, which made Charles McCarran laugh.

No sooner had Alan reached his apartment than John Walters came knocking. His expatriate friend, John felt as Alan did about the war, though John intended to return to America, if ever the opportunity came to do so lawfully. Stocky, oval-faced, bright-eyed though not handsome, John was a poorly-adjusted soul, his unhappiness in large part the product of a neurotic diffidence. He was intelligent, a summa cum laude at Baylor; Yale had offered him a scholarship. Common sense John possessed in rather less measure. Alan could not understand John's wish to return to the United

States, and, although he had not acknowledged this to himself, he held it against him.

"Tricky Dicky's won, huh, Alan?" John was disconsolate. He sipped from the single can of beer Alan knew he would drink.

"Dicky is prexy. Who cares?"

"I care. Humphrey is more likely to grant amnesty."

"That's true. Keep your spirits up, John. Ohio and Illinois are still out. If Hubert can carry them, he still might win."

"He's winning in Texas. I never would have believed it."

"Nor I. George presents the horsesh__ country's electorals to the Demos on a stained platter." John, who was from Abilene, was accustomed to Alan's designation of his state, and found it funny.

"The war will go on, whichever wins, I think," John said.

"Still some bamboo shacks to bomb."

"I don't see how there could be many left."

"It's odd to be so interested still in American politics," Alan said. "I've scarcely given Canada's as much as a perfunctory look. No sons-of-b like LBJ up here, I hope."

"You know, I think we tend to de-humanize our leaders whom we dislike. They're men, like us, after all."

"What is there to de-humanize in Johnson?"

"Come on, Alan. He's a human being. He made a mistake."

"Mistake? That goes beyond the outer limits of euphemism, John."

"Have it your way, then. I'm not saying I forgive him, either. Only trying to make the point he isn't infallible." Alan opened himself another beer, and the image of his old friend Jim Riley suddenly entered his head. Jim was the best beer-drinking buddy Alan had ever had. Jim hadn't responded to his letter. Didn't old friends realize how much that hurt?

"You shouldn't be so bitter," John said. "For one who has done so well up here, so quickly. Most of the guys have a hellish time. They don't have the luck of a mentor, like you."

"I'd like to get to know some of them," Alan said. "I'm writing an essay about our generation, and an important part will be the portrayal of the exile. If I am not typical, then I ought to find whoever is."

"Believe me, you're not. Neither am I. We're better educated, for one thing, although I would say many of the guys are either college grads or have some college. The ones I know, anyway. The biggest difference is that we have jobs."

"How are things at the center these days?" Before John could answer, there came a knock at the door. It was Jeanne McCarran.

"Hi, Alan," she said. Her eyes were glassy, something he had noticed on at least one previous occasion, and her blouse wasn't buttoned right. But she was steady on her feet, and sure of her words.

"Your blouse is buttoned wrong," Alan said in a low voice.

"You fix it," she whispered back, kissing him lightly on the cheek and sweeping right past both of them into the bathroom.

"Whoosh. Whoever that was, I don't think she even saw me," John said.

"Haven't you met her?"

"No."

"Her name's Jeanne. She's my mentor's, as you call him, daughter."

"Is she your girlfriend?" John asked.

"No." The election returns came on, and it began to look as though Humphrey would not catch up. John's heart sank. Alan offered another beer, but John declined. Five minutes passed, and still Jeanne had not reappeared. Apprehensive, Alan thought he had best investigate. He knocked on the bathroom door, and, getting no answer, opened it. She was sitting calmly on the edge of the bath. Alan went on in, and Jeanne kicked the door shut behind him.

"Who is he?" she demanded.

"A friend of mine," Alan said with disbelief. "What on earth are you doing sitting in here like this?"

"I have been waiting for you to come in and tell me who that is," she said. Alan thought the remark made no sense whatever.

"Well, come on out, for God's sake, and I'll introduce you."

"Get rid of him, please," Jeanne demanded, just as Alan opened the door; he could only hope that John had not heard her.

"Jeanne McCarran, John Walters," Alan said.

"Hi, John," Jeanne said, extending her hand for a brief, unsatisfactory shake. Alan sat on the sofa-bed, and Jeanne sat practically on top of him, giving John the impression she desired. Alan rose.

"He doesn't like me very much, John, as you can see," Jeanne said.

"He doesn't like anyone very much," Alan grumbled.

"May I have some of whatever there is?" Jeanne asked. Alan did not think she needed a beer, but he retrieved one for her, thinking she would drink very little, in any case. "Alan came to Canada from the States, John. He says he came because of Vietnam, but actually it was for sex. We Canadian girls are all they say, right, Mr. Young?"

"Wrong." Alan frowned at her.

"Who is the new president of the great U.S. of A?" Jeanne said.

"Nixon, it looks like," said John.

"I don't care," Jeanne said. "Alan's convinced me McCarty was the only decent one, and he got left in the cold."

"McCarthy," said Alan.

"What do you do, John?" Jeanne inquired.

"I work at the U.S. Refugee Center, here. I'm an expatriate, too."

"Really? I'll bet that's how you two met."

"Yes. As a matter of fact, Alan's one of my closest, expatriate friends." The fact was, Alan was one of only two.

"Which state are you from?"

"Texas."

"Wow!" Jeanne exclaimed. "Where's your horse, John?"

"Don't have one," said John.

"Texas big, John?"

"It is quite large, actually."

"Oh, Texans don't really brag, like everybody says, do they?"

"It's nearly a thousand miles from El Paso to Orange, Texas, on the Louisiana line," John said gravely, plainly pleased that his state's reputation had reached at least to a Canadian girl in Quebec. "That's farther than from New York to Chicago."

"That is truly impressive," Alan cracked.

"What do you do at the refugee place, John?" Jeanne asked.

"Help advise the guys just arrived," said John. "It's sort of an undefined job, I guess you'd say. Not all that professional an organization, I guess I'd have to admit. There's three of us, plus two guys who help out sometimes, but unpaid. The head guy is a lawyer, named Paul Kelly. In truth, almost all the exiles go to Toronto."

"Who is Kelly, anyway, John?" Alan asked.

"All I know is, he was with a law firm in Boston, and he decided to come up here and help the exiles. He's strongly against the war. I don't know much about him, though, he's a remote sort. I know the other guys at the center better. Kelly knows the situation up here pretty well, and he has knowledge of Canadian law, which obviously is important. He's good at keeping morale high, among us."

"So he's the boss," Jeanne said. "What do you do, again?"

"Like I said, I advise, mostly. My major at Baylor University was philosophy. The only thing you can do with a philosophy major is teach. I'm in school at the moment. I'm a long way from teaching, though. Actually, I'm going back to the U.S., if I can, someday. Lawfully, that is. That's why I'm for Humphrey, since he might grant amnesty. No chance Nixon will."

"But what kind of advice, John, do you give?" Jeanne said, stubbornly pursuing her line of inquiry.

"Oh, you know, things like housing, jobs, that sort of stuff. Frankly, on paper I guess you would say we don't do very much. We can't. If there are no jobs, there are no jobs. We do provide emotional support. This can't be measured, but that doesn't mean it has no value. I was just telling Alan that most of the guys who come up here are not half as lucky as him. They drift, completely cut off from everything they have ever known. They're unemployed, undirected. Sometimes they end up in trouble with the police. It's bad. Well, we're there, to help if we can. The center is a place to congregate and be with others like yourself."

"Do you provide meals, or beds, or something?" Jeanne asked.

"No, we haven't the budget for that," John said, "but we do direct the guys to places like the Salvation Army, where they can get a good meal."

"Well, that makes sense, doesn't it?" Jeanne said, not sounding particularly persuaded herself.

"I'd say so," John said.

"Although I don't see how having a cot or two could cost very much," Jeanne said.

"Suppose not," John said, "but the office is pretty small, there's no place for a cot."

"Must be small, all right," Jeanne said. "Cots don't take up much room."

"No, there's no place for a cot, really," John insisted. "Wouldn't you agree, Alan?"

"I would, yes," Alan said, thinking the conversation aimless and perfectly inane.

"What must a girl do around here to get noticed?" said Jeanne. "Take her clothes off?"

Alan gave her a reproachful glance, to which she countered with an expression that clearly said, "I'm only kidding."

Feeling he was in the way, John rose to leave.

"You're drinking my beer, Alan!" Jeanne exclaimed.

"That's true," Alan said, his opinion she didn't require it evident in his tone.

"Look, Alan, I don't need a lecture."

"I have to go," John insisted, now feeling very much in the way.

"No, don't go, John," Jeanne said. "Alan and I aren't going to fight, and you're not intruding. I've been shooting 'speed', and now Alan's playing daddy." Neither to Alan nor John did she sound as if she and Alan were not headed for an encounter. What Alan had come to suspect—that she was using drugs—Jeanne had confirmed with one hasty remark.

"It's not that I think I'm intruding," John stammered. "I just have to go, that's all."

"Well, any friend of Alan's is a friend of mine," Jeanne said, extending a hand for John to shake. He did so.

"I'll call you later in the week, John," Alan said, seeing him out the door. Alan turned to face Jeanne, who was prepared for his ire. "What's the idea, Jeanne? Is there something about this apartment? What about the 'speed'? I have suspected …"

"G_damn you, I want you so bad I ache, and all you want to talk about is draft dodgers and presidents and now, what I do with myself. Would you just leave me alone?" Jeanne crossed her arms in a huff.

"I don't think you're being fair, Jeanne." Alan remained calm, thinking how very attractive she was sometimes, how trying on other occasions.

"I apologize," she said, meaning it. "Do I owe John an apology, too?"

"Will you tell me about the 'speed'?"

"Honestly, Alan, it's none of your business."

"Tell me just the same."

"You're worried I'm screwing myself up?"

"Yes."

"I appreciate that, but I'm a big girl now. I can take care of myself."

"I know that, too," Alan said wearily, recognizing the futility of pursuing the matter.

"It's good you drank my beer, Alan. I don't even like the stuff. I'm sorry for making that scene in front of your friend."

"Forget it. John's a loner. He'll take any friends he can get. Even kooks like us."

"You're more of a kook than me, I think," Jeanne said sweetly. She gazed at Alan and smiled. "But you're such a nice kook. Has it occurred to you I like you very much, Alan?" It had begun to, in fact.

"I like you, too," Alan said, hardly realizing he meant it. Jeanne wished desperately that Alan would ask her to stay the night, but she was certain he would not. Rather than risk another argument, she thought now a propitious time to depart. Alan accompanied her to her car, and there they exchanged "goodnights" and parted.

One evening, Marcel and Alan went out on the town. Marcel had boasted of his ability to hold his beer, but Alan doubted his French-Canadian friend was a match for his old chum Jim Riley, in this department. They met at Alan's apartment and soon exhausted his supply. Alan said that wouldn't do, to which Marcel suggested they go to a bar he liked downtown. They drove to a seedy district, an area of gaudy neon, raucous, dirty bars and flophouses. On a tiny stage, a girl in panties and bra was jerking to the sounds of a jukebox and trying not to appear apologetic. As on each Friday night, the place was crammed with men ranging in age from eighteen to eighty, all huddled furtively in their whispering groups around the tables. It was extremely dark, and Alan, not knowing his way around, stumbled on someone spread out on the floor.

"There is a man lying on the floor over there," he thought it wise to inform the shapely girl who was leading them to their seats. Her brassiere hid little. Alan estimated she could not be a day over sixteen.

"He's asleep. That's where they sleep."

"Oh." Alan felt a bit stupid.

"What do you want to drink?" Alan chose a double martini; Marcel, a pair of beers. They stared at the gyrating dancer, but this soon produced ennui, for she was neither physically appealing, nor able to dance erotically.

"Gads, what a lousy dancer," Alan said.

"They should get her off stage and put our waitress up there."

"Agreed."

"Why doesn't she take it off?" Marcel said of the dancer. "It is the only thing that might save her."

"On the contrary, it's keeping it on that's saving her."

"How do you reach that conclusion?"

"Heard melodies are sweet, but those unheard are sweeter."

"Come again?"

"I thought you said you know a prostitute here, Marcel. There are no prostitutes here. Just miserable men, and that ridiculous dancer."

"The prostitute I know works at another place. We shall go there next." Next was preceded by two more rounds apiece; Alan, returning to beer, poured it down like water.

"Beer and boobs, I'd say," Alan said, now drunk. "Both of which that waitress of ours keeps jabbing in my face. One of these times I'm going to take her up on it. The little flirt. Any girl can look delicious in a bra like that. A fourth of a bra, that is." Marcel, who seemed none the worse for wear, suggested they move on to Bozo's. They drove what amounted to walking distance to an anonymous hotel whose bar was called Bozo's. In his condition, Alan could not make out the sense in that, and he was having some difficulty in holding his head up. Bozo's was even darker inside than the other bar, and it had a piquant odor about it, as well. Girls in various stages of undress were scattered everywhere. Nona spotted Marcel almost at once, and, as she was unattended, she came right over. She kissed him as though he were her lover returned after a long absence and whispered something into his ear.

"I taught her French," Marcel said. "She can say 'hello' and 'more money', and she knows all the dirty words."

"An eclectic choice, Marcel," Alan sputtered. He couldn't make her out very well in the darkness, and his head was spinning besides, but from what he could tell, Nona was good-looking. It was her lips that caught his eye; they were smeared with lipstick, yet Alan could tell they required no embellishment. Such was their allure, a wild desire to kiss her gripped Alan, and, had not another girl appeared to attend to him, he would have. Alan brushed her off.

"If we sit at a table, you must at least buy her a drink, Alan," Marcel observed, and Alan thought the remark a strange one, since they were seated at a table.

"What's the idea of disappearing for so long, Marcel?" Nona pouted. "Are you two-timing me?" Alan could not keep from laughing at this remark. "Who's the clown, Marcel?" she said in a sarcastic reference to Alan.

"Why, I'm Bozo, sweetheart," Alan answered, "and you're fired." Now, it was Marcel who laughed, rather loudly, and the prostitute, miffed, elected simply to ignore Alan entirely. This suited him. It was alcohol he was interested in. Alan drank on in silence, watching Marcel, whom he thought treated Nona as though she were his quarry. A random passerby —another customer— received Alan's order for a refill, prompting Marcel discreetly to ask Nona to get Alan another drink.

"I hope you do not mind being here, Alan," Marcel said. "She is a fine girl, really. You are not looking too well, actually. Maybe you should stop. Would you mind if we left you for a short while?" Alan thought he perceived a jumble of unrelated sentences.

"Not at all, Marcel." The portent of nausea swept over him. Alan wished Marcel would get on with it. The pair disappeared, and Alan, abruptly certain he was to be ill, and soon, rose to go to the toilet. But in his exigency, and in so hopeless a state, he found quite impossible clearing the obstacle seated beside him, the faceless prostitute who had been his undesired companion from the start. He heaved all over her.

"You b_____!" she screamed, attempting to free herself from beneath him. In response, Alan vomited again, this time copiously. "God!" shrieked the girl, still trapped. "Somebody help!" Alan muttered an unintelligible apology as yet another spasm shook him, and the desperate girl, succeeding in shoving his inert bulk to the floor, managed what had become a truly pointless escape.

It was almost three the next afternoon before Alan stirred from his bathroom floor sprawl. Though he was shaky and pale, the worst was past. He even chuckled on recalling Marcel's observation on their way home, that he had thrown up on half of Montreal, and his own grim quip in return, "Only half?" The phone rang, and, after an exchange of "hellos" with Jeanne, Alan dropped the receiver, so uncertain were his hands. On discovering his condition, Jeanne insisted he permit her to come over. He refused, saying he would be all right, but her insistence won. She came at five, at which time he was feeling no better, though no worse, and fixed him soup and tea, which she had brought, as he possessed neither. He was thankful Marcel and he had finished his supply of beer, for the mere thought of it in his refrigerator made him queasy. Jeanne stayed for two hours, caring for him as a devoted wife might, without a hint of *quid pro quo*. So gentle was she, Alan was reminded of the good days with Jane Harsfield. Jeanne left at seven, but not before Alan had asked her for a date.

Word came that week, the last in November, from both McGill and Sir George Williams universities. Two rejections. As always, the notes were exceedingly courteous. "We regret we must reject your application for admission. It is impossible to accept every qualified applicant. Thank you for your expression of interest. Best wishes in whatever you undertake." Alan was crestfallen. His grades were good. He had felt sure he would be accepted at Sir George Williams. Hadn't John said as much? Now what was he to do? He had mapped his future, and now a new plan had to be forged. He could not go on substituting indefinitely. Well, there were other universities in Canada, he considered, although at this late date it would be impossible to get into one by spring. But the truth was, Alan had never been greatly enthused by the idea of teaching in college. He was not unhappy at Duval High. In fact, he was rather enjoying himself. Alan remembered Dave Hillsborough's words, that the real reward in teaching, communication with the student, was denied the substitute teacher. That, Alan had agreed, was true. Full-time teaching was the only way to go. Thus Alan, who had long looked condescendingly upon high school teaching, began seriously to consider making a career of doing just that. His first resolution was to speak with his friends on the Duval faculty, Dave, Marcel and Margaret.

Margaret Page was thirty, divorced and tall; she stood at five feet ten barefoot, a circumstance which uncharacteristically caused her some chagrin. Alan did not mind her height and told her it was of no consequence. Margaret was attractive, though not beautiful. She had pretty brown eyes and brown hair, what there was of it, and thin cheeks which tapered into a chin that protruded just slightly. Her bosom was large, and her back long, as were her legs, which were well-shaped, although her calf muscles were clearly visible when she walked. Margaret and Alan had a purely sexual relationship. They shared a mutual respect, both acknowledging theirs was a strictly temporary arrangement, a fill-in until something better came along. Alan had made a point of bringing this out into the open early on, to Margaret's dismay at the time, though she had come to appreciate it. Whether, however, it was the honesty of their relationship, or the fact it would not last, which most contributed to its success, was impossible to say.

Margaret Page was not stupid. She had found the profit in adversity and was determined not to repeat her mistakes. Her speech had a way of inspiring confidence, and Alan, while not convinced she was as sensible as she proposed, had nonetheless made her his closest confidant in Canada, Charles McCarran excepted.

He had asked her for dinner the same night, and she, after feigning irritation, accepted cheerfully. As it was a bitterly cold night, Margaret wore her heaviest black suit, which Alan said would be ideal for a funeral, beneath a heavy coat. High heels Margaret never, never wore, for she regarded them as an obscenity. Prodigality found expression in her use of lipstick; she insisted she wore so much because she liked lots of lipstick, and, while Alan admired that kind of reasoning, he disliked so much lipstick. Her hair Margaret wore short and flat, which Alan thought made her look boyish, at least from the neck up. She would have it no other way. Long hair was a terrific nuisance, she said. Once, he had suggested she might not appear as tall with longer hair, but the hair remained short. In truth, Margaret was dreadfully lazy. She might sooner find another husband with a little more effort, but she was unwilling to make it. She rarely knocked herself out in her teaching, either, doing what she knew was enough to get by, and no more. Competent though she was in the classroom, her refusal to go the extra step precluded her entry into the ranks of the most admired and best loved among the Duval High faculty. Margaret could not care less.

"A nightcap and then away you go, Alan, dear," she announced when they reached her apartment. "You can't have everything after such short notice." Alan reclined on the couch, kicked his shoes off and lighted himself a cigarette.

"Anything you say," he said. "Would you like a cigarette?"

"No. A gin and T for you?"

"A Margarita, please."

"That's what you think," she laughed.

"Indeed it is."

"Rather sure of yourself, aren't you?"

"It is the only way to be."

"Do you want a gin and T?"

"I'd like a nice glass of egg nog, I think. I'll have the Margarita for dessert."

"The Margarita is the main course, or nothing at all."

"So be it, Cleopatra. You've a nicer ass than any asp.' He went over and kissed her and slipped his arm around her waist.

"You've a thing about my rear, you know. A thing."

"I know. I can't get my mind off it." Alan patted her buttocks. "Too bad I'm not a Velasquez."

"I assume you are referring to the Naked Maja. Goya painted that."

"No, that's a frontal view, I'm sure of it. Goya had no eye for tail, and Vinny cut off his ear. Let's forget the nightcap, madcap," he whispered into her ear, his tongue pursuing the sound. She swooned and returned his kisses, kissing his lips and cheeks and eyes and nose. He fumbled with the buttons of her suit, finally letting her do the lion's share. From there they stripped themselves and got into bed.

"You are the silliest person I have ever known," Margaret said.

"Roll over on your stomach, for a change." She obliged. He entered her and they came to a quick climax, then a slower, better one, before saying another word. Alan rose, located himself a cigarette, assumed the lotus position at the foot of the bed, tickled the soles of her feet with the cigarette before permitting it to assume its proper function, and launched into his planned discussion about Duval High.

"I have a surprise for you, Margaret," he said. "I'm thinking of full-time teaching at Duval."

"Full-time? I thought you were going to go to graduate school."

"They turned me down." Alan couldn't help feeling a little ashamed in admitting it.

"They turned you down?" Margaret was annoyed with herself for having failed to see that coming. "I'm awfully sorry, Alan. I can't see why they would turn you down."

"I can't either, but it's academic, now. They did, and that's that. I'm serious about Duval."

"I think it's a terrific idea. Duval isn't a bad place, all things considered. I think you would like it. Full-time teaching, that is. It is much more satisfying than substituting. You'll feel more like you're part of the school. You'll be able to become better acquainted with the students. Substitutes really don't even have their own students, have they? The pay is better, by a good deal. In every way, it's better." Her genuine interest touched him, but Margaret was saying nothing Alan hadn't already considered himself.

"What I want to know, though," he said, "is how I should go about obtaining a position on the faculty. From where I am, I can't just walk in and say, 'Here I am.'" Margaret laughed. "To get on full-time by spring is impossible, I'm certain," Alan continued, "but I don't mind substituting another term. It's just that I wonder whether I have a chance of getting on, full-time, by next fall. There's almost surely a waiting list. Besides, I doubt I'm fully qualified."

"How did you get the job you have now, then?" it occurred to Margaret to ask.

"A friend," Alan said hesitantly, unprepared for the question. That, he thought, must do.

"Well," she said, wondering whom he knew, "if your friend could do it once, can't he do it again? You might even make it by spring. Duval requires a degree, which you have, and education credits, which I think you told me you have, and certification, which is no big problem, and, gradually, it's coming to require a Master's. I mean, that's the direction of things. That day is still a long way off." Alan recalled Dave Hillsborough's having said the same thing. Alan had, in fact, considered going to Charles McCarran, but was loathe to do this. He wanted things square this time. "Then there are other high schools, as well," Margaret continued, thinking perhaps Alan did not want to talk about his unnamed friend. "There's junior high, too. If you can't get on at Duval."

"Oh, I'd hate to leave Duval," Alan said. "I've made friends there."

"You'd make friends elsewhere, you know."

"Yes, I know that, but I might lose the ones I've got." Alan leaned over and kissed her. "I don't know the system. Is Duval hiring? Or are there any potential vacancies?"

"You mean, is anyone about to get fired?"

"No, I mean retire. Or get fired, sure." Margaret sat pensive for a moment. She knew Marcel Pirmont was perilously close to losing his job, but they had dated, their unhappy finish notwithstanding. "There's McDougall."

"Who?"

"Kenneth McDougall. He teaches physics. He has not one but two Master's degrees. Quitting to take a position in Toronto. Leaving in June."

"How does that help? I don't know how to teach high school physics, or any physics, for that matter."

"It doesn't help, but it did answer your question."

"You are impossible," he said, laughing. "Good company, but a lousy adviser."

"Good company? That must be a euphemism."

94

"Whatever for?"

"You fraud."

"I thought I was the silliest person you've ever known."

"That, too. A silly fraud."

"A fraudulent silly, you mean, my broad Philly. Oh, that's poor. How about Fraulein Sally?" Alan shook his head. "Worse." He paused to think. "Succulent dilly. That's it. But now I've forgotten what it is."

"I'm sure we all have," Margaret sighed. She got out of bed and went to the refrigerator.

"Believe it or not, I feel like a glass of milk. Would you like some milk, Alan?"

"Whatever is that?"

"Premature egg nog, exceedingly warmable."

"Milk makes me violently ill, I'm afraid," he said.

"Your childhood must have been hell."

"It was," he laughed. "Still is."

"You are an unusual person, Alan. Sometimes I feel I hardly know you. I think you are complex and unsettled."

"Are those related?"

"For you, they are. They both characterize you."

"Complex and unsettled. Is that good?"

"Well, it's better to be settled than unsettled, I think, but I'm not being critical, only observing. A wise person once told me a young man cannot make a serious mistake before he is 35, and I believed him. I still think it's true. So being unsettled at the moment isn't a bad thing."

"A young man cannot make a serious mistake before he's 35? That doesn't strike me as the truth."

"The idea is that when you are a young man, the world is yours. Naturally you make mistakes, but as long as you are young, you can get around them. That's the essence of the thought."

"I'll remain a skeptic," Alan said, far from convinced, for he had a vague and disquieting notion he had already made some profound and irreversible mistakes.

"Okay," Margaret laughed. "Would you like to stay the night?"

"I thought you'd never ask." Alan kissed her and thought maybe she was the best friend he had in Canada. She fell asleep soon after intercourse, but Alan, restless over the problem of securing a full-time faculty slot at Duval High, stayed awake for some time. As he lay there, Margaret sleeping peacefully, her back to him, he began also to think about Jeanne McCarran. It struck him how much more frequently he was thinking of her than before, and what a contrast there was in his feelings for her and those he had for Margaret Page. He found he was eagerly looking forward to Friday evening with Jeanne, and he wondered if he was not falling in love with her.

Come Friday, Alan still had not made up his mind what to do about getting the proposed Duval job. He taught that day, reflecting all day long on the ills of substitute teaching. He saw the same faces often enough, but the nature of substitution made intimacy with the student impossible; students did not take the substitute seriously. It was the same back at West Los Angeles High, he remembered. Substitutes were exploited. On reaching home that afternoon, Alan resolved to see someone in the public school offices the next morning. In his mailbox was a letter from Stefan.

Santa Barbara
Dec. 9, 1968

Dear Alan,

You sly dog. I was to be your best man. Now you've off and done it, and I'll never be your best man. You'll be lucky if I send you a fork. OK, I'll be serious. The way you talk about Jeanne, it sounds as if I may not be far off the mark. They say short romances are best, however. Are you Cupid-struck?

School marches on. Bear is unquestionably a subversive. Every day he has a new plan for overthrowing Nixon and making McCarthy president. He swears he has a letter written to you, incidentally. The new humanities building is finished, at last. Most of my classes are in it. Modern, but like everything else these days, it lacks personality. The old science building reeks of formaldehyde (as you know), but those grand old hardwood floors give it personality. Kind of an indefinable thing, personality. There's more long hair, here on campus, than ever. Looks like Nixon's election won't change that. The big war moratorium in S.F. on the fifteenth was called a success. Can't see how they figure that, since the war continues.

I hope I'm not betraying a trust. I received a letter from your folks, asking me for my perspective on your existence up there. I was very surprised to get such a letter. Anyway, I wrote back and said I thought you were getting along very well and not to worry. I didn't say I thought they'd fret even if you became Prime Minister, or President, or whatever it is. The letter (theirs) wasn't easy to handle. I hope what I said satisfied them. Don't tell them I told you, Alan Canada.

That girl you knew here last year. Remember her? (Jane.) I ran into her the other day, and she asked about you. She mentioned she got a letter from you way back in the fall, and she said you had sounded unhappy. In an exceedingly perfunctory way she asked me for your address, and I obliged. I think you can count on not hearing from her. Anyway, you being hitched now, what difference? (Happy Honeymoon!)

I'm making application several places for law school, but the school I want to go to is Minnesota. I'd like to take my degree there, practice for a few years in the Twin Cities and ultimately go into politics there. The Democratic Farm-Labor Party is dominant in the state, and progressive. My parents are excited by the thought of my returning home and have promised to help, if I can't get a scholarship or loan. The "shabby system," as you described it a couple of letters ago, will never be changed by moratoriums and marching in the streets and anarchy. I agree that it's shabby, but I think reform must come from working by the rules. Sen. Kopinski at your service.

Can't think of anything else at the moment. Have a good holiday with your folks over Christmas, but don't forget to keep a tight lip about their letter. Did Shakespeare ever use that phrase?
Stef

Alan found this letter more perplexing than anything else. He thought Stefan was obliquely criticizing him. Stef? Alan couldn't believe it. All the facetiousness about his having married puzzled Alan; he racked his brain trying to remember what he had said in his last letter, in vain. He resolved to make a copy of letters thereafter, or perhaps discard the old policy of never re-reading. His friend's decision to go into politics irked Alan, for such was his contempt for that realm, it annoyed him his best friend would want such a thing.

It began to rain. Being from Los Angeles, Alan was unaccustomed to rain, and he did not like it. It depressed him. He took a long, hot bath, mulling over Stefan's letter, and, at eight, arrived at the McCarran's.

The McCarrans were out, and Jeanne wasn't ready, so Alan's host for the moment was Rickie. As usual, Rickie wanted to talk football. Weren't the Alouettes having a miserable season? Alan scarcely knew who the Alouettes were. He had not attended a football-minded college and had never cared much for the sport.

Jeanne finally appeared, some ten minutes overdue. In her Navy blue suit, with her muskrat fur and white scarf, she was lovely.

"Your little brother has footballs on the brain," Alan told her, once out the door. "This is a rare malady, heretofore believed confined to the wasteland south of here, but it seems the disease has moved north. He's driving me crazy, if you want to know the long and short of it."

"When you were fifteen, you weren't driving anyone crazy?"

"Only myself." They went to the nightclub at the posh Duquesne, where a highly-touted comedy team of three had been appearing for some time. As things turned out, their humor relied almost entirely upon the bedroom and the bathroom. Alan was unamused, for the show seemed tasteless to him. Raucous laughter persisted throughout, though, and the applause at the conclusion was long and loud. Once it had died down, Alan sought to apologize. He was interrupted by a nearby, inebriated patron, who was shouting "encore" at the very top of his lungs. The man was rapidly removed, with what discretion circumstances allowed.

"That," Alan said, "is the first genuinely funny thing that has happened here tonight. They have a simply vulgar show, which everyone enjoys, then worry about appearances and etiquette when some drunk starts shouting a perfectly innocent French word."

"You need not feel bad about it, honey," Jeanne said. "Who would have believed the Duquesne would have a show like that? It makes no difference to me. Being with you is enough."

"Another drink?" Alan asked, thinking about the term of affection she had used.

"They're terribly expensive," Jeanne said. Dinner had not exactly been a bargain-hunter's dream either, Alan thought. "I'll have another, if you want one." Jeanne did not want more alcohol. She was not a drinker, having found other means of intoxication more to her liking.

"Too expensive is right. Let's skip it. This lascivious joint doesn't deserve my support."

"I'd like to talk with you, off by ourselves somewhere," Jeanne said. "Why don't we go for a ride."

"I'm for it." Once in the car, however, they lapsed into small talk. Alan could see that she was procrastinating. He felt he knew what was on her mind and admitted to himself he was eager for her to get to it.

"Will you behave yourself if we stop at my place?" he asked. They were in the neighborhood.

"Of course," she said, not liking his remark in the least. Once inside his apartment, she declined alcohol. "Why do you enjoy hurting me, Alan?" Jeanne sat on the sofa-bed and tucked her feet beneath her.

"Hurting you?" Alan was taken aback. "I wouldn't hurt you."

"You do all the time. Or don't you see?" He didn't. "You ask me over when you're sick, you ask me out, you bring me here, but you never act interested when we are together." Alan considered he had not asked her over the day he was sick, that she had practically barged in. "I want you, Alan. You know that as well as you know your name. I'm falling in love with you, or maybe I have been from the start. I thought it was just sex, but it isn't." From across the room, Alan looked intently at her, biting his lower lip. He didn't know what to make of it. He had anticipated she would say just what she had, he wanted her to say it, had all but prayed she would. But he was unsure of his own feelings. "May I have a cigarette?" she asked.

"I don't know what to say," Alan faltered, extending the pack of cigarettes. He could not think where to go from there.

"It isn't so serious, Alan," she said sweetly. "Your mother hasn't died. Somebody wants you, that's all."

"I understand that, Jeanne." It occurred to him the right response would sooner come in ten seconds than ten minutes. "You're the first girl who has ever said what you did, to me. Love is such a complex thing. I knew a girl back in college, and we were very close, but I never could quite decide if it was love." Alan hesitated. He was irritated with himself. He had always thought of himself as articulate, and now he was stammering. "What makes you think you love me?" he thought to ask, thinking it an intelligent remark.

"You are unlike any of the other fellows I know," Jeanne said. "You are the first guy I have ever known who I couldn't get to go to bed with me. It's still beyond me. You are also the first guy I've found myself thinking about constantly. I like being with you, always. I like it very much. Surely, if nothing else, that shows?"

"Well, yes, but all that isn't necessarily love. It might be that you find me some sort of novelty and challenge."

"It isn't that you're different that appeals to me. It's what is different. You bring new ideas to my head. You always seem right to me, somehow—or nearly always, anyhow. As for the challenge, I admitted already about the sex thing, but that's over. Okay?" Jeanne could hardly be more gentle and patient. Her mind was clear, she knew exactly what she wanted to say. Alan did not.

"You know I enjoy being with you too, Jeanne, but I don't think that is the same thing as love."

"I never said it was. Is that what you make of all I have said?"

"No, of course not. I didn't mean to have implied that. I only feel that love demands caution and ... well, caution. Impetuosity would be a mistake."

"Yes, it would. I am not being impetuous." Jeanne did not think Alan was making good sense, and she disliked what he had said. She thought there was no place to go with their conversation, and suddenly she was ready to go home. "I'm rather tired," she added, and, try though she had, she failed to conceal her displeasure with him.

"I don't mean to annoy you, Jeanne." Couldn't she see he would declare himself, if he could? It would make everything so placid and pleasant and happy, he thought. But he could not do it. At her doorstep, he kissed her lightly on the cheek, and their evening was over.

The next morning, Alan went to the administrative offices of the Montreal Public Schools. Closed. What ever happened to working on Saturday? he wondered. Although very cold, it was bright out; Alan decided to take a walk around downtown. Soon it became evident it was too chilly, and he entered a café. Armed with Stefan's last letter, as well as some stationery, Alan, over three cups of coffee, composed a reply.

Dear Stef,

Oh, the bliss of matrimony. Yes, Jeanne and I severed the Gordion by tying the knot. How did you guess? I of course had intended for you to be best man, since that is the best capacity a best friend can fill for a brotherless bridegroom. Balderdash! Whence the gobbledygook?

I'd have you truly preoccupied if I had just been able to procure a fake invitation, but that, the lady said, "isn't done." Humorless old biddy. Sweet sixty and a virgin and taking it out on everyone.

You say Bear is a subversive. How do you figure that to be news? I'll tell you what's news. He hasn't learned to write. I've given up on him (and it hurts).

Jane was her name, and you are right in that I being hitched now, she is of no great importance. As for my parents, I don't think you betrayed a trust. They will worry about me from now on.

Anyway, I am closer to you than I am to them. I wonder if they realize that? They must have an inkling, having written to you. They are flying in day after tomorrow.

I dismissed Jane too quickly. You know, Stef, she and I were very close for a few months, in there somewhere. She was eager to be with me, and I with her. You remember. Then, all of a sudden, it went to pieces. Not gradually. She just turned ice cold. I think her father may have had a hand in it. I met him twice, which was not enough to learn much about him, but Jane hinted he held against me my lack of direction. Maybe he gave her an ultimatum. Still, she liked me. It's hard to see her turning so cold in deference to her father's fatuity.

I'm re-hashing this because I want to be serious about Jeanne McCarran. (Never mind the usual first paragraph nonsense.) She's in love with me, and I think maybe I am with her. We went out last night, and I knew she was going to say, "I love you" (she did), and if she had not, I would be miserable. Now, trying to be objective (I can't dismiss all the animosity running in my veins for Jane), I feel closer to Jeanne, I think, than I ever did to Jane. (Do you suppose the similarity in their names means something? Naw.) It is a difficult thing to write about. I liked being with Jane, I didn't want our relationship to end, but I never felt moved to verbal intimacy, and neither did she. With Jeanne, I am steadily feeling otherwise. With Mom and Dad coming, I'll be out of town for several days. (I want to get away. We're going to Quebec City or Vancouver.) This will give me some time to think about things. What do you think? Whew! A difficult topic, that one.

About law school. What can one (you), or even a handful, of senators who have integrity do against the madding crowd? I don't mean to discourage you, it just seems so uphill to me. Sisyphus should have had it so bad. I'm glad you have at least picked your home state. (At last, I see the good in Minnesota—besides Gene, that is.) All that remains is for me to move to Winnipeg, and we'll practically be walking distance.

Windsor is so perfectly halfway between St. Paul and Montreal. I wish we were getting together over the holidays. Patience, they say, is a virtue. Maybe so, but trying.

Alan Canada

Among all, Alan's humor was best appreciated by himself. Writing to Stefan, in particular after receiving a letter he felt was not quite right, was a catharsis. His thoughts were always clearer, once written. This done, he could quit thinking about Jeanne McCarran for a while, forget what problems he anticipated his parents would bring, and turn his attention to the burden which most weighed him down. Alan now admitted to himself, aloud, he was glad the public school offices had been closed. He knew that, even if perchance he had the prerequisites for a full-time teaching position, there was doubtless a waiting list. Possibly, too, the schools would not hire an American exile, full-time, although this had not been a bar to substitute teaching. Alan reasoned it wasn't his fault the graduate schools had rejected him, for his grades were good, and he was competent to do the work. They had wrecked his plan in one fell swoop. It was up to him now to make his own breaks. Full-time high school teaching would be both rewarding and fun, he had decided, and the thing to do now was to go to Charles McCarran. Alan knew how much Charles liked him, and he knew Charles would be pleased that he was seeing Jeanne. Perhaps, Alan reflected, he was in love with her. Maybe they would marry. That would please Charles immeasurably, no doubt. Going to Charles, it was clear to Alan, was the only intelligent course.

Before Alan had the chance to speak with Charles McCarran, his parents arrived, and for the next eight days, he was wholly occupied with them. Once having gotten a good look at the condition of his life in Montreal, both were more than willing to do whatever their son wished. He said he wanted to leave town. Marcel Pirmont had told him Quebec City was very French, and it was near. Vancouver was said to be scenic, but it was distant. Money was no object on this luxury cruise, however; when Alan chose Vancouver, out of nostalgia for the West Coast, his father had no objection. The family spent Christmas together at the best hotel in the city, and, except that they were in a hotel rather than at home, their Christmas was much like any other they had had together, in recent years. Alan wished his parents understood him, a sentiment they shared, although this did not occur to him. But he had tried explaining and knew it was useless. Neither mentioned as much as once their son's momentous decision of the past summer. They were reasonably pleased with his situation, they were happy to find he was content. They had no objection to his becoming a teacher, if this was what he really wanted. On Christmas Day, Alan wired Jeanne and all the McCarrans a "Merry Christmas," and he gave his parents modest, thoughtful gifts. They presented him with five thousand dollars. Alan was instantly furious, but with a supreme effort, concealed his anger and feigned gratitude. Such a gift, so wretchedly excessive, represented to him a giant step backward in their understanding of him. Could his parents not grasp that he was truly on his own, now? Had they not implied they understood, by saying they were encouraged? Had they paid no attention to what Stefan had told them? Were they thick-headed? Alan's disappointment was aggravated by the belief that money was always the "easy" present, and a poor substitute for something which, though less costly, imparted love. His anger gave way to a taxing frustration, and, although he hid this, a strain was placed on the last days of their visit. Hardly had their plane vanished from sight, he mailed their check back to them, enclosing a polite note; then, relieved, Alan boarded his flight to Montreal.

He had not been home an hour when the telephone rang. He answered, hoping it was Jeanne.

"Well, hello there, stranger," she said.

"Jeanne!" Alan was delighted.

"When did you get back from wherever you have been?"

"I just got back. I've been in Vancouver, with my parents."

"What were you doing in Vancouver, of all places? It's clear across Canada."

"I wanted to get away from Montreal for a few days. So we went there."

"You got away all right."

"Did you get my wire?"

"Yes, and we were so pleased." Jeanne was ecstatic he had sent it to "Jeanne and family," but she kept still about this.

"How was your Christmas?"

"Nothing very special, I'm afraid. It was fun seeing Charles, my older brother. Christmas is the only time he ever comes home. He and dad get along even less well than I do with him."

"Mine was pretty ho-hum, too," Alan said. "My folks are okay for a few days, but I don't think they know me from Adam, so after very long, it gets tough."

"I'd like to have met them," Jeanne said wistfully. "I'm glad you're back, Alan."

"So am I. Why don't we get together New Year's Eve? Are you free?"

"Of course I am. What shall we do?"

"I'm recently spoiled on fine hotels and champagne, so we'll go to a fine hotel and have champagne."

"Whatever you say," Jeanne said, not understanding. Could he mean they would get a room?

"Only kidding," said Alan. "New Year's is for parties. I'll see if I can't arrange something with some friends."

"I know where there's a party."

"People you know, you mean?"

"Naturally." Jeanne saw she was on the brink of committing a mistake. "I'd really rather be with your friends, Alan. I'm not very close to the people giving the party."

"Okay," Alan said, seeing straight through her lie to the tact. "I'll make some phone calls, and call you back later." The New Year, however, was only four days off; Dave had plans of his own, and Marcel said he knew no one to ask. Alan suggested Katie Reinhart, an algebra teacher at Duval he knew was single, and figured Marcel must know.

"Not my type," Marcel said. Alan realized Marcel's horizons presently ended at that brothel. The call was a mistake. Alan then called John, whom he knew was not the partying type, but Alan was desperate now. John accepted the invitation enthusiastically, but admitted he didn't have a girlfriend at the moment. Alan assured him he would find him a good blind date. He called Katie, but she was booked. What about Margaret? he asked himself. He was annoyed with himself, for getting into such a corner. Even if Margaret was free New Year's Eve, she was hardly suitable for John Walters, and vice versa. Not to mention the awkwardness. The four of them would not be much of a party. Alan thought for a minute to call Jeanne and consent to her friends' party, but, having called John, it was too late for this. Impulsively, he rang Margaret, who wasn't busy, only embarrassed that she was not. She accepted, after the usual fuss over the late notice. Who was John Walters? That she could ask offhand. It hurt, Margaret had to admit to herself, to ask who Jeanne McCarran was. Alan was surprised he had never mentioned her to Margaret, and, detecting the pain in her voice, which also came as a surprise, he did what he could to ease it. He thought to say something more of John, but the right words eluded him. That the three of them would come for her at half past eight ended their conversation. Now, laughing at himself, at the farce he was arranging, Alan called John to advise him he had found him a date. Alan said little of the woman with whom John was to spend the evening. Finally, he called Jeanne, with whom his candor prompted a gentle suggestion that they make it six; she knew a couple she thought would like to join them. Feeling that two more, even if strangers, would improve the party's prospects, Alan readily consented. The party would be at his apartment. Her friends must bring their own liquor. Snacks and mixes he would provide. Alan told Jeanne it was going to be a most unusual party.

Alan had had two glasses of champagne before he reached the McCarran residence. It was New Year's Eve. The evening would be a disaster, Alan felt certain, and that the mess was his fault caused him unending self-reproach. He wished, as well, that he had not already begun to drink, but if Jeanne noticed, she didn't let on. By the time they reached John's, Jeanne was aware of Alan's gloom, and, as John, armed with a bottle of champagne, sauntered out to the car—Alan had honked for him—she leaned over and caressed Alan's cheek, kissed him on the cheek and whispered a few endearing words. The trio then fetched Margaret. The furthest thing from an ingenue, Margaret sized John Walters up within a minute, and was appalled. She thought only if there was plenty to drink would the evening ahead be better than staying at home, New Year's Eve or no New Year's Eve. If John was timid, however, he was not dull, and, before they had reached Alan's apartment, Margaret had actually worked up some enthusiasm. Alan thought it the most wonderful absurdity ever. It perked him up to where he all but forgot his apprehension.

"I don't know why I always get so sentimental on New Year's Eve," John said as the four disembarked at Alan's residence. "It's foolish, really. It's just another day."

"Oh, I don't think so, John," Jeanne said, as though the two were old friends. "Everyone gets sentimental. Don't you find it sad, the end of a year?"

"I certainly do," Margaret said.

"Is everyone going to bawl?" Alan asked.

"Now come on, Alan," Margaret said. "You're not so hard-boiled as not to feel a pang or two, are you? 1968 was a good year, I think."

"Are you kidding?"

"Alan's still bitter," John ventured. "I still get goose bumps listening to the national anthem. Ours, that is."

"Theirs, you mean," Alan said harshly. "Yours, theirs, not mine!" Alan's tone made everyone uncomfortable. John, who knew well enough of Alan's sensitivity on the issue, sought immediately to close the subject.

"I know we differ on this," he said, "but it isn't worthy of argument."

"Who's arguing?" said Alan. "I'm through with the United States, you aren't. Just a matter of taste, you might say. Who wants a bourbon and soda?"

"I'll have some of John's champagne," Margaret said. She and John sat on the sofa-bed, and Jeanne opted for the carpet, near the front door. Alan busied himself with the bourbon he wanted and poured champagne for the others. In came the other couple, Ted Bennington and Odette Pau, both students at McGill University, both friends of Jeanne, both carrying a bottle of cheap wine, and both more than a little intoxicated already. Jeanne embraced them and accomplished introductions. Odette's gaze fixed upon Alan and reverted only when all began to notice. Ted went to the bathroom, Jeanne re-sat on the floor.

"I understand you are from the U.S. and are writing a book," Odette said to Alan, as he placed her bottle of wine in the refrigerator. "What's it about?" She had a sensuous voice, but she was not pretty. She wore jeans and a red blouse that was barely adequate, tucked in as it was, to accommodate her bulging breasts. Her jeans were excessively tight, making the contour of her buttocks easily discernible. Her nose was large and pointed, and her mouth full.

"It isn't about anything," he said to her.

"Existential, you mean?"

"Nope, not existential. Not, period. I am not writing a book. Who said I was?"

"Nobody," Odette giggled. "My icebreaker, you see."

"Ah. Does it work?"

"Yes."

"Let's join the others."

"I would rather not. Ted doesn't do anything but go to the toilet, and you're so gorgeous."

John found himself reluctantly caught up in conversation with Ted. Odette was busy pumping Jeanne for information about Alan, and none too discreetly, though in truth even dead sober Odette Pau was wholly incapable of discretion. Margaret was left out, and Alan, wishing to speak with her, winked across the room at Jeanne and sat beside Margaret.

"I want to ask you something," he said.

"Do I like John?"

"Do you?"

"He's different."

"I figured you might think that. You aren't angry, I hope."

"Only with you, Alan dear, for saying that," Margaret said pointedly. Her remark, however, was accompanied by a smile, and, in any event, Alan was too occupied with his own thoughts to consider how he had insulted her.

"Now don't laugh, Margaret. I am not trying to cast you in a mommy role, or be corny, either. You've been in love. How do you know when it's the real thing?"

"Alan, dear, I didn't know," Margaret said. "You never gave me an inkling. Oh, my!"

Margaret clutched her breast with both hands, in mock astonishment.

"I am trying to be serious, Margaret."

"Oh, for heaven's sake, Alan. I've never known anybody half as saucy as you, and you pick tonight, of all nights, to be profound. It's your party, you know."

"I'm the party killer, huh?" She nodded yes. "Well, I'll not have that, but look, Margaret, I do want to talk with you about this."

"Maybe later, Alan dear," Margaret said. "We must join the others." The others were occupied with a conversation about sex positions.

"I like being on top," Odette said. "Takes longer." She gazed at Alan, who returned a disapproving gaze and put his arm around Jeanne. He could not remember having met a person he liked less on first impression. "What do you like best?" Odette asked him.

"Take all the furniture out of a room, wax the floor real good, then get on top or bottom, as you prefer, and slide around like cats," Alan said. Odette's jaw dropped. She wasn't sure Alan wasn't serious. "You must try it sometime," he added encouragingly.

"How would it be like cats?" asked Ted, who was bleary-eyed and drunk.

"It just would be," Alan said curtly. "Do you mind?"

Ted nodded he did not mind, with a kind of mournful apology.

"This wine is just too tiresome!" Odette said. "What are you drinking, Alan?"

"It's bourbon and soda. You can have some, if you like."

"I like," said Odette. "Just the soda, though. I abhor bourbon."

"Serious?"

"What do you think?"

"Incapable," Alan muttered.

"What?"

"Unthinkable, to drink mere soda on New Year's Eve." The evening had begun to assume surreal dimensions, for Alan. He had not had a moment alone with Jeanne since they picked up John. She must have been thinking the same thing, for she came to help him mix Odette's cocktail.

"Hello, stranger," she said.

"A fine pair those are," Alan said huffily.

"I've never seen Odette so obnoxious."

"The heck you haven't."

"Honest, I've never seen her act this way."

"I don't believe you," Alan said, exasperated. "Friends don't just suddenly act some bizarre way. Not mine, at least."

"That's not very nice of you, Alan. Odette is my friend, and she can be most amiable."

"Okay," he said. "It isn't important. What a weird party. The mismatch of all time, John Walters and Margaret Page, cooing like lovebirds, and everyone else at each other's throat." Alan laughed at it. "Except Ted, that is. He's not at anyone's throat. What's his problem, anyway?"

"Ted's very drunk," Jeanne said. "Honey, do you think I'm at your throat?"

"I didn't mean you," said Alan. "I wish Stef were here."

"Cheer up. Things could be worse. What difference does the party make? We're together, and that's all that matters to me. Put up with the others, and when everybody has left, we can whisper sweet nothings to each other. How's that?" Jeanne had forgotten John and Margaret did not have their own transportation.

"I think I like you very much, Jeanne." Alan drew her close. "Why don't you make the divine Odette quit putting her hand on my thigh?"

"I didn't know she was. I'll make her quit, all right."

"I'm only kidding," Alan said sheepishly. "Just trying to make you jealous." Jeanne gazed tenderly into Alan's eyes, knowing she had won him.

Nineteen sixty-nine was but minutes old when Ted and Odette left. He was hopelessly inebriated; Odette would have to drive. She was angry with him and frustrated over having been rebuked by Alan. Her departure brought a sigh of relief from everyone who remained. Even Jeanne had lost patience with her, although Odette's behavior really was not much divorced from the usual. With their departure, the gathering became enjoyable. The two couples talked and drank in a group for some time, until finally Alan managed to get off alone with Margaret, who alone among them was tipsy.

"Are you drunk?" Alan inquired.

"Of course. Aren't you?"

"Not really."

"Alcoholics are made New Year's Eve."

"I've heard it's the saddest day of the year for prostitutes."

"Why is that?"

"I haven't the slightest idea. It's just something I've heard."

"I shouldn't think prostitutes ever have very happy days."

"Probably not," Alan said, remembering the misadventure with Marcel. The recollection still made him a bit queasy.

"You know, prostitution is a two-way street," Margaret said. "Nothing makes me more furious than a vice squad. The stinking hypocrisy!

Prostitution is an economic proposition. The basic rule of economics is supply and demand."

"Let's change the subject," Alan suggested, not the least interested in the woes of the harlot's life.

"What do you have in mind?"

"The subject I brought up a few hours ago."

"Which one was that?" Margaret had forgotten it entirely.

"I want to talk about love, Margaret."

"Oh, yes, I remember. You were declaring your love. On your knees, Alan, dear."

"Margaret, can you be serious?"

"I'll have to think about it." Exasperated as he was, this made Alan laugh. "You think you love her, is that it?"

"I think, maybe, so. I'm not sure. It is so difficult. That's why I wanted to talk with you."

"Do you want my honest opinion, Alan?"

"Of course. Nothing else has any value."

"I firmly believe in two theories on love. One, true love comes at first sight, so to speak, or not at all. Two, true love leaves no room for doubt."

"Come on," Alan said, looking at her as though he thought she was crazy. "Love at first sight? That's storybook stuff."

"You asked me to be honest. That's what I'm doing. I believe whole-heartedly in what I said."

"Was it love at first sight with you and ... what's-his-name?" Alan could not recall Margaret's ex-husband's name.

"Yes."

"What went wrong?"

"That's none of your business."

"So it isn't. Sorry."

"Perfectly all right."

"Well, I don't begin to believe your theories, Margaret, but I asked for it."

"I didn't think you would. It doesn't matter. You and Jeanne are none of my business."

"I'm glad you and John are getting along so famously."

"Don't be preposterous. We're getting along because I had the sense to drink plenty. He's sweet, but he's not for me."

"He's a virgin, don't you think?"

110

"What a stupid remark, Alan. Why don't you ask him that?" As if to oblige, John now joined them, sneaking his arm on the sofa behind Margaret's shoulder.

"Off you go, Alan," John said. "You can't steal her." Alan thought John was making a perfect fool of himself. Feeling sorry for Margaret, and finding irksome John's refusal to drink more than a thimbleful of liquor per hour, Alan made up his mind to fix him a drink that would lay him flat. Alan knew the best way to manage this was with punch, and it happened that he had two large cans of fruit juice in the refrigerator, which would serve admirably.

"Let's switch to punch," he announced, and then, rhetorically, "okay by everybody?" Alan selected for John the largest glass he owned. Into it he poured a generous quantity of gin, then added the fruit juice. Not much of a punch, but it sure as heck is going to pack one, Alan chuckled to himself. He tasted it to ensure the liquor was concealed, for he had implied to the group the punch would be "innocent." Alan added more gin, tasted again, and found the gin still could not be detected. Good old gin! Then, it seeming to him John might be suspicious about having the only large glass, Alan poured his own drink into the ample, empty can of fruit juice.

The beverage was cold and good, and John, in his unsuspecting thirst, drank most of his quickly. Jeanne was strangely quiet, Alan thought, but the other two jabbered away. Entirely occupied with his scheme, Alan waited impatiently for John to ask for a refill. At last he did, and Alan handed him a concoction identical to the first. But it happened the first, potent as it was, and so rapidly consumed, had had its effect; John, unsure of his grasp, knocked over the new installment before managing a single swallow.

"I'm sorry, Alan," he said, blushing with embarrassment.

"It's nothing, John," Jeanne said. She retrieved a towel from the bath.

"I don't want anybody to think I'm drunk," John said. The room was beginning to move on him, a sensation he had never experienced.

"I've done that lots of times, John," Margaret said. "Don't worry about it."

"I think we should go," John told her. Margaret thought so, too, and Alan, not satisfied his plan had succeeded, fished ruefully into his pocket for his car keys.

"You needn't take us," Margaret said, seeing the reluctance written across two faces. "We'll get a cab." John rather liked the idea, and Jeanne liked it so much she could hardly contain herself. When the taxi arrived, Alan saw them out the door, accepting John's effusive thanks and Margaret's determined leer. They left not a great deal soberer than the earlier pair. Alan closed the door and returned to his spot beside Jeanne, on the floor.

"I love you, Alan."

"Jeanne ..." but he left it at that, and kissed her passionately on the lips. He hugged her, squeezing hard until she cried out.

"You brute," she said, smothering his face with kisses.

"Will you stay the night?"

"Every night," she whispered breathlessly. He kissed her and explored her mouth with his tongue, and his hand worked its way down her blouse, unbuttoning as it went. She ran her fingers through his hair and caressed his nape. He unfastened her bra and, cupping her left breast, blanketed it with kisses, converting its nipple. His hand ran up her thigh, teasing just short of the moisture and heat. He worked it beneath her panties until it found its destination. She dug her nails into his back. He tugged at the zipper of her skirt, and, managing, she, with a little skillful squirming, was free of it. She reclined on her back, arching her hips, desperate for him to get out of his pants. She couldn't wait. She shot up and embraced him with all her muscle, crushing herself against him, kissing him passionately, biting his cheek.

"Hurry, Alan, hurry, or I'm going to 'come' right here."

"I can't very well finish ..." Alan pulled out the sofa-bed and then lifted her in a single motion upon it. In another moment, he was stripped and over her. "You're taking the pill?"

"Yes!" Jeanne didn't think she could wait another second. Alan penetrated, and, jerking wildly, Jeanne reached orgasm quickly, with a gasp. Working at it, Alan nearly succeeded in making their climax simultaneous.

"I love you, Alan darling," she said, her arms limp over his back. Jeanne was perspiring profusely.

"I love you, too. Very much, Jeanne." Alan was aware he had never said those words, and it struck him he had missed a whole world. Jeanne smiled blissfully and, tucking herself neatly in his arms, ardently whispered her affection for him. He was even more declarative. But it was the length of the day, rather than their explosive sexual release, that had left both too spent for further lovemaking. Soon, they were fast asleep.

CHAPTER 4

Alan rose first, and, observing her sleeping, it seemed to him the most natural thing on earth to be in love with her. The long, doubt-racked prelude now seemed an aberration. Alan thought he was the happiest he had ever been in his life. She stirred, and, upon opening her eyes, found herself looking into his. They exchanged tender "good mornings" and "I love yous." They had coitus, with delicious leisure. At breakfast, Alan related his plan to speak with her father, about getting a full-time teaching position at Duval High. Jeanne was surprised and distressed that he had been rejected by the graduate schools at McGill and Sir George Williams universities.

"I'm not half as smart as you, darling, and McGill took me."

"It's their mistake," Alan said confidently, "but one of no consequence. I have decided to make a career of teaching in high school—really. What I want is to get started, as soon as possible." Jeanne didn't see why her father could not help Alan again, as indeed Alan, too, had reasoned. It was marrying Alan, however, which occupied her mind, and, while he did not realize it, she was hardly in their conversation. As for Alan himself, he viewed getting a full-time teaching job on the Duval faculty as the last hurdle in the exhausting task of choosing and securing a vocation. He felt lasting contentment was near, and he was inexpressibly eager to get there.

When Alan went to Charles McCarran with his favor to ask, he announced forthrightly that he was in love with Jeanne. Oddly, he was as eager now to make the declaration as he had been unwilling only days earlier; it was as if there was no middle ground. McCarran, who had secretly hoped for just this, was overjoyed. He told Alan he would do what he could for him, cautioning that full-time teaching was quite another matter from substituting, and that chances were Alan must live with the status quo a

113

while longer. Alan responded that he would leave the matter entirely to him. Alan asked no questions, reasoning he deserved a break. He said he did not mind substituting another semester, and left it at that.

Even without having been told, Charles McCarran would soon enough have understood, for Jeanne and Alan spent every spare minute together. Long ago the hours she kept had ceased to be discussed, so that her staying the night with Alan produced no dissent in the McCarran home. It was Alan who changed the arrangement, for he felt Charles was uncomfortable with it, although the older man had said nothing. The lovers took to spending available afternoons together in bed. Come nightfall, Alan took Jeanne home.

"Why, if you aren't a prude," she objected. Alan nonetheless had his way. Marriage, in the back of his mind, was the only thing she thought about. Always, it had seemed to him an enormous step, demanding caution, but now that he felt he had found his love, Alan wanted to cast aside his old opinions and simply marry her. It was only that discarding such long-held ideas did not come easily. What Alan needed was a little time. The patience the situation required she wholly lacked, however. After several, futile efforts to get him to talk at any length on the subject, Jeanne quietly ceased taking birth control pills. She became pregnant almost at once.

Margaret, meanwhile, angry with Alan for what struck her, in the sobriety twelve hours of sleep had brought, as a fiasco in which she had played the fool, went to Marcel. The two had dated at one time, but he had brought their relationship to an ignominious end, leaving hard feelings on both sides. Marcel's job at Duval was in jeopardy now because, in his apathy and discontent, he had come to handle carelessly his private life, which was no longer so, and which the school board felt unsuited one of their teachers. Margaret doubted she could say anything that might save Marcel his job, but she reasoned if he knew his friend Alan Young was squeezing him out, he might shape up. The truth was, Margaret cared not a whit if Marcel found himself out of work; what drove her was her wish to block Alan. She knew herself and could see it was revenge she sought. Too, she was almost certain Alan was unaware of Marcel's precarious position. This critical point Margaret's injured pride had succeeded in dismissing as of no importance. She went straightaway to Marcel and told him Alan's plan, as she imagined it.

114

"What makes you think my job is in danger?" Marcel said, not very pleasantly.

"Half the school knows it, Marcel. I didn't come here to play games."

"Then why did you come?"

"To warn you and try to help you. Alan Young has a powerful friend, and he is going to get him your job."

"I do not believe a word you have said. Alan is not the type to stick a knife into a friend's back."

"I wouldn't have thought so, either, but ..."

"Perhaps you came for love?" Marcel said suggestively. He shot his arm around Margaret's waist and zoomed in for a kiss, which she just averted.

"Stop that, Marcel! What's the matter with you? I don't love you."

"I think maybe you do."

"Honestly, Marcel, what are you talking about?" Margaret couldn't believe her ears. Alan's groping inquiries on love came to her, and she remembered John Walters' slobbering on and on in the taxi about how much he loved her. Only a reluctant, devastating candor had put an end to his maddening importunity. "How unreasonable can men be?" Margaret continued, as if in soliloquy. "You are all so stupid and vain. You are enslaved by your libido. Have you no self-knowledge? You think all women are falling all over themselves for you. You shout love and stumble into marriage without once thinking about what motivates you. You don't even know what the dickens you are doing, and all the while, in your fantastic vanity, you think yourselves the stronger sex. It is the best joke on earth."

"Get yourself screwed, Margaret."

"That's eloquent of you, Marcel. I'll tell you one thing for sure. Alan is ten times the man you are, any day of the week."

"I'm so glad you came," Marcel said sarcastically, opening the door for her. She departed without another word, berating herself for coming. Her anger with Alan subsided, and she found herself hoping fervently he would get Marcel's job, and wondering whether a man alive had the sense God gave the meanest beast.

Now the fact was, Duval High, Dave Hillsborough included, was increasingly eager to be rid of Marcel Pirmont. His private life was considered a scandal and an outrage. However, it was the feeling of the school board his dismissal in the middle of the term would create more problems than it would solve, and, therefore, the decision had been made to retain him until June, regardless of the difficulties.

Into this situation came Charles McCarran. Charles McCarran was a fighter. His brush with the blacklist, as an apprentice architect, had proved an intense learning experience, stamping permanently into his mind that "might made right," and to trust no one. Though not an opportunist by nature, Charles was a shrewd and resilient individual. Some years ago, his firm had submitted what proved to be the next-to-lowest bid for design of a new elementary school. Unexpectedly, he got a phone call in which it was made plain his bid, very close to the low bid, could still prevail, provided he slip $5,000 under the table. The job was a lucrative and coveted one, and Charles had toiled greatly on it. He could not resist. By sheerest accident sometime thereafter, he not only had discovered the $5,000 had gone directly into the pocket of L. Emile Dumas, an influential member of the school board, but had the means to prove it. He had never dreamed he would ever "use" this knowledge, but he could never see Dumas, or read his name in the paper, without remembering. Alan had unwittingly given him the excuse, and Charles had talked himself into it with surprisingly little difficulty.

Charles McCarran was a failure as a father. His eldest son, Charles, left home for trade school in Sherbrooke practically on the day his secondary schooling came to an end. He neither wrote nor phoned home, and rarely returned. Jeanne, at McGill, was immersed in drugs and promiscuity. Rickie, the boy, was stepping unmistakably into his brother's footprints. But it would be unfair to place upon the shoulders of Charles McCarran the entire, or even the greater part, of the blame for the breakdown of the family, for his fault lay primarily in his refusal to confront his wife. Languid, childish, self-absorbed, she was the scourge of the family, yet he loved her stubbornly and would not consider divorce. In sticking it out, Charles had lost his children. Thus, when Alan happened along, in the emotional context of a barroom brawl, Charles McCarran had interpreted it as nothing less than his chance to guide a troubled youth right. Indeed, Alan's early perception of Charles as a surrogate father was accurate. Now, with the promise of eventually becoming Alan's father-in-law, Charles had all the motivation he needed to make a call on L. Emile Dumas.

"Look, McCarran," Dumas said with hostility, "you blow the whistle, you go to jail, too." McCarran had heard this from him before and, although

116

the favor was bigger this time, he knew Dumas was just sounding off and would cooperate. He was right. Dumas saw that it would not take much to discredit Marcel Pirmont. The problem lay in "selling" Alan, a mere one-term substitute. Before the school board, Dumas praised Alan Young lavishly, relying in no small measure on fiction. He said Alan's work at Duval High was inspired. Why, Alan Young was a born teacher! He had already won the respect and admiration of students and fellow faculty. Alan Young was dependable. Alan Young's private life, in sharp contrast to Pirmont's, was above reproach. This point was particularly emphasized. Alan Young had the necessary qualifications—it happened he did—and could therefore start immediately.

"Slipping Mr. Young in now will be a ripple, compared to the waves Mr. Pirmont is making," Dumas told his fellow board members. It was asked whether Marcel would have grounds for a lawsuit. A clause in his contract, something about "unprofessional behavior," would foreclose a suit, should Pirmont be foolish enough to go to court. The fact was, Marcel didn't have a case. Both Dumas and McCarran were confident of success. Alan was qualified, and Marcel's conduct was highly exploitable. "Why Alan Young?" was a question never really explored in any depth. In short order, the coup was accomplished.

The first to reach Alan with the news was not Charles McCarran, but Dave Hillsborough. Dave was upset; he was even more curious. He demanded an explanation. How had Alan done it, and why? Caught by surprise, Alan thought for a minute Dave was playing a joke. He most surely did not sound like he was joking. Dave became angry, thinking Alan was pretending. This, in turn, brought a burst of temper from Alan.

"Look, Dave," Alan said, calming himself. "It's true I wanted to get on full-time at Duval. We've talked about it, haven't we? But I wouldn't take Marcel's job. You know me better than that. I didn't even know Marcel was going to lose his job. You never mentioned it. Nobody ever did."

"I have always believed you are honest, Alan," Dave said. "It's difficult to believe you were so much in the dark." Dave was momentarily silent. "Yes, I believe you. There's a funny business in the works here somewhere, though, and I intend to get to the bottom of it. Marcel has been a friend for a long time." Well, it was true Marcel was a friend, Alan reflected, but the hint of satisfaction in Dave's voice, the artificiality of his righteous indignation, was not lost on Alan. Devoted to teaching, Dave Hillsborough was the least likely to tolerate Marcel's debauchery. There was no denying it tarnished the profession. Dave was sorry for Marcel, would make an effort to remain friends, but he was glad Marcel was out at Duval High.

Alan called Charles. The latter was disappointed someone had reached him first with the news. Alan wanted to know what the dirty business was. His voice was almost harsh. Charles McCarran had no idea how to respond. He thought Alan the most feckless person he knew. He felt Alan had no right to be angry with him. Alan acknowledged this, too, however. Alan was shocked at himself, realizing now what he had sanctioned, and how he had rationalized it. He saw there was only one decent thing he could do, only one thing that could salvage him his friends and his integrity. He had to refuse the job. He told Charles this, in so many words. The latter was speechless, and then he exploded in anger. Alan, ignorant of the facts, apologized for putting him on the spot, but this was not nearly sufficient for Charles, who perceived that if Alan balked now, the whole affair could blow up in his face. After such an intense campaign of persuasion at the school board, and with all arrangements made, it would be very awkward, perhaps impossible, to explain Alan's caprice. Charles told Alan he would be humiliated, if Alan backed out. Scarcely aware of himself, he said he would take whatever steps were necessary to ensure Alan never saw Jeanne again, if he refused the job. The last thing Alan ever expected to hear from Charles McCarran was a threat, and, as he did not know of the trouble he was causing, Alan knew not what to think or say. Jeanne was no real concern, the father's role in such matters a thing of the past, but to humiliate the man who had been his benefactor—even, judging by Charles' remark, to make an enemy of him—Alan desired least of all. It was a terrible dilemma. Alan again asked Charles to explain why it was crucial he take the job, and in reply he received the same lie, delivered this time with venom. Quickly, Alan's mind analyzed his predicament. He judged that his friends at Duval High might never believe he had not been out to "get" Marcel. Stefan would believe him, he thought ruefully, but not these friends. Without a doubt, his friendship with Marcel would come to an ugly end; he might lose Dave and Margaret, too. The word would spread at Duval, and he would be no one's colleague or friend.

On the other hand, to alienate Charles McCarran was to cheat the man who had knocked himself out for him ever since his arrival in Canada, indeed—Alan recalled the first, hellish fortnight—perhaps saved him.

While he could still have Jeanne, everything would be more difficult with a hostile father-in-law. Alan berated himself for what he concluded must have been gross self-deception, recognizing that he would not be where he was, had he been willing to be patient. He looked at his future. He wanted to teach, and he needed the much more substantial salary full-time teaching would provide. He wanted to settle down. Marcel was on his way out, anyway, and it was true he had not known, whether or not his friends believed him, whether or not he became an outcast on the faculty. But Alan could not talk himself into it this time, for there was no circumventing what for him was the crux of the matter: Taking the job was tantamount to approving cutthroat tactics. No, it meant more, it meant being a cutthroat himself. The realization horrified him. Mustering his resolve, Alan told Charles he would not take the job under any circumstances, come what might. It was a categorical refusal, delivered so strongly there was no mistaking it. Charles cursed him, reiterated his "disenfranchisement" and slammed down the telephone receiver.

Events began to happen quickly. McCarran phoned Dumas and explained the situation. The latter laughed long and hard, but McCarran sat patiently through it, and when the other had sobered and admitted the reality of the danger, he was ready to consider what course was to be taken. Time was of the essence. They had to get someone else in place of Alan immediately, at the same time finding an excuse for his no-show. Done quickly, the strangeness of it would be overlooked. Delay would arouse more and more curiosity. Finding a replacement for Alan was not a problem, according to Dumas, as there were always unemployed teachers. Irate, Charles said he knew that. What explanation for Alan's behavior was there? Dumas worried. The board had been told he was keen on the job. They had been told he was a superb candidate.

"People will believe anything, Dumas," said Charles, further annoyed by the man's naivete. "The important thing is that we—you—must act today. Every moment of procrastination imperils us." Charles was fearful he could not make Dumas understand the importance of this, and he was even afraid Dumas might just sit on it, in which case the nasty business could come to light. There would be two arrests. This was a fear born of panic, however; it was groundless. They came up with an excuse for Alan, and at once Dumas went into action. Alan was dropped, and, within two days, someone else had been hired, and the bizarre affair was on its way to being forgotten. Except by Dave Hillsborough. Dave's private investigation was beginning to earn him publicity at complacent Duval High, but, in his zeal, fed by the ego-boost he was getting, he was too loud too soon. Dumas got wind of what he was doing, and Dave was discreetly advised that his further pursuit of the matter would result in quick and permanent expulsion from the public schools. Though an important member of the faculty, Dave did not have a protected job, and thus was without the bargaining power he had flattered himself he possessed. If "they" tried to ruin him, he reasoned, the whole thing would be exposed, but it would be an ugly proceeding, and somewhere along the way he could get hurt. The thought of being out as a teacher was more than he could bear. Dave reasoned shady dealing is part of any front office, and that one was best advised not to try to fight it. Marcel was finished, but by his opprobrious conduct, he deserved no less. Dave thought himself a fool for having plunged so mindlessly into the intrigue. Quietly, he ceased his investigation, and the matter was over.

After missing her period, Jeanne McCarran decided on a pregnancy test. She could hardly believe it might have happened so soon, but she crossed her fingers and hoped against hope it was true. In front of her in line at the free clinic, operated by the provincial government, were two of the unhappiest-looking girls Jeanne thought she had ever seen. It was plain both were hoping for the verdict opposite what she desired. Jeanne found this perplexing. Her turn came, and within a few minutes, she knew she was pregnant. Jeanne was ecstatic. She couldn't get to Alan quickly enough. She was confident he would marry her, now. When her father had told her she was not to see him again, she had only laughed in his face, for it was years since she had paid the slightest heed to his injunctions, and least of all on earth was he going to deprive her of her man. She anticipated Alan would be startled and then upset, so she prepared herself. She reasoned it would be but a brief storm, and then he would marry her. There would be no other course for him, and, anyway, she felt it was what he wanted, only could not quite make up his mind to do.

She caught him with her news at a bad time, for Alan was smarting from her father's rebuke and despairing over their unhappy end, he was cognizant he was out of a job and, he was hurt by Marcel, who said he wanted no more of him, that it made no difference to him that Alan had turned down the job. This seemed to Alan the ultimate injustice. Jeanne and Alan embraced, and he began explaining the rupture with her father when she broke the big news, which made instant poppycock of everything he was worrying over. Alan did not shriek, it did not occur to him either to kiss or strangle her, he merely sat at the table, arms folded across his chest.

"Many fantastic things have been said to me," he said calmly, staring at her, "especially lately, but that is undoubtedly the most fantastic of all. No, it is grotesque. That's the word. It's something right out of Poe. You haven't done that really, of course. Not just when everything was so right for us. I know you don't really mean it, Jeanne." Alan shook his head. It could not be true. Not two weeks ago, he had believed the end of problems was in sight, and now he could see nothing before him save a redoubtable array of difficulties. Things could not turn around like that. What was happening must be a nightmare, this the latest and worst episode.

"Yes, I mean it, Alan darling. I don't understand your saying it's grotesque, just when everything was right for us. Everything is right for us." Jeanne tried to kiss him, but he spurned her, and turned away from her momentarily. She remained silent.

"Hon, we had it made," he finally said, turning back to face her. "We got through all those troubles and found we loved each other. In fact, come to think of it, any two people who could weather all we did and still come through must be deeply in love." Jeanne wondered what troubles Alan meant, but dared not interrupt. "We were going to marry, with your dad's blessing, and I was going to teach at Duval, and eventually, yes, we were going to have a family." With this Alan's voice broke, but she embraced him and held tight, whispering every loving word she had ever heard and covering his face with tender kisses. Alan wrapped his arms around her, and, denouncing his self-pity, told her passionately he loved her. "Talk about scandal," he said. Alan laughed aloud. "Wait till Stef hears this one." Again he laughed, thankful for having Stefan. "Wait till mom and dad hear it," he said in afterthought, and then, in further afterthought: "Wait till your dad hears it!"

When the news broke, Stefan kidded Alan. If Alan didn't care, then he wouldn't, either. If Alan was happy, then he was, too. Judge and Mrs. Young were scandalized at first, but soon enough this wore off to a great extent, for their son, after all, was in another city in another country. Besides, both were glad he was to marry, for it would settle him down, and it was apparent to both this was what Alan most needed. It was Charles McCarran's reaction that surprised Alan. He accomplished an about-face. No doubt that the business with L. Emile Dumas had come out satisfactorily made a difference, yet it was his daughter's pending marriage that really healed the wound. As for the circumstances, McCarran only roared at how Alan had been snared. He did privately resolve not to offer to help Alan again, as it had caused him only trouble. Charles McCarran could not quite figure Alan out, but he liked him, and he was immensely pleased that he was to join the family. Adele McCarran, who in all this time had not come to know Alan, thought it was high time Jeanne married someone.

It was, of course, expedient to marry as soon as possible. Alan announced that under no circumstances would he consider a ceremony without Stefan as his best man. In school at Santa Barbara, with semester-break now past, and lacking the means for such a trip, Stefan, it appeared to everybody except Alan, must be omitted; his inclusion just wasn't practical. Alan calmly countered by saying that Jeanne and he might have ten babies before he would marry her, unless Stefan could be his best man. Now unemployed, Alan could ill-afford the cost of flying his friend to Montreal. Nevertheless, he was prepared to pay it. Charles McCarran made clear he did not believe this expense should be borne by the father of the bride, an unnecessary opinion, since nobody was suggesting it was. Dorothy Young told her husband to give in to their son's whim and pay for Stefan's trip, and he consented.

A wedding date was set, and invitations hastily mailed. John Walters would be present, and so would Margaret Page, and Dave Hillsborough, who, with Alan's refusal to take the job Dave knew he wanted so badly, was friendly again. On Jeanne's side were her brothers and most of her crowd at McGill University. Judge and Mrs. Young arrived, ahead of Stefan; Alan met their plane and hugged his mother warmly. He could not explain it to himself and cared even less to try, but, somehow, he wanted to show them off to everyone. No mention had ever been made of the check he had sent back, and no one mentioned it now. Painfully aware of how society-minded both were, his mother in particular, Alan had worried they would be loath to accept Jeanne's early pregnancy. If, however, this made the slightest difference to either parent, the feeling was well-concealed. Alan decided they were feigning nothing, that they really did not care that their grandchild would be born less than eight months after their son's marriage, which to Alan was a most glorious mark in their favor.

This general euphoria ground to a devastating halt when Alan's mother met the bride. Impressed by Jeanne's good looks and charm, Robert Young thought Alan had found himself a jewel, but Dorothy Young had required only two minutes to reach a firm conclusion about Jeanne McCarran, and, after complaining to the deaf ears of her husband, she went directly to their son. She told him Jeanne was a hussy. She was as blunt as she could possibly be. Alan was dumbfounded. He said that, given a month of hard thought, he was certain he could think of nothing that could matter less to him than her idiotic opinions about the girl he loved. Alan, too, was as candid as the tongue permitted.

"Alan, darling, I am only trying to do what is best for you."

"In that case, I suggest you get on the next plane for L.A."

"Do you want a wife who will never be faithful to you?"

"You don't even know her," Alan shouted. "You've been here three days. You don't know what you're talking about. You just want to wreck our marriage so you won't lose your little sonny. You will never understand I'm grown, never, never."

"I will not have you shouting at me, Alan."

"I'm not shouting," Alan shouted.

Certain she was right about Jeanne McCarran, and desperate, Dorothy Young pleaded again with her husband.

"She's poor white trash, Bob. It's as plain as day. What's the matter with you, that you don't see it?"

"Alan and Jeanne are in love, Dorothy," Robert Young said. "Can't you see that? Anyway, Alan wouldn't marry a slut. You're mistaken about her."

"You men are dense past all belief. Don't you realize it may not be his child she's carrying?"

"No, I don't realize any such thing. You are certainly being unfair to Alan, I think."

"Won't you please just talk with him, Bob? For our sake, as well as his. Trust my intuition, please." Robert Young thought it very unreasonable of his wife, but her pleading carried the day; he agreed to speak with their son. She warned him of Alan's extreme sensitivity.

"How did it happen, old chap?" father asked son, as gingerly as possible. "Did she say she was taking the pill, when she wasn't?" It was a good guess.

"Exactly right," Alan said. "Standard procedure these days, I suppose." Alan was lighthearted. He felt a certain, rare bonhomie with his father. He was not prepared for what was coming. When it came, he blew up.

"Why did you come?" he shouted vituperatively. "You aren't parents, you're antagonists. Mom tells me she's a whore, and you tell me she's pregnant by somebody else and that I'm stupid. Normal parents do not relate to their children in this fashion. They love them, instead, like Jeanne loves me. If you weren't so warped in the head, you could see that."

"I don't believe either of us has said she doesn't love you, Alan," the judge said calmly. "We are only thinking that, in view of the fact Jeanne was willing to trick you, as you admit she did, then maybe you aren't the first, you understand."

"Oh, I understand," Alan said loudly. "I understand. No, I'm not the first, any more than she's my first. That's archaic. What has it to do with anything? Nothing." Alan abruptly mellowed almost to a plea. "Don't the two of you give me credit for anything, dad? Do you work at being estranged from your son?" Alan stalked from the room before his father could reply. He had Jeanne and he had Stefan, and he figured they were enough.

Of the discussions with his parents, Alan told Jeanne not a word. Together, they went to meet Stefan's plane. Alan's anger subsided, for here he was with his wife-to-be, and Stefan would arrive shortly—a wonderful bonus, for the agreement Alan and Stefan had made their last time together, in St. Paul, had remained only a resolution, with no foreseeable fulfillment. Stefan arrived, and shook hands with Alan before turning to do the same with Jeanne.

"A hug, if you please, from my fiancé's best friend," she said. Stefan obliged, blushing.

Stefan thought she was very attractive, and she thought he was very unattractive.

"Let's forget the others," Alan said, putting one arm over Jeanne's shoulder, and the other over Stefan's. "Let's just go have a private ceremony and forget there's anybody else in the world." Alan had said this facetiously, but suddenly it struck him as the perfect vengeance.

"Suits me," said Stefan, "but who are we boycotting, exactly?"

"Every other biped that exists, Stef," Alan said in earnest, emotion in his voice. "No exceptions."

"Even the brightest simians?" Stefan inquired gravely, which made Alan laugh uproariously and joyfully.

"They can have their bananas," he said, and the game was on.

"What if they don't like bananas?" Stefan asked.

"That's against the rules," said Alan.

"Ah, but it is said some have no regard for the rules," Stefan said solemnly.

"Let them eat cake," Alan said.

"Marie had it with cream, for breakfast," said Stefan.

"Then she's lost her head," Alan said.

"And her breakfast, too?" said Stefan.

"That I cannot say," Alan said. It was Stefan's turn, but for fear of being rude, he chose to defer to Jeanne. Naturals for one another, Alan and he could erase their separation in a moment. But now there was Jeanne to think of, to get to know. Stefan knew he would never have his friend to himself again.

"Alan has often told me you are as loony as he is, Stefan," she observed, "and I can see it was no exaggeration." Alan smiled and kissed her on the cheek.

"I like to think of myself as the loonier, actually," Stefan said, "but certainly this is debatable. I'll give him that much."

"I wish the three of us could just go off," Alan said. "Others seem important when I'm with them, but they recede into oblivion when I'm with either of you." There was such passion in these words, both those with Alan realized he was troubled by something, and both made a mental note not to forget to ask him about it, when the other wasn't around. This was hardly necessary, for more than once in the hour the three had together, Alan repeated his fervent wish.

Her dissatisfaction with Jeanne McCarran unabated, Dorothy Young now went to Stefan. She and her husband knew something of him, as Alan had brought him down to Los Angeles several times, from Santa Barbara. She reasoned nobody could reach her son if Stefan could not, for it was plain to her Alan was closer to him than either to her or her husband. Stefan refused her unequivocally, seeing selfishness behind her claim she sought what was best for Alan. But the seeds of discontent were planted; Stefan, recalling Alan's early letters, and feeling that perhaps Alan after all was being deceived, decided to approach Jeanne. Uncharacteristically, he did not think out what he was doing. His prudence failed him. Jeanne, stupefied and outraged by his insinuation, fled to Alan in tears. Alan refused, simply, to believe what Jeanne had to say. Infuriated by his response, she dared him to face his friend with it, a challenge Alan accepted.

"I'm sorry, Jeanne, if I have insulted you," Stefan said, when confronted. "It was inadvertent." Stefan, a little alarmed, nevertheless did not yet fully appreciate his blunder. His words left Alan thunderstruck, for with them, Stefan had corroborated her.

"I cannot believe you accused Jeanne of that!" Alan half-shouted. "You are the best friend I have on earth. So how in the …"

"Jeanne, may I have a word in private with Alan, for a minute, please?" Jeanne only glared at Stefan, so he grabbed Alan by the arm and pulled him out of earshot. "Look, Alan, you don't suppose I would act against your best interests, do you? Best friends stick by their friends, no matter what. I'm happy for both of you, immensely happy. I raised the issue only because your mother …"

"My mother!" Alan interrupted. "So, she put you up to it." Alan was incensed with his mother. "Good grief, Stef. You sold out. I'd never have believed it of you." Now, his gross error became clear to Stefan. He realized he had jeopardized his bond with Alan for the sake of a point Alan would never see. He wondered how he could have been so prodigiously stupid. Groping for the right words, Stefan apologized copiously to both Alan and Jeanne, admitting he had made a terrible mistake he himself could hardly believe. Alan accepted his apology immediately and unconditionally, and Jeanne pretended to accept it. Convinced the real villain was his mother, not Stefan, Alan found he was gladder than ever to be living so far from her. He was eager for the wedding, to be rid of her. Of them, for his father was little better.

Despite its prelude, the wedding went well. Dorothy Young grimly accepted it. Adele McCarran ignored everyone, although she did smile at least as often as her counterpart. The two fathers beamed. Judge Young was newly enchanted by Jeanne, and thought his son had done well by himself. He dismissed his wife's suspicion and forgot her harangue. As for Alan himself, he felt he was the happiest he had ever been. Gazing into his bride's luminous eyes, Alan found he was indifferent to the grievances he harbored against those present. There was Margaret; Marcel's parting shot had been to inform Alan of her visit. There was Dave, before whom Alan had had to prove himself. There was John, whose failure with Margaret still rankled, and had produced a new, if only occasional, coldness toward Alan, who he felt "sided" with Margaret. There was his mother. Cupping her soft cheeks in his hands, Alan kissed his wife, and the ceremony was over.

At the reception, Alan had an idea. He was through in the Montreal Public Schools. His acquaintances he could do without. Stefan would be in law school in Minneapolis. Why couldn't the two of them move to Winnipeg, where Stefan would be but a few hours' drive? There, they could make a fresh start. Alan felt Jeanne would be agreeable, since she was not close to either of her parents. Also, Alan disliked her crowd at McGill, and, without fully realizing it, he wanted her away from them. He asked Stefan what he thought of the plan, and the latter, interpreting it as full and lasting forgiveness, again reproached himself for his blunder. Stefan was enthusiastic. He said he was reasonably sure he would be accepted at the University of Minnesota School of Law. Jeanne, too, was receptive, as Alan had anticipated, although she was not anxious to be near Stefan, and began to wonder, groundlessly, over the relationship her husband had with him. It seemed to her off-balance. Without the insult she still bore in mind, by the fact Stefan was a rival, of a sort, it was doubtful they could ever be close. Jeanne loved her husband and had no intention of sharing him with anyone.

Jeanne and Alan honeymooned in Quebec City, said to be one of the nation's most charming cities, French to the core, filled with fascinating architecture—according to Alan's father-in-law—history on every corner, wonderful restaurants. These lovers saw none of it. When, inevitably, it came time to return to Montreal, two hearts were equally heavy.

In the rush to marry, there had not been time to secure a larger apartment; this became their first task. Worse, Alan was unemployed, and, while they had received generous wedding gifts from both families, little was in the form of cash. Then, too, Jeanne was unhappy about going back to school. It was this, however, which decided them. Well into the spring semester, Jeanne was best-advised to finish, as many an employer required, at the least, two years of college credit. They would get another apartment, far across town from home, she insisted, and Alan could find some job, surely. Then, come June, if it still seemed sensible, they could move to Winnipeg—or somewhere. It was the intelligent thing to do, Alan admitted, much as he wished to leave Montreal now. The prospects for employment being as barren for Alan as they were, whatever improved Jeanne's chances was to their undeniable advantage.

Jobs for someone of his education and experience were not numerous. Alan could not find work. The new apartment they had obtained was costing nearly double what his old one had, and Jeanne, busy with her studies at McGill, lacked the time to try her chances in the job market. Apparently there was nothing to do but wash dishes. In desperation, Alan decided to try the American exile's organization, but Paul Kelly said the organization didn't have the resources to be of much help in the job-hunting department.

"We have to have our priorities," Kelly said. Alan wondered what priority could come before putting food on one's table. "In your new neighborhood, with its better class of people than where you were, I would think you might have greater opportunities."

"I suppose so," Alan said, although he wasn't perfectly sure what Kelly meant. In any case, it was certainly not the same thing as getting him a job. Not until that evening, back home, did it dawn on Alan he had not mentioned to Kelly his change in address. How, then, had he known? It disturbed Alan. He told Jeanne, who suggested John Walters might have told Kelly. That was possible; John had stopped by once, since their move. Yet it seemed to Alan an odd and a significant thing. He remembered Kelly's having said, when he first arrived, that the organization tried to keep tabs on the exiles, in case of accident. That made sense, yet Alan could not shake the feeling something was not right. It was as though he were being spied upon. Alan made a note to ask John if he had told Kelly, the next time he saw him. Alan had remained cordial with John, as indeed he had with Margaret and Dave, reasoning that if they were not Stefans, they were better than no friends at all.

Unemployment was damaging Alan's self-respect, and it was not salubrious for his marriage, either. There was nothing to do but settle for whatever he could find, which translated into becoming a waiter at an expensive restaurant near where they lived. The humiliation was almost intolerable for Alan, and, while Jeanne did what she could to make him feel better about it, this was little help. Compassion and tenderness and encouragement came easily for her, for she loved Alan deeply. Entirely wrapped up in him, and needing no more, Jeanne was content. Alan felt he loved her, and, although he really did not, by eschewing doubt when it arose, their marriage continued smoothly. Only Margaret Page saw beneath the surface, only she knew Alan was deceiving himself. Naturally, he saw much less of her, for their relationship was sharply altered, and he was no longer at Duval High School, nor indeed even in that part of town.

In May, having finally finished his essay, Alan sought to get it published. It had been a joy to research and write. Titled "The Lost Generation, 1947-1967," the essay argued not that his was the only lost generation, only that indisputably it qualified as one. Alan's introduction set the tone:

> A famous writer who wrote books about Spain and found himself one day in Idaho described his generation as "The Lost Generation." The author was Ernest Hemingway. He was speaking of his compatriots, the famous "expatriates" of the 1920's, F. Scott Fitzgerald, Gertrude Stein, Hart Crane, Malcolm Cowley, John Dos Passos, Harry Crosby, and others, writers who abandoned The Village, in disillusionment, for Paris, where, for a while, the emptiness of such vogues as Dadaism nonetheless seemed far more meaningful than an America devoted to the dollar and oblivious to art. Art for art's sake was their credo, and certainly some among them history has shown to have been great writers. What they lacked was a suitable milieu, a place, if you will, to call home. What about today's exile, ignored or maligned, the American generation born at the close of World War II, the child of the Nuclear Age and the Cold War? Is not his a lost generation? Is not an exile always and but an exile?

> This was the generation conceived in the years immediately following the global war, the war which the United States, the arsenal of democracy, had won. However, out of this war there emerged a new foe, the Soviet Communists. Now the duty of the arsenal of democracy became to hold back the Communists. While the child of the Cold War was a mere tot, the war in Korea was fought. The Red Scare and the McCarthy Era peaked, and the U.S.A. was running scared. Each morning in school, this generation heard the National Anthem and recited the Pledge of Allegiance. In school, these were told that the Communists were evil, that Nikita Khrushchev was the wickedest of men. This was said again and again, until it was believed.

This generation believed it straight through high school, and then into college, but now the country was again at war, in a tiny, distant, unknown land called Vietnam, again holding the line on Red aggression. Or was this it? For now, this lost generation filled the universities, from sea to shining sea, and, for the first time, it came to question what before had been accepted as the gospel truth. A veritable Pied Piper, ironically another Senator McCarthy, entered the scene, and with his tunes he enchanted children of the Nuclear Age.

The lost generation began to see the American effort in Vietnam as something quite divorced from what it was said to be. It perceived the effort to be a sham, a deceit, an obscenity. For it became clear that the Viet Cong posed no threat to the American democracy, and, ergo, that American military power was being used just to slaughter them. This was much the most difficult of all realizations, for to the lost generation, it was not merely unacceptable, it was absolutely *unbelievable.* This is the important point. Vietnam diametrically contradicted all that these had for so long been told. America would not, *could* not, do such a thing. Thus, by the thousands, by the hundred thousands, Vietnam disillusioned, and left upon each an indelible scar.

Alan first selected, as a possible medium for publication, the literary journal at Sir George Williams University, but the policy there was never to accept unsolicited manuscripts. Undeterred, Alan then journeyed over to McGill. The publications office was located in the basement of the most-decrepit, best-hidden building on campus, to be found only by the most dogged explorer. Inside was not encouraging: Stacks of paper on desks, shelves, the floor; a clutter of pencils, pens, erasers, carbon copies; a trio of the most ancient of typewriters; filing cabinets dynamite would not open; a blackboard which would never know chalk again. A man in an ill-fitting suit materialized from behind a desk and asked Alan what he wanted. Alan's answer produced a look of uncertainty. It happened the gentleman was the secretary, and a new one at that. He apparently had no notion of what to say to Alan, whose faith in the endeavor was rapidly evaporating. The day was saved by a young woman who came in. Alan explained the nature of his errand to her and immediately got an appropriate response. The editor was out, she said, but she would see that he got Alan's essay. How long was it? Approximately 4,000 words. The McGill Review accepted unsolicited manuscripts, she said, which was not a guarantee of publication. There was no remuneration. Alan said he knew these things, putting the woman off a bit, which in turn irked him. Indeed, the place both irked and puzzled him, but, as it was either risk it or abandon it, he silently relinquished his manuscript and, smiling at the staring pair, departed.

Word came from Stefan. The law school at the University of Minnesota had rejected him. He was accepted at both UCLA and Hastings, the latter in San Francisco, so it would be one or the other of these. Alan was stricken, for he had practically picked the Winnipeg neighborhood to which he intended to move Jeanne and himself. How was it possible Stefan had been turned down by the school in his home state? This was his surest bet, supposedly. Again, plans had to be changed.

The graduate schools of the Montreal universities had made it clear they did not want him, he was permanently unwelcome at the employment office of the Montreal Public Schools, waiting tables was not something he could live with much longer. What could he do? Jeanne would soon complete her second year of college, but the thought of her as the family prop caused Alan pain; that was his duty, not hers. Her pregnancy was now apparent, and, while he could not deny his excitement at the prospect of becoming a father, their financial worries had him resenting the way she had tricked him. When Stefan's letter came, Jeanne, who had become opposed to the idea of moving to Winnipeg, made the mistake of opening her mouth. There was a scene. She questioned whether she came first. He said he resented that. She said he had never approved of her friends. He said that was because none of them merited approval. She said she never wanted to see Stefan again, that she had not forgotten how he had insulted her.

This was more than Alan could bear. Recalling the incident for the first time, he blurted that maybe Stefan had a point. At this, Jeanne broke down in tears. Did he believe that, too? Yes, she deceived him, but only because he would not do what she knew he wanted to do. Had he not realized that from their first night together, on New Year's Eve, she had never so much as wanted to be with another man? Wasn't he at least that perceptive? Alan apologized, saying he had not meant what he said, that he had always believed her. She said she did not believe he really loved her, that he would not care if she left him for her friends at McGill. He said that was absurd, and he forbade her to have anything to do with them. She said she resented his hypocrisy. He was prepared to steer their lives around what an unworthy friend thousands of miles away in another country was doing, but he would not let her go near her friends, as though they were a plague. He said they were worse than a plague, and he said he would not tolerate further criticism of Stefan.

Out of defiance, Jeanne began again, on the sly, to run around with her old McGill friends, the crowd that called itself The Rapprochement. But the fact was, Jeanne no longer cared for these friends. They seemed childish, now. It was Alan she cared for. Yet she saw now, too, that her husband did not love her. She would not be faithless, as indeed she had not been since the new year; for all the rancor, the baby she carried was Alan's. But unstable as she had been before marrying, and with the realization hers was an unreturned love, Jeanne began again to founder. Her reacquaintance with The Rapprochement served only to worsen her condition, for Alan was correct in his appraisal of them as self-destructive. Her clandestine re-association lasted, however, only one month; she did not like them, as before, and she refused to play the games. Jeanne wanted only her husband. Chastising herself for her weakness, she left them for good one day, making up her mind to do everything in her power to make Alan happy and their marriage a success. Which was no more than what she had been doing, all along.

But their union was unsound. Alan began to understand his feeling for his wife was not love. He tried to remember how he had felt before, thinking he must have fallen out of love. Somehow, he found he could not remember how he had felt before. It baffled him. His work at the restaurant was freshly humiliating each day. Alan was miserable every minute he spent there. His immediate superior had taken a dislike to him, and now habitually faulted his work and sought to belittle him in front of the manager. An attempt to make an issue of Alan's status as an exile had, however, proved unsuccessful. Alan thought if only he could find a decent job, things would improve. Again, he gave consideration to another city, a new start. Montreal seemed a quagmire to him. He would miss his father-in-law, if they moved. Alan felt Charles McCarran was his best friend, after Stefan, and he was closer to Charles than his own daughter was. The unpleasantness between them over the job at Duval High was long forgotten, by both. In retrospect, Alan thought he had mistreated Charles. Alan, however, could not help reflecting, sometimes, on the difference having that full-time teaching position would have made. He reminded himself of the folly of brooding on the past.

"What is it you want, Alan?" Charles asked him the night Alan mentioned he and Jeanne might leave the city. The older man naturally did not want them to go. "I think that is what you need to ask yourself first."

"I can't stand being a waiter, Charles. It's demeaning. If I just had something I could stay with. Something permanent, so that the two of us could feel settled. I'm exhausted with this state of limbo, and now that the baby is coming …"

"You and Jeanne are happy, aren't you, Alan?" Charles said.

"Oh, yes," Alan replied, figuring he probably was not fooling Charles McCarran. The first few months they had been happy, but Alan, for all his efforts, could not recall when or how things had changed. Had it been actually getting married? Was that what had spoiled it? Alan told himself this couldn't be right, since they had been happy after marrying, too. He clung to the belief a solid, respectable job, one to which he could commit himself, would restore everything that had somehow gotten lost.

"What about Jeanne doing some work, if possible, until the baby comes?"

"She might find something, Charles, but you know how it is. I don't want her being the breadwinner." Alan half-laughed. "You know, it's a funny thing. In that essay I told you about, that I wrote, I drew a portrait of the average exile. I did not think I was very average, but now, I'm beginning to resemble that portrait, like Gertrude did Picasso's portrait of her."

"Who is Gertrude?"

"Gertrude Stein. She was a literary figure in the early part of this century. An American. She is in my essay, as a matter of fact." The essay was yet another thing that had gone wrong. Alan had been advised by the McGill Review that his piece was unsuitable for their publication and would be returned to him, but they had not returned it.

"Have you ever thought of writing for a living, Alan? You like it. What about the newspapers?"

"Charles, do you think I can just walk into the front office of *The Gazette* and announce, 'Here I am, fellows'?" Alan laughed ruefully at the notion.

"I don't see why not," said Charles McCarran. "Others have."

"You know, I would have liked teaching," Alan said, but this made Charles frown, and Alan, seeing there was no place at all to go with it, dropped it.

133

"I should hate to see the two of you leave. It is for you to decide, of course, but I don't see any real advantage in moving."

"Just the idea of fresh air. I guess."

"You and Jeanne have some money, don't you? I mean ..."

"I know what you mean, Charles." Alan appreciated Charles' frankness and made certain this showed in his response. "We're still okay, but the baby is going to mean finding a cheaper apartment. Jeanne can't work, she'll be at home with the little one. We may have to sell the car, and that won't bring much. I bought it second-hand. We'll have to cut corners wherever we can. I'll probably have to take a second, bad job." Alan was in despair. Charles McCarran had not realized how distressed Alan was over their financial plight. He had an inspiration. He could replace one of his secretaries with Jeanne. It would cause a small stink with his partners, no more. Charles knew Alan would not for a moment agree to a handout, but he reasoned his son-in-law might consent to this, and it was better than a loan.

"If it is all right with both of you, Alan," Charles said, "Jeanne can work for me, until the baby comes. We need some additional secretarial help." His father-in-law's offer made Alan smile.

"You always bail me out, don't you, Charles?" he said. Both were silent, momentarily. "I'll speak with Jeanne about it. It would buy us a little time, and that would help a lot."

"Then you don't mind staying in Montreal?"

"The grass is no greener elsewhere, I'm sure. As I said, it was just the idea of fresh air. I think it is more reasonable to stay here and have Jeanne accept your offer." Alan acknowledged to himself it was a delusion getting away would be a panacea. Charles was grateful they would stay where he could be of assistance. As for Jeanne, she was not enthusiastic about working for her father. This Alan had anticipated, but no persuasion proved necessary, for she said she would do it, and she made a pact with herself not to complain. Once again, thoughts of moving were discarded.

In California, Stefan graduated. Alan received a letter from him.

Santa Barbara
June 12, 1969

Dear Alan and Jeanne,

My last letter from dear old St. Barbara-by-the-sea. I am going to miss this place. I can remember arriving four years ago and marveling at the sun and the warmth. People said it wasn't cold in the winter, and I asked them then what was it.

Commencement put me to sleep. Some numbskull in the California Senate gave the big speech. Same song and dance as after high school. The future is in your hands, etc. Seems like somebody could think up something else to say. Some big shot in our class spoke, too. He had a list of credits a mile long, but I swear I never saw the guy once until he got up on that stage. In high school, you have to play football, be on student council and date a cheerleader, if you want to speak at commencement. In college, be obscure.

I'll be in San Francisco for the next two weeks, looking into housing, checking out the school (again). Then, back to St. Paul for the summer. Too bad you two didn't move to Winnipeg, after all. We might have gotten together some weekend over the summer. Guess I'd have been the one to make the trip, huh? I still can't believe I didn't get into the U of M law school. They are going to be sorry at the U of M one of these days, when, as the senior senator from the Golden State, I introduce a resolution to abolish the Big Ten for lack of sound judgment. The Big Ten turns into The Little None. Guess that would be the end of the Rose Bowl, wouldn't it?

Alan, you mentioned in your last letter that you are unhappy being a waiter. It got me to thinking about what you might do. Long-term, that is. You have a flair for writing. Have you ever thought of journalism? You got a couple of articles published in "The Intelligencer," if I remember right. That essay you sent me, on the lost generation, is really good. (Did you get it published?) I think you should try to get into journalism, in short. Incidentally, I think you put your finger on it in your essay. Too bad the President isn't a reading man. Nixon is a zero. The joke here is that he's going to reveal his secret plan to end the war as soon as he finds out what it is. Every night on the news they give a body count for the number of casualties over the past 24 hours. The North Vietnamese always have lost about ten times as many men as the South Vietnamese and U.S. combined. So how come the war isn't over? Reagan is Nixon's number one boy. If Washington can tell lies, Sacramento can, too. Well, when I get into politics, there's going to be some changes. This, I understand, is going to take some time. Everybody says the first year of law school is awful. Come to think of it, didn't your dad go to Hastings? Maybe he could give me a tip or two?

Can't think of anything else at the moment. Write to St. Paul. Maybe sometime over the summer we can work out a rendezvous at Windsor? I'd like to see both of you before I tackle law back out here in September.

Stef

P.S.: Army physical notice came.

Alan thought it singular that two widely-separated persons had suggested the same thing to him within the space of a week. Deciding it might be worth a try after all, he acted on Charles' counsel and went to the newspapers. Alan even dropped in at one of the French-language papers where, since he spoke no French, he could not possibly have been hired. He wasted his time. There was nothing for him to do but continue waiting on tables, and bear it. Working for her father, Jeanne was making more money than her husband, but this made absolutely no difference to her, only to Alan. Realizing the importance of having the money, Alan shrugged his shoulders and dismissed, as best he could, his inadequacy as a provider.

Jeanne was not much of a cook, at least so far, but this did not inhibit Alan from socializing. From time to time, he invited Dave Hillsborough or John Walters or Greg Harding, his one friend from Le Gourmand, or even Margaret Page, for dinner. Jeanne, too, had a few friends, outside The Rapprochement, who came now and then, but Alan did not particularly like them either. He thought his wife's tastes in friends stupendously bad, but he knew she deeply resented his passing moral judgments on them, and thus, excepting the ones he had known in The Rapprochement, he refrained from this conduct.

This evening, he had invited both Margaret and Dave. Alan wished to speak with them about the public schools, for he thought there might yet be some way to get back into the school administration's good graces, if he went through the proper channels. Dave said bluntly that "Alan Young" was persona non grata at Duval and, necessarily, higher up. Margaret, no less frank, said "once fired, never re-hired" was the unwritten rule in the schools and, for that matter, in practically every office.

"I wasn't fired," Alan protested uselessly.

"Yes, you were," said Dave. "Technically, you were given Marcel's job, so when you refused it, you had to be fired. It's a legal technicality."

"I never even signed a contract," Alan said.

"Doesn't matter," said Dave. Alan could not comprehend how he could have been fired from a job he never had. It seemed to him every bad thing happened, if it possibly could.

"What keeps you single, Dave?" Jeanne asked cheerfully, changing the subject, for she felt there was no sense wasting another minute on the previous one.

"The right girl hasn't come along," Dave said.

"You can't wait forever, you know."

"Can't afford to be too choosy, is that it?"

"I should say not," Margaret said, making everyone laugh. Her skill at self-effacement was a quality Alan had long admired in her.

"You're hardly an old maid, Margaret," he teased.

"That's from your perspective," she said.

"I wonder that the right two people ever find each other," Dave said. "I have known many women, but not one I thought I could love and marry." Alan was dubious of this claim, since Dave had never seemed to him interested in anything but skiing.

"It requires a good deal of flexibility and maturity, Dave," Margaret said. "I'm not much of a believer in love, to tell you the truth. It isn't love that makes a marriage work. It's maturity."

"You've become hard-boiled in your old age, Margaret," Alan joked.

"No, I mean that. I was in love with my husband, and I am sure there are other men I could love. I hope I do. But I think the idea of love is beaten to death. People develop ulcers over it. Am I in love? What is love? Why can't I fall in love? How love makes me suffer! It's meaningless. Young people marry for sex, not love. They think it's love, they even call it love. The girl gets pregnant, because that is the female function, and they have a child, or two. Then, because they are themselves children, the marriage breaks up. They blame it on love, on not being in love anymore. That isn't it. The problem is, they aren't adults. They are in over their heads. Somebody shut me up."

"You think the female function is just to have babies?" Jeanne asked, astonishment in her voice.

"Did I say that?" Margaret responded, clearly implying she felt she had not. "What I meant is, every female wants to bear children. If my former husband … well, never mind. We had some bad luck, I guess you could say, or I would undoubtedly be a mother today. Aren't you eager, Jeanne, to have your baby? Aren't you ecstatic you are pregnant? Of course you are."

"Yes, I am," Jeanne said. "I thought I heard you say that the only function we women have is to have children."

"Not the only function, but certainly the chief function," Margaret said. "It's simple. What is a uterus for? The fetus. It has no other function. Women have a biological urge to be pregnant. If we didn't, homo sapiens would come to an end. It's Darwinian, really. Unused organs eventually atrophy. That goes for the uterus as much as for a flipper, or whatever."

"A flipper?" Alan said gratuitously.

"Please don't think I'm taking anything personally," Jeanne said, "but I don't agree with you."

"Hardly anybody ever does," Margaret said, laughing, "and it would surely be presumptuous of me to think I am right, and everybody else is wrong." But Alan could see Margaret thought exactly that, and his perception was accurate. Margaret was so wonderfully sure of herself, he reflected. Alan wondered if he had married the wrong woman.

"Will you drink them if I mix a batch of heady screwdrivers?" he inquired of the company, snapping himself out of his reverie.

"Mix away, headier the better," said Margaret. While Alan was at it, she succeeded in breaking away from the others. She joined him in the kitchen. Margaret could see that Alan was unhappy. "What's wrong, Alan? I've never seen you so subdued and quiet. Where is that irreverent soul I once knew?"

"He's dead," Alan replied, abruptly very nearly whimpering. Alan just fought it back, as a torrent of regret and self-pity swept over him. What had happened to the simple, unfettered, carefree days?

"Alan, whatever it is, it can't be as bad as all that."

"You are lousy at platitudes, Margaret."

"I suppose so," she said, wondering which platitude she had uttered. "How can I help, Alan?" Margaret took his arm. "I really want to help."

"There is no way. I'm just feeling sorry for myself. When things begin to go wrong, they go very wrong. Adversity feeds on itself, I think."

"If you would like to stop by, some afternoon," Margaret said discreetly, "on your own, that is, you would be welcome." Margaret did not think this would be like Alan, yet she felt he might be receptive.

"Don't be silly," he chided gently. "I couldn't do that now." Alan appreciated her offer, however, and considered he had certainly misjudged her as a friend. He reproved himself for not having remained close to her, since marrying. Always, he had been so confident of himself, and now he was confident of nothing. He could not so much as identify a friend. He was as a man, lost in a mist.

Since the day Alan asked him if he had informed Paul Kelly of his change in address, John Walters had been secretly looking into the matter. John was certain he had not told Kelly of Alan's move, but he had elected not to reveal this to Alan, and had only said to him, offhandedly, that he couldn't remember. John was persuaded something was amiss, for on several previous occasions, he had entertained vague suspicions of espionage on Kelly's part. This incident was the proverbial straw that broke the camel's back. How had Kelly learned? John sought to keep his imagination in check, yet couldn't help wondering if Kelly was somehow in cahoots with the government in Washington, spying on the exiles in Montreal, or maybe even in all of Canada. No, couldn't be true, John reassured himself. Mustn't get paranoid. Nonetheless, he was resolved to take action. He moved cautiously, taking no one into his confidence, for he knew not whom to trust. Besides, if trickery was involved, John wanted the credit for exposing it. Thinking there might be many U.S. agents in Canada, he decided not to ask questions in Montreal. Instead, he wrote a friend living in New York, not a particularly close friend, and asked him if he would mind checking to see if a certain Boston law firm had once employed a certain Paul Kelly. John gave no reason for the favor. His New York friend, mildly curious, obliged, writing back that Davies, Schwartz, Franklin & Ross had indeed once employed Timothy Paul Kelly, Esq. John was surprised, for his paranoia had prevailed. He had talked himself into believing Kelly was engaged in illicit activity.

The question continued to nag John, for there was no explanation for Kelly's knowledge that Alan had moved to another apartment. John decided to go one step further. On the faculty at Harvard University were many outspoken "doves." John selected the man he had always most admired and wrote him, describing Kelly and explaining, as fully as he could, the several "mysterious incidents," as he characterized them. Quietly, discreetly, an investigation was begun, in Cambridge. It revealed that Timothy Paul Kelly, 34, was born in Springfield, Massachusetts, on Feb. 18, 1935, graduated from Boston University School of Law in 1959, and practiced law at Davies, Schwartz, Franklin & Ross from 1959-1962. After that, Tim—the name he had always gone by—vanished, until turning up in July 1967, in Montreal, where he organized the American Expatriates Center. The center's funding came from a potpourri of anti-war causes and foundations, whose aggregate contribution came to slightly more than $80,000. That was all there was. John's Harvard contact advised him to drop the matter, since, John's suspicions notwithstanding, there was not a shred of evidence of skullduggery. While it was odd that Kelly's whereabouts for five years could not be determined, and that he had once gone by his first name but now used his middle name, this did not add up to much, and it proved nothing. John agreed, but after brooding on it for several days, he changed his mind and called all four Montreal newspapers. One of them expressed a mild interest and asked John if he would consent to an interview, which he gladly did, on condition the newspaper would not reveal him as its source, if Kelly was contacted. Subsequently, the paper attempted unsuccessfully to speak with Kelly, who absolutely refused an interview. With this, the paper chose not to pursue it. John was informed of this decision. Though far from satisfied, he could see no way to proceed; the best he could do was resolve to watch Kelly more closely. One day he called Alan, and told him most of what had transpired.

"It's strange, don't you think, Alan, or have I lost my perspective on this?" John said. "People don't disappear for five years, unless they're secret agents, or something."

"I don't know, John. You and I have disappeared, in a manner of speaking, wouldn't you say?" Alan thought John was jumping to wild conclusions, and, in any case, was so absorbed with his own difficulties, he could not work up any real interest in it.

"What would you do, if you were in my shoes?" John asked.

"Well, I suppose you could confront Kelly, but it would be awkward. You might end up looking pretty ridiculous."

"I thought of doing that," John said, "but I think there's more to lose than gain. Right now, I know something Kelly doesn't know, so I have the advantage. Think I'll just stick with the status quo for a while, and watch Kelly's every move."

"Sounds good, John," Alan said.

"Thanks for your thoughts, Alan. Remember, don't mention this to anyone. Okay?"

"Okay, John," Alan said. Their conversation ended. Alan felt if anything was peculiar, it was Kelly's shift from first to middle name; still, this was probably nothing more than a harmless eccentricity. Alan had too much else on his mind to bother with it. It did alter his opinion of John Walters, whom he had come to regard as an idler. Again, Alan thought he was wrong about a friend, and now more than ever he fretted over his inability to trust himself and his judgment.

Alan wrote to Stefan:

> Dear Stef,
>
> Outside of you, Stef, I can't tell a friend from a foe, love from sex, up from down. I've lost track of myself. I can't trust myself. Everything conceivable is going wrong. I can't get work, except for this cursed waiting on tables. It's wrecking my self-respect, or maybe it's already wrecked, pick your tense. My wife is making more money than I am, working for her dad. I am not in love with her. This is the worst trap any man can ever get himself into, I'm convinced. I think I used to be in love with her, but something changed. Now, I'd rather be with another woman (Margaret, the tall one). She has invited me over, if you get my drift, and while I never supposed in a million years I would consider adultery, I am. An afternoon now and then with Margaret would be a godsend. It is not that long till the baby arrives, which may help my marriage, although we are going to be pressed financially. In a moment of insanity, we moved into this apartment we have now, which is ten times too expensive. I can't remember why we chose it. I can't remember anything. Life is blurred.
>
> I have just re-read this letter. I am not suicidal, even though I might sound like it. I just feel cornered, like there's no way out. But they say it's always darkest before the dawn.

Responding to your letter, I'll see if I can't be more optimistic. Your nostalgia over Santa B is a sure sign of a future
at the state funny farm. Just the same, I would give a lot to be
back there, now. All commencement speakers are trite. It's a
requirement. The valedictory at my high school made the girls
cry. I was too busy with two friends and two six-packs. Abolish
the Big Ten, you say. Okay with me. Abolish the country, while
you are at it. Whether or not I have some writing ability is
irrelevant, since there is no niche for me in that field. None,
zero. Nixon doesn't read. Obviously. Reading requires thought.
As Learned Hand once said, thought is the most difficult,
yet most important, of human endeavors. Well, something to
that effect. Dad used to talk about Learned Hand, that's how
I happen to know about him. What a weird name. First year
of law school is tough. Dad wanted me to go to law school,
naturally. You remembered right, he went to Hastings. When
you get back to California, you might call him. I'll do it for
you, if you like.

I wish we were in Winnipeg, where we could get together.
There's a very good reason to stay here, though: Jeanne is making money. Maybe, just maybe, we could swing a weekend in
Windsor, next month, say. I could leave for a few days, as I'm
due a vacation from Le Gourmand. Will let you know in next
letter. For God's sake, write.

Alan

He did begin seeing Margaret. His first visit they only talked, reminisc-
ing, philosophizing. They even discussed adultery, and she could see the
battle Alan was having with himself. The second visit, Alan and Margaret
did most of their talking in bed. To him, it was not the improper, but the
proper, thing to do. He felt close to her, much closer, he thought, than
ever before. It seemed to him now that the mutual pleasure of sex was the
highest communication between a man and a woman. Alan told Margaret
that he had not felt the same harmony with Jeanne, even in the best days
of their courtship, that he now felt with her.

"Alan, you're closer to me now than you used to be," Margaret pointed
out, not believing what he had said. "I don't care for you any more than I

ever did. We talked before, yes, but you came for sex. Now, you come for more. Our relationship isn't the same. I think you're forgetting that." That was true, Alan had to admit, and again his thoughts were of the good times with his wife. Had they connected? Yes, they had. Lots of times. He had loved her once. The torment gushed in again, and Alan wondered how he could be in bed with another woman. Censuring himself, he made up his mind never to do this again. But his resolution failed, again, and again, Margaret offered no discouragement. She liked Alan. She had always found him amusing and she lusted after his ardent kisses. She was a little sorry for Jeanne, but not very sorry. They would be careful, and, with a little luck, she figured Jeanne Young would never be the wiser. Indeed, Margaret judged that if Alan's wife ever did discover their affair, most likely it would be from Alan himself.

Stefan wrote.

St. Paul
Aug. 21, 1969

Dear Alan,

So, you're not suicidal. Shall the whole world rejoice? We await your answer, breathless. Now read on. I've spent a good deal of time on this letter. It is not the product of impulse.

You may not be suicidal, but a cry baby you are, that's for sure. A big one. By saying, "I'm not suicidal," aren't you asking for sympathy? I think so. To my knowledge, you have indulged in self-pity only twice (when that girl quit you at school, and when you were here last year). Both times, you quickly shook yourself out of it. So, what's the story now?

I'll tell you what it is. You have given up. You have lost your self-respect. I'm not sure what brought this about, although I know being a waiter is part of it. There's honor in every job; it's your attitude toward it that's the problem. So, what else is news? Well, judging by your comments, I'd say your marriage is in trouble. What's caused this?

You and Jeanne were Romeo and Juliet. Now, you claim you don't love Jeanne. You even want to get in the sack with somebody else. Adultery, Alan? You have made Jeanne your scapegoat. She tricked you. Okay. That was wrong. But she loves you, it's written all over her, and the same was written all over you. You told me you were *glad* she had deceived you. You told me the thought of becoming a father was exciting. Now that the going has gotten tough, you choose to scapegoat. That's a cheap shot, Alan, and you are not one to take cheap shots. Destiny lands its blows. You've taken some hard ones. Who hasn't? Always before, you took it in stride. Now, you're collapsing. So, how about it?

Stef

P.S. #1: Could we meet in Windsor, before I return to California Sept. 7? You and Mrs. Young, I mean. I can come anytime.

P.S. #2: I talked with your dad long distance about Hastings. We talked mostly about you, if you want to know.

P.S. #3: Who says postscripts are just for forgetful old ladies and infatuated teenagers?

But Stefan, who thought he knew Alan best, was wrong. Alan had never loved Jeanne, if Margaret alone knew it. All the same, the letter made a strong impression on Alan. He did not see how he could talk himself into feeling for his wife what he did not feel, he was aware another couldn't accomplish this for him either, but he could be upstanding. Stefan, Alan thought, was right: He had loved Jeanne, and during that time he had been the happiest ever. Perhaps it would return.

Wondering at his adultery, Alan went to see Margaret. He found her in her bathrobe. Impatience permeated her voice. Once, twice, three times she said she understood. He said he appreciated her understanding. They agreed they would remain friends. At her door, Alan smiled knowingly, and, thinking his wife sixty times the lovelier, he winked at Margaret and was gone before she could say another word.

He made yet another resolution, somehow to see Stefan, in Windsor. First, he secured from the restaurant his vacation allotment. Then, he told Jeanne how it was to be: He would spend two days with Stefan in Windsor, then he would meet her in Quebec City. They would stay a week, in the same hotel, same room if possible, as they had on their honeymoon. Damn the expense. Resigned to Stefan, she agreed without argument. She very much doubted Quebec City would be the lark it had been for them, but she saw this initiative as Alan's clumsy way of saying he wasn't giving up on their bond. Jeanne loved Alan. She blamed his distress, their distress, on the job he could not live with. Eventually, he would get a good job, and things would improve. Too, she felt the birth of their child would help make them close again. Jeanne was optimistic.

Going to Windsor was an expense they could manage. A week in Quebec City, at Deauville House, was not. Alan knew perfectly well they couldn't afford it, and so did Jeanne. But the former felt it was the only way he could justify seeing Stefan, while the latter was for anything which might bring him back to her. Thus, less than a week before Stefan was to be in San Francisco, Alan and his old friend finally accomplished the Windsor rendezvous. The circumstances were not what Alan had expected. He was supposed to be in graduate school. Instead, he was a waiter. He was supposed to be single and fancy-free. Instead, he was locked into marriage, about to become a father. He was supposed to be happy …

It was Stefan who, back in college, had relentlessly pointed out the inevitability of being drafted, come summer, provoking Alan at last to take the Naval Reserve exam. It was Stefan who had urged Alan, on more than one occasion, to do the expedient thing, always to no avail. It was Stefan who believed he understood his friend as no one else did, and who felt now he must find the right words of encouragement.

Alan arrived first, in his car, and, waiting for Stefan at the Windsor bus depot, he could easily see the towering skyscrapers of Detroit, across the river. It was the first time since leaving that he had set eyes upon the United States. His mind went back, back to the induction notice, and what he had done with it. He chuckled even now at the recollection, wishing he could have seen the recipient's face. He thought of his parents' reaction to his decision: Despair, tears. Such a display of emotion had surprised him. He thought of the days with Stefan in St. Paul; it had been an enchanted time, as a stay in a never-never land. He thought of the flight to Toronto, of the pause in the very city he gazed at now, of the steps he had taken on that soil, of his arrival in Canada, of the rain and the hotel and the drunken man and the fistfight and Charles McCarran. It seemed an infinity ago. What had happened, that he had become so miserable?

Stefan arrived. Just seeing him had a steadying effect. Stefan was like a rock in a tempestuous sea. Before they had exchanged a word, Alan found himself wishing there was some way he could talk his friend into staying.

Stefan wanted to know where Jeanne was; Alan made an excuse. Stefan was irritated that Alan had left her in Montreal. Badinage failed, for Alan was incapable of holding up his end. The days, only two, passed slowly. Alan thought his friend preoccupied with law school, and he resented this. In truth, they scarcely spoke on this. They went to a movie, tacitly agreeing something was needed to kill time. Never before had these two together had too much time on their hands. At last it came time for Stefan to return, and Alan, far more miserable than ever, groped for an explanation. Sitting together over a final cup of coffee, at the same coffee shop as two days before, Stefan embarked upon his speech.

"So, what of our visit? Just like old times? It hasn't been, has it? For two days, I have watched you and listened to you, Alan, and now I have got something to say. Something I noticed long ago, but only recently found the appropriate words for: The Rival Hypothesis. It's something I ran across boning up for law. Do you know what it is?"

"Just what it says, I assume," Alan said, annoyed at the prospect of a sermon.

"Exactly right. Alan, it is your big problem in life. Your Achilles' Heel. It's as certain as anything in the world that you never see The Rival Hypothesis. No one could possibly be more consistent. What have we talked about? Your dissatisfaction with your marriage, your dissatisfaction with your job. How did all this come about? By your not perceiving The Rival Hypothesis. You mentioned Detroit, over there. Okay, let's go back. You know better than to think I would criticize your coming to Canada. I've never quarreled with that. But what were the events leading up to this? First, there was the Army. I told you, you were going to be drafted, two autumns ago. Remember? Finally, I got you to take the Naval Reserve test. You flunked it. A mysterious ear ailment I had never heard you mention once. Thinking back on it, I almost wonder whether the Navy doctor wasn't looking at somebody else's chart, by mistake. You are not an invalid. Okay, you flunked the Navy physical, which was a catastrophe, since then you became convinced you would flunk the Army's, too. You never considered The Rival Hypothesis, that you would pass it. Then, you applied for C.O., and again, you never considered The Rival Hypothesis, that it would be rejected. Then, you came to Canada, intent upon grad school. That plan went awry, why? Because something you never considered happened: They rejected your application. Then came Jeanne. I'll have to play the devil's advocate here. You fell in love, and she got pregnant. Your mother met her, and made up her mind she was carrying somebody else's baby. I made the colossal mistake of not realizing, first, that you would never consider it, and, second, that your mother was totally wrong in her appraisal of Jeanne. She was never pregnant, until it became a specific means to a specific end, namely, marrying the man she loved. Therefore, except in theory, there is no rival hypothesis here. The point is, you would not even consider it in theory, much less practically.

"Okay, to the future. Yours, that is. Mine is to be wasted in the arena of American politics. You have the sense to scorn that which deserves nothing more. Where are you headed? Two items are giving you endless grief: Your job and your lack of love for your wife. Repeatedly, something you have said was a sub-head under one of these two. I wrote in a letter to you recently that I thought you were making a scapegoat of Jeanne. I was right about the scapegoat, wrong about the victim. It's your job you've made the scapegoat. You're blaming everything on it. You say it has cost you your self-respect. The Rival Hypothesis is unemployment, Alan. Look at The Rival Hypothesis, and it will salvage you your self-respect. Which won't, however, make you feel any differently about Jeanne. This is a separate matter entirely.

"I said I was playing the devil's advocate, when I mentioned love. Frankly, I don't place much stock in the idea of love. I'm on shaky ground here, since I've never been in love, much less married. Love was invented, they say. I don't think it's love that makes for a successful marriage. It's things like realism and responsibility and effective action. And effective worry. You're not even worrying effectively. You're mired in self-pity. You said yesterday you think misfortune breeds more misfortune. I never thought of that before, but it strikes me as profoundly true. Being down and out becomes half-pleasant. You enjoy cursing the Fates, and you sit back half-eager for the next blow. If it doesn't come, you manufacture one. Things deteriorate instead of improving. That's where you are. I say, 'effective worry'. If staying on with Jeanne is intolerable, then get a divorce. Don't just brood on and on. Otherwise, stay with her. You are about to be a father. Isn't that enough of a reason to maintain your marriage? Doesn't your child deserve a father?

Plus, you have a beautiful wife who adores you. Most men would envy you. Quit fretting over whether it's love or not. There may not even be any such thing. Yours is a bright future, not a dark one. See it for what it is, Alan."

"I didn't need a pep talk, Stefan," Alan said quietly. Stefan could not remember the last time Alan had addressed him as 'Stefan' rather than 'Stef'. "I dislike spurious self-effacement. All that about how much wiser I am for not going to law school and into politics, when that is all you've talked about for two days. I don't think your word choices always reflected constructive criticism. I'd never have believed it of you." Alan choked the last of it out.

"Then I apologize, if you think that," Stefan said forthrightly. "This will only aggravate you, I suppose, but I anticipated you might respond as you have. After all, either you would hear me, or you would not. You didn't. I'm still your friend. I can be no more lucid than I have been. Possibly I didn't say anything valid." Alan remained silent. "Well, I guess there's nothing more to say ... I'll drop you a line when I get settled in San Francisco." Still Alan said nothing. "I hope you and Jeanne have fun in Quebec City ... so long, Alan." Thus they parted, Stefan bereaved at the realization even he could not reach his friend, and Alan stooped under the heavy new burden. But their bond was too strong. Stefan and Alan had been so close for so long, it would take more than one misunderstanding to undo things. All the way to Quebec City, Alan deliberated on their visit. He figured time and distance had worked against them, that naturally he could not expect things to remain as they had been back in Santa Barbara. Those days, those years, which he had thought would never end, now seemed to him to have an aura of magic about them. Alan longed with all his heart to be back there. The present returned. Yes, Stefan was different now, but Alan reasoned he was still his great friend. He wished he could return to Windsor and smooth over the raggedness of their parting. Too late. On he journeyed, and on he thought. Remarks Stefan had made began to come back. Responsibility was what counted, not love. Alan remembered Margaret's having said something similar. Surely a tremendous responsibility—the greatest for any man, Alan reflected—was about to be his, the rearing of a child. His heart leapt. This was a great thing! Why hadn't it seemed so, before? This was all he needed, this certainly would set things right again with Jeanne. This would turn everything around. Alan laughed aloud. What a wonderful thing, that soon he was to be a father! All of a sudden, he was eager to be with his wife; he accelerated the Volkswagen, and, as more of Stefan's words seeped in, the transformation continued. Maybe there really was no such thing as love, despite the fact everybody spoke of it. Yes, he had heard it was invented. By one of the English romantic poets, wasn't it? He would re-commit himself to Jeanne, and be happy with her and the little one, and not again worry over the issue of love. What counted was not shirking responsibility. He never had before, he wouldn't now. That was what mattered. Still something else came back, the scapegoating. Yes, he blamed his job, but he still had his self-respect, if he wanted to have it. It was as easy as realizing it; in that instant, it was back. Alan cried out with joy, and then cursed himself that he could have been so stupid as not to have understood Stefan while they were together. Bitter was his reflection as, momentarily, the fear he had lost his friend gripped him; then, realizing this was not so, he became fiercely angry with himself. When would they see each other again? There was no telling.

"How dumb can I be?" he said out loud. Alan shook his head. "I never gave him a chance. What must he think?" Alan's mind went to work on ways he could make it up to Stefan, and this absorbed him as he drove on. Upon reaching the outskirts of Quebec City, he turned his thoughts to his wife. Unexpectedly, the nagging question of love came back. Could it be it did not matter? This was difficult to accept, for he could not reconcile how he felt now toward his wife, with how he had once felt. If "before" had not been love, then what was it? There was no answer. Well, the thing to do was to press on, quit fretting, assume the responsibilities he knew were his. Alan reached Deauville House and, with resolve if not passion, prepared to meet his wife. Jeanne was there, right on time, awkwardly draped in one of the plush chairs in the lobby. The highly visible load she bore, which Alan had come to resent, which had fostered repugnance, even, he rejoiced at seeing. He wanted to pat her there. Alan's was an about-face so marked, she noticed it immediately, and, although no believer in miracle, Jeanne found herself quietly thanking Stefan, for whom she had no use on earth. Their rapprochement, the object of the proposed five days of a duplicated honeymoon, was accomplished in the first five minutes. Alan took her in his arms and kissed her and caressed her cheeks, thinking neither on love nor onlookers. No less his now than ever, for it was true she had loved him from the first, Jeanne left it all to him. The point in staying at Deauville House no longer existed, they should save their money and go home, he said. But it was his vacation, and Alan thought it would be fun to stay a couple of days, since this time they might even discover the charms of Quebec City. He announced they would stay two days, and this they did, cutting quite a figure about town, a man and a decidedly pregnant woman, tripping gaily about like … honeymooners! The days proved perhaps the best they had ever had together, and certainly the best in a long time.

On return to Montreal, Alan made up his mind to find a second job. They were going to need the income; that alone was the important thing. He would settle for whatever he could find. What he found was an opening for a concierge at a hotel near their apartment. Also, Alan resolved again on a teaching career. This decided, he began writing to every graduate school in Canada. He reasoned he would be admitted somewhere, surely, and they would move to that city, and he would make ends meet by working while attending school.

September turned October. Alan thought by the look of his wife the baby would come any minute. He was restless, she calm, which, he reflected, was just as everyone said it would be. The fact was, the baby was still weeks off.

They had John Walters by one evening, for dinner, and husband and wife spoke of nothing except the baby. John departed thinking Alan absurdly sentimental, and woefully domesticated. When John reached his apartment, two men jumped him as he emerged from his car. One held him from behind, and the other, an especially big and powerful man, broke his jaw with one well-delivered punch. Devastated, and bleeding profusely, John was at their mercy, but they were finished with him. John just managed to get himself inside, and, staggering to the telephone, succeeded in dialing Alan. Then, knowing he could not speak, he was able, by supreme effort, to mumble his name until Alan got it.

John was three days in the hospital; his jaw had to be wired, and 37 stitches were required. Alan came by each evening to see him and, when he was released, drove him home. He also called John's parents, in Texas, to assure them their son, although seriously injured, would be all right. (They came nonetheless.) Alan wanted to know who had done this. He felt a certain responsibility, John's having been with him on the evening of the attack. John doubted he would recognize his assailants. The entire episode had lasted less than a minute. The two men had said almost nothing. John was left with no clue whatever as to their identity. Nevertheless, he did not believe it was a random act. Attacks like this occurred seldom in Montreal.

John said he suspected Timothy Paul Kelly had somehow learned about his probe, and this was retaliation, probably by the Central Intelligence Agency. To John, it all added up to revenge, despite his having nothing to implicate Kelly—who came by twice while John was hospitalized—let alone evidence that the men who attacked him were government agents.

"I suppose I did have it coming," John said. Alan was thunderstruck.

"What in heck do you mean by that, John?"

"I broke the law of my country, and now I have been victimized by lawbreakers from my country. What does the Bible say? 'As ye sow, so …'"

"You didn't break any law," Alan interrupted, close to anger.

"Of course I did. So did you. We both ran away."

"Look, John," Alan said firmly. "That's nuts. It's the government of the United States that broke the law. The Vietnam War has never been declared by Congress. It's a totally illegal war. It probably violates every international convention, too. You're not the criminal, the president of the United States is."

"Have it your way, Alan," John said dispiritedly. "You always do." John was tired, and the last thing his convalescence needed was an argument.

CHAPTER 5

THE LAST WEEK OF THE MONTH WAS HECTIC. TWICE, JEANNE THOUGHT the time had come, only to find it was a false alarm. At last, on the 28th, Jeanne announced she was positive this was it, and once again they left home for St. Bonaventure Hospital. The third time proved the charm; Jeanne was admitted, and Alan, after completing the necessary forms, was directed to the waiting room. There, he encountered two other men, both older. Both were reading magazines months old. The idea of reading, or even being sedentary, was inconceivable to Alan. Back and forth he paced the room.

"Suppose you could hold still, friend?" one of the pair asked him. "You are about to drive me up the wall." Unaware he had been addressed, Alan did not break stride. "I say, would you mind sitting?" the man continued, himself standing. "You are making me dreadfully nervous."

"Who, me?" Alan said. "I didn't realize you were talking to me. What did you say?"

"I asked you if you would kindly sit down."

"Can't. I don't see how you two guys can be so, er, placid."

"First-timers?" the other man inquired, smiling.

"Are you kidding?" said the first man. "This is my fourth. An accident, she insists, but I'm not so sure about that." The other man laughed.

"And what about you?" he asked Alan. "Surely this is your first?"

"Yes. It shows, I suppose?"

"Yup."

"Well, sorry if I'm disturbing you fellows. I've got to walk."

"You are not bothering me," said the second man. "I remember my first time. I was about your age, and just as impatient." The man stood and offered

Alan his hand. "Congratulations. There are a few moments in life which are very special, and it is your good fortune to be experiencing one right now. Not that I'm not thrilled, mind you, but the first time is in a class by itself."

"Yes, congratulations," said the first man, also shaking Alan's hand, "and please quit that infernal pacing." Alan in turn congratulated both men, but still did not think he could sit down.

"You hoping for a boy or a girl?" the second man asked Alan.

"Oh, a boy, I suppose. Doesn't really matter. A daughter would be nice, too."

"I think most young men want a son first. I know I did, but it wasn't until the third that the missus obliged. This will be my fourth, also."

"Must you?" the first man protested, as Alan resumed pacing.

"Yes, I must," Alan said curtly. "All right, I'll try the hall."

"Why wouldn't you indulge him?" the second man asked the first, after Alan's departure. He was annoyed by his peevishness. "You could see he was a little tense. Doesn't really know what he's gotten himself into, but which of us does?"

Out in the hall, a nurse had intercepted Alan. She was a petite brunette.

"Can I help you?" she asked him.

"No, thanks. Just getting a bit of exercise." Alan was becoming exasperated.

"I'm afraid that isn't allowed in the corridors." She gave Alan a sympathetic smile. "Are you an expectant daddy, by chance?" It wasn't a great guess, since this was the obstetrical ward.

"Yes," Alan said, "and I just can't sit quietly at the moment. Got to pace."

"In that case, pace away," the nurse said, winking, "and congratulations." Her language brought a grin to Alan's face. "If anybody gives you any lip, send 'em to me."

"You're the only person in this hospital with an ounce of sense," Alan said.

"I've known that all along," the nurse replied.

There was a mix-up of some kind. "X" thought "Y" had reached Alan with the news his daughter had been born, and "Y" thought "X" had. Fully forty minutes elapsed before their physician himself, Stuart Hamilton, located Alan.

"You are the father of a beautiful baby girl, my good man," he said heartily, shaking Alan's hand. "Seven pounds and six ounces and doing wonderfully, as is mom. Congratulations!"

"Thank you, thank you, doctor," Alan responded, beaming.

"Your wife is expecting you," Hamilton said. Alan had no way of knowing Jeanne had been waiting for him for forty minutes. He had no way of knowing she had planned to delay on having Mary brought to her, until he had joined her, but had lost patience and asked for Mary. He had no way of knowing the baby reached her arms only a minute ahead of his arrival. All he knew was, when he walked into the room, she was absorbed with their child as only a mother with newborn can be. She hardly noticed him, and when she did, it was not warmly.

"Where have you been?" she said sharply. "I've been waiting and waiting."

"You have?" he responded, taken aback.

"Yes, I have, Alan. I wanted to ..." She dropped it, and returned her full attention to the baby. When Alan came over to kiss her and take his first look at Mary, she acted as if she didn't want to share their daughter with him. She made an unkind comment. Unexpectedly, the resentment over how she had deceived him, and even the suspicion whether he was the father, which he had truly dismissed, was back, all of it, with a vengeance, and just like that what was to have been the most joyful moment of their lives together went horribly sour. After a brief interval, in which there was further recrimination from her, prompting ugliness from him in return, Alan found an excuse and left. Hardly was he out the door, Jeanne burst into tears.

When Alan came to get his wife and daughter the next afternoon, Jeanne was contrite. She had considered her conduct and, while still not understanding the long interval between her asking for him and his arrival, she felt she had behaved badly, and was ashamed of herself. She apologized immediately and hugged him hard. Alan, in return, was unmistakably short. They rode home in complete silence, but on getting into the house, she broke into sobs.

"What is it, Alan? Why are you being so awful?"

"What do you mean?" he said with a hint of feeling offended.

"You're being mean to me. Don't pretend you aren't."

"You're imagining things," he said pointedly, himself surprised by how easy this behavior was proving.

"I am not imagining things. You are being mean to me!" Alan left the room.

There ensued a period of days of a hellishness beyond exaggeration. Alan stayed cold and unapproachable, although he was a dutiful father and, when his in-laws stopped by, his familiar self. He seemed to go out of his way to do his part with the baby, all the while treating Jeanne with unabated scorn. She tried to tell herself it wasn't happening, that indeed she was imagining this conduct, but her heart knew better. After a week of ceaseless unkindness from her husband, Jeanne collapsed utterly, emotionally and physically. She began shrieking, locked herself in the bathroom and sobbed by the hour, and even became neglectful of Mary. Night after night there was almost no sleep for her. She became feverish. Alarmed, Alan called their doctor. Jeanne was put on medication and showed improvement, though she was not well. Alan himself was coming undone, for he, too, needed rest. He began swallowing her sleeping pills indiscriminately. Three weeks into Mary's birth, he collapsed, totally spent, into the most troubled sleep of his life.

He was running, running faster than he had ever run, faster than he could imagine he could run, surpassingly fast and yet, his pursuer was gaining. Alan was terrified. He urged himself on, despite an aching side, faster faster faster. Where was he? In a jungle, a steamy thicket of plants and ferns and fronds and trees uncounted, threatening to trip him at every step. A real din, too, with the ceaseless shrieking of monkey and cawing of a million parrots. Must be the Amazon, but what was he doing in the Amazon? Alan looked back to find his pursuer, whoever he was, drawing nearer. He lunged desperately forward, and suddenly it was clear the cacophony wasn't birds, it was guns. There were thatched huts, and men and women and children, and fighting, men in uniforms, a terrific battle with automatic weapons and flame throwers and helicopter gunships swooping down. A woman grabbed a small girl and flung her to the ground, covering her. They were Asians. Vietnam! This was Vietnam! Alan saw bloodied men falling all about him, there were screams, the village was aflame. He tripped and nearly fell, looked back, and to his inexpressible horror, saw that his pursuer, now only a few feet away, was President Johnson! He was lunging at him, tackling him! The president had a document, a folded sheet he opened with a snap of his wrist and thrust in Alan's face. "I believe this belongs to you," the president said in his unmistakable drawl. His draft notice! Alan beheld it in horror and instantly began again to run. He looked back, and now, the president was grinning at him, a terrible, unnerving grin, but matching him pace by pace! Alan ran still faster, but again he was caught and tackled, and the president repeated, "I believe this belongs to you." Back up again, running, running again, the battle raging all around, tackled again, "I believe this belongs to you ..." Alan, utterly out of breath, "please, please Mr. President ..." somebody begged, must be him! Up again, running, and suddenly everything went blank. Where was he? No more jungle. He was in some kind of room, it was a court, a courtroom! He was in a courtroom!

"Mrs. Young, will you tell the court what you next observed your son, the defendant, do, after he opened the envelope?" It was his mother, testifying in court! Testifying against him!

"He put the envelope down, got up from the table, and walked into his bedroom."

"Mom wasn't even home," Alan whispered frantically to Billings, "let alone following me around the house."

"Hush, Mr. Young," said Billings.

"What did he do in the bedroom?"

"He went into his closet and emerged momentarily, with a shoebox."

"And what did he do with the shoebox?"

"He opened it, took out a box of crayons and went back into the dining room."

"I think it was the breakfast room," Alan whispered. "I think."

"Please be silent, Mr. Young."

"But don't you need to know?"

"Where his draft notice remained on the table?" the prosecutor inquired.

"Yes."

"What did he do next?"

"He opened the box of crayons, took one out and wrote something on his draft notice."

"Which crayon did he select?"

"Objection. Immaterial and irrelevant."

"Overruled."

"Which crayon did he select?"

"The red one."

"And then what?"

"He put the crayon back in the box and returned to his bedroom."

"What did he do when he returned to his bedroom?"

"He put the box of crayons back into the shoebox and put the shoebox back in his closet."

"And this shoebox was among items you had saved from his boyhood and adolescent years, and stored in his closet, is that correct?"

"Yes."

"Could you give the court some idea of what other items were in the shoebox?"

"Objection. Relevance."

"Overruled."

"What else had you saved over the years?"

"Oh, school things, like a blue ruler he had cherished, and a protractor, and an attendance award, and a drawing of a horse he did in first grade, and report cards, things like that. His tassel from high school graduation."

"Thank you. Mrs. Young, was your son agitated as he was going about defacing his draft notice?"

"Objection. Leading."

"Sustained."

"Was he upset while he was inscribing his draft notice?"

"Objection."

"Overruled."

"No, he was not upset."

"Would it be more accurate to say he was calm and measured, as if the entire process was premeditated?"

"Objection. Leading the witness."

"Overruled. You may continue."

"Yes, it was as if he had planned the whole thing."

"Thank you, Mrs. Young. No further questions."

"Counsel?" the judge addressed Alan's lawyer.

"Thank you, Your Honor." Anson Billings approached the witness stand. *"Mrs. Young, you have testified you were home the afternoon of July 29th and observed your son open an envelope that had come in the mail, which contained his draft notice, and that thereafter he inscribed something upon it with a crayon, is that correct?"*

"Yes."

"And you mentioned that your son selected the red crayon for his purposes, is this correct?"

"Yes."

"How did you know it was the red crayon?"

"I was just a few feet away, I could plainly see it."

"A few feet in which direction, Mrs. Young?"

"Objection. Relevance."

"Overruled. You may continue."

"A few feet in which direction?"

"I don't know what you mean by direction."

"Were you in front of your son, or behind him, or to the side?"

"The side."

"Which side?"

"I don't recall."

"In the dining room, did you say?"

"Yes."

"Could it have been the breakfast room, Mrs. Young?"

"Objection. Materiality and relevance."

"Overruled. You may continue."

"Well, I'm not certain," his mother stammered. *"I used them interchangeably, you understand."*

"Used what interchangeably, Mrs. Young?"

"Objection."

"Overruled."

"Used what interchangeably?"

"Breakfast room and dining room."

"So sometimes when you say, 'breakfast room' you mean 'dining room,' and sometimes when you say, 'dining room' you mean 'breakfast room'?"

"Yes."

"That could get confusing."

"Objection!"

"Sustained."

"So you're not sure if it was the breakfast room or the dining room, and you're not sure if you were to your son's right, or to his left?"

"Objection. Immaterial, incompetent and unclear."

"Overruled."

"Are you asking me two questions?" Alan's mother was remembering the prosecutor's having warned her about the compound question.

"Yes, but I'll re-phrase, if it will help."

"Please."

"You're not sure if your son was in the breakfast room or the dining room?"

"No. It was the dining room."

"All right. And you're not sure if you were standing to his left or his right?"

"Not sure."

"What did he write on his draft notice, Mrs. Young?"

"I couldn't see."

159

"You couldn't see? You were close enough to identify he chose the red crayon."

"So?"

"So you could see which crayon, but not what he wrote?" There was sarcasm in Billings' voice.

"Objection! Badgering the witness."

"Overruled."

"Is that right?"

"Right."

"And you didn't crane your neck to see?"

"Objection, Your Honor!"

"Sustained."

"Weren't you curious, Mrs. Young? After observing your son's actions in such minute detail, as you have testified, you ..."

"Objection!"

"Overruled. You may continue."

"Weren't you curious, Mrs. Young, what he wrote with that crayon?"

"Certainly I was curious." Dorothy Young was curt. *"I just couldn't see, as I told you."*

"Mrs. Young, aren't you customarily at the Women's Club Tuesday afternoons?"

"Objection. Relevance."

"Overruled. You may continue."

"Aren't you?"

"Would you please repeat the question?"

"Aren't you customarily at the Women's Club Tuesday afternoons?"

"Yes, but... yes."

"But what, Mrs. Young?"

"But I wasn't there that Tuesday."

"Are you certain of that?"

"Perfectly."

"Is attendance kept at the meetings?"

"Objection. Relevance." The prosecutor was becoming exasperated.

"Overruled."

"Is attendance kept at the meetings?"

"As a rule."

"Your Honor, the defense offers into evidence Defendant's Exhibit 9, the attendance chart for the meeting of the Women's Club, Tuesday, July 29th."

"Counsel?

"No objection." It was a formality. Both sides had seen and stipulated to all the exhibits before trial.

"Mrs. Young, do you recognize this attendance chart?"

"Yes."

"And is this the chart kept at meetings of the Women's Club?"

"I believe it is."

"Would you please read the eleventh name on the list?"

"Dorothy Young."

"Is that you, Mrs. Young?"

"Yes."

"If you weren't there, Mrs. Young, as you have testified under oath, then you arranged to get credit for attendance by having somebody sign for you?"

"Objection! Objection, Your Honor! Counsel is slandering the witness."

"Sustained. Let's have no more of that, Mr. Billings."

"I'm sorry, Your Honor. Mrs. Young, how do you account for your signature on the attendance chart, if you were not in attendance?"

"Objection!"

"I'm going to allow that. Overruled." Dorothy Young remained silent.

"Mrs. Young?"

"How dare you suggest I had someone sign my name. How dare you!" Dorothy Young was furious.

"You haven't answered the question, Mrs. Young."

"Oh yes I have."

"Very well," Billings said, smiling with satisfaction. "No further questions."

"Counsel?" the judge addressed the prosecutor, who was wincing with alarm that his witness had briefly lost control.

"Thank you, Your Honor. Mrs. Young, could your memory be faulty and you did attend the meeting of the Women's Club July 29th, but were back home when the defendant showed up?"

"Objection. Leading."

"Overruled. You may continue."

"Quite possibly."

"Could the meeting have been an unusually short one, or adjourned early for some reason?"

"Objection. Leading the witness."

"Overruled."

"Possibly."

"*Lack of a quorum, for instance?*"

"*Objection, Your Honor. The prosecution is putting words in the witness' mouth.*"

"*Overruled. You may continue.*"

"*Yes, yes, I remember now, we did lack a quorum that day.*"

"*And this accounts for your getting home earlier than you might have otherwise?*"

"*Yes.*"

"*Thank you. No further questions.*"

"*Counsel?*"

"*How long did the meeting last, Mrs. Young, roughly?*"

"*Objection. Materiality.*"

"*Overruled. You opened the topic, counsel,*" the judge reminded the prosecutor.

"*I'd say less than an hour.*"

"*How long did it take to ascertain there wasn't a quorum?*"

"*Objection. Relevance.*"

"*Overruled.*"

"*Not long.*"

"*How long is 'not long'?*"

"*Objection.*"

"*Overruled. You may continue.*"

"*A few minutes.*"

"*What did you do the rest of the time?*"

"*Talked, I suppose.*"

"*Mrs. Young, you testified earlier that after your son inscribed his draft notice, he returned to his bedroom, put the box of crayons he had used back in the shoebox, then put the shoebox back into the closet?*"

"*Objection, Your Honor. Redundant. Witness has already testified to these facts.*"

"*Overruled.*"

"*Yes, that's right.*"

"*Had your son removed any other items from the shoebox to get to the crayons, like the protractor you mentioned?*"

"*I don't remember.*"

"*The crayons were conveniently right there on top, then?*"

"*I didn't say that.*"

"*Objection to this entire line of questioning, Your Honor,*" *the prosecutor said* strongly.

"*Overruled.*"

"*Mrs. Young,*" *Billings resumed,* "*were the crayons right there on top?*"

"*That seems unlikely,*" *Dorothy Young responded impatiently.* "*I have no idea where the crayons were. Alan put everything away.*"

"*Thank you, Mrs. Young. No further questions, Your Honor.*"

"*You may step down.*"

"*The State calls Stefan Kopinski.*" *Alan was thunderstruck. Wasn't it enough his own mother had testified against him? Was his best friend to do the same? Stefan was sworn in and answered the same perfunctory questions as everyone, giving his full name, spelling his last name, giving his address, date and place of birth, etc.*

"*Now Mr. Kopinski,*" *the prosecutor said,* "*please tell the court how long you have known the defendant.*"

"*Approximately five years.*"

"*Where did you meet?*"

"*At college, the University of California at Santa Barbara.*"

"*Your freshman years?*"

"*It was my freshman year. Alan—er, the defendant—is a year older than me, so he was a sophomore.*"

"*I see. Were you roommates, then?*"

"*We were in the same dormitory, Creighton Hall, but not roommates.*"

"*Did you become close friends?*"

"*Best friends. Alan became my best friend, and I think he would say the same of me.*"

"*Objection.*"

"*Overruled.*"

"*You just found a lot of common ground, was that it, that cemented the bond?*"

"*I don't know that it was common ground so much,*" *Stefan said after a pause,* "*but there was a kinship of spirits, I guess you'd say. Hard to pin down. We just took to each other.*"

"*Thank you,*" *the prosecutor said to Stefan in a clipped fashion, as a reminder he was only to answer the question.* "*Now Mr. Kopinski, did the defendant visit you at your home in St. Paul, Minnesota in August 1968?*"

"*Yes.*"

"*Was he living in California at the time?*"

"*Objection! Relevance.*"

"*Overruled. You may continue.*"

"*He was living in California?*"

"*Yes.*"

"*About how long was the visit?*"

"*Objection! Relevance.*"

"*Overruled.*"

"*About how long…*"

"*Four or five days.*"

"*He stayed at your home, correct?*"

"*Yes.*"

"*What occasioned the visit, all the way from California?*"

"*Objection.*"

"*Sustained.*"

"*What brought the defendant to your home in St. Paul?*"

"*Alan—the defendant, I mean—was on his way to Toronto, Canada. He had been drafted, and he was going to Canada to avoid the draft. He stopped in Minnesota to see me on his way.*"

"*Did you invite him?*"

"*No, he invited himself.*"

"*You had no objection to his visit?*"

"*No. We were best friends, as I said.*"

"*What did you do during his visit?*"

"*The usual things. Saw some movies, had a couple of picnics in Como Park, talked a lot.*"

"*Was it a happy time?*"

"*Yes.*"

"*Happy for both of you?*"

"*Objection. Calls for a conclusion.*"

"*Overruled.*"

"*I think so, although Alan was a bit preoccupied at times.*"

"*So when it came time for your friend, the defendant, to leave, it was somewhat difficult?*"

"*Somewhat. It was inevitable.*"

"*Did you take the defendant to the airport?*"

"*Yes.*"

"*Did you chat together on the way?*"

"*Yes.*"

"*Do you recall anything in particular you discussed?*"

"*Yes.*"

"*Would you tell the court what that was?*"

"*Alan asked me …*"

"*Objection! Hearsay.*"

"*Overruled. You may continue.*"

"*Alan asked me if I could guess what his last act on American soil would be.*"

"*Then what?*"

"*I said I couldn't guess, so he told me.*"

"*And what did he tell you?*"

"*He said he had his draft notice in his pocket, then he pulled it out and showed it to me.*"

"*Thank you, Mr. Kopinski.*" The prosecutor betrayed his exasperation with Stefan's stubborn refusal to wait for the question, as rehearsed. "*Your Honor, the State offers into evidence State's Exhibit No. 12.*" The prosecutor handed Alan's notice of conscription to the judge, who looked at it and handed it back.

"*Counsel?*"

"*No objection, Your Honor.*"

"*You may continue, Mr. Hawkins.*"

"*Thank you, Your Honor. Mr. Kopinski, how did you know the draft notice was the defendant's?*"

"*It had his name on it.*" The prosecutor showed Stefan the document and pointed at a certain line.

"*Would you please read this paragraph to the court?*"

"'*To Alan R. Young, By order of the Department of the Army, you are hereby notified of your conscription into the Armed Forces of the United States. You are ordered to report for induction promptly at 10:30 a.m. August 9, 1968 at Building 6, Fort Wilson, California, at which time you will be inducted into the United States Army. Failure to report is a federal offense punishable by imprisonment in a federal penitentiary for not less than five years.*'"

"*Is the notice signed?*"

"*Yes.*"

"*Would you read that to the court, please?*"

"'*Signed, Clark Clifford, Secretary of Defense.*'"

"*Now Mr. Kopinski, is there anything else at all on this document, which you have not read?*"

"Yes."

"Would that be the red lettering across the face of the document?"

"Yes."

"Would you please read what is written?"

"After you, chum."

"After you, chum?"

"Yes."

"Anything else?

"No, nothing else."

"Thank you, Mr. Kopinski." The prosecutor took the draft notice and walked over to the jurors, holding it in the middle at the top and ensuring each got a good look at it. "Mr. Kopinski," he resumed, "did you ask the defendant if he wrote 'After you, chum' on his draft notice?"

No."

"Why didn't you ask him this?"

"He told me."

"And if he hadn't told you, would you have concluded it was more or less implied?"

"Objection! Leading the witness."

"Sustained."

"Mr. Kopinski, did you understand that by the word 'chum' the defendant intended Clark Clifford, the Secretary of Defense?"

"Objection!"

"Overruled. You may continue."

"Yes."

"And is it your belief the average person would also conclude this was a reference to Secretary Clifford?"

"Objection!"

"Overruled."

"Yes."

"Mr. Kopinski, would you say the defendant also was using the term 'chum' in the familiar, mouthy sort of way?"

"Yes."

"Did the defendant say anything else about what he had written on his draft notice?"

"Yes."

"And what was that?"

"*Objection! Hearsay.*"

"*Overruled.*"

"*He said he intended 'chum' to include the president, since he was Clifford's boss and the real perpetrator of the war.*"

"*Objection!*"

"*Overruled.*"

"*Did he use that very word, 'perpetrator'?*"

"*Objection, objection! Your Honor, the defense wishes to go on record with a continuing objection to this line of inquiry. It is all hearsay.*"

"*Duly noted, counsel.*" *The judge turned to the prosecutor.* "*You may continue.*"

"*Yes, that was the word he used.*"

"*Why is the judge letting Stefan say all those things I didn't say?*" *Alan whispered to his lawyer.* "*None of this happened, I don't think.*" *He couldn't seem to remember for sure.*

"*Well, Mr. Young, a good deal of testimony is going to be admitted which otherwise wouldn't if you were testifying,*" *Alan's lawyer replied, a little testily.* "*As I have explained to you.*" *Alan scratched his head. What was Billings talking about?*

"*What do you mean, if I were testifying?*" *Alan whispered.*

"*Counsel!*" *the judge remonstrated,* "*you are out of order.*"

"*Yes, Your Honor.*" *Billings turned to Alan.* "*You have got to be quiet.*"

"*But I have to know what you meant?*"

"*You're not testifying, Mr. Young. We've been over this a thousand times.*"

"*A thousand? I don't even remember once.*"

"*Mr. Young, hush. This is no time for games, for games, for games, for games…*" *stuck again, repeating, repeating. Alan was ready to scream.*

"*Counsel!*" *The judge was sharp.*

"*Sorry, Your Honor.*"

"*Now Mr. Kopinski,*" *the prosecutor said,* "*was there anything else to further confirm the defendant intended that President Johnson be a recipient of the ugly message he …*"

"*Objection!*"

"*Sustained.*"

"*… of the message he wrote on his draft notice?*"

"*Yes, there was.*"

"*And what was that?*"

"*The envelope.*"

"*The envelope?*"

"Yes, Alan—the defendant—took an envelope out of his pocket and showed it to me." The prosecutor returned to the prosecution's table and picked up an envelope. "Your Honor, the State offers into evidence State's Exhibit No. 13." He handed the envelope to the judge.

"Counsel?"

"No objection."

"State's Exhibit No. 13 received into evidence," the judge said, handing it to the recorder for official stamping. The judge then returned the envelope to the prosecutor, who then handed it to Stefan.

"Is this the envelope, Mr. Kopinski?"

"Yes."

"Would you please read to the court how the envelope is addressed?"

"Johnson, White House, Washington."

"Johnson, White House, Washington?"

"Yes."

"Anything else at all?"

"Yes."

"And what is that?"

"The return address."

"Would you please read that, Mr. Kopinski?"

"A. Young, Toronto, Canada."

"A. Young, Toronto, Canada?"

"Yes."

"What did the defendant do, after showing you the envelope?"

"He put his draft notice inside, and sealed it."

"Then what?"

"He said…"

"Objection! Hearsay."

"Overruled. You may continue."

"He said mailing it was his last act on American soil."

"Was there any further conversation between the two of you, with regard to this 'last act on American soil'?"

"Yes."

"And would you tell the court what that was, Mr. Kopinski?"

"Alan—the defendant—asked me if I understood that by 'after you' he meant he would go to Vietnam after the president and the secretary of defense went."

"And what did you say?"

"I said I understood that."

"Anything else?"

"He asked me if I thought the president and the secretary of defense would get the message."

"And what did you say?"

"I said I wouldn't worry about it."

"Mr. Kopinski, how would you describe the defendant's mood at this time?"

"Objection! Calls for a conclusion."

"I'm going to sustain that."

"Was the defendant sad over what he had done?"

"Objection!"

"Overruled."

"Was the defendant sad over what he had done?"

"I would say no."

"Remorseful?"

"Objection!"

"Overruled."

"No, not that either."

"Was he cheerful or elated?"

"Objection!"

"Overruled."

"Sort of. More pleased with himself than anything else, I would say."

"Thank you, Mr. Kopinski. No further questions."

"Counsel, you may cross."

"Thank you, Your Honor." Alan's attorney got up and walked over to the witness box, Alan having repeated to him he had no recollection of the conversation Stefan had just related. "Mr. Kopinski, are you originally from St. Paul, Minnesota?"

"Yes."

"But you live now in California, is that right?"

"Yes."

"St. Paul and Minneapolis, I believe they are known as the Twin Cities, is that right?"

"Objection! Relevance."

"Overruled. You may continue."

"Yes, the Twin Cities."

"Big cities, are they?"

"They're pretty big, I'd say."

"Lots of traffic, I'll bet?"

"Objection!"

"Sustained."

"How was traffic when you were driving to the airport?"

"About like always."

"And that would be?"

"Moderate to heavy."

"Tough keeping up with population growth?"

"Objection! Relevance and foundation."

"Counsel," the judge addressed Alan's lawyer. "I'm going to sustain the objection and bar further questions along these lines, unless you can demonstrate their relevance."

"Your Honor, I'm going to do just that with my next question."

"Very well, proceed."

"Tough keeping up with population growth?"

"I guess."

"Yet, despite this heavy traffic you were negotiating, you could take your eyes off the road and read your friend's draft notice, line by line?"

"Objection! Testifying for the witness."

"Overruled. You may answer the question."

"Well, there's stoplights, and there's really not that much to read."

"Mr. Kopinski, you testified it was a happy time. You presumed to know your friend's inner feelings?"

"Objection!"

"Overruled."

"You presumed to know your friend's inner feelings," Billings said before Stefan could respond, "yet you also testified your friend was preoccupied?"

"Yes, I think he was."

"And was he happy when he was preoccupied?"

"Objection!"

"Overruled."

"Well, maybe not when he was preoccupied."

"So which is it, Mr. Kopinski? Was your friend happy, or preoccupied?"

"Objection! Badgering the witness."

"Sustained."

"Mr. Kopinski, you testified you and Alan were best friends, is that right?"

"*Yes.*"

"*Particularly in college?*"

"*Only in college, really. We've been widely separated since then.*"

"*Very well, only in college. And that was for three years?*"

"*Yes.*"

"*Would you say you knew your friend as well as his parents, or even better than his parents, during this time?*"

"*Objection! Relevance.*"

"*Overruled. You may continue.*"

"*Maybe. I really couldn't say.*"

"*Would you say your friend Alan Young is a man of conscience?*"

"*I don't know what you mean by 'conscience.'*"

"*Are you unfamiliar with that word, Mr. Kopinski?*"

"*Objection!*"

"*Sustained.*"

"*Did your friend struggle with ethical issues, like the draft and the war in Vietnam?*"

"*Yes. We all did.*"

"*Do you recall a mutual friend of yours and Alan's, Kenneth Hatcher, who went by the nickname of 'Bear'?*"

"*Yes. He was Alan's friend.*"

"*Not yours, too?*"

"*Well, yes, but basically Alan's. Bear and I didn't run around together, except with Alan—the defendant.*"

"*Do you recall a restaurant near the college campus, called Arvino's, which the three of you frequented?*"

"*Objection! Relevance.*"

"*Overruled.*"

"*Yes, we went there sometimes. Good pizza.*"

"*Did the three of you discuss the war one evening at Arvino's?*"

"*I suppose we might have,*" Stefan shrugged. "*Can't really remember.*"

"*You don't remember your friend Alan having told you his father ...*"

"*Objection! Hearsay.*"

"*Overruled. You may continue.*"

"*... having told you his father offered to help him beat the draft, but he refused, because it was dishonest?*"

"*Yes, I remember that.*"

"And did you have an opinion on the matter?"

"I don't recall for sure, but I think I suggested he should listen to his father."

"Alan, then, refused to do something dishonest, but it didn't bother you, did it, Mr. Kopinski?"

"Objection!"

"Sustained."

"Mr. Kopinski, isn't it true you yourself received a Notice to Report for Physical…"

"Objection! Relevance."

"Sustained. Mr. Kopinski is not on trial here, counsel," the judge remonstrated Alan's lawyer. *"I'll not warn you again."*

"I'm sorry, Your Honor." Billings hesitated, returned to the defense's table, sat down and sorted through several documents. *"No further questions."*

"Nothing further, Your Honor," the prosecutor said.

"You may step down," the judge said to Stefan.

"The State calls John Walters." Alan couldn't believe it. Was John also to testify against him?

"Do you swear to tell the truth, the whole truth, and nothing but the truth, so help you God?" John was asked by the bailiff, his left hand on a Bible, and right palm in the air.

"I do." John sat down.

"Please state your full name, and spell you last name, for the court, Mr. Walters," the prosecutor said.

"John Luke Walters, W-A-L-T-E-R-S."

"And what is your date and place of birth."

"October 14, 1945, Abilene, Texas."

"And do you still live in Abilene?"

"No."

"What is your current place of residence?"

"Montreal, Canada."

"Mr. Walters, are you acquainted with the defendant?" The prosecutor pointed at Alan.

"Yes."

"Did you and the defendant also meet in college, like the previous witness?"

"No. I went to college in Waco, Texas."

"Where did you meet the defendant?"

"In Montreal."

"And when was this, Mr. Walters?"

"We first met in the fall of 1968, I believe."

"Tell the court how you and the defendant became acquainted."

"We met at the American Expatriates Center, in Montreal. It was a place where guys who went to Canada to avoid the draft could go."

"I see. And were you, then, Mr. Walters, in Canada to avoid the draft, like the defendant?"

"Yes." John could not help feeling mortified in making the admission, although he knew perfectly well the prosecutor was going to ask him the question.

"You in fact had a job at the Expatriates Center, did you not?"

"Yes, I did."

"And the defendant come to the center one day, and that's how you became acquainted?"

"Yes."

"What did he come to the center for?"

"Objection! Relevance."

"Overruled."

"To find out about housing, jobs, that kind of thing. Alan had just arrived in Montreal."

"So the center was something of an informational service for draft dodgers like the defendant, is that right?"

"Objection!"

"Sustained."

"Did you and the defendant become friends?"

"Yes."

"You saw each other frequently?"

"I wouldn't say frequently. Now and then."

"Mr. Walters, do you remember one evening in particular, when you were over at the defendant's apartment, and his girlfriend arrived unexpectedly?"

"Objection! Asks for a conclusion."

"Overruled. However, counsel," the judge cautioned the prosecutor, *"the court's patience isn't indefinite. Establish soon where the State is going with this witness."*

"Of course, Your Honor."

"Yes, I do remember that evening."

"How does it happen you remember that evening particularly?"

"Because of Jeanne's, his girlfriend's, now she's his wife, bizarre behavior."

"What did she do that was bizarre?"

"When she came in, she did not say a word, but went straight into the bathroom and closed the door."

"Then what?"

"Nothing. She stayed in there until Alan finally went in and got her to come out. When I got to know her bet ..."

"Just answer the question, please, Mr. Walters," the prosecutor interrupted. "As an expatriate, like the defendant, did the two of you sometimes discuss the war in Vietnam?"

"Nearly always."

"It was something you shared?"

"Yes, and no."

"What do you mean by that?"

"Well, unlike Alan, I love my country and want to return."

"Objection!"

"Sustained."

"Mr. Walters, did the defendant that evening say anything about his draft notice ..."

"Objection! Hearsay."

"Sustained."

"In discussing the war, did you and the defendant ever discuss conscription?"

"Yes."

"Did you ever talk about your draft notices?"

"Objection!"

"Overruled. You may continue."

"Yes, we discussed them."

"Did the defendant say anything to you about his having defaced his ..."

"Objection, Your Honor! Leading and prejudicial."

"Sustained."

"What did the defendant say to you regarding his draft notice?"

"Objection, Your Honor! The defense wishes to go on record objecting to this entire line of questioning. It is all hearsay."

"Duly noted, counsel. Witness may continue."

"He said he wrote a message on it and mailed it to the president."

"No, I didn't," Alan whispered to his lawyer. "I absolutely didn't tell John that."

"For the last time, hush, Mr. Young."

"Did he say anything else?"

"No. He seemed to be expectant, waiting for me to say something."

"And did you say something?"

"No."

"Then what?"

"He asked me if I was curious about the message."

"What did you say?"

"I said sure, I was curious, although I really wasn't very."

"And what was his answer?"

"Objection! Hearsay."

"Overruled. You may continue."

"He said he wrote, 'After you, chum.'"

"Thank you, Mr. Walters. No further questions, Your Honor."

"Counsel?"

"Just one question, Your Honor." Billings ambled over to the witness stand. *"Mr. Walters, were you the unfortunate victim of an assault one night in the parking lot at your apartment?"*

"Objection! Relevance."

"Overruled. You may continue."

"Yes."

"Do you know who attacked you?"

"No."

"How many attackers?"

"Two."

"Were you injured?"

"Objection! Your Honor, the defense has failed to show the relevance of this testimony."

"Overruled. This is your witness, Mr. Hawkins, and I'm going to allow him to respond."

"Yes, I was injured."

"How were you injured?"

"Broken jaw."

"I'm terribly sorry. Were you also robbed?"

"No."

"Do you recall how long the attack lasted?"

"Few seconds."

"Were you taken to the hospital?"

"Yes."

"Were the men caught?"

"Not to my knowledge."

"How did you get to the hospital?"

"Alan took me."

"You mean the defendant, Alan Young?"

"Yes."

"You phoned him, didn't you, Mr. Walters, when you got inside your apartment? He was the first person you thought of, your best friend, who ..."

"Objection."

"Overruled."

"... who dropped everything when you called, and came and got you, and took you to the hospital, and oversaw your stay, and called your parents in Texas to assure them you were okay, and took you home when you were released, didn't he, Mr. Walters?"

"Yes."

"I'd call that a pretty good friend," Billings concluded with a decided edge in his voice.

"Objection!"

"No further questions of this witness, Your Honor."

"Counsel?" the judge turned to the prosecution.

"Nothing further, Your Honor." John stepped down from the witness box, looking guiltily at Alan, whose return gaze was uncomprehending.

"The State calls David Neil Hillsborough, Your Honor, Your Honor, Hillsborough, Your Honor, Your Honor, Hillsborough, Your Honor, Your Hon ..." like a broken record, stuck again, repeating repeating ...

CHAPTER 6

Alan woke and gasped loudly, waking Jeanne. He was in a cold sweat, and she saw instantly he was in a panic.

"Oh, Alan darling, what's the matter, what's the matter?" Jeanne cried plaintively. Alan lay inert beside her, his mouth voicing unheard words, his face the portrait of unbearable anguish. "You've had a bad dream," she surmised, her hand gently caressing his cheek. Alan muttered something unintelligible. "You always dream when you sleep on your back."

"What?" Alan stared at his wife, disoriented, his eyes enormous, as though in an hypnotic trance. "Dreaming!" he exclaimed, staring at her wildly. An indescribable relief began coloring his face. "It is just a dream. A nightmare! Running through the jungle, running, I was being chased, chased by, by the president, President Johnson, running so hard but he caught me every time, he had my draft notice, there was a trial, my mom testified against me, Stef, too … all a dream!"

"Sounds like a whale of a dream, all right. Go back to sleep, darling, it's the middle of the night." The bedside clock read 3:18.

"Oh Jeanne," Alan said earnestly, taking her hands, "I've had the strangest, most nightmarish, yet wonderful dream." There was peace in his voice, despite his difficulty grasping that anything so real could be purely imaginary. Alan's relief, indeed, was measureless, but relief was only part of it, for the dawn of understanding was arrived, bringing illumination where before darkness ruled, insight to replace confusion. The terrible searching, seeking, agonizing, up one blind alley and down another, the endless hunt for explanation that had led nowhere, was over, his unconscious mind having harbored the truth all along. It was incredible. "Got to get up, got to get this on paper, before I lose it," Alan said, tossing the covers aside. Everything began falling into place. Where previously not a single piece to the puzzle could be made to fit, now the proper slot for each was apparent, and the puzzle was solved. It was more than simple, it was embarrassingly simple.

Alan realized he had fallen asleep, but no deep slumber this, rather, the fitful sleep borne of exhaustion and the swallowing of potent pills in inadvisable quantities. As he scribbled down the elements of his dream, an equanimity flooded his soul, and along with it, the sure knowledge he could handle what lay ahead.

"I've made a mistake," Alan said to himself. "I can fix it." He was going home, taking his family with him, returning to give himself up, to go to prison, to serve his term as the only proper way of one man's taking his stand on an issue affecting all.

"Jeanne," he said, his voice momentarily failing him, "how can you forgive me?" He looked straight into her eyes. "I've been so mean to you, how can I have behaved so badly, can you please forgive me?" Alan eyes abruptly filled with tears, and try though he did, he could not keep them from coursing down his cheeks.

"Darling Alan," she responded, and took his head to her bosom. "Nothing to forgive. I love you, and always shall."

"What you're proposing isn't sensible, Alan," Charles McCarran said when they visited later that day. "I'm sure you can see how much Jeanne needs you. How can you be so selfish?" His father-in-law refrained from accusing him yet again of brutalizing his daughter with his thoughtless behavior, but the questioning went on. "How can you take care of your wife and child if you're in jail? Your drastic move may make your conscience feel better, but it accomplishes nothing else. I think you're still making the mistake of looking back, Alan. You must forget your past before you can move forward. The Vietnam War is on the other side of the world and isn't your concern. Your wife and daughter are your concern."

"You know perfectly well I'm not abandoning them, Charles," Alan said. Conversations with his father-in-law, he reflected, had tended to be variations on a theme, this one no exception; Charles was always telling him what to do. "Jeanne and the baby can live with my folks and visit me regularly, and it will be only for a few years, and I'll be thinking about them every day I'm in jail and counting down the days till I'm out." Much remained to be worked out here, Leavenworth, for one thing, being in Kansas rather than California.

"You're asking me to support your family, that isn't right." Charles had had more than enough of Alan's obsession with "right and wrong." The older man was not unkind, but he meant to block this newest foolishness if possible. He saw no difference in Alan's conduct, the usual ingredients all in place: Fervor, immense conviction, intransigence, deafness to the views of others. Charles McCarran doubtless knew, too, he was wasting his breath. All the same, he did try, repeatedly, to change Alan's mind, for he wasn't keen on his only daughter's removal thousands of miles to another city in another country, particularly considering her fragile emotional state, to say nothing of the prospect of dealing with her loony husband's determination to throw himself into jail for the indefinite future. Alan's unreason seemed to Charles to be reaching new heights.

"Jeanne is in no condition to make a move like this, Alan," he chided. "Surely you ought to reconsider? Aren't you putting yourself before your wife? That's not like you. Jeanne isn't even well."

At one point in their fruitless discussions, Alan almost mentioned his dream to Charles, but opted finally for silence, reminding himself of his father-in-law's incapacity to work with ideas and abstractions. Charles McCarran's dismay and frustration did not, however, translate to Alan's parents. After all, they were getting their son back, totally unexpectedly, the business about going to prison notwithstanding.

"You face life-long ostracism," Robert Young admonished his son, "pre-emption from voting, the most basic right of every citizen. Your conviction will be a blot on your record all your life, will compromise your ability to find work every single time you try. You will never be able to erase the black mark. You want to do right by your country, Alan, but that country hasn't done right by you and is only going to kick you in the stomach. What you propose comes down to a matter of principle and absolutely nothing more." Life in prison, harsh, hazardous, Robert Young hardly considered; all his words were robbed of their usual conviction by his joy over getting his boy back.

The change in Alan was soon evident to everyone. It was as if he had received a magical injection, routing his malaise and his wife's, too, for there was no question Jeanne began to improve. Just the same, her recovery was going to take time, and Alan did not balk when she decided he should go first to California, that she would follow with Mary as soon as feasible.

Nothing was going to happen immediately with the federal authorities, anyway; Alan noted he could turn himself in at his pleasure, and then a legal proceeding must follow. He might even find work in the meantime. Jeanne, who had longed to get out of Montreal, was thrilled about moving to California and, while concerned about her husband's jailing and its consequences, knew he could not be dissuaded. Besides, she loved Alan.

Alan wrote Stefan.

Dear Stef,

Do you believe in miracles? I didn't, either. I have had a dream, Stef. It was last Tuesday night. I was beat, exhausted, hadn't slept much. You can't imagine—well, you can—how tough it's been. Jeanne has been in another world, largely due to my awful conduct. (She's much better.) Stef, this dream was more real than reality. I was in Vietnam! Running desperately through the jungle, with fighting all around. I was being chased by—are you ready for this?—the president! He had my draft notice, and he waved it in my face. Next thing I knew, I was in a courtroom, on trial, and my mother was testifying against me. Then, guess who? You! Then, John Walters. The detail was fantastic, the attorneys, their arguments, what people looked like. My lawyer said my dad hired him, because he was the best in Montreal. It was tremendously dramatic. I trust they're teaching you in law school to talk, talk, talk. My lawyer, can't remember his name, said if I was convicted I would spend five years in jail.

You will appreciate the irony of my having dreamed I might be imprisoned, in a minute. I haven't been able to live with what I did, running away, coming to Canada, running out, I should say, but only my unconscious mind knew this. No, certainly I have not changed my view on Vietnam, the farthest thing from it. I handled it wrong, is what it all comes down to. To register my protest, one man's protest, against the atrocity we're committing, I should have allowed myself to be arrested, as others in my position did. I simply didn't realize this at the time. I didn't understand, I wasn't smart enough, I wasn't moral enough. I remember Marcel Pirmont's having said—this wasn't in my dream—that I hurt the United States by leaving, and at the time, I thought this a dumb remark, but, lo, I haven't forgotten, and Marcel turns out to be right! I walked out on my country. I walked out on our men in Vietnam. Yes! By coming to Canada, I opposed not the war, but them. I'm ashamed. I just didn't know. I thought I was escaping unjust imprisonment, yet, ironically, for all its immensity, Canada has had invisible bars, it has been my jail. Call it a gigantic irony if you like, I'm destined to be jailed in San Quentin or some place, still, in a true sense, it's prison I'm leaving. Life is a set of contradictions, but I am more sure of myself now than ever, and I am content as I have not been.

My dad, of course, is issuing his customary advice about how misguided I am. He says I'm going to be "ostracized." Does he think I expect brass bands to be playing when I step off the plane in L.A., a great celebration for the hero protester, coming home to face the music and do what he should have had the sense to do all along? As usual, my father-in-law, who means well, thinks I'm cockeyed. He cannot understand, no matter how much I explain, whereas you understand totally without explanation. I should hire you to act as my interpreter with him.

I have no illusions, Stef, none at all. I goofed in coming to Canada, but it was an honest mistake, and I'm doing something about it. Don't you see, if thousands of us, tens of thousands, would go to jail, the war could be stopped! I'm not talking just about those who ducked the draft, like me. I'm talking about those who got deferments. We are in a war, a national crisis, and there should be no deferments. Every man has a duty. By exempting some, we've created "us Americans" and "them Americans." No good! Are we a country, or not? My point is, men with deferments must refuse to accept them, thereby forcing the government to draft them. Refusing conscription, too, they would have to be prosecuted. The courts and jails would be packed, they couldn't possibly handle it. Going to jail is the moral choice, the exercise of citizenship, but our society is so hugely selfish and immoral, everyone's thought is only of how to save his own neck. "We the People" indeed!

I've been so blind … even going to Vietnam would have been more appropriate than what I've done. The nation is so blind… this isn't World War II. Why can't Americans see the truth about this dirty little war? But who am I to talk, it is only just now I have achieved a full understanding. What, after all, does one know when he is 21? It is the older generation which must bear a heavy burden of responsibility. They've let this happen.

Your thoughts would be welcome. Jeanne and Mary will remain in Montreal for a while, but as soon as I settle various commitments, I'll be booking my flight to L.A. (I'll stay here through the holidays.) As you said that awful time we met in Windsor, Jeanne loves me without reservation, and she has given us a wonderful daughter. I can't wait to show her off!

I'm a lucky man, Stef, as I think you also said.

Alan

Stefan read Alan's letter carefully. At first, he could make little sense of it, for he had fallen into the habit of doubting his friend's logic. Wasn't Alan yet again exhibiting his knack for making a bad situation worse? Moreover, it was Stefan's opinion the only thing more ridiculous than a dream was someone who would assign it significance. He re-read the letter, and found he was vexed by Alan's implied censure. Stefan had his deferment and, to be sure, it would take a better argument than Alan's to get him to surrender it. Not until later, much later, did Stefan discover what he did not wish to discover. A better argument than "it's the right thing to do" was always required, but there could never be a better argument. Between these merciless absolutes man was trapped, eternally. Not this man, Stefan reassured himself.

The January day was sunny when Alan's jet touched down at the Los Angeles International Airport. Gazing out the window at the activity, the many planes—"Delta," "United," "American," "Air California," "Western"—the cluster of airport buildings, the tall southern California palms shrouded imperviously in the smog, Alan grinned. This was home, and it was so instantly familiar, every bit of it, and so natural, for a fleeting moment, he disbelieved he had ever left, or that all that had intervened had ever really happened. Then reality set in, and with it came his unshakeable resolve. At the gate, his mother embraced him, and then his father, too. Lumps in throats, words were few, but they linked arms and, with neither misgiving on a countenance nor hesitation in a step, proceeded down the long corridor to the baggage claim. Only that night was there any mention of Alan's decision. Although the family had explored the subject in more than one long-distance telephone call, Alan wished to make a couple of points again, in his parents' presence; and, there was tacit agreement they could not settle for chitchat the night before Alan gave himself up. He explained again to his mother and father the critical difference between paying the price a law exacts by its violation, and running away. They agreed. He expressed again his belief men with deferments from service had to refuse them. Alan's parents found this notion of such surpassing nonsense, neither commented upon it at all.

"As for our soldiers, they're heroes," Alan went on. "At least to the extent as in World War Two, if not more. We had to stop Hitler, but our guys are being wounded and killed in Vietnam, just because it's politically advantageous to Nixon." Alan took a deep breath. "I don't know what, in all the world, could be more immoral."

"You are mistaken, Alan," his father said. "This war has already brought one president down, and you may be sure that isn't lost on Nixon. If he doesn't find a way to end it soon, he's finished, too."

"End it soon!" Alan exclaimed. "He could end it tomorrow. Declare we have achieved our objectives, and order the troops home." This was a view some critics of the war were espousing.

"The proof the president can't do that is that he hasn't," his father said, with slight irritation. Alan shook his head. He had heard reasoning like this from his father all his life, and long ago concluded it had something to do with being a judge. "The president must do what is expected of him. Like all of us, actually. Trust me on this one."

"Don't people in the military accept the risk they might become involved in fighting, dear?" his mother said.

Alan let it go. He was through with arguments. His parents could believe whatever they pleased. The important thing was, he had the answer now to the question that haunted him, a question as terrible, in its way, as the one haunting the nation. Alan turned to his father, with a final consideration.

"I'm going to need a lawyer, dad."

"I've already thought of that, Alan. I'll get you one, if you will let me."

"The best in L.A.?" Alan asked facetiously, enjoying his private joke.

"Well, I can't guarantee that, Alan, but I'll certainly get you a good one."

"Just teasing you, dad. What I'd like is for you to get me three or four names. Reasonably priced. I'll pay for my own lawyer. You and mom are doing enough by agreeing to look after Jeanne and Mary."

"Just as you prefer," his father said.

"Thanks, dad." A silence ensued. There seemed little more to say. Alan rose from the table. "Guess I'll call it a day. Tomorrow will be a big day." He shook his father's hand, and hugged his mother. "Goodnight."

"He puts up a brave front," Dorothy Young said, "but this war has destroyed him."

"I've thought so, too," Robert Young said, "but now I'm not so sure."

"How can Alan hope to recover from this?"

"You know, Dorothy," Robert Young said after a pause, "I admire what Alan has done." He had not yet shared with his wife a step he was mulling. "It has made me realize I have not thought well of our son in some time. That's a peculiar attitude for a father to have, don't you think?"

"You did what you could," Dorothy Young said unpersuasively. "Alan remains immature. He speaks of how the war has broken his generation's heart. Does he think that makes them special? Many things break our hearts, but we don't let it stop us."

"I've been wondering," Robert Young said unresponsively, "if I could do what Alan is doing, if I were in his shoes."

"You would never have found yourself reduced to such a choice," Dorothy Young said with conviction. Her husband made no answer, as he wasn't perfectly sure this was a compliment.

They changed topics, but soon, they were back to Alan. Nothing could be resolved.

"I'm going to bed," she finally said. "Are you coming?"

"In a few minutes," he said. Dorothy Young departed up the stairs, leaving her husband to the last of his coffee, and his own reflections.

At the local office of the Federal Bureau of Investigation, early the next morning, Alan had a shock when his file was opened, and there was his draft notice, with the ignoble message he had inscribed. Alan winced, for he required no reminder of an unworthy act in which he had actually taken pride. A man in his middle years, wearing a shoulder holster, asked Alan a series of questions. He was treated with kindness. The interview lasted less than ten minutes. At its conclusion, Alan was arrested for failure to report for conscription, in violation of federal law.

CHAPTER 7

JEANNE MOTIONED TO THE WAITRESS, DESCRIBING A SQUIGGLY "W" IN the air with her fingers. Despite this indication it was her check she wanted, she got more coffee from the waitress, when she finally arrived. She seemed to be doing nothing but circulating around the restaurant with a coffee pot.

"You'll need just a wee bit more before you hit the road again, hon," the waitress said, topping Jeanne's cup. "Can't be nodding off, like your little girl there, in all the St. Louis traffic. She's a honey. What did you say was her name, again?"

"Mary," Jeanne replied. "Thanks for the coffee, but it's my bill I really want now, please."

Mary Young, indeed, was blissfully asleep. Nearing her second birthday, she had always been a wonderful child in this respect, seldom requiring her mother to rise at a small hour. Just as well, too, Jeanne might have reflected, considering the long year she had spent with her in-laws, during most of which she had a night job that kept her out of the house until two in the morning. Among the sources of friction between her and her mother-in-law, this had certainly been near the top of the list. The entire year had been a dreadful mistake, but it had had about it an inevitability not lost on Jeanne.

Her destination, the Rodeway Inn, was on Market Street, "more or less downtown," as Randy had put it. "You really can't miss it. It's about a twenty-story hotel, and it's circular. Very distinctive. No other hotel around, either. It's kind of by itself." Jeanne secured Mary in the baby seat and embarked for St. Louis, 23 miles away. It was late afternoon, Friday, but as she was headed directly east, the sun was behind her. Traffic began to pick up when she crossed the interstate, but most of it was coming in the opposite direction, as the business day was coming to an end. She passed a business district on her left, frantically looking for the Grand Avenue exit. None to be seen. Jeanne had no way of knowing the cluster of nondescript buildings she had just passed were those of Clayton, a suburb which was not accidentally prospering proportionately to the decline of the old city on the Mississippi. Jeanne got off the freeway at the next exit and began searching for Grand Avenue, but after several futile minutes, decided to pull into a gas station and get directions.

"Grand Avenue," said the attendant, a young man of about 25, "is in St. Louis. This is Clayton. Get back on 1-40 by going down this street, Ecklund Road"—he pointed outside—"and turning left at the first stoplight. The on-ramp is right after that. You got to keep going quite a few miles. Stay on 1-40. You'll see the Grand Avenue exit all right, can't miss it. Downtown St. Louis is just ahead, but you want to exit before you get downtown."

"Thank you very much," Jeanne replied.

"You need gas, or anything?" the young man said, in the hope of stalling her departure. It didn't work.

Into the city she proceeded, passing signs for Washington University, zoo, historical society, art museum. Past Kingshighway, a name she liked, more buildings. "Bigger city than I thought," she said to herself, although in truth, she had not thought about the city one way or the other until now. Finally the Grand Avenue sign came into view, a relief, but now she found herself behind a semi-trailer also exiting the freeway. Jeanne remembered she was to turn left on Grand and continue heading north until she reached Market, where she was to turn right. The big truck, however, blocked her view of Market Street, the first street after she passed over the freeway. Jeanne continued north, vaguely aware she may have missed a street, but thinking it wouldn't have been the one she wanted. Through one intersection after another she went, until she was well into north St. Louis. She knew she was going the wrong way, as the neighborhood had become residential. She turned around and pulled into another filling station. Mary, awake in her car seat, was becoming restless.

"I'll be back in half a second, Mary," she told her daughter, reaching back over her seat to touch her on the cheek. Mary would commence talking within two months, but for the moment, it was still baby talk.

There were three persons in the service station, two men and a woman. Both men looked to be in their twenties and wore Shell service station uniforms; the woman, perhaps twenty, may have been a customer, Jeanne wasn't sure. The three were engaged in an easy-going banter which abruptly halted when she walked in.

"Could you tell me which way Grand Avenue is?" she asked no one in particular, cognizant she had interrupted a conversation.

"You're on Grand Avenue, ma'am," one of the men said.

"Market Avenue, I mean," Jeanne said, "Market Avenue." Silence.

"There's Market Street, about a mile down Grand, if that's what you mean," the other man said. He pointed the direction.

"That's it, Market Street," Jeanne said. "I'm getting confused."

"Straight down Grand, just before the freeway. There's a light, it's a big street."

"Less than a mile, I'd say," said the first man. "What's the street just before Market?"

"West Pine," the girl contributed. "I think."

"Let's look at a map," the first man said, withdrawing one from the rack. Another customer came in, a middle-aged man, somewhat overweight. Greetings were enthusiastic, and it seemed to Jeanne that she was the only one who wasn't acquainted with everybody.

"Listen, I've got a child in the car, I need to get going," she said. "Market's a mile down the street, just before the freeway, you said. I think I crossed it, but didn't see the sign. Thanks so much for your help."

"You're welcome, ma'am." Two voices.

Back in the car, Jeanne was exasperated with herself. She was sure the street she had missed was Market, which indeed it was. She turned east, and almost immediately the Rodeway Inn came into view. Just a matter of following directions, she said to herself.

Jeanne got a room on the twelfth floor, facing south. The view did not impress her. Just another city, and certainly not as impressive as Montreal. Jeanne wished she could reach Alan, but that was out of the question. There was still no getting used to it, really, after more than a year and a half. She fed Mary and then rested. Tomorrow would be a big day. Jeanne was resolute. She had the weekend to find an apartment, no less no more, and with the help of Randy Collins, she was very determined to make it happen. Of course, it could all come to nothing, despite their best efforts, but she was characteristically optimistic. She wouldn't settle for just anything, but adequacy, not perfection, would be her criterion. How complicated could finding a one-bedroom apartment be, after all? She had done it on her own in Leavenworth, hadn't she? St. Louis was bigger, and the apartment-locating service seemed like a good idea, but it was still a pretty basic assignment. A thunderstorm woke her sometime in the night, but Mary was undisturbed. Jeanne was soon asleep again, too. When the hotel wake-up call came at seven, it was raining hard.

Jeanne dressed Mary in her smart, green frock, and opted herself for her Navy blue suit. This was a day to look good. Unlike the previous day's adventure, she found her destination without difficulty, and entered the front door at Randy's office promptly at 8:30.

It had been the third Monday in January 1970, Alan turned himself in at the Federal Bureau of Investigation in Los Angeles. His parents, back at the house, frustrated by their son's refusal to permit either of them to accompany him to the FBI, embarked upon one of the most serious discussions of their lives, although it was not getting in the way of breakfast.

"You wouldn't do this when it really might have mattered," Dorothy Young scolded her husband, "and now, the mind you couldn't make up is still full of contradictions. Bob, not twelve hours ago, you were lauding Alan's decision. Now, you're calling it 'the mistake of a lifetime'. What will it be tomorrow?" Robert Young let his wife have her say. He knew she wasn't really so very angry with him, only vexed by their son's behavior, and deeply worried.

"Dorothy, let's not look back. It's water under the bridge, and in any case, Alan would never have consented."

"Well, that's the problem now, too, isn't it?" his wife rejoined. "He's more determined than ever. It's perfectly hopeless. I can't imagine how we could have persuaded ourselves to have this talk."

"I can admire what he's doing and still consider it a mistake, can't I?" the judge said. "I don't see those as mutually exclusive. I think one thing we must do is find someone Alan will listen to. What is the name of that college friend of his?"

"Stefan Kopinski," Dorothy Young said. "He's in law school at Hastings, remember?"

"Yes, of course, let's begin with him."

"Bob, don't you suppose the two of them have spoken already, probably more than once? No harm in trying, but I don't see this as working."

Dorothy sighed deeply. What was going to work? That was the question, and neither of the Youngs had an answer.

"I'll call Duncan when I get to the office," the judge said. His wife put her hand affectionately on top of her husband's, which was palm down on the breakfast table.

"Please do," she said gently, but firmly, in the hope of reinforcing her husband's resolve. This was unnecessary, for there would be no hesitation this time. When Robert Young reached his office, he had hardly greeted his staff and grabbed his coffee before he was dialing Duncan Sutliff. A retired brigadier general, Duncan Sutliff, at 70, was still very much in his vigor, a well-known figure in West Los Angeles circles. The judge had known Duncan nearly ten years, as a fellow member of the West L.A. Rotary Club, where Duncan enjoyed a reputation as something of a raconteur. He was, among other things, an exceptional speaker whose periodic talks on global affairs, from a military perspective, were among the most esteemed of any addresses given at the club; they dependably produced a good turn-out from the membership and always met with enthusiastic applause and a spirited question-and-answer period. Occasionally, the news media were even present, or at least were invited, when Gen. Sutliff was addressing a matter deemed newsworthy, but more often his talks took the longer view rather than focus on current exigencies.

Just what Duncan might have to say about the judge's personal exigency was another matter and, his resolve notwithstanding, Robert Young could not help a certain nervousness, for broaching his topic, or plea if that was the term, would inevitably cross a line never contemplated by their friendship. If Duncan took it wrong, if the whole business was anathema to him, it would alter their friendship permanently. The judge had thought about this, of course, at great length, and finally selected the general as the person to call, not least because he was reasonably confident Duncan Sutliff would not be unsympathetic, and, above all, could be relied upon as the soul of discretion, regardless of how things worked out.

Duncan's wife Louise, whom the judge knew, though not well, answered. Her husband had been a little under the weather the last couple of days and was still asleep. Could it wait? Of course. Robert Young left his number, a trifle miffed at himself for calling the elderly couple before 8:30 in the morning; he may have gotten her up. He wouldn't second-guess his judgment, though, since something deep inside him knew that delaying until midday, after the demands of the day had commenced, might have changed the calculus. Now he could turn to the day's assignments clear-headed, knowing his call would be returned. The die was cast, even though he had not even reached Duncan, let alone said a word of what was on his mind. It was a great relief.

His secretary, an attractive, curvy brunette in her mid-thirties named Alice Simmons, buzzed him, having noticed the light on his phone line had gone out. Alice was relatively new to the office, but fit in well and was a perceptive individual who indeed had rightly surmised, just by the way the judge had come in and greeted her, that he was preoccupied.

"The magistrate judge wants to speak with you, judge, but I'll be happy to hold the call, if you're busy." Alice was gracious, but not obsequious, a trait common to judges' staffs.

"No, that's fine, please put him through, Mrs. Simmons."

It wasn't until 4:30 in the afternoon the judge heard from the brigadier general.

"Sorry to be so long getting back to you, Robert," Duncan Sutliff said. "One thing after another, and suddenly the day is gone."

"Perfectly all right, Duncan," the judge replied, not quite concealing that he regarded this as a not-entirely-satisfactory excuse, since the general, after all, though a busy retiree to be sure, was nonetheless retired. Duncan, if he detected this, let it go. "Something rather important on my mind, actually, so I did want to try to reach you today." At this, the judge had to laugh a little at himself, since it was hardly urgent. Alan, who had given himself up, was free on personal recognizance and, while the machinery of the criminal justice system was now in motion against him, he would not find himself at the gates of Leavenworth tomorrow. The judge shuddered. This was what must be averted. This was the purpose of the conversation.

"I'm all ears," Duncan Sutliff said.

Suddenly, it all gushed forth, like a dam burst. Robert Young didn't bawl, exactly, but he could hardly restrain himself as the long-suppressed tension within him found release. He was shocked at himself, but he wasn't sorry. Wasn't his whole life a holding back, an exercise in restraint? Well, what man's isn't, he considered, but perhaps that of a judge peculiarly, for in the courtroom, except on rare occasion, he could not say what it pleased him to say, no matter how great the temptation.

190

"Well, Robert," the general said when the judge had reached his conclusion, breathless and almost giddy, "if I'm hearing you right, your boy's finally done the right thing, and now you and Dorothy, for some reason, don't want him to do it. I don't quite understand, frankly." Duncan Sutliff was perplexed. How many times, particularly in the beginning, when Alan had first gone to Canada, had he engaged in conversation with Robert Young and seen the judge shake his head in resignation over his son's inexplicable decision? Hadn't the general, along with most of the judge's friends, responded with a measure of sympathy, if not acceptance, for weren't they parents, as well, and who could control a headstrong boy of 21? "You sound like you wish your boy had not come back from Canada, but I know for a fact that isn't true."

"Then I just haven't made myself clear," Robert Young said, getting to the point, although he had already made it. "Yes, Dorothy and I are delighted Alan has returned, that goes without saying, and that he's recognized an error and, as you said, is doing the right thing. The problem, Duncan, is that he's jumping from the frying pan into the fire."

"How's that?"

"Going to prison ... since he didn't ... going now, after one mistake, it's a second mistake, and he'll ..."

"How is it a second mistake, if it wouldn't have been the first time?"

"Because now Alan will have two black marks on his record. Ran away to another country to avoid serving, then came back and became a felon. He'll have no chance when he gets out of Leavenworth, to get ahead. Don't you see? In a sense, it really would have been better for him to have stayed in Canada."

Duncan Sutliff still wasn't sure he did see, but there was no sense going around and around.

"Robert, I'll see what I can do," he said. "Just to recapitulate, you're asking that Alan be permitted now to enlist, and that he receive a guaranteed assignment stateside. No Vietnam. So you, we, have two distinct objectives. What if we can swing "a," but not "b"?"

"No good, Duncan. It's a package. Got to have both."

"Well, I'm just saying, no guarantees. This is a pretty unusual request for a pretty special dispensation." The general could have used another word, indeed, almost had, and this was not lost on the judge, who wondered nonetheless if what he was proposing was really all that uncommon. Yet

191

Duncan was surely right he could not guarantee a thing. There simply was no good choice available to Alan; this is what it came down to. The judge held firm, and the general, for his part, kept his mixed feelings about the whole idea to himself. He personally felt the strategic value of defeating the Communists in Vietnam was not worth the costs, particularly in view of how clumsily the war had been waged. Just the same, American boys were dying in Vietnam, and along comes a judge, of all people, prepared to skirt the law in order that his wayward son might serve, further provided the Army condescends to meet his terms regarding that service. It was monstrous, really.

"So you'll get back to me, Duncan?" the judge proffered.

"I'll do that, Robert. Must give this some additional thought, naturally." The judge wondered if he was leaving the door open to outright refusal. There was one more thing to say.

"Listen, Duncan, I should add, I don't know that Alan will consent to this, you know he's stubborn, won't listen to anything he doesn't want to hear. I haven't approached him, obviously, but he's pretty determined on this jail thing, and frankly probably will not listen to his mother or me, not that we're expecting you, on top of everything, to talk him into it, but thought you should have this extra piece of the puzzle, before you start making phone calls."

"Maybe we're putting the cart before the horse, then?" the general said, sensing the project was doomed if the judge had not so much as breathed a word of it to his son. "Wouldn't it make more sense if you sounded him out a little first, you think?"

"Duncan, I've sounded him out for years. He's not going to listen to me. I have someone in mind to speak with him, although I haven't talked with that person yet either, I started with you and, needless to say, I am asking a big favor and if you would want to follow through and actually speak with Alan, you'd be more than welcome." This did not seem the optimal arrangement, however, because the general and Alan were strangers. The general thought so, too, but it appealed to his vanity that he might make the necessary arrangements and then reach the boy when his own father could not. Both men were momentarily silent, Robert Young reflecting that his friend must be thinking he was acting impulsively in the hope of carrying out an extraordinarily harebrained scheme that was not even legal, which, in fact, wasn't far from what the general was thinking.

"Robert, I'll see what I can do," the general hesitated.

"Duncan," the judge said, perceiving his hesitation, "why don't I speak with Alan first? You sit tight a few days until I get back to you. I think this is the best way to proceed." There was no good way to proceed, let alone a best way, which was more than apparent to both men. The retired military man remained persuaded that doing nothing until, and if, the proposed beneficiary's consent was secured, was sensible. Something in the judge's voice told him Alan Young's cooperation was unobtainable.

"That works for me, Robert," Duncan Sutliff said. Their conversation ended. The judge turned the recording device on his phone line, which was always "On" unless he turned it off, back on. He was relieved to have made the call and would not now persecute himself over having made himself vulnerable, even if it was ultimately all for nothing. "Probably will be," he muttered to himself. "So be it." Dorothy couldn't nag him about it further, and there was something to be said for that. He was confident of Duncan's discretion, however matters turned out. Again it occurred to him what he was proposing was probably not all that uncommon. Wasn't he a judge, and hadn't he been a litigator for years before that? What deals hadn't he seen made? Why, he'd made more than a few himself! It rather staggered him, unexpectedly, that he'd sunk so much worry and misgiving into the matter. Not to mention, as a federal judge, he had a sinecure the envy of kings; even in the unlikely event the whole business found its way into the newspaper someday, he'd be all right. He'd weather the storm.

The judge and Mrs. Young were having a small dinner party that evening, so there was no real opportunity to discuss the day's news, but the judge did mention he had called Duncan Sutliff, and Dorothy Young was warmly appreciative. Later that evening, after the party, she asked her husband when they might expect to hear from the general.

"Oh, it's still our move," Robert Young said. "Didn't I tell you when I got home? We decided it makes more sense to talk this through with Alan and get his OK before Duncan proceeds."

"I'm not so sure about that," Dorothy Young said, obviously disappointed by this development. "I just think we stand a better chance if this talk with Alan isn't approached on a tentative basis. Wouldn't it be better, when we sit down with him, to say, 'Now, Alan, these arrangements have been made, there isn't going to be any nonsense about this, you're enlisting at such-and-such a time and place, you're doing this, period'. Instead of, 'Would you consider this, please, and if so, we'll see what can be done'?"

"Game, set, match," the judge said, vaguely wondering why he had not let her handle it all along. "Dorothy, I can't ask Duncan to stick his neck out before we have reasonable assurance Alan will cooperate." Dorothy Young sat at her mirror and began removing her make-up. She was 55, unquestionably still an attractive woman, despite a rough menopause not quite played out. She was first and foremost Mrs. Robert C. Young, wife of the district judge, but she was not only this, not by any means. Dorothy Young moved in numerous circles in West Los Angeles, sat on sundry boards and committees, favoring those of a philanthropic rather than an artistic nature, and was widely admired as a loyal friend and someone you could always count on. If Dorothy Young said she would be there, she would be there. She was solidly practical and generous with her time and her purse.

"I suppose you and Duncan are right, Bob," she said with resignation. "I was only thinking we want to do everything we can to maximize our chances, when we speak with our son." She resumed at the mirror. "What can I do, at this point?" The judge shook his head. "Why don't I give Mrs. Alan Young a call?" This took the judge by surprise, since he knew his wife did not particularly approve of their daughter-in-law. "Or maybe it would be better if I wrote her a letter?"

"What would you say?"

"Dear, Alan may lack judgment, but he does have a conscience. Throwing himself in jail for years will be very hard on Jeanne and Mary."

"True, but what does contacting her accomplish? It's Alan who must understand this. You can write her, sure, but I wouldn't count on results. Not to mention, she's already told us she supports Alan's decision completely."

"I know she does. I'm just looking for something else, some other avenue of attack, to break down Alan's resistance."

"Alan and Jeanne appear to have an excellent marriage," the judge observed. "I think she's even more devoted to him than vice versa."

"I think she is devoted to him, but it doesn't really have much to do with our problem, has it?" Dorothy Young said. Her daughter-in-law's devotion to her son, be it of unprecedented scope, was not altering her fundamental disapproval of the woman.

"Alan knows you aren't exactly enchanted by the choice he made in a wife," the judge said pointlessly.

194

"Choice!" Dorothy Young was incensed. "What choice? She deliberately deceived him, and he did the only honorable thing. That's not my idea of choice."

"He should have known better," the judge said, shaking his head. Their son didn't know better about anything. He was like the character in that French story, stumbling wide-eyed from one outrage to the next, eternally dumbfounded by human nature.

"I am not hostile toward that woman," Dorothy Young said. "I hope this isn't everyone's impression. My goodness, I don't intend that, Bob?"

"Hostile is too strong a word, but let's face it, you've been pretty consistent with your criticism, Dorothy. It really is time to back off. She's moving here, remember?" Dorothy Young had not forgotten an arrangement that promised difficulties.

"When are we going to speak with Alan?" she asked, steering the conversation back to where it had begun.

"Actually, we're not. I think Toby's the choice." Toby was Toby Barton, Esq., Attorney-at-Law. Robert Young had decided on him as Alan's defense counsel. Toby Barton could talk a jury into anything, surely he could talk some sense into his client?

"Who's Toby?"

"Toby Barton. Has a criminal defense practice, over in Santa Monica. Building quite a reputation for himself. He's argued several cases in my court, so I've seen him in action. He's a younger fellow, early forties I'd say. Kind of an informal manner, though not necessarily in the courtroom. I think he and Alan will hit it off."

"That sounds wonderful," Dorothy Young said. Her husband really was moving forward with this! "Have you called him?"

"Haven't. I wanted to chat with the general first. Tougher call first. No reason Toby won't be happy to take the case." Very happy to score points with a federal judge, Robert Young didn't add. The call to Toby was made the next day, and, yes, he would be delighted to take the case.

"There is this one, uh, wrinkle, I'd like to go over with you, Mr. Barton, before you sit down with Alan. Perhaps I could stop by your office after work?"

Meanwhile, the Vietnam War dragged on, as the Nixon Presidency entered its second year. It seemed to Alan Nixon was as intent as his predecessor in the White House on prosecuting the war, even as the demands to stop American participation became more frequent, strident and broader-based. Alan himself was terribly at loose ends. Living at home, even if of a relatively brief duration, wasn't felicitous. It was unbearable being separated from Jeanne and Mary, and their long talks on the telephone were a poor substitute for being together. In a real sense Alan was and was not back home, for what had intervened was not a dream, he had a wife and daughter, and he belonged with them, or, rather, they belonged with him. He told Jeanne he didn't know when the trial was to take place, but it was important to have her support, and that he loved her.

"You do have my support, dear Alan," she said during one conversation. "You've always had it and always shall. I love you so much."

"I know you support me," he replied. "I just meant your support ... and physical presence." Jeanne more than understood. She missed Alan in that way, too, but her period of illness, notwithstanding it had been short-lived, had been intense, and she was still not recovered, even entirely from the effects of the medication. She remained emotionally fragile, too, and it was not lost on her being separated from her husband was inhibiting her recovery here. She, too, was back at home, and the arrangement for her was just as unreal as Alan's. It was home she had so desired to escape, and had escaped, and now, strangely, she was back. Neither of her parents, however, was engaged in pretending their girl had come home and it was a return to the good old days, since, for one thing, there hadn't been many good old days, and, more fundamentally, their daughter was a wife and mother whose place was not with them, but with her husband, no matter his circumstances.

Charles McCarran was far from reconciled to Alan's latest folly, but it was done, and he knew his daughter must get well and get to her husband's side, just as soon as possible. Privately, he despaired over the prospect his daughter faced, life with a man of an unsteady temperament, given to wild whims and fanciful notions which were just fine to harbor and act upon, if you were a bachelor living out alone in the woods somewhere, but for a married man, for any married man, let alone the one his daughter had chosen, dreadful. Alan, he feared, would never be a dependable bread-winner, never settle down to the dreary quotidian, but would always rebel against the order of things, and inevitably gravitate from job to job, for what employer welcomes this kind of unpredictability? All of this was not to forget, of course, the little matter of spending several years in prison first. That, Charles reflected sardonically, would certainly add to the appeal of an already equivocal employment prospect. Jeanne was stuck with this, and not one thing could be done about it. The silver lining was that Alan had manifestly made Jeanne happy, for there was no doubting her love for him was genuine and deep. For one of his children to have found domestic happiness, in view of the turbulent environment in which they had been nurtured, was not to be sniffed at. There was still hope for Rickie, too, but the older son, Charles, had moved away, embittered, years ago, and evidently meant it when he said he was never coming back. He hadn't. It defeated Charles, this family failure, for he was unaccustomed to failure, and while his marriage had had its challenges, on balance he felt it had worked out satisfactorily. Was it that Adele really had not wanted to have children? What woman doesn't want to have children, he asked himself. Adele had been an adequate mother, but not a wonderful one. It was beyond Charles' perception that some motherly instinct had not attained full flower in his wife, which all three children had more than understood, and which consequently had drawn them closer to their father. As the children had gravitated toward their father, their mother's coldness and isolation became more pronounced. It was a beast that fed upon itself. Jeanne's predicament, to be sure, offered a new avenue for maternal love, but at this point a massive gesture from her mother would certainly be required to make a believer of Jeanne, and if it was forthcoming, it hadn't happened yet.

The vicissitudes of marriage still lay ahead for Stefan, now well into his first year of law school at Hastings in San Francisco. Law he loved, as he had expected, and he was excelling, but his circumstances otherwise displeased him. For one thing, he did not care for the city, although he couldn't say just why. Was it the bus rides from his apartment each day, and the four-block walk from his door to the bus stop? It was straight uphill, every step of those four blocks, on the return trip, and at 11:00 p.m., after a long day and evening of study in the law library, waiting for the bus and then facing those four blocks was a trial. It was often close to midnight when he found himself at last trudging past the Leyba Street Café, which seemed never to close, and the petite city park with its familiar historical marker about John C. Fremont, to his apartment. Still, blaming the city was ridiculous. Who dislikes San Francisco? Plus, had he really become acquainted with the place? Hardly. The cable cars were overrated, to be sure. No colder experience on earth than riding on the outdoor platform on one of those contraptions—and this from someone from Minnesota! Chilled to the bone, yet the dang things figured in one way or another on every travel poster, you could depend on that, and who knew how many tourist dollars they generated? A fair number of those dollars went into keeping the anachronisms in good repair, Stefan reflected with some satisfaction. What really had soured his experience with the city was his living arrangement, and the law school, as far as Stefan was concerned, was the culprit. Hastings' limited dormitory space had filled quickly, although Stefan himself was partially to blame, for he had delayed his enrollment decision pending word on his application to the University of Minnesota School of Law. He was left with having to hunt for a place to live, in the great city. His apartment's location was what ultimately made it so unsatisfactory, and yet, finding it at all had proved as taxing and miserable a task as Stefan could remember. Indeed, when he found it, he had the feeling he had found the last available apartment in the city.

A fortnight's stay with a widow who rented a room in her home had preceded the apartment hunt. One Ida Witherspoon by name, she claimed to have rented to a string of Hastings students over the years, and the location, it was true, was good. Mrs. Witherspoon's late husband, Burt, had been an engineer, and their son, Burt, Jr., lived in Los Angeles. They had a daughter, too, Ellie, who lived over in Richmond and had three kids. Seemed ideal, but Mrs. Witherspoon was strict about guests and noise and kitchen privileges and even watching TV, and after two weeks it was more than apparent it wasn't going to work. Stefan embarked on the frustrating, time-consuming search for another habitation. He must have seen close to two dozen apartments before settling on The Maplewood, the least expensive of all he saw and, with one exception, the most distant from the law school. No help for it, he would like it, like the neighborhood, make the trip each day, if only once, make the arrangement work. The apartment itself wasn't so bad, a one-bedroom with a reasonably spacious living area, a nice kitchen and even a window in the bathroom; it was bigger and better in every respect than Alan's first apartment in Montreal. Stefan was on the ground floor of a three-story building, not his preference. There was no view in a city of spectacular views. There would be one attempted break-in while he was there.

It was Wednesday evening the judge and Toby Barton met. Toby had a hearing downtown at 3:00, so he and the judge had arranged to meet at

198

Anthony's Tavern and Grill, near the federal courthouse, at 5:00. Toby had almost been late for the hearing, despite long experience with Los Angeles traffic. It was raining, as it does in Los Angeles in the winter, making traffic worse, and he had made the mistake, at La Cienega, of getting off the clogged freeway in favor of Wilshire, equally clogged. There was no mystery to the Los Angeles traffic nightmare, as far as Toby Barton was concerned. In a city with four million motorists and three million parking spaces, one million people, around the clock, were behind the wheel, looking for a place to park. Simple arithmetic, that's all there was to it.

The judge opted for coffee, and so did Toby who, for no good reason whatever, was momentarily nervous. It passed.

"Mr. Barton," the judge said, after several minutes of chitchat which had accomplished that Toby Barton would be called 'Toby', not 'Mr. Barton', yet it was 'Mr. Barton' again momentarily, signaling to the attorney the judge was beginning now in earnest. "Thank you for making the time to meet with me. It's pretty important." This was a little forced, but there was no hesitation in manner or voice. "My son Alan, who is 23 years old, has just returned from Canada, where he went when he was drafted, after college." Robert Young paused to swallow some coffee. The two men looked each other squarely in the eye. "He has come back and given himself up and is presently free on PR bond. He needs a lawyer." The judge halted there, for the moment.

"Why did he leave in the first place, judge?" Toby inquired. "Matter of principle?"

"Very definitely. I should have mentioned Alan attempted to obtain conscientious objector status, but this was turned down. It was not a half-hearted effort, but a very sincere and concerted one, I must say. Nobody except a religious fanatic, of course, ever gets the C.O., and Alan couldn't throw that in."

"I see," Toby said, although he didn't really. This was unfamiliar ground. "What brought him home?"

"Well, he claims to have had a drea—" Their waitress came by with more coffee, an interval just sufficient for the judge to realize that, try as he might, explaining his son's goofy dream was impossible. In any case, the attorney would hear it all, in excruciating detail, no doubt, from Alan himself. "Toby," the judge re-commenced, "what we're dealing with here is someone who is young, and inexperienced, and who has terrible judgment, and who has done some crazy things, but Alan isn't crazy."

"Stubborn and strong-willed, I gather," Toby said.

"You don't know the half of it, counselor," the judge replied, "but all in due course." Their conversation consumed more than two hours. They switched from coffee to a cocktail, and the judge had a Caesar salad. The restaurant was busy, as it tended to be, except on weekends, when downtown Los Angeles was significantly less inhabited. Robert Young was pleased by Toby's responsiveness and more persuaded than ever he had made a good choice, which, however, raised an issue.

"Who is my client, judge?" Toby asked. "You're calling the shots, you're paying the bills, but when I meet with Alan, as I'm sure you fully understand, I must do just that, meet with Alan."

"Toby, Alan is your client, obviously, and he's paying your fees, for the record, assuming we can, uh, he and you can agree on them. Alan's not exactly wealthy. Alan's calling the shots, as you put it. I'm meeting with you today because I know you and he doesn't, and he needs a top criminal defense man. Believe me, I have every intention of stepping out of the picture now. Alan doesn't want me in it, he's not interested in my opinions, doesn't listen to them. If our mutual goal is what is best for Alan, my withdrawal from further participation is that, definitely, so you've no cause for concern over who your client is." Toby now felt foolish. Had he actually elected to explain a basic tenet of the attorney-client relationship to the Honorable Robert C. Young, U.S. District Judge? "Toby, I'll give Alan your name and phone number. It's up to him after that."

"That's fine, judge, and let me just make absolutely sure I've heard you correctly. You've warned me my first obstacle will be to persuade Alan of the advantage of entering a plea, and the second will be to get him to accept this anticipated arrangement whereby we get a suspended sentence with enlistment as a term of probation. You feel reasonably confident Alan will be amenable to the plea, since he has no case for pleading 'not guilty', nor any intention, if he had, of doing so, and, moreover, the very fact he expressed a desire to hire an attorney evidences, you feel, his appreciation of the predicament he's in and the advantages of representation. As to the second obstacle, you are much less confident and in fact have suggested Alan will categorically refuse to consider enlistment, and it's pretty much up to me to figure out a way of talking him into this. Does this pretty much sum it up?"

"You've nailed it, counselor," Robert Young said, and Toby Barton smiled and rubbed his hands together, for he relished a challenge and felt he had prevailed against tougher ones than this.

"Again, however, judge," he said, "let me emphasize we can and will negotiate for a clean slate in the end, but I would be surprised if we aren't looking at some jail time first." The rain had ceased by the time they shook hands and parted. Los Angeles was a different city after rain. The precipitation magically cleared the air, temporarily, and, lo, snow-covered mountains, invisible the rest of the time, suddenly appeared to the northeast. These were the San Gabriels, and while they weren't visible now, since it was dark, the judge knew they would be on the near horizon in the morning. First-timers in the city, he had always reflected with amusement, must think they are having an hallucination, the first time those mountains appear, dazzling and unimagined. It was like that family trip, by train to Portland, one summer when he was a boy. They had taken the Daylight, which ran along the coast, to San Francisco. The train was painted orange and red. Couple of days in San Francisco, then the ferry across the bay to Oakland for the train north. It was the overnight train, and in the night, something woke the boy, and when he looked out the window, there, astonishingly, like a wonderful dream, was a towering, snow-draped peak! It was Mt. Shasta, although Bobby Young, at ten, didn't know it yet. To this day Mt. Shasta, which he had not seen again but once in all these years, was special to the judge, and recalling that first moment seeing that mountain, so unexpectedly, in the moonlight, gave him goose bumps. It was a boy's wonder, carrying over into wonderless adulthood.

Father was all business when he presented son with Toby Barton's card. "I think the two of you will hit it off, Alan, and Toby will represent you vigorously. He's expecting your call."

"Thank you, dad," Alan replied. He had a moment's weakness as the reality of what lay ahead, tangible in the form of the business card he held, hit him, and just for a moment half-hoped his father intended to come along, when he met with Toby Barton.

Alan was pleased that Toby Barton's office was in Santa Monica. He liked Santa Monica. Part of the affection was certain associations with boyhood and going to the beach, but it wasn't only this. He liked the town's vintage air, for it was one of the older seaside towns, although he could never be persuaded there had actually been a time when one left Los Angeles and drove through unpopulated country to reach Santa Monica. There was nothing fashionable or ritzy, to Alan's way of thinking, about Santa Monica, it was just a plain, slightly faded place, and this he found appealing. Not that there weren't palatial homes to be found, but wealth didn't dominate the place as it did other precincts, like Beverly Hills. Alan was in for a shock, however, when he reached the law offices of Barton & Kline, LLP, housed in a bank, not coincidentally one of the fanciest buildings downtown. His heart sank as he walked in the front door, for he couldn't see how he could afford this, and he wasn't going to accept a dime from dad. The receptionist, an attractive blonde with an unfortunate scar, or birthmark, on her lower right jaw, which, though it was small, drew the eye, welcomed him warmly, as though he had been there many times before, and told him Mr. Barton was expecting him and would be with him momentarily. It was nearly fifteen minutes, though, before Toby Barton appeared. The receptionist offered coffee, but Alan declined. He passed the time alternating between going over what he wanted to say, and speculating about the elderly couple, silent and stoic, seated opposite him in the small waiting area. What could be their legal problem? Neither looked as if he had too many more summers before him. Probably a will, Alan concluded. Maybe they want to change it. Must already have one.

Toby, wearing a sports jacket over a turtleneck sweater, gave Alan a hearty handshake.

"Come in, Alan, it's a pleasure to meet you. It's a pleasure to meet Judge Young's son! I can see the resemblance." (There was little resemblance; Alan took after his mother.) "Would you like some coffee?"

"No, thanks," Alan said. He felt the lawyer should have called him 'Mr. Young'. He would then have insisted upon 'Alan', but it should have been 'Mr. Young' initially.

"Coke?"

"Coke would be great," Alan responded. He took a seat. The entire south wall of Toby's office was a window, floor to ceiling, and the view was the Pacific Ocean. Glorious!

On his desk, inviting a client's grasp, was a handsome, oversized gavel. A woman, not the receptionist, brought Alan his Coke and coffee for the lawyer, and they got down to business. Alan told his story, a good deal more than he needed to tell, consuming twenty-five breathless minutes, with nary an interruption from Toby. When he was done, it was the lawyer's turn. He was coldly prepared, and, unlike his client, there would be no rambling.

"Alan, let me say first, it's not a sure thing I can reduce your jail time by a single day. There is no sure thing in law. Your voluntary return is our trump card, of course, and we'll play it at the appropriate time. Your obvious earnestness, your inexperience, to be perfectly frank, and your contrition, all will benefit us. It's unfortunate, on the other hand, that you inscribed your induction notice, but this was a rash and immature act that would be damaging only if we ever found ourselves in front of a jury, which we won't." Alan couldn't agree more with Toby's characterization of his defacement of his draft notice. It gave him pain every time he thought about it, a childish, stupid gesture that was an acute embarrassment to himself, and which could never be erased from his record. "Nonetheless, I think we can aim for as much as a year to eighteen months off your term. The government, of course, has an open-and-shut case, so you might wonder why they would be willing to give ground at all, but there are a number of reasons, not least among them that this war is becoming so politically unpopular." Toby paused to take a long sip from his coffee. It came in a large mug with "Stanford" inscribed. "There is, however, another possibility here, not to be overlooked, and if we can realize it, you might not spend an hour behind bars."

"Really?" Alan couldn't believe his ears.

"Enlistment."

"Enlistment?" Alan wasn't understanding. "Enlist in the Army?"

"Exactly." The attorney could see that his client was struggling with an idea with which he had not been presented and which had never occurred to him.

"How could I do that?" Alan shook his head. "I couldn't do that, Mr. Barton. I'm against the war. I wrongly went to Canada, in order not to be forced to take part in the war, I'm back to do the right thing and go to prison, and you're saying I go to Vietnam after all, like none of this happened?"

"Something like that, Alan, although you would not go to Vietnam. Part of the bargain would be a guarantee of stateside duty."

"Oh, I see," Alan said. He shook his head.

"This is the ideal solution, Alan. Going to prison isn't the hot idea you seem to think, if you'll forgive my bluntness, and it will seriously affect your prospects in later life, in terms of jobs, social acceptance, and so forth. Instead, we get you probation, you enlist, serve your country, obtain an honorable discharge, and the little deviation to Canada, although we can't make it go away, becomes just a little deviation, not a big deal. You'll come out just fine this way, I'm confident of that."

"Mr. Barton," Alan said, taking it all in, "I don't know if this is your idea or my father's. I have my suspicions. This is unacceptable. You see, it's dishonest. Like going to Canada. That was dishonest. There were only two honest choices for me—for any man—when I was drafted. Serve, or refuse to serve, but pay the consequences, whatever they be, under the law. This, actually, is also to serve one's country, though nobody sees it that way. This arrangement you've described …"

"Alan," Toby Barton interrupted. "Listen to yourself, because you just summed it up perfectly, don't you see, when you said nobody sees serving prison time, in this context, as serving your country. That's the truth for sure, and it's why the course you want to take is such a mistake. Nobody, Alan, nobody, is ever going to buy into this fine distinction you make between going to Canada and going to jail. Nobody is ever, ever going to pay it the smallest notice. The only thing anybody will ever look at is whether you put on the uniform, when asked. They aren't going to ask what you did after you put on the uniform, so it's just as good to sit behind a desk here in Los Angeles as to be in Saigon. They're just going to look to see if, when required, you did put on that uniform."

"It's dead wrong," Alan responded. "It's opportunistic, it's selfish, hugely selfish, it's taking advantage of my position, since I'm not some poor kid from East L.A. who can't afford a big-time lawyer and whose dad isn't a judge, because that's involved, isn't it, I just know it is. I could never do this, Mr. Barton. I know you're trying to do your best by me and I appreciate that, but I'm going to prison. I need a lawyer because, quite frankly, I can't see myself standing by myself in the courtroom against the district attorney."

"Well, that's wise," Toby Barton said.

"Plus, I do want you to see if you can get my sentence reduced," Alan added. "The longer I'm in prison, the harder it is going to be on my wife and daughter."

"May I just suggest, then, that you talk this over with your wife, before reaching a final decision? You are exemplary in putting her interests and those of your child first. Shouldn't she be involved in a decision as important as this one?"

"She has been involved," Alan said. This was true only up to a point. "I can talk with her some more."

"Please do, and may I expect to see you again not later than Monday? The government isn't going to wait on us."

"Could be as soon as tomorrow," Alan said. Tomorrow was Saturday. "Look, Mr. Barton, I think it's fine for you to represent me, I mean, I accept your representation, except we haven't even talked about your fee, so I accept provided I, um, can afford you, but I'm not sure at all I can go along with the enlistment idea, so those would be my terms."

"I understand," Toby Barton replied. "Why don't we worry about fees when I see you again Monday? I'm sure we can work something out." Both rose, and they shook hands. "It was a pleasure meeting you, Alan. Please give your dad my regards."

"I'll do that." On leaving the office, Alan bade the receptionist goodbye, noticing that the elderly couple he had seen previously had disappeared, but three other persons, all younger people, two men and a woman, obviously not together, were waiting their turn. He drove home mulling not the enlistment idea itself so much as his father's probable role. Should he make a scene? He grew angrier the more he reflected on it. It was like that $5,000 his parents had given him for Christmas, that time in Vancouver. When was that? Two years ago. Well, two Christmases ago, but it was really little more than a year. All that had happened in that tumultuous year, and the wondrous dream that had brought the clarity he had sought so long, was repudiated by this unbelievable enlistment notion. It was as if his parents had elected to ignore that any of it had transpired. How would they feel if he took a year of their lives and blotted it out, erased it, negated it, denied it? Alan just couldn't believe it, and had dismissed altogether the possibility the whole thing was Toby Barton's doing. He drove on, but as he neared home, he found his anger yielding to resignation. Pointless to be confrontational again. He knew what he would and would not countenance, so what was there to discuss, let alone argue over? Indeed, he reflected, his father had made a point of telling him his dealings with Toby Barton were confidential, protected by the attorney-client privilege, and it would be smarter to keep them that way. So, his father wasn't even expecting discussion! That simplified matters.

"Meeting with Mr. Barton went well," Alan announced resolutely when he got home, his voice unmistakably imparting there was little more to be said. "I accept his representation, if we can agree on fees. Somehow, that's the one thing we didn't discuss. I'm going to see him again Monday, so we can work it out then."

"I'm so glad, dear," his mother said, a sentiment his father echoed. Hardly more was said. They were not about to grill their son, having come fully to appreciate this would accomplish nothing, and more than likely backfire on them. If Alan wanted to talk, they would listen; if not, they would sit in silence.

Jeanne and Alan spoke every day. Tonight, she called him. He was surprised when she made an impassioned plea he consider Toby's idea. She was dreading the years of separation, not to mention the plan for Mary and her to live with her in-laws while Alan was in jail. This enlistment option, totally unexpected, was the solution!

Alan wouldn't listen, however, and Jeanne, who loved not least about Alan his stubborn honesty, gave it up. Alan had a restless night, nevertheless. The way Jeanne had implored him kept coming to mind. She always just consented, so this was a development. He thought about Stefan, too, and knew perfectly well where he would come down on the question. But his equivocation was short-lived. When he met Monday afternoon with Toby Barton, the first issue was the enlistment option. Alan said it was out of the question.

"I'll have to seek representation elsewhere, Mr. Barton," he said, "if this remains on the table. I'm your client, or your prospective client, and while I am happy to hear and consider every possibility, I make the decisions." The attorney replied that he understood perfectly, and could not agree more. Alan Young, as his father had cautioned him, was strong-willed, and it was readily apparent to the lawyer Alan was not to be dissuaded. So be it. Agreement on a fee proved no problem, since Toby Barton had decided he would cut his fee by fifty percent, more if needed, for Judge Young's son; it would pay a dividend in the long run, no doubt about that, and while the judge was going to be disappointed his son would consider no course except imprisonment, Toby was confident this would not come as much of a surprise. Over supper Monday evening, Alan told his parents he had hired Toby Barton.

"Mr. Barton did surprise me," he said off handedly, "with the idea I might be able to enlist, despite having dodged the draft, and serve in the armed forces without going to Vietnam." Alan's parents' hearts were suddenly in their throats. "He wasn't explicit how this would be arranged, but I got the impression he could do it. Wouldn't even have brought it up, otherwise, I suppose." Alan waited for reaction.

"Well, there's an interesting possibility," his mother choked out when it was apparent her husband would not, or could not, speak up. "What do you think, Bob?"

"I ... I ... that is, uh, interesting," the judge stammered, struggling not to betray them. He was none too pleased how his wife had put him on the spot. "What did you say, Alan?"

"Out of the question, of course. I informed Mr. Barton this would turn everything I have learned and believe in upside down. Not sure he agreed, pretty sure he didn't, but he consented. I'm his customer, after all."

"How would it do that?" Alan's father wanted to say. He did not. It would only launch a battle that was doomed. His mind was already shifting from the present conversation to the unavoidable one with Duncan Sutliff. "Well, Duncan, you recall that talk we had, about my boy, well, never mind, Duncan, forget it but thank you but please do forget it and especially forget I ever mentioned it." Something like that. Less said the better. Duncan was always going to look at him a little differently around the tables of Rotary. In the privacy of their bedroom that evening, Robert Young awaited his wife's recrimination. It never came.

"I hope," Dorothy Young did say, "you are not supposing I find fault with your silence at the table." She put her arm over his shoulder and kissed him. "You might just as fairly fault me, Bob. You've carried this burden. Alan isn't going to listen to reason, we both more than know that, and I think we did the sensible thing to stay out of a shouting match. He's going to jail, maybe it'll all work out somehow in the end, in any event, we are powerless to prevent it from happening." Her voice cracked with the last sentiment. The judge kissed his wife.

"Thank you for that."

"What are you going to say to Duncan Sutliff, Bob?"

"Don't worry about that. I'm just glad Duncan had the good sense not to take this further prematurely." Duncan Sutliff was ultimately glad, too, but not without a pang of regret. Robert Young's favor was one he could accommodate. This was hardly the first time a young man of privilege had sought to avoid military service in time of war. Hadn't Henry Adams, in England in 1861, expressed a wish to return to Massachusetts and enlist, but the choice was his, and he never got on the boat? The judge's request had presented the opportunity, never unwelcome, to wield a bit of power. The general was sorry to lose this opportunity. On the other hand, part of him disliked the whole business, for it was dishonest, no use saying it wasn't, and Robert Young's sorry excuse for a son could take his cowardice and sit in a jail cell, where it could keep him company. "Sorry I couldn't be of service, Robert," the general said gingerly, adding under his breath, "but this, after all, is why we have jails."

Alan entered a plea of guilty in United States District Court on March 12. He was sentenced to 44 months incarceration at the federal penitentiary in Leavenworth, Kansas, and was to give himself up to the federal marshal on March 24, making his release date approximately Thanksgiving, 1974. He did the calculation in his head and reckoned he and Jeanne would make that one very special Thanksgiving. Toby Barton had managed to get sixteen months shaved off his term, which certainly pleased Alan greatly. If only, he reminded himself harshly, he had understood this was the correct step, when it was the correct step. It was a self-censure that would dog him, though with diminishing fury, for a long time.

Meanwhile, Jeanne and the baby had arrived in Los Angeles, and Alan and Jeanne were sharing his bedroom at the house, an arrangement with which no one was entirely comfortable, but it made no sense to find an apartment when Jeanne and Mary were going to live with the Youngs during Alan's imprisonment. This uneasiness was destined to increase with Alan's departure, for Mrs. Young and her daughter-in-law were not close. Dorothy Young, it was true, had ceased believing Mary was not her son's child. To be sure, the move into their home would have been unthinkable, absent this concession. But she remained adamant in her belief her son had been tricked into marriage by a promiscuous woman, and now, by some malicious twist of fate, that very woman was come to live under her roof!

Alan bade his parents farewell outside the U.S. Marshall's Office, and Jeanne, Mary in her arms, accompanied him inside. They made it quick, but it was an exceedingly tender moment as they exchanged their love and mutual commitment. Alan took the baby in his arms briefly, and found himself unexpectedly near tears, but he fended them off. They parted, and

Jeanne returned to the waiting automobile. From the moment she climbed into the back seat, Dorothy Young having remained in the passenger's seat in front, a tension was present that was evident to all. Jeanne was spared the sharp exchange that had preceded her getting into the car.

"Please get in back, Dorothy," the judge urged. "It will make all the difference if she finds you sitting where Alan was, don't you see? Hurry."

"I'll do no such thing. You get in back. I'll drive. You can't order me around like that. How dare you!"

"Fine, then, be ugly about it. I know what you think of Jeanne. One thing for sure, you never change your mind, once it's made up."

"You get in back," Dorothy Young shouted, actually pushing her husband toward the door. "You think you know everything, you think it's such a great idea, you do it."

Randy was running a little late, and as she waited, Jeanne's thoughts inevitably gravitated back to what had preoccupied her for days: The decision to move to St. Louis. She could not help but engage in second guessing, sitting there waiting, staring out the window at a decidedly stark urban scene. There didn't seem to be anyone about. Well, it was Saturday, maybe that accounted for it. Her job was good and it was vital that she keep it, and this was the overriding, determinative factor, she reminded herself. While it was unlucky the branch office in Kansas City was cutting back on staff, Jeanne, on the other hand was among the lucky ones selected to be relocated to St. Louis, rather than laid off. But the move obviously meant a major change in her life. St. Louis was hundreds of miles from Leavenworth. She got to see her husband every other Sunday afternoon at the prison, and they had good visits, without a glass partition between them, like in the movies. How could she leave him? When would she see him again, if she moved? Could she afford it? Where would she live? St. Louis was a large city, unlike Leavenworth, with all the complications that implied.

"There is a dilemma, I'm afraid," she had told her boss. "I'll have to leave my husband. I would really appreciate it if somebody else could be transferred, so I could stay here."

"I'm afraid that's not possible, Mrs. Young." Curtis Monroe didn't inquire why moving would mean leaving her husband, and Jeanne hadn't volunteered the information.

"Well, my, ahh, husband and I haven't really talked about it, as of yet, but we will, and if it's all right, I'll let you know our decision in the next couple of days."

"I realize this a difficult decision for you," Monroe said, "so we're happy to give you a couple of days, but no more." He in fact was a bit annoyed by Jeanne's response; wasn't she being offered the transfer, when she could be losing her job?

"Thank you," Jeanne replied. She half-laughed, internally, at the ridiculousness of their conversation. What would Monroe have said, if he knew her husband was in prison and not about to get out, that to the extent, in view of this weird fact, there was any stability at all in her family, it was due to sheer grit on her part, that she had had to do everything by herself in a foreign country and that her own mother-in-law had been inexpressibly mean to her on more occasions than she could count? Well, this was a bit exaggerated. The United States, after all, wasn't precisely a foreign country for a Canadian, Jeanne Young wasn't the only woman with a husband in jail, and she certainly wasn't the only woman persecuted by her mother-in-law. Moreover, though Jeanne could not be honest with herself here, she had been equally hard on Dorothy Young.

Jeanne surprised Randy by agreeing to the fourth apartment he showed her. It had taken less than two hours, from the time she arrived at his office! He was impressed by her 'take charge" approach. They returned to his office and accomplished the paperwork. Now it was back to the hotel; Jeanne didn't get lost this time. The hotel wasn't far from downtown, and as she drove east, the Gateway Arch loomed on the horizon. She vaguely noticed it. The decision she had just made so consumed her, she found herself turning into the hotel's parking lot with no memory at all of the drive. Jeanne McCarran Young could not know the very neighborhood she had just left would be her home for the next thirty years.

The return trip to Leavenworth was uneventful. It was about a six-hour drive, provided one did not get lost in Kansas City, which had happened on the way over. This time Jeanne managed. She had become cool-headed. Her marriage and all it had brought had made her a more self-confident person than she had ever imagined she could be. Reinforcing this strength and resiliency was an advantage lacked by many: Jeanne had a clear focus in her life, from which she would not be deflected. Alan and Mary were her purpose. She loved her husband, no matter what, and would always be guided by this. It was not unlike what faith makes possible for some persons. Jeanne would no more be spared trouble than the next person, but her love for her family would see her through, time and again. Sadly, Alan, the great beneficiary of this affection, would seldom appreciate it. They were opposites, in truth. Alan was without his wife's practicality and common sense; Jeanne lacked her husband's imagination and proclivity to consider the "big questions." These differences, however, were exceeded by another. Whereas Jeanne wasn't a deep thinker, knew it and admired and loved this quality in Alan, he faulted his wife for her inability to be abstractly intelligent. Alan, in short, did not love Jeanne as she loved him, and this would be a constant down the years.

This was Jeanne's Sunday to visit Alan at the penitentiary, and as she got Mary ready, she was humming. The decision was, of course, made, they were moving to St. Louis. The hard part was over. Alan would agree, and even if he didn't (but he would), she thought merrily, hers was a husband not in the most advantageous position to thwart his wife's wishes! Their visits were happy occasions for Jeanne, even if the conversation flagged, as it sometimes did. This was not due to any malaise in Alan, who, like every inmate, struggled initially but had found ways to cope and, because his conscience was clear, was relatively adjusted to his circumstances. He spoke sparingly of prison life with his wife, but if he had said more, he would have told her he had not met with unkindness or persecution from other prisoners, but had, on occasion, from the guards. He had been punched, to be sure, but the abuse was mostly verbal. He had made the mistake, early on, of discussing his views on the war and why he had come to prison, which met with derision and mockery. Not all the guards were hard on him, but those who were, were pretty constant about it. Soon enough, Alan accepted the futility of argument or protest and gave it up. He was in the minimum security section of the prison and had limited contact with prisoners of more volatile propensities; if he had been around them, his appreciation for the harshness of prison life, and the hazards of a guard's life, would have been greater.

Alan was not the only inmate incarcerated for refusing conscription, but conversations with others like him, approached enthusiastically in the beginning, had run their course, and Alan was not close to a single one. By all rights, this should not have been the case, especially with Benjamin Sanders, who was from Atlanta, and who saw exactly eye-to-eye with Alan on the ethics of war protest. Ben, unlike Alan, had not gone to Canada, having understood what he had to do from the start. It still bothered Alan he had been so wrong for so long, and he was a bit in awe of Ben. With the complete support of his family, Ben had met with fewer obstacles than most, particularly in dealing with his father. Ben and Alan had had some good talks and respected each other, but they were not close. Ben would return to the family business, furniture repair and restoration, when he got out, and this was his one and only objective, which Alan had grown tired of hearing about. He was decidedly less interested in football, too, specifically, the Georgia Tech football team, about which, it seemed to Alan, there could be very little Ben Sanders did not know. Alan's nearest confidante was, in fact, a middle-aged man named Ray Wallace, who had stolen a quarter of a million dollars from his employer, and spent every dime. Ray was of a sanguine disposition and not in the least remorseful.

"They treated me as badly as one human being can treat another and deserved it, let me tell you," he said with vehemence. Ray was given to speaking his mind and reminded Alan, on a regular basis, that principles were the worst curse that could befall any man and that he must discard them at first opportunity and be untroubled thereafter. Alan protested, naturally, and heard in return the familiar refrain: "Nobody gives a damn about your ethical nuances, for Chrissake. You think everybody went to college and studied Plato? Nobody went to college and studied Plato." On one occasion, he told Alan an anecdote: "There was this young fellow hired by the Census Bureau and sent out to Oklahoma to gather data. He was in the Panhandle, the old Dust Bowl, where there's no water, no vegetation, not a speck of green, just the good, brown earth. Been there?" Alan nodded he hadn't. "There was a rancher standing out in his corral in his dust-covered spats and cowboy hat, and the young man went up to him. 'Excuse me, sir', he said to the rancher, who was sixty if he was a day and had a couple days' growth of beard, 'but I'm with the US Census Bureau and I'd like to ask you a few questions'. The rancher nodded okay, and the young man fired off his questions, how many in the family, how many sons, how many daughters, how many acres the ranch was, did he have a mortgage, how many head of cattle, and so forth. Finally, he was finished, and just to make a little conversation by way of conclusion, he said to the rancher, 'You know, sir, I've been doing this census here in Oklahoma for some weeks and was over in Tulsa before this and I've learned a lot of things about Oklahoma. Did you know there's more lakes in Oklahoma than Minnesota?' The rancher scratched his stubble, looked at the horizon, doing about a 240-degree turn, turned back to the young man, and said, 'Well, meebe so, son, but it shor don't look like it.'" Ray Wallace paused.

"Nice story, Ray," Alan said.

"Get the message?"

"I think so, but tell me, anyway."

"This moral point you are always making, about coming to jail after doing the wrong thing, 'running away' as you put it, and how the difference is so important. It's foolishness. I mean, maybe you're right, like the kid in the story, but what you did never is going to look right. It's always going to look like you didn't serve your country when your country asked you to. That's the analogy."

"I am serving my country," Alan said bleakly.

Prison life was, among other things, a matter of adjusting to a routine. Alan had done this. There was no space. There was certainly no privacy, even in the latrines. Chores were abundant and, after the initial distaste-fulness, proved welcome, since they kept him busy. Alan located the prison library soon and, in unoccupied hours, could be found with his face between the covers of a book, which earned him some predictable nicknames. All in all, he was managing, but he reminded himself, his sentence was of a manageable duration. He could not conceive how inmates serving sentences running into decades, kept their sanity.

On her visits, Jeanne brought Mary with her, of course, and Alan had the opportunity to hold their daughter, unless nursing became imperative. More than once, a new diaper was necessary.

"Wouldn't have wanted you to miss out on that experience, honey," she was given to saying. Fact was, he was about to start missing out on it, since she was moving to St. Louis. "So I really think, and I've thought a lot about this, Alan, all the way across Missouri, I think there's really no choice, I have to go. I can come back once every month or so, maybe." She grabbed and held his hand, leaving him with one arm holding Mary. "It won't be the same, I know, and it won't be for Mary, either, and she'll begin to understand, if she doesn't already, that her dad is in and out of her life, and, yes, I'll find a way to make it work, until you're out of here." On a later visit, she described their new apartment to him in great detail, regretting she had not thought to take pictures; they had a cheap camera, which, however, took good pictures.

"Is the neighborhood safe?" Alan asked. "St. Louis is a big city, and all big cities have bad areas." It was a daunting future, and Alan wasn't taken with the idea of his wife and their infant daughter moving to a considerable town where they did not know a soul, and starting over.

"Yes, silly," Jeanne said cheerfully. "Randy wouldn't have shown me apartments in bad neighborhoods," she reassured him. "I've done this before, you know." She had moved from California to Kansas on her own, found a place, found a job. Alan gave Mary, who was dozing, a kiss on the forehead, and suddenly gulped hard. Separation loomed again, and it was unwelcome, but he knew Jeanne was right in her decision and it would be their decision, and he knew, too, she would pull it off. Alan may not have loved Jeanne as she did him, but an admiration for her self-reliance was developing. She had developed a toughness, too. Maybe, he reflected uncomfortably, she was tougher than him? No question the year with his parents had effected a change.

"What can I do?" he asked. "What can I do to help you with this move?"

"Get out of jail?" Jeanne had not said this unkindly. She was well-aware Alan wanted to help, but, realistically, there just wasn't any way. "I'll be all right, honey," she said yet again.

Jeanne gave notice to her landlord, and began packing. This would not take long. She and Alan owned no furniture to speak of, and even their personal belongings were exiguous. She had a Volkswagen and reckoned, between the trunk and the interior space, she could get everything in, which did not prove true by a long shot, obliging her to rent a U-Haul. It was a cloudy Saturday when she finished the last of it. She fell back onto the sofa, more weary emotionally than physically, and sipped from a cup of tea while the rain splattered intermittently against the windows. Jeanne wondered when her married life would begin to be normal. Alan faced two more years in the penitentiary. What would he be like when he was released? Was it her imagination, or was he becoming increasingly distant during their visits? Would their marriage survive this test at all? What would he do with himself when he was free again? Alan was without ambition. She could hardly get him to talk about it. He said he was reading a book about accounting. He could become an accountant, he said. Accountants were always in demand. There must be plenty of opportunities in a big city like St. Louis for an accountant. But there was no fire in his voice. Jeanne knew intuitively he was not serious about it, and she was right. Her father had once impulsively called her husband a "ne'er-do-well," and there was a creeping fear in her heart dad was right. Was all the responsibility to be hers? Finding a place for them to live, caring for Mary, earning a living?

Alan and Jeanne had the tenderest of partings the next afternoon, but not before another lecture from him about a woman alone in a big American city.

"I have never set foot in St. Louis," he said, "so you're already ahead of me in that department. Like every big city, Jeanne, there are going to be neighborhoods you just have to stay out of. I don't know where these are in St. Louis, but it's important. If you get in a bad area, don't get out of the car, just keep going, sooner or later you'll find your way back to familiar landmarks."

"Alan, darling, didn't we have this conversation yesterday? Wasn't I in Los Angeles, without you, more than a year? Wasn't I in Montreal, which is a very big city, all by myself, before you swept this girl off her feet?" Jeanne smiled sweetly.

"Not the same thing. I know a thing or two about Montreal myself, remember, and it's not unsafe the way U.S. cities can be. Plus, you weren't alone in L.A. This is different." Jeanne agreed it was different, grudgingly.

"So how big is St. Louis? Big as Montreal? I doubt it. Montreal's the biggest city in Canada."

"Glad you asked," Alan said. He began thumbing through the almanac he had borrowed from the prison's library. "Here it is. 'St. Louis, largest city in Missouri, on the Mississippi River, major commercial and manufacturing center, founded 1764, point of embarkation for Lewis & Clark Expedition, 1804. Site of Louisiana Purchase Exposition, 1904. Population 1950: 856,623.'" Alan closed the almanac. "Pretty big city, wouldn't you say? St. Louis is famous for its role in the westward expansion. The Gateway Arch commemorates good old Manifest Destiny. Good jazz and blues, too."

"Jazz sounds good," Jeanne said. She didn't know what he meant by whachamacallit destiny, and didn't care. "Maybe some good clubs?"

"I'm sure. Lots of good jazz in St. Louis." Alan could not, however, think of the name of a single jazz composer. "You're talking Mark Twain territory, too," he added. "Life on the Mississippi."

"It'll be fun to see the famous Mississippi River," Jeanne said. "I didn't know St. Louis was on the Mississippi."

"You didn't know St. Louis, Missouri, is on the Mississippi River? Jeanne! Everybody knows that."

"Not quite," Jeanne said drolly.

"Huck Finn on the raft, with Jim? Tom Sawyer? Come on, sweetheart, you've read Mark Twain, haven't you?"

"Not that I can recollect."

"Boy, if I had known what an ignoramus I was marrying ..."

"Well, I guess I'm smart enough to stay out of jail," Jeanne said, immediately regretting it. How had that slipped out? Alan swallowed hard.

Jeanne drove out of Leavenworth punctually at 6:00 the next morning, with Mary strapped securely in her baby's seat. She knew it was six hours to St. Louis. It was sunny. She tuned in a rock station and sang along as the miles clicked by. She had saved a little money in Leavenworth, not quite $3,000, and she received money intermittently from her family. Her in-laws had promised they would send money, if needed, but to date she had not asked for a cent. She had made no mention of this to Alan, but he talked with his parents periodically, and, in what represented a reversal of his previous position, had extracted a pledge to help them if necessary, which, similarly, he had not mentioned to Jeanne. The secrecy aside, there was a tacit understanding among all concerned that Jeanne and Mary Young would not be left to starve while the family's breadwinner languished in a prison cell.

Jeanne would accept the financial help and not be fussy about it, or feel guilty. She could not know it, but her lot would improve with the move to St. Louis. For Alan, the two remaining years in Leavenworth would be a time of decreasing morale. The interminable drudgery of prison life, the terrible sameness of the days, began to tell. More than ever, he wondered how individuals like Frank Greven and Ronald Ulmer, a pair of inmates with whom he was vaguely acquainted and who he knew were in Leavenworth, respectively, twenty years and for life, kept their balance. He wasn't forgiving their misdeeds, but long incarceration was a singular fate. These stood outside the tumult of life, like a person sober at a party where everyone else is inebriated; they were apart, unlike others. No question, Alan concluded, lengthy incarceration demanded a profound emotional adjustment the average person couldn't imagine. He knew he had had to make an adjustment of his own, but his sentence was relatively short by comparison.

Nevertheless, his last two years were sufficiently long, compounded by the fact Jeanne's planned visit every other month proved impossible.

The last two years in law school dragged for Stefan, particularly the third, when, like his classmates, he became consumed by an eagerness at last to be done. He had excelled at Hastings, making Law Review, but, while he did not lack ambition, neither had he found a bailiwick that "grabbed" him and, notwithstanding he would graduate fourteenth in his class, faced the same obstacles finding a position as everyone. He would not miss San Francisco, where he was limiting his job search, although a romance during his second year had made the time fly by. Her name was Gloria and she was a free-spirited woman, four years older than Stefan, who had left her native Colorado for the "uninhibited Barbary Coast." She lived and worked in Oakland, which Stefan was to come to know, temporarily, better than San Francisco. They had met one Saturday afternoon at an art exhibit in San Francisco which Stefan, in need of a break from his studies and looking for something different, had abruptly decided to attend. Gloria was a brunette, not quite a beauty but possessed of a ravishing figure and, equally seductive, a devil-may-care attitude. Despite his cautious nature, Stefan would need five months to discover Gloria might or might not have a husband back in Aurora, Colorado. The mere possibility was more than enough; it sent him into a cold sweat, and he broke off their relationship decisively. It could have turned ugly, had Gloria elected to be confrontational. She didn't. After all, law student Stefan Kopinski had never been a long-term investment.

Stefan's difficulties in finding work after graduation were partly his own fault. He had served an internship at a San Francisco firm the summer between his second and third years of study and stood a chance of receiving an offer from them, but he was determined not to remain in the Bay Area. Accordingly, he concentrated his job search on the southern part of the state, focusing on Los Angeles, Santa Barbara and San Diego. He had ruled out returning to his native Minnesota, to his family's disappointment, as this was thought to have been the plan. At some point he could not identify he had decided there was much to be said for California living. Hadn't California been his home since finishing high school, wasn't his best friend a native who would eventually return, which, surely, would cure their present estrangement? Wasn't it nicer to live in a place where one was not obliged to remain generally indoors between November and April? Stefan

217

found amusing that his home state was defined by its winters, as nothing else; invariably, it was the climate first remarked, whenever he mentioned where he was from.

In truth, Stefan had mixed feelings. The fact he had studied law in a different state didn't really matter, if he decided to return to Minnesota. The most compelling reason to return was his parents, whom he loved and who loved him. On the other hand, they were a mere three-hour flight away. This, finally, decided him. When, however, the job search converted from weeks to months, Stefan began looking at opportunities in Minneapolis, and the letters went out. The news delighted his family, but it wasn't to be. Each response was negative, and discouragement began to set in. Finally, one day, it occurred to him Alan's father might be of assistance. He contemplated sending Alan a letter first, but decided this would consume time unnecessarily, and went ahead with a short letter directly to Judge Young. Was the judge, by any chance, in the market for a law clerk? If not, did the judge know of someone who might be hiring and looking for an enterprising young lawyer with ambition and talent?

In his letter, Stefan did not bother with introducing himself beyond a simple sentence, as he was reasonably certain Alan's father would remember him as his son's closest friend, about whom he had undoubtedly heard on many occasions, not to mention he had stayed at the house three times, and they had met again in Montreal, at Alan's and Jeanne's wedding. Stefan was right; no introduction was required. The judge scratched his head upon receiving the letter. He did not need a law clerk, but Dan Bryant, down the hall, did. How ironic, the judge told himself. He had always hoped, in a father's way, his son would follow in his footsteps. A clerkship for Alan would dependably have been available when he finished law school. But it wasn't his son who was finishing law school, rather, it was his son's best friend, now a candidate to occupy the position of surrogate. His own son, instead, was somehow in prison. Mr. Kopinski, the judge told himself, is an estimable young man, no doubt, and Alan's friend, but he is not my boy. There was something unpalatable about the idea, and the judge elected not to follow up with Stefan, who, not having heard, proceeded to pick up the phone one afternoon and call the judge's office.

Robert Young didn't have to take the call, but he did, and, impressed by Stefan's doggedness, and feeling remorseful about succumbing to an unworthy impulse, he told him he knew of an available clerkship, and would mention his name to Daniel Bryant. Stefan, meanwhile, should of course send a letter and his resume and references. That's all it took. Not three weeks later, Stefan was in Los Angeles, law clerk to Daniel L. Bryant, U.S. District Judge. It remained for Stefan to kick himself, again and again, for not having recognized what he knew, that "pull" was what mattered, and not being shy about asking a favor. There was a lesson in this, and Stefan Kopinski was a quick study. His three years clerking for Judge Bryant would be a valuable experience, and would open more than one door for him. Before those doors started opening, however, the big one in Alan's life, the one out of prison, would finally open. This would happen in August 1974. The day was August 24. Alan had been on the phone, several times, the preceding week with his lawyer, Toby Barton, with whom whole years had gone by without so much as a Christmas card. Alan would be released three months before his release date, free and clear. No probation. He had been a model prisoner, never made trouble. Packing, obviously, did not take long. Alan had a small suitcase into which everything went except his orange prison suit, his daily attire for the duration of his stay. "Not going to miss you," he muttered as he shed the garb for the last time.

At noon on August 24, Alan left Leavenworth, Toby Barton at his side. The latter had flown in from Los Angeles to handle the paperwork, primarily, but also to be with his client on a day of celebration. They were practically strangers. Waiting at the gate were Jeanne and Mary, and his parents. Alan wore a suit Toby had secured for him and would surprise his parents with a full beard he had grown; Jeanne had seen it and, while she much preferred him without the facial hair, she had remained silent, surmising growing the beard may have provided him some sort of solace while in jail. She intended to speak up now, for whatever good it might do. So would Dorothy Young.

The joy of the occasion trumped everything—family tensions, unhappy recollections, disappointments, misgiving, frustration. There was only undiluted joy and tears, even from Robert Young. It was a sunny, warm summer's day in northeastern Kansas, and it was a time for celebration. Airline tickets, three nights at the Mark Hopkins in San Francisco for Jeanne and Alan, had been discussed. Judge and Mrs. Young would pay all expenses and handle baby-sitting chores. Crazy not to do this, Jeanne begged Alan, but he vetoed the plan, saying they did not need a trip to admittedly the country's most romantic city to re-kindle the romance in

219

their marriage, which indeed was correct, and while the champagne at the Top of the Mark probably would have arrived with more flair, the resumption later that day of their marriage at the Holiday Inn in Leavenworth left neither with any complaint.

Alan's father gave him a check at their parting. This really made more sense than an expensive trip, although his parents had intended both. There was no surprise, as before; the check had been discussed in advance, and Alan not only hadn't balked, but was deeply grateful. Jeanne had a job and it was going all right, but he must find work, now, must find a career, and how long it would be before he was on his feet was impossible to say. Only sure thing was, it would not happen quickly, so the financial assistance was most welcome. There had been talk of Alan and Jeanne returning to California, but Jeanne was very determined, she had a good job and only sour memories of her time in southern California, and although she scarcely articulated it to herself, she knew deep down the friction between herself and her mother-in-law was permanent. Dorothy Young, for her part, would have agreed. They got along wonderfully well, widely separated. Jeanne, it was true, was not particularly keen on St. Louis, but she was wise enough, too, to know one makes his life, wherever he is, and she had made a life for herself and Mary in the Missouri city, taking it one day at a time. She was justifiably proud of her accomplishment and would not turn her back on it. Alan also was inclined to favor St. Louis. Returning home had a certain sentimental appeal, and, despite the wide gap that had developed between himself and Stefan, he reckoned they could obliterate it by resuming contact, but these considerations must decidedly take a back seat to what was best for his daughter and his wife, which translated into joining them and becoming a part—a contributing, reinforcing part—of the life she had created for them in St. Louis.

Across Missouri, they discussed subjects great and small. Alan insisted upon a slight deviation at mid-point, to see Jefferson City.

"Quaint, don't you think, that the state capital isn't even on the main highway between the two big cities?" Alan said.

"Maybe in Jefferson City they're glad to be a little cut off from the crowd."

"Still, it's the capital, it ought to be on the highway."

"Ottawa's between Montreal and Toronto, our two main cities, and I don't think anybody goes there unless he has something to do with government," Jeanne said. "But maybe you saw it when you went to Montreal?"

"I flew, honey, from Toronto to Montreal."

"That's right."

"Come to think of it, though, that time I saw Stef in Windsor, I must have gone through Ottawa. Don't remember it. I sure do remember the time with Stef, though. We had a miserable visit." Jeanne didn't respond. She had heard him speak many times of the trip to Windsor, and however unsatisfactory the visit with Stefan may have been, she had always been grateful for something, she knew not what, because Alan had been a changed man when he arrived in Quebec City.

They both liked Jefferson City—"Jeff City"—picturesquely situated on the Missouri River. It began with a simple but satisfying lunch at a diner. Missouri was very green and very humid, but they were both accustomed, at this point, to the swelteringly hot Midwestern summer. The domed capitol itself easily dominated the landscape, was walking distance from the diner, and there was no objection from Jeanne when Alan suggested they go see it up close.

"Might even be open. I'm sure we can get a crash course on Missouri history, and it should be nice and cool inside." They tried walking hand-in-hand, but pushing the baby stroller over a rough sidewalk with one hand proved awkward, so Jeanne withdrew her hand from his. The capitol was open; the security guard directed them to the desk where they could pick up materials about the building, the city and the state, and informed them they could even take a guided tour.

"Or, you can just poke around on your own," he said, "if you prefer."

"Believe we'll do that," Alan replied. There was really no reason for them to rush, they both reflected, since St. Louis was only two more hours. Alan's life would doubtless turn hectic soon enough; why not relax while he still could? They did linger, and Alan, who had been brushing up on Missouri facts and history in preparation for the move to St. Louis, was delighted to find corroboration in the corridors of the state capitol for what the almanac had imparted. After more than an hour, they agreed it was time to go. They would visit Jefferson City again, though not for many years, but this unplanned excursion, coming so very soon after Alan's release from years in prison, with Mary merrily in tow and green and steamy Missouri all around, would be a happy memory for both of them, always.

Ahead, now, lay St. Louis. Alan had no idea, really, just what to expect, despite Jeanne's having spoken of the city many times. She was not enchanted by it, though there was nothing particularly objectionable, either. The great Gateway Arch she had finally discovered; Jeanne thought it was not worth all the fuss. The city made much of its history, but it seemed to her not to be compared with that of her native Montreal. As for scenery, St. Louis had neither southern California's mountains nor ocean, so there was simply no comparison at all here. There was one lovely park near her apartment, with statues and fanciful gazebos, where she took Mary on Sunday afternoons; the rest of the city was pretty much a wash, as far as Jeanne was concerned.

Not for Alan. He loved St. Louis from the moment he saw it.

"After where you've been, the North Pole would look good," she cracked.

"It's under water."

"Ice."

"Water." Fact was, Alan had not been much of anywhere. He knew the strip of land between Los Angeles and Seattle well, and he knew Montreal, but not much else. There had been two trips to New York, with a side trip to Washington the first time. He had never been anywhere in the Midwest except Minnesota. St. Louis was a blank slate, and almost everything that filled it would be wonderful.

"We have to see the Arch first," Alan insisted. "Then we'll go home."

"No, honey," Jeanne protested. "I'm tired. Mary's tired." It was getting late afternoon, and Jeanne wasn't in the least interested in sightseeing.

"Just the Arch, I promise. How can you drive into St. Louis and not see the Arch? Like going to San Francisco and skipping the Golden Gate Bridge."

"You can see it from the freeway when we exit at Grand. Before that, even."

"You're not going to let me drive down to it and see it up close?"

"No." She meant it. They were in the city, now, and, suddenly there it was, straight ahead.

"Look at that!" Alan exclaimed. "The Gateway Arch! St. Louis, Gateway to the West! Wow! It really doesn't look that big, though."

"It's big, very big. It's still miles away." Alan was trying to take in the increasingly interesting urban landscape while negotiating traffic. They skirted the southern rim of Forest Park and crossed Kingshighway, Alan noting the imposing cluster of medical buildings fronting the park. "Barnes Hospital, Jewish Hospital, St. Louis Children's Hospital." On they went, but only a short distance farther. At Grand, Alan exited. There again was the Gateway Arch, visible straight ahead. It still didn't strike Alan as impressively large, but it remained at some distance. He'd find out another time. They crossed the Mill Creek Valley, Jeanne recalling her very first trip to the city; it was here at Grand she had turned the wrong way and become temporarily lost. Now, they lived hardly a mile away. The apartment was on Utah Street, a pleasant, tree-shaded street lined on both sides, for the most part, with tidy, brick homes. They were on the third floor of an old, grayish brick building, dating from the 1920's. Jeanne had finally taken pictures, but it was still a bit of a shock to see just how drab the edifice was. There was another, identical apartment building adjacent, on the west, and their apartment being on the west side of its building, they had a view primarily of the twin building. The apartment was not without its amenities, as Alan was about to discover, not least among them that it was spacious, with high ceilings, hardwood floors, an ample bathroom, and an endearingly cranky set of radiators as reliable as the building's brick itself. It was somewhat dark inside, however, and was going to stay that way, since windows faced only west and north. Jeanne had made the best of it, had made it their home, and so it would continue to be, Alan told himself as he surveyed the premises, finding proof of the presence of a woman and small child evident everywhere, in items large and small. The neighborhood was safe. It was a sensible, even a good, choice, despite the distance Jeanne was from her workplace. (Her first job, a relatively short drive from the apartment, had lasted only a matter of months after she relocated to St. Louis.)

Jeanne had bought a bottle of wine, and she cooked steaks, and they dined by candlelight and made love well into the night, and Alan, a bit groggily the very next morning, embarked upon the process of becoming a schoolteacher, this choice in career having prevailed largely by default. Stefan had it better, Alan told himself. Stefan knew he wanted to be one thing and no other thing, a lawyer. He would doubtless be an excellent one, and he would not be plagued by philosophical torments. Putting the Vietnam War behind him, getting on with his life and his responsibilities, Alan knew was imperative; it was also more easily said than done. Stefan had not responded to his letters in a long time, and Alan wondered if their friendship had come to an end. Maybe being in prison accounted for the loss of communication, Alan tried reassuring himself, knowing all the while incarceration had not foreclosed receiving mail.

His first stop was the administrative offices of the St. Louis Public Schools, housed in a nondescript building of uncertain vintage, deep in the bowels of the city. Because Jeanne had to have the car to take Mary to the day care center and then get on to her job, Alan was reduced to the bus, and it was a long journey. Within days, he would buy a used Pontiac. Nobody at the school office seemed very interested in helping him, and "Mr. Potter," the Assistant Superintendent who was in fact the person with whom he needed to meet, was available only by appointment. Alan wondered why it had not occurred to him to make an appointment.

"I'd like to make an appointment, then," he said to the young woman who was more or less paying attention to him.

"Mr. Potter's secretary isn't here right now. You'll have to speak with her."

"Will she be coming in soon?" he asked. It was 9:00 a.m.

"I couldn't say. She usually gets here right around now. You can wait over there." She pointed at a trio of upholstered chairs definitely in need of replacement. "Shouldn't be long."

"Well, thank you," Alan replied. "I will wait." Will wait, he reflected, not for an interview, but for the only person in the office apparently able to arrange the interview. It was a typical municipal office. The walls needed painting, at least two of the neon lights were not functioning (one flickered from time to time), the whole place needed a good dusting and vacuuming, the windows did not look as if they'd been washed in a year. A typewriter clattered somewhere, but people were milling about, desks were cluttered, an air of languor pervaded the office. Alan fought off a growing sense of dismay. After another ten minutes, Martha Overby arrived, and a good thing happened. She said she would just check to see if maybe Mr. Potter could fit Alan into his schedule. Indeed, if he could come back at 1:30, it would happen! Alan thanked Mrs. Overby and said he'd be back. What he would learn before day's end was that he would have to obtain a teacher's license from the State of Missouri, which would mean going back to school for two years. Alan was not surprised by this.

"Any way to do it faster? Go to summer school, take extra courses during the semester?"

"Actually, you can do that at Harris-Stowe, and be done in 18 months," R.L. Potter replied. "It's a lot of work, though."

"I think I could manage it," Alan said. He was sure he could manage it. Nobody was looked upon with more condescension than an education major, he distinctly recalled from his college days. He was not free of the bias, himself. Now, he was going to be an education major! One more arrogance to discard and never dwell upon again.

Luck was with Alan. The fall semester at Harris-Stowe Teachers College had not begun, and if he applied immediately and passed a necessary test, he could get in and, yes, as he had been told, there was an 18-month program, so he could potentially have his license by January 1976. Alan was elated. He could take the entrance test right then and there if he wanted, or come back another afternoon.

"With your credentials, Mr. Young, there should be no difficulty," Potter observed. Alan took the test that day. There was nothing to it, he didn't miss a single question and was reasonably sure of this when he turned his test in. Alan had given much thought to teaching while at Leavenworth. He wasn't terribly fired up about it, it's true, but he wasn't terribly fired up about anything. He knew for certain one thing only, that he was going to stay out of sales. He knew he had a competent mind and could have handled accounting, or law, but his heart was not in it, and he was not prepared to give his days to something about which he was lukewarm. He felt high school teaching would not occupy all his time, and in the unlikely event it did, he had concluded it was the one thing to which he really might give his heart. The stint teaching in Montreal had given him a taste for the vocation, and he had found it not unsatisfying. It had also persuaded him of something he rather suspected already, and this was that he wanted to teach high school, not college, if teaching was his choice. Alan reflected unfavorably upon his four years at the University of California, when he thought about it at all. He shook his head in disbelief, for it seemed to him he hadn't learned a thing, nor could he remember vividly so much as one of his professors. He did remember a number of his high school teachers. Maybe it was vanity, wanting to be remembered by his students, maybe the belief he could reach them, if they were to be reached at all, more probably in adolescence than thereafter, maybe it was the knowledge to teach at the university level would mean getting his doctorate. For whatever reason, he had chosen high school, and was sticking with it. In short order, Alan found himself seated in a classroom at venerable Harris-Stowe Teachers College, a student again. His classmates were preponderantly black women. Alan would soon learn the history of Harris-Stowe, anything but just another, run-of-the-mill teachers' school, for this one, like so many St. Louis

225

institutions, had a copious past. Moreover, it was a good teachers' college. Graduation day would prove as promising as Alan's first encounter with the local school system had not been. Indeed, he landed a mid-year job, despite having no seniority, teaching English to 9th graders at Roosevelt High School. He was a union employee and was eligible for tenure after only three years.

Teaching was hard at first. It wasn't the subject matter, but the technique, that eluded him. His colleagues of some experience told him this was perfectly normal, that nobody stands in front of a room full of teenagers and begins communicating with them immediately. Alan did not mention he had taught before, however briefly and only as a substitute. He was not reticent about admitting, if asked about his past, he had been in prison, and explaining why, but the time in Quebec had come to him to seem such an aberration, he preferred not to say a word about it. It could be completely dismissed and forgotten, he told himself half-seriously, but for the small fact of a wife and daughter. Gradually, his confidence grew, and the initial struggle in the classroom greatly diminished. Something about the "fit" at Roosevelt was not satisfactory, however. Alan got along fine with his colleagues, including a crusty old veteran named Jack Marty, who was less than pleased by Alan's having "ducked service," as he put it, but they got along nonetheless. He was not a favorite among the students, though not disliked, either, but he attributed this to his inexperience. He was teaching what he wanted to teach and at the level he wanted to teach it, and yet ... and yet he continued to be dogged by a lack of motivation. This wasn't the kind of thing he could hide, and although he was competent, this shortcoming was noted on his evaluations, and it was apparent, as well, to the young people he instructed. Nor did he exhibit enthusiasm for the committee work and other extra-curricular chores that came with the job, which he felt were largely a waste of time. He was certainly not alone among faculty in harboring this opinion, but unlike others, he complained. Gradually, a perception developed that Alan Young was something less than a "team player," that he was in teaching for himself only and would do only the minimum required to get by. At an informal gathering marking completion of his first full academic year at Roosevelt, in May 1977, there was applause, but it was perfunctory. It was in this same year that his father faced an unexpected and serious surgery, for which Alan went to Los Angeles. His relationship with his parents was not unlike his teaching; it was satisfying yet, mysteriously, something short of rewarding. Something was missing, something elusive but essential. Alan could not identify it. There were occasional visits, in each direction, but after 48 hours, everybody was glad to be back at the airport. Neither of his parents shared his affection for St. Louis, which struck them, in his mother's words, as old and dirty, but Alan was so taken by the city, they kept their views to themselves. Jeanne's parents, too, came at Easter their first year, and again the next year. Adele McCarran was warmer than Alan remembered her. In fact, with the maturity of her children, she had become a more sedate and happier soul, which was especially evident to Jeanne. Charles McCarran was pleased to find Alan was earning a gainful living, but he continued to suspect his son-in-law's emotional stability and dreaded the day would come when he heard from his daughter that the family's breadwinner wasn't earning the bread any longer. Not that there was the remotest possibility of doing anything about her choice in husband. To Charles and his wife, it was more apparent with each visit how deeply in love their daughter was with Alan.

After being laid off, Jeanne had gotten a job as receptionist at a roofing company in the suburb of Kirkwood. It was a family business, not large, and she was the only woman on the premises, although an older woman, who turned out to be the owner's wife, popped in from time to time. Jeanne, in fact, was more than the person who answered phones and customers; she did a little bit of everything, including giving rides, which could be irksome. The company did only residential roofing and was a busy, lively and even cheerful place. Nobody was getting rich, exactly, Jeanne Young emphatically included, but work was steady and, if there was seldom talk of raises, there was a Christmas bonus each year, in which the company took special pride. They threw a party, naturally, and everyone got something, even when the company had not had a particularly good year. Checks were distributed by the owner himself, Wilhelm Schlenker, each employee was recognized and, in special cases ("five years," "perfect attendance,") praised; indeed, it was almost as if the company looked for some excuse to honor its employees. Not to say there wasn't criticism from time to time, or that the job could not be harsh, or the owner arbitrary, but Jeanne, like most employees, accepted criticism when warranted and never thought about it again when it wasn't. The Christmas bonus invariably left a glow that was good for months. Unfortunately, the job involved a commute of nearly 30 minutes, each way, which did not include the stop to leave Mary at the day care center. Jeanne had tried, initially, to see if she could bring Mary to the office, but the owner had balked, and even if he had not, the unsuitability of the arrangement would soon have become evident. Jeanne would have preferred to remain at home with Mary, but fate had decreed otherwise, and she was not one to mope about how things turn out. "When the Lord closes a door, He opens another," she remembered. Growing up in the Roman Catholic Church, Jeanne had not been religious; her father's insistence upon Mass regularly had indeed proved an alienating factor in adolescence. Now, however, with the hand she had been dealt, Jeanne had returned to her faith. It had sustained her in many a lonely hour. Her parish was St. Matthew's in south St. Louis; it would become Alan's, too. They would learn that the Catholic Church was a formidable presence in the city.

Alan gradually came to understand what it was about Roosevelt High School he disliked. Expectations were low. Something had certainly changed, and not for the better, since he had been in high school himself, notwithstanding it was not so very long ago; he had graduated in 1964. Yet it wasn't the same. He remembered his own, 9th grade English class distinctly. A large chunk of the year had been devoted to a single work of fiction, *Great Expectations*. His teacher, Regina Garland, was a spinster who had devoted her life to teaching 14-year-old boys and girls, and she was extremely good at it. That one Dickens novel, to which so much loving care had been devoted, had made a permanent impression upon Alan, and, he had no doubt, many of his classmates. Indeed, he dated his interest in literature from this experience. Dickens was not being taught until 11th grade at Roosevelt High. The nod to Shakespeare was limited to *Romeo and Juliet*. *Evangeline* was still around, and *The Canterbury Tales*, but not *The Rhyme of the Ancient Mariner*, and not *The Vicar of Wakefield*.

"How can Coleridge and Goldsmith not be taught in high school?" he barked on more than one occasion. "I mean, when are you going to read *The Vicar of Wakefield* if not during these years? How can you limit Shakespeare to one play? What about *Macbeth*? *Julius Caesar*? *Twelfth Night*?'"

"College," was the reply.

"No," Alan said, with a growing stridency, "not a good answer. Shakespeare is fine in college, I'm sure, I studied Shakespeare quite a bit in college, but I doubt I would have if I hadn't gotten a pretty good taste earlier. *'Et tu, Brute'* and *'Friends, Romans, Countrymen'* and *'Tomorrow and tomorrow and tomorrow creeps in this petty pace'* belong to adolescence. This stuff makes an unforgettable impression at sixteen. Isn't that the idea? To plant the seed when the soil is at its most fertile? Why has the long-time wisdom of teaching Shakespeare in high school been dropped?"

Nor was the retrenchment occurring only in the English curriculum; it was across the board. Less learning was going on, demonstrably less, and a good deal more time was being devoted to what was called "remedial education," and to discipline. Alan was astonished upon hearing from veteran teachers that students were increasingly prone to talk back in class, or just get up and walk out. Then, his turn came, and he did not handle it skillfully.

Gerald Ford was president. If the value of an educated mind was important to him, he was keeping it to himself, Alan reflected. He was restoring stability after Richard Nixon's resignation, and bringing this turbulent period to an end must, after all, come first. Alan had followed with great interest the events leading up to the fall of Nixon, starting with the Watergate break-in and culminating in his speech to the nation. He was not sorry to see Nixon humbled. Nixon had prosecuted the war in Vietnam even longer than Lyndon Johnson had, while prevaricating, like his predecessor, over the purpose of the war and its prospects. The war had lasted nine years, while never being declared by Congress, had cost more than 50,000 young Americans their lives, left countless others wounded, to say nothing of Vietnamese casualties, and done untold damage on the home front, where unrest, especially but not exclusively on college campuses, had reached its zenith at Kent State University, in Ohio. Alan's generation, the "baby boomers," was the most devastated by the war, but it had dragged on so long, so stubbornly resisted every chance at resolution, it had finally affected vast numbers of Americans. Alan was puzzled and angry over the lukewarm reception the returning soldiers received. It was a national disgrace their heroism and sacrifice were hardly acknowledged. His opposition to the war and conviction he had finally done the right thing in going to jail remained intact and unchanged, but Alan was simultaneously by no means unsympathetic to the viewpoint a war, if it's going to be fought, should be fought to win. There was truth, he felt, in the allegation U.S. forces had been held in check by Washington, almost as if the president was reacting to some impulse within him telling him the whole business was misbegotten from the start and therefore should be undertaken half-heartedly. If the troops had indeed been held back to some degree, with all that that implied about increased danger for them, and now found that their reward, on return from a battlefield they were not permitted to dominate, was to be ignored, then what ignominy, Alan thought, could exceed this? The despair and damage of Vietnam seemed utterly without mitigation, reinforcing yet again his belief in the course of resistance he had ultimately adopted. He did not ask himself why it required reinforcement, but deep in the recesses of his mind was a remark Jack Marty had made one day. Jack had said something about an 18-year-old kid, hypothetically, with a girl back home in Cleveland, and Saturday afternoons at the soda fountain, and monkeying around with his pals, and college before him, maybe a career in medicine, or maybe trade school, and going to the Indians' games with his dad, his whole life, in short, before him, cut down on the beaches of Normandy, alone and far from home, denied even the consolation of knowing his sacrifice was not in vain.

"You can never impeach that, Alan, so don't even try. Nobody can ever impeach it. Not even God."

"I don't want to impeach it," Alan had protested. "I'd have been there."

"Sure?"

"Sure."

"Good, because you can't impeach it. You can say whatever you like about the path you chose, and maybe in some way you're right, too, it's a different time, a different war, but what that 18-year-old kid did is unimpeachable." Alan knew Jack was right. He knew it then, and he knew it now, and it caused him unrest, whenever it came to mind. That 18-year-old kid was not a soldier among ignorant armies, clashing by night. He was a soldier in an heroic army that had shed much blood to bring down a criminal maniac. He was a soldier in an army that was the epitome of moral courage.

In California, it was Stefan's final day, clerking for Judge Bryant. The great unknown did not lie before him, because he knew perfectly well what he was going to do, namely, become the best lawyer ever to be hired by Martin & Yates. What Stefan did not know was, the judge would say something to him, something unaccountably nonsensical as far as he was concerned, that would stay with him across the ensuing decades and, despite an unreliable memory, ultimately matter very much.

Book Two

CHAPTER 8

D EBRA KOPINSKI POURED HERSELF A GLASS OF MERLOT, TURNED ON the stereo and plopped down on the carpet in her favorite spot, back against the wall. It was the girls' weekend with their worthless father, she had the place to herself. Kind of nice, really, she had even begun to look forward to these alternate weekends. She gave up trying to balance the goblet on the carpet and retrieved a book, upon which the glass sat more or less securely. How funny! The carpet sported multiple stains, including one no arrangement of the furniture could hide, what was one more?

She surveyed the room. A hopeless clutter. How had so much of the girls' clothing migrated into the living area? Could only mean they'd run out of space in their own rooms. Got to get them to clean up, Debra told herself for the thousandth time. She eyed apprehensively a stack of unopened mail. Mostly bills, no doubt. Wouldn't be the first time she was late. One day the lights wouldn't come on, the toilets wouldn't flush. That would be a pretty big clue for the girls life wasn't so peachy. Not that they didn't know it already.

Debra took a gulp of wine. It went down nicely, leaving a warm feeling. The music was comforting, too; she was listening to Pat Boone, a favorite. Debra closed her eyes, telling herself when she opened them again, the room would be perfectly clean. She opened them and noticed two of the sofa's three cushions had split open. What was the matter with the third? The lampshade was torn, too, come to think of it. She kept it facing the wall, where it was effectively concealed. Debra went into the kitchen for something sweet to munch, and the skillet, with its memory of dinner's macaroni, greeted her from the sink. Ought to wash it right now, before it becomes encrusted. She was too weary. Ought to get a maid, one day a week, even one morning a week. She could afford it, why not? Lisa was too young to be a great help, and her older sister, Linda, was hostile.

Linda, in truth, was far more than hostile. Hardly an adolescent, she was confused and wretched. Her mother, she felt, was to blame for the divorce. She had started drinking, on the sly. Since this was beyond imagining, Debra detected nothing.

Debra was on her own. A maid could make a big difference. A few phone calls, how difficult was that? Thank God for one thing. Her friends didn't care how her apartment looked. Heck, Tina Buchanan's place was worse, if anything. She and Tina should be closer. They were in the same predicament.

Debra understood life is much the same, day after day, and she accepted this. What she could not accept was the complete absence of playfulness and spontaneity. Let alone romance. Oh, there were evenings out, now and then, flops without exception. You just couldn't get very far into a conversation before he asked for the grenade.

"How has an attractive woman like you managed to stay single?"

"Did I say that? Geewhillikers."

"So you, um … ?"

"Divorced."

"I'm sorry." Pause. Count the seconds.

"So, um, do you, um, have you, uh, um … do you …"

(Come on, big guy, you can spit it out.)

"Um um do you uh um have, um … do you …"

"Have children? Why yes, I have a child. Actually, I have two. Two childs." Ka-Boom.

It wasn't fair, what had happened to her. It wasn't right, in fact, it was very, very wrong. Debra turned to her one dependable resource, her faith, and this helped, but was it asking so much, for a bit of balance? Everything was such a struggle. She needed an agent of change, but there was none except herself, and she was so spent, physically and emotionally, how could she ever bring it about? She felt locked in, powerless. Debra remembered a job she had once had, at a restaurant. She washed dishes and glasses, the same dishes and glasses, and knives and forks and spoons, the same knives and forks and spoons, 400 of them, the same 400 knives and forks and spoons, every night, the same 400 to scrub all over again, as if this time was the first time. They would never go away, there would never be one fewer,

400 every cursed, everlasting night. Who could do this indefinitely? Yet this was her life now, was it not? Every day brand new yet not new in the slightest regard, just a drab, soul-destroying existence from the moment of consciousness until its dissolution.

Still, when it came to the joylessness of her days, the disputes with Stefan took the cake. He was dependably ugly with her. Shocked and dismayed, Debra resolved not to respond in kind, but her resolution was not as strong as his determined enmity, and in time she discovered she could hold her own nicely, thank you. One visitation weekend, she was three hours late retrieving the children, arriving at 9:00 in the evening rather than 6:00. Both Stefan and Sharon Kopinski were furious, and it mattered not in the least Debra had called to say she would be delayed.

"We had plans," Sharon said curtly. She was in her robe, children in tow.

"Must have been a pajama party," Debra observed.

"Oh, you're a riot, Debra," Stefan said.

"The girls must be thrilled to know you can't wait to unload them when the clock strikes six."

"I told you, we had plans," Sharon said.

"I don't think you did."

"You're calling me a liar, Debra?"

"You know, I don't think this conversation is appropriate in front of the children."

"You're a fine one to talk, then, with that crack about unloading them." Debra herself regretted the remark.

"Look, I'm sorry, okay? Let's not argue this way."

"You started it."

"How sweet of you, after I apologized. Are you determined to have the last word?"

"That would be you, Debra," Stefan said.

"We had a dinner invitation, Debra, if you must know," Sharon said. "We were looking forward to it. We had to call and cancel at the last minute. It was embarrassing."

"How awful, dear, but I just know you'll get over it."

"Why don't you go, please?" Debra took each child by the hand.

"Tell you what," she said. "How about I come three hours early next time, and we call it even?"

"Just go, please." None of the adults, in truth, wished to carry on this way in front of the children.

"What a witch," Sharon said as Debra and the girls went down the walk. Sharon knew she had said it loudly enough to be heard.

CHAPTER 9

A S FAR APART AS THEY WERE NOW, BOTH DEBRA AND STEFAN WOULD have been amazed to know how fondly each remembered their early years together. They had lived in a modest apartment the first three years of their marriage, but it had had only one bedroom, and when Debra became pregnant, they had the excuse they needed to go shopping for a home. Stefan, it was true, was not yet a partner at Fulton & Shaw, LLP, but he was confident the day would come, and neither Debra nor he could see the sense in continuing to sink money into a rental. They had reviewed their financial situation carefully, recognizing that taking on a mortgage and the expenses of a child at the same time might be unwise, but you couldn't wait on life, could you, no, you had to leap, if you looked first, you never would leap. Wasn't that what someone had said?

They found a tidy, brick home on a street of tidy, brick homes at the edge of "respectable" Pasadena. The Rose Parade would not be coming down 14th Street. Debra set to work immediately converting a house into a home. A handsome, Navajo basket on a living room perch, a pair of tall, slender, blue candles on the table, a bowl of dried roses in the bathroom, an eye-catching, floral bedspread, a fern in the kitchen Stefan accusingly claimed was the source of tiny, flying bugs the existence of which Debra never conceded, a wreath, generally of religious import, perpetually on the front door, depending on the season. More than once over the ensuing years a visitor might be heard to remark on the "lived-in quality" of their residence. Stefan could not know the very opposite would characterize his future home.

"Methodism" would be her reply if Debra were asked to name one thing that had defined her growing-up years. Her mother was an ardent

237

Methodist, and her grandmother, and her great-grandmother. For all Debra knew, her family could be the first Methodists in California, and California was better for it, indeed it was. Scattered throughout the homestead were family photographs which, if you looked closely, you would discover were taken, generation upon generation, at the same place: First United Methodist Church of Alhambra. Needless to say, this was the venue for one of the more recent set of photographs, Debra's wedding. Debra had thought nothing of this "family tradition" as a child; once an adult, it seemed to her obsessive, almost a mania.

Debra's mother had taken her to church every Sunday. Mrs. Morrison was given to saying she just did not feel right, all week long, if she missed church and Sunday school. On those rare occasions when circumstances dictated otherwise, there was always something going on during the week. Was this not also an obsession, never to allow more than seven consecutive days to transpire without a trip to church? Then there was the choir, in which Grace Morrison sang, as her mother had, and it didn't really matter she couldn't sing, nobody else in the choir could, either. Mrs. Morrison was president of the Women's Guild, serving a term of an apparently indefinite duration, for when she looked back, Debra could not remember her mother's ever having not been president. Then there was her reply, whenever asked how she was, "I am blessed." Who said that? Whose mother said that? Debra, at eight, did not know she would herself adopt the practice one day. Mrs. Morrison tithed, too, and may it be said, did so religiously. Then there was the trip to the poor farm in San Pedro every Sunday afternoon, where her mother performed the work of a saint. Nothing had had as profound an impact on the impressionable girl as these journeys. Debra remembered distinctly wondering what in heaven's name a "poor farm" could be. Was it a ramshackle old barn housing a few pitiful chickens and a skinny cow or two?

Debra navigated it all and finally reached college, where she did one thing decidedly practical: She left home. It was off to university in San Jose, where she majored in Home Economics and joined a sorority. Alas, she failed to find a husband, which as far as Grace Morrison was concerned, was the single reason for any girl to attend college.

"These years are your best chance, Debra," her mother reminded her every time she came home for a holiday. "You must believe me. Remember, I met your dad at a Greek Social, as they were called in those days."

"Why wouldn't I believe you, mom?"

"I know you do. I just worry about you."

"Try not to, please. When Mr. Right comes along, I'll be ready."

"Debra, sweetie, Mr. Right doesn't come along for any girl. You have to find him."

"That really hasn't been my experience. When a guy thinks you're after him, he vanishes."

"Yes, I know that. The trick is to chase him without letting on."

"You'll just have to leave this to me, mom."

"All right, sweetie. You know I don't want to intrude in your life." Debra rolled her eyes. "Just don't be too picky. A girl has to be a gambler, in this world."

Debra decided to return to Los Angeles after college. She felt, correctly, she could meet her formidable mother on even terms now. She would not live at home, that went without saying. She found an apartment and a roommate.

Debra and Stefan met at a fundraising event for a local charity. It was one of those occasions not designed for conversations of any substance, since people mostly were strangers. The pair spoke less than ten minutes, but Stefan stole plenty of glances at her the remainder of the evening and, as the event was concluding, approached her, expressed how much he had enjoyed their chat, and said he would like to see her again. She said she would like that, too.

Debra Morrison would never be a beauty. It was the shape of her face, primarily, which formed an almost perfect oval. This was not an asset. She tried grooming her hair in a dozen styles to offset this disadvantage, settling finally on parting her hair on the right, enabling her to drape her long locks across the left side of her forehead, down to the shoulder. This successfully offset the symmetry of her face. She was a brunette, her deep brown eyes had a bewitching quality about them, and she had a wonderful figure she was not at all shy about using to every possible advantage. If the estimable John Wesley, Esq., disapproved, too bad!

Fact was, Stefan Kopinski was as awkward with women as he was adroit in the courtroom. His fumbling manner was not lost on Debra, who responded with a "take-charge" approach that proved as marvelously effective as it was ironic, since if there was one thing Stefan always was, it was in charge. This was not really so mysterious, in truth. Stefan had to be at the top of his game at all times. Literally every minute in the courtroom, he pressed his advantage and probed for the weakness in his adversary. Not a word, not a gesture, escaped his notice. When he stepped out of this arena, he wanted nothing more than to let it all go. Accordingly, when a plain but sprightly Methodist girl crossed his path, he had neither the desire nor the will to resist her leadership.

Debra's father, Henry Morrison, known to everyone as "Hank," painted houses. Hank was brawny, basically good-natured, with a thick mustache that drooped over his lip, a strong voice and a hearty, painful handshake. His grammar was not so good, though Stefan never could quite decide if the double negatives and subject-verb disagreement were not sometimes for effect. "Went" and "gone," in any case, he never got right, and Hank had a special fondness for "ain't." Hank loved bowling and belonged to a league, he hunted pheasants, and he rooted for all the L.A. teams, which seemed to Stefan, who had little interest in sports, numberless. Hank and Stefan may have seemed opposites, but they were on good terms from the beginning, and Stefan grew to have admiration for Hank Morrison and his family. Roles in the Morrison family were well-defined, almost to the point of caricature, and objections, had there been any, would not have gotten far. Hank earned a living, Grace fixed supper. Hank had nights out with the boys, Grace had nights in with the kids. Grace submitted to Hank, when Hank required submission. Homework was shared, in a manner of speaking; Hank kept the house shipshape, Grace helped the children with their school assignments. Hank followed politics, Grace did not. Hank voted for Eisenhower, and Grace voted the way Hank did.

Debra and Stefan had courted a little less than a year before he popped the question. They had been intimate almost the entire time, for once she had determined she would make Stefan her husband, Debra had thrown caution to the wind. She had felt this would land him, and she was correct, for Stefan had never known a relationship like this, and he wasn't sure he deserved it. Regardless, it was happening, and those months, their intensity, the pleasure, the novelty, the astonishing realization he had found a woman who desired him, Stefan never remembered without shaking his head in disbelief.

There had been a trip to St. Paul, eventually. Mr. and Mrs. Kopinski were mildly disappointed by Stefan's choice in a wife, for they felt there was little remarkable about Debra Morrison, and both were put off by her excessive dwelling upon her faith. Somehow, she weaved it into every conversation. They remained silent. It was useless to intervene, and, anyway, they might be wrong. Moreover, they could see their son had found an eminently sensible and decent girl who would be true and would take care of him, and wasn't there something to be said for that?

Happy families, it has been said, are all alike, unhappy ones unhappy each in its own way. Had Stefan been acquainted with the thought, he'd have said it's the other way around. For the bitterness that consumed Debra and Stefan was common to every failed marriage, while their early years together had a luminosity which belonged to them alone.

Saturday mornings meant grocery shopping. The excuse for waiting till Saturday was that Stefan could help her with the bags. It was a poor excuse, Debra could handle them herself, but they pretended it was a good excuse, because Stefan wanted to go with her! A boring chore became silly fun. Debra generally sent her husband in search of some basic items, like milk and eggs. She went faster when he wasn't hovering. One morning, she sent him in search of "Ceylonese coconut oil." There was no such thing. After several minutes' search, Stefan asked an employee affixing prices to merchandise with a stapler-like mechanism, where he might find it.

"Not familiar with that," the man said doubtfully. "Sounds more like a product you might rub on your skin. You know, something for women."

"Righto, thanks," Stefan replied. "A product for women!" He went off in search of Debra. "I think I smell a skunk, here." What the devil was inside a coconut, anyway? Coconut milk? Check. Coconut meat? Check. Coconut oil? No check. Here was merriment! His wife, not really very strong in the imagination department, had pulled a fast one.

"Thought I'd lost you," Debra said when he materialized. "I'm nearly finished."

"Couldn't find the coconut oil," Stefan said. He was going to play along.

"Should be with the shortening. Did you look there?"

"Looked everywhere. I even asked a clerk for help." Debra almost laughed.

"What did he say?"

"Never heard of it," Stefan said mournfully. Debra again had to fight breaking into laughter.

"Now that is strange," she said.

"I'll watch the basket, if you want to go look for it yourself."

"No, honey, it's not that urgent. I'll get it another time."

That night, as Debra brushed her teeth, Stefan took her teddy bear from its place on the pillows and put it in the refrigerator. When Debra came to bed, she noticed immediately.

"What have you done with teddy?" she asked accusingly.

"Teddy was running a fever. I had to act quickly."

"Yes?"

"Teddy's in a cool place."

"Did you take teddy outside?"

"Cooler." Debra thought about this momentarily, then jumped out of bed and made for the kitchen. She opened the door to the refrigerator.

"Teddeeee! Teddeeee!" She shoved teddy into the oven and returned to the bedroom.

"Teddy better?"

"Teddy better. Teddy in the oven." She jumped into bed and a shoving match ensued. Then they were intimate. Intimate again, and again.

"My parents were right about you," he joked.

"Too late!" she said merrily. They gazed lovingly into each other's eyes. They were lovers, truly and wonderfully lovers. Stefan wondered yet again at his luck.

Debra was an accomplished cook and loved to cook, and soon, instead of the simple fare that had sustained him through his bachelorhood, Stefan was feasting on chicken fricassee and veal Marsala. It was all wonderful. He had never eaten like this, not even at home, he told himself (which wasn't so). Debra beamed with pride, and he beamed at his wife's happiness. That was the secret, right? Making her happy, rather than expecting her to make him happy? And vice versa. So simple, nobody got it.

"Stefan, honey, that's not the place for the sofa." There was no sting in Debra's criticism. Her husband simply wasn't putting the loveseat where it belonged, opposite the front window. He wanted it at an angle, which anybody could see gobbled up needed space. "We can't have a nice view out the picture window where you have it." Calling it a picture window was fanciful, but Debra wasn't going to call it anything else. It was the biggest window in the house, and it was in the living room.

"Don't you think it's going to be too bright, directly in the path of the sun?" Since their home faced north, this was not a realistic concern. Stefan discovered his back was starting to ache; he felt like he had been moving the loveseat around the room for hours.

"It won't be too bright, and if it is, we move it. Simple." Stefan obeyed orders without further dissent and put the loveseat opposite the picture window. He chuckled recollecting the best piece of marital advice he had ever encountered, on that peerless venue of contemporary American communication, the bumper sticker: "I'm the boss, my wife said I could be." That was worth a year of marriage counseling. Stefan had no way of knowing such counseling lay in his future, and if you had told him so, then and there, he'd have scoffed happily at the very notion.

Choices were actually fewer with the chairs. They had only two, aside from their dining room set of four. Both must go against the east wall. Round table between, rectangular table in front of the picture window. Lamp on the round table, plants on the rectangle. Neither Stefan nor Debra had a green thumb, but it was on her list. Second lamp in their bedroom. The lamps were a matched set, faintly blue with a floral design. They did not look expensive, and they weren't. The same went for a pair of landscapes they had purchased at a "Starving Artists" Sale. They were attractive, large enough to command the walls upon which they were hung. A forest, blazing with autumn's colors, and a desolate but beautiful seascape. Family pictures were confined to the bedroom. Their one extravagance was an Oriental rug for the living room floor. This was not their extravagance; the rug belonged to Debra's parents. On loan until their son-in-law-the-lawyer made his first million.

The kitchen had a window over the sink with a view of their neighbor's house. The small bathroom had little to recommend it. There was no window, just as well, considering it would have looked out on the neighbor's living room.

The second bedroom, of course, would be the most important room in the house. It would contain a bureau and the crib. They shopped together for the crib, Stefan at every step more hindrance than help, wondering if it would be a boy or a girl, delaying on the choice of curtains, depending, but no worry about the wallpaper, it was an insipid pattern of multi-colored, parallel lines, equally disagreeable to either gender. They'd get it replaced, someday. An expense that could wait.

Those years in their "Swiss cottage," as Debra's mom described their home, which in no way resembled a Swiss cottage, Stefan would never get out of his head.

CHAPTER 10

STEFAN, TO BE SURE, WOULD WEATHER THEIR DIVORCE, WHEN IT CAME, without losing much sleep. Debra was the opposite. She'd be spared nothing. Disbelief, denial, anger. Disbelief was dominant. The whole idea of divorce was profoundly unreal to her; her mother said it was a "sin." Sin or not, here was the man who had professed his love across the years and with whom she had shared everything, turned on her as no apostate ever before, exhibiting a meanness in the term's fullest sense and with a vengeance. How was this possible? Was it theater? Were they play-acting in some depraved drama? Like being friends with your doctor. At the office, being examined, the friendship was weirdly suspended while the roles of physician and patient were assumed, but the moment the examination was over, they were Jim and Susan again. Debra could not get her bearings, she would be helpless in the face of husband-turned-antagonist, compounded by the fact Stefan hired a lawyer. She had to have one, too, for this would be a fight, she had rights and she would not have them stripped from her! Heavens, what if he tried to take the children? She would fight him to the highest tribunal on earth.

Not to worry. Stefan wasn't interested in having the children. He wanted out.

"Believe me," he said sometime before a judge would decide the terms of their divorce, "we don't want a judge deciding the terms of our divorce."

"Really? Would that be because you want me to agree to your terms?"

"No, Debra. I'm willing to compromise. It's just better we handle it ourselves, and I don't see why we can't. We're reasonable people. A third party will make choices neither of us likes."

"You have shown no willingness to compromise, so why you are blubbering about it now is peculiar, to say the least. It has taken me a long time to understand this, but you're not even my friend, let alone the man I married. I'm done with these conversations."

So to the courtroom they eventually would go, Debra herself armed with a lawyer, where more anger and more hypocrisy lay in wait, and, supremely, the harshest of ironies, for virtually every critical decision hinged upon what was "in the best interests of the children," when incontestably not divorcing was far and away what was in the children's best interests. Debra found it inconceivable. How could this not be understood? Who made these laws? What happened to common sense? It was stupid, contemptibly stupid, and Debra would say so, using those very words. Neither judge nor another soul batted an eye. "Zombies, you're all zombies," Debra would declare. At the adjournment for lunch, she was in for remonstrance from her lawyer.

"You must not do that again, Debra, no matter how strongly you feel. Remember, almost the first thing I told you, never answer more than the question. Never blurt something out in a courtroom. The man you married has cast the past aside without a trace of sentiment, and you must do the same, imperatively. Recall the good times, if you must, when this is over. Do you understand?"

"Yes, sorry. Won't happen again." Debra wasn't sure which good times she was recalling.

It had been overhearing a colleague describe his wife as "frumpy" that had presaged the trouble to come. What did that mean, exactly? It wasn't flattering, he knew that, and when he consulted the dictionary, he found "dowdy, unattractive." This unhelpful and unwelcome term had been overheard at a popular cafe where the associates customarily gathered on Thursday evenings to discuss work, obviously, and the partners, obviously, and, by golly, each other's wives, apparently. Stefan had gone to the men's room and heard the remark just as he returned. Even if he hadn't heard it, the embarrassed silence would have given him a good hint he had been the subject of conversation.

Neither the silence nor the embarrassment lasted long.

"So, counsel," Ernest Boyd said, addressing all, "what conclusions may we draw from Roth's having called Katherine 'his sweet little lay?'" Laughter. Roth was Bernie Roth, an associate.

"Beauty, counselor, is in the eyes of the beholder," Doug Hooper said. "I find nothing sweet about Katherine. I wouldn't trust her as far as I can spit."

"Agree," said Jay O'Leary.

"You don't have to look at 'em in the dark," Ernest said.

"They're not looking at you, either."

"He didn't call her his sweet little lay. It was sweet little lady."

"Nah, it was lay." The men had to leave it at that; one of the female associates arrived.

"Hey, guys," she said. Eleanor Llamado was in only her second year with the firm and often seemed unsure of herself, a condition she would overcome.

Stefan Kopinski, on the other hand, was, if anything, too sure of himself. At Fulton & Shaw, he had fallen into the employment law practice when another associate had abruptly left the firm. Stefan was ambitious and seized his new role with zest. Like all the associates, he was expected to work 12-hour days, and he did without a murmur of complaint. Companies, for the most part, were his clients, since the firm largely handled defense rather than plaintiff's work. Stefan didn't care, either way. Employment law would be his field of expertise, and no one would do it better.

It was one thing, of course, to hear one of his fellow associates say something uncomplimentary about his wife. It was another when Debra began to be noticed by the partners. No good could come of this. Just when he began to grasp his wife was unpopular, Stefan could not say. Nobody had come right out and said, "I don't like Debra Kopinski." No, of course not. It was more insidious than that. Malcolm Fulton, who was "Of Counsel" and had lung cancer, remarked on Debra's absence most of the evening at the country club fete, which, he was "constrained" to add, was not the first time.

"She didn't feel well," Stefan had replied. "She went to lie down."

"Nothing serious, I hope," Fulton said, making little effort to hide the doubt he harbored there was a thing the matter with Debra Kopinski. She was just an unlikeable woman, increasingly disinclined even to try to contribute to conversation. This was unfortunately true. The more Debra felt she was being given the cold shoulder, the more resentful she became, and the more resentful she became, the more she got the cold shoulder.

Miguel Ordoñez, who had just made partner, said Mrs. Kopinski refused to say "hello" to his wife or to him, indeed, walked right past them, staring straight ahead, as if they were not there. Fred Shaw said he had met with the same conduct.

"She is unfriendly, period. I would like to know why."

"Know what she said to me?" Art Feinberg said. "By way of greeting? One guess, I'll give you one guess." Nobody could guess. "Have you been born again? Yeah. I say hello, how are you, that's her response. Incredible."

"Not surprising, really," Fred Shaw said. "She goes on about religion all the time."

"You think that's normal, to ask somebody if he's been born again, even before you say hello?"

"Beats drop dead." This from Ordoñez. Everybody laughed.

Stefan heard none of this, it was the office scuttlebutt, which, needless to say, he was certain to hear. At first, he reacted with sharp disagreement. How dare them? Debra was his wife, she was none of their business. He was mistaken about this. Wives were part of the package. Certain things were expected, nay, more than expected. They were required. Appearance, attitude, expressed opinions … you got it right, or you didn't. Stefan, gradually, conceded to himself Debra's willfulness was producing difficulties. The day came when he brought it up, for he could no longer pretend nothing was amiss.

"Everybody noticed, Debra."

"Noticed? What are you talking about?"

"Please don't get defensive."

"I repeat, I don't know what you're talking about."

"You just flat out disappeared at the Fulton's party. Dinner over, you vanished. I finally go hunting for you all over their house. Now that was weird. I find you reading in their study. Pretending to read. Sitting there by yourself. Do you think some folks might find that rude? Or might find it peculiar? Do you want people to think you're peculiar? What am I supposed to say?"

"There you go, as usual, worrying about yourself. So typical of you, dear. You don't care about me, or my feelings, it's all about you."

"Have no idea what you mean, Debra." Stefan shook his head.

"People aren't nice to me, okay? Alberta asked me how I was, and I told her, and she asked me who blessed me, and I said Jesus Christ our Lord, and she uses a four-letter word. Is that okay, is it? How about I use that word with her?"

248

"Alberta drinks too much. She's three sheets to the wind when she gets to a party."

"Oh, so that makes it all right? She's vulgar with me, but, geez, she's drunk, and I'm the one everybody says is ... is ... what did you say?"

Then there was the flap over fur. Wearing your fur coat in the winter was *de rigueur*, notwithstanding it was seldom cold enough in Pasadena for fur. Debra had a sable jacket. They had gone together to get it, at a famous department store with a branch in L.A. Browsing through the furs, Debra noticed there were no price tags. When she asked the saleswoman about this, the reply was, "If you have to ask, dear, you can't afford it." This was not said unpleasantly, and it made Stefan and Debra laugh. Now, it was tears. Debra refused to wear her fur. This made her conspicuous, because every other wife, without a single exception, had fur on her shoulders. What was the issue? Was she making a political statement? Debra paid little attention to politics. She had worn her sable, now she wouldn't.

"I just don't want to wear it anymore." That was the first explanation.

"It's too hot." Second excuse.

"I think I might be allergic to fur." Not allergic to the fur on other women's shoulders, apparently, just her own. Where was the wheezing, the runny nose? This was no excuse, there was no excuse. Fur was expected, and Debra wouldn't wear it.

Stefan, in truth, was not entirely unsympathetic with his wife's way-wardness here. There was something fatuous about the insistence every woman wear fur to social events in the winter months. One of those dumb, unwritten rules you absolutely cannot defy.

"I wear a tie, don't I, Debra? Every single day. Know something, ties aren't all that comfortable. By golly, too bad, men wear ties, professional men, I'm a professional man, I wear a tie. How about I go to court one day, representing my client, representing my firm, no tie? No way. But you, you have to be different. You're gonna have your way, aren't you? Even if it means undermining my career. Stubbornness, when it goes over the line, is a weakness, not a strength. A vice, not a virtue."

"All about you. Your career. Undermining your career. That is so idiotic. Your career depends on if you're a good lawyer, which you are. Not what I wear. Just so idiotic." Stefan retreated in dismay. He still had not accepted the futility of these conversations. Reason was his strong suit, indispensable for a lawyer, but inside his own home, he could not use it effectively. Nor was Debra done. She brought it up again, the next day.

"If you keep harping on the fur coats, Stefan," she said out of the blue, "I'm going to give my sable away."

"Well now, why don't you just do that, Debra? Why don't you just hurry on over to Goodwill? Don't you know they're short on fur coats?"

"Shut up." Debra, however, did begin wearing her sable again. She did cease saying, "I am blessed." She quit disappearing at parties. What she could not do was blend seamlessly in. Debra was a wretched conversationalist. "Small talk" utterly eluded her. The day arrived when it was the Kopinski's turn to throw a party. Four couples were invited. One came.

"This evening was a major embarrassment for us," Stefan said later. "It won't be easy to fix."

"Oh please, there's nothing to fix. Anyway, small parties sometimes are best." Debra knew the evening had not been successful.

"Debra, we have to make concessions. You alienate people. Important people. You don't even try."

"Try what?"

"Try to be … to … play the game, Debra. You gotta do that better. You're so rigid. So … so unaspiring."

"I suppose you are upset about my talking about God's grace, aren't you?"

"Did you have to go on and on about it? Explaining how it's not earned? Did you notice, when you were done, neither Bob nor Nanette said anything? There's a big clue in that. Nobody cares. It's a subject that makes people uncomfortable."

"You are so hypocritical, Stefan. Nanette goes on and on about her daughter the orthodontist. Nobody objects. Why can she do it, and not me?"

"Because, Debra, Nanette Osborn plays the game, perfectly, all the time. She spends on her clothing and always looks terrific, she goes to the beauty parlor, there's never a hair out of place on her head, she …"

"She's perfect and I'm not," Debra interrupted. "Got it dear, say no more." Debra had gotten the last word, but she was not happy with herself. The party had been a flop. Maybe Stefan was right she was … what had he said … alienating people? She must try harder. Money was not a problem, she could get her skirts and blouses at Saks. Maybe Nanette would go with her. They could have an afternoon together. Go to the beauty parlor together. All it took was a phone call. As for her relationship with her husband, their conversations increasingly were arguments and, yes, she liked getting the last word. Debra got out her Bible. Which psalm was it her grandmother had constantly quoted? Debra couldn't find it, too many psalms. It wasn't the 23rd. Then, she found it! It was the 19th! She could hear her grandmother now, reciting it. Debra asked herself if the words in her mouth, when she and Stefan were fighting, were acceptable to the Lord. She resolved to remember the psalm if she and Stefan had another row, but she did not.

"You mustn't allow your faith to flag," said her pastor, Walter Cormack Stone, whom she admired very much and who was something of a local celebrity, with a weekly radio show. Debra was not shy about stopping by the church, unannounced, for a chat with Pastor Stone, and if he was there, he invariably made time for her. She was a parishioner to cultivate. "Life without the Lord is not worth living. It is reduced to a short, savage struggle."

"Kind of seems like that's what it is with the Lord, too, pastor," Debra said. "My marriage has become a struggle. My husband and I never used to fight. Now we often do. I'm worried. I don't know where to turn."

"That isn't true. You've come here. Why don't you bring your husband with you? We'll talk."

"He'd never come."

"Why don't you ask him just the same? He might surprise you."

"Pastor, if there is one thing Stefan has quit doing, it's surprise me. His behavior is as predictable as the sunrise."

"Have you considered marriage counseling?"

"He'd come here first." The clergyman sighed resignedly. What was the point in these talks, really? She had an answer for everything.

"Do not allow your faith in our Lord Jesus Christ to fail," the pastor said, after fully another half hour of unrewarding conversation. He placed his hand gently on her shoulder. "Remember always you must believe in order to see, not the reverse. This is the very essence of faith, and it does change your life. Pray and pray again, and our Lord will answer your supplication, and show you the way."

"Thank you, thank you. I'll do my best." And for a while she did. Then came the day when she timidly suggested to her husband they accept Pastor Stone's invitation to come together to speak with him. "You'll like him, dear, really you will."

"I do not require religious instruction," he said scornfully. "I get enough of that from you."

"Religious instruction?" Debra said sarcastically. "Is that really what you think we'd get from the pastor?"

"What else?" Stefan said.

"Maybe some ideas on how we can be closer," Debra said hopefully.

"I don't think so."

"Of course you don't, Stefan," Debra retorted.

Some days later Debra, upon realizing her visit with Pastor Stone had given her the incentive she needed to look into marriage counseling, got out the phone book and began going through the names. There were many, but aside from wanting a woman for sure, and convenience of location, she had no criteria for making a selection. All had letters after their names, representing advanced degrees. She picked a woman named Madeleine Ullstater, because she liked the name. Sounded vaguely French, maybe that would be helpful. Debra made an appointment and met Ms. Ullstater one afternoon about ten days later. Ms. Ullstater's office was downtown. Once inside the building, the very first office Debra passed, and there were many, sported a sign, "Therapy You Can Afford." The affordable therapist's name was there, too, but rather decidedly not what you saw first. Ms. Ullstater's office was one flight up. Debra took the stairs rather than the elevator, her heart sinking with each step. She was gratified not to find "Marriage Counseling For Every Budget" on the door. She took a deep breath and went inside.

She was in a small waiting room. Four chairs. No receptionist. A clock. A ceiling fan, not turned on. One of those dreamy Maxfield Parrish landscapes on one wall. A coffee pot. Smelled fresh and good. Paper cups. A platter of cookies. Music, maybe a little too faint, wafting around, the sort one always hears in medical offices, and quasi-medical offices. No magazines or newspapers, nothing at all to read. How, Debra asked herself yet again, can I have persuaded myself to do this? She might have bolted, but just then Madeleine Ullstater opened her office door.

"Mrs. Kopinski?" she asked, extending her hand. She had incorrectly emphasized the first, rather than the middle, syllable in "Kopinski." Her manner was gracious, if a trifle florid. She was a brunette, and her hair was in a ponytail. She wore a well-cut suit with a corduroy skirt, a turquoise necklace and matching earrings. She was certainly a contemporary of Debra's, if not indeed a few years younger. Debra had expected an older woman.

"Yes," Debra said, shaking hands.

"Won't you come in?" Debra sat in one of two, leather chairs. "Did you get yourself a cup of coffee and a cookie?"

"No, thank you. I don't drink much coffee. Usually just when I get up in the morning."

"That's my preference, too," Ms. Ullstater said. "Now how can I help you this afternoon?" Her voice had a soothing, patient quality, but carried a note of authority, as well.

"I don't really know," Debra faltered. "My husband and I aren't getting along too well. Our marriage used to be wonderful. Not anymore. Got to find a way to turn things around, but I'm out of ideas."

"Does your husband want a divorce?"

"I don't know," Debra said. "I'm beginning to think, maybe, maybe he does."

"You used the word 'wonderful.' So your marriage wasn't merely good at one time, it was wonderful. This is very encouraging. Can you tell me a little about those wonderful years?"

Debra embarked upon an answer, beginning with their courtship, bringing herself once to tears, but recovering quickly. She became more businesslike the further she went. She spoke virtually uninterrupted for fifteen minutes. Her portrait of her marriage was markedly favorable to herself.

"You said you think your husband uses his work as an excuse to get out of the house," Madeleine Ullstater said. "Do you ever go by his office?"

"No. I have no reason to."

"Surely you could come up with some excuse?"

"Forgive me, but are you suggesting he might not be there?"

"I'm not suggesting anything. I merely thought it might be useful, in that you could be reassured he really is working those long hours. I've worked with lawyers, and long days, and Saturdays at the office, are not unusual."

"I believe he goes to the office, I just don't believe he's necessarily working. It's his refuge. He'd rather go there and read *The New York Times* than be with his wife and daughters."

"That's not uncommon," the counselor said kindly. "I would like to meet your husband. Very often, the first appointment is with the wife alone. Men just don't call marriage counselors, in my experience. However, it is also my experience that both husband and wife must attend. After a few sessions, I am in a position to meet each party independently. So I would like to suggest you bring Mr. Kopinski with you next time, even if he's kicking and screaming all the way."

"I agree it has to be both of us." Debra shook her head in dismay. "I really am not sure I can talk him into it. He might consent to one meeting, so I'd leave him alone afterwards. Could you give it your best shot, if I can get him here once?" Madeleine Ullstater laughed.

"I don't believe anybody's ever said that to me before, Mrs. Kopinski. I will give it my best shot. And if you can't get him to come, but you would like to continue coming, that would be more than fine."

"Thank you," Debra said. "By the way, my last name is 'Ko-PIN-ski,' not 'KO-pin-ski.'"

"Sorry."

Debra was out the door. She liked Madeleine Ullstater, even if she wasn't completely persuaded she had not implied Stefan was running around on her. Debra did not have an explanation for the trouble in her marriage, but her confidence Stefan was faithful was not misplaced. His jealous mistress was his law practice, not a tart he had tucked away somewhere.

How was she to get him to agree to counseling? Their conversations were often unpleasant, and certainly not productive. Where to begin? Should she be conciliatory? Debra felt this was the role she always assumed, in the face of his hostility. Why not try the opposite? Approach it as though there was nothing to discuss, it was going to happen, he would cooperate. Could she pull that off? Might help to have an actual appointment in place, and soon. Next day. Of course, he would have his usual excuse. He would have to be at the office, they'd have to see Madeleine Ullstater another time. Yet, hadn't he hinted at a willingness to meet with a marriage counselor? Debra couldn't remember. She would approach their conversation in the spirit of conciliation. This was her strong suit, this was the part she knew best.

Stefan knew what was coming and had already made up his mind. He'd go with her—once—to see someone. Debra's suspicion was right on the money. Once would shut her up.

CHAPTER 11

I T WAS A SATURDAY STEFAN'S FATHER-IN-LAW ARRIVED AT HIS HOME. HE had not called first, and Stefan wasn't home. The housekeeper said he was probably at his office, where he usually went on Saturday. Hank Morrison inquired if the office was on Sims Road? She didn't know. His daughter wasn't home, either, or the matter could be resolved immediately. Hank was glad Debra wasn't there, however. He did not wish to be sidetracked this morning.

"Got a phone book?" he asked. Ridiculous, looking in the phone book for the professional offices of his son-in-law. He located it readily. Hank thanked the housekeeper and headed out the door. He was a little irked with himself, for now he remembered how often Debra had complained Stefan was never around. Always at the office. Including weekends. Worked all the time. Hank pulled into the parking lot at the Sims Road Professional Building, which did not look very special from the exterior. A four-story office building, one of three in a row in a small office park. They were a matched set. In the lobby, Hank looked at the directory and found Fulton & Shaw on the third floor. When he reached the front door of the office, he discovered it was locked. He gazed inside and could clearly see there was nobody at the reception desk. Closed on Saturday, of course they were. Hank was annoyed with himself, again. How was he going to get Stefan, who undoubtedly was inside, to let him in? No doorbell. Hank knocked on the door and then on the window, too. Knocked hard. No response. He was turning to go, when his son-in-law appeared.

"Hey Hank." Stefan was all smiles as he let his father-in-law in, though just for a second he wondered if he was carrying a gun and meant to use it. "Prominent attorney found shot in his office. Saturday morning, nobody around. Police have no leads." Stefan had pretty much forgotten this conversation with Hank was inescapable. Apparently, this was to be it.

"Hope this isn't an inconvenient time?" Hank said. "I should have called first." He didn't mean this. He meant to surprise Stefan.

"No, not at all. Just doing a bit of catching up. I like to come here on Saturday. Wonderfully quiet." Stefan led the way down the corridor to his office, Hank peering into other offices as they walked. All were extravagant. An abundance of leather and mahogany. Even Hank was impressed. He was not intimidated. When they were seated, Stefan thought to ask if he'd like a cup of coffee. There was a coffee maker, and Stefan was reasonably confident he could make it work, if required. Hank declined. They engaged in chitchat for several minutes, the usual subjects. Stefan knew why Hank had come, and Hank knew Stefan knew.

"I expect you've guessed what's brought me here this morning," Hank finally said.

"Yes."

"Tell me Debra is wrong, that you aren't really planning to get a divorce."

"Hank, forgive me, but is my marriage really any of your business?"

"It's Debra's business, and I'm her father."

"So that gives you the right to pass judgment on my marriage?"

"I'm not here to pass judgment on your marriage, Stefan."

"Very well. What can I do for you?"

"Stefan, a man doesn't walk out on his wife and children," his father-in-law said bluntly.

"I'm not walking out on them. Debra and the girls would be very well provided for. They wouldn't go hungry or be destitute."

"In your world, it all comes down to money, doesn't it, Stefan? Money will fix everything. It won't fix this." Here there was a pause in the conversation.

"I think that's a bit harsh, Hank. I hope you are not suggesting money isn't important in your world. I'm sure it is." Another pause.

"Stefan, I'm not here to talk money. I'm here to say something to you, man to man." Hank Morrison looked straight at his son-in-law. "A woman's family is her life. When you and Debra stood at that altar, what did she do? What every woman does. She turns her life over to the man standing next to her. Whither he goeth, she goeth. It's up to him. He's in charge. He makes the decisions. She obeys. That might sound unfair, but she gets back the best thing in a woman's life. Know what that is? Fulfillment as a wife and mother. All women want this. Understand? Your marriage is an important item in your life, but your law practice is your primary focus. It's Saturday morning, and where are you? Your law office. Makes my point for me. Debra doesn't have a law office, does she? No. She has her marriage."

"Good thing Janice isn't here."

"Who's that?"

"An associate we hired not long ago. She's a feminist. Familiar with the term?"

"Not really." He wasn't there to learn about feminists.

"They believe all differences between men and women should be banished. You should hear what she calls pregnant women."

"What?"

"Pregnant people."

"Have no idea what that means."

"I think the idea is, they're both pregnant. I'm really not sure. Don't worry about it."

"So when she has her baby, does it find milk at his breast, too?" Hank said.

"I believe she's single. She's young, Hank, just a few years out of school. I'm sure that's where she got her ideas."

"She's wrong. Men and women aren't alike."

"Maybe not, but you're swimming against the tide."

"Stefan, let's get back on subject."

"We are on subject. Your notions about marriage are out-of-date, Hank. And let me tell you something else. Debra isn't happy. So do you want her to stay in a relationship where she's unhappy? That what you want for her?"

"So you're doing her a great big favor by getting a divorce, because she's so unhappy. Now ain't that swell? I really expected more of you." Stefan did not like this remark. He was prepared to bring their talk to a quick conclusion if Hank was determined to be insulting. As if he sensed this, Hank relented. "Look, Stefan, I didn't come here to be … to have an argument. You and I, we've always gotten along, haven't we?" Stefan nodded. "All I came to say is, a man doesn't walk out on his wife and kids. It's … it's cowardice." This was the word Hank was hell-bent on getting out of his mouth, and now he had. He had no idea if Stefan had heard it from someone else, but by God he was going to hear it from his father-in-law. "I don't know why any man would choose … that."

"Again, that's your opinion, Hank. Doesn't make it so, just because you say it."

"Yeah it is so. It's one of the verities. True yesterday, true today, true tomorrow."

"All right, Hank, I'll give it some thought," Stefan said. He wouldn't, and both knew it. Stefan got to his feet. "I'm going to have to get back to work, now." Stefan extended his hand, and they shook warmly. "I'll walk you to the door." At the door, they shook again, perfunctorily. Hank had the last say.

"We're through, Stefan, if you do this." There was no doubting Hank meant this, and had he known the extent of his elder granddaughter's peril, his language would have been far stronger.

CHAPTER 12

DEBRA RESPONDED TO THE DOORBELL, AND THERE, TO HER SURPRISE, stood Sharon. The latter did not make a habit of dropping by for a friendly little chat, for the very good reason there would be no friendly little chat.

"May I come in?" she asked.

"Yes," Debra stammered. Sharon stepped inside, though Debra wasn't being very accommodating about making room for her.

"All the way in?"

"Yes," Debra said, almost giggling at Sharon's remark. She had no practice with this response, or it might have come more easily. "How are you, Sharon?"

"I'm good, Debra," Sharon said, surveying the room. It was a mess. Debra couldn't care less if it surprised her. "And you?"

"Fine. What brings you here? Is Stefan sick?"

"No, nothing like that," Sharon said, sitting on the sofa. "He showed me the letter from Sperry-Bault Clinic. I'm assuming you got a copy, as well?"

"Of course, everything comes to both of us."

"Debra, as Linda's and Lisa's stepmother, I—" Sharon paused to get the words she wanted— "have tried to be sensitive to yours and Stefan's wishes, and never stick my nose where it doesn't belong. I have viewed my role as a secondary one and tried to play that part, despite no experience as a stepmother, let alone an actual mom. I hope you will agree with me that I have tried."

"I think you've tried lately, Sharon," Debra answered with conviction, "but not at first."

"Perhaps," Sharon said. "In any ..."

"No 'perhaps' about it, Sharon," Debra said with more conviction. "You deliberately tried to alienate Linda and Lisa from their mother. They told me things, not that I would not have seen it for myself."

"What did you ever see, Debra?" Sharon said curtly. She was not going to sit there and be falsely accused, even if it meant aborting the purpose of her visit. "Please, let's look forward, not back. I am so terribly worried about Linda." There was ample cause for worry. Linda's hostility toward her mother had long since become spite. The girl lived now at a detoxification center, where her addiction to alcohol was not being addressed successfully. Linda had been drinking, undetected, for years. It had all finally come to light when a motorist had called the police after spotting a woman staggering down the side of a street one night.

"There will be another incident at Sperry-Bault Clinic," Sharon said. "You know there will. It isn't working for her, Debra." Debra shook her head. Sharon was undoubtedly correct, there would be another incident. Linda was going to find a way to get herself kicked out, just as she had done at her first placement.

"Do you have some kind of plan?" Debra said resignedly.

"Actually, yes. Linda isn't going to get better if we don't initiate a radical intervention. She's going to get worse. She might die." Sharon gasped at the thought. She had not felt sure she could express it. "I've been doing some research," she continued. "There's quite a few places around the country for troubled teenagers. A lot, really."

"Sharon," Debra cut in. "Sperry-Bault Clinic is for troubled teenagers. That's where Linda is now." Sharon reached into her purse and withdrew a brochure. It described the facilities and programs at a place called Auburn Hills. She handed it to Debra.

"I want you to look at this, Debra. Could we move to the table?"

"If you like." No enthusiasm in Debra's manner, although she was mildly curious, and perceived in Sharon's manner a purposefulness to which she was unaccustomed. "Shall I put on the kettle?" she found herself saying.

"That would be nice." Debra got up to go in the kitchen. "Wait," Sharon said, rising, "let me handle the tea, just tell me which cupboard it's in. You take a few minutes to read this brochure."

"Cabinet to the right of the stove." Sharon put the kettle on, Debra read. The program at Auburn Hills did not strike her as materially different from the one Linda was currently in, nor its predecessor's. Moreover, the one she was reading about now was in another city, Portland, Oregon. Surely Sharon was not seriously suggesting Linda be plucked from her present placement and removed to a distant city? This made no sense.

Over tea, the two women spoke in a way they never had, but which was very much what Sharon intended. Sharon, after a good bit of back-and-forth, conceded the program at Auburn Hills was not unlike the ones in California. Whether a higher level of tolerance for wayward adolescent behavior was really in the offing was questionable; they couldn't tell by the language in the brochure. To be sure, both the residence where Linda was now, and the previous one, were highly structured and remorselessly no-nonsense. Boundaries were what most of these kids had never had. Not so behind these doors.

"If this place is no different from the others, what's the point?" Debra reiterated. "You can't be serious. It's in Oregon. We'd dumping her in a place far away. How will that make her feel loved?"

"Debra, hear me out," Sharon said patiently. "Stefan and I are not going to fetch Linda from Sperry-Bault Clinic. This time, it's us." Debra did not like the word "fetch." Wasn't it your dog you told to go fetch a ball?

"Us? The two of us? Have you forgotten Linda despises me?"

"Then she'll have to despise me, too, since we shall be inseparable."

"You've discussed this with Stefan, presumably?"

"Not yet," Sharon said without trepidation. "Stefan, as always, is in the middle of a trial. I don't have to tell you how that goes." Debra nodded in ready acknowledgement. "It doesn't really matter. He's thrown up his hands in despair, he's as lost for answers as we are. He won't balk at this." Debra wondered if their marriage was foundering. Sharon usually gushed over her husband. The two women would certainly agree Stefan had put his career before them both, and the children. He was consumed with ambition, and absolutely nothing could be done about it.

"We go get Linda, before she is expelled from Sperry-Bault Clinic. We fly to Portland. I considered driving, but it's a long drive, and nerves might fray. We enroll Linda at Auburn Hills, unless there's something really objectionable about the place. We make it clear she is dealing with both of us from now on."

"Oh, Sharon dear, I … I just don't know … this doesn't make sense … I'm so afraid …" It was well Sharon wasn't afraid, since there was enough fear in Debra for both of them. "Maybe we should try bringing Linda back home," Debra said, not meaning it, for when this had been tried, the results were horrendous.

"Nope, we are going to Oregon."

"Really, this makes no sense at all, Sharon," Debra said, shaking her head. Sharon wasn't fazed. Nothing was going to be resolved right away, she understood that. She would not give up, and little by little, Debra's resistance would weaken, until it was gone!

Which is precisely what happened.

The day came to go to Sperry-Bault Clinic. To get their daughter. They went together. Debra's faint heart was fainting.

"Sharon, why don't you go to Linda's room without me," Debra said, once the necessary paperwork to withdraw Linda from the facility had been completed. Debra was petrified Linda would make a scene.

"Very well," Sharon said reluctantly, "but this is the very last time Linda sees her stepmother unaccompanied by her mother." Debra stared at Sharon. She was certain there would be a scene. So what? Why the same old dread? She had lost count how many scenes there had been, including in some very public places. It was all so utterly hopeless. Debra fought back tears.

"You brought her?" resounded from down the hall, after Sharon entered Linda's room. "Why? I don't ever want to see her again."

"You are coming with me, Linda," Sharon said resolutely. She was perfectly calm. "Your mother and I have a plan that involves the three of us. This is going to work, and you are coming with us, right now."

"I hate my mother." This, too, echoed down the hall.

"I am aware of that, honey. Everyone in the building is aware of that, I imagine." Sharon instantly wished she had not said that. So stupid. "I'm sorry Linda, I didn't mean that."

"You're probably right," the girl said, unoffended. "I'm not the only one in here who hates her mother, I can tell you that. This girl named Trudie won't even say her mother's name."

"And you, Linda?"

"Debra, Debra, Debra," Linda said sarcastically. "How's that?"

"You get an A-Plus." Sharon said. "Let's go. Give me your arm."

"No," the girl said, so her stepmother took it. Her mother, in the lobby, was in a near-panic. She rose as she saw them approach.

"Oh, Linda," she choked out. There was no further resisting the tears.

"Hello mom," Linda said indifferently. She resisted her mother's attempt at an embrace. "Let's not get carried away here." This injured Debra, exactly as if this time were the first time.

"Linda, darling, how are you, dear?" Debra tried at least to take her daughter's hand between hers, but this didn't work, either.

"Okay, I'm okay." Silence. "What's the plan?"

"Linda," Sharon said, "your mother and I do not believe this place is right for you. Would you agree?"

"You're asking me that?" the girl said incredulously. "Of course I agree." She couldn't stand the "joint," as she termed it.

"That's what I thought," Sharon said with a wink. "We're going to try something else, but with the understanding from the start this will be a long-term commitment by all three of us. Understand?"

"I am not drinking in here, if that's what you mean. They go through my stuff every 30 minutes, how could I?" The girl had somehow managed to smuggle a flask of vodka through security at her first placement. The vodka was found, and she was expelled the same day.

"I'm not sure what you mean by that, honey? I didn't mean to imply that, if I did."

"This joint is run like a prison."

"Linda, we have been doing a bit of looking around, you might say." Debra reflected Sharon's use of the plural was a bit much, since she had not been involved. Sharon, in any event, was not to be corrected. "We have found a different environment for you. We think it has great potential for you."

"I'm listening." Not listening in a good humor, but listening.

"We are flying to Portland, Oregon tomorrow."

"You're joking, right?"

"Not joking. Portland, tomorrow. Your mother and I are confident we have found a place more suitable for you. Less prison-like. Doesn't that sound good?"

"I'm not going to Portland, Oregon."

"Yes, honey, you are."

"No, honey, I'm not."

"Dear," said Debra, "please don't mock your stepmother."

"Where does dad figure in this? I want to talk with him. How come he's never involved?"

"Honey, you know he's involved," Sharon said. "He is for whatever will hasten your recovery. Goes without saying."

"I'm getting better here. I don't want to start over."

Sharon had reserved three seats in a row on their flight. Linda would literally be between her mother and her stepmother. Was she going to like this? Probably she will make a scene, Sharon imagined. Let her. They were going, if she sat there and screeched or sulked all the way. Linda would discover having her mother beside her would not contaminate her after all. Linda, however, was silent for virtually the duration of the flight. She was civil about including her mother, when she did say something, but both Debra and Sharon got the message pretty quickly she wasn't eager to chat, and since speaking with each other meant rather awkwardly speaking across the girl, nobody said much of anything. Sharon felt foiled in her bid to have an affectionate exchange among them. At least Linda had not simply ignored her mother in favor of her; that would have been a wretched outcome. As for Debra, she spent the flight peering out the window and wondering how she could conceivably have let Sharon talk her into this. A scatterbrained stunt. Sharon was expert in that department. Couldn't succeed, a certain fiasco. This was the word she came back to, again and again. Linda, who had not made up her mind about the venture, nevertheless began to relish a trip. There had been a family road trip to Seattle, and they had visited Portland, but Linda remembered nothing. What was Portland famous for? Anything? How big was it? Not as big as L.A., for sure. Linda had a notion Seattle was bigger, too. It was probably super-conservative, Linda told herself, not that she gave much thought to politics one way or the other. She was way too busy drinking. Oregon wouldn't be California. California was California. You could do anything you wanted. You could always find an accommodating liquor store.

As the flight neared its end, Linda spoke up.

"What's the name of this place I'm going, again?" she asked her stepmother.

"Auburn Hills, honey," said Sharon, "and it's where we're going. You are not alone."

"You mean you're staying, too?" Linda didn't know it yet, but she was half-right.

"You know what I mean, Linda," her stepmother said gently, but firmly.

"Today? Are we going today?" It was mid-afternoon. Although neither of her caregivers detected it, there was a slight note of fright in the girl's inquiry. The reality of her stepmother's determination began to sink in.

"Not today, honey. It would be late before we could get there. My goodness, we have to find the place, first. I told them tomorrow, but even that could be changed, if we decided maybe to do a little sightseeing, first. Would you like that?"

"Not really," Linda replied, but she immediately felt she might have hurt her stepmother's feelings, these being the only feelings with which she was concerned. "On second thought, I'm game. When else am I going to go sightseeing, after I'm incarcerated?"

"You are not being incarcerated," her stepmother said unpersuasively, since she was being incarcerated.

"Whatever," Linda said morosely. She was exhibiting none of the brashness she ordinarily did. Of course, it had been a while since her last drink. Debra felt she should speak up, say something to her daughter, something encouraging, if only she were not completely discouraged herself. Fortunately, Sharon wasn't discouraged in the least. These two women had never been close. Given circumstances, how could it be otherwise? The trip would be a revelation for both of them, especially Debra.

They took a taxi to the hotel. How many rooms? Sharon had this worked out, too. Two rooms. Linda could choose with which parent she would stay. She chose Sharon.

"Why don't we rest briefly, freshen up and have dinner?" Sharon said. "We can ask at the front desk for a restaurant recommendation, or maybe we just eat here at the hotel?" Both Debra and Linda nodded assent. They retired to their respective rooms. Debra flung herself on the bed, more tired than anything else, but this was not merely physical fatigue, it was emotional exhaustion. As she lay there, the futility of the enterprise seized her yet again, and she became weepy. Her daughter was lost in a labyrinth; was there no way out? What they were attempting in Portland wasn't new, only the place was new. Linda couldn't handle it this time either. Debra had never considered the expense of dealing with Linda's illness as anything but money well spent, but the unnecessary trip to Portland seemed money wasted. A thought crossed her mind. Doing the normal, rational, conventional thing had produced only failure. What harm was there in trying something abnormal, irrational, unconventional? Their lives could hardly be more upside-down than they presently were. Debra had no idea where this thought had come from. Was Sharon thinking similarly? Coming to Portland wasn't rational. There came a knock on the door. It was Sharon.

"I have something for us, in my purse." She withdrew two small bottles of liquor, the sort available on an airplane. She held them up. "Bourbon or gin. What's your pleasure?"

"Where did you get those?" Debra asked.

"On the flight. Bourbon or gin? I'll go down the hall and get us some soft drinks."

"Where's Linda?"

"In our room. I think she'll be all right for a little while. She's watching TV. We are going to succeed with that girl, I promise you, Debra. But we can't have a drink in front of her. So come on, no more delay, time to celebrate, you want the bourbon or the gin?" Debra picked the bourbon, and they had a highball together, all of twenty minutes. Debra was more accustomed to wine, and the hard liquor, consumed quickly and on an empty stomach, did wonders for her humor. It was more than this, however. This improbable adventure Sharon had kicked up was making her unexpectedly happier. That it was well-planned was becoming apparent to Debra.

This elation would be brief. Linda was not to be found in the other room. She had bolted for the bar the moment Sharon left. Both women knew instantly this was where they'd find her. They flew down the stairs into the lobby and into the bar. There sat Linda, at a barstool, with a drink in her hand. When she spotted her mothers, she hastily drained the glass. Double vodka on the rocks. To be exact, her second double vodka on the rocks. Two + two = four. Linda had entered the bar and made straight for a barstool away from other customers. When the bartender had come over to her, looking skeptical about her age, Linda had needed exactly four seconds, by word and gesture, to convince him he was perfectly willing to risk the establishment's liquor license, not to mention possible prosecution.

"Oh Linda, how could you?" her stepmother said despairingly. Her words were robbed of any moral force. She was to blame. What a blunder, what an enormous blunder! It didn't help, either, that she and Debra had been sneaking a drink themselves. Debra herself couldn't speak. She was sobbing.

"Leave me alone," Linda said. She was ugly. "Both of you."

"We are going back upstairs, Linda," Sharon said firmly.

"I want another drink," Linda screamed.

"No way." Sharon reached for her stepdaughter's arm, but Linda swatted it aside. Was there going to be a scene? Debra was frantic. The bartender approached.

"Is there some difficulty here?" he said under his breath, giving Linda a knowing eye. She returned his look with one of contempt. Evidently he had believed she meant to keep her end of the bargain. Men were such asses.

"Double vodka, rocks," she demanded.

"Linda, you are coming with us, right now," her stepmother said with conviction. She turned to the bartender. "How dare you serve this minor alcohol. How could you do this?" The bartender, a man in his thirties, good-looking, didn't reply. He left.

"Come on, Linda," her stepmother said. "We're done here." Since more alcohol was out of the question, Linda had to give in.

When they got back to their rooms, Debra knew she must do something. She felt Sharon's confidence had been badly shaken. She did not pause to consider she had never worried before about her confidence, or, for that matter, much of anything else. A forceful step had to be taken, at once. What this was Debra didn't know, but it was imperative she act.

"I erred, Linda, dear," she said gently. "I am at fault. I hope you will forgive me. Your stepmother and I are going to see you through this, no matter what. Let's not even dwell on tonight's ... on tonight. In the morning, we are going to the clinic and enroll you, just as planned." Debra turned her gaze to Sharon.

"Just as planned," Sharon managed to say.

"Now, I am going downstairs and get us all sandwiches," Debra said.

"I'm not hungry," Linda growled. The alcohol, after a period without it, had tasted inexpressibly good, and the only thing on her mind was, how to get her hands on more.

"Nobody is going to force you to eat, honey," Sharon said.

Debra was away fifteen minutes. When she returned, she had, besides the food, her nightgown. The second room had become unnecessary. It was Sharon who was close to tears.

Breakfast went all right. At 8:55, a cab deposited the three of them in front of Auburn Hills. The building was imposing. Sharon thought it looked even grander than it had in the brochure. Three stories tall, four Ionic columns in front. It was white, maybe too white. The front lawn was impeccably manicured. An American flag flapped in the breeze. A second pole sported another flag, that of the state of Oregon. Inside went the threesome: Sharon, largely recovered from the previous evening and more resolute than ever; Debra, filled with curiosity; and Linda, convinced this would be exactly like her previous two incarcerations. She was between her mother and stepmother, and the latter had put her arm around her shoulder as they went up the steps and through the door. All were momentarily dismayed, for this was indeed another asylum, it could not be mistaken for another thing. For a moment, Sharon regretted not having made an initial trip by herself, to check things out. She recovered quickly and approached the front desk with determination. This time would not be like the others, it would not, it would not!

"May I help you?" the receptionist said.

"Good morning," Sharon said. "My name is Kopinski. We have an appointment with Mr. Nussbaum at 9:00." The receptionist, a nondescript woman in her middle years, ran down the appointment log.

"Yes, here you are," she said. "Won't you take a seat? Mr. Nussbaum will be with you shortly." She handed Sharon a clipboard with a sheaf of papers. "You will need to complete these first. I will also need to see your proof of insurance." So far so good, no surprises. Indeed, the paperwork was uncannily similar to that at the two previous facilities where Linda had been.

"Shall I complete these forms, Debra, or would you prefer ..."

"Why don't you go ahead?" Debra said, her voice cracking. Were they really going to leave her daughter here, and fly home to Los Angeles?

Sharon completed the forms, answering every question as fully as possible, including information about previous institutionalizations, if any. None of their damn business, she muttered to herself, but she answered the questions. Linda was hurting, she needed help, they were going to pay a substantial fee for this help, where did they get off asking these intrusive questions?

Questionnaire completed, Sharon returned it to the front desk. Shortly thereafter William Nussbaum appeared. He was the Deputy Director. Introductions were accomplished, Nussbaum noting all three women had the same last name. They embarked immediately upon a tour. Nussbaum liked to start with this, then retire to his office for more perfunctory matters, like payment considerations. The tour generally left people impressed, particularly those becoming acquainted with such a facility for the first time. This wasn't even the second time for the family Kopinski. Sharon began to be discouraged, as the sales points made in the brochure, which had sold her, became one by one no different from those of any other such facility. She fussed at herself again for not having made a trip of her own first, caught herself doing this, and stopped. They came upon an especially attractive garden, studded with roses. They took the serpentine walk through the garden, pausing at the fountain. Everything was trim and neat and orderly. William Nussbaum greeted one "resident" after another. He knew everyone. At last, they arrived at his office, where indeed payment was the primary subject. Nussbaum also explained policies in detail, not neglecting behaviors by residents that could result in expulsion. He was methodical, first to last.

"Are there any other questions I can help you with?" he concluded, implying the decision to enroll Linda was a done deal. Debra and Sharon looked at each other. There was really nothing to hold them back, but each thought the other might have an issue. Sharon spoke up.

"We are impressed, Mr. Nussbaum, with Auburn Hills. Thank you for the tour and for your time. I think we'd like to discuss this among ourselves, at this point. Perhaps we could plan on speaking with you again tomorrow?"

"That would be fine, please take your time," William Nussbaum said. He was disappointed. His sales pitch usually closed the deal.

"Well, Linda," Sharon said when they got back to their hotel. "What do you think?"

"You mean I can say 'No'?"

"Honey, your mother and I don't want to force you to do something you find really unpleasant, but short of that, don't you think this place could be good for you?"

"I've done this twice already."

"Dear," Debra ventured, "your stepmother has gone to a tremendous amount of trouble, all for you. This trip, all the arrangements, all the leg-work, her doing. She is totally invested in your recovery."

"Your mother, Linda, has paid me a compliment. She has left no stone unturned, either. Yes, you've done this twice before. Let's not look back. This time is going be different, and I'm going to keep saying that." Sharon paused. She had left something unsaid. This was the moment to say it. She was nervous. Would Debra object? Might she feel she was being ... being replaced? Go for it.

"I have a little announcement to make," she said tentatively. She gulped. "Honey, I'm staying for a while in Portland," she said to Linda. Sharon looked at Debra. Facial expression told all. Her misgiving was groundless.

"You are!" Debra exclaimed. "My goodness, that's wonderful, Sharon. That is so wonderful." The women found themselves embracing. "Linda dear," Debra said to her daughter, "think of the sacrifice your stepmother is making to be with you. She's leaving her life in Pasadena. She's leaving your father. All for you. She's making a very big sacrifice."

"No, Debra," Sharon remonstrated. "It is not a sacrifice. Definitely not. It is what I want to do. What I am giving up is nothing compared to what I am getting."

"I don't believe that," Debra said.

Linda wasn't sure it was wonderful, or a magnificent sacrifice. But she had no choice except to surrender. Sharon embraced her warmly, and when her mother attempted the same, Linda was receptive.

Two days later, Debra returned to California. An emotional moment for her and Sharon was in store first.

"Sharon, thank you," Debra said, using a word she had seldom used with Linda's stepmother, "for your commitment to Linda's well-being. I thought this experiment, if that's the word, was crazy, yet I'm starting to feel good about it. You are making a major sacrifice, away from your husband, away from the busy, active life you have in Pasadena. It is a sacrifice, even if you refuse to call it that. I would not have done it for you."

"You would too, Debra, and it is not a sacrifice. I am only embarrassed it has taken me so long to realize how much more important Linda's health is than anything I am doing in Pasadena. Stefan will be all right, I guess I don't need to tell you that." They both laughed uncomfortably. "I'm not far, two hours by plane. I can always come back, if something urgent were to develop."

"I suppose so," Debra said, "but I am holding to my opinion."

"Thank you, Debra, for coming to my rescue when I made that colossal mistake."

"Our mistake," Debra said. Not another word was required. There would be a warm embrace when they reached the airport, and with that, Debra flew home, and Sharon climbed into a cab, and the great unknown.

On the flight back to L.A., Debra's remaining defenses against a full-fledged panic attack crumbled. She was literally flying away from her daughter! How could she have agreed to this? Linda wasn't ever going to get well, she was a lifetime commitment. The happy days of her daughter's girlhood flooded over Debra. Those ridiculous ballet lessons! If there was something a six-year-old could not do, it was stand on her toes and accomplish a pirouette. Debra had watched the class with amusement, fighting to keep from bursting into laughter. There was Girl Scouts. Linda had been a good Scout. She had won her share of awards for her achievements. Linda had a talent for drawing. She was one of the star pupils in art class. With only a pencil, she drew landscapes of remarkable vividness. Her teacher encouraged her without being too restrictive, feeling Linda should have relatively free rein to draw as she wished. The idea was to see how far her youthful imagination and talent would take her. Her sister Lisa couldn't draw anything, and moreover exhibited no particular talent. She was steady rather than impetuous, not given to moodiness or volatility. She was the superior student when it came to grades, she loved to read and indeed had her head between the pages of a book perhaps too often. Both sisters were outgoing and made friends easily. Birthday parties were festive and well-attended. Debra reflected on the enormous luxury she had had. Her husband earned a living, she was able to give her undivided attention to her daughters. However, a pattern, perhaps inevitable, had evolved. Stefan became the absent father. Oh, he was there, and the girls were not denied a commanding father figure, but it was clear to all he was ambitious and would allow nothing to stand in his way. Stefan had found in law what he had expected to find, an inexhaustible vocation at which he could excel, and prosper. Law was just right for Stefan, he had a "head" for it, from the beginning. But he would be an associate for seven long years, and every decision he made those seven years hinged on his advancement. The price was steep: He missed his girls' girlhoods.

Sundays excepted. After church, which occasionally even included Stefan, the family had had brunch at the country club, then an activity of some sort, even if it was only a quiet afternoon at the park. Stefan, under stern orders to participate, had genuinely enjoyed these outings, rather to his surprise. Nothing about them was exceptional, and therein lay the secret. For him, these Sunday excursions were a complete departure from his routine the other six days of the week. They gave him a chance to catch his breath.

There had been no serious illnesses, praise God, though Lisa had a nasty case of chickenpox when she was nine, which somehow her sister

271

escaped. No accidents or broken bones, even when the girls got bicycles, which they did not ride recklessly, nor race against each other, for here, as in other pursuits, Linda was just sufficiently older, Lisa could not compete. The only exception was scholarship. The younger sister had the edge here. Linda, when she became a teenager, also became boy-crazy; Lisa followed suit, but not to the same degree. Scholarship continued to matter to her. She was good at all subjects, and loved science best. (She would graduate from UCLA with a degree in Biochemistry and a 3.8 GPA.) They had been a contented, young family, the future before them.

Meanwhile, Stefan was displeased with his wife. He accused her of a "peremptory move." She reminded him she had told him she was going to remain in Portland for a while. He could not deny this, but now that it had happened, he objected. A wife should not leave her husband. The decision to put Linda in a residential facility in Portland was perfectly idiotic. A futile, idiotic, unnecessary expense.

"Stefan, calm down," Sharon said, when he had finished. "I have not left you." She reflected it was nice to discover he really would notice she wasn't there. "I can hop on a plane anytime and be there in two hours. It takes that long to go anywhere in L.A. I believe Linda's very survival is at stake. I am totally committed to beating her disease." This was a point of contention, since Stefan did not go along with the school of thought alcoholism is a disease. He began to say something, but she cut him off.

"Darling, you must not object to what I am doing. I haven't done much with my life," she said emotionally, "I definitely never expected to have a stepdaughter. But I have, and that stepdaughter is in desperate need. Help must come from me, you can't do it, Debra can't. I can. I could not find a real purpose on my own, but this one has been extended to me, I accept it, I embrace it, I will fulfill it."

"How am I going to explain your absence?" The Kopinski's elder daughter's troubles were not common knowledge, but some in their crowd knew.

"Just say it's a family matter. It's nobody's business." What family didn't have its issues?

"Yes, that will do," Stefan agreed. "Did you ever think I might miss you, though?"

"I already miss you," Sharon answered, almost meaning it. She loved Stefan, in a manner of speaking, she liked the life she had, but she was seized by the mission she had undertaken, and it pre-empted every other consideration in her life.

Sharon settled back in an armchair in her new abode, a hotel room, and chuckled. Her stepdaughter was securely ensconced at Auburn Hills, about four miles distant. Their journey had begun! She was going to learn a thing or two herself, before this was over. Like how to cook. Sharon never really had, before marrying Stefan, or after. They had a cook. Stefan would be fine. She'd be going to the supermarket, selecting meats and vegetables, and fixing herself meals in the kitchen in her room. She had a suite, with a sitting area, two bedrooms, and, naturally, a big-screen television. Sharon watched a fair share of television, and if pressed, would be obliged to admit she was hooked on one of the soap operas that populated so much of daytime programming. Her accommodations were functional, not much else. The view from the main window was the parking lot. She was on the second floor. The hotel included a fitness room, but no swimming pool. Sharon kept fit, she had a weekly regimen, back in California, she would resume it, here in Oregon. Her figure was undeniably alluring and she meant to keep it that way. She had tried yoga, not cared for it, but held to the belief rigorous exercise was good for soul as well as body. It was only nights she was dreading. She had no place to go. Depending upon how long she would be in Portland, she might join organizations and become integrated, at least to some degree, in the life of the community. After all, she had no idea what sort of place Portland was. It wasn't a big city, like Los Angeles, but there must be places to go, museums, parks, concerts. It would be fun discovering them. All the same, she found herself saying to herself, more than once, "Sharon Kopinski, what have you gotten yourself into?"

Auburn Hills had a policy, strictly enforced, there be no "outside" contact for new residents, the first two weeks. The objective was to establish a relationship of trust between resident and clinic, uninterrupted by the familiar, external world, meaning family members. The facility took pride in its programs and methods, and its recidivism rate was enviably low, but permanent recovery from addiction to alcohol nonetheless involved a time-tested regimen with which Linda was only too familiar. She had never seriously attempted the 12-step program, and was very certain she could never succeed at it.

Linda would have a therapist, deemed a "mentor" in the parlance of the institution. This person's name was Priscilla Skevington, she was a highly trained therapist who had been with Auburn Hills seventeen years. "Skevington," as she was called, as last names were used, was 52. She was as homespun as they come, a wife and mother, educated but not of a scholarly bent, and very good at what she did. It was Linda's good fortune to have been assigned to her.

"Linda," she asked her at the first session, "I want to ask you something. Our goal is permanent sobriety. This means never taking one more drink. It means attending Al-Anon meetings, when you leave here, at least once a week, preferably more, for the rest of your life." Linda had heard every bit of this before.

"Impossible. I can't do it."

"You most certainly can, and will. Because you know something, Linda, while lasting sobriety will be difficult, no use saying it won't, there is one thing much more difficult. Can you tell me what that is?"

"No. I guess I don't understand."

"What I am saying is, the life you are living is harder, much harder, much more demanding, than becoming sober is. It might not seem so, but trust me, it is. As difficult as beating your addiction to alcohol will be, not beating it is more difficult. The moment we start you on the road to recovery, and this is that moment, every day, every hour, every minute of your life will be easier, not harder. Now doesn't that sound good?" This was Priscilla Skevington's set speech, not in the least customized.

"Good luck." Linda's rejoinder was not said harshly.

"Luck won't have much to do with it, Linda. We won't need it."

The next fourteen days were horrible. Linda was frantic for a drink. She threw fits. She screamed vulgarity at Skevington and everybody else. Auburn Hills, to her astonishment, was prepared to allow her to scream all she wanted. Linda was going to have to find another way to get herself thrown out. The days ticked by. Linda was hoarse with screaming, but she went on, she made threats. "I will hurt you," she told Priscilla Skevington, swinging her fists in the air. The therapist was unfazed. "Did you hear me, Skevington, I will hurt you." A fist came close to her therapist's face.

On the fifteenth day, Linda had a visitor. Her stepmother. Linda was in her robe in a chair in her room, but she rose to greet Sharon and share an embrace. Sharon was nearly overcome with emotion.

"Where you been?" the girl asked. "L.A.?"

"No, honey, I've been right here in Portland. I'm not leaving you. I've been getting a look at the town. Some fun places for us to explore together."

"You must be eating at a lot of restaurants."

"My room has a kitchenette." Sharon laughed. "I'll bet you didn't know your stepmom could cook?" Linda did not know this, since in all the visitation weekends she had spent at her father's home, she had never known her stepmother to prepare a meal or, for that matter, wander anywhere near the kitchen.

"You're cooking?" Linda was incredulous.

"Had a very nice lamb chop last night. Directions said to cook it silly, so I did. Made some potatoes, too. Nice red wine." Oops!

"We had chicken, I think. It was okay. Food here isn't bad, really." Better not be, Sharon thought, considering what they were paying.

"And what about you, honey? Okay, too?"

"I suppose. Skevington is great, I like her a lot."

"Yes, I spoke with her and like her, as well. She is wholly committed to you."

"She puts up with a lot." Linda didn't elaborate. Sharon, in any case, knew how the last two weeks had gone. For her part, Linda was beginning to take it all in. Here was her stepmother, who apparently had moved to Portland and was prepared to remain until she was well. That would be forever.

"Am I eligible for parole yet?" Linda inquired.

"Not yet, honey. Patience, patience. That day will come." Linda could not hide the doubt on her face. "Why don't you tell me about your first two weeks? I'd like to hear more about Priscilla Skevington. What does she have you doing?" Sharon mused she was asking questions, like her husband the litigator, the answers to which she already knew. "Your mother and father will be expecting my report."

"So you're in this together?" Linda said. This was not correct. Her father wasn't precisely "in it." He had consented, but had no other role, at least not so far. He remained impressed by his wife's initiative, as indeed was Debra, who was closer to dumbfounded.

"Yes and no, honey. Don't worry yourself over that. Just know the three of us are absolutely united, and committed to your recovery. As is the staff here at Auburn Hills. You are the absolute priority in many lives." It was a nice spiel and Linda did not doubt its verity. But, did she want to recover? Did she want to forgive her mother?

"There's not all that much to say about my life in here. It's the same 12-step program. Did you really think it would be something else? You read about this joint before sticking me in it, right?"

"Yes, honey, you know I did. I don't believe I promised you would not face challenges similar to before." Sharon was a little displeased with her stepdaughter's seeming indifference to her efforts. She wondered if Linda had the curiosity to ask her what she had been doing all day long in a new city where she knew nobody. Linda did not ask. Sharon had gone shopping, and then done more shopping. She had visited the renowned Rose Garden and walked around the downtown district. Portland had numerous bridges over the Willamette River, a couple of which were interesting in their construction. Mount Hood she had looked for in vain, as it was overcast every day. She had not made it over to the Columbia River Gorge, she was deliberately saving this for Linda; they would see it the first time together. All in all, she did not find anything particularly remarkable about Portland, it was really just another city. The question now arose in full force: What was she going to do with herself? Until now, she had not concerned herself over this. She was too preoccupied with her stepdaughter. Now she was here, she had made good on her resolution, she must occupy herself with something. She was resourceful, she had interests, she must choose something. Indeed, she told herself, while her stepdaughter's plight was paramount, she must strive for balance, not permit it to absorb her completely.

She joined a health club, where she could spend as much time as she wished. She began to make friends. Sharon had always had a knack for this, and it did not let her down now. She joined a cooking class, where she spent Wednesday evenings. Unfortunately, the class was for advanced chefs, the meals were esoteric rather than basic; it wasn't for her. She found another class, where she was surprised to discover four of the seven enrollees were men. Two were divorced, the other two were bachelors. At one of the stores she visited, she had bought yarn and embarked upon a sweater for Linda. Sharon had not knit in some time, but like learning to ride a bicycle, it was still in her. What she did not remember was what a source of relaxation, and accomplishment, knitting was. She wondered why she had stopped. Her life in Los Angeles, especially her life with Stefan, she saw from a new perspective, which she had not expected. To her, her life seemed choppy and disconnected, a life not exactly purposeless, but unfocused. In this assessment she was not entirely fair to herself, which she came to understand. Had she been frivolous at times? Unquestionably, but who hadn't been? She was a woman of substance, too. Didn't her present endeavor bear witness to this?

For both Sharon and Linda, the unorthodoxy of the relocation to Oregon began to dissipate. Linda began to appreciate her stepmother's sacrifice, devotion and iron resolve; it was the last, particularly, that gave the girl heart. Sharon established a regimen, consistent with the rules of Auburn Hills, whereby on a daily basis she maintained contact with Linda, be it a full afternoon together some Sunday, or merely the message, "your stepmother phoned," delivered at a strategic point amid the day's activities. Sharon learned everything she could about Linda's routine. One Sunday, she secured a special dispensation to take Linda on a "field trip." Sharon had chosen the trip to the Columbia River Gorge she had been saving. They could make a full afternoon of this. Linda inquired how her "other parents" were doing. She even joked about one friend she had made who was effectively an orphan, whereas she had three parents.

"Can I have one?" the girl had said enviously, and Linda had, of course, offered her mother.

Sharon told her stepdaughter there was little in the way of news from California. Sharon noted her mother and father worried terribly about her.

"I reassure them you are doing fine, honey. You are, you know." Calls between the households in California and Oregon were random but not infrequent, especially in the beginning. Sharon was gratified by her husband's interest. Sharon was childless. While her child-bearing years were not over, the chances she and Stefan would have a child were remote. Her elder stepdaughter's collapse had become so profound, so dangerous, Sharon had been given not only an opportunity at motherhood, but a singularly meaningful one, however surrogate. She would make reconciliation between mother and daughter a goal, too, bearing in mind nothing was to stand in the way of the primary objective, restoring Linda's health.

The trip to the Columbia River Gorge went well. Linda was thrilled to be out of the joint and back in the real world, as she put it. She found the Gorge itself "gorgeous." Could this be where the word came from? "Gorgeous Gorge" she said repeatedly. They had BLT's at a coffee shop, and were back at Auburn Hills by the curfew, six o'clock. Linda could hardly bear to part with her stepmother and go back inside.

"This isn't the last time we will do this, honey. It's the opposite. It's the first time." Sharon embraced and kissed her stepdaughter.

Less than a week later, Linda let loose with one of her tirades against her mother. Sharon was filled with dismay. Abruptly, she lost patience.

"Linda, listen to yourself, would you, please? You make these awful accusations, what a bad, unloving mother you have, how she abused your father, how she destroyed your home. Does your sister feel this way, too? I wonder. Your mother, Linda, loves you, and the reason you get so worked up about this is, deep down you know this. Otherwise, what's the point? You wouldn't care."

"Oh bull," Linda said. Sharon nevertheless felt she had struck a responsive chord. By golly, she would chip away at her stepdaughter's professed contempt for her mother until it, like her addiction, was gone!

Linda's treatment plan continued reasonably well, and slowly, ever so slowly, she began to improve. She let up on the fiery denunciations as their futility became apparent. Not all on the staff were tolerant of her behavior. She was young, yes, so were others, she was miserable, yes, others were miserable, she was not desperate, like others, for a parent's love.

On the parental front, Debra had elected to wait six weeks before going back to Portland. She had decided to create a buffer of sorts, largely out of respect for what Sharon had undertaken: Six weeks with her stepmother and without her mother. These were the longest 42 days in a life that had been characterized by long days for a long time. The separation from her daughter was unendurable. On the side of the refrigerator, affixed with a magnet, she kept a calendar. She marked each day, at its conclusion, with a red X. Whether this was making the days pass more quickly Debra was uncertain. They dragged interminably. She spoke often with Sharon and was gratified by what was described as progress, although it was hard to tell for sure. Debra and Stefan spoke, too, not enthusiastically, but there was a tacit agreement they would keep each other informed of what was going on in Oregon. Stefan was adapting to his wife's absence with less difficulty than Debra was to their daughter's.

Sharon asked herself one day if Linda's less frequent condemnation of her mother stemmed from her own, manifest unwillingness to listen to it, or if the girl was understanding something she had not understood before. The former seemed more probable. There would be another outburst, in any case, just when Sharon had reached the hopeful conclusion she had heard the last.

"You cannot hate your mother unless you love her," Sharon was now given to telling her. Her stepdaughter grappled with this. Wasn't it a contradiction? Chipping away, chipping away. Sharon's siege was unrelenting. She was aghast at the sheer immaturity of her stepdaughter, and began to see this as the basic vulnerability from which other ills had developed. Linda was so young, really, so overmatched by circumstances. Sharon suspected the divorce had started her stepdaughter's spiral. When the topic came up, the girl invariably blamed her mother.

"Honey, it was your father who divorced your mother," Sharon responded. "Don't misunderstand, I am not blaming your father, he is my husband and I love him, but the divorce was his idea, not your mother's. This is the truth, he'll tell you so himself."

"Don't you think I know that?" the girl would answer, impatiently. "Mom treated dad shabbily. She was the cause. It amazes me how long he put up with it."

"Honey, I haven't a magic answer for you," Sharon said. "I don't believe there is one. People divorce, it's part of life. I hope it never happens to you, but it happens. Only your parents know, if even they do, what undermined their marriage, yet you, at your tender age, stubbornly persist in your belief what went wrong, when you don't really know. This isn't helping you, it's only embittering you, but this line of thinking has become so habitual I don't think you even realize it." Sharon was certain Linda wasn't hearing this from her for the first time, as she had heard her therapist say something along very similar lines. "It's long overdue, honey, that you acknowledged to yourself you've tormented yourself long enough, you're going to forgive, forget and move forward. You are an attractive, young woman with a wonderful life before you."

"I prefer to torment myself," the girl said. She wished her stepmother would quit calling her "honey" all the time. It ceased to mean anything.

Something else her therapist had said was that she suspected Linda blamed herself for the disintegration of her parents' marriage.

"This is far from uncommon, I'm afraid."

"I have never heard Linda say she blames herself," Sharon said strongly. "She blames her mother."

"That's correct, but it's a defense mechanism to conceal her own sense of fault. She isn't even aware of it, it's subconscious." Sharon found this troubling. She was not sophisticated in such matters, but she had spent far more time with her stepdaughter than her therapist had, and she had never detected by word or deed any "concealment" of self-blame. Was this responsible? Wasn't her therapist potentially creating an issue? Did Linda really need this heaped upon her? Stefan, she reflected, would demand evidence of self-blame. She should, too, but the therapist would just make some excuse. She already had. It was "subconscious." Sharon wondered where to turn. Debra? She didn't want to demand a different therapist; anyway, she'd probably say the same thing. Sharon was determined to resist this.

"Linda," Skevington said, "cannot make a full recovery until all the conflicts within her have been identified and resolved. Her drinking, as in so many cases, is her response to her acute unhappiness. It's anesthesia. What does anesthesia do? Takes away the pain. In the case of alcohol, of course, it's a false god. Alcohol is a depressant. When it becomes an addiction, you have Linda."

"I agree about the alcohol," Sharon said. "All the conflicts within her, that's another matter. We all have conflicts within us, all our lives, that aren't identified and resolved. Linda will never leave this place (Sharon almost blurted "joint" and rather wished she had), if this is the case."

"It's no good sending her back into the world with outstanding issues," Skevington said. Sharon let it go at that. She remained uncomfortable. A thought occurred to her that places like Auburn Hills had a stake in keeping patients as long as possible. All about money. So maybe they cooked up issues? This seemed terribly cynical.

As for Stefan, he was starting to adjust to bachelorhood. The peace and quiet were welcome. It wasn't that his wife introduced havoc into the household, despite her penchant for half-witted projects the half-wittedness of which she eventually realized, but not before having sunk time and money into it. The couple didn't fight, their marriage was as calm as his with Debra had turned tempestuous, they even found an occasional interest in romance. It was the lull in his social life Stefan perceived to be what contributed most to his serenity. Here, he had to admit an unexpected sympathy with his ex-wife. The round of parties and "in-kind" obligations were interminable and taxing. But you had to do it, period, and Debra would not. What had he been told, finally, at the firm? "Your wife's intransigence is holding you back." That cryptic remark translated to, get your house in order if you want to succeed here. Stefan's initial defensiveness, in response, had not gone over well. The rebuke from the senior partner had stung. Stefan felt he was being singled out, that other wives had their shortcomings. Plus, this wasn't really the issue. His marriage and his profession were to be kept apart.

Lisa came every other weekend. No change here, and yet, there was change. Her sister wasn't with her. His wife wasn't with him. Stefan had his younger daughter to himself. Heavens, what would they do? Where would they go? What would they talk about? Stefan found himself almost wishing Debra would stay rather than drop the girl off on Friday afternoon.

"How does a movie sound?" Stefan ventured.

"I'm for that, dad!"

"Pizza first, or afterwards?"

"First, since I'll eat tons of popcorn and then won't be hungry."

"I should have thought of that." On the other hand, going to the movie first would give them something to talk about over pizza. "Let's see the movie first," he said. "You can have a small popcorn." It turned out there was no small popcorn, only large and larger, but Stefan still felt pizza after the movie was better. He laughed at himself, not entirely comfortably. Here was the redoubtable Stefan Kopinski, Esq., litigator extraordinaire, on the horns of a dilemma. Pizza and movie with his daughter, or movie and pizza?

"I think mom's over you, dad," Lisa announced one weekend. Her mother, Stefan felt, was a topic best avoided, so this caught him off guard.

"What do you mean, Lisa?" he sputtered. "Is she seeing someone?"

"Don't think so, but she talks about you less." She had not meant this unkindly. Still, it hurt.

"What about your old man? Do I talk about your mother less?"

"You don't talk about her at all, dad."

"Dear me," he responded. "Anything in particular she used to say, and doesn't now?" Stefan was mildly curious. Very mildly.

"She used to talk about the old days more." By this the girl meant the years before the divorce. "Not that I remember them that well. Probably Linda does." Lisa had been seven at the time of the divorce; Linda, ten. "Dad, when is Linda coming home?"

"When she is completely well, Lisa."

"I know that."

"Then why ..."

"Mom says she's better. She talks with Sharon." Lisa and Linda both called their stepmother by her first name. This had been Sharon's choice. Nobody liked "stepmom," and "mom" was out of the question. "She goes to Oregon sometimes. I want to go, she says 'maybe someday,' which means 'no.'"

"Perhaps for the time being that's best, Lisa. Nobody is trying to keep the two of you apart, I'm sure you know that. Your stepmother is in charge, she's there, and both your mother and I talk with her, so she'll let us know when you can go up there with your mother. The day will come. Unless your sister gets back here first!"

"The trip would be fun," the girl said irrelevantly. "How did Linda get so sick, dad?" she said relevantly.

"People get sick, Lisa."

"I know that."

"Your sister started drinking," Stefan said advisedly. "Your mother and I didn't know. She was just starting adolescence. It's a tough time." Now why had he said that? Lisa herself must deal with adolescence; why tell her it's hard? Start her drinking, too? God forbid. "Challenges differ, same way people differ. You haven't had the challenges your sister has because, well, you're Lisa and she's Linda. Adolescence is generally a tough time for girls and boys." Hadn't he just said that, and wished he hadn't? The girl disliked the observation. It was such a pat answer. Adults seemed to have a set of answers they could summon for each question, but they were never satisfactory, never on the mark, always a deflection from the real issue.

"Everything seems to break," Lisa said. "Is that the way it is, until we die, dad?"

"Lisa, good heavens," he almost scolded her, "that is far too bleak an outlook on life from one so young." Stefan reflected he might have expected such pessimism from his other daughter, given circumstances, but not this one. A presentiment seized him. Was Lisa also destined to crumble? This simply could not be allowed to happen. He reminded himself to redouble his vigilance over his younger daughter. It defied his comprehension how neither Debra nor he had picked up on the clues their 12-year-old girl was often drunk. She and a schoolmate had smuggled liquor from their respective homes, initially as a lark, but it had become something else altogether. How could they have missed it? How was this possible?

282

CHAPTER 13

THEIR DIVORCE, WHEN IT HAD COME, HAD BEEN A WRENCHING ONE. Stefan had said, as he was going out the door one workday, he wanted to have a chat that evening. Debra was not particularly alarmed. These portentous announcements only meant he wanted to bring some shortcoming of hers to her attention. He gave his wife a peck, which had pretty much become the sum total of the physical affection now shared by the couple. At the office, a colleague noticed Stefan seemed preoccupied.

"Everything okay?" he asked.

"Yes, sure," Stefan responded. "Why?"

"Seemed like your head was in the clouds."

"No, I'm fine, but thanks for asking." Everything was A-OK, if you did not count the divorce he would be unloading on his wife that evening. Stefan's mind was indeed elsewhere all day long as he fretted over the forthcoming conversation. He felt his wife had no right to be surprised by what he would say, that their marriage had been on the rocks for so long, she knew perfectly well, at this point, he might ask for a divorce. On the other hand, she might not see it coming. Debra's willfulness affected everything she did, why should their looming divorce be different? She will have willfully refused to consider it, he said to himself. This conversation would be a trial. Figuratively, that is. Stefan was very determined they would stay out of court. For one thing, the courtroom would create far more discord and hard feelings. Stefan's practice had only rarely extended to what, in a triumph of euphemism, the profession now called "family law," but in his limited experience, he could not recall a single instance where the parties, no matter how dedicated initially to peacefulness and cooperation, had not dissolved into acrimony and finger-pointing. It just came with the turf, and he and Debra would not be spared. There was another reason to stay out of court. A judge would order sale of their home. Stefan had no intention of allowing this to happen. He was perfectly ready to give Debra the financial aid she would need, but he was keeping the house. Of course, this meant writing her a big check. Stefan was reasonably confident Debra didn't care about the homestead; this was his ace, and he would play it at the right moment.

He pulled into the garage, ruefully remembering a remark one of the partners had made. "Right house, right car, wrong wife." What a trifecta! He had finally surrendered, yet still had not quite dismissed what he felt was a shameless intrusion into his domestic life. It was extortion, wasn't it, to have given him the choice of his career or his marriage?

The table was set for dinner. It always was. The savory smell of a roast in the oven wafted through the kitchen and dining room. Debra was upstairs but had heard him arrive, and came down. They exchanged a peck identical to the one when he had left that morning.

"How did your day go?" she asked. Debra had not forgotten she was in for a serious conversation of some sort, and thought she was ready.

"Something smells good."

"Chuck roast. Potatoes and carrots. Yum."

"Yum is right." Dinner proceeded uneventfully. Each had a glass of wine. After dinner, Stefan said there was something he wished to discuss.

"You mentioned that this morning," Debra said. "I'm all ears." Stefan's heart sank. His wife obviously did not so much as suspect what was coming.

"Let's go upstairs, shall we? Magdalena can handle the clean-up." Well of course she would handle the clean-up; she did every night, didn't she? Misgiving seeped into Debra. Was her husband sick? If so, would he have kept that from her? She doubted this. Was he in love with another woman? She doubted this even more. Was he more than usually upset with her? Over what? As they proceeded upstairs, separation, let alone divorce, had not crossed her mind. Their marriage, it was true, was in the doldrums. What marriage did not find itself in just such straits, from time to time? Perhaps he had secured a month off at the office, and they would be off on that idyll to Tuscany everybody dreams of, and nobody does.

Debra sat at her vanity, in their bedroom, Stefan on a chair. Here goes, he told himself, swallowing very hard.

"Debra, I want a divorce." (Gosh, that wasn't so hard!)

"What?" stammered his wife. "A divorce? You can't mean that, Stefan, for goodness sake."

"I do mean it. Our marriage has become toxic for both of us." This was carefully rehearsed.

"It most certainly has not," she said firmly. "We need to work on getting back the spark, I'll grant you that. Maybe if you were not so busy ..." this wasn't the place for criticism ... "we need to find more time for each other. We need to put each other first, like years ago, when we met."

"That's the point, Debra. It is years ago. Not weeks, not months. Years. Our relationship has been stale for years."

"We are not in a relationship, we are married."

"Very well, our marriage has been stale for years."

"Is stale the same thing as toxic?" Debra said combatively. She was not sure why she had said that at all, but this was unfamiliar territory.

"Stale and toxic. Both. We have to act. We are both still going strong, but that won't last forever. We must free each other to find somebody else."

"No."

"No? No, what?"

"No, we aren't divorcing. We married. We have children. We are staying married."

"I won't be dissuaded, Debra. I have given this a great deal of thought, needless to say, and I believe very strongly this is best for both of us, and for the girls. Do you think our arguments have escaped their notice?"

"If you're serious, I believe we should seek spiritual guidance. Divorce is a sin, Stefan. Do you want to commit a sin?"

"Religion stays out of this." Stefan here strayed from the script, which wasn't smart.

"Very well, let's get marriage counseling. I'll be sure to tell our counselor in advance not under any circumstances to introduce religion."

"Sarcasm won't help."

"Stefan, I suppose I might consider a temporary separation, if nothing else works. This would be a last resort." Debra did not mean a word of this.

"I said I won't be dissuaded. Counseling is useless."

"How do you know this? It's just your opinion. Do you have some evidence for it? Have you done some research?"

"Please, Debra, let's not argue."

"You're the one who's arguing."

This was going nowhere. Stefan looked around their sumptuous bedroom. The scale was majestic. Over 1,200 square feet! Their bed ... enormous ... beyond enormous ... Henry VIII had not had this bed. A button rang the buzzer downstairs, summoning the domestics. Neither used it much. Debra wasn't comfortable with it, and Stefan regarded it as something women use. Help with their toilette, that kind of thing. Stefan required no help, and he wasn't going to have breakfast in bed, either. Too time-consuming. His life was at the office, he could have breakfast in bed on vacation.

Their bedroom was the second biggest space in their home, larger even than the den, itself palatial. Their living room, at 1,900 square feet, was the "show-stopper." The ceiling was 18 feet high, with a dozen beams, each a sequoia. The magnificent fireplace, which was occasionally used, would heat a lodge. Bookshelves lined the south wall and even contained books, not that Stefan or Debra had read them, or even knew what was there. Debra had found a place where books in bulk might be purchased for just such a showy arrangement. Alice Adams and Anna Karenina stood side by side, absorbing dust, neither's fate in any danger of being discovered by the inhabitants of the residence. A spacious picture window faced west, catching the evening sun and basking the entire room in the golden, California light. The sunlight in California had a special glow, Stefan had long ago discovered. Nothing like it back home in Minnesota. It had a wondrous clearness. Unfortunately, the notorious Los Angeles smog often dimmed it.

"Debra, look," Stefan said with as much gentleness as he could, "our divorce does not have to be a contentious, ugly business. There is no reason for us to have a contested divorce. I want to be generous, I see no reason we cannot talk our way through it, as two reasonable adults."

"Are you through?" she said impatiently.

"What does that mean?"

"It means, if you're through talking, then this conversation is over, since I have no intention of agreeing to a divorce." Stefan shook his head in amazement. Didn't she, a lawyer's wife for crying out loud, know her consent wasn't required? Hadn't they known couples who had divorced? Surely this had come out in conversation? It was impossible Debra could be so ignorant.

"Either husband or wife can get a divorce unilaterally, Debra. You know this, don't you?"

"Unilaterally? Is that lawyer-talk?"

"No."

"Are you saying you can divorce me without my agreement?" Debra could not hide the tremor in her voice.

"That's what I'm saying. It's the law." Debra pondered this momentarily.

"Stefan, we made a promise at that altar. Are you reneging on that promise?"

"Marriage is a civil commitment, not a religious one. Plenty of people don't get married in a church."

"But we did, didn't we, and I don't remember your having objected. We made a promise to each other. That promise we recited at that altar together means more to me than whatever the law is."

"Debra, couples grow apart. The legislature doesn't legislate morality. It is a creature of the times. The laws governing divorce are a response to the direction marriage has taken in our society."

"I have no idea what you are talking about, and neither have you."

"I can't say it more plainly."

"Let's see," Debra said. "Do you take this woman to be your lawfully wedded wife, to have and to hold, to love and to cherish, for better for worse, for richer for poorer, in sickness and in health, till death do you part?" Debra amazed herself with her recall, since she thought she had it pretty nearly right. Stefan was not a little amazed himself. "You said that to me, Stefan. I said it to you. I believe the word 'lawfully' is in there. How do you explain that?"

"It sounds nice. Unenforceable."

"Those are stirring words, I think. They stir me. They are glorious, inspired words. Noble words. It is so sad, so very sad, Stefan, you don't understand this. You are educated, you are intelligent, yet this eludes you. How can I make you understand it?"

"You have your marriage vow. I'm sticking with the statutes of the great state of California." Stefan did not like the condescension in his wife's words.

"To be sure, you've worshipped at that altar in a way I haven't at the one you mock."

"Whatever you say."

"I have to have some time to think," Debra said after an interval. "Why are you in such haste? We need to talk, we need to see our pastor, we need to get counseling. What about Linda and Lisa, Stefan? Have you thought about them?"

"Of course I've thought about them. It's outrageous for you to imply otherwise. They will be fine."

"No, they will not be fine. A divorce will destroy this family. I have no career, like you. What am I supposed to do? Starve?"

"I have already told you I intend to be generous. You and the girls can continue living at the same level to which you are accustomed. This is not an issue."

"I need time to think."

"I don't want a fight, Debra." With this, a long silence ensued. No eye contact was made. Debra left the bedroom. Half an hour went by, then another. Stefan kept his composure. He read a magazine he kept on his bedside table. Finally, his wife reappeared. She had been crying and was determined not to resume their conversation until her tears were gone, but no sooner had she begun to speak, they were back.

"You can't do this, my dear husband. I don't know why you are unhappy. You don't even seem unhappy. Mostly, you're not even around. We eat meals together, we go to parties, where we immediately separate, like we were strangers. You work all the time, I appreciate this, we live comfortably, yes we could be more … more …" Debra ran out of inspiration.

"Debra, I will always be here for you. You will never be destitute." He would ignore her tears, if possible.

"What about our daughters?"

"We already discussed them."

"Ohhh, no we did not already discuss them. We're going to, though. Linda is ten. She's so vulnerable. She's not being spared what girls must deal with. Not that you would understand that."

"I wish you would stay away from the sarcasm."

"You're not even here. Do you know how old Lisa is? Do you, Stefan?"

"Well she's seven, now isn't she? Three years younger than Linda."

"That's right, and do you think at seven she can handle the obliteration of our home?"

"What? Is a bomb going to explode? That would be obliteration."

"I don't mean the house, now do I?"

"Linda and Lisa will continue to have two loving parents. Nothing changes. Except maybe for the better. The turmoil in our marriage has been perceived by both Linda and Lisa. It's toxic. I know I said that before, but it bears repeating."

"No wonder you chose to become a lawyer. You are going to destroy our daughters' lives, and you've found a way to turn this into a positive."

"Have no clue what that means. Why don't …"

"Why don't we call it a night?" she interrupted. "Maybe it doesn't take two to have a divorce, but you still need two to have a conversation, and I'm done."

"We'll talk tomorrow," he said conciliatorily. They did not, however, return to the subject the next day, or the next. Stefan could see his wife's mood was volatile. What she might be dreaming up he could only imagine. He figured she was waiting for him to bring up the subject again, then she'd let loose. Let her. However protracted the divorce would turn out to be, he was seeing it through, he was prepared. And it could be protracted. If they found themselves in court, it could take years.

Debra phoned a friend, a lawyer she had once known. Ironically, this was the individual who had invited Debra to the event where she met Stefan. How are you? Long time no talk! How are you? What have you been up to? Gosh, how long has it been? Too long! Debra worked around to the purpose of her call. Did the law indeed permit either party to a marriage to dissolve it without grounds?

The answer?

"Irreconcilable differences," the lawyer said. "Those are the grounds for divorce."

"Irreconcilable differences?" said Debra. "What does that mean?"

"Nothing really, but it's the law."

"What a bad law," Debra said disbelievingly. Good heavens, couldn't "irreconcilable differences" be anything? "You know something," she blurted in frustration, "we both prefer to sit in the same chair in our den—a glider. Is that an irreconcilable difference? Is it? Or how about this: I believe divorce is immoral. I assure you Stefan disagrees." Well now, she had let the cat out of the bag, assuming it had ever been in it. Anyway, what did it matter if Elaine knew the marriage under discussion was hers? Didn't matter in the least. "How about we disagree if there's an Easter Bunny?" Debra said. "Would that qualify?" She was almost gasping for breath.

"Debra, I can tell you're upset, but you're putting yourself through all this for nothing. The law is what it is, laws reflect the times." The attorney spoke with patience. Her practice did not include Family Law, but she knew many family lawyers, and had never heard Debra Kopinski's condemnation from so much as one of them.

"I suppose," Debra said, vaguely remembering her husband had said something akin. She still didn't understand it. "Thank you so much, Elaine," she said.

"I don't think I've been much help."

"Yes, you have."

"All the best, then. Debra."

"Same to you, Elaine."

When Debra and Stefan resumed their chat, the former was prepared. Debra was going to try to talk her husband out of the divorce, first, and if that failed, as she believed it would, she was determined, second, that their divorce contain certain, specific terms and, third, if he was unwilling to agree to those terms she, Debra Kopinski, would hire a lawyer and take her husband to the Supreme Court, if necessary.

Debra wanted to know, conclusively, if there was another woman. Stefan said he had recently met a younger woman, whose name was Sharon, and they had had a couple of evenings together.

"She has her own life. I have mine. We don't have strong feelings for each other, and she has absolutely nothing to do with our splitting up." This was true, and Debra accepted it. Her husband might no longer love her, but he didn't love somebody else. There was a measure of consolation in this. A very small measure. Stefan did not mention Sharon had told him there would not, under any circumstances whatsoever, be the slightest romance between them as long as he was married. Indeed, she had all but said they would not be seeing each other again, under the present arrangement.

"I appreciate your openness," Debra said, "and I believe you. Golly, how have we reached this point, where we must assure each other we don't doubt the other's sincerity?"

"I have never doubted you, Debra."

"Stefan, you intend, I think, to go forward with this divorce. It will destroy our daughters, and I realize I said that before, but it just seems like something you can't say too many times, but it's not too late, it doesn't have to happen. So many bad things do happen, a serious illness, for example, that can't be avoided, but this can, and that's why it is so frustrating I can't get through to you."

"The girls will be fine, Debra. They will still have us, loving them, taking care of them, just not in the same household. But you're right we have been through this before. Let's not again, please."

"So tell me," Debra said, an edge now in her voice, "how does this work, exactly? Do they spend six months with me, and six with you?"

"No, Debra. You will have physical custody, subject to visitation. We will share legal custody."

"And what does all that legal babble mean?"

"It isn't babble. It means they will live with you, but I will have them every other weekend. This is the customary arrangement. We alternate holidays."

"What if I decide to move to … Chicago?"

"Are you planning to move to Chicago?"

"No," she said bitterly.

"We will share legal custody. This means we have an equal say in the fundamental decisions affecting the girls, like their health and their education."

"How perfectly dreadful."

"What do you mean? It's what we're doing now."

"It is not."

"Other couples have faced similar challenges and made it work, and we will, too."

"The challenges are unnecessary. We are creating them."

Stefan's determination to keep the dissolution of their marriage amicable and out of court failed almost at once. Debra was an even-keeled woman, he had told himself. She would be hurt, yes, but she would recover. He failed utterly to reckon on a woman scorned …

"Why do you want the house, dear?" she said acidly. "I'm keeping the girls. Does little old you need all this space?"

"Debra, you don't even like our house. You've said so many times." (This was true.)

"I like it now."

"Be reasonable. You can find yourself a nice condo that will suit you and the girls perfectly. We're going 50/50, so if I keep a major asset, like the house, you in return will get a liberal settlement. You can find yourself a really nice place. You are going to be well-off."

"You can get yourself a really nice place," Debra replied. "On top of everything you're piling on me, I don't need the huge hassle of finding another place to live."

"Let's table the house and discuss other things," Stefan said. He knew Debra was just stirring the pot, she did not want the house. His wife's humor was ugly, and right now she meant to make a dispute of everything. The bitterness of their conversation would be difficult to overstate. Debra's anger seldom abated, producing anger in return. Why had it turned out this way? Her maintenance and child support awards would be generous. This met with ridicule. She said she would not agree to visitation rights for him, she would demand total physical custody. He was walking out on his children, he therefore forfeited subsequent contact.

"You want to have it both ways, don't you dear?" she said. "I'm afraid not."

"You're just being vindictive, Debra."

"You are throwing your family to the wolves, and you accuse me of being vindictive? How hypocritical of you."

"That's at least the twentieth time you have taken something I've said and thrown it back into my face. It's the ruin of our marriage, your defensiveness is, and your character, too."

"Are you finished? Because I have a thing or two to say about your character, dear."

"This conversation is not doing either of us any good," Stefan said. "Let's stop until we can do better."

"Suits me. How will we know when we can do better?" Stefan let the question go. She wanted the last word, fine with him.

CHAPTER 14

D EBRA'S JET LANDED AT PORTLAND. SHE WAS BESIDE HERSELF, WITH
equal measures of joy and apprehension. Sharon had said she would
meet the plane; she had not said if Linda would be along. Surely she
would be! Linda knew her mother was coming, that was no secret. The
plane pulled up at the gate, and Debra's anxiety, already through the roof,
nearly overwhelmed her. She told herself she would not get off the plane,
she would fly right back to California. She'd pay for the return ticket right
there on the jet. She'd ask the stewardess to inform any party who might
be waiting for her she wasn't on the plane. Hmmm ... did that add up?
She could hide! Duck into the restroom. Lock the door.

"Ma'am, is anything wrong?" a stewardess inquired.

"Who, me?" Debra stammered. "No, no nothing's wrong. Just, uh, just
a little nervous."

"Can I help?"

"Thank you, I'll be fine." Must be behaving oddly, for her to have noticed,
Debra mused. Got to get off the plane, somehow. She made her way down
the aisle, each step a tug-of-war against the invisible force pulling her back
into the plane. Here was the terminal! Debra looked frantically at the many
faces, and there, front and center, was the other Mrs. Kopinski. Beaming!

They embraced warmly. Two grown women who, considering the context, could hardly have been candidates for a friendship, and for a long time
they were not friends, but now there was a bond, a sturdy bond. A mutual
admiration. A mutual purpose.

"You didn't bring Linda?" Debra gasped, after they had exchanged
enthusiastic greetings. Debra looked around hopefully. The apprehension

was not gone, but Debra wished desperately to look upon her daughter, and risk a hug, many hugs.

"She planned to come. We've been talking about it for days. At the last second, she got cold feet. Don't be disappointed. She is eager to see you."

"I thought, I thought you said ..." Debra's thought trailed off. She had not concealed her disappointment.

"Now, now," Sharon said, in a tone she used with Linda. Not really appropriate with her mother. "It's going to be wonderful, I know it is," she said reassuringly. "I would not tell you so if I did not mean it." Sharon was reasonably confident she meant it.

"She's afraid," Debra said.

"Linda is a lot of things. Yes, she's afraid, but less afraid. Yes, she's confused, but less confused. Mostly, she's still a kid. She needs dependable, absolute support, and she's getting it." Sharon herself sighed deeply. Her stepdaughter's recovery was going to take dependable, absolute support for the rest of her life.

They went first to Sharon's place, to unload Debra's luggage. Sharon had a spare bedroom, but with Linda coming for the weekend, they were short one bed. A sofa in the living room would suffice. Sharon would take it. It was not all that comfortable, but never mind.

The errand accomplished, they headed for Auburn Hills. Debra furtively swallowed a pill. It was a sedative, she had been taking them for some time, one in the morning, one at bedtime. This was neither, but she followed the regimen scrupulously, and had skipped the tablet that morning. She wished she had a glass of wine and wondered vaguely if drinking wine in the middle of the day would set her upon the calamitous path her daughter had taken. That's why they call them "winos," right? Her daughter, her flesh and blood, was a wino! Debra shuddered at the very word.

"I expect she'll be waiting for us in the lounge. Excited?"

"Thrilled," Debra replied. Yet again she was faint-of-heart, but now she chastised herself. No more of this! No time for weakness! The two women entered the main reception area. Sharon was immediately recognized.

"Linda is in the lounge, Mrs. Kopinski," the receptionist said, smiling broadly. She welcomed the occasion, for it was a happy one in a sea of unhappiness.

"Thanks, Doreen," Sharon said. Down the corridor they went, through the double doors into a genuinely lovely, cheerful lounge with big windows capturing as much of Portland's unreliable sunlight as there was to capture. Linda had chosen a chair facing the door, so she could see them the minute they entered. She was as uncertain of herself as her mother. Should she jump to her feet? Dash over to her mother? Not get up? She got up and waited for her mother, who lurched forward with an indelicate but helpful push from Sharon. They embraced, mother and daughter, mother reluctant to let go. When they did, she cupped her daughter's cheeks in her hands.

"Oh Linda, oh my goodness …" the tears burst forth.

"Mom, don't cry, mom." Linda herself was not going to cry. She had used up her quota of tears for a very long time.

Debra was alarmed by her daughter's appearance. She was thinner. She was pale. Her hair was lackluster. Her eyes were lost in their sockets.

"My goodness, Linda dear," her mother said, "I don't believe they're feeding you very well."

"They're taking good care of me, mom," the girl said.

"I think a little more fat on those bones wouldn't hurt."

"We'll get started on that tonight," said Sharon, who had materialized after having kept her distance. "We're going to a wonderful seafood restaurant I found. Reservation for three at 6:30." It had required some searching, but Sharon had found a place without a liquor license. (The alcohol in her habitation she had placed in a locked cabinet.)

"Sounds like a plan," Linda said. The restaurant was not near the residential treatment center, though Portland was far more compact than Los Angeles; it was not a long way.

Dinner came off without a hitch. Debra reveled in being with her daughter, while at the same time fearing something would go wrong. Something always did. No matter. Enjoy the evening. Enjoy the moment. What possible point was there in worrying over what might happen? If Linda started being abusive, she'd deal with it then.

Back at her residence, Sharon announced she would sleep on the sofa.

"You're the guest, Debra," she said. Oh, no! How could she have called Linda's mother the guest? What a contretemps! Sharon quickly corrected herself, but if Debra was annoyed, she gave no indication.

"I will not take your bed, Sharon."

"I will take the sofa," Linda said. "I have the strong, young back, okay?" The three eyed the sofa with some unanimity it was the worst choice. "Mom, you take the spare bedroom."

"No. I've had a long day, I could sleep on the floor."

"My abode, I get my way," Sharon said. "I take the sofa. Debra, if you don't take my bed, Linda and I are going to pick you up and deposit you there, and lock you in. Right, Linda?" This settled it. Linda actually giggled.

Come morning, the girl's guard was up. This was apparent immediately. Debra kept silent. Breakfast was not festive. Linda was not hostile, but she was not amiable, either. Determined not to allow last night's goodwill to dissolve, Sharon thought to take Linda by the arm, march her outside and state bluntly: "Your mother has come all the way from L.A., she loves you, weren't you happy being with her last night, open your heart, sweetie …" She resisted the impulse.

Sharon brought up the day's itinerary. Linda recollected Saturday mornings at her father's, when she and Lisa were there on visitation weekends. What was discussed? The day's itinerary. What shall we do today? My goodness, it was Saturday morning now! Her sister would be sitting at that breakfast table with dad, discussing the day. Poor sis! Dad probably took her to his office.

Sharon had selected the art museum. Linda had exhibited a measure of talent once upon a time, for painting, though she had not so much as picked up a paint brush in many years; if her hands clasped anything, it was a quart of vodka. Going to the museum suited everyone. It turned out the museum was largely devoted to modern art. Debra did not care for it at all. As they stood before a large canvas that depicted, according to the caption, "Suns Over Sea," but was in fact several wobbly yellow circles at the top of the canvas and a narrow strip of blue at the very bottom, Debra spoke up.

"Unlike you, my gifted daughter," she said, almost risking putting her arm over Linda's shoulders, "I have no ability to paint, yet I do believe I could paint that."

"Then why haven't you?" Linda rejoined. Debra was taken aback. Her daughter's retort was confrontational. Sharon thought so, too. Here it was, the two parents thought, independently. Lasting harmony was a phantom, these occasions were destined to blow up. "Guess that didn't come out quite right," Linda went on. "Not criticizing you, I was only saying it's one thing to say you could paint that, and another to do it." This helped, a little.

"I don't know when I'd have had the time," Debra said. "It would not have occurred to me I was painting."

"That's what is called inspiration," Linda said. The confrontational tone was back. Was the girl determined to belittle her mother? Sharon's mind raced. What if Linda got loud and mean? They'd be asked to leave.

"You are so much more knowledgeable than me, dear," Debra said. "I can only stand before a painting like this and gawk, whereas you bring a more informed viewpoint. Why don't you consider painting again? Those landscapes you drew so long ago, when you were a schoolgirl, were good. Better than that, any day." Debra pointed at the offending painting.

"Maybe I should," said the girl. "Maybe it would help me get sane again."

"You are in no danger of insanity, Linda," her mother said.

"Then what am I doing in that asylum?" Linda said, confrontationally.

"I don't seem to be able to say the right thing," her mother faltered. Ah, here was her mother's defensiveness, rearing its ugly head for the millionth time. Boy I've missed that, the girl reflected. It all came back in a rush. Why couldn't her mother see this weakness in herself? It drove all who met her away. The miracle was her father had tolerated it as long as he had. You could not have a normal conversation with her mother, the defensiveness would emerge, she would dependably get her feelings hurt, interpret something said to her as blaming her, now the victimization role, which she had perfected, this unbreakable pattern, why oh why couldn't her mother see it in herself? Debra announced she wanted to get off her feet for a few minutes, but, "don't worry about me, dear," that's right, you've wounded me, I want to be left alone. The resentment she harbored toward her mother flooded over Linda. She did not say a word. Debra, about to weep, withdrew; once outside, she wept without restraint.

"She just ... just ... started up with her usual blame game, like she always does," Linda said. "I can't stand it!" Sharon responded by leaving the girl and going in search of Debra. She was very displeased with her stepdaughter.

"This wasn't a good idea," Debra told Sharon, sharply. The tears were drying.

"We could go somewhere else."

"I don't mean the museum. I mean coming to Portland."

"Oh, Debra."

"Forgive me, Sharon, I know you meant well, please don't misunderstand. Linda is never going to forgive me. I've got to find a way to accept that. I'm going to get a cab."

"A cab? Where are you going?"

"Home."

"Oh, Debra, you can't do that. We can patch the misunderstanding, we'll smooth it over. What about last night? It was wonderful, no?"

"Not that wonderful."

"Oh, Debra, please. What does abruptly leaving accomplish?"

"What do you want me to do, Sharon?" Debra said harshly. "Go back in there and listen to my estranged daughter find another way to take something I say and hurl it back in my face?" Sharon didn't respond. "I try to understand her hurt, her pain. That's how she got hooked on alcohol, isn't it? Because she was in so much pain."

"She's still a child, Debra. Her life has been horrific for a long, long time. Don't take this wrong, but maybe you expect too much?"

"Do I, Sharon? It's my fault, in other words?"

"I'm not even talking about fault, Debra."

"I have loved that child every moment of her life, as any good mother does. I'm not saying I'm special. I don't expect her to throw her arms around my neck and tell me she loves me. She doesn't even say 'mom' or 'mother' to me, in case you haven't noticed. No, I'm not expecting a lavish display of affection. But it's one thing not to say, 'I love you' and another to look for opportunities to inflict injury. I really don't see why I must keep putting up with that."

"Your clothes, all your things, are at my place. You can't get in. Shall I give you my key? But then you must wait for us. You don't even have a flight. Are you going to sit in the airport for hours? Oh, Debra, this is no good. I had a movie planned for the three of us tonight."

"All right, Sharon," Debra said, relenting. It would be terribly insensitive to Sharon if she aborted the weekend. Linda would just have to put up with her mother a little longer, she told herself with a certain, grim satisfaction.

"Oh, I'm so glad, Debra." They embraced. "Let's go get Linda."

"Maybe she's lecturing somebody else, huh?" Debra said.

"She'd make a fine docent," Sharon said, and they both laughed. Sharon drew a deep breath. The day was saved, the crisis averted. Until the next one.

On their way out of the museum, they ducked into the gift shop. Linda thought if she could find something inexpensive, her mother could take it back to her sister in L.A. Nothing was inexpensive. While Linda browsed, Debra leafed through a book about the museum's collections. She turned to the page where the painting, "Suns Over Sea," was described. "The artist, known only to his copious public as 'Maurice,' typically asks his viewer to think existentially. Why one sea, when there are many, why many suns, when there is one?" Debra chuckled. Talk about inspiration! Here was inspired nonsense! Who took this seriously? Well, the museum took it seriously. The gift shop took it seriously, to the tune of thirty dollars for the book. Maurice's "copious public" took it seriously.

The film was still "on" for the evening. It was good fun, nothing objectionable. They stopped at a coffee shop for a late burger.

"I was thinking about that museum," Linda said. "I don't agree with your opinion, but you're entitled to it." She was looking at her mother, which gave both women a clue whom she intended.

"Thank you, dear. You really didn't have to say that. I'll try to be more open-minded." Her daughter's remark touched her, for it indicated this had been on her conscience. This was, however, precisely as close as they would get to reconciliation. Conversation flagged. The strangeness of the situation took hold. Sitting in a coffee shop at 10:00 at night in a town called Portland in a place called Oregon. The girl, troubled; her mother, heartsick; her stepmother, driven. What had the weekend accomplished? Did it matter if nothing was accomplished? Should each of them evaluate the weekend and give it a pass/fail grade? Should they just let it be?

Back in California, Lisa's visitation weekend with her father would not conclude the following day, as it generally did, since her mother was away.

If his daughters' alternate weekend visits, pursuant to the divorce decree, had produced days of forced gaiety, now, with one daughter absent, the challenge of making the time as fluid and "normal" as possible was even greater. With both girls, they could amuse each other. With one, it was all up to dad. For all his quickness on his feet, his ability to speak persuasively even without a minute's preparation, Stefan hit a wall with his daughter. She was in school, why not ask about that? Did she have a hobby? A boyfriend, maybe? Was she stable and level-headed and smart enough not to step in her sister's footsteps? Ask her mother about that one. What did she aspire to do with her life? No, she was still too young for that question. Would she like to go to a movie? Ask about that, movies were good, movies were dependable. They had yet to come away from a real stinker. For her part, Lisa shrugged off the artificiality of these visits as easily as a duck shakes water off its back. Her sister's disintegration had frightened her. She would not meet the same fate. She would find her own path. Lisa was indeed level-headed. She believed in herself. This, perhaps more than anything else, distinguished her from Linda.

"Don't be so uptight, pop," she occasionally remarked. This invariably produced a smile from her father, who went right on being uptight, however. He was thankful his divorce had not estranged him from his daughters, as it had mother and elder daughter. This baffled Stefan, in truth. Debra had proved a lousy wife, no argument there, but he believed she had always been a good mother. A superior mother. Lisa loved her mother, Linda despised her, or professed to. What explained it? The therapists, and at this point nobody was still keeping count, all had their own ideas, naturally, and maybe they were good ideas, yet Linda's virulent hostility persisted. Stefan was a pragmatist, he did not deal in ideas so much as he dealt in results. His older daughter's unending meanness toward her mother rendered the professionals' explanations, no matter how demonstrable on paper, valueless, as far as he was concerned. A lot of money had gone down a hole. Linda's alcoholism, in a sense, was simpler. She had to quit drinking, permanently. That was the cure, it was the only cure, either it happened or it didn't. Her hatred toward her mother was infinitely more complex. And now, where was she? Some place in Oregon, for God's sake. Another of Sharon's whims. How had she conned him into it? (Same way she always did.)

The remainder of the weekend in Oregon passed without incident, and Monday morning, back in Pasadena, Debra was at Stefan's door at 8:00. Lisa, who did not doubt the love of father, mother and stepmother, was relinquished by the first to the second.

"How was your trip?" Stefan inquired.

"It was all right. Linda was in good spirits, most of the time. I seem to have said a thing or two that upset her, but all in all it went well." This sounded prepared to Stefan, but he felt, correctly, Debra was disinclined to be open with Lisa present.

"I can sit in the car while you talk, if you like," the girl volunteered, as though reading her parents' minds.

"No, dear," her mother said. "Time to go home. I do hope the two of you managed to stay out of trouble."

"We got into as much trouble as we could," Stefan said, "didn't we, Lisa?"

"If you say so, pop."

Debra expected many questions. They were not forthcoming. Lisa was more curious about Oregon than she was her sister, it seemed to her mother.

This was not true, but Lisa had come to accept her sister's recovery would be a lengthy process, with little likelihood for a dramatic breakthrough. She would get well with steady, but small, steps. So it was Oregon she asked about, but not really all that much.

Back in Oregon, Sharon was meeting with a counselor. She wasn't clear on the difference between counselors and mentors. Was Linda really and truly better? The counselor, one Annie Cuthbert, said she wanted to delve deeper into Linda's anger toward her mother.

"Do you know the history of Linda's caustic antagonism toward her natural mother?" she asked Sharon. "Did it precede the divorce with her husband?"

"I have no idea," Sharon said. She was exasperated. "How do you ever know a thing like that? I could have issues with my own mother. We all could. Who's to say?"

"Can't address a problem until you've identified it."

"Forgive me, but Linda is here to be cured of her alcoholism. Before it kills her, for God's sake. Issues with her mother, what's the deal? We're not paying for that."

"Nobody is losing sight of the primary objective," Cuthbert said, "but as I said, what is driving her to drink must be determined. Otherwise, she's really not cured. You can't kill a weed by trimming its branches. You must uproot it."

"Well, I hope this comes out right," Sharon responded, although she didn't care if it came out right or not, "but theoretically you can keep uprooting interesting little clues until you've gone all the way back to Linda's birth. Maybe her mother had a Caesarian? Maybe this traumatized Linda?"

"This process is frustrating," Cuthbert said, keeping her composure in the face of Sharon's mounting impatience. "Progress is fitful, setbacks are inevitable. Don't lose courage. We will win." This sounded to Sharon like a set speech, and she was right. Still, it would be unfair to condemn it on this basis. Rehabilitation was always problematic. Curing alcoholism was a life-long endeavor. Linda would never cease attending Alcoholics Anonymous meetings. No matter the occasion, no matter the temptation, she must never take one swallow of alcohol again. As for her contempt for her mother, this, too, could be addressed only to a certain point, and then it would be up to Linda, to look into her own heart, to decide affirmatively not to continue to hold these feelings. Rehab, finally, was only the starting point.

And the bugaboo? Suicide. It was a devilish business. How does anybody, Sharon was to learn, reach the point where only self-destruction will answer? In a case like Linda's, far from uncommon, the alcohol ceased to be what it initially was, an evanescent escape from the misery in one's life, and became itself a way of life. When you are drunk all the time, you are not drunk at all, Sharon was told. Keeping a bottle of vodka in your refrigerator and pouring yourself a glass at eight in the morning, as Linda had been doing, no longer seems strange, let alone ruinous. A depressant, alcohol leads one deeper and deeper into despondency and hopelessness. Unless this vicious process is arrested, the day must come when the alcoholic quite literally cannot go on. He is gutted, he has neither the physical nor spiritual capacity to continue.

"It's suicide, eventually, whether you deliberately overdose, or succumb to the ravages of alcoholism," Cuthbert informed Sharon. It chilled her to the bone. She had never known an alcoholic. The ladies she ran around with, the crowd to which she and Stefan belonged, lead lives of measure. If anybody was a drunk, he was getting away with it. Sharon seriously doubted it. They were reasonable people, living in life's zone of safety, the middle, far from the poles. They steered clear of the emotional jolts that might upset one's equilibrium, they never allowed an excess of emotion, they didn't cry, they didn't laugh. They ate their vegetables and got a good night's sleep. Sharon unexpectedly remembered a woman she had once known, what was her name ... started with an "A" ... Amy! Amy was always a trifle giddy, not entirely serious, especially about herself. She dressed maybe just a bit suggestively, she flirted with every man in the room, including husbands, but wives were not concerned about Amy's batting her eyelids at their husbands, nobody took Amy seriously. Sharon wondered if Amy had been an alcoholic? What had become of her? She was married, had kids. Had she leaped off some cliff? Short of that act, Sharon found herself, just for an instant, envying Amy.

It was so unfair, and awful, what had befallen her stepdaughter. She was going through hell, and she was faultless! Why was life this way? She was just a girl, how could she possibly handle the torment that had been meted out to her? She could not. She could only suffer.

One day, Linda asked her stepmother what she was doing at Auburn Hills and, without waiting for a reply, answered her own question.

"I get it," she had said. "Two poisons in my life, booze and my mother. She's five thousand miles away, and no one in this joint will give me a drink. What a plan!"

"You are half-right, honey," Sharon answered, ignoring the girl's humor. "Your mother is not a poison in your life. You have chosen to believe that, that doesn't make it so. You can just as easily not believe it."

"You know," Linda said, "you two are such great pals now, or seems like, but you used to hate each other. I remember your fights, you don't? So does my sister. We used to talk about them."

"You've just made my point for me, honey. Do you see?"

"No," Linda pouted.

"You said," her stepmother said with infinite patience, gratified by how the conversation had somehow placed the argument in her lap, "your mother and I used to have fights. I can hardly believe it myself, now, but you are right, Linda. Maybe they were not exactly fights …"

"They were fights."

"Yes, I guess, but let's not lose our way. Your mother and I had fights, now we don't. We have become friends. We decided not to quarrel anymore. We changed. You can change too, honey. You just have to want to. You don't have to keep those hard feelings you have for your mother. You just decide to love her again, as you once did."

"I get your comparison, but how do you get yourself to think a way you don't want to?"

"Honey," Sharon said breathlessly, for hadn't her stepdaughter cracked the door open, ever so slightly, "one of life's realities is that we have to do things we don't want to do. My goodness, I don't have to tell you this. You don't want to be in Auburn Hills. But we can think as we wish. This is what your therapists call "attitude," and they are correct. Nobody can take this away from you. So when negative thoughts toward your mother arise, you tell yourself, I don't have to think this way, I can just as easily decide I am going to think of my mother in a positive, loving way. You might surprise yourself. Haven't you found sometimes, when you had to do something you did not want to do, it wasn't so bad after all? Maybe it even turned out to give you satisfaction? Imagine waking up in the morning, and realizing how much your mother loves you, and then realizing this heavy burden you're carrying, this burden of resenting and blaming her, is one you can be free of, just by doing it!" Sharon stopped there. She was out of inspiration, if she could even call it that. Her stepdaughter, after all, had heard this from her before.

"It's so hard," the girl said, her voice faltering.

The months went by, until, at last, Linda's stay at Auburn Hills had run its course. The facility seldom kept clients longer than six months, because by this time, "Maximum Institutionalization Improvement" ("M-Double I") was reached. The first and most necessary step in getting an alcoholic off the bottle was simply to separate the individual from access to liquor and then, over a period of months, restore the body's health and free it from its toxic dependency on alcohol. This accomplished, there really was not much to be gained by continued residency. Linda would keep seeing a therapist, and imperatively attend meetings of Alcoholics Anonymous.

It was time to go home. Debra had come to Portland. The "red tape" required for releasing Linda was monumental. Debra met with no fewer than five of the members of the professional staff. Assessment of Linda's condition was generally favorable, although Annie Cuthbert felt recidivism was more likely than not to occur.

"No alcohol in your home," Debra was sternly warned.

"I do enjoy a glass of wine, now and then," she said.

"If you must. Keep it under lock and key. Your daughter will know what's in that locked drawer, count on that. You will accidently leave the key where she can get it, it's inevitable. When you are asleep, when you are in the bath, when you are away. She will watch for her opportunity. If she gets her hands on the alcohol, this would be very, very bad."

"So you're saying she's not cured at all?"

"Lead her not into temptation. That is what I am saying." It was Priscilla Skevington speaking. "Make certain she starts going to AA meetings right away. By all means go with her. She has got to stick to this, from now on. This sounds hard, it is hard, especially for a youngster. Returning to drinking is not an option."

There would be no gala farewell that evening for mother, daughter and stepmother. Sharon wanted out of Portland as quickly as possible after Linda's departure from Auburn Hills, and accordingly had booked tickets for the flight to Los Angeles late that afternoon. She had also arranged for Stefan and Lisa to meet their plane.

Linda was in high spirits. Portland was all right, what little of it she had really come to know. Mainly, it wasn't home. Seeing her dad and sister again she was anticipating with relish. Once airborne, the flight attendants began going through the aisle with refreshments. Coffee, tea and soft drinks were available, as well as liquor, for purchase. The attendant reached the row of seats where the women were. Linda, as on the flight to Portland half a year earlier, was in the middle. The bottles of liquor were in plain sight, almost within reach.

"Would you like something to drink?" the stewardess asked Sharon, who was in the aisle seat.

"Coke, please."

"And you, miss?"

"Coke also, thank you." Debra opted for nothing. She wanted the stewardess to be done and out of sight, along with her bar. Debra recalled the warning. Do not place temptation in your daughter's path. Here was temptation. Debra had already made up her mind she would not keep wine under lock and key. There would be no alcohol in the house. But how could she keep all temptation from Linda? There was no earthly way. Her older daughter would be exposed to alcohol every which way she turned. Would she have the strength to stay well? Debra caught her breath, almost audibly. Linda had been such a happy, well-adjusted girl, with the carefree life every child deserves. It had exploded, been blown to smithereens by Stefan's decision to get a divorce. He was the culprit, now and forever, and there he would be at the airport, all smiles.

Greetings, in any case, were enthusiastic, especially between sisters.

"I almost forgot what you look like!" Lisa said jubilantly.

"You did not."

"You look a lot more grown up, actually."

"So do you."

"I thought you were never coming back."

"You wish."

The family of five had dinner at a festive Mexican restaurant, this being Linda's specific request.

"The enchiladas in Portland are vile," she said, making everybody laugh.

"So what did you eat?" Lisa asked.

"Plain old chow, sis, but hardly ever Mexican food."

"I don't imagine Portland has much of a Mexican population," Stefan said.

"I think maybe they have a lot of people from Sweden there, but I'm really not sure," Linda said.

"Sounds reasonable to me," her father said. "Might be some Russians, too. They were in the Northwest at one time. Even here in California."

"They have a few, nice museums and some really great parks," Linda said. "Portland is famous for its roses. They call it The Rose City."

"Rains frequently, though," Sharon said. "Good for the flowers, at least."

"Daddy, how come you never take me to great parks?" Lisa teased.

"Didn't know that's where you wanted to go." Since finding a place to go was the enduring challenge of visitation weekends, a park might have made sense, if the Kopinski's backyard were not as big as one.

"I'd really like to hear some live music," Linda said. "It's been a while." Los Angeles was full of bands.

"Yeah, dad," Lisa said.

"You girls can go through the paper and find a concert, and your step-mom will be happy to take you."

"Awww," from both sisters.

Sharon collared her husband later, when they were alone.

"Linda must start attending AA meetings, immediately."

"I know that. Will it really be different from before?"

"Stefan, I have just spent half a year living out of a hotel room in another city. It hasn't exactly been a picnic. I have had some kind of contact with Linda every single day, even if it was only leaving a message for her at Auburn Hills that I called. Now we are back in L.A. I am not going away. I hope she likes me. I am going to be involved with her ongoing recovery on a daily basis. She has been cold sober for 187 days, by far the longest stretch since she started drinking. Her body is completely rid of the toxicity which had overtaken it. It doesn't need a drink. All we have to do is make sure it never wants one again, either."

"We've been here before, seems to me," Stefan said, not without hope. "What can I do? Was my role a subject of discussion at Auburn Hills?" Sharon hardly knew how to respond. Her husband could begin by paying more attention to his daughter. Love, support, encouragement. How hard was this to understand?

"Linda needs the same thing I have needed, but miraculously have found. A purpose. She must find one. Otherwise, I believe she will slide back into her previous existence. One of the professionals at Auburn Hills practically said this will happen, although the others were more hopeful." Sharon did not include that Annie Cuthbert had said Linda was at a "tipping point" and that if she ever returned to drink, she might be irretrievable. This view, too, was not the consensus.

"How many ... what did you call them ... mentors ... did she have, for God's sake?"

"I know of five, at least," Sharon said. "What difference does it make? Let's get back to finding a purpose for Linda."

"Obviously she must go back to school. She was enrolled at Cal State. Did she actually finish a semester? I can't recall."

"I am pretty sure she didn't. I agree, getting her back in school is paramount."

"Have you talked about this with her?"

"Of course I have. We've talked about everything. A hundred times."

"And?"

"She's confused, Stefan. She agrees one day, and the next, going back to school is the last thing she wants to do."

"She needs staying power."

"Yes, but if you have a purpose, a goal, you acquire staying power."

"I agree with that."

"Stefan, now that I've returned, I intend to get back into the swim. We might start with a romantic evening, what do you say?" Sharon looked at her husband demurely. "But I am making Linda top priority. I don't care what might be on our social calendar, she comes first. If there's an AA meeting the same night as a social occasion, I'm going to the meeting. Things were simpler in Portland, in a way. Linda was my only priority. By golly, we'll move back to Portland, if it takes that." Sharon's determination was beyond any doubt. Stefan perceived that his flippant, dilettantish second wife, who, unlike wife number one, fit so well into the expected mold, had become his older daughter's guardian angel, her best chance to stay well, to survive. Indeed, it would soon become apparent to him Sharon was fundamentally changed. The responsibility she had assumed, and the leadership she had exhibited, were unimpeachable.

"What can I do?" he repeated.

"Come with us to the AA meetings," she said. "Let's play it by ear. I know you've got to put work first, but let's be on the lookout for chances, where maybe we haven't before." Sharon was winging it.

"Fair enough. We could alternate on the AA meetings. You go, I go."

"We both go, the first time for sure. Okay? We aren't just going for support. We're playing cop."

"What about Debra?"

"She's completely in agreement. It remains to be seen if six months at Auburn Hills has altered Linda's relationship with her. I know it was addressed, as part of her treatment."

"Sounds hopeful," Stefan said ineffectually.

"This is going to work, darling," Sharon said reassuringly. "Others face this challenge and succeed, and we shall, too." Sharon sounded to herself like a broken record; she felt she was saying this to everyone. Could it be her real audience was herself?

"Thank you, Sharon," Stefan found himself saying. He did not add, "I love you," but perhaps it was implied.

Lisa, the forgotten daughter, was herself exhibiting signs of discontent, after having stayed on an even keel while her sister was disintegrating. Her therapist, Gail Monrovia, whom she had been seeing faithfully, pursuant to the court order, attributed this to adolescence.

"Lisa," she told Debra, "is basically stable. Indeed, I would call her remarkably so. She has witnessed, from a perspective no one else has, the horrors her sister has endured, and deep down, it has scared her silly. Adolescence is … well, adolescence. We've all been there. I think this is a time to be especially vigilant."

"Ms. Monrovia," Debra said, "I could not be more vigilant. I have been vigilant since the day Lisa was born."

"I wasn't impugning you as a mother," the therapist said.

"Well!" Debra huffed. She said no more.

"As I said," Gail Monrovia continued, nonplussed, "I do believe Lisa will take it in stride. Even so, adolescence isn't childhood. Feelings are exaggerated, and we are vulnerable, in a way we have not been, to huge mood swings. While I have detected no resentment in Lisa over the disproportionate attention her sister has received, you may want to watch this closely. She understands, obviously, why her sister has been favored, if that is the word, but she may nevertheless feel she is second fiddle. So watch for signs."

"I have given her unconditional love every day of her life," Debra said.

"Of course you have, Mrs. Kopinski, I did not mean to imply otherwise." Gail Monrovia had met before with this irritating tendency of Lisa's mother to become defensive on the slightest provocation, or no provocation. She could use a little therapy herself.

"So what should I be on the lookout for?" Debra said, not quite amiably.

"Sullenness, withdrawal, bursts of anger, remarks like, 'It's always Linda, don't I exist?'"

"I can honestly say I have not heard her say that."

"Good. Points to what a good mother you are."

"Thank you."

Lisa, finally, did not grow up too fast, as her sister had, for Linda had been defenseless against the massive encouragement introduced by the divorce. Boys became important, but grades stayed important. She was a scholar, and Lisa would become, when college rolled around, something of a political firebrand, embracing the "feminist" movement, which she gleefully observed shocked her "anachronistic" mother. She was wrong. Her mother, by this time, was shock-proof.

Stefan accompanied Sharon to Linda's first AA meeting, after her return to Pasadena. It was the group to which she had belonged, and several faces were familiar, even after half a year. This was not really surprising. Such meetings tend to have regulars, despite spotty attendance. Whether or not actually articulated, there was a "this is my last chance" aspect to these sessions, which gave them a decided, no-nonsense character. Meetings took place Monday and Thursday evenings; attendance at both was strongly recommended. Most of the attendees were men; Linda was one of only two women in her group, and the other woman was middle-aged. Confidentiality was required, but this had not prevented Linda from mischievously informing her stepmother on one occasion that "another female" in the group said her father was drunk all the time and more or less lived at the bus station, "if you ever want to meet him." A middle-aged man named Joseph was the nearest thing to a confidant for Linda. Joseph was mild in word and manner. He had a bushy beard. He was a machinist, or something like that, Linda wasn't sure. (What was a machinist, exactly?) He had started drinking when he was about Linda's age. He had been an alcoholic for thirty years. He lived alone somewhere, his wife had moved out long ago. He was unemployed, now. Linda figured he must be on welfare. Linda liked him. He was gentle, and he had a sense of humor. He once announced to the assembly he had grown weary of the term "wino" and would thereafter insist he be called a "sommelier." Linda had no clue what the word meant, but when she found out, she laughed to the point of tears.

"My name is Linda, and I'm an alcoholic." Her father took a deep breath. This was sobering, this was what that word was invented for. Here was his very own daughter, making this chilling admission to a roomful of complete strangers. How, conceivably, had this come about? The early years, the girls as toddlers, his wife, whom he had adored, his dream of becoming a litigator. A dream he had realized. Sentimental Stefan was not, but as the recollections flooded over him, as he witnessed his daughter's terrible vulnerability, he was almost overcome. His second wife, sitting impassively beside him, had dedicated herself unsparingly to her stepdaughter's recovery. Stefan reached his arm behind her and rested it upon her shoulder, and they exchanged a glance. This was not the only AA meeting Stefan would attend, but it was the one he would never forget.

"Dad, did you spot any promising new clients at the meeting?" Linda teased him on their way home. They all laughed, but Stefan missed the underlying insight, that his work was his life, not only as far as he was concerned, but everyone.

Linda must return to school. This was the consensus among her three parents. Linda hated school. Most of her memories were of tedious classes. She had discovered they could be rendered less tedious by being inebriated. The next casualty was attendance itself, as she had descended into debauchery. Going back to school amounted to starting over. First term, freshman year. Her friends had scattered. Some of them are probably at AA meetings, too, she reflected grimly. Sharon had considered the risk Linda would take up again with those with whom she had gotten drunk, and she was adamant about not allowing this to happen. She was gratified when she encountered little opposition from Linda.

With her stepmother's assistance, Linda was enrolled again at Cal State. The school had an art department. Sharon and Stefan had grasped the one, slender straw they had, Linda's drawing talent. Maybe it could be revived.

"Contented persons are seldom artists," he observed.

"What are you saying, Stefan?" Sharon said.

"Artists aren't contented. They're tormented. They suffer. Suffering propels one to maturity. Linda's ordeal has given her a window on suffering. This will make her a better artist, if she can be persuaded to go in that direction." Stefan's utterance made little sense to him, and none at all to Sharon.

"Suffering propels one to maturity?" Sharon exclaimed. "Where did you come up with that? Linda has suffered, but she certainly isn't mature."

"Maturer," Stefan said, unsatisfactorily.

Linda received massive support. Her parents, all three of them, closed ranks. Nobody articulated it, but they shared a deep fear their disputes really might have contributed to Linda's disintegration. There would still be disputes, to be sure, but they would be invisible to Linda. She would not slip away from them again. Even Lisa did her part, serving as a "listening post." That Lisa had escaped the scourge that had nearly killed her sister neither Stefan nor Debra nor Sharon could explain, but they were nevertheless deeply grateful. Linda, of course, might have dragged her sister into dissipation. She had had no wish to do so, and was in too much of a stupor most of the time, anyway. What compared with that first, cold shot of vodka, straight out of the refrigerator, first thing in the morning? So sweet, nothing better. Put you on top of the world. Made you clever, insightful, you could take on anything. Linda, like most alcoholics, was nothing at all like drunks depicted in the movies, happy-go-lucky and lovable. The drunker she became, the more sullen and vulgar. Then, inevitably, came the day, when it took a second shot of vodka to accomplish what one had. This was the road to hell. Thankfully, Linda had never had an accident while driving, a minor miracle considering she lived in Los Angeles.

On a date one typical evening, Linda had been drunk when her date arrived. They went to a restaurant which had a beer-and-wine license, but not hard liquor. Linda disliked wine, chiefly because her mother liked it, and beer meant frequent trips to the ladies' room. They ordered beer, and Linda promptly poured half the contents of the bottle onto the tablecloth, before realizing she had missed her glass.

"Oops," she said, with a wink. "Now they'll get a real liquor license." Her date, William by name, did not know she was an alcoholic.

"Are you drunk, Linda?"

"I hope so."

"Do you feel like staying?"

"Sure, I'll eat. What are we having?"

"Pizza. Venezia is a pizza restaurant."

"Well now, that makes sense, doesn't it?"

"A little food would probably do you some good," William observed apprehensively.

"Hey, I'll be fine, guy," she said. "Bring on the pizza." She barely managed one slice. At her door, she was unsteady on her feet. He got her inside and onto the sofa, where it was apparent she was going to pass out. She was helpless, but the thought of taking advantage of her was out of his head as quickly as it had entered. Instead, he took a seat and watched her for twenty minutes. He could see she was going to be all right. She just had to sleep it off. He left.

That was then, and this was now. At the community college, Linda gave up her half-hearted attempts at drawing. She wanted to break fresh ground, to sever every link to the past. No more booze, no more hard feelings toward her mother. Linda could not forgive her mother. Her hostility was diminished, if for no other reason it wasn't worth the effort. Forgiveness was another matter. All those years of church-going, all those lessons in turning the other cheek. So easy to say, so hard to achieve.

Having given up art, Linda decided to become a nurse. This meant years back in the classroom, it meant perseverance. The reward would be self-sufficiency in an ever-expanding field, where jobs were more available than in many disciplines. It was a good choice. It met with enthusiasm from her parents, who were equally pleased by how she had decided it herself. Linda enrolled in the pre-nursing program at the college. Alas, she could not find the motivation. One day her father idly suggested law school, noting women were enrolling in vastly increasing numbers. His servitude to the profession was more than enough to dissuade her here. Lisa was much the better candidate for law. Linda kept at it, though, went to her classes faithfully, but all the while she was searching for something else.

Compounding her lack of motivation, Linda, back in school, was in an environment in which alcohol was inescapable. What college student did not drink beer? Linda began seeing Thomas Minden. The pressure on her was immense.

"A sip of beer won't hurt you," he said. Linda resisted. She took the issue to her stepmother. Sharon was prepared.

"Guess what, my beloved husband?" she said one morning soon thereafter.

"What?" Stefan was wolfing down the last of a stack of pancakes. He didn't much like the sound of "beloved husband." Something was afoot.

"You get to play father, big time." What could his mean? Sharon drew him to her and kissed him affectionately on the cheek.

"I'm playing father now, no?"

"Yes, darling."

"I'm listening," he said when she had not continued.

"Linda has her first boyfriend since her recovery. His name is Tom. She's told me a little about him. He's also a student at the college. He's probably a very decent young man, but he's also a freshman in college." Here she paused. "A lot of drinking goes on."

"No question about it," Stefan said. "Linda knows she is going to be around alcohol. All her life. She knows she can't touch it."

"She's so vulnerable. College is such a drinking environment. It'll never be this bad again, but she must get through this stretch."

"Is there something you think I can do?"

"Darling, Linda has miraculously gotten well."

"Not miraculous, you did it," he said. She appreciated his compliment immensely.

"Stefan, you must speak with her. This is where you can be influential in a way neither Debra nor I can. It's a father-daughter talk." Sharon could be very firm indeed these days, and she was now.

"Maybe so," Stefan said. He wasn't persuaded. "What do you expect me to say?"

"I don't know, darling, but I think you will."

"I'll give it some thought, later. Got to go." She gave him a smooch. Stefan, who won far more often in court than he lost, wondered how he could win the challenge his wife had presented him. What would shelter Linda from the boozy world of college? He could speak with her, certainly, but was there really some brilliant argument she hadn't heard before? The social whirl of college, was she simply to stay home, except for classes? Might as well put her in a convent. He had a notion his older daughter had already pre-empted that. He wasn't going there, for sure ... Anyway, would no social life not encourage a return to solitary drinking? Better to let her face the pressures of Saturday night. Stefan dreaded the conversation. Maybe, he told himself, it wasn't what he said that mattered, so much as his insistence they talk. Maybe that was what Sharon was getting at, when she insisted this was a father-daughter occasion. Stefan vaguely knew he had been something of an absent dad, but he did not doubt he had always, by word and deed, imparted to his daughters he adored them. Maybe a trip with Linda? San Francisco for a weekend? Why not? Stefan looked at his calendar. Packed, as always. Never an idle hour! He relished it. He had known law was for him, as far back as debate class, in high school, at which he had excelled. Now, he was a manifest success. He earned $250,000 a year. No, the San Francisco trip was impossible, unless they could get a flight late Friday afternoon. He broached the idea with Sharon.

"You never take me to San Francisco," she joked. This was not true. They took extravagant trips.

"Be serious."

"What will you do when you get there?"

"Have the big talk."

"I don't know," Sharon said. She thought there was too much drama in the plan, and not enough plan. Wouldn't dinner at some local spot Linda liked make more sense? Sharon expressed her opinion.

"How about I give her the choice?" he said weakly. He didn't know what was best.

"No, don't do that. This is no time to be wishy-washy. You've got to be in command."

"You're right, we won't go north. Plenty of places here."

"Agreed."

In the end, they went to a coffee shop Sunday afternoon. Linda knew to expect something.

"Sharon and I have been a bit concerned," her father said, "about this fellow you're seeing."

"Don't be," Linda said matter-of-factly.

"He's a fine young man, no doubt, but Linda, we're so concerned about your being pressured ..."

"Please don't be, dad," his daughter interrupted. "Tom drinks, of course, I've told you, but I do not. I know I can't, even once. He accepts this, more or less. I haven't been in the sack with him, either, if that's your worry." Stefan actually blushed.

"Well," he said, chuckling, "I'm sure your stepmother will be glad to know that, too."

"I knew this was her idea."

"She loves you and wants what is best for you. The same goes for your dear old dad."

314 ·

"Look, I really, really appreciate your concern, and Sharon's, but you know what, I guess I've kind of surprised myself, but I'm okay. You might as well believe me, because I'm telling you the truth, and if I were back to drinking, no way it would escape Sharon's notice. She knows when I sneeze."

Stefan retreated, encouraged and strongly inclined to believe his daughter in her assertion she was doing all right. When he spoke with his wife, he gave her a full report.

"I do believe she understands this isn't a game anymore," he said. "It's life and death, and if not dying, going back into treatment yet again. Almost think she'd rather die."

"Despite all the drinking she is going to be around, you think we can trust her?"

"Do we have a choice?"

Linda was required to keep a journal. She was on the honor system, however. She did not have to divulge its contents. Her latest entry:

"Big talk with my dad today. Very unusual, two of us, Sunday lunch. Went to Blatt's. Greasy spoon I like. He wanted to take me to dinner at some fancy-pancy place, but no way I was going to sit across a table from him for three hours. Good talk. He's totally worried I'm going back to booze. Not exactly the first time I've written that, huh? Told him not to worry, my boyfriend drinks enough for both of us. Told him we're not sleeping together, but no way this would have bothered him as much as the drinking, if we were. Actually, I appreciated our talk. That he wanted to. He and Sharon are being terrific with me. I'm positive she put him up to it. They love me. That matters a lot. All for now."

For years, Linda had ignored how she looked. Among other things, her hair was unkempt. When you are lying on the bathroom floor, how your hair looks is not on your mind. Gazing into a mirror one day, she had an inspiration. What was to prevent her from going to beauty school? She was never going to finish her studies in nursing. She floated the idea to her stepmother, who was strongly supportive. It seemed an excellent choice. Linda wasn't really suited to a profession.

Getting into beauty school was a matter of paying tuition. Sharon and Linda did a bit of happy searching together. There were numerous possibilities. They visited two schools, both liking the second one better. In short order, Linda was enrolled. Linda would "graduate" in eight weeks, if only she stayed with it. She took to beauty school as a fish takes to water.

315

It was indeed just the thing for her. Sharon was overjoyed. Here not only was her reward in having stood by her stepdaughter through hell, but the focus for Linda she so needed. Purpose would be a strong shield against the temptation to return to drink. Debra, too, was thrilled by the choice, which she termed "God-given." She wondered why she had never thought of it herself. She shared Sharon's confidence it was just right for Linda.

And it was.

CHAPTER 15

M ONDAY MORNING. THE PARTNERS BEGAN THE WEEK AS THEY ALWAYS did, seated around the conference table at Fulton & Shaw. The talk was desultory before they got down to business. Among the topics were new cases, and among them was a suit against one of the firm's top clients, Gordon-Jessup Company, a big insurance firm. Stefan got the case. It was his client, and defending employers sued by aggrieved, former employees was the core of his practice. In this case, the former employee was a man named Mike Huxtable.

"Just another poor stiff who couldn't cut the mustard," Stefan remarked upon being handed the file.

Mike stood impatiently in line, although there was no reason to be impatient, he wasn't late for anything, indeed, had no place to go, and really did not even want to leave the store. His therapist was given to telling him his attitude was everything, that if something annoyed him, it was because he let it annoy him.

"It's all up to you, Mike. A given set of circumstances isn't upsetting per se, it's upsetting because you make it so." Lawrence Dietrich liked to use that phrase, "per se," he used it all the time. "Is life worth living? Not per se. You have to make it worth living, Mike."

A voice barked over the drugstore's PA system. "Help at Register Two. Help at Register Two." Mike found it amusing. Every time he came to McFarland's, there was a line at the cash register, presumably Register One. Inevitably, help was needed at Register Two, or that at least was the way they worded it, since it was really Register One where help was needed, wasn't it? Dutifully, an employee materialized at Register Two until the crisis passed, then with equal dispatch vanished until "Help at Register

Two" sounded again, which would not be long. Why not have someone at both registers? What was that employee doing that was so much more important, even though it could be interrupted constantly, than providing speedy service at the cash registers? Were aggravated customers good for business? Mike laughed under his breath as the pert, youngish clerk took the post at Register Two and announced, "I can help somebody over here."

Mike Huxtable, 41 and adrift, seized greedily these days upon anything that might make him laugh. He had lost his job, unexpectedly, six months ago and, despite every effort, he remained stubbornly unemployed and, indeed, was now wholly without prospects. A development he was keeping from Charlotte, his bride of eleven years and the mother of their two sons, Andrew, 10, and Todd, 7. Charlotte knew, of course, as a wife does. Did he really suppose she didn't notice he was home most of the time, had ceased putting on a suit and going for an interview, did not even bother getting out of bed sometimes, even to see his boys off to school?

"Andrew sees how you've changed, Mike, he's worried, he asks me, 'What's wrong with dad?' He needs reassurance from you as well as from me. Todd is probably picking up on things, too. I think we underestimate children."

"How do you want me to reassure him?" Mike would respond. "Lie? Tell him everything's swell? You just said we underestimate children. How would it be better to deceive him, if he knows he's being deceived?" Now did that make sense? Mike mulled it. Charlotte shook her head in resignation. She had no answer. Maybe there was no answer. At least they were still talking. At least their marriage wasn't becoming shaky, not yet, but wouldn't this inevitably happen if Mike's present circumstances persisted? How did the old saying go? It never rains but it pours.

Just ahead of Mike in the check-out line was an elderly gentleman engaged in a struggle with the case containing his glasses, which obstinately refused to snap open. His hands were the problem. They shook involuntarily, he no longer had complete dominion over them, and today they simply were not going to oblige him. He fumbled the case and it plopped down on the point-of-purchase candy rack, landing squarely, wouldn't you know, on Butterfingers. Hah! Another chance to laugh.

"Could I help you?" Mike said, grabbing the case, which, however, now that he held it, he did not know what to do with. Opening it seemed inappropriate.

318

"Thanks, young man, if you could just pry that contrary thing open, I can take it from there." Mike opened the case and the gentleman reached for his glasses, hands trembling worse than ever. He nevertheless managed to get them on the bridge of his nose and then, painstakingly, over each ear, whereupon he smiled triumphantly at Mike. "Cussed things," he said. "Don't ever get old."

"I'm already old." Mike didn't say it. It wasn't true at McFarland's, to be sure. Mike had noticed on an earlier visit he was literally the only man in the store between 25 and 65, and he had made sure the same was true today, wandering the premises and looking down each aisle. Yup, all the men in town, every last one of them, himself excepted, between 25 and 65 were at work, where they belonged, pursuing purposeful lives, building reputations, fulfilling their responsibilities as breadwinner. "I'm the loser," Mike muttered to himself.

Mike was an insurance salesman. He was with the Gordon-Jessup Company, known to everyone as "GJC," had been for nine years. He was based at the company's branch office in Pasadena; the home office was in San Bernardino, and there was talk of moving into the booming Los Angeles market, but so far it was only talk. The firm dated to 1952 and billed itself as "Your one-stop choice for all your insurance needs in the Inland Empire." Mike felt the slogan was prosaic, but it had brought customers through the door since 1952, hadn't it? He had found his niche in insurance, and thought he had found his niche at GJC, too. He was a "producer," he was dependable, he did his job well and brought enthusiasm to it, he felt his work was important, he was a "team player," he was respected in the community. How could he have been summarily fired one afternoon, after eight years and 344 days of dedicated service? How could this happen? What about his family?

Mike paid for his merchandise, a can of shaving cream, and left McFarland's. He had managed to consume a half hour there, browsing the familiar aisles aimlessly, leafing through the magazines, looking for something, anything, to occupy him. Drugstores once had soda fountains, he remembered. No more. Whose idea was it to get rid of them? McFarland's was a functional, charmless place, but it had become something of a refuge for Mike and it was on the other side of town from where he lived, so there was little risk of encountering one of Charlotte's friends from the "wives' set." They had pretty much been dropped, in any case. It was a narrow little

319

world, and one of the sharpest lines of demarcation was employment. If you didn't have a job, you were out of luck. Not that their friends could be blamed, it was just the way things were.

What now? Mike climbed wearily back into his car and tossed the ignition keys onto the passenger seat, where they bounced once and landed on the floor. Why start the engine? He had absolutely no place to go. Mike draped his arms over the steering wheel and stared blankly out the window. "Ought to have tried shoplifting the shaving cream," he said to himself. "Then I'd get noticed." He chuckled. "Sweetheart, I'm in jail. Come bail me out. Or better still, don't." Now there was a plan. Three square meals a day, and they'd put him to work doing something. License plates, wasn't it? No more humiliation, every day, every single day, no more pretending, no more forced smiles, rejection, failure. It almost made sense.

The Huxtables were getting by, only because Mike's father, in San Diego, was sending them $2,000 each month. It was called an interest-free loan, but everybody knew Lloyd Huxtable would never ask for the money back. One of those little fictions strangely necessary in certain contexts. Like the word the president of the local service club used when he met with Mike. "You're in transition, and there's really no classification, I'm afraid, for that." What the heck was "transition" supposed to mean? In any event, he had not been asked to resign. He was a loyal member of Rotary, an "impact" member active in the life of the club, and he was popular. Mike wasn't too clear on why the conversation with the president had been necessary at all, probably some dumb rule or other, but it had gone all right, and he certainly wasn't going to dwell on it. The matter would resolve itself, eventually, since Rotary, after all, was a businessman's club. Members, accordingly, were expected … to be in business! Not lying around the house all day long. From his brother, John, and his sister, Meg, he had no reasonable expectation of financial assistance, and none was forthcoming. There was plenty of sympathy, for whatever that helped. John was still in San Diego. He fixed computers and was a confirmed bachelor. Meg, the oldest, had married a welder from Houston, where she lived and devoted her entire existence to him and their four children. She rarely came home. Mike shared with her husband, Sonny, a passion for college football, USC and Texas respectively, but this was the limit of their common ground. Mike's mother Beverly, whom everyone called "Bev," devoted her life to her husband and children. Charlotte's dad, Eugene Foster, worked for the Southern Pacific Railroad in Los Angeles. He was a widower. Eugene and Mike had always gotten along well, and Mike was correct in his surmise they need only ask, and they could count on him for help. He wasn't about to ask.

Charlotte did not have a college degree. She had not worked since Andrew was born and had no marketable skill. That she was going to have to do something was beginning to sink in. As for her husband's predicament, she had decided to give it six months, and if he still had not found work, they would talk. It was time for the talk.

Mike retrieved the ignition keys and started the car. To go where? He couldn't bear to return home, having left only 45 minutes ago. He had deliberately skipped breakfast that morning so he could go to Madge's for one of their terrific Belgian waffles with pecans and whipped cream, not that spending ten dollars on breakfast made sense. He had resisted the football magazine at McFarland's, he should do the same with the waffle. He drove in the direction of Madge's, irresolute, knowing he could turn on Rhime Drive, or at 22nd Street, and be pointed homeward. He turned at 22nd, drove around the block, putting him back on Hayes, and proceeded sans indecision to the coffee shop. He bought a *Los Angeles Times* – what was another fifty cents? – and went inside.

Mike simply could not understand what had happened to him. His therapist posited that he had been unhappy at work, and thus brought on his discharge, however unwittingly.

"I've seen this many times, Mike," Dietrich said. "We sabotage ourselves."

"I wasn't unhappy, Larry," Mike responded. "Just the opposite. You weren't there, watching me each day, for nine years. Who stays on a job for nine years, if he's unhappy?"

"Plenty of people," Dietrich said. He wasn't backing down. Mike's situation was far from uncommon. The telltale signs were there, not least among them Mike's total refusal to utter a single word of praise for a certain colleague. Mike was unaware of this pattern. Lawrence Dietrich was gradually piecing together the nature of Mike's relationship with Randall Galloway. He felt there was blame all around, but when, if ever, Mike would be willing to accept this, was the question.

Mike had his Belgian waffle with pecans and whipped cream, washed down with three leisure cups of coffee, and although there was no inspiration in the newspaper, it was an otherwise satisfactory way to pass an hour.

Arrangements were made. Charlotte's sister, Cheryl, would come for Todd at 5:00; it would be up to Charlotte to come pick him up at 9:00. Andrew was having an overnight at a friend's. Charlotte had prepared halibut, with French-style green beans, mashed potatoes and apple cobbler a la mode. She had decided against candles, since that sent the wrong message; romance was the last thing on the evening's agenda. They were going to discuss Mike's future, if it killed them. Charlotte didn't anticipate unpleasantness, but if it happened, so be it. They had agreed to have this conversation, although neither had dreamed half a year ago it would come to pass. Charlotte's vague misgiving over a possible argument was misplaced. Mike felt equally strongly it was time to talk – and act. They didn't wait to finish dinner to embark. Mike produced a sheet of paper upon which he had listed the options available to them. Charlotte was immediately encouraged.

The first option was to hold to the status quo. They almost laughed over this. They were having this conversation because the status quo had become untenable, weren't they?

"Still, it's an option," Mike said unseriously.

The second option was for Mike to take temporary work of some sort, almost anything, while he continued searching for a position in his field. This suddenly made so much sense, Charlotte couldn't fathom why he hadn't done this all along. Well, because they had figured he'd get another position in no time, yes, that explained it.

"Problem is," he said, "these jobs tend to require no training or experience, pay badly and don't generally attract people at my station in life. I'd almost rather starve." Mike had not mentioned he actually had received an offer; it was for part-time work, not in his field and with no prospect of advancement, and it paid less than what he was getting from the state. The unemployment checks were done, now, too, making their conversation all the more imperative.

"It isn't a question of just you starving," Charlotte said, not unkindly. She rubbed his arm. "Mike, shall we all starve? I'm not asking you to flip hamburgers, but you've got to recognize you may have to settle for something really odious. It wouldn't be forever." Unless it was.

"I know that, I do, I understand that. I've been giving some thought to the medical field, but I'm really jumping ahead of myself here to the next option, the fourth."

"Medical field?"

"Yes. Obviously I wouldn't be a doctor, but there are jobs in medicine. Medical technicians, for example. It's a growing industry. Only thing I guess I'd rule out is nurse, you know, never could go for that." Charlotte didn't inquire why nursing was off the list, since she knew. Not even complete ruin could get Mike to give up that prejudice, and there was no use saying a word about it.

"You'd have to go back to school?"

"Yes. That's why I consider this option four. Basically, it means switching careers. Starting over."

"How many more years in school?"

"Two. At least."

"How could we afford it?"

"We'd have to get a loan. Believe it or not, I'm pretty confident I could, Charlotte. I've spoken, informally at this point, with Javier Rodriguez, he's in the Rotary Club, you've met him, he's a good guy, he knows I'm, well, a good guy, too, we've golfed, I really think I could get a loan. Even though he's not even at our bank. It would be better, needless to say, if he were. Guess I could move our money, before it's all gone."

"So we'd fall into further debt, is that prudent?"

"We're not in debt," Mike said reassuringly.

"Thank goodness," Charlotte responded, just averting a *faux pas*. She knew perfectly well her father-in-law wasn't expecting them to re-pay him.

"It's a risk, sure," Mike said, "if I finished school and couldn't get a position. I think it's unlikely. Might even be a real advantage to have reached my middle years, life experience, you know, and as I said, it's a rapidly expanding field."

"Could you get into school right away, or would there be a long wait, or some requirements you don't have?"

"Haven't looked into that carefully yet, but I'm pretty sure these technical, vocational colleges have relatively few entrance requirements."

"That actually sounds good, Mike, really promising." Charlotte tried her best to sound positive, but a sigh escaped anyway. "What was option three, since we skipped it?"

"Option three is for me to open my own business," Mike said, failing to conceal completely the note of doubt in his voice. Charlotte, having nearly made one mistake, brought all her tact to the table, wholly unnecessary, since Mike shared her secret view, which neither would ever express, that

323

he just wasn't cut out to be the boss. Mike was the classic number two. He excelled in this role, and would not in the other.

"Wouldn't opening your own business require a lot of money?" Charlotte said by way of suggesting she had some qualms about this choice.

"Well, yes, but remember, Javier is good for a loan." Unless he wasn't.

"Okay, great," Charlotte said unpersuasively. She fought for composure. "This is progress, darling! What's next?"

"Two more options. Fifth, we get out of California and start over somewhere."

"Doing what, Mike? Where?"

"Well, I'm not really very serious about this, am I, but it is something we could do, no matter how impractical." Fact was, Mike had idly thought how pleasing a really fresh start might be, but he recognized it wasn't sensible.

"So we'd find ourselves in some hole, like Phoenix, not knowing a soul, no family? Definitely not a good option, that one." Charlotte had said this disapprovingly. "What's next?" Next was last.

"Lawsuit," Mike said.

"Lawsuit? What does that mean?"

"I sue GJC."

"That would cost a fortune, Mike, and what makes you think you would win?" Charlotte's tact was out the window.

"I'm presenting options. I got the name of a lawyer over in South Pasadena who apparently doesn't charge for the first meeting. He represents people in circumstances like mine. I could meet with him just to see if he thinks I have a case, couldn't I?" Charlotte shook her head in despair. Her husband's situation was hopeless. She was near tears.

"Don't cry, sweetheart," he said, "it's going to work out for us, believe me." He took her into his arms. "I promise you we're going to get through this, we absolutely are."

Mike had made up his mind to speak with Felix Webb, whether Charlotte approved or not. He had no real expectation it would lead to anything. Indeed, he had virtually settled upon option four, the loan from Javier Rodriguez to finance a return to the classroom, culminating in a great new career in medical technology. Nonetheless, he would chat with Felix Webb, Esq.

Another day, another excursion to McFarland's. Mike considered the soap situation. There were exactly a dozen choices, each trumpeting its

324

superiority. How much difference can there be in soap? Shampoo guaranteed to control dandruff. Right. If it did that, there'd be no more shampoo. Probably gives you dandruff, Mike muttered. He reflected what it would be like for someone from an impoverished land suddenly to be plopped down amid this crazy abundance. He'd think he was on another planet. In a real sense, he would be. The prices were amusing. Every item $8.99, or $20.99, or $5.99, or $14.99. Hadn't he read the government was planning to phase out pennies? Disaster for merchants! Who's going to spend nine bucks for shampoo when it used to be $8.99? "Stop the anti-penny crusade! Cents make sense!" Now there was a winning slogan, and it had just popped into his head. A young woman materialized and got in Mike's way. What, was she a real customer, planning on a purchase? Mike reminded himself others in the store might actually be there for a purpose. Not merely "others." Everyone. Everyone was at McFarland's for an express and specific purpose, except him. Mike Huxtable was expressly, specifically purposeless. "Everyone understand that?" Oops, he had nearly said it out loud. The woman made her selection and flashed him a smile. Had she lingered with that eye contact? No doubt about it. What girl didn't dream of a passionate tryst with an unemployed drifter? And talk about romance! Who needs a chance encounter in Venice when you can meet at McFarland's, where it's neon-bright and the janitor has cordoned off a section in order to mop the linoleum? Mike discovered it was time to get out of McFarland's and wasted no time in doing so. He'd be back.

He was back, and back and back and back. What had begun as an occasional excursion was practically a daily one now, at least Monday through Friday. The place was no longer a drug store for Mike, it was his sanctuary. He didn't need a cabin in the woods. McFarland's served admirably. Inevitably, he was approached one morning.

"Sir?" Mike was addressed. The man introduced himself. Marcus Fields, floor manager. Marcus was a young man. He was not impressive in manner or appearance. In particular, the tie he wore, a slender, black one, was both wrinkled and had a spot on it, and, Mike reflected, would best be removed at once, if the man had any gumption about how he looked.

"We've sort of noticed," Marcus said haltingly, "you're here a lot, if you don't mind my saying so, and you never really buy much of anything, and you're just kind of wandering up and down the aisles all the time, and other customers have noticed, you know, and asked who's that guy, you know, and I'm not saying obviously you're bothering anybody don't get me wrong, but this is a business, you know ..."

"Look," Mike interrupted, since the floor manager was plainly incapable of finishing the thought. "I, I," Mike faltered. "I just need, I just need a place to go. For the moment. I'm looking for work, I was in the insurance business, and I haven't been able to find a job, but I'm looking, okay, you might not think so since I'm here so much but I am, and I just sort of fell into the habit of stopping in here, can't even explain it really, but if I'm driving off customers, and I do sometimes make a purchase myself, but if I'm driving off customers, I'll quit coming, but I'm not really doing that am I, that's hard to believe."

"You're not driving off customers," Marcus Fields said with unmistakable sympathy. Gosh, could anything be more pitiful than a man reduced to poking aimlessly around a dreary store in search of some undefined comfort? "Just felt like we should talk. Mind if I ask your name?"

"Mike Huxtable."

"Look, Mr. Huxtable, I hope you find what you're looking for." The floor manager didn't realize the double meaning in his remark. They shook hands. Marcus Fields, a good ten years younger than Mike, would relay the substance of their conversation to Mr. Brice T. Howells, whose idea it had been in the first place to confront the mystery man whose countenance dominated the security cameras. Marcus Fields had not wanted to be sent on the errand at all.

Meanwhile, Mike was a bit shaken by the conversation. Had he told that earnest young man his name, his occupation, his plight? Mike steered clear of McFarland's, but only for a few days.

Another destination was the post office. Here, again, Mike had been obliged to find a location other than the convenient one blocks from where they lived, since it was all-too-likely he would run into someone from their former crowd. One day, he had. It was Alicia Minster. Alicia and her husband owned a chain of supermarkets, and were fabulously successful. They had two children, or was it three? Alicia had plenty of those sparkling minerals on her person, even on a trip to the post office.

"We understand you're in transition, Mike," she said. Was that the royal "we," perhaps? Alicia was pretty regal all right. It was almost funny, this ridiculous euphemism, this code word current in business circles and apparently fashionable now with wives, as well. Couldn't they get "unem-

ployed" out of their mouth? "How are things going? How are Charlotte
and the boys?"

"They're well, thanks. Thanks for asking, Alicia." He wasn't fooling her.
Alicia was, in fact, irked with herself for having embarrassed him, however
unintentionally. But what else was there to say? What did it matter, in any
case? Their ticket into the social circle was his job. The longer they didn't
have a ticket, the more remote the circle became. The day would come (and
did) when he'd meet Alicia Minster, and there would not be so much as
a nod of greeting.

At this post office, Mike would not run into Alicia or any of them. He
was miles from home. The postal clerks, on the other hand, recognized
him when he came in. More envelopes, more and more, but more had
become less as time went by, as places to send a resume became fewer.
Mike figured the clerks knew he was mailing resumes, the envelopes were
always the same, addressed to businesses across the Los Angeles basin, and
anyway, what was a man in his prime doing at the post office at 10:00 in
the morning, if he had a job?

Then came the day, as the hopelessness of her husband's situation deep-
ened, when Charlotte, returning from a part-time job she had procured,
sons with her, was met with a note on the kitchen counter. "Back later."
Charlotte was frantic instantly.

"What's for supper, mom?" Andrew asked.

"I'll fix something in a minute."

"I want spaghetti."

"All right then, spaghetti it is." Charlotte was glad for the suggestion,
since her mind was elsewhere. The phone rang. Mike.

"Hi sweetheart, I'm in Hollywood."

"Hollywood, Mike? What are you doing there? Did you have an interview?" This she very much doubted, but one could hope.

"Not really. Just drove over for the heck of it. Long time no see."

"It's after six, Mike. Aren't you coming home?" Though worried,
Charlotte had not been completely successful hiding the impatience in her
voice. She thought her husband sounded inebriated.

"Not sure that's a good idea, 'cuz I'm a little woozy. Had a couple of
drinks." It was more than a couple, much more.

"Oh, Mike, how could you, how could you do this?" Now the impatience was at the forefront. "How are we going to make it when you pull a stunt like this?"

"It's not a stunt," Mike snapped back. "I think you'd be pleased I have the good sense not to drive."

"So where are you? At a pay phone?"

"No, I got a room. I'm in a motel. Everything's fine."

"Nothing is fine, Mike. I'm coming to get you."

"Are you crazy? It's an hour's drive, both ways. What about the boys? That's just dumb, Charlotte."

"You're who's dumb, Mike." She was sorry at once she had said that. "I am sorry. I don't mean that, Mike. I am just so worried about you. I don't care if it takes an hour. I'll see if Irene can watch the boys, if not, I'll bring them with me."

"It will be nine o'clock before we get home. Assuming you can find me. Assuming you don't have an accident, or something worse happens. You're always saying not to compound things, yet that's what coming for me is."

"Mike, going off to Hollywood and getting drunk is compounding things."

"Be sensible, Charlotte," Mike said, followed by an inspiration: "One of us has to be."

"Mike, listen to me for a minute, would you? I want you to come home because your sleeping off a binge in a motel room in Hollywood is another step away from the normal life we had. It's another step away from Andrew and Todd. It's another step from your ever getting back on your feet. Please, Mike, this isn't a prepared speech, it's seat of the pants, but you have got to come home now, and that's all there is to it. You've had the sense to understand you can't drive, thank God. I'm coming for you, no further discussion."

"You don't know where I am," Mike observed dryly.

"Fine, I'll go to every motel on Hollywood Boulevard till I find you."

"Who said I'm on Hollywood Boulevard?" That did it. Charlotte burst into tears, which did not foreclose his next inspiration: "Who said I'm alone?"

"You know something, Mike?" Charlotte blubbered. "I don't care. Sleep it off. Come back when you feel like it. If that's tomorrow, fine. If it's never, that's fine, too." She did not mean that, and Mike certainly knew it.

"I'll come back tomorrow, sweetheart. Promise."

"I love you."

Remorseful, Mike decided to get some sleep. No pajamas, no toothbrush, but those things didn't matter. His night was far from over, however. Nausea swept over him as soon as he lay down. The room was spinning. Still, he tried to get to sleep, closing his eyes, ignoring the symptoms. He said a short prayer, and sleep did come, until a loud noise outside his window put an end to it. It had sounded like a car crash, but he wasn't sure. In any case, he was awake again, and he felt he could not fight his way back to sleep, so he rose, threw some water in his face, slipped into his clothing and went outside. He was mildly curious about the noise, and thought maybe a bit of fresh air would do him good. Then, he could return to his room and get back to sleep. He still wasn't sure he wasn't going to throw up, but if he did, he would not be the first to have done so on Hollywood Boulevard. It was one in the morning, and the street was populated. Traffic was heavy, but when wasn't it in L.A.? What surprised him was the quantity of pedestrian traffic. Mike passed a man in a suit, then a second. Funny time for a suit. Two young men, neither in a suit and one without a shirt, were pushing each other, harmlessly. Four, no, five, more young men, college boys, drunk and boisterous. Much profanity. A young woman, none-too-clothed, gave him an inviting look as he walked by. Next thing he knew, she was walking beside him, and had slipped her arm in his.

"Looking for a date, cowboy?" she said.

"A date? I don't think so." What, were they going to a movie? Mike strode purposefully forward, despite her clinging to him. After a brief interval, she fell away. Unexpectedly, he came upon a parking lot which, wondrously, he recognized as the one where he had parked. It seemed a long time ago.

"Damn," Mike said to himself. "I'm going home right now. I can drive, I can go slow." Mike fished into his pocket for his car keys. Not there! He tried the other pocket, knowing perfectly well he never put them there; he kept his wallet there. No wallet! It was gone, too! I've been robbed, he told himself. But when, how? That girl! No, she hadn't touched him. Yes, she had! She had taken him by the arm! Mike was in a panic. He headed back down the street, walking fast. Where was the girl? He reached the spot where he thought she might have been. Long gone! Mike tried to gather his wits. "I'll go back to my car, I'll be there when she shows up," he told himself, "if she hasn't already got it." He started back down the sidewalk, toward the parking lot, but somehow remembered his car keys did not identify the car. It was safe, if he stayed away from it! Just the opposite of what he was doing! Got to think clearly. What she had was his wallet, his money, his credit cards, his driver's license, his address, his house key. She knew where he lived! Got to call Charlotte! Mike fairly ran back to his motel room, but he couldn't get in. That key was gone, too! She had taken everything! How was it possible he hadn't realized it? Catching his breath, he went to the lobby and, as calmly as possible, told the clerk he had misplaced his room key. The clerk obligingly gave him another, hardly noticing Mike was disheveled and smelled like a distillery. Mike got to his room, grabbed the phone and began frantically dialing Charlotte when he saw keys and wallet were right there, next to the phone. He hung up before the call went through and collapsed in relief on the bed, overwrought and almost tearful. He was safe, his family was safe, the car was where he had left it, nothing was irretrievable. He did not know it at the time, but this misadventure had frightened him badly. It would not be repeated, and his homecoming the next morning was joyous, to say the least. Charlotte asked no questions.

Mike made an appointment with Felix Webb, after confirming the first half hour, as advertised, was free.

"The thing is, Mr. Huxtable," Felix Webb said patiently after some minutes had been devoted to getting acquainted, "we have to have something to hang our hat on. I can't stand up in front of the jury and say you were fired because of your age, with no evidence to support the claim. Evidence is crucial."

Mike was frustrated. Hadn't he already told Felix Webb age had nothing to do with his losing his job? How could he have put it more plainly? "It wasn't my age. Age had nothing to do with it. I got a new supervisor, who hated my guts. That's the reason."

"That is not actionable, I'm afraid, Mr. Huxtable," Felix responded. So why were they discussing it again? "Are you very certain nobody ever said anything age-related? Something about your being an old guy, old coot, old snot, old snoot, old sport, greybeard, set in your ways, over-the-hill, tired, need new blood, no energy, no new thinking, no drive, no enthusiasm, no ambition ..." Felix might have sounded like he was rambling, but he was not; he was throwing out words carefully chosen, to see if a single one might trigger a recollection in Mike's mind. He went through the litany slowly.

"I'm not an old guy, Mr. Webb. I'm 41. Why would anyone call me old?"

"That's old, as far as the law is concerned, and that's what matters. Isn't that why you decided to consult with a lawyer in the first place?"

"Yes, but we can't just make something up." Felix Webb did not answer immediately. Of course they could make something up, provided a jury could be persuaded to believe it. Mike had been replaced by a young, single woman. This helped their case, but not enough.

"My age isn't implicated, if a remark or gesture that could be interpreted as age-related is required," Mike said decisively. The meeting obviously was coming to nothing. It was demoralizing to be told the law offered no recourse, but Mike was so demoralized already, this was not a big deal. "I'm on my own," he told himself, by no means for the first time.

"Firing you and hiring a young woman is something," the lawyer said. "We haven't touched on reverse discrimination, but there could be something there." The attorney wasn't going to explore this without starting the meter.

"Reverse discrimination?" Mike said. "What's that?" Legal doubletalk, no doubt.

"Well, it's a possible claim, but I regret we are running out of time. If you would like to continue with our discussion, it will be necessary to make another appointment." Felix Webb said nothing about his fee, knowing Mike Huxtable would understand his meaning.

"Of course," he said. Both men rose, and Felix Webb extended his hand.

"Best wishes, Mike, if I don't see you again," the lawyer said cordially, using his first name for the first and only time.

"Thanks, thanks much," Mike said. He was out the door, out of the building and, consulting his watch, discovered 29 minutes had elapsed since he went in. The attorney had this down to a fine art.

Mike had no place to go. He decided to drive. He had taken to doing this, and Los Angeles was perfect for it. There was that excursion along the coast, one day, from Malibu to Palos Verdes. He had had a really good cheeseburger, with bacon and chili, at that place in Manhattan Beach, what was it called? He'd been east to Palm Springs, where nothing would have been affordable, even if he were not out of work. He'd gone down to San Juan Capistrano once to see if he remembered it from his boyhood, having grown up in nearby San Diego. It wasn't familiar, but still kind of thrilling. Nobody could explain the swallows. Today, he elected to drive the length of Wilshire, from downtown to the ocean. He'd find a coffee shop in Santa Monica for a late lunch and take the freeways back to Pasadena. Yes, this would consume the day nicely. As he drove, he reflected on the meeting with Felix Webb. The attorney, naturally, had wanted the facts.

"Don't leave a thing out, no matter how trivial it might seem," the attorney had said. Mike had focused on the days leading up to his dismissal, and said relatively little of his tenure at GJC. Had he emphasized the antipathy of his new supervisor, Randall Galloway, who was solely responsible? Yes, he was confident he had. For Mike Huxtable was absolutely convinced this, and this alone, explained his fate. How had the two of them gotten off on the wrong foot? Mike prided himself on his skill at getting along with everybody. You had to be a "people person" in the insurance business, and he was, undeniably. When it had become apparent Randall was giving him the cold shoulder, Mike wracked his brains for an explanation. Had he said something? Done something? Should he just come right out with it, with Randall?

"I think you're imagining this, Mike," said Harv Tobiason, a trusted colleague he had decided to speak with. "Randall is capable and fair-minded, and he's been around the block. What purpose would a vendetta against you serve? He's only been here a short time, you hardly even know each other. Why don't you go grab a beer somewhere? Talk sports and women. Can't go wrong there."

"I beg to differ. I think we could go very wrong."

"Wronger than you are now?"

"Just can't see it, Harv."

"Okay, then. Every office has its personality issues. You can't let it affect your work." Now what did Harv mean by that? Was this a lecture? Perfectly asinine to say a thing like that to him. Nevertheless, a day or so later, Mike approached his new supervisor and suggested a beer.

"No can do, Mikey. Got tickets to Lakers-Celtics. Not even an earthquake could keep me away." Randall grinned. "Mikey!" The condescension was unmistakable. Hadn't he asked not to be addressed that way? Yes! Proof Randall didn't respect him and wasn't a colleague or friend. Of course, Mike wasn't the only one for whom Randall had a demeaning nickname. "Mikey," for that matter, was pretty tame. (Mike had mentioned this to Felix Webb, who asked if this nickname had anything to do with age.)

Envy. Dishonesty. Spite. Mike Huxtable had his vices, but not envy, not dishonesty, not spite, and he could not deal with them in others. It was not just a matter of their defeating him, he could not accept how someone ostensibly a friend could act that way at all. A bitter experience long ago, when he was a Boy Scout, had left an indelible mark. Mike's father was a Scout and had remained involved in Scouting all his life. On the back of his business card he had printed the twelve traits of a Boy Scout. He was understandably determined that his son become a Scout, and among his most cherished photographs in the family album was one of Mike, flanked by his beaming parents, in his uniform, wearing his merit badge sash. Mike, like his father, had made it to the top, Eagle Scout. It had been more of a struggle for the boy, who had stopped at the minimum, twenty-one merit badges, while his father had earned thirty. As an adult, Mike had dropped Scouting. An incident, when he was 14, had soured him on it forever. His troop was on a week-long camping trip. Unluckily, he had drawn Richie Culverson as his tent-mate. The two had gone to school together always and never gotten along. During the course of the camping trip, Richie had found an opportunity to remove $10 from the pocket of Mike's trousers. Reasonably certain, when he discovered the theft, that Richie was the culprit, Mike had gone to the scoutmaster, who comforted him as best he could but noted he could not accuse Richie without proof, and anyhow, a good Scout wouldn't do such a thing, so Mike, could you be mistaken? Nope. Mike knew darn well he wasn't mistaken.

"My mom gave me that ten dollars just before I left for camp," he said tearfully. "I was saving it for the last day. Richie took it. He took it!"

The troop went into town the last night of camp for a gala supper and awards ceremony, and Mike, not having mustered the resolve to confront Richie in the privacy of their tent, faced him. This was his last chance.

"You took my ten dollars, didn't you, Richie?" They were standing in line at the side of the stage, where the awards were being presented. Everyone was getting at least one.

"What are you talking about?" Richie responded angrily.

"My ten bucks. It was in my blue pants. You took it when I wasn't in our tent, didn't you? I know you did, Richie." Mike was indignant.

"I didn't. You're a liar, Mike."

"You are. You're some Scout, Richie. Lying and stealing. Give me my money back."

"Hey, watch it there, Mike. I might have to punch you." This really wasn't the place for a tussle, but they began shoving each other. This was noticed. "Mike Huxtable" was called from the podium.

"It's on your conscience," he said to Richie, as he went forward to accept his award.

Mike was correct Richie had taken the ten dollars. He was wrong his conscience would suffer.

As the family's resources dwindled, Charlotte Huxtable discovered the world of discounts and bargains and sales extended well beyond grocery story coupons. It took some hunting, which was becoming an obsession, but it was worth it: Five dollars off any full service car wash priced at $15.95 or more (they would wash their cars themselves); $2 off any medium pizza, $3 if it's a large pizza (eating at restaurants was out, indefinitely); professional maid service, $4 discount for first cleaning, with coupon (Charlotte could keep their home spotless, thank you); professional rug cleaning, guaranteed to remove all odors, including those of pets, $10 off with coupon (ditto); 10% off any purchase of four new tires, limited time offer (always a limited time); new roof, save as much as $1,000 (roof was okay, but boys had to stay off it); $5 off your next dry cleaning, valid until 4/5 (clothes would be washed, dried, pressed, mended, and given all other necessary care at home, thank you); backyard play sets, save $25 on installation (school playground equipment would suffice); spiffy up your home with new blinds featuring cordless lift system, up to $300 off (their windows had curtains, not blinds, thank you); cigars and pipes, $3 off any purchase of $30 or more, offer expires 10/6 (no smokers at the Huxtable residence); deluxe buffet at China Gardens, $2 off any adult dinner, limited time offer (no eating out, indefinitely, remember?); deluxe manicure, $5 off with coupon, acrylic file, $3 off with coupon, offer expires Saturday (Charlotte kept her nails impeccably); bathtub refinishing, $20 off with coupon, offer expires 1/31 (what was bathtub refinishing?); lawn mowing, 10% off with coupon, "Make your home the talk of your neighborhood" (three men in the Huxtable family, they'd keep their home the talk of the neighborhood); face lift, $4,000 value, up to $250 off, valid until 11/15 (Charlotte liked how she looked, and would so continue, even in the highly unlikely event she ever had $3,750 for a face lift); "We purchase jewelry, gold, silver, platinum, up to 5% off with coupon, offer ends soon" (Charlotte would hold on to her wedding ring if and until they were actually without food). This but a smattering. Groceries remained the primary focus: Ground beef, 80% lean, sold in package of 2 lbs. or more, $2.69 per pound; ribeye, bone in, $6.29 per pound; fresh Atlantic salmon fillet, $6.89 per pound; boneless chicken breasts, $3.89 per pound; red seedless grapes, $1.39 per pound; pork loin back ribs, previously frozen, $5.89 per pound; almond milk, $2.89; strawberries, 16 oz., $1.29; tomatoes, $.95 per pound; mini peeled carrots, 16 oz., $.95; large avocados, 4 for $5; red onions, $.95 per pound; green bell peppers, $.65 each. Charlotte was discreet. She kept her coupon booklets well out of sight, in the back of a drawer in the bedroom dresser, and did the clipping when nobody was around. Mike's self-esteem was so shaken, anything that might remind him of the family's straits, in turn bringing on his developing self-blame, was to be avoided. Inevitably there were slip-ups, but for the most part, Charlotte got away with it. The expertise she developed became a matter of pride. After Mike got the job at the bank and the family began to recover, Charlotte went right on with the bargain-hunting. She came in for some kidding, when a coupon for some absurd item was noticed, happily putting up with it because she knew the last laugh, her immense success at cutting costs, was hers. She had saved the family thousands of dollars.

One day, she found a "consignment" department store in neighboring Alhambra, where the merchandise seemed a cut above what one usually found in second-hand clothing stores, and no more expensive. This became a frequent destination. The establishment seemed to have no name other than "Consignment Store." The merchandise was not always dependable. Socks she purchased for the boys developed holes in the heels immediately. A blouse she bought for herself tore under the arm when she reached for a jar on a kitchen shelf. Generally, however, the clothing was sturdy. The shop never wanted for customers.

Some of the savings, on food items particularly, were noticed by the boys and their father. It couldn't be otherwise.

"Mom, I don't like this milk you've been buying," Todd complained, making a face. "Tastes yucky."

"Me either," Andrew chimed in.

"People in India are starving," said their mother.

"You always say that," Todd said. "Why can't we have the old milk?"

"This is healthier, that's why."

"It's cheaper, huh?" Todd said.

"Nothing wrong with that, is there?" The boys weren't fooled. The family's belt-tightening was not confined to food, it extended to every aspect of their lives. Charlotte had sat down with them from time to time and explained in vague terms how their father had unfortunately been laid-off temporarily, "these things happen," he would get another job, but in the meantime, they had to be careful with their money.

"I expect the two of you to understand this," she admonished, "and you can help your father about these little sacrifices we have to make right now by remembering not to make a fuss about them."

Problem was, not all the sacrifices were inconsequential, as far as the boys were concerned, and they didn't remember they were not supposed to rebel. Andrew, especially, had made a fuss about the denial of a new pair of shoes for soccer. Used shoes he would not accept, that's what he had on now, wasn't it? A new pair would cost more than $100. While Mike and Charlotte were endeavoring to cut corners as seldom as necessary, regarding the boys' lives, the price of the shoes was out of the question. If Andrew couldn't make do a while longer with the shoes he had, then no more soccer. He kept playing in his old shoes, but they were badly worn, and finally he was forced to leave the team. It was a very hard time. Andrew was sulky. Not my fault dad lost his job, he told himself bitterly. When he did return to soccer, after a two-year hiatus, it was not the same, it was not as good. He was at a different school, he was on a different team, his old friends were gone. His interest in soccer was the casualty, to his parents' considerable dismay. It was just this kind of outcome they most sought to keep from happening, as the result of the calamity visited upon the household. They recognized their sons were vulnerable, that their emotional health was at risk, and it worried them endlessly. Although therapy could not be regarded as anything but a luxury, both boys saw a therapist. Andrew was unquestionably the more affected by his father's circumstances. Particularly difficult for the boy to absorb was the loss of the group of friends he had run around with since before kindergarten. He fought his resentment but to no avail, and his powerlessness added to his frustration and misery. The therapist warned that the younger brother, Todd, might be "internalizing" the effect the family trauma was having on him, that he could be experiencing sadness and conflict of his own. Neither Mike nor Charlotte felt this was so.

"Just be vigilant, that's all I'm saying," the therapist, an expert in child psychology, said. "If you see signs of trouble, we'll deal with it. If not, so much the better." This seemed sensible enough, for both parents. It was Andrew, at his volatile age, who was the concern.

"The rebellion he is exhibiting," said the therapist of Andrew, "is actually pretty normal, though usually it comes later, in the middle and later teenage years." Charlotte did not like this remark. She preferred to think of her sons as exceptional rather than like the common run. Mike wasn't bothered. Hadn't he rebelled against his parents, especially his father? Hadn't he been a teenager? Mike, in any event, was the passive parent in these conversations, he was too shattered by what had befallen him and had to rely on Charlotte to see it through. She more than met the challenge, finding initiative and strength within herself she did not know she had. She was absolutely engaged in the boys' struggles and, indeed, could be provoking and intimidating.

"You came on a little strong there, sweetheart, don't you think?" Mike said on one occasion, after Charlotte had challenged a remark made by Patrick Dooley, MSW.

"Did I?" Charlotte was unconvinced.

For his part, Mike felt it was almost as if some malevolent force was steering him from one setback to the next. What could he do? Was there a critical step he hadn't taken, a phone call he hadn't made? Good heavens, how many had he made, each with the same, bitter result?

"Your resume is impressive, Mr. Huxtable, and we talked about it at some length, but finally felt your strengths do not quite match up with what we are looking for." Wrong set of strengths, wouldn't you know?

"We hired somebody else."

"Not qualified."

"Don't remember seeing a resume." Mike said he'd send another, although he kept a log and could see for himself he had sent them one. "No need, the position has been filled."

"Sorry, but a background in insurance is unrelated to our business." Must remember to haul out the resume and add that line about his years peering into volcanoes.

A thick skin never developed. Each setback stung as badly as the last. Had his wounds been visible, he'd have looked splotchy, like a leper. Besides Lawrence Dietrich, Mike saw a psychiatrist occasionally, when a prescription needed filling. He had gone through a prolonged bout of insomnia and was determined to keep that malady from recurring; a tablet he took nightly just before turning in definitely was helping. Mike was prepared to spend money on doctors, for it was imperative he maintain his health through his ordeal.

How many miles had he put on his car, driving to interviews across the length and width of Los Angeles? He had spent a pretty penny on gasoline all right. All for naught. There had been an interview in the San Fernando Valley someplace. It was a job in retail, which held no appeal whatsoever for him. But here he was, in his suit, primed for the interview. A month later, having heard nothing, he phoned.

"Oh yes, Mr. Huxtable, sorry we had not gotten back to you, you were our second choice." Well now, wasn't it just jim-dandy to know that!

How many times had he gone up and down the Help-Wanted columns in the Sunday newspaper? This was L.A., a big city, the Sunday paper was downright heavy. Surely it would be filled with opportunities? Yes, there were many ads, and yet not many. His method was to put a checkmark beside every possibility, even if farfetched, but the hopefulness this engendered would be dashed upon further scrutiny, when the lion's share emerged as clearly unsuitable. Not infrequently, even the ones on the short list came down to two, or one, or none at all.

"Did you find something good today?" Charlotte would ask hopefully, as Mike leafed through the paper at the dining room table, pen and scissors at the ready.

"Here's something," he'd say, and she'd come to look over his shoulder. Now and then, it would be something to which she could agree enthusiastically. Far more often, what enthusiasm she could muster, was forced.

"All they can say," she'd remark, rubbing his shoulders affectionately, "is no." Which they did.

Mike did not limit his job search to the newspaper. He began a subscription to the local trade magazine, a monthly journal which carried a small number of ads in each issue. Mike responded to nearly all of these. Nothing. He was puzzled. He was experienced, he had a solid reputation, what stood in the way of an interview, at least? Was GJC saying something about him? This he dismissed as paranoia. He could not catch a break, though. Month by month, the family's savings account dwindled. The $2,000 monthly from his father kept them afloat, but it was not enough.

Charlotte had never been able to secure full-time employment. Fact was, she didn't want full-time employment. She felt the boys were her priority, that her husband would find work again. As the months dragged by, she grew more and more impatient with her husband. Why couldn't he get a job? Did he make some awful gaffe at interviews? What was the problem? Charlotte held her tongue, most of the time. Speaking up generally made matters worse.

At GJC, Mike's replacement, Cecilia Ingram, had left after less than a year. She was a young bride. Her husband was well-to-do. She had never needed the work at all. They would start a family, they would prosper. Her months at GJC contained neither highs nor lows, she had done passably. Since she had been paid significantly less than Mike, the firm had come out ahead. Clients overwhelmingly asked no questions. As long as they felt they were getting their money's worth, they could have Frankenstein for their account executive, for all that mattered. The firm had sent a letter to selected clients with a false explanation for their long-time employee's departure, something about seeking greener pastures, "We wish Mike well." The letter was pro forma, designed to be forgotten immediately by its readers.

One morning, Mike got a phone call from a former colleague at GJC. Mike was into his third year of joblessness. The $2,000 monthly from his father-in-law had ceased after twelve months.

"Hey, Mike, Jerry Hauser, remember me?"

"Sure, Jerry, how are you?"

"Life is sweet."

"Keep it that way."

"Thought I'd call, see how things are going for you, maybe have lunch?"

"Things are going okay," Mike lied. He and Jerry Hauser had not been close, and if Jerry really cared how he was doing, he'd have called long before this.

"You find something or still looking?" It was the middle of the morning, Tuesday, and Mike Huxtable was home, so Jerry was in a position to answer his own question.

"Still looking. Long process."

"That's tough."

"Beginning to think being 44 isn't helping, either. Experience is not an advantage."

"How so?"

"You think some guy in his thirties is going to hire a guy ten years older who knows more than he does?"

"I suppose not. Fudge on your age."

"It'd take more than that."

"Well, look, let's have lunch, you want to? Really get caught up."

"Sure." Mike wasn't terribly eager to have lunch with Jerry Hauser, but it would be a place to go, and maybe something positive would emerge.

"How does your calendar look?" Jerry tried to imply Mike was busy.

"Guess your schedule is fuller than mine, Jerry. Any day works for me, really, except Thursday." He saw his therapist on Thursday.

"Noon tomorrow work for you?"

"Just fine."

"Schaffer's. New place over on 2nd. Been there? Gourmet sandwiches, very good."

"I'll be happy with a cheeseburger, but sure, that sounds good."

"See you tomorrow."

The restaurant wasn't even in Pasadena. Mike, unexpectedly, had trouble finding it and was a few minutes late. Maybe Jerry didn't want someone from GJC walking in on them? Can't be seen fraternizing with that loser, Huxtable. "Cynical of me," Mike chided himself, but it wasn't cynicism.

Their greeting was warm, but by halfway through their meal, they were hunting for conversation. Jerry deflected Mike's questions about the office. The latter, in the contemporary parlance, was "history," gone, dead, forgotten. Jerry's objective, in any event, was not to answer questions, he had a favor to ask. He needed a letter of recommendation.

"You want a letter from me?" Mike said disbelievingly. Wasn't he the one without a job? Mike himself had called a former colleague, shortly after his discharge, and asked for a letter, despite knowing this was against company policy. If a discharged employee got a glowing recommendation, what did that do to the company's claim he was fired for poor performance? Invitation to a lawsuit. So letters were a thing of the past, and if the result was kicking a guy when he was down, too bad.

"We didn't really work together that much, Jerry," Mike said.

"Why would you say that? We were a team at GJC."

"Oh please, Jerry, that's not true."

"Hey, you got laid off, it happens. Times get better, who knows, you might find yourself back at your old desk."

"I don't think so," Mike said with exasperation. "Jerry, look, I'm happy to write you a letter, it's kind of weird, but I'm happy to, but I have to be honest, and I can't really say that much about your work, not in an informed way, since we didn't really work together much."

"You write what you're comfortable with, buddy, I'm sure it'll be good."

"Mind if I ask, before we say goodbye, what's got you looking for another job? You sounded like things at GJC are fine. What did you say? Life is good?"

"I just feel like there's no harm in having an up-to-date resume, you know?"

"Sure. I know, believe me." Thus ended their luncheon. In the car on the way home, Mike could not help laughing at the silliness of his life. It was better than crying. Out of work, utterly without prospects, he was serving as a reference for an employed ex-colleague.

Meanwhile, Andrew was becoming more and more unruly. "Anger issues," Patrick Dooley said, as if this were sufficient explanation. Andrew was not recovering, not by a long shot, from the loss of his schoolmates of long standing. He was seething with resentment against both his parents, his father especially. He was to blame, he lost his job, and no excuse served. The youngster simply lacked the emotional capacity to deal with such a wrenching experience. This, too, his therapist noted, not that Mike and Charlotte Huxtable didn't know it themselves; it was far too apparent to miss.

"How come dad lost his job?" he snapped at his mother. She never had a satisfactory explanation. "All my friends' dads have jobs." She asked him how he knew that. "I just do."

"Your father is having a hard enough time, Andrew, without your being so upset with him." Charlotte caught herself. Heavens, had she accidentally implied the boy was contributing to the family's vicissitudes? How many times had she been warned by Patrick Dooley never to say something that could lead a child to believe a family catastrophe was his fault? "Andrew," she added hastily, "please don't misunderstand. You are not to blame, your brother is not to blame, for what has happened to your father. We just have to accept it and try … try to be … understanding." Mother hugged son. Charlotte Huxtable was trembling with fear she had made a terrible mistake.

"It's not fair!" the boy protested.

"Oh, Andrew, I know it isn't fair. Life isn't, always. You could be hungry. You could not have a home. You could not have your parents. Your life could be so much worse."

"Count my blessings, yes, I know."

"Right."

"I already feel better," the youngster said sarcastically.

As time passed, Andrew's anger subsided into an unrepentant sullenness which, if anything, was more difficult to deal with. The downward trajectory of the family defeated him. His respect for his father went out the window. At school, he could not stare his new classmates in the face. He felt they were all looking at him as if to say, "We know all about your dad, we know he's a failure." This was all in Andrew's head, and his therapist had tried repeatedly to get Andrew to understand this, without success. The only thing that was ever really going to work was his father's getting back on his feet. Instead of this, Andrew found his father sprawled on the sofa, day after day, still in his pajamas well past the time he should be at work.

"Your friends feel bad for you, Andrew. And let me tell you something else. They have problems of their own. You said you can hardly bear to eat lunch with them. Andrew, they are not sitting with you pondering your father's predicament. Believe me." Patrick Dooley's words met with an unintelligible reply.

One day, Charlotte suggested Mike take Andrew on an excursion, a "male-bonding" weekend.

"Can't force these things," Mike said negatively. "Anyway, we can't afford it."

"You don't want to, in other words?"

"Did I say that?"

"What it sounds like."

"I guess ... I still think it's forcing it."

"It was just a thought," Charlotte sighed. "There must be something happening in southern California you and Andrew would enjoy. You could overnight at some nice motel and come back Sunday." What sort of diversion would they both like? Rather, what sort of diversion would Andrew like? He didn't like anything these days. There was an amateur car racing event at a track in Bakersfield, come to think of it. Mike knew of it because he knew one of the drivers, an acquaintance he had not seen in some time, but who had encouraged him to attend an event. Charlotte said "Go" when

Mike mentioned it as a possibility. Bakersfield was within reach, a room and supper would not be an extravagance. It seemed worth a try.

Mike wasn't sure what to expect. What sort of cars would Steve and the others be driving? Was it like NASCAR? Indianapolis? Surely not; these were amateurs, fellows who liked to get together and race. The races were "meets," this was the "Bakersfield Meet." It was a hobby, as Steve had termed it, weekend fun during "the season." Winners got a trophy, but Steve said the purse seldom exceeded $1,000. There were rules, and they were strictly enforced. No liquor was allowed at the track. Any driver found with liquor on his breath was expelled immediately. The cars had to meet certain specifications, mostly out of safety considerations and to ensure no driver had an advantage. To Mike, they looked like little more than souped-up soap box racers, but they were not as flimsy as they appeared and could reach speeds of 80 miles per hour. Accidents were rare, and rules infractions were seldom a problem. There just was no money in it.

Andrew was enchanted! Pure fun with, yes, an element of risk, but a small one. One driver lost control and almost flipped his car, but was unhurt. Steve and another driver in the field of nine were much the best, lapping the others and racing neck-and-neck to the very end; Steve finished second. The purse was $1,000 which, when expenses were factored in, came to approximately $300 for the winner. The cars were one-seaters, unfortunately, or Steve would have taken Andrew for a few laps around the oval. Steve found himself answering a battery of enthusiastic questions. Mike promised they would catch another race, possibly the "Riverside Meet," next month. They had burgers for supper and watched TV. There was no "heavy talk" whatsoever. The weekend trip was a success, which Charlotte could tell before Mike said a word.

Next month, they were in Riverside. The weekend this time was not as good; how could it be? There was no real trip, since they were not leaving town. The day was gray rather than sunny, as it had been in Bakersfield. There were sixteen cars and a purse of $1,200. Everything seemed less fun, somehow. The track was nicer than the one at Bakersfield, with a roof over the spectator stands; in Bakersfield, the bleachers were exposed and somewhat dilapidated. The novelty was gone. Steve's car gave out when the engine overheated (always a problem), and he failed to finish. Mike had got them a motel room, but wished he hadn't. He regretted not having Todd along this time. The younger brother must be feeling his older brother is

343

getting all the attention these days, Mike told himself ruefully. If it was not one thing, it was another …

Still, the weekend went all right. Andrew did not exhibit the intense fascination he had at Bakersfield, but something more important was in the making. The racing had reminded Andrew how many interesting endeavors life offered, of which he was totally ignorant. His father even gained back, although it would not last, some of his son's lost esteem. As for Mike, he was deeply grateful to Charlotte, whose idea the weekend trips had been, and he said so.

"No thanks required," she replied. "I am just so very, very happy this worked. We have to keep exploring, Mike, keep pushing forward. I know you're demoralized, aren't we all? We've got each other, we've got the boys, we've got our health, knock on wood, you will find work." Would he? Mike believed the longer his joblessness stretched, the less likely he was to get a job. He had no prospects.

They took in a college basketball game in San Diego. As Todd was going to a friend's birthday party and staying overnight, there was no problem with leaving him out. The game was boisterous.

"Are we going to stay with granddad and grandmother?" Andrew had inquired before they left town.

"No, but we'll swing by tomorrow for lunch."

"Could I walk down to the beach by myself?" It was no distance from their room, but it was dark.

"What are you going to do there?"

"Just get my feet wet, dad."

"You be back in half an hour, tops."

It was a lovely evening, warm but not too warm. Mike's hometown had an agreeable climate, maybe too agreeable, since there was little seasonal change. Mike's mild apprehension about Andrew's going to the beach alone was unfounded; he wasn't alone. People were milling about up and down the beach. Andrew loved the ocean. The ceaseless waves captivated him. He took off his shoes and socks, rolled his trousers halfway up his shins, and walked into the surf. He thought San Diego's beaches were better than L.A.'s. Bigger waves, better sand. Faithfully within a half hour, Andrew returned to the motel. Why couldn't his father find a job? The question nagged him unmercifully.

"There's no harder job than looking for a job," his mother would explain, but when was his dad looking? Actions speak louder than words, he remembered having been told, and this was confirmation.

When father and son got back home the next day, a rejection letter awaited Mike. "Thank you for your interest in working for The Ortmann Company. Unfortunately, we do not have an opening at this time. Best wishes." Mike was sure he had read those very words before. Many times. Oh, well. He felt the weekend had been a mixed success, and this rounded it out perfectly.

"How was your trip, Mike?" Charlotte asked.

"Fine. Nothing special. We enjoyed the game."

"And your family?"

"Also fine. They send their regards."

"I hope you remembered to give them mine."

CHAPTER 16

O NE THING MIKE HAD NOT SHARED WITH CHARLOTTE WAS HIS DE-
termination to see Felix Webb again. He knew this time the lawyer
would charge his fee; it was $210 an hour. Mike felt he had not completely
probed his possible case, and knew he was not going to be satisfied, until
this was done. He'd tell Charlotte later, or never. Maybe he had a good
case? Maybe he could win a lot of money?

"Tell me in the greatest possible detail about your last day at GJC,"
Felix Webb said.

"It was Friday. That might have tipped me off, since that was the preferred
day for firings. But I had no reason … it was late afternoon, after just about
everybody was gone. Believe me, that place empties fast at 5:00, especially
on Friday. Must have been around 4:30. Ideal time. I was involved in some
dismissals myself, before my turn came. Firings weren't that uncommon
at GJC, to tell you the truth. An acquaintance actually told me one day
that getting sacked at GJC was a badge of honor. Just said that out of the
blue. Trying to make me feel better, I guess." Mike shook his head at the
recollection. "Didn't work."

"Did this individual ever work at GJC?"

"Not to my knowledge. Maybe he knew something about the firm. It's a
big company, you must be familiar with it?" Felix Webb wasn't. "Anyway, it
was around 4:30, and Randall Galloway asked me to come into his office."

"He phone you?"

"Yes."

"Do you remember his exact words?"

"Not really. Just come see me, or something like that. Nothing out of
the ordinary."

"All right, then what?"

"I went to his office." Mike paused. Had there been any clue he missed at the time? He could think of nothing.

"Please go on."

"I went in. I didn't close the door. Doors usually stayed open at GJC. Not for a termination, though."

"Then what?"

"I was surprised to find Ann was right behind me. She just appeared out of thin air. She closed the door behind us."

"Ann?"

"Ann Weller, HR."

"That was a tip-off, perhaps?"

"Not really." Mike felt the lawyer was asking useless questions. Running up the fee.

"Was Ms. Weller customarily present at terminations?"

"Couldn't really say. She wasn't at the ones where I was involved, I don't believe. There weren't that many, where I was involved."

"Did GJC always have a third person present for terminations?"

"I don't know, Mr. Webb. I didn't fire people."

"Did you ever recommend someone for termination?"

"Once, reluctantly. This particular individual just was not suited to the job. I'm pretty certain he was not surprised. He knew it wasn't working out. Truthfully, I think he was relieved to be out of there. Best for him, in the long run."

"The exception, not the rule."

"Oh, definitely."

"Although nobody should be surprised to be fired," the lawyer said.

"Nobody should be surprised to be fired?" Mike caught his breath. "It was the surprise of my life." The attorney smiled sympathetically.

"Who spoke first, once you were all seated?"

"Had to be Randall." It was the type of question Mike found vexing, the answer being so apparent.

"What did he say?"

"He said things weren't working out."

"His exact words?"

"I think so."

"Tell me about Ms. Weller."

"She was an older woman. Been with the company a long time. A really nice lady."

"You were friends?"

"I was friends with everybody. Except Randall. I wasn't around Ann much, she was in the human resources department. But we were friends, definitely."

"How many HR people?"

"I don't know, Mr. Webb. I think three. I had very little contact with them." What difference did it make? The note of exasperation in Mike's voice was not lost on the attorney.

"How about a cup of coffee? No charge."

"That sounds good." Mike wasn't amused by the lawyer's remark. Coffee was obtained, and Felix Webb disappeared. Mike was left alone in the lawyer's office. This was peculiar, and Mike wasn't comfortable. When they resumed their conversation, there was no explanation from the lawyer where he had gone.

"You may wonder why I ask some questions," the attorney said, for Mike's building exasperation was impossible to miss. "There is purpose in all of them."

"I understand you want to know everything, Mr. Webb," Mike said. "I'll do my best." He did not, however, believe some of the questions weren't off the cuff.

"That's all any of us can do. Now let's get back to your conversation with Randall and Ms. Weller. Tell me what else you remember."

"A silence took place. I was thunderstruck. Totally in shock. Nobody said anything."

"Who finally spoke up?"

"I did. I asked Randall what he meant by that. Things aren't working out. What did he mean? Afraid we're going to have to let you go, Mike, he said. He said Mike, not Mikey. Definitely."

"His exact words?"

"I think so."

"Then what?"

"I believe I said something to the effect he couldn't be serious, I was almost at my ninth anniversary working at GJC, I had a family to support. I was in total shock, Mr. Webb. Miracle I could speak at all."

"Then what?" Felix Webb was passionless.

"Your family is your responsibility, Mike, not the company's."

"His exact words?"

"Yes," Mike said, grinding his teeth. "I'll never forget that."

"Then what?"

"I asked for an explanation. Said I deserved that much. Said 'things aren't working out' meant nothing."

"Then what?"

"Very well, he said. There are serious performances issues. Your performance is poor, Mike."

"His exact words?" Mike was ready for this, by now.

"For sure he said poor performance. Can't swear to the rest."

"Can you recall anything he said at this point that could be construed as age-related?"

"Nope."

"Then what?"

"I asked him what performance issues?"

"What did he say?"

"Let's not prolong this, Mike. I think you know where your performance has been inadequate."

"His exact words?"

"Oh I don't know if those were his exact words, Mr. Webb. Pretty hard to keep your head when you're being told you no longer have your job."

"I understand," the lawyer said sympathetically. No you do not, you most certainly do not, unless you've been there, Mike told himself. "Then what?"

"I think Randall handed me the severance agreement." (This had come up at their initial meeting, and the attorney had read over the document sufficiently to confirm it was the standard agreement.)

"Then what?"

"Randall explained the agreement to me. This took several minutes. I was in a daze."

"Then what?"

"Randall stood up. Ann did, too. Randall extended his hand. I shook hands with him, and with Ann. I was in a daze. I think he wished me luck. Don't know how I can remember anything. I went back to my office and got my things. I left my keys on my desk. I noticed Randall and Ann were still conferring in his office as I left."

"Did you speak with anyone on your way out?"

"No. Everybody had left." Mike looked spent. They spoke several more minutes, but the attorney saw that the best he was going to get had been got. He wrapped things up.

"I'll consider what you've told me, Mike, and get back to you without delay. I must tell you I am not very encouraged about your case, to this point. Of course, we may discover something. May I call you in a couple of days?"

"Sure. I'll be home," Mike said dispiritedly.

Felix Webb's dilemma was a familiar one. His client had no money. He was out of work, wasn't he? What worse time could there be to consult with a lawyer? Webb took cases on a contingency basis occasionally, but his client must have a far stronger claim than Mike Huxtable's even to consider this. With Mike, it was strictly money "up front." While Mike hadn't spent much yet, the next step, "discovery," would cost a bundle. Yet Galloway's deposition was essential to bring an informed assessment of the strength of Mike's case to the table. It was a vicious circle: Mike needed to know whether he had a case before he started writing checks, and Felix Webb needed the checks before he could determine if Mike had a case. What to do?

The attorney felt he needed a full day for the deposition. He would also subpoena pertinent records from GJC. There were the interrogatories, as well. Additional depositions might be necessary, not to mention GJC would want to take Mike's. Felix Webb added it up, his fee plus costs. One thousand, two thousand, three thousand, four thousand, five thousand...

When they next spoke, by phone, Mike thought he was ready for the attorney's quote. He wasn't. Webb detected this readily.

"I appreciate it's a chunk of money," he said. "So talk it over with your wife, Mike, and let me know. How does that sound?"

"Fine, I guess. Charlotte and I will discuss it." Presenting the attorney's quote to Charlotte, who didn't know of this meeting with Felix Webb, was going to be tricky. Mike wanted to go forward with the deposition of Randall Galloway. Even if it came to nothing, he would relish sitting across a table from that weasel and watching him squirm under his lawyer's probing inquiries.

"Have you gone completely off your rocker, Mike?" Charlotte said. She wasn't angry. "We are pinching every penny, and you want to throw thousands of dollars away on a legal fee?" The measure in her voice was as unnerving as anger would have been.

"It's not thousands, sweetheart." Which simply wasn't true.

"Mike, I'm not going to threaten to leave you. I know I can't talk you out of this, so go right ahead. When we finally go under, and we will, then I'm leaving." Mike was stricken with fear. Charlotte meant every word.

Mike decided to drive down to San Diego one morning and get his parents' thinking. The trip turned into a phone call, and the proposed lawsuit met with stiff opposition. A futile waste of time and money. Both were blunt with their son. Both could see the real problem was their son's idleness. What was the old saying, something about the Devil ... Mike's father, at one point, said they could not help him with the expenses of a lawsuit, although Mike had said nothing to suggest he expected this. Nothing could be more completely out of the question.

Mike called Felix Webb. He told him he wanted to sue. The attorney said he would proceed immediately, but not before he had made sure his client was clear on financial arrangements, which would be put in writing for his signature.

"Who are we up against?" Mike inquired.

"Their lawyer, you mean?"

"Yes." Mike wasn't sure why he'd asked, since it was unlikely he'd ever heard the name he was about to hear.

"Stefan Kopinski," Webb said. "He's tough." Mike grimaced. "So am I," Webb added.

The deposition of Randall Galloway began promptly at 9:00 on a Tuesday morning at the law offices of Fulton & Shaw, LLP. Felix Webb had informed Stefan a full day would most likely be required. The two attorneys were acquainted, but had never squared off in court.

The deposition dragged along uneventfully, with much attention to matters of zero relevance, to Mike's way of thinking, including a surfeit of pointless matters, such as where Randall Galloway had gone to college. They stopped for lunch. Mike asked his lawyer how he felt about the morning and got a positive response. Fact was, the lawyer was saving his big guns for the afternoon session, when Galloway would be tired and impatient, and therefore more apt to slip. Stefan Kopinski, of course, had cautioned his client accordingly. Mike also inquired about the seeming contradiction in objecting to a question and then answering it, whereupon Webb explained the process to him. At 1:00, they resumed.

"Tell me, Mr. Galloway, where did you work before coming to GJC?"

"Objection, relevance," Stefan Kopinski said for the twentieth time, or was it two hundred? "You may proceed."

"I worked for Giles, Inc."

"How long were you there?"

"Let's see, from approximately February until September."

"About eight months, then?"

"About."

"What sort of company is Giles?"

"Pharmaceuticals."

"What was your job title?"

"Vice President."

"What were your duties?"

"Objection. Answer the question."

"I was primarily tasked with finding ways to make the company more profitable."

"That's important, isn't it?"

"I would say so."

"Is one of the ways you make a company more profitable firing people?"

"Unfortunately, sometimes it's necessary. Nobody likes to lay people off."

"Eight months, then, at Giles. And about the same at GJC, before Mike Huxtable was let go, would that be correct?"

"Approximately."

"That about your limit, Mr. Galloway? Eight months?"

"Objection."

"Where did you work before your eight months at Giles?"

"Objection. Answer."

"I was with The Fitzsimmons Company."

"What did you do there?"

"Objection. Answer."

"I worked with management on lots of things."

"Any of them related to bottom line?"

"Sure, some."

"Did you recommend anybody for termination?"

"May have. I don't really remember."

"This is your life's work, and you can't remember?"

"Objection. I object to counsel's sarcasm. Don't answer."

"How long were you with Simmons?"

"Fitzsimmons."

"Fitzsimmons."

"Couple of years."

"Could you be more precise?"

"No, I could not."

"You're something of a free-lancer, then, aren't you, Mr. Galloway? Stop by a company for a short while, clean up the mess and move on. Never stay anywhere too long. Have gun, will travel?"

"I would not agree with that."

This give-and-take went on for another hour. A five-minute break was taken, and they resumed.

"Now would it be accurate, Mr. Galloway, to say you characterize terminations as layoffs?"

"No, that would not be accurate."

"So a termination and a layoff are not the same thing?"

"A termination is a termination, a layoff is a layoff."

"Either way, somebody's out of a job, wouldn't you say?"

"Right."

"Now you previously said Mr. Huxtable's job was eliminated, did you not?"

"I don't remember that."

"Well, is someone else doing his job now, or not?"

"Not to my knowledge."

"Objection," Kopinski said. "I object. Counsel is putting words in my client's mouth."

"If someone is doing his job, then Mr. Huxtable wasn't laid off, was he? He was fired."

"I never said he wasn't fired. He wasn't doing his job."

"What would be an example of his not doing his job?"

"Unreliable. He was often late for work."

"Was Mr. Huxtable a salaried employee?"

"Yes."

"Are salaried employees on the clock?"

"No."

"That's the essence of being salaried, isn't it, Mr. Galloway? You don't punch in and punch out. Your time is your own."

"There is an expectation at GJC that everybody be at his desk at 8:30, more or less, including persons on a salary. This goes for every company. You can't just wander in when you feel like it."

"You on a salary, Mr. Galloway?"

"Yes."

"At your desk 8:30 sharp?"

"Yes."

"I see. That is your idea of a performance issue, then?"

"One of many."

"What else, Mr. Galloway?"

"Mr. Huxtable quit wearing a coat and tie every day."

"Everybody else got on a coat and tie every day?"

"I couldn't say. We're not talking about everybody else."

"Any other performance issues, Mr. Galloway?"

"His desk was sloppy. He was warned repeatedly."

"Sloppy desk? Papers scattered, that kind of thing?"

"Yes."

"So that's a performance issue?"

"I would say so. It's insubordination, too."

"So, tardiness, even though he was salaried, no coat and tie, sloppy desk. That right, Mr. Galloway?"

"He lost a blue chip client, Harlee Enterprises, for your information."

"It was his fault?"

"Yes, it was his fault. His client, his responsibility."

"When did this happen?"

"Before I got there."

"So you don't know."

"Not precisely."

"You know for a fact the client left because of Mr. Huxtable, even though you weren't there?"

"I know an account executive is responsible for his accounts. This was his account."

"Do clients ever leave for a reason totally unrelated to their account executive?"

"It can never be unrelated. It's his account."

"Nobody else ever lost an account?"

"I'm sure others have. But the first rule of business is to keep your clients, so losing any client is serious, and this was a blue chip account."

"Blue chip. Is that really what you call them?"

"Yes."

"How long had Harlee Enterprises been in GJC's stable?"

"I don't know. A long time, I'm sure of that."

"So Mr. Huxtable must have been doing something right for a long time?"

"I don't know if he was the account executive all those years."

"Have you ever spoken with anyone at Harlee Enterprises?"

"No, I would have had no reason to."

"Somebody at GJC tell you Mr. Huxtable was responsible?"

"I don't recall."

"You don't recall. So Mr. Huxtable may or may not have lost a client, you really don't know."

"No, he lost it. Not may or may not have."

"This is your case for poor performance?"

"Hardly. He lost other accounts, too."

"I'm listening."

"I can't name them, but he did."

"Seems like you could name them, Mr. Galloway."

"Objection," Kopinski said. "Counsel, you're mistaken if you think your constant sarcasm and mockery will be tolerated."

"I'll be sure to make a note of that, Mr. Kopinski," Felix Webb said. He resumed with Galloway. "In nine years with an organization, Mr. Galloway, doesn't every account executive bring in his share of accounts, and lose one now and then?"

"He lost them all the time, not now and then."

"Yet you forgot to bring a list."

"Objection!" Kopinski said irately.

"So for nine solid years, Mr. Galloway, they kept him around, even though he was constantly losing accounts?" Galloway said nothing. "Any other performance issues, Mr. Galloway?"

"He lost the Bancroft & Matthews account. Also a blue chip account."

"I see. And this was another long-time client?"

"It was a prospective client the firm had been after for years. We finally got them in the door, Mr. Huxtable had a presenting role, and he blew it."

"So this wasn't a present client, it was a prospective one?"

"That's what I just said."

"How do you lose a prospective client?"

"If you're Mr. Huxtable, you find a way."

"What happened?" Felix Webb liked that he had apparently hit a nerve.

"Your client showed up for the presentation with a blood stain on his collar."

"A blood stain? What do you mean? A shaving nick?"

"That would be correct. On his white shirt. You couldn't miss it. You couldn't see past it."

"Good grief, Mr. Galloway. You were present for the presentation and couldn't take your eyes off it?"

"I wasn't present, but I saw it. Like I said, it caught your attention."

"You weren't in the presentation?"

"I didn't have to be. It's irrelevant."

"And in what way was this a performance issue?"

"It was extremely unprofessional."

"So GJC didn't get the account because Mr. Huxtable nicked his chin shaving?"

"I know this client placed particular value on everything being just so. But even if they didn't, Mr. Huxtable was sloppy and unprofessional."

"You didn't answer my question. Did his nicked chin cost GJC the account?"

"It didn't help."

"I see, it didn't help. How was his presentation, in terms of its substance?"

"I told you, I wasn't in the room. Bert Haggard told me it didn't go well."

"That would be hearsay, Mr. Galloway, but as long as you've brought it up, who is Bert Haggard?"

"Another account exec at GJC."

"Was he in the presentation?"

"Yes."

"What did he say?"

"He said he was disappointed."

"Disappointed? With what?"

"Your client."

"In what way?"

"Condition of his shirt collar."

"Did he say he was concerned it could have affected the presentation?"

"I don't recall precisely."

"You remember the morning. You remember the prospective client. You remember the presentation you did not attend. You remember the condition of Mr. Huxtable's shirt collar. You remember speaking afterwards with Mr. Haggard. But you can't remember what he said?"

"Objection. I object to counsel's badgering of my client."

"I object to your constant, disallowed intrusion into this proceeding, counsel. You are not being deposed, Mr. Kopinski."

"My objections would be less necessary, Mr. Webb, if your questions were appropriate."

"Mr. Galloway, did you speak with anyone from Bancroft & Matthews about my client's shirt?"

"No. Why would I? I would have no reason to speak with them."

"So aside from your own notion, the only person with whom you spoke about my client's shirt was Mr. Haggard, and you can't quite remember what he said?"

"That's what I said."

"You suppose Mr. Haggard's memory might be better than yours?"

"I object," Kopinski said. "Don't answer."

"Ever nick yourself shaving, Mr. Galloway?" Felix Webb inquired.

"Don't answer that either," Kopinski instructed his client.

The deposition continued in this vein the rest of the afternoon. It would be necessary to resume the next morning.

"Tell me, seriously," Mike said as Webb drove them back to his office, "we didn't just spend half a day talking about a nick I got shaving?"

"I don't believe it was half the day, Mike."

"Not really the point. The whole thing was just … stupid. Dumb. Sorry, that's how I feel. I'm certainly not saying you're dumb."

"I do understand." Felix Webb's mine was elsewhere, on what he wanted to do in the morning.

"It just seemed like very much about very little." Mike was thinking about the money he was spending on a ridiculous discussion.

"*De minimis non curat lex,* Mike."

"Latin, I gather?"

"Correct."

"And it means?"

"The law does not concern itself with trifles," Felix Webb said solemnly.

"The law does not concern itself with trifles!" Mike shrieked. "Is that what you said? We spend a whole damn afternoon talking about how I nicked my chin, which I don't even remember by the way so maybe they made it up, and you're telling me the law does not concern itself with trifles!" Mike laughed, but it was a bitter laugh, not a joyful one. "I'm out of a job, I'm ruined, and the law does not concern itself with trifles. Oh man." Mike couldn't go on.

"You must remember, it doesn't really matter what we think. It matters what a jury will think. What might seem trifling to you might not be at all to a jury."

"So you're telling me in the jury room twelve honest men are going to take a word of this seriously?" Mike was thoroughly demoralized. This was utter nonsense, contemptible nonsense, and tomorrow meant more. The attorney drove on in silence.

"Now Mr. Galloway," Felix Webb commenced the next morning, "are you acquainted with a GJC employee named Cecilia Ingram?"

"Yes."

"In fact, you hired her, did you not?"

"No."

"You had no role in her hiring?"

"I recommended her."

"So you had a role in her hiring, did you not?"

"A limited one."

"Now Mr. Galloway, who is Ms. Ingram's supervisor?"

"I am."

"What are her job duties?"

"Objection. Relevance. Answer the question."

"She sells insurance obviously," Galloway smirked.

"Commercial practice?" Felix Webb kept his temper.

"Some."

"Are any of her duties akin to what Mr. Huxtable's were?"

"There's some overlap, I expect." Here Felix Webb produced a pair of business cards. One was Mike's old card, and the other was Cecilia Ingram's.

"Would you kindly look at each card and read them aloud?" Webb said. Galloway complied. "Aside from their names, the only difference is the word 'associate,' would that be correct?"

"Yes."

"So Ms. Ingram is the Associate Account Executive. That is the title beneath her name, correct?"

"Yes."

"Whose associate is she?"

"That would have to be your client."

"Obviously." Webb smiled expectantly. "But if you don't have an account executive, you can't very well have an associate account executive, can you? No. You can't have an assistant chef without a chef, you can't have a co-pilot without a pilot, wouldn't you say, Mr. Galloway?"

"Objection. I object to this badgering, this is unacceptable, counsel. Do not answer."

"I object to your objection."

"Why don't you do that."

"Now Mr. Galloway, since Mr. Huxtable no longer is employed at GJC, where he was an account executive in the Commercial Underwriting Department, but Cecilia Ingram is employed at GJC, in the same department, that would make Ms. Ingram the de facto account executive, would it not?"

"Not necessarily."

"Are you aware that Mr. Huxtable and Ms. Ingram spoke one day?"

"No."

"So you don't know she was over at Pasadena Construction in his capacity, doing his job?"

"No."

"Who sent her there?"

"Nobody, necessarily. Her job must have required her to be there."

"You are her supervisor. Don't you keep track of where she is going, and why?"

"Not for every little thing."

"You knew Mr. Huxtable's job, didn't you? How could you recommend he be fired for poor performance, if you didn't know what performance was expected of him? You must have known his job duties, cold. Yet all you can say about the employee now occupying his position is, her job duties must have required her ... what did you say ... required her to be somewhere?"

"Oh please, this is immaterial and irrelevant," Kopinski said. "I object."

"Mr. Galloway, are you aware that my client asked Ms. Ingram how things were going, and she told him how things were going, and it became completely obvious to him she had been given his job?"

"Object. Hearsay. Don't answer."

At: 11:30, Felix Webb concluded. Back at his office, Mike had just one question.

"Can we win?"

"Mike, you must permit me now to finish going through your file, and consider everything Mr. Galloway has said. I will get back to you before the end of the week."

Mike had no choice but to be content with this. He did repeat he was not in a position to keep spending, unnecessarily. The long and short of it was, neither the gender claim nor the age claim was strong. Being a reverse discrimination claim, the gender claim suffered from the weakness it ran against the grain. White males were not supposed to be plaintiffs. It was not unheard of for such a plaintiff to win a lawsuit, but the climb was steeper. Add to this they had no evidence of gender bias, aside from Ms. Ingram's being a woman. Moreover, male employees outnumbered female by four-to-one at GJC. Not good for their argument. As to the age claim, Mike was over 40, so he met that requirement. But he had no direct evidence, not one word or act, that could be a starting point in making a case. Felix Webb thought the company's claim Mike had performed poorly could be attacked, but he had to get past summary judgment first, and the attorney reluctantly decided this would not happen. The one possibility remaining was to take Ms. Ingram's deposition. Might be some interesting revelations, if he could depose her. Otherwise, it was time to talk settlement. Webb called Mike and gave him his assessment. The latter did not even ask what another deposition would cost, he could do the math himself at this point. It was his turn to tell the lawyer he'd get back to him. Mike wanted to speak with Charlotte, but he could not bring himself to do it. It was pointless. Another deposition was out of the question. It would just lead down another path ending in futility. Monday morning Mike called Felix. They explored settlement options and agreed Felix would offer to settle for $19,500. They would come down to $16,500, no lower. One day later, the attorney called Mike. The company would agree to add one month to the severance package, which currently stood at two. It was very much a "take it or leave it" counteroffer. Felix strongly urged Mike to take it, and got a strong reply. Mike felt the counteroffer was insulting, he couldn't imagine accepting it. Felix said this was not the way to look at it, that they had pried something out of the company, that this represented a victory.

Mike's mind raced. He had spent $6,000, at least, on Felix Webb, and the bills weren't finished. He must sign an agreement precluding any further legal action, not that there was such a thing. He had burnt his bridges at GJC, where he had idly pondered he might get his job back, if Randall Galloway were to leave. This was his lawyer's idea of a victory! He accepted the counteroffer, shook hands a final time with Felix Webb and went home to face the music. He didn't really believe Charlotte was going to leave him, but it wasn't going to be fun. Mike took a look again at his options. Launching his own business was his next choice. A home office would be necessary; a lease was completely out of the question. He'd get some business cards and letterhead, those wouldn't cost much, and he'd send a letter to every one of his former clients and solicit their business. Who knew? He might pilfer one or two. His clients had been loyal to him, he had taken good care of them, the allegation his performance had been poor was false. A home office posed numerous challenges, however. He'd have to convert the den, which was the family room. The boys, in particular, spent time in there, since that's where the television was. He'd have to have some sort of exterior sign, come to think of it. Another expense. A separate phone line was advisable. More cost. Prospective clients had a natural inclination to avoid going into someone's home. A home office inevitably suggested somebody operating on a shoestring. Mike floated the idea by Charlotte, who had never asked for the numbers on the litigation initiative; the money was spent, she knew they had lost money. Forget it. The scolding Mike anticipated never happened. Instead, Charlotte had embraced him with great affection, when it was over.

"You had to know, now you do, it's all right, I love you," she whispered in his ear. Had to know? Had to know what? What did he know he hadn't known? It was ambiguity, inconclusiveness, nothing was clear, nothing was "known." Except that he had the best wife in the world.

"I love you, sweetheart," he said.

Charlotte offered no resistance to the home office idea. It wasn't going to work, her husband wanted to try, so be it. A kind of resignation had come over her.

Thus, Mike opened an insurance business at his home. He spread the word in every way possible, including mailing his business card to a select group of his former clients. He followed up in each case with a phone call. Mike served on two local boards of directors and was active in two charities, and here, too, he distributed his card. After three months, he took stock. He did not have a single account. He told himself he would give it another three months, then see how things were going. His tight discipline, putting on a suit each morning, sticking to a workday, was ebbing fast. He resumed sending out his resume. Three more months went by, he had acquired two clients. Neither was remotely a blue chip account.

CHAPTER 17

I T WAS A FRIDAY AFTERNOON. MIKE MADE HIS TRIP TO FIRST STATE BANK. He went twice a month, on Friday, to deposit Charlotte's paycheck. The family's savings had fallen from approximately $140,000 to $4,922.15 When that was gone, they were done. Mike went inside the bank and filled out a deposit slip. Standing in line, he noticed a sign, between the teller cages. "Teller Wanted." Mike saw it, read it, thought nothing of it. It had not registered at all, he was so robotic now, so removed from reality, the words were meaningless.

The line creeped forward as his eyes wandered aimlessly around the familiar lobby. The rack of brochures advertising the bank's services, the ceiling fans spinning lazily, the digital clocks. Whatever happened to real clocks, Mike mused. The line moved again, and Mike's gaze reverted to the sign. "Teller Wanted." He was out the door before even fully realizing what he was doing. He drove like a maniac home. He dashed upstairs, threw off his clothes and put on his remaining presentable suit, fought with the tie but got it secured, gargled some mouthwash, ran heedlessly down the stairs, very nearly tripping, grabbed a resume from his desk drawer and drove frantically back to the bank. It was late afternoon, it was Friday, the position, assuming it had not been filled and they just had not gotten around to removing the sign, might be gone by Monday. He was going to get this job, or die! A bank teller. So what if it didn't pay well! So what if it was totally without prestige! So what! Mike swung wildly into the first available space in the bank's parking lot. Don't think I ran over anybody, he said to himself.

He checked his tie in the mirror, it was straight, he leaped from the car and fairly ran back into the bank. Was the sign still there? He was momentarily panic-stricken the job had been filled in the 45 minutes he'd been gone. It was still there! Still open! Mike paused to gather his wits. He was back in the lobby, they wouldn't close with him there. With whom should he speak? Oddly, in the tightly-knit community in which he lived, where an acquaintance was around every corner, he did not know a banker here. All strangers. He went over to the executive department and asked a woman at the front desk, presumably the secretary, if he might speak with someone. By a stroke of luck, he didn't think to mention his errand, or she would simply have handed him an application and asked for his resume. Instead, she assumed he wanted to open an account.

"Please take a seat, sir. Someone will be with you shortly." Mike sat down. Next to him was seated another gentleman. Drat the luck, the gentleman was ahead of him. He would get the job. How to barge in front of him? Mike was literally trembling, almost feverish. Got to settle down, he said to himself, got to think clearly. This guy could be here for any number of reasons. Ten minutes went by, and, sure enough, the secretary came over and told the gentleman a banker would see him now. Mike fought for self-control. Finally, his turn came. He was ushered into the executive suites. The contrast with the lobby was striking. These floors were carpeted, wood paneling was everywhere, handsome paintings decorated the walls, the lighting was subdued, a quiet atmosphere prevailed. Mike was introduced to Victor Franciscus, identified as a vice president. Oh no! Mike was seized with panic. Here he was in this bank officer's office, with no purpose except to hand him his resume. Franciscus was undoubtedly anticipating Mike wanted to discuss getting a loan. Certain humiliation loomed.

"How may we be of service today, Mr. Huxtable, is it?" Victor Franciscus said. He was on the tall side, and his manner was hearty and winsome. He was also a decade younger than Mike.

"Actually," Mike said, clearing his throat. "I just wanted to apply for your teller position, and I guess I shouldn't be doing that in here, but the receptionist asked me to take a seat, and so, here I am." Mike managed to smile, sheepishly. But he had spoken strongly, without apology. If he was consuming Victor Franciscus' valuable time, it would not be much of it. Mike reached into his coat pocket and withdrew his resume, and extended it to the banker. "My resume." Both men were still standing.

"Yes, ordinarily Sheila would be the one to give this," said Franciscus. "Your interest in the position is appreciated." That was his cue; time to get the heck out of there. A heavy moment passed.

"Mr. Franciscus," Mike found himself saying, "I did not really mean to meet you, I mean, to contrive to meet you" … not what he meant, either … "just to fork over a resume, which obviously Sheila should have been given, my mistake, but could I just have a moment with you, considering I'm in here, I promise to be quick."

"Won't you sit down?" Mike sat down gratefully. Victor Franciscus took his seat, behind his ample desk. Behind him, on the wall, was a captivating depiction of a countryside, vaguely French in appearance, complete with a small light above it. A picture frame was on the desk, but its back was to Mike. Family picture. There was also some sort of device, a globe slowly turning. Mike thought it might be attached to a clock, but he couldn't see that, either.

"My name is Mike Huxtable, Mr. Franciscus. I have a wife and two boys. I have a bank account here. We've banked here for years. We're very happy with the bank. Wonderful, superior service."

"We always like to hear that," Franciscus said. This gave Mike just the moment he needed to take the plunge.

"Mr. Franciscus, I used to be in the insurance business. I worked at GJC for nine years. Maybe you're familiar with the firm?"

"I've heard of it.'"

"Long story short, they brought in this new guy, I'm not even going to say his name, and he just plain didn't like me, and one day, I got fired. My work was excellent. He was just a mean so-and-so, he had the power to throw me out of work, since he was my new supervisor, and he did." Franciscus said nothing, but could not help wonder why someone whose work was so stellar had lost his job. "Long story short," Mike resumed, "I have gone through absolute hell since then, I can hardly imagine how to describe it, I have a family, I couldn't find another position in insurance anywhere, I've wondered if they were saying something about me, I finally opened …"

"Mr. Huxtable, forgive me for interrupting, I do understand your … your situation, your … dilemma, if I may call it that. I am actually waiting for a conference call, so if you don't mind." Victor Franciscus rose and extended his hand, Mike jumped to his feet and did the same. "Do fill out an employment application and you can do that right here and give it to Sheila, and I assure you it will be given fair consideration."

"Thank you for your time and interest, Mr. Franciscus," Mike said with deep sincerity. "I need this job, I want it desperately, I'll be the best teller First State has ever had." Mike was completely overwrought. He left the office and returned to the bank lobby. Had he made a fool of himself again? "May I have a job application, please," he asked Sheila, "for the teller position that's open?" Mike found a seat at a table and started upon the application. The expected inquiries were all there, including: Have you ever been fired from a job? If yes, please explain. Explain? How about, the jerk who was my new boss didn't like me, like we were schoolboys or something, so he sacked me. Mike wrote, "layoff." He finished the application and returned it to Sheila. Heading for the door, he remembered why he had come to the bank in the first place, to deposit Charlotte's paycheck. He got back in line.

Meanwhile, Dan Simpson, another vice president, had gone into Victor Franciscus' office to participate in the conference call. Their offices were adjacent, and Simpson had witnessed the conversation between his colleague and Mike. He had not heard much, but enough to know the visitor had been making whatever his point was with great earnestness.

"Who was that guy?" Simpson asked Franciscus.

"Fellow looking for a job. Apparently he got past Sheila. Sounded desperate. Said he got fired, hasn't been able to find work, he's in insurance."

"What's he interested in? We got anything but that teller slot?"

"That's it. Told me he'd be the best teller we ever had." The two men looked at each other. Although it was unlawful, First State, like many businesses, was guilty of gender discrimination. In the teller's cage, greeting the public all day long, which was preferable: A curvaceous young woman with just the right blouse on, or a paunchy, balding, middle-aged guy? Who was kidding whom? "I'm sure he'd do the job well," Franciscus added. "There's not that much being a teller."

"When were we planning to quit accepting applications?" Simpson said.

"No set date. We can quit when we want. Sheila has a stack of resumes."

"We'd catch it if we just hired this guy, if that's what you're thinking," Simpson said, surprising Franciscus, since his colleague had surmised what he was unaccountably contemplating.

"Maybe. But didn't you ever want to be a hero?" Simpson had no reply. "You're right," Franciscus continued, "we go through the resumes, but this guy is on the short list, far as I'm concerned."

"Sure, fine with me. We really do need to get that slot filled." At this point, the two bankers were advised the conference call unexpectedly was postponed until Monday.

"Now that's a kicker," Franciscus said. "We could have been out of here." Without hesitation, he picked up his phone and rang Sheila.

"Sheila, did that fellow who was just here fill out an application?"

"Yes, sir."

"About how many applications would you say we have at this time?"

"Three dozen, at least. I can count them if you like."

"No, not necessary." A wild idea was coursing through Franciscus' head. "I don't suppose Mr. Huxtable is still in the bank?"

"Yes, he is, Mr. Franciscus. Over in the line to see a teller." It was now late Friday afternoon, a time many people found themselves in the bank, and the line wasn't short. The wild idea in Franciscus' head got wilder. Toss the resumes. Go out there and hire Mike Huxtable right now. The banker was surprised to discover his heart was racing. Not much did that, anymore, and he was only 33. What had seized him, that he wanted to hire this forsaken individual on the spot? Was any other person in that stack of applications any less needy? Weren't they all out of work? What Franciscus also knew, however, was that Mike Huxtable stood no chance if it came down to the applications. He would never get an interview. Interviews for a teller! Who wouldn't stay a year!

The president of the branch bank, Tom Briscoe, would likely be displeased. On the other hand, wasn't there something to be said for hiring somebody who might actually stick around?

"Sheila, would you kindly ask Mr. Huxtable to see you before he leaves today?" Franciscus said. "Then call me."

"Certainly, sir." If Dan doesn't want to be a hero, that's his choice, Victor Franciscus told himself. He was going to be one. Within a few minutes, Mike found himself back in the bank officer's office. There was the French countryside he had not expected ever to see again, the globe going around and around. Mike could hardly contain himself, since it seemed a good omen Franciscus had asked to see him again. He tried to stay calm. How many times had his hopes been dashed? Expect nothing, that was best.

369

"I'll bet you didn't suppose you'd be back in here, did you?" Franciscus said with good humor. He had looked over Mike's resume and his application. Mike Huxtable was far too qualified for the position.

"Not hardly," Mike gasped.

"Please be seated." Mike sat where he had been only shortly before, fighting to catch his breath. "Your resume is impressive, Mr. Huxtable. Frankly, I must tell you, your credentials are well beyond what is required to be a teller."

"I know that, Mr. Franciscus."

"The pay is about half what you listed as your salary when you left GJC." (It was a bit more than half.) Mike knew this too, since the teller's salary was listed on the application. "Opportunities for advancement are close to nil. We don't even have a head teller." Both Franciscus and Simpson had been lobbying for some time for this position, to no avail.

"I know that, too. It's better, much, much better, than where I am now. I've been out of work for so long, earning nothing." Mike wished he had not said that. Made himself sound like a loser.

"Still want the job?" Victor Franciscus said, smiling, looking Mike in the eye.

"Yes," Mike all but shouted. "Yes, Mr. Franciscus, yes."

"When could you start?"

"Right now!" Franciscus laughed.

"That won't be necessary. Think you could be here 8:00 Monday morning?"

"Oh yes. Definitely. I'll be here."

"You're hired. See you then." Franciscus rose, Mike rose. They shook hands.

"Thank you. Thank you, Mr. Franciscus. Thank you." Mike was in a dream. He flashed past Sheila on his way out, saying, "see you Monday," he got out the door and shouted "yahoo" and then headed for his car, not exactly running but not walking, more of a hop, skip, jump, skip, jump, skip, hop, hop, jump. He unlocked the door, climbed in, closed the door and let out a blood-curdling yell, pumping his fists. If the roof had not been metal, they'd have gone through it. "I got a job, I got a job, I got a job."

Mike was still dancing when he got home. He waltzed around the empty house, "tra la la tra la la tra la la." This was bliss! This was catching that touchdown pass, first kiss, "I love you" from your future bride, first job, first promotion. This was Rolls Royce, Mona Lisa, Taj Mahal. Mike couldn't quit singing with ineffable joy. What would he say when Charlotte got home? Celebrate! Dinner out tonight! It had been forever since they'd done that. Mike calmed down long enough to give a little thought to his wardrobe. He'd need a new suit! (Tellers were not required to wear a suit.) New shoes! (Well, yes, although a teller could be barefoot and nobody would know.) Haircut! (Tomorrow.) Confidence! (Restored.) Where was Charlotte, anyway? Getting the boys from school, everybody bracing for another weekend of intense strain and hopelessness. "Boys, your father is struggling, I expect you to …" to what?

Mike chirped some more. Chirp. What fun it was going to be to tell Andrew and Todd the family's interminable nightmare was over at last. They could do things again, have things again. Raise their heads with their classmates, feel good about themselves. So much wretchedness for so long, gone! Mike reflected upon his new job. What does a teller do, exactly? It was arithmetic, no? That, and excellent customer service. He could do those things, oh yeah. Must be some training, but how demanding could that be? Numbers had to add up at day's end, for sure. Addition and subtraction. Learned that stuff in grade school, hadn't he? All those succeeding years in classrooms, for what? Ruin.

Of course, the salary was lousy. Advancement was problematic. Even if they finally got around to having a head teller, and he eventually got that job, it wasn't going to constitute much more, and no place to go from there. Oh bother! Why worry over these considerations? Hell with them. Charlotte arrived with Andrew and Todd, each lumbering from the car with his satchel. Such a familiar scene. Charlotte opened the back door and Mike seized her, and hoisted her into the air.

"I got a job, sweetheart, I got a job!"

"Oh, Mike, you got a job, oh, what wonderful news!" Charlotte couldn't believe it. She was thrilled. So were Andrew and Todd. "Tell us about it, oh my gosh, I can hardly believe it, it's so wonderful." It was unbelievable. So much time had elapsed, Charlotte had given up on her husband's ever finding work again.

"Well, the whole thing is just sort of miraculous," Mike said breathlessly to his three eager listeners. "You know how I go over to First State every other Friday to deposit your check, Charlotte?" She nodded. "Well, today, while I was waiting in line, I saw this sign, advertising for a teller position.

Hardly aware of myself, I ran out of the bank, came home, put on a coat and tie and dashed back to the bank. Well, I found myself in this bank officer's suite, he's a vice president no less, told him I was interested in the teller position, well, he must have been impressed even though we talked hardly at all, he took my resume and told me to fill out an application with the receptionist, which I did, then I started to leave but remembered I needed to deposit your check so I got back in the line and, next thing you know, the receptionist tells me Mr. Franciscus, that's his name, wanted to see me again, so I'm back in his office, and he offers me the job, right there on the spot! I report to work eight o'clock sharp Monday morning." Mike stopped to catch his breath, which needed catching. "Can you believe that?"

"You're going to be a teller?" Charlotte said, not quite concealing her misgiving. It did not seem like much. Mike detected this.

"Charlotte, maybe it's not a great job, heck, I'll be on the clock, think of that, but it is something. Maybe I can advance, why not, I know I'm not going to be on the banker's track, that's okay, maybe I can get on it after I've been a teller for a while, who knows, it doesn't matter right now, all that matters is, I have a place I have to be at eight Monday morning! We're going out to supper, by the way." This they did, the four of them, and Charlotte, though not able to cast aside completely her doubts, found her husband's wild joy infectious, and the evening was a great success.

Mike did not report for work at eight o'clock Monday. He was there at seven. He had risen at six and hummed his way happily through a shower, shave (nickless) and breakfast. Charlotte, Andrew and Todd were agog with joy, watching husband and father float around the house. It was simply too wonderful, almost unbearably so, after so much misery. Mike might someday, with perspective regained, give himself the credit he was due for having held the family together. To be sure, nobody else would ever do this, including even his admirable wife, who could never quite shake the belief her husband could not be blameless, for so drastic a step as job loss to have befallen him.

As he expected, the bank, at seven, wasn't open. He was obliged to wait. He had stopped en-route and bought himself an expensive latte, and he was enjoying it, swallow by swallow, as he stood beside the hood of his car, merrily observing the workday coming alive. The bank was at the far end of a shopping mall, not actually a part of the mall, but close enough the mall's parking lot was convenient for bank customers. Little by little, the lot began filling up with automobiles. The sixty minutes he waited for the bank to open, an eternity only three days ago, zipped by, as he watched the increasing activity, knowing he was part of it again, at long, long last. Sheila drove up. Her name was Sheila Inwood, and her title was Secretary, though she did a little bit of everything. She waved cheerfully at Mike in recognition as she emerged from her car. For just a moment before they spotted each other, Mike toyed with the delicious fantasy it was all his imagination, that he was trapped in another purposeless morning, loitering in a parking lot. He could be arrested for that, couldn't he?

"Good morning," Sheila said brightly. "Been waiting long?"

"No, just a few minutes. Nice morning, isn't it?"

"Beautiful." They went inside. Mike wasn't nervous, exactly, but he had been out of the swim so long, he was awkward now, and decidedly not as sure of himself as he had once been. He feared his manner was clumsy. Sheila motioned for him to take a seat, the same one he had occupied Friday. It was unreal, to be sitting in the lobby in which he had been countless times as a customer; now, he was an employee. Was this happening? Had he taken a job as a bank teller? Who makes a career out of bank telling? Mike decided that wasn't the word. "Tellering?" He gazed around the lobby. So this is my new home, he said to himself. I will be the best teller in the bank's history.

"Mr. Huxtable?" Sheila beckoned.

"Mike, please."

"Yes, of course, we're on a first name basis here. I'm Sheila." She handed him some paperwork. Ordinarily, he'd have looked upon it as a chore. Not today, not a chance. He couldn't wait to get going. Mike knew some sort of training lay ahead, he knew little else, but this, too, he awaited eagerly. It was training for his job, wasn't it? His new job. His new career. Let the training begin! Sheila, who had left him to the paperwork, returned.

"I want to introduce you to Mary Fullerton, our head teller," she said. "She'll be your immediate supervisor." Head teller? Immediate supervisor? Mary Fullerton turned out to be a matronly sort, middle-aged, whom Mike had seen now and then on his banking errands. He didn't like the way she wore her hair, in a bob. Not appealing on a woman her age, he thought. He reckoned she was about his age, perhaps slightly older. Mrs. Fullerton took him around to meet the other tellers, or "customer support staff," as she referred to them. There were two young women, both very attractive; one was attending college at night, and the other was a wife and mother.

Mike recognized the latter, who also recognized him. There were two men, as well, one also in school, and the other, closer to Mike's age though still younger, who handled duties at the drive-up window. Everybody was warmly welcoming. "You'll like it here." "You'll fit right in." And: "Welcome to the right side of the teller positions." Chuckles all around.

"Thank you so much, Mrs. Fullerton," Mike said after the introductions. "I can't tell you how glad I am to be here." Mike mused over the trick posed by being simultaneously a teller and his own customer. It was the bank's policy to require all employees to be bank customers, which Mike felt was objectionable, but if it had meant getting the job, he'd have moved his money from the Bank of England, if he had money in the Bank of England. He was about to discover there was more to a customer support staff person than addition and subtraction. He didn't ask Mrs. Fullerton if it was all right to identify himself as a teller, which seemed infinitely preferable. "Customer support staff," when you came right down to it, was an absurdity. Wasn't the fellow spraying lettuce in the produce section at the supermarket customer support staff? The cashier? Neither had Mary Fullerton asked Mike to address her as "Mary." Accordingly, he hadn't. She would hover just behind him all day long all week, as he worked his station. Her remarks, he thought, were all of a critical nature, but he let it go. He'd do the job better when she wasn't there. For this was a job Mike Huxtable could do in a heartbeat, which left him both elated and dismayed. Challenges would be few. Rather, it was going to be a terribly repetitious, daily grind. It was nevertheless his salvation, his family's salvation. When he looked back on those lost years, he was genuinely frightened. Yet here, he was once again an "employee at-will." His fate at GJC could be repeated, no matter how much of himself he threw into the job. Mike believed Victor Franciscus had liked him, everything pointed to this, but whether he was the individual Mike ultimately had to please, he knew not. He never saw Franciscus again. The banker was transferred to another branch some months after Mike began. It was really very peculiar. The bankers must have another door into the inner sanctum. (They did.) He seldom saw them at all. A customer came in one day who gave Mike a start, since at first glance, Mike thought it was Randall Galloway. A strong resemblance, but it wasn't him. Mike wondered what he'd do if Galloway were to walk in. "What was in it for you, big shot?" he'd ask him. That ought to get the conversation going.

Something else Mike never saw again was the sign at the bank advertising for a teller. It was odd. He was told it commonly was posted when a slot was open, but he had never spotted it before, and he didn't see it again. It was as if it had been up one day only, his day.

Since Mike was an hourly employee, he was expected to be punctually at his post at 8:00 and out at 5:00. Overtime was out of the question. He had half an hour for lunch and two fifteen minutes breaks, one in the morning and one in the afternoon. This was a sharp contrast to his salaried position at GJC, but he had been an executive there. Every Wednesday, called "hump day," donuts materialized; his turn would come, and when one week he brought bagels, he was not popular.

"They're healthier," he proclaimed, which did not increase his popularity.

The job was humdrum, of course it was. Conversations with customers were perfunctory. Even when somebody came in he knew, it had to be all-business. Like a barber's life, in this respect. A lifetime of brief, insubstantial conversations, forgotten immediately.

Four weeks into his new job and still utterly joyful, Mike drove down to San Diego. It was Saturday. He had an envelope in his pocket, and in it five hundred dollars. He had called in advance to make sure his parents would be home. Lloyd and Beverly Huxtable were both in their sixties. They were not poor, but neither were they wealthy, and the $24,000 they had sent their son had taken a swath out of their savings. It was not regretted. What was money for, if not this? Hardly a thing money bought was worth having, when you came right down to it. They would never ask for a cent back. Their son's new job seemed insubstantial. Had he shared with them his wages, any remaining doubts would have ended. Nevertheless, a job was far better than no job, and Mike could continue to look for something else, couldn't he? They would bring this up, and he would nod in agreement, knowing in his heart he was not going to keep engaging in that futility again anytime soon, if ever. He was drained.

They had a happy afternoon, the three of them, over sandwiches and coffee. Life was good again. When time came for Mike to head back to Pasadena, he reached into his pocket for the envelope.

"I want you to have this," he said to them, handing the envelope to his father. "Refusal will not be accepted." Lloyd Huxtable took the envelope and opened it, surmising it contained money. He removed the bills, one, two, three, four, five.

"It's not much, but it's a start." Mike's voice abruptly cracked. "You saved us. We would have gone under for sure. I don't know how to thank you. There's no way." He had to stop. His parents themselves were deeply moved. Nobody spoke momentarily. "I love you," Mike sputtered. He embraced them both. "Time to go." This, too, had been difficult to get out. Mr. and Mrs. Huxtable glanced at each other. They had never intended repayment. Were they going to take the $500? If they didn't, there would be no further offer. If they did, Mike would keep repaying. He'd probably never get close to $24,000, but something was better than nothing. They had only a moment to choose.

"Mike," his father said, "you do not owe us anything." He put the bills back in the envelope and handed it to their son in a manner that would not brook resistance. "We have been clear on this from the beginning."

"We love you," his mother said. "All of you. Do bring your family with you, next time you visit." Mike drove home. All the way, he asked himself if he could ever be the parent his parents were. Todd, he felt, had weathered the storm, but Andrew was another matter entirely. He was a teenager, those years were inescapably challenging, yet his behavior at times was so erratic, Mike and Charlotte were worried. They'd get that call one night, from the police, about an accident on Interstate 45 … inevitable … could they lock him in his room until he was 21?

Mike, first and foremost, was determined to bring zeal and excellence to his new job. Maybe he had sat on his laurels at GJC? Deep down, he didn't think so, but he began second-guessing himself anyway. He could not lose this job, too, no matter what was required. The job wasn't demanding; his skill at taking the initiative, taking on responsibility, leadership, found little opportunity for expression. On the other hand, everybody was cordial, he did not feel the tellers on either side of him were competing with him, as indeed they were not, "teamwork" really meant teamwork. The secret hostility of putative colleagues, hardly unique to GJC, was all but absent, and this was a huge plus. Mike was eligible for benefits, even the retirement plan, after a year's service, and he would get raises annually, though they were small. His life, in a word, was restored.

CHAPTER 18

CHARLOTTE COULD SEE THE ENORMOUS DIFFERENCE IN HER HUSBAND and did her best not to lament, even privately, the inadequacies of his position. Todd continued on an even keel, perhaps in part due to his older brother's growing dissatisfaction, which he witnessed in a state of increasing terror. For Andrew's resentment and anger were growing, not diminishing, with his father's return to work. It was counterintuitive, it was utterly unexpected, it was awful, but the boy's respect for his father, in a state of collapse these many years, was wiped out when he became a bank teller. Sharp exchanges between father and son became even more frequent.

"What do I tell my friends now, dad? You cash people's checks? Is that what I say? Customer hands dad check, dad cashes it, customer hands dad check, dad cashes it. Do you have to go to school to do that?"

"Do not speak to me that way, Andrew," his father admonished. "You don't know a thing about my job. I'll have you know there's much more to it than cashing checks."

"I'll bet, huh dad. You sweep the floors, too?"

"You go to your room, Andrew, and you stay there until I say."

"I don't think so."

One day, in a heated exchanged laced with profanity from Andrew, Mike, to his utter astonishment, slapped the boy. Andrew slapped back. Andrew was 15, a sophomore in high school.

"Go pack your bags, Andrew," his father said sternly. The slap was the last straw. "We are driving to CBA tomorrow and enrolling you." CBA was California Boys' Academy, not precisely a military school, but something very close to it. Uniforms, bugles, marching. A high wall surrounded the premises. The academy was about 200 miles north of Los Angeles. The administrative offices would not be open Sunday, but never mind, they were going.

"No way, daddy-O," Andrew scoffed. He had heard this threat before. He failed completely to realize striking his father was way over the line. A vulgar shouting match ensued. Todd was sent to his room. "Whatcha going to do, daddy-O," Andrew mocked, "tie me up and put me in the trunk?"

"If necessary."

"You can't make me go."

"That's what you think."

"That's what I know."

"Why do you even want to stick around, if life with your old man is so unbearable?" Mike did not mean this, but it was said. Andrew responded with another vulgarity and went to his room.

"You hit dad, Andrew," his brother said to him in breathless astonishment. "You hit dad. How could you do that?"

"Didn't you see him hit me first, Todd? Didn't you? You were right there."

"It's not the same." Todd was scared. Was his brother going to be sent away?

Downstairs, a conversation in its way not dissimilar, proceeded.

"Mike, what came over you? You hit Andrew in the face. My goodness." Charlotte was badly shocked.

"He hit me, Charlotte, didn't you see? Our son hit me."

"I know he did. He never did that before. You must forgive him right now. He's not going to CBA."

"Yes, he is going to CBA. This has been brewing for a long time, now it's happened. CBA will be good for Andrew."

"It will not. We are not going to do this. Andrew's not a bad boy. Our troubles have affected him. We yanked him out of school once, he lost his friends. He's halfway through tenth grade. You can't seriously propose we do this."

"I'm not seriously proposing it, Charlotte. I'm doing it."

"You're all worked up. Please calm down."

Mike was up first the next morning. He had some toast and coffee and was literally on his way out the door when Charlotte appeared. The boys were still asleep. There had been no apologies after the preceding day's events, and Mike was steaming beneath a calm exterior.

"Wherever are you going at this hour on Sunday morning, Mike?"

"California Boys' Academy."

"Mike please. We are not sending Andrew there."

"I am going up there, Charlotte, and I am going to speak with somebody, and see the place and get the lowdown. Then we'll discuss it."

"Mike, it's Sunday. There isn't even going to be anybody there."

"Of course there will be. It's a boarding school, isn't it?"

"That doesn't mean the offices will be open. At least call first, if you're determined to do this." This was a good idea, but Mike was going to CBA, regardless.

"It's a three-hour drive, sweetheart. I'll be home for supper."

"What shall I tell the boys?"

"I don't care what you tell Todd, but by all means tell Andrew where I've gone."

In a little more than three hours, Mike found himself at the gates of CBA. It was an impressive campus, comprised of three, massive, three-story buildings, forming a very broad "V." The middle building had a clock tower. The buildings were brick, a dark, purple brick. The look wasn't ominous, exactly, but nobody would call it exuberant, either. There was a parade ground on the east side, but Mike couldn't see it, because of the wall. There wasn't a soul in sight. Mike pulled up to the guard station.

"Good afternoon."

"Good afternoon, sir."

"I've come to speak with the ..." Mike stumbled ... the principal? ... probably not right ... "the principal?"

"That would be Major Van De Graaf. I'm afraid offices are closed today. Open at seven in the morning."

"So there's nobody I could see today? Kind of important, and I've come all the way from L.A. Wife and I want to enroll our son here."

"Like I said, not much doin' today. Everything's closed." Oh, what a fool's errand this had been, Mike thought. "I got some pamphlets in the drawer here, if you'd like to take one," the guard said. He reached around and withdrew one.

"That'd be great," Mike said. The guard handed him one. It was a two-sided, promotional piece such as one might find touting the wonders of Yosemite Park.

"They got a whole lot more stuff about CBA in the administration building."

"Well I will just have to come back, but this pamphlet is better than nothing, thanks." Mike turned around and pointed the car southward. Three more hours, and for his efforts he had this pamphlet, if you could call it that. You folded a pamphlet, didn't you? Nothing to fold.

Driving the three hours home, Mike wondered that he could have concocted such a fiasco. Should have listened to Charlotte. He wouldn't admit the place had been closed, well, not to Andrew. The pamphlet was proof he'd made the trip, at least. Mike decided he would apologize to his son. He was horrified that he had struck him. He was overwhelmingly determined he would not allow the family turbulence Andrew was causing to throw the family further off balance. Hadn't they gone through enough those agonizing, desolate years he was unemployed? Were those years what had turned a loving son into the sullen, tempestuous 15-year-old Andrew had become? Certainly Andrew's therapist believed there was a connection, but it all seemed a bit too pat for Mike, and Charlotte, too.

Mike got home, it was nearing five, Charlotte was fixing Sunday dinner. Mike was forthright with her. She responded they could talk at their leisure later. Pulled pork was top priority.

"As you boys know from having heard it from your mother, I drove up to CBA today," Mike said when they were at the table. "It really is not that far." Mike addressed both boys, but he was looking at Andrew. "I liked what I saw, but, Andrew, your mother and I will speak with you about this another time. If you'd like to take a look at this pamphlet in the meantime, you're welcome to." Father handed son the pamphlet, thinking Andrew might tear it in half. "Andrew, we are keeping you at Fillmore High until the end of this school year, for sure." Mike paused. "Now Andrew, I want to say to you, in front of the entire family, because the entire family was present yesterday, I want to say to you, I am sorry I slapped you, I have no clue how that happened, but it was very wrong of me, and I solemnly promise you it will never happen again. I love you very much." With this, mother and brother looked expectantly at Andrew, who said not a word. Mike was more than prepared for this, and let it go. Andrew was 15, he couldn't be expected, could he, to bring himself to apologize? Mike wasn't even disappointed, and he assuredly had no intention of nursing a grudge or allowing his son's unacceptable conduct even to linger in his memory. The subject changed, and dinner proceeded uneventfully.

Mike was at his post at the bank in the morning, more grateful than ever for the work. The family was going to be a contented, prosperous one again, if he had to move heaven and earth to accomplish it. Turned out, far less would be required. Andrew read the pamphlet carefully, admired the illustrations. He liked the look of CBA! He was counting down the days, literally, on a calendar, until he reached his 18th birthday, when he could do what he wanted; it was still far away, but if he could spend even part of that time somewhere other than home, all the better. To be sure, CBA was a different cup of tea from Fillmore High School. Andrew was confident he could handle it. Neither Mike nor Charlotte, of course, had any way of knowing Andrew's thinking, and they remained at cross purposes over sending their son to reform school. Charlotte accused Mike of wishing to punish Andrew for his having hit him, which met with a firm rebuke from her husband.

"The boy needs structure, Charlotte, we've spoiled him I suppose, the discipline we try to impose upon him is only futility, as you well know, but if he spent his last two years in high school at CBA, it might do him a world of good. What is reform school for? Reforming behavior. Andrew's behavior needs reforming."

"Looks to me as if you have made up your mind already, Mike. Do we have to make this decision today?"

So many considerations went into the decision, at one point Mike entertained the notion flipping a coin might be best. Charlotte continued to balk at the idea. Just when it looked as if no decision could be reached, Andrew surprised his parents with the announcement he would like to go to CBA. Mike and Charlotte were thunderstruck. Mike asked for a day off and drove back to CBA, this time with his son. They met with the R.L. Van De Graaf, U.S. Army, Ret. They toured the facility.

"Does having been at reform school affect a kid's chances of getting into college?" Mike inquired.

"Not at all," Van De Graaf replied. "It's that grade point average that matters. We have a recruitment weekend here every spring. Various colleges have booths. We also have a non-college track, with various employers occupying booths. We mean it when we assert we get boys back on course and keep them on course, even after they've left here." Can't very well argue with that, Mike reflected. While the tension in the Huxtable household had actually abated somewhat, it remained abundantly clear to both parents their

elder son was discontented. CBA was within easy striking distance of L.A.
For that matter, if things did not work out, Andrew could be withdrawn
and re-enrolled at his present school. They'd forfeit the tuition, not an idle
consideration, for CBA was no bargain. Mike reminded himself again
money spent on bringing their sons up soundly, seeing them to maturity
and self-sufficiency, was money well spent. Since he was working again,
they could afford CBA.

It was not an easy decision, but in the end Andrew did enroll at CBA.
From the start, he liked it. The regimen was harsh, it did have an unmistakable military air about it, and making good grades, while important, was not
as important as discipline. Andrew's bed had to be made to specifications,
he wore a uniform and was responsible for keeping it spotless, he learned
to march, learned to chant, he ran the flag up the pole at reveille when his
turn came, he didn't have to cook, the institution had chefs, but he had
his turns cleaning the dining room and the kitchen, he risked swats if he
was disobedient. It wasn't a public flogging, just a well-placed whack on
the rump in the major's office. Everybody got one sooner or later, Andrew
not excepted. He was certainly not spared latrine duty. There was a firing
range on the campus, and all boys learned to shoot. In the gymnasium
and the swimming pool, exercises were mandated. Andrew did them, did
everything, without complaint. He liked it. His parents visited like clockwork and were immensely gratified by their son's progress. They took to
bringing Todd along. His brother's enthusiastic description of life at CBA
was not infectious.

Come recruitment weekend his senior year, Andrew participated actively.
He had been considering going to West Point, but his two years at CBA
did not serve as a springboard, as Andrew believed. Nothing prevented
him from enlisting, if that was what he wanted. Andrew thought he might,
someday, but he wasn't really keen on it. It was the pitch he got from one
of the recruiters, a fourth-generation family business based in Tacoma,
Washington that was a small but well-respected player in the Alaskan
crab fishing industry, that seized his imagination. A high school diploma
was required, he had to be at least 18, he had to meet certain, minimum
physical requirements, lifting primarily, and he had to be able to stand on
a slippery deck in a maelstrom and not commence to throw up. This last
item seemed funny to Andrew, but Cavanaugh & Sons was very serious
about it. The recruiter, a gentleman who went simply by "Mick," was an "old

sea salt," as he winningly, if unoriginally, called himself, he had been with Cavanaugh & Sons since he was not much older than Andrew Huxtable, he loved the way of life and spoke of it in such a gripping, wonderful way, Andrew was sold. His parents, when he told them of his decision, were less enthusiastic. The longer he put it off, the harder it would become to go back to school, and they wanted him to finish school. His mother urged him to go to college and get his degree, and then if he wanted to fish for crab, he could do that for a while.

"You are still very young, Andrew," she told him. "You have all the time in the world. You can always stick a fish hook in the water, but that college degree is so important, in terms of your later prospects. You are going to encounter many closed doors without a degree. Many good jobs."

"Mom, I hope you don't think you catch crabs by sticking a fish hook in the water," Andrew laughed.

"Well I really have no idea," his mother replied. "Crabs are in the water, I got that much right."

"Yes, you did."

"Is it safe?"

"Yes, it's safe. A whole bunch of guys do it, don't they?"

This conversation with his parents had none of the friction that had come to characterize such exchanges. Andrew, both his father and mother observed, was remarkably more grown, in just two years. He was bigger, stronger, surer. He spoke with conviction. And they realized, not only did he want to take this job, he was going to take it. He would soon reach legal age, and then they could not prevent it, in any case.

Crabbing proved brutal, unforgiving work. It was seasonal, so there were months of ceaseless work, then months of doing virtually nothing. Andrew learned the ropes quickly and did his job well, but he didn't love it, as he had expected he would. The camaraderie was the best part; the men were devoted to each other, to each other's well-being, and there was a real *esprit du corps*. A great deal of horseplay and rough language were part and parcel of the job. Andrew thought it was excessive, and he wasn't the only one. The work, despite the extensive safety measures taken by Cavanaugh & Sons, contained an inherent element of danger. By far the greatest risk was a man overboard. Chances of rescue were not good, unless the lost man was spotted immediately. Andrew found it amazing a man in the sea, only a moment earlier on ship, could disappear so fast. Fortunately, there was no such incident during his employ. But men did get hurt. After a year, Andrew had had enough, but Mick met with him and told him the first year was notoriously hard, the secret was not to give it up, the job got easier as it became more familiar, and many a time he had talked a man expressing Andrew's very sentiments into giving it a further chance, with positive results. Andrew agreed to a second year. The pay was good, in view of the job's hazards. Andrew met a woman by the name of Ursula, who moved in with him. She was not alone; she had a daughter, three years old. Ursula had never married. When Andrew asked her where the father was, she was evasive but finally said she thought in Seattle somewhere. She was an attentive mother. She was six years older than Andrew.

His second year with Cavanaugh & Sons was better, and he signed on for a third. Then, it happened. Somehow, his sleeve snagged in the cage as it was being lowered into the water. Automatically, the hydraulic system shut down, but Andrew did not escape injury. He was not at fault, no one was, it just happened, but he blamed himself just the same. He went on worker's compensation. When the doctors determined "Maximal Medical Improvement" ("Double M-I") had been reached, Andrew was declared to have 85 percent use of his wrist. He opted to take the permanent partial disability benefits, to which he was entitled, in a lump sum. He wasn't embittered, he didn't feel he was cheated, despite knowing 85 percent was inflated. Andrew could no longer make a fist with his left hand. His crabbing days were over.

He loved the Pacific Northwest, he loved the outdoors. A degree in forestry became his goal. He had lived in Washington long enough to qualify for in-state tuition at the University of Washington. One day, when he reached their apartment after school, he met an unknown gentleman. The man was short and had a hearing aid and a beard and wore a New York Yankees baseball cap.

"Andrew, meet Bill," Ursula said. She was standing just behind him. Bill extended a hand for a shake. He looked nothing like Andrew had supposed. They had an amiable, brief conversation. What it amounted to, Bill was back, and Ursula had made her choice.

Andrew pursued his studies at the university sedulously. He had been a good student before the turmoil at home had sidetracked him. Now, it was all back. He could do well, he knew he could, and he did. Andrew believed he had "found" himself, his true nature, his calling. This wasn't necessarily so. He had felt the same way hauling crabs from the sea, but never mind. The important thing was, he was pursuing a goal, he would have a career, he would do useful, important work. The ragged years, the rupture with his father, he couldn't forget, but he could put it into perspective. His father's failure still nagged him, but it also served as a motivation. He wouldn't end up that way. He would be successful.

And he was.

CHAPTER 19

A S THE PLANE LANDED, STEFAN REMINDED HIMSELF ANEW HOW IRRItated he was by the journey. How had he allowed himself to be talked into it? He had met Jeanne Young only once, briefly, in another country and another lifetime, and here he was, in St. Louis, expected to recognize a face he had seen only in the photographs Alan had occasionally sent across the years. Since Stefan had not done the same in return, indeed, had sent nothing at all because communication between the old college friends was remorselessly one-way, Jeanne had even less chance of knowing him. If, however, Stefan had not been completely ignorant how Alan Young had gone about filling his days, for thirty years, he'd have known that Alan, among other things, had done some tutoring.

Emily Abernathy was sixteen and in her junior year at Saint Louis University High School. Emily wasn't very big. She stood four feet eleven, and while her parents were holding out for at least one more inch, it looked less and less as if it would be forthcoming. As for Emily, she didn't care. If she was short, she was short. If she wasn't a beauty, she wasn't a beauty. Emily wasn't homely, either. Nor as shy as one might initially suppose. Emily would have her share of boyfriends.

The tutoring was her mother's idea. Mrs. Abernathy valued the life of the mind and was determined to instill this in her children during their critical, school years. Accordingly, they attended one of the best high schools in the city, and because English was her weak point, Emily had a private tutor. Upon whom she had a crush, which Alan knew.

Alan had had a brief and unsuccessful career with the St. Louis Public Schools, after which he had interviewed for a position with Saint Louis University High School, where he had a brief and unsuccessful career.

Indeed, neither position was anything remotely approaching a "career." Alan hated classroom teaching, it was too hidebound for him, too many rules, too many misplaced priorities, too much wasted time. Although this was subconscious and he was therefore not aware of it, classroom teaching took him back to Canada, and since this, like every one of his memories of Canada, was odious, he had squelched it. He had begun tutoring almost in anticipation his position with SLUH would be ending, and when it did, it did not spell the end of tutoring, too. He had taught junior English at SLUH and, as a tutor, accepted students only in their last two years of high school. Preposterously, the tutoring caught on, and Alan developed a roster of students. He took a course and obtained a certificate declaring him to be trained and certified, and he got a business card, which he tacked onto bulletin boards in strategic places like laundromats. He even devised a fee schedule, to which he did not adhere scrupulously and which, in any event, would not have put food on his table if he had rigorously enforced it and tutored from dawn until dusk every day of his life.

Alan had considered returning to school, but he would need a loan, which was problematic, and, besides, he had no real ambition, and never had. In college, he had idly considered becoming a Shakespearean scholar, but much had intervened, and now he did not even remember the thought. His father-in-law would certainly have said Alan was well along in fulfilling his prophecy, that his daughter was stuck with a ne'er-do-well for a husband, but this, ultimately, was not entirely fair to Alan. He would recognize, eventually, he must have a real job, and he would get one, or, to be precise, one and then another. His best position would be at the Northside YMCA, where he would stay seven years, working in every capacity except Life Guard, for which he was unqualified. He became friends with many staff and parents. He particularly admired "Mr. Berkeley," Terence Berkeley, a long-time employee absolutely devoted to the welfare of the young men who came through the door. Alan learned from Terence about the city and its changing demographics. Indeed, it was this that finally brought his job at the "Y" to an end. The exodus by residents from the neighborhood could not be checked, and since this meant fewer and fewer patrons at the "Y," costs had to be cut. Alan's job was among the casualties.

Alan had selected *Great Expectations* for Emily. He saw her twice a month, this was the fifth month. They had reached the novel's conclusion, or, rather, pair of conclusions, and tutor had an assignment for pupil.

"What did we discover in our last session about the story, that makes it highly unusual?"

"Two endings!" Emily cried.

"Right," Alan said, "and you said you prefer the second ending, while I like the first better."

"Yes."

"All right, Emily, what do you say to my contention it was an artistic mistake for Dickens to re-unite Pip and Estella?"

"I don't see why, if he was going to have them meet again, why it wouldn't be just as good, artistically, for them to stay together."

"That's an excellent answer, but so many books end at the altar, *War and Peace* for example, why didn't Dickens make good on his initial plan to have them meet again, but then part for good?"

"I'm not sure I understand what you mean by many books ending at the altar."

"Marriage. So many books end with marriage."

"I didn't know that."

"So Dickens adopted a different course. That was my point."

"I understand now."

"Do you remember what we discovered was the reason Dickens wrote the second ending?"

"The book was written in segments for a magazine."

"Serialized."

"Yes, I knew I had the wrong word, but couldn't remember the one you used. The book was serialized, but Dickens was a very popular author, and his readers didn't like how he ended the book, so he wrote the ending they wanted."

"Exactly right. Dickens is the most famous novelist Great Britain has produced, he was a masterful storyteller, and he wasn't going to let artistic integrity prevent him from obliging his readers' wish. Some other authors, for whom getting the novel right artistically was the most important thing, would never have made the concession Dickens made."

"They weren't as popular as Dickens, though, were they?"

"Indeed they were not, Emily, generally not by a long shot," Alan said. "All right. We are going to wrap up Dickens next time and turn our focus to poetry. I want you to read "The Eve of St. Agnes" by Keats and be prepared to discuss it, but first, I want you to identify a possible, third place Dickens could have ended *Great Expectations*, and write an explanation, not longer than one page, why this would make a better ending than either of the two, existing endings. I'll give you a hint: Estella doesn't figure in it at all."

"I'm not sure I can do that, Mr. Young," Emily said doubtfully.

"Yes you can," Alan said. He himself felt neither of Dickens' conclusions was satisfactory, though the first was decidedly superior, and that the author should have concluded his story a chapter earlier, when Pip, thoroughly chastened, realizes he has been wrong about Herbert, too, wrong in believing he lacked business acumen, and that the fault might have been his, not Herbert's, all along. They had spent five months on the novel, tutor and pupil had, and Alan had scattered clues along the way in anticipation of giving Emily this final test. He was confident she'd get it right. She did.

No, Alan and Jeanne Young were never going to be rich, nor was either particularly interested in the accumulation of wealth. Alan had had everything growing up, and now, he didn't particularly want anything. Jeanne wanted only her husband and their daughter. She did not share her husband's enthusiasm for St. Louis, and she vaguely wished, from time to time, they had a nicer, more convenient apartment. If they never did, so be it. When Alan got his first job, with the public schools, she had quit working to devote herself fully to Mary. They made ends meet, without putting much away. When Mary entered first grade, Jeanne decided to return to work. She got a loosely defined job as receptionist and "Jane-of-all-trades" at one of the television stations, and when that position, which she knew the moment she took it would not last, ended, she quickly found another of a similarly ephemeral nature. Jeanne could take care of herself, in and out of the workplace. Had not she been the family breadwinner, while her husband languished in prison, year after year? Had not she taken work, albeit with her father, long ago in Montreal, when the best her husband could do was wait on tables? The girl who had fallen madly in love with the American expatriate the minute she saw him had grown into a capable woman, wife and mother, with a good head for finances, a shrewdness about business practices, and a full appreciation for the ways of men, her own husband not excepted. Jeanne knew no truer words were ever spoken than, "Men have no morals when it comes to women," which she remembered a friend of her husband's having said, and she had hotly disputed, back when they were still in Montreal. Turns out the worldly Ms. Page was right! It baffled Jeanne why so many women could not understand something so basic. Then she would remember she was once one of those women. But the bafflement remained.

Their modest apartment was not without its advantages. Jeanne had had the gumption to consult a lawyer before entering into the lease, and through him had managed to acquire a rental at a fixed rate for the extraordinary term of fifteen years. Utilities were extra, but so far, they had been reasonable, although the cost of winter heating and summer cooling climbed steadily. The former they might have spent less on, but for concern Mary might be cold; the stifling St. Louis summers, on the other hand, demanded any available solution. Then, too, their apartment had only one spare bedroom, which Alan and Jeanne reckoned might discourage visits from relatives, as it meant moving Mary out. Among things they shared was gratitude for the distances separating them from their respective families. Although St. Louis was actually closer to Jeanne's hometown of Montreal than to Alan's, Los Angeles, there was no direct flight, and the required layover in Chicago, plus the international barrier (which in actuality amounted to very little), really did cut down on visits. The first time they had come, at Christmas, Alan's father-in-law had found almost nothing favorable about their situation, from his son-in-law's indifference to "getting ahead;" to his daughter's forlorn life in their dismal flat; to the city of St. Louis, which, as they were leaving, Charles McCarran declared to be, in his professional judgment, the sorriest looking city he had ever laid eyes on.

"There is not one building in this city you would ever want to look at twice," he declared. "Even Toronto is better." From the Montreal architect, this was the ultimate insult.

"What about the Arch?" Alan said. "Where else can you stand on 630 feet of air?"

"You can have that, too." They had taken the trip to the top, and it was not a thrill.

Ronald Bailey was a senior at SLUH and another of Alan's pupils. Ronald complained to his tutor he never had the right answer when called on in class, and consequently disliked reading.

"Every book has some sort of theme, and I never know what it is. My classmates do, but when the teacher calls on me, I don't know. I just mumble something, and then somebody else is called on, and he gets it right." The boy was obviously upset by his presumed inferiority.

"Ronald, I'm sure you are just imagining that you are the only one who doesn't know the answer. You don't suppose you are my only student who has told me this, do you? You are far from alone." Ronald felt a little better to hear this. At the moment, his English class was focusing on the short story, reading Saki, de Maupassant and Somerset Maugham. Ronald didn't much like Saki or Maugham, but he loved de Maupassant, especially *The Diamond Necklace.*

"It's one of the most famous stories in the world, Ronald, so your enthusiasm for it shows you're a pretty fair critic," Alan said.

"If you say so, Mr. Young," Ronald said haltingly, but he was pleased by the compliment.

Another day it was David Hewitt. Tutor and student were reading *Don Quixote*, and although Alan was skipping the pastoral stories and Part Two, it was nonetheless a big project. When finally they had finished, finished with the adventure, finished with the hilarity, tutor was ready with his question.

"How do we explain, David, how a story about the biggest birdbrain in literature has lasted four centuries, remains in print, and has even given birth to a Broadway musical?" David didn't know. "What makes Don Quixote different from Sancho Panza?"

"Sancho Panza doesn't think a windmill is a giant."

"Correct. That's where we start. Sancho Panza sees things for what they are. Now let's take this a step further. Why does Don Quixote not see things for what they are?"

"He's eccentric?" Alan had to laugh at his student's remark.

"You put that as well as anyone ever has, David. Yes, Don Quixote is eccentric. The question is, why? What makes him eccentric?"

"I think it's because he always tries to do the right thing."

"Yes! That, David, is right. Don Quixote always tries to do the right thing." Alan was delighted by his student's grasp of the novel. (Maybe tutor could take a measure of credit?) "This brings us to the essential, core issue. "We must once again ask, why? Why does he always try to do the right thing?"

"Because he's better, morally?"

"And what makes him better, morally?"

"He was born that way?"

"No, not that. Something else. You're so close. Think about it. Think about his behavior, on every occasion. He strives to do the right thing. So ..." Tutor left the blank for his student to fill in, but here David was stumped.

"You'll have to give me a clue, Mr. Young."

"David, Don Quixote has made a decision, hasn't he? He has decided he's going to live in the world not as it is, but as it should be. He's going to inhabit the world in which every man strives to do the right thing. He's going to live in the world in which every man responds to the best impulse within him. He's going to live in the ideal world we can imagine, but exists only in our imagination. Don Quixote moves into that world. He makes it his world. So far so good?"

"So far so good," student replied.

"This decision by Don Quixote results in his being mocked and ridiculed, but maybe, just maybe, he is secretly envied. What do you suppose?"

"Mostly mockery, I think."

"Agree completely. That last line, though, when the barber is delivering the eulogy, let's look at it: 'To live a fool, and yet die wise.' The author gives us a hint, I think, that Don Quixote figured out something very big. Think about that last line, and let's give it some further consideration next time you're here."

For Jill Robbins, the assignment was *The Mill on the Floss*. Alan called Maggie Tolliver his favorite heroine in fiction.

"Why does Maggie resist Stephen? He's tricked her onto the boat, hasn't he? That was wrong, but he knows, doesn't he, she is as passionate about him as he is about her. He's finally contrived to get them alone together, and yet she won't yield. I want you to write a paper, not more than three pages, defending Maggie's choice. Because it's the worst choice among those available to her, isn't it? Yet she makes it. She consciously, deliberately makes the worst choice. You defend it. Three pages, tops."

Alan considered having a monthly, or perhaps quarterly, event, where a number of pupils would be present, and everybody would have the opportunity to become acquainted and learn from each other. This, for the time being, was only an idea. Space was an issue; their apartment was small. Alan favored moving Mary into their bedroom. She was still a girl, he insisted they could make it work. Jeanne would not consent. It was ridiculous. Mary must have a room of her own. The only alternative was to make space in their living room, itself not large. They moved the furniture around, allowing

Alan to have an "office," as he described it, against the east window. It did not impart professionalism, but it must do. Jeanne's love for her husband trumped everything. He was the love of her life, he had rescued her from her unhappy home in Montreal, she had deceived him, yes, she knew he had not forgiven her completely but maybe he would someday, meanwhile, she had everything she wanted.

Early afternoon one day, between jobs and having had both scheduled tutorials cancelled, Alan ambled over to the Missouri Botanical Garden. This was one of his favorite destinations in town, and he had secured a membership, as he had at the old subscription library downtown and at the historical society. Jeanne had objected to these expenses, but Alan was bonkers about St. Louis, and he had his way. Alan had little interest in sports, so what could have been a tremendous expense was avoided. It was not easy to live in St. Louis and ignore the Cardinals, but Alan managed it. Jeanne had heard from more than one acquaintance there were only two seasons in St. Louis, baseball season and "waiting for baseball season." Baseball was everywhere. The team's logo was a cardinal perched upon a baseball bat, and during the season, wherever you turned, there it was, on uncountable shirts and caps and buttons and pins and cups and plates and signs and banners and flags flapping from car windows ... there was even a mortuary in town where you could be buried in a casket adorned with the cardinal on the bat! Once, Jeanne had found herself speaking with a gentleman she barely knew, and when she remarked she did not really care one way or the other about the Cardinals, he had uncivilly told her she was in the wrong town.

At the Garden, Alan liked to sit in the café and grade his pupils' papers. He sometimes wrote a letter to Stefan, a vain attempt to maintain a correspondence. Stefan threw them away, unread. He had no interest whatever in maintaining contact with Alan. The exasperating phone calls had finally ended, when Stefan had all but come out and said they were unwelcome, but the mail kept coming. Alan would not accept their friendship was over. It couldn't be more one-sided.

Alan got out his pen. He had asked Bill Trudell, who was a senior at SLUH, to read "Dover Beach" and write a short paper analyzing the poem. Bill's first line grabbed his tutor's attention: "When one has finished Matthew Arnold's 'Dover Beach,' he is left with a unique question: What is this poem about?" Alan shook his head and began writing in the margin.

"Bill, you ask yourself that question after you finish any poem, so there is nothing unique about it." Then he added: "You must think all the time."

Two elderly women at another table in the café drew his attention. Both had snowy white hair and bonnets, one pink and the other light blue. Their conversation was animated. Sisters, perhaps? Old friends? Widows? Husbands gone, children grown, now alone. Maybe they were retired schoolteachers? Teaching was what women did in their day, wasn't it? Spinsters? Or maybe they had gone into nursing? That was the other avenue for women. Alan fairly stared at them, which neither noticed. They were indeed elderly, their skin massively wrinkled and leather-like. The more he watched, the more he became persuaded there was a slight, involuntary tremor in one lady's head. Had her friend noticed? A sign of mortality, appearing in one, not the other! Or maybe it was nothing new, and they had discussed it frankly? What were their names? Alan decided on Mildred, with the shaky head, and ... and ... Betsy! Yes, Mildred and Betsy. There was something formidable about old women. When they reached those distant decades, they were fearless. Nothing rattled them. Alan pondered which of the several gardens they preferred? Victorian Garden, of course! Alan's personal preference was the Japanese Garden, called Seiwa-En, which billed itself as the largest such garden in North America. Who cared, for goodness sake? Why did everything always have to be the biggest, the fastest, the grandest, the best-est. Boasting wasn't his adopted city's way, and he liked that very much. Although his family's annual vacation trips were generally to the national parks, they had gone one year to the Upper Peninsula of Michigan, via Chicago. Alan remembered Chicago as full of superlatives. Tallest building, busiest airport, biggest (or was it oldest?) aquarium. Silly. What he failed to acknowledge was that St. Louis had once been larger than Chicago, had once been a place teeming with ambition and progress and, yes, chest-thumping. But Chicago had overtaken St. Louis in the contest for supremacy in the interior, and St. Louis had never really recovered.

Alan had never been to New York, or Philadelphia, or Washington or Boston. The only place east and north he had gone was Montreal. Nor had he been south, although there would be a trip down the Mississippi to New Orleans. It was California, Quebec, Kansas and Missouri. St. Louis was his spiritual home, and he loved every aspect of the place. St. Louis could do no wrong. Alan did not see the city in perspective. He always saw only what he wanted to see. The stark fact was, St. Louis was chock full of trouble, with many parts of the city simply abandoned and boarded up. Crime was a problem, education was a problem, city services were in a state of collapse as the tax base eroded. St. Louis was an independent city, not a part of the surrounding county, and had lost more than half its population in a generation. Yet Alan was utterly captivated. He decided the city's history was the finest in the country. Manifest Destiny! That stirring term to describe the westward expansion to the Pacific, thereby creating a country spanning a continent! And what was St. Louis' role? The Arch, the Gateway Arch, the starting point westward! Lewis and Clark. Zebulon Pike. John C. Fremont. No responsible history of the United States could ignore the role St. Louis had played.

Alan explored St. Louis alone. He was not an absent father, he shared responsibility for Mary, but this was the only thing 50/50 about his marriage. Jeanne would not, in any case, have cared to learn about the city. She was neither curious nor inquisitive. This suited Alan. He loved setting out on a Saturday morning and spending the day poking about town. Alan's nature had changed. Growing up, he had been outgoing and sociable. He made friends easily. He was well-liked. But the tumultuous move to Canada and the ensuing, chaotic eighteen months there, followed by the return to America and imprisonment, had taken an enormous toll. Alan had become obsessive and self-absorbed. He constantly questioned what he heard, what he read, looking for some ethical clue, some answer to a weighty issue. He preferred sitting at a table at the botanical garden, musing over the lives of two old women, to an evening at the movies with wife and daughter. Years later, as an adult, Mary would look back at her girlhood and wonder why her mother had never grabbed her by one arm, a suitcase by the other, and left for good. She could not decide, however, if the imbalance in her parents' marriage was something she appreciated at the time, or came to understand later. Nevertheless, she knew her father loved her as completely as did her mother. Mary's memories for the most part were good ones. The summer trips west, for example. Yellowstone was her favorite park.

"How does the geyser just keep erupting, same way, same time, over and over again?"

"Nobody knows, Mary. What do you think?" She looked puzzled, gave up on answering.

"What causes the mud to bubble?" Dad had looked this up in advance and produced an answer daughter found eminently satisfactory. They stayed at the classic inn at Old Faithful; Mary loved it. The whole place was made of wood. The bathrooms were down the hall. Now that was funny!

At Carlsbad Caverns, Mary was astonished. She refused to leave. Her parents almost had to drag her back to the surface. It was cool, down in the earth, and sweaters were useful, but back in the New Mexico sun, they were the last thing one wanted.

"Do the caves go all the way down into the middle of the earth, dad?"

"They might," her father said. "There might be life down there. There might be lakes and streams and food for people to eat, and a moon just like ours."

"How could there be a moon?"

"Would you like to read a book about some people who go to the earth's center?"

"Yes!" Back home, father bought daughter the Jules Verne story, which absorbed her for weeks.

At the Grand Canyon, father explained that the cliffs had been formed by the river at the bottom. They made the journey down. On mules!

"That river made all these cliffs!" daughter exclaimed. "How could it do that?"

"Well, it took millions of years, Mary."

When they crossed the Continental Divide, after a visit to Glacier Park in Montana, Mary asked what it was, having seen the sign.

"Divides the continent, just like the sign says," father said.

"I don't know what that means."

"It means, Mary, that the rain that falls on the west side of the divide empties into the Pacific Ocean, and the rain that falls on the east side empties into the Atlantic Ocean." Mary was silent. What could this mean?

"Somebody watched the raindrops falling?" she said.

"Every last one of them," her father joked. "The entire length of the continent." He could barely stifle a guffaw.

"How could anybody do that? The raindrops wouldn't even keep flowing. They'd disappear."

"They'd evaporate," mom threw in helpfully, herself struggling with the concept. Alan looked up at the sky. It was clear.

"Too bad, but I don't think it's going to rain, or we could watch." The Continental Divide! Mary could not take it in. How did this work? Who could have ever figured it out? Did that person walk the whole length of the continent? Her dad, she knew very well, was not past pulling her leg, and she was pretty sure she had detected some merriment in him.

"You made that all up, huh, dad?"

"No, Mary, not a word." She wasn't sure about this answer, but if it wasn't so, what explained the sign?

They floated upon Great Salt Lake, Mary asking how salt got into the water.

"Same way it got into the ocean, Mary, only the concentration is greater here. That's how you can float."

"Can I drink it?"

"No. It won't end your thirst, in fact, you'll be thirstier." Mary rather thought she'd try it.

The journeys to the national parks were an unmitigated success, with wife as well as daughter. Jeanne's experience with her adopted country was limited to the year in southern California, an unhappy time, the relatively brief time in Kansas, no picnic either, and St. Louis. The parks, however, were glorious. Even more glorious was how these trips converted her husband into another man. He was attentive rather than self-absorbed. It was as if he left all his preoccupations and doubts in St. Louis for fourteen magical days. Then, back to reality with a man whose life, she understood as no one else could, was mostly in his head.

"Some time we should go to Banff in the Canadian Rockies," she said. Her timing left something to be desired, since this came out not at Glacier, but at the Grand Canyon. Jeanne had been to Banff with her own family when she was growing up, and remembered the trip fondly. Was there something about nature that propelled people into their best behavior? Back in Montreal, the family's issues returned like clockwork.

Then there had been the trip to New Orleans on the paddlewheeler. Alan never shut up about Mark Twain the entire trip. What American schoolboy didn't read *Tom Sawyer* and *Huckleberry Finn*? But they weren't the same, were they? (Another of Alan's tutoring assignments.) Tom bamboozles his friends into whitewashing the fence for him, Huck chooses eternal hellfire rather than betray Jim. Both good yarns, but one was more than that. What made their trip most memorable, however, was a romance Mary, now fifteen, struck up with a boy of the same age, also a single child traveling with his parents. He was attempting, without much success, to quell his rage over his parents' having dragged him on the boat with them, when he met Mary. Then the trip flew by, for both. They even braved a kiss at parting, which wasn't terribly memorable, since they had closed their eyes too soon and barely touched each other's lips. His name was Robert and he lived in Kenosha, Wisconsin, and despite grand avowals, Robert and Mary would never see each other again.

Chapter 20

Iₙ ᴛʜᴇ ᴀɪʀᴘᴏʀᴛ ᴛᴇʀᴍɪɴᴀʟ, Sᴛᴇꜰᴀɴ ᴡᴏᴜʟᴅ ʜᴀᴠᴇ ᴡᴀʟᴋᴇᴅ ʀɪɢʜᴛ ᴘᴀsᴛ Jeanne, no recognition either way, had she not been holding a home-made sign with "Stefan" written upon it. The woman holding the sign was a complete stranger. Jeanne Young was 51. She had kept her good looks and her figure, there was not a trace of gray in her hair although her robust brunette might not be natural, she had her share of wrinkles but they weren't overwhelming, and she looked exceptionally smart in a plaid skirt.

"Jeanne!" Stefan said, having overcome the impulse to walk right past her and get on the next plane back to California. They embraced warmly. Jeanne Young was completely persuaded she had never laid eyes on this man. He could be Stefan Kopinski or the King of Siam.

"Welcome to St. Louis, Stefan," she said earnestly. "I am so glad you're here."

"Thank you, Jeanne, it's wonderful to see you again."

"Been awhile, hasn't it?" she said.

"Not since Montreal, I believe, when you and Alan married," Stefan said. They both knew perfectly well this was it. How was it she and her husband's oldest friend had met only once, way back in 1969? The year she had spent in L.A., he was there, wasn't he? No, he was in San Francisco.

"Seems like a million years ago," she said, with which he heartily agreed. That distant occasion, when they had actually managed to have a spat, was utterly unreal now.

"You don't look a day older," he said, which in any other context would easily have qualified as flattery, but since he could not remember how Jeanne Young had ever looked, it was perfectly honest.

They were strangers, to be sure. Stefan would have known something of Jeanne, if he had not ignored Alan's communications over the years. For her part, Jeanne knew Stefan was a lawyer, and had two children, and had he divorced? She wasn't sure. That was all she knew.

Another thing Stefan would have known was his friend's belief Jeanne had "wrecked" his life. That was the term Alan used, invariably. Jeanne understood perfectly. She had tricked him, he had done the honorable thing, and the result was, he was trapped in a marriage he hadn't sought. Alan felt cheated. Jeanne could not get him to see it any other way, for this was her husband's weakness, he could not concede a viewpoint other than his own. She was left with no choice but to accept it, and hope that with the years his anger would subside. Alan would not leave her, she could be confident of that, which left her with a husband often cold and unresponsive. In return, she loved him.

Alan was unfaithful, too. Even back in Montreal. Nothing wrong with a fling, the French had the right idea about these things, he had a way with women, and he wasn't going to abandon his family. Women tended to cling, whereas he, a man, just wanted … well … he was a man. Men weren't made for just one woman, were they? No. A woman never had two men in her life at the same time. Men were the very opposite. Did an occasional affair make him a bad husband? (Heck no, he was a bad husband, with or without adultery.)

"Your first time here?" Jeanne inquired as they climbed into her car.

"Yes. St. Louis is somewhat off the beaten path."

"Not as far as Alan is concerned. He thinks it's the center of the world."

"Bit obsessive about it, is he?"

The two fell silent. Jeanne might have pointed out a landmark, but they were in the county not the city, and there weren't any landmarks. There was very little appealing about suburban St. Louis, and even Alan seldom wandered there. As they drew nearer their destination, Stefan pondered yet again what he would say. What was he going to say? What was he supposed to say? He knew Jeanne's views on her husband's situation and was largely in agreement. Still, it remained far from certain what the best course was. Was there one? Misgiving seized Stefan momentarily. This stranger driving him around a strange city to meet a lost friend, now a complete stranger, and he was expected to come up with some magic formula that would set everything to rights again.

402

"Anything you want to go over, before we get there?" Jeanne asked, as though reading his mind.

"What worries me is what you have called his 'fragility.' I don't want to say something that might make matters worse." They had discussed this issue on the phone. It was Jeanne who had called Stefan at her husband's urgent behest.

"He's crazy in the hospital and nothing is working, and he begged me to call you," she had said frantically. Even so, it had taken every ounce of cajolery within her to persuade Stefan to come to St. Louis.

"It can't get worse," she said now to Stefan, "it can only get better. I can't imagine you could say a wrong thing. You and Alan have something unique, and that is why it's so important you came. Stefan, you can say things to Alan nobody else can, including me. You kind of have a free ticket, you might say." Free ticket? Not sure what that meant. Did Jeanne really not know how little he had said to his old college pal in a quarter of a century? Stefan had dismissed Alan as indolent, not to say peculiar, long before this recent talk of "destiny." While he had never come right out and just said to Alan, our friendship is over, he had sent the message so unequivocally, anybody else would long ago have understood. Stefan had never responded to a letter, to a Christmas card. He had never phoned Alan, not once. Alan had been back in southern California at least twice, and Stefan had lied and said he was in trial and could not spare so much as an hour for lunch. Yet Alan had never given up on the friendship, such as it was, and now it was from his reluctant friend something, preferably a miracle, was expected.

"Righto," Stefan said, "except you know, Jeanne, Alan and I have not been that close in recent years."

"I'm aware of that," she said. As a loving and attentive wife, Jeanne, in fact, was perfectly aware of how one-sided her husband's friendship with Stefan was, and deep down, she resented his presence now. He was an unworthy friend. It was just that nothing else had produced results, and maybe, just maybe, this would … somehow …

"One thing I would like to review with you," Stefan said, "although you did mention it on the phone. Would you recall again exactly what you remember from that night?" The lawyer in Stefan wanted to be clear on her version, before he asked Alan for his. It seemed unlikely, but perhaps a revealing discrepancy would turn up. You never could tell.

"We were watching TV. We usually do in the evening. I fix supper and kind of half-watch. I was in the kitchen. Not really listening, but then I heard Alan say my name in a queer sort of way, like he needed help. I ran into the living room, and he was lying on the floor. Well I panicked and put my arm under his head and called his name over and over and asked him what was wrong. I could see he was conscious, he wasn't turning blue or anything, so I helped him to his feet. He sat down on the sofa but he wasn't speaking so I could understand him. I was afraid it was a stroke so I called for an ambulance and we went to the ER and, well, the doctor said it wasn't a stroke which was a huge relief. It was clear something was wrong, though. They decided Alan should be transferred to the mental hospital. He's never been back home."

"Gotcha," Stefan said, as Jeanne pulled up at a large, red brick building, an old building, with a quartet of Corinthian columns below a portico, and a quaint dome on top, painted green.

"What a pile!" Stefan exclaimed. "Is this the hospital?"

"This is it."

"Seems extraordinarily big."

"It's for everybody in Missouri who's … who's mentally ill." She hated the place.

"Aren't you coming in?" Stefan said. It was obvious they could not leave the car where she had stopped.

"He knows me," she said drolly.

"Okay, then," he said. Apparently their conversation was over. He got out of the car. Where was she going? Home? Timbuktu?

St. Louis State Hospital was indeed housed in a grand, old building. Still, it was a hospital, and hospitals were not cheery places, they were dreary places. Remodeling and modernization were evident. Chairs and sofas in the lobby looked new and inexpensive, the lighting was muted, the wallpaper deliberately bland. Stefan couldn't decide if it was blue or purple. He approached the reception desk and introduced himself to an ample woman with a name tag reading "Norma." He stated his business. Presumably, Jeanne had made arrangements. Norma pointed to a corridor on her left after he signed the guest register.

"Down the hall and through the double doors. Room 105. Coffee is complimentary, and you can purchase soda pop or snacks from the vending machines. Enjoy your visit."

Enjoy his visit! What, was this a resort? Couldn't Norma take him to Alan? There was another woman at the desk. But no, he could go on his own, and buy himself a Coke. Stefan took a deep breath and started for Room 105. He was an experienced and capable litigator, equal to the demands of the courtroom, and he was consumed with apprehension over a meeting with an old friend who liked him a lot.

Alan occupied a room for two, but the other bed was vacant at the moment. His was the first, next to the door. Stefan walked in, and there, propped up against a pair of pillows in his hospital garb, was a man in his middle years, somewhat on the heavy side, with a Clark Gable mustache that looked very much better on Clark Gable, sipping some beverage or other from a straw, and reading a magazine. This was Alan. Stefan did not know him. The reverse wasn't the case. Stefan still looked like Stefan. He had not gone to seed, which was Stefan's first impression of Alan. He looked like an older man who had led a dissolute life and was paying for it now.

"Stef!" Alan shouted loudly enough for all St. Louis to hear. "You've come!" Alan leaped from his bed with an agility that belied his girth and gave Stefan a fierce embrace.

"Hey there, Alan, how are you?" Stefan muttered when their embrace was done. "How are you, man?"

"A whole heckuva lot better than half a minute ago, I'd say!" Alan was beaming. If his doctor or any member of the staff had wandered in at the moment, they'd have sworn they were in the wrong room. Alan Young, suffering from acute depression brought on by "suicidal self-hatred," was never, never cheerful. Alan now took Stefan's hand and shook it vigorously.

"Well get back in bed, I didn't mean to get you up."

"Heck no, I'll take the chair. You take the other one." They sat. "Jeanne just drop you?"

"Yes. Not sure where she went."

"She'll come back later. We are going to have a long visit first." Long visit? It was past five. Stefan intended to be back in his hotel room by nine, ideally sooner. Of course, there was already a kink in that plan, since his ride had disappeared.

"So how are you, Alan? Can't really quite believe I'm here. Jeanne said you could use a bit of cheering up, and that's my role."

"Aw, Stef," Alan said, but abruptly couldn't get another word out. Stefan, meanwhile, was marveling at the name by which Alan had always addressed him. Nobody else, not his parents, not his brother, not his wife number one, not his wife number two, not his partners at the firm, not another soul had ever called him "Stef." It had an instantly salubrious effect on Stefan now, for it made Alan real to him, as he was not in the physical sense.

"Alan, you ..."

"It's this destiny stuff, Stef. We all have one. Most of us never are shown what it is. I have been. It's knocked everything out of me." This Stefan did not grasp. What's the use in a destiny, if you don't know what it is? He caught himself. Don't try to figure out statements like this one, stick to the purpose of the visit. If only he knew what that was ...

"Alan, Jeanne explained this destiny stuff, as you call it, but I don't really get it. I wish she was here, so we could both hear what you have to say together. Anyway, tell me what you mean, because I didn't come all this way not to say something to you, but you go first."

"Now Stef, how long a flight is it from L.A. to St. Louis? Couple, three hours?" Closer to three.

"Okay, not long by air," Stefan laughed, "but by camel, yes."

"What do you think of my adopted town?" Alan said enthusiastically. Enthusiasm would have floored his doctor, too. "Guess you haven't really seen much yet, though." Not seen much yet? Did Alan think he was hanging around? He had a flight early the next morning.

"Right. A freeway through suburbs. Could be anywhere."

"Did you see the Arch from the plane?"

"Didn't have a window seat, unfortunately." It was overcast, as well, and the flight path had not taken them near downtown.

"You can see it tomorrow. It's not going anywhere."

"Actually, Alan, I have to get back tomorrow. Thought Jeanne told you?"

"Tomorrow? You're leaving tomorrow?"

"Alan, I barely managed these 24 hours. I'm preparing for trial."

"Gosh, Stef, we were going to have a real visit. I can't believe you're not staying." Alan was crestfallen. Stefan was unaffected.

"In my experience, Alan, short visits often are the best," Stefan found himself saying. Alan remained distressed. "Look, we have plenty of time. Jeanne will be back, I suppose the three of us are having dinner here. Really, don't be upset, we have time."

"Don't really have much of a choice, have I?" Alan said, gathering himself.

"Tell me about this destiny stuff, Alan. That's why I'm here." Stefan was now in earnest, and he meant to be blunt. Alan detected this. Hadn't his old friend come because he was an old friend? Alan embarked upon an explanation. Stefan had heard it all before, from Jeanne, over the phone. He was not expecting a revelation, and none was forthcoming. They were in Ontario again, in Windsor, Alan searching for an answer, Stefan expected to deliver it. But this wasn't Windsor, Stefan had no memory of ever having gone to Windsor, or it might have served him as a dress rehearsal.

"It was June 30, evening," Alan said. "I turned on the TV. Jeanne and I always listen to the news. The announcer said, 'The remains of the Vietnam War's Unknown Soldier, recently exhumed from Arlington National Cemetery, have been positively identified.' I took an interest, strange, because I haven't given five minutes' thought to Vietnam in 25 years. Anyway, I say to Jeanne, 'Be weird, wouldn't it, if he's from St. Louis?' and she says 'Small chance' with which I agree. It's not even a small chance, this country has 300 million people and this city has 300,000 of them. How big a chance is that? The announcer says, 'The remains are those of Air Force 1st Lt. Michael Joseph Blassie of St. Louis,' and the next thing I know I'm lying on the floor and the medics are tending to me. They revive me and take me to the ER. Jeanne says I'm incoherent but I am not incoherent, Stef, I am perfectly coherent and my mind is crystal clear. The long and short of it is, Lt. Blassie did his duty, and I ran away instead of doing my duty. I ran off to Canada with a head full of baloney. Do you know my dad once told me to my face he was disappointed in me? I was speechless. Lt. Blassie was shot down in 1972, while I'm sitting in my cozy little jail cell congratulating myself on what a great guy I am. I've saved the country if only those 300 million people would follow my sublime moral leadership. What a load of baloney that is." Alan paused. "Can you really disagree with me, Stef? With my conclusions? If you can, I'd like to hear it. The floor is yours." Alan had spoken with an eerie calm.

"Alan," he said, "You might be the first person who ever called a jail cell 'cozy.'"

"Not taking it back," Alan said.

"I'm not asking you to." Alan's self-condemnation was tiresome. It was almost as if he was half-enjoying himself. "I also think it was unconscionable of your father to say what he did," Stefan added irrelevantly, which prompted Alan to say some more things about his father. Stefan feigned

407

interest. It was getting on toward dinner time, and Stefan had not had a bite to eat since leaving L.A. "Why don't we grab some supper?" he suggested. "You hungry?" Alan was agreeable. There was still no sign of Jeanne. They went to supper. Alan took some pills. Their topic was lost. Alan began throwing questions at Stefan. He asked him about his family. Alan knew Stefan had divorced his wife, Debra, who had had two daughters by him. Stefan obligingly answered Alan's questions about the girls, staying away from the older girl's alcoholism. "Some emotional issues, such as teenagers have." Alan didn't know Stefan had remarried.

"What's become of Debra?" he asked. Alan had never met Debra, never met Sharon, never met Linda, never met Lisa. Just names.

"Doing all right." Stefan wasn't going to say much about Debra.

"None of my business, Stef, but can't say I'm not curious what could have produced a divorce, I mean, that's pretty drastic, and doesn't really sound like my oldest friend. She do something?" Doesn't really sound like my oldest friend! Now what did that mean? Since he didn't know beans about his oldest friend.

"Kind of a religious nut. They're Methodists, her family, and they want you to be, too. They should be missionaries, come to think of it."

"She was too religious?" Alan said. "Can't divorce over that."

"I didn't say that."

"I don't know anybody who's very religious. Religion is diminishing, I think." Alan turned thoughtful. "Funny, the things we remember. When I was growing up, there was this sign downtown, 'JESUS SAVES.' It was on two lines, fit perfectly since five letters in each word, and it was lit at night. Probably atop the Rescue Mission, can't remember. Strange, to think of it at all."

"Jesus saves. Debra could relate to that."

"I wonder what became of that sign," Alan said nostalgically. "Long gone, I'm sure." Whether the city was the better for it was an open question.

"Downtown L.A. is in a permanent state of construction," Stefan said. "I seldom go there."

"I wonder if Pershing Square is still there," Alan said. "Hope so. They can't turn everything into a parking lot."

"Pershing Square?"

"A whole city block that was a park. Beautiful. Lots of lush foliage. Sidewalk preachers. Probably a Communist or two. Very impressive when you're ten years old."

"I wouldn't be surprised if it's gone. Los Angeles doesn't look back."

"There was this big hotel, too, the Biltmore. Faced out on the park. My mom took me inside one time. Huge lobby, the way hotels had in those days. I don't know why we went inside, except to see it, I suppose. Wait, we went in the elevator, too. They had operators. Some kind of wheel the operator turned with a handle. Operator called out the floors. I remember that like it was yesterday." A smile actually crossed Alan's face. This was happy reminiscence. "And there was this weird little train, Stef. Forget what it was called. I'll think of it in a minute. It went up a hill downtown. They had this track, and the train went up from the bottom station while the train at the upper station headed down. Just one track, but in the middle there were two tracks, and the trains always met there. Otherwise, they'd have collided. I always wondered how they met right there in the middle, every time. I was ten. The whole thing was on a timer, obviously."

"Obviously," Stefan said. He had not come to St. Louis to listen to Alan ramble about growing up in Los Angeles.

"So where were we?" Alan said, sensing his friend was uninterested in the features of downtown Los Angeles in the 1950's. "You got a divorce. What happened, though? Debra doesn't sound like the type who'd run around." This produced an unceremonious guffaw from Stefan.

"I think you could safely bet the ranch on that."

"Well, I didn't mean to pry."

"No problem. We had irreconcilable differences. That's all you really need to establish. Divorce is no-fault in California. Pretty much everywhere, I'm sure."

"So you don't have to have a reason to get a divorce?"

"No."

"And your new wife? What did you say her name is?"

"Not that new anymore. Sharon's her name. Sweet woman, I'm lucky I found her."

"She work? Got kids?"

"No, and no. Sharon keeps busy, though. She's always dabbling into something, and she is a tremendously social woman. Loves to go to parties, and have them. She has a life of her own, and sometimes I feel like we're

409

just passing each other in the night, but we're devoted to each other. She's a good wife. And stepmother." Stefan had said about as much as he intended to say about his domestic affairs. They spoke of sundry, inconsequential matters. Stefan steered clear of St. Louis, which once would have been an inexhaustible subject, but Alan had said, when they spoke in his room, he felt the city he loved had "betrayed" him, and Stefan had not liked the sound of that, whatever it meant. Well, it meant nothing, that's what it meant. Ditto the poetry he had suddenly thrown into the conversation, out of nowhere; so typical of Alan. What was it?

"The rose of all the world is not for me, I want for my part only the little white rose of Scotland, that smells sharp and sweet, and breaks the heart. Hugh MacDiarmid." Stefan had made the mistake of asking what it meant. "Can't explain poetry, Stef. You have to get it yourself." Now that was irritating. Yes, by golly, that was irritating. Stefan wasn't pleased by the onslaught of questions, either. His family wasn't his friend's business, and he certainly had not come to St. Louis to talk about them.

"So tell me something about your work," Alan said. "You haven't said a word. I know you're just being modest, that you have a great reputation. I knew back in college you'd be a great lawyer." What a dumb remark; Alan hadn't known that.

"I'm a partner in a law firm, handle defendant's side employment law mostly. I did some real estate in the beginning, and tax, but gravitated to employment law, and that's where I've stayed."

"So you represent companies, right, against unions?"

"No, Alan, that's labor law. Employment law is new." Stefan definitely was not going to get into a discussion about his practice. He said a few words about protected classes, and discrimination, and harassment, and employment at-will, and retaliation. "You have honest plaintiffs and you have liars," he concluded.

"Glad you're the lawyer, Stef."

"Alan, look, it's getting late, do you want to hear what I've come to say, or not?" (They had returned to Alan's room.) Stefan didn't wait for a reply. "You speak of your terrible and unique destiny. You've used that phrase more than once, haven't you?" Alan nodded. "Alan, you have had a coincidence in your life. We all have them. We all have them. You've had others, haven't you, this isn't the first. Yes, they momentarily leave us startled. We even think, sometimes, God is sending me a message. No, God isn't sending

410

a message. There is no message. It's just a coincidence. That's all, just a coincidence. It is the sum total of what we are dealing with here. You and you alone have decided to turn this happenstance into this destiny business, that's absolute nonsense. It's nonsense, Alan. But you know, Alan, I can say this, your wife can say it, your doctors can say it, but it's all for nothing if you do not decide, at some point, decide yourself, for once in your life, to listen to a voice besides the one in your head. When you do this, you'll get out of this place, you want that, don't you? I am telling you, as your friend of long standing, you have taken a meaningless coincidence and decided to make it the turning point in your life. You are shut up in this building, you know why? Because you're a suicide risk, Alan. That's why they count your pills every day. Did you think about that? That's why they have you on the ground floor, so you can't jump from a window. You have created this hell for yourself, this torment, all over nothing. Your wife, Alan, loves you. You are putting her through hell over this nonsense, she's worried out of her mind. You want to play these mental games, fine, provided you're a bachelor. You're not a bachelor." Stefan paused. Alan said nothing.

"Alan, I want to tell you something. A colleague of mine at the firm handled a fraud claim recently. Jury believed the plaintiff. Except for one woman. This woman, according to my colleague, wouldn't be dissuaded. Eleven to one. They adjourned overnight, reconvened in the morning. Know what happened?"

"No, what?"

"She gave in. She changed her mind. Or, to be exact, she didn't change her mind, but she recognized eleven to one is eleven to one, and maybe she was wrong, and although, deep down, she didn't think so, she was going to defer to the judgment of eleven other thoughtful, intelligent people." Stefan paused, but not long enough for Alan to speak up, because he wanted to finish. "Now, why do I tell you this? Because I want to make a prediction. I want to predict what you are going to say. You are going to say she sold out, aren't you? She was false to herself. Untrue to her principles. Made an indefensible decision, ethically. Am I right, Alan?"

"You know you are," Alan said sadly.

"My dear old friend," Stefan said, actually taking Alan's hand, "this woman, in my opinion, did the ethical, not the unethical, thing. She was willing to say to herself, internally, privately, maybe I'm wrong. She listened to that voice, and she responded to it. Very few people can do this. We all know we're right, all the time. This is logically impossible, of course, but we go right on believing it anyway. Alan, please consider that you could be wrong. If you will do this, I do believe it is your first step in recovering your life. You can do this. You have a strong support system." Stefan didn't specifically include himself here. "I want you to think about this, will you promise me you will?" Alan seemed not to be listening. A long, not entirely comfortable, silence ensued.

"I'll think about it, Stef." More silence. "I will, Stef, promise. I'll think about your visit. Why wouldn't I? I'll think about everything you've said, I will." Alan was sinking again. "Coincidences, you're right, there's a lot of coincidences. Thinking differently. Thinking about that woman who changed her mind. I still think she was wrong. Not thinking about destiny. All that stuff about your work. At-will divorce and privileged classes. I've been listening, believe me."

"It's no-fault divorce, Alan, at-will employment." Stefan started to add protected, not privileged classes, but why bother? Ridiculous.

"Same thing, wouldn't you say?" Alan said.

"Same what?" Stefan said. Jeanne appeared at the door.

"Hello, boys," she said. How had their evening gone? Well, very well. Get all caught up? Yep, sure did. Talk about anything important? I'll say. Stefan was determined farewells would not take long. He consented to a hug from his oafish friend amid pledges to keep in touch. They would keep in touch the same way they always had, unilaterally. Stefan felt he had accomplished whatever objective his journey was, and he was emphatically done.

"I wish you could stay another day or two, Stefan," Jeanne said on the ride to the hotel. "It would mean so much to Alan." She said this out of politeness. She knew Stefan would not stay. That he had come at all was incredible.

"I have to get back." They had had this conversation. He wasn't having it again.

"I understand." Jeanne drove on in silence. Stefan was content to say nothing, his mind already in his office the next day. Jeanne, surely, would ask about his visit with Alan, and his answer was prepared.

"What do you think about Alan's condition?" she said with just a hint of exasperation. Couldn't he speak up without her inquiry first? Was that asking so much?

"I have no way of answering that because, unlike you, I do not know how Alan has been. Really, this is the question I should ask you. Do you see progress? Alan for the most part struck me as lucid. He was very anxious, he was even shaking at one point, and his mind wandered, yet for the most part I could understand him. He's so thoroughly fixed upon this destiny business, and it's so irrational, I don't know what will work. I spoke as strongly as I could, that's what I came to do, and it's all I can do. I wonder if hypnosis might be attempted. Has this been considered?"

"It's been considered. His doctor thinks it could backfire. Make things worse. We've also talked about something even more drastic, ECT. It could cause him to lose his memory ... which might be a good thing, but what if he woke up and didn't know who I am?" Jeanne was at the point of tears.

"I'm no expert, but I don't believe that's a risk." Or was it? Stefan wasn't sure.

"Did he call himself an Oboe Among Clarinets?"

"Yes." Stefan had forgotten that asinine self-definition.

"Any thoughts on that?"

"Not really. Alan is completely self-absorbed. You and I and everybody, we're just accessories. Please don't misunderstand, I don't mean to be insensitive. This is just the way Alan is. He's forever wondering about philosophy and morality and what the right thing to do is. As if there was such a thing. Nine times out of ten, one path may be better than another, but not absolutely better. It's all gray." Jeanne could not disagree.

"Know what he used to call himself, before Oboe Among Clarinets?"

"What?"

"Deep In Shallow Water." Stefan gasped. Another idiocy. How could this woman put up with this boor, let alone love him with all within her?

"There again, that self-absorption," Stefan said.

"His doctor, doctors that is, say these self-designations are significant. They say it's indicative of Alan's isolation, how he subconsciously wants to be different, to be alone."

"I concur. Alan has always wanted to set himself apart." Stefan realized he was speaking as if he had known his friend over the past quarter century, when he had not.

"What really worries me," Jeanne said, "I see him slipping away from me, and I can't stop it." Now the tears burst forth. "I love Alan, I can't bear to lose him."

"We'll pull him through, Jeanne," Stefan said, resting his hand upon her shoulder.

"Thank you for coming." They drove on, silent again. Then she spoke up. "Alan's conversation with himself, as his doctors say, about his destiny, did you say anything about that to him? Or did I ask you about that before?" Had she? Stefan himself couldn't remember.

"It's a meaningless coincidence. That's what I told him."

"What did he say?"

"Well, let's see." Stefan paused. "Don't recall his exact words, but obviously he refuses to accept that. I mean, that's what this is all about, isn't it? His so-called destiny?" Jeanne could think of nothing to say. Stefan clearly had no answer. No one had an answer. There wasn't one. Stefan continued. "You are really on the horns of a cruel dilemma. Alan needs to be busy, so he doesn't spend his days ruminating. Yet lying in that hospital bed, what can he do, but ponder? He gets worse, not better. But if he's released, the consensus, as I understand it, is that he'll kill himself. What's he going to do, spend the rest of his life there?" Jeanne was crying. Her love for her husband was closer to worship. A husband lying in a hospital bed, filled with self-loathing, more dependent than ever on her. When hadn't that been the case? She was the family prop. He had gone to prison. Then what? Who was he? Alan had no career, no profession. A bum. She worshipped a bum. Absolutely no explaining it, Jeanne's love for her husband was like a force of nature, a law unto its own, impervious to logic and common sense, unassailable and inexhaustible.

They neared the hotel. Traffic was sparse. It was after 10:00. Stefan spoke up.

"Alan should be released, I think, whatever the risk. It's worth it. He has no life at all in that place, playing mind games all day long, I mean, what's the point?"

"Won't you stay another day, Stefan?" she asked. She knew he wouldn't. Stefan was cold. He wasn't interested in being her friend, any more than he was her husband's. He'd put this trip behind him before St. Louis disappeared from the plane's windows.

"Can't, sorry." She pulled up and stopped at the front door. No more talk. "Keep me posted how he's doing." She extended her hand and he took it between his. No hug. Sayonara. Abruptly, the falseness of his friendship overcame her, and she nearly gave it expression. Stefan didn't give a damn.

He didn't want to be kept posted. And she wouldn't keep him posted. Stefan entered the lobby and drew a sigh of relief exceeded only by the one Jeanne drew as she drove away.

On his flight the next morning, Stefan spotted the Gateway Arch from the window. His trip to St. Louis was complete.

CHAPTER 21

A S STEFAN BECAME MORE KNOWN AMONG HIS COLLEAGUES, HE BEGAN cutting back on his litigation practice and spending more time "schmoozing." He was a senior partner, he was expected to know the right people, including in Sacramento and Washington.

One of the ways he went about making and keeping important connections, a "network," was to speak at employment law conferences. He was in demand and not infrequently found himself in Chicago or New York or Key West or San Francisco. An annual conference in San Francisco, which he never missed, was his destination now. He always flew, but this year, he was driving. He was to give one of the plenary talks to the entire conference, then speak at a pair of what were termed "break-out" sessions, of which there were fifty-eight to choose from. The conference featured the usual smorgasbord: Do's and Don'ts of Criminal Background Checks; Federal Whistleblower Claims; The Bermuda Triangle: FMLA, ADA and Worker's Compensation; Same-Sex Harassment After *Windemere*: Plaintiff Counsels' Perspective; The Equal Pay Act: Why Are Women Still Short-Changed?; Common Mistakes in Drafting Separation And Release Agreements; The Five Critical Steps in a Sexual Harassment Investigation; FMLA Basics. And so forth. Among the faculty of at least thirty, he was sure to run into many colleagues. The conference itself typically drew upwards of six hundred participants.

He could count on certain staples, too. Craig Kearney, which rhymed nicely with blarney, would tell the jokes, his métier; Arthur Vigil and Louann Polk would handle "housekeeping" matters, terrific bores; Peter Rivers would give away his "signature lollipops" at his firm's booth. There would be dozens of booths. Then there was San Francisco. Tons of wonderful restaurants. What was that place on Geary Street? Best dim sum restaurant in town, and Stefan didn't even care that much for Chinese food. Catch the "world famous" drag show at Finisterre's? Pass on that. Ride a cable car again? Shucks, yes. Rub shoulders with the tourists. You'd find a few of them at Fisherman's Wharf, all right; no native would go near that place. Stefan enjoyed the city's crowded, busy sidewalks. It was a heady city, more like New York than L.A., to Stefan. Los Angeles started with cars. It wasn't that there weren't some great places to go. You just couldn't get there without an automobile. You could sit at your desk and look out the window at a coffee shop not three blocks away, but could you get there on foot? Impossible.

The conference held no surprises for Stefan, which was fine. He hadn't expected any. Robert Cornish from the Equal Employment Opportunity Commission in Washington gave a good talk, as did Judge Darnell of the Ninth Circuit. Senator Milhaus presented his annual summary of the legislative session. Stefan knew Rick Milhaus well, and when they found time for a chat, did not disagree with his opinion the session had been a bust. The conference, which billed itself as the "Biggest and Best in the West" had, in truth, become unwieldy. What had begun years earlier as a true lawyers' conference had ballooned into an event that drew hundreds of human resources personnel, the preponderance of them women. It was well they attended, but it had changed the focus of the conference somewhat, and Stefan decided he liked it better before.

Stefan schmoozed and networked with his usual gusto, and when the conference concluded, he pointed south. He went along the coast, stopping at Monterey for a night, then down to Santa Barbara for another night. It would be an easy sprint home from there. When was the last time he had been in Santa Barbara? He couldn't remember. There wasn't much not to like about Santa Barbara. A prosperous community that somehow had escaped the uncontrollable growth of Los Angeles. Just a beautiful town, and that included the university campus. Stefan opted for a bit of nostalgia. If you had asked him why he wanted to visit the campus, he'd have fumbled with an answer just as he had when Sharon inquired why he was driving to the San Francisco conference rather than flying.

Finding the school wasn't difficult, but finding a place to park was close to futile. He finally pulled into a ramp that wasn't even on the campus proper. He headed into the campus. This was where he had gone to college. Those four years seemed very distant now. What was the name of his dormitory? Creighton Hall, that was it! He set out to find Creighton Hall, and did find it, but the building had been razed and replaced by a modern monstrosity four stories high, still called Creighton Hall. It looked much bigger than the building he remembered. He didn't go inside. The campus was not familiar. It was getting on to lunch time, and he thought he might grab a sandwich somewhere. The Student Union would have sandwiches, if he could find it. He would find it. This was the purpose of his having driven, not flown, to the conference in San Francisco. This was the purpose of his having elected to spend a night in Santa Barbara, when Los Angeles, only a stone's throw away, could easily have been reached. This was the purpose of his making a beeline to the campus from his hotel. He was going to find the Union, and he was going to find something very specific in the Union.

He had to ask directions. He went past the bookstore. It seemed very much larger than he remembered, and filled with merchandise besides books. He saw sweatshirts inscribed with UCSB, green, blue, red and brown. Caps, too. Backpacks galore. No surf boards. How come? Stefan decided the bookstore was new and not in the same location as before. He wandered on, more or less keeping to the directions he had been given. The Anthropology Building, the Liberal Arts Building, the Administration Building. Abruptly, there was his destination. A boy and a girl emerged just as he reached the entrance. They were pawing each other with considerable determination. His hair was in what Stefan decided was a bouffant. It was bright orange. Each wore a backpack. Stefan looked a moment too long and got a look from the boy that clearly said, "What are you staring at, dude?"

The dude went inside, where plenty of students were milling about. He encountered one "fast food" restaurant after another. Stefan told himself these definitely were not there before, and he was correct. He mulled a hamburger but feared indigestion later. Students were everywhere, including not a few sitting on the floor, momentarily relieved of their backpacks. One young man with a thick, black beard was listening to music through ear jacks while idly consuming a quantity of French fries, most of which he had carelessly allowed to slip out of a small sack onto the floor. No environment could be more casual. Stefan had the impression he had wandered not into a school building but a summer camp. Could be in California, Europe, anywhere. Nothing hinted at scholarship or purpose of any sort, it was just sprawl on a sofa, or the floor, and do whatever you wanted. Stefan spotted a sign indicating the way to the cafeteria. That seemed improbable, that they still had a cafeteria, in view of the fast food invasion, but it was precisely the cafeteria he was searching for. There had been two lines, one for those settling for the *plat du jour*, the other for those preferring the *a la carte* selections. The two lines were not alike. The *a la carte* offerings were extensive and not a little more expensive than the *plat du jour*. Despite his having long ago dumped his college pal and forgotten his college days, Stefan had never been able to shake free from his memory one thing: Alan had always taken the *plat du jour*, not the *a la carte* meal, when they ate together, which was every day. Alan, unlike Stefan, could afford the more expensive meal, but he always opted for the plainer fare of the *plat du jour*. Such a strange thing, this memory, but Stefan cherished it, and he wanted to find if the cafeteria was still operated in this manner.

He was in for a major disappointment. The cafeteria consisted of tables and vending machines. It was where you could bring that hamburger you just bought, and purchase a candy bar from one of the machines. No food was served, no *plat du jour*, no *a la carte*. Stefan remembered there was a table by the windows he and Alan had favored. He spotted several tables by the windows, but they meant nothing. He decided on a cup of coffee from one of the machines. Sandwiches were also available, but they did not look appetizing. He took a seat. The chairs were plastic, the tables were Formica, the cups from the vending machines were Styrofoam. A coed working at her computer glanced at Stefan and went about her business. Was she working on her term paper? Playing a computer game? Stefan remembered there had been pinball machines and pool tables in the Union, somewhere. You could play these games now electronically, or "virtually" in computerese, so the real things probably had gone the way of the dodo bird. Hadn't there been a sign, "Mind your pool stick." Now that was a strange thing to have popped into one's consciousness. Alan and Stefan had seldom played pool; neither was much into games. Two girls at the table nearest the vending machines rose to leave. One was a head taller than the other. Both were blondes, and they wore their hair identically, short, straight, cropped. As they walked out, arms linked, Stefan noted what was inscribed on the back of each shirt. On the shorter girl: Butch Cassonova. On the taller: Sin Dance Kid.

Those had been good years, 1965-1969, when he was an undergraduate. Stefan had taken school seriously. He wondered if this was what he could not quite put his finger on, about this casual campus where he was now, versus the one he had known thirty years earlier. A reduced seriousness? He had worked hard and made his grades. Stefan had decided while still in high school he would become a lawyer, and he never swerved from this goal. This was such a contrast to Alan. Stefan remembered Alan as a goof-off. Alan crammed for tests, but the rest of the time, he never cracked a book, or at least not while Stefan was around. And Stefan was around. They had been inseparable. Poor Alan, Stefan reflected, sipping his cappuccino, which wasn't half-bad. Lying in that horrible hospital bed, the textbook "basket case." Alan had his good days and his bad days and his very bad days. He'd never leave. He was incoherent, he spoke nonsense, he'd throw an absurdity or something irrelevant or a line from some book into the middle of a sentence and then flash a silly smile. Who knew what was in his head? Yet Jeanne remained true. Stefan found himself mirthful again over the craziness. He toiled and brought home the bacon and had had two wives, each in varying degrees indifferent. Alan did nothing, well, no, he had spent some time behind bars, and what did Jeanne give him? Unconditional love.

Stefan's summary of his friend's life was not entirely accurate. Alan had brought home the bacon from time to time. His two teaching positions had produced a real paycheck ... his job at the Northside YMCA, a good, steady job he had held many years, until it was converted into a volunteer position ... his work at the bookstore, where he thought he was going to be around books and was, in a manner of speaking, working in the mailroom and largely packing and unpacking boxes and maneuvering a forklift, which was amazing fun to drive ... his work at the suburban newspaper, where he thought he'd be using supposed journalistic skills but was placed in the circulation department, where he was useless ... his work at that hardware store, where he had stayed several years, also a sales job but since the products were widely known and of proven quality, they could withstand an inept salesman ... his interest in alternative medicine and intent to learn acupuncture, prompted by a brief affair with a Chinese woman, but then came the blow ... the destiny ... a life obliterated ...

Stefan reflected on Alan's incarceration. How long had he been confined at Leavenworth? Was it five years? Stefan felt it had been something less. Alan had returned from Canada and all but demanded the government lock him up! Some ethical point, some nuance, so typical of Alan. What had it been, exactly?

Stefan sipped his coffee. What was it nagging him? He couldn't seem to rise from his seat, as if an invisible hand restrained him. Two young men came in, joking back and forth. "Alan and me!" Stefan reflected. How could they have been such close friends, indeed, friends at all? Stefan felt the person Alan Young had become was someone with whom he would never have become friends. Like a relative you really can't stand but, by virtue of the blood connection, qualified as a dearly beloved cousin. The girl working so assiduously at her computer caught his eye again. Maybe she had a hot date later? Stefan had not had many hot dates in college. Alan might be lazy and unambitious, but he was assuredly better with the distaff population. Well, until that Canadian girl deceived him. He was too trusting. So absurd, so avoidable, running off to Canada in the first place, escaping the draft, getting tricked, marrying, husband and father until one day, oops, made a mistake, high-tailing it back home, going to prison, going to make everything right, meanwhile wife and daughter can fend for themselves, nothing would be allowed to stand between him and the penitentiary!

One of the boys gave one of the vending machines a solid whack. Then they exchanged high-fives, and one departed left; the other, right. Just like the two cafeteria lines! Left for *plat du jour*, right for *a la carte*. Stefan's memory was fighting for something, something he knew but didn't know, something that was there but not there, he needed the key, the key would unlock the memory. The boys, the cafeteria, the food choices. Alan's taking the *plat du jour* was like … like something … it was like … what had someone said … taking the *plat du jour* was like … it was like … like something. He could not get it to form in his mind. A man about his age came in, purchased a sandwich and left. Probably a professor, Stefan mused. "You may remove your backpacks!" must be the first utterance of every lecture. Stefan remembered a class he had had that met Monday afternoon for three hours. A pre-law course. Oddly, most of the students were girls, and the professor was a woman, too. He thought she favored the female students. This was well before the great change in the profession. The student body at law schools now was about half male, half female. Stefan figured he wouldn't live to see the implications for the profession, but the female lawyers he knew were very good at what they did. Divorces, that's what they did. Who was that obnoxious lawyer Debra had hired? She was a she, yes indeed.

Stefan reached for the letter in his jacket pocket. He had not opened it, but it was from Alan. It had a St. Louis postmark. Why had he brought it with him, when he had long ago quit reading Alan's periodic letters? Was having just been in St. Louis, a matter of months ago, the reason? Stefan didn't ask himself.

> Dear Stef,
>
> Gosh it was great to see you again after such a long long time. I just can't tell you how much helped me!!!! Jeanne thinks so to. We can't let so much time go by between a visits. Next thing you know we'll be old. (I have to pinch to realize how many sores and scores are behind me now. Ghastly!!!! I have been thinking about our conversation. I was listening to you!!!! I remember everything you said. For example, to be busier. Yes!!!! Doctor has made a changes in my pills, he does this sometimes. I actually sleep okay. Jeanne is my angel. I know this has been an ordeal for her. I'm really sorry about your divorce, but those things happen, uh? Maybe at-will divorce isn't such a hot idea. I don't like meditation, not relaxing. Tou are supposed to say the same word over and over again called a mantra. I don't find it relaxing, either , but they make me do it. I recite Keats hahhahhah. Who are these coming to the sacrifice, oh mysterious priest???? Come back come back come back. Stef, you are my oldest friend and always will be.
> Alan

Stefan put the letter down. What a mess. He finished his coffee. What was he doing here? In all the years he had been in southern California, he had never made the simple drive from Los Angeles to Santa Barbara. Why, it was a half-day's excursion! Nothing to it! Yet he had never done it, never crossed his mind. It had taken a road trip to San Francisco, and here he was now, at the former cafeteria at UCSB, with a letter from Alan, which he had deliberately, he now realized, brought with him on his trip, to open here and, moreover, actually read. What explained it? Stefan was a little shaken by his own, odd behavior.

He put the letter back in his pocket. Time to go. He took one last, fond look around the place. Such a dear memory, those meals with Alan. Every day, every day, they ate together, and Alan took the *plat du jour*. Every time. Stefan asked himself, yet again, why this meant so much to him? He carried the memory around like a great treasure, and it was thirty years ago, and he remembered hardly another thing of his college days, but he remembered this. Why? He shook his head. What was it about the *plat du jour* and … what … something about the *plat du jour* … there were two signs, weren't there, one identifying the *plat du jour* line, the other *a la carte* … something about Alan … taking the *plat du jour* … something said … something was … similar … something was similar …

Stefan reached home. He was oddly tired. Three days on the road, but none of the drives had been arduous. It was mid-afternoon; Sharon was off somewhere. She hadn't left a note, but he hadn't said for sure when he'd be back. Wives were a burden. If he had not married Debra Morrison, the wrenching divorce would not have happened. "Get a divorce, Stefan." "Do it now." "You want to make partner, don't you?" "She's holding you back." So he got the divorce, and he found the right wife. "Good move." "That's the ticket." "She's sharp." "She knows the score." Yes indeed, Sharon was so indispensable to his professional progress, she could move to Oregon and stay there indefinitely, and nobody had said a word.

He began sifting through the mail on his desk. Amazing how much had accumulated in a week. He was restless. Not as young as he used to be, maybe the trip was more fatiguing than he realized. The mail was mostly bills and solicitations. Stefan decided on a swim at the health club he had joined. He did not much like exercise, but swimming was relaxing and not too demanding, and it was said to be the best all-around exercise. His palatial home included a swimming pool and, for that matter, an exercise room outfitted with all the latest equipment, but he could not get himself to use either. It was paying dues at the health club that worked. He was just out the door when Sharon arrived.

"Hey, you're back," she greeted him.

"So it appears."

"Good trip?"

"Like always."

"Big conference?"

"Several hundred. It's bigger every year. Not necessarily better."

"They don't always equate, do they?"

"Nope."

"Looks like I caught you headed out the door. Going to Wright's?"

"I was, but I'm not terribly committed to the idea."

"Oh go on," Sharon said. "I'll ask Magdalena to whip together something. How about enchiladas? Be ready when you get back." Stefan gave his wife a peck. She was a good wife, and he felt, correctly, she regarded him as a good husband, but absence had a way of making the heart grow fonder, and Stefan sometimes wondered if the long stay in Oregon might not have been only for Linda's sake. Stefan reached Wright's Fitness Center and ran into Judge Lowry immediately. There was no coming to Wright's without meeting friends and acquaintances; the place was so successful, a competitor was building a facility within a matter of blocks.

"Greetings, counselor," the judge exclaimed. "How's tricks?"

"Gettin' by, gettin' by." The men shook hands. "How are you, judge?"

"If I were any better, I couldn't stand it." It was the kind of remark that defeated further remark. Hugo Lowry, to be sure, had presided over more than one trial in which Stefan was litigating, and Stefan had fared generally well in his court. The judge did not, however, enjoy a particularly strong reputation in the legal community. For one thing, although he was not even elderly, he had a way of snoozing in court. It was kind of hilarious, really. The judge would doze off, usually in early afternoon. This created an "After you, Alphonse," situation. Who would wake up the judge?

"Is the judge asleep?" would start to circulate among the jurors.

"I believe he is," Stefan had actually once said, when a woman in the juror's box had asked him.

"Can he do that?"

"The judge can do whatever he wants, ma'am." Stefan slinked away, laughing under his breath. One of the lawyers generally solved the problem with an "accidental" rap on the bench, bringing Judge Lowry back to life. Hugo Lowry, in any case, could not be budged from his position. Every four years, he must run for re-election. He always won easily. One opponent had tried to make an issue of his dozing, to no avail.

Stefan had his swim, glad now he had gone to the trouble, it was invigorating. He toweled off, without further greetings, dressed and headed for his car. At the exit, whom should he meet but Judge Lowry again.

"Stay well," said the judge. Stay well?

"See ya," Stefan replied. He liked the judge. He was all right. He liked a little siesta after lunch himself, come to think of it. A judgeship was a very good job, generously paid, and you got to scold lawyers. Generally secure jobs, too, although state judges, unlike federal, must deal with elections. Still, there was nothing like incumbency. Stefan recalled a young man, literally half a dozen years out of law school, who had not spent a day of his brief career in a courtroom, who was appointed to fill a term of a judge who had passed away. Totally unqualified, but when the election rolled around, he won. He was the incumbent. All in all, though, federal judges had it better. They could be removed only for moral turpitude. Stefan found himself thinking of his mentor, Judge Bryant. He had gone on to that great courtroom in the sky. Had Judge Young? This was Alan's father. The two judges had had adjacent offices in the U.S. Courthouse. It was Judge Bryant who had the key to the riddle Stefan couldn't solve.

Magdalena's enchiladas were peerless. Stefan said he had made sure to eat well in San Francisco, and he had, but he had not had a Mexican plate.

"I'm going to catch up on the mail," he mentioned when they had finished supper.

"I'm going on upstairs," Sharon said.

Stefan sat at his desk. He clicked on the lamp. Vanity, that's what Alan had called it. His vanity in dodging the draft by going to Canada, then vanity again in going to jail. When all the time what he should do was right in front of him. Answer his country's call, go to Vietnam. Gracious, it seemed so distant, already, but it was less than two generations. In two more, the war would cease to exist, just as if it had never happened at all. The anguish that had gone into it, a nation divided, the protests, first on college campuses, then everywhere. Those students he had observed that afternoon at UCSB, what was their knowledge of Vietnam? Only what they had read in their textbooks. And what might that be? Had the editors remembered to include a paragraph about the "domino theory" and "peace with honor?" The war was forgotten, and along with it, the lies two presidents had told.

Stefan opened his desk drawer and withdrew the letter he had placed there when he got home. What an ungodly mess. Well, it pointed to an afflicted mind. Stefan sorted through it. It wasn't entirely hopeless. Could Alan really mean to amend his own thinking, to discard his bottomless self-persecution and forgive himself? Stefan doubted it. The need to be busier. Well of course he needed to be busier. "At-will divorce." Where had

Alan come up with that? Stefan could only surmise he must have mentioned at-will employment at some point, and Alan had confused the concepts. "Tou?" What was "Tou?" Stefan stumbled only momentarily. Should be "You." Recites Keats. Now that sounded like Alan. Stefan tossed the letter into the trash can.

CHAPTER 22

T HE KOPINSKIS WERE HAVING GUESTS, AND STEFAN WAS GETTING THE liquor ready. Their wet bar, to be sure, had cost a pretty penny, in fact, almost 1,200,000 of them, but it was handsome, no question about that, a sea of marble and stainless steel, and they used it frequently, didn't they? The Kopinskis indeed entertained often, and a good thing, too, that between them they had a large number of friends, since they had run out of things to say to each other.

Not that their marriage was failing; it wasn't. Indeed, Stefan had acquired a new respect for his wife, since her return from Portland. Her mission accomplished, Sharon herself had, to some degree, fallen back into her old ways, though she would never again be indifferent, as she once had been, when it came to her stepdaughters' welfare. Stefan watched her turn into their driveway. There were three garages, two housing BMW's; the third was empty at the moment, but German automobile manufacturing would get the nod, if filling it became necessary. Sharon's afternoon errand had been to the studio where she was studying violin. It was all a lark. She liked her teacher, found him amusing. The Pacific Ocean would evaporate before she strummed one right note.

Still, she practiced from time to time, which made the 8,500 square feet of their home advantageous, since Stefan could get out of earshot. She parked in the driveway and emerged with her violin. Sharon was a "looker," flirtatious and beautiful. Debra wasn't a "looker," she wasn't flirtatious, she wasn't beautiful. She was older, and she had had two children. Sharon was flighty and unpredictable. Debra wasn't flighty, and she wasn't unpredict-able. Stefan drew a deep sigh. He had it all. A partnership with a prosperous law firm, a hefty income, wife and family, beautiful home, second home at

Vail and no mere cabin this, but another palace, luxurious vacations and not merely to London and Paris but Cape Town and Singapore. When, that is, they could actually take vacations. For work consumed Stefan Kopinski's life, and lent an unbalance to it. A psychologist might have conjectured Stefan hid behind his work to avoid confronting something in himself, and perhaps he would be right, but it was a moot point in any case, since Stefan would never consult a psychologist.

Sharon was displeased over how the violin lesson had gone and wasted no time imparting this. "Fifteen minutes early!" she exclaimed irately. "Paolo ended my lesson fifteen minutes early. Claimed he had a commitment in Hollywood he had just not been able to re-schedule. 'Paolo so sorry, Paolo try very hard for Meeses Kospeenskee, so mush talent, Meeses Kospeenskee, so mush beautiful.' Can you beat that? I have my suspicions. Anyway, he said he'd take the time off my bill. I'm sure he won't and is just supposing I'll remember the endearing kisses on each cheek and forget it. Not a chance!" She would forget it.

"How'd the lesson go, before he aborted it?"

"Poorly. He seemed preoccupied. Young Italian, hot-blooded, and I think his dates are all boys, that's what I think. Needs to get his hair trimmed, too, it's shaggy, although of course he wears it that way for a reason."

"No doubt," Stefan contributed, never having met the violin teacher, and not in the least interested how he wore his hair. "How long have you been taking these lessons? Several months, no?"

"Why do you ask?" Sharon replied, her guard up.

"Matter of curiosity."

"Paolo thinks I have great potential, for your information. He used to play for the orchestra in Turin. He's a very accomplished musician, plays with an orchestra in Hollywood, forget the name of it. He could play for the L.A. Philharmonic, if he wanted to."

"Why doesn't he want to?" Stefan asked with a hint of impatience.

"That's his business, isn't it? Probably the Philharmonic's a little too conventional for his tastes. Very eclectic, Paolo's tastes." His wife stuck out her tongue at him. "He could have a hundred reasons for preferring to stay where he is." Stefan changed the subject. His wife found her teacher exotic, and this explained the lessons. It would pass, like all her other expensive pastimes, and she would know just as much about playing the violin on the last day as she had on the first. Stefan chided himself for his impatience with his wife's whims. She was a wonderful wife in many ways, perhaps most emphatically in the total support she gave her husband. Debra had failed at that. Yet Stefan knew their relationship was never going to be the same as his had been with his first wife. There had been something inexpressibly special about his first marriage, until, that is, it fell apart. Their first home, a shack, really, compared with his present residence … so he was moving forward, wasn't he? Why did he gaze back longingly at circumstances manifestly inferior? Wasn't life more and better of everything, always? You couldn't hold still, since nobody else was.

"Darling, would you splash some Scotch on these ice cubes?" Sharon said, handing him her glass. "They're looking kind of naked." Stefan might have guffawed, if he had not heard it a score of times before. Cynthia Brewster and her husband, Atlas, who had arrived, had heard it, too, but they must exhibit a tact Stefan could eschew, so they managed a chuckle apiece. Stefan poured his wife another drink.

The Brewsters and another couple, Roy and Libby Magnuson, were the Kopinski's guests this evening. The doorbell rang, in came the Magnusons. The usual talk ensued. These occasions were a chore when you came right down to it, and every one of them would have agreed, the likeliest holdout being none other than Sharon Kopinski, if asked. Chore or no chore, it was required, it was the Kopinski's turn in the cycle, and the lobster was ready for the pot. They had hired a caterer, of course, responsible for the meal and the table, which was impeccable.

It was all right with Stefan, these get-togethers, perfectly all right. What did it matter if the conversation never changed? Over drinks, the men would discuss the stock market, and sports though not golf since Stefan did not play and not politics since Roy, unaccountably, was a Democrat, but yes women, even if the wives overheard, and the latest developments in the local business and professional communities. The women would discuss children and clothing and clothing and children, plus a bit of gossip of their own, primarily who was getting divorced, and there would be mirth but not jokes because women did not tell jokes. At the table, seating was boy-girl, boy-girl, boy-girl, with Stefan and Sharon at the ends, and the conversation became general.

"Sharon, this lobster is divine," Cindy Brewster said.

"Do I get credit for turning on the oven?" Sharon said. Laughter.

"Lobster doesn't go in the oven, Sharon." Laughter.

"It does the way I cook it." Laughter.

"What makes a great Chardonnay, 'cuz this one is?"

"From the Hilliard Vineyard. Napa, or Sonoma. Napa, I think."

"Very, very nice."

"Don't you love Napa? We go there every time we're in San Francisco."

"Our own little hideaway is a quaint little inn called The Bluebird. Have you been there?"

"Doesn't ring a bell."

"The last time we were in San Francisco, a beggar lying on the sidewalk suddenly jumped up just as we were walking by, and it startled me badly, but he didn't say anything or stick out his hand. Just jumped up suddenly."

"Was that at Union Square? We've quit going there. I don't feel safe."

"Where was it, Roy?"

"Truthfully, I don't recall."

"You don't remember that man who leaped into my face?"

"No. You must have been with somebody else." Laughter.

"Roy's memory is failing. Alzheimer's." Laughter.

"Sometimes it's best not to remember." This from their host. Laughter. It was all right with Stefan, this witless banter. Was a business lunch any different? The gab around the tables at the club? The same, lame conversations, week after week, year after year. But it was all right. Sharon was all right. Hadn't she accomplished her purpose, the "trophy wife?" Stefan did not doubt Atlas Brewster and Roy Magnuson sneaked looks at Sharon's neckline. But it was all right.

Everything was all right. Stefan was in trial. Everyday life was swept aside with a vengeance. The case involved an allegation of sexual harassment. Gordon-Jessup was his client.

"Just the facts, ma'am," Stefan would be saying, recalling Joe Friday, although Stefan would not be saying those words precisely. The facts may be simply stated: Susan Etzold was employed by the Gordon-Jessup Company, "GJC," a large insurance firm. She was 28 years old. Susan was a blonde, with pale blue eyes, "bedroom blue" as her boyfriend liked to say, and she had a sensational figure. Susan worked out at a gymnasium two nights a week, as she was determined she was going to keep herself trim and fit. She was partial to short skirts and had the legs for them, which she kept bare most of the time. Hose were for special occasions. This didn't include work. She liked to sit with her legs crossed, which hiked her skirt invitingly up her thigh.

Her boss was Gregory Hesse. Gregory was 50. Married, three kids. Fourteen years at GJC. He was rather decidedly middle-aged, with a seriously receded hairline, a second chin in the making, and an expanding "beer belly." He was good-natured and popular. Gregory was also having more and more trouble keeping his eyes off Susan Etzold's legs.

"Mr. Hesse," according to Susan Etzold, had come into her office on a certain Tuesday afternoon, immediately pulled up a chair right next to the one in which she was sitting, thereby placing himself very close to her, surprising her, and, after a minute or two of conversation, had put his hand on her thigh and run it quickly up her leg to her panties, reached beneath them and begun molesting her, and then whispered in her ear she could expect a substantial raise, since her work really was excellent, but she would in return agree to sex with him. His hand, she said, was still under her underwear, and he was panting nervously.

"Why didn't you remove his hand, Ms. Etzold?" Stefan asked her.

"I did!" she exclaimed. "I most certainly did."

"Before he touched you."

"It happened too fast. And he didn't touch me, he molested me."

Not much of this was true. Gregory Hesse had placed his chair next to hers, not his practice, and he had succumbed to the temptation to rest his hand on her exposed thigh. His hand had remained there only a moment.

"My goodness, I am so very sorry, Susan," he had said, ashamed and embarrassed. "I just lost control there for a second. My sincere apology." Gregory had looked Susan in the eye when he said this, risen and left her office quickly. He avoided her for days, but could not continue to do this. He said he stopped by her office one day not long thereafter and apologized again for his conduct. He had meant this sincerely. Gregory Hesse was an honorable man.

With this, he had felt the matter was closed, although he recognized restoring the professional relationship he and Susan had had might take time. Susan, meanwhile, had consulted the company's employee manual and found the language about the stern consequences of sexual harassment. She was required to report the infraction, without delay, to her immediate supervisor, but since this was Gregory Hesse, she took her allegation to the next person up the ladder, Sal Allsworth. Susan didn't work with Sal, but she believed, correctly, he was the individual to whom she should report the matter.

The company acted quickly. A woman whose business was the investigation of sexual harassment claims in the workplace was reached. Her name was Suzanne Beeler. She was good at what she did, and Gordon-Jessup invariably called on her in these situations. For the next 72 hours, Suzanne was a constant presence at Gordon-Jessup. She was swift and thorough. She conducted several interviews, although it really came down to two, and perused the relevant files. Satisfied with her probing, she met with Roderick Jessup at Gordon-Jessup. Roderick had his attorney, Stefan Kopinski, with him. Stefan had one question. Suzanne was ready for it.

"Who's lying?" he asked her.

"The woman," she said.

While this was taking place, Susan Etzold was demanding the company fire Gregory Hesse. She claimed she was "traumatized." She asked for time off. She threatened to hire a lawyer. None of this came as a surprise to Stefan Kopinski or Suzanne Beeler. Susan Etzold was following a familiar script.

"Ms. Etzold," Suzanne told Roderick and Stefan, "was nervous and evasive, when I met with her. Frequently, she said she could not exactly remember something, even though the alleged harassment had occurred less than 48 hours earlier. I met with Ms. Etzold Thursday morning. Gradually, however, her memory began to improve. She was beginning to suspect her vagueness was a mistake, I think." Here, Suzanne Beeler consulted her notes.

"Ms. Etzold," she continued, "used the word 'guaranteed' twice. The big raise was guaranteed. I asked her if Gregory mentioned a sum? No. I asked her if she had then asked him how much the raise would be. No.

"Seems to me she'd have asked. I asked her what else Gregory had said, and at first she could remember nothing, but then she abruptly recalled his having called her a hot babe. I asked her when he said this, and she replied she was pretty sure it was while he was touching her, although she did not use that word, she said 'molesting,' and then she was more explicit and said she remembered now, he had said, 'You are one hot babe.' I asked her to be more specific about the time and place of the proposed tryst, and she couldn't remember, but after I had elicited from her Gregory had indeed come purposefully into her office and seated himself practically in her lap and by gosh he had been looking lewdly at her for some time,

434

come to think of it, and so I inquired, if he was lewd and purposeful and sat down right next to her and ran his hand up her leg, didn't he have a specific plan, like the amount of the big raise, and where and when their assignation would take place, and she began to remember, oh yes, it was to be Saturday afternoon, he had said, and the place was the Hotel Liverpool. That's one of those flophouses over on Ardmore Street. Well, it became increasingly obvious to me she had not had the time to put together a solid story and was fumbling her way through it. I asked her why she had not reported his lewd ogling, since it had been going on for a while, and she replied she must have been in denial, that she didn't want to believe her boss was looking at her that way. At this point, she got out a Kleenex and dabbed at her eyes and sniffled, but I do not believe she was really crying, I saw no tears. After this little act was over, she became aggressive. She said, you're a woman, have you ever been traumatized like this? You haven't, have you? Well you're lucky, she said. She expressed amazement she could even talk about it. She demanded that Mr. Hesse be fired at once. She said she could not believe the company could expect her to work in the same office with him another day. She said something again about how traumatized she was, she used this word several times."

"Let me ask ..." Stefan began, but Suzanne wasn't done.

"I believe this woman is lying, gentlemen," Suzanne continued, "but it is not my impression she is an opportunist so much as she is a relatively young woman, she is 28, who has started something and doesn't know what she has gotten herself into. She cannot very well come forward now and admit she's made it all up, can she?" Here, the woman in Suzanne exhibited a bit of sympathy for Susan Etzold, which both men detected.

"And Gregory?" Stefan commenced. "What did he have to say?"

"He's the one in shock, not Susan," Suzanne said. "He's the one who's traumatized. He's crazy scared he's going to lose his job and maybe get prosecuted. He's a decent guy, this comes across strongly. I asked him if he had been ogling Suzanne and he replied, forthrightly, that while he did not much like the word 'ogle,' sure, he had been looking at her, and he challenged me to find one man in the office who hadn't. 'Who do you think she wears the short skirts for?' he said." Suzanne paused.

"Gregory frankly admits he put his hand on her thigh. Mid-thigh. This is not an issue. He told me he apologized instantly and promised her it would never happen again. He said, more than once, he could not believe he had done this, and that he was ashamed of himself. He said his hand was on her leg before he knew it, that he had no recollection of having thought about it first. Said if he had, he'd have gotten out of there. I asked him if he customarily went into Ms. Etzold's office and sat down next to her, and he replied this wasn't uncommon, that they worked together. I asked him if it was necessary to sit so close to her, and he said, again forthrightly, he could not deny he liked sitting where he could see Ms. Etzold's legs. He repeated here he was sure he was not the only man who liked looking at her legs. It was as if he was saying, look, men are this way. He did not actually say this, just my impression. I said this did not justify his having run his hand up her thigh, and he responded, quickly and very strongly, that he had done no such thing, he had only put his hand on her thigh and then immediately removed it. 'You must believe me,' he said earnestly. 'I did not run my hand up her thigh. If that is what Susan is saying, she is not telling the truth.'

"Gentlemen, I agree. Susan Etzold is not telling the truth."

The company put Gregory Hesse on paid administrative leave during these three days, but in view of Suzanne Beeler's conclusions, he was brought back to work. Susan Etzold promptly resigned. Her attorney would add "constructive discharge" to her claim of sexual harassment, "constructive discharge" meaning that, given the circumstances, she had been forced to resign, not done so voluntarily. Her primary claim nonetheless remained that she had been subjected to unlawful sexual harassment. She named both Gregory Hesse and Gordon-Jessup as defendants; it was the latter she was really after, since this was where the "deep pockets" were. She sought damages of $500,000, to include front and back pay, intentional infliction of emotional harm, loss of consortium despite not even being married, and medical expenses including hospitalization by a psychiatrist she had consulted. She remained under his continuing and close (and expensive) observation, according to her complaint. Where or when she might work again was impossible to say. Her life was a shambles.

Stefan seldom lost a summary judgment motion, but he lost this one. Ordinarily this would set settlement negotiations in motion, but he advised Roderick Jessup against settlement. He felt he could win in front of a jury. "It's what my gut is telling me," he said. Stefan didn't know why he used that expression, except that it was currently in vogue. The only thing his gut ever told him was, too many enchiladas. After some discussion, Roderick elected to defer to Stefan.

"Now Mr. Mower," Stefan began, "would you tell the court where you are presently employed?" Mower was Rolfie Mower, Susan's live-in boyfriend.

"Objection, relevance." This from Susan's counsel, Edmund Autrey.

"Overruled."

"Where are you presently employed, Mr. Mower?"

"I am not at present employed," Rolfie said, in a manner that implied he was proud of the fact.

"Are you looking for work, Mr. Mower?"

"Objection, relevance."

"Overruled."

"Are you looking for work, Mr. Mower?"

"Of course I am."

"When are you engaging in this activity, Mr. Mower?"

"Objection, relevance."

"Overruled."

"Mr. Mower, when do you look for work?"

"Whenever I see something good in the paper."

"So you look at the ads in the paper, and if you see something good, you give them a call?"

"Yeah, or I just go over there sometimes. I'm a handyman, you see."

"Get in your car, then, and look for work during the day?"

"Correct."

"Where do you live, Mr. Mower?"

"Objection, relevance."

"Overruled."

"I got a place of my own."

"What's the address?"

"Well I'm not living there right now."

"Where are you living?"

"Objection, objection."

"Overruled."

"I'm staying at Susan's place."

"I see. So you and Ms. Etzold are living together, at present?"

"Not all the time. She makes me real mad sometimes, and I leave."

"Go back to that place of yours?"

"Correct."

"Mr. Mower, I am going to read from a transcript of Ms. Etzold's deposition, where she testifies under oath, you are living together and, what's more, you are home all day long, essentially doing nothing. Not looking for a job, just hanging out." Stefan read the relevant passage from the transcript.

"So?" Rolfie Mower said. "I never said I look for work all the time."

"Mr. Mower, when you are not looking for work, do you maybe sometimes pop open a can of beer and watch a little TV, until Susan gets home?"

"Objection. Your Honor, this is completely irrelevant."

"Overruled."

"Yeah, sure, I do that sometimes," Rolfie replied. "Any law against that?"

"What do you like to watch? Those daytime game shows?"

"No way."

"Sports, maybe? Do you like sports?"

"Yeah I like sports."

"So you watch sports, like baseball and football?"

"Correct."

"Now Mr. Mower, did you and Ms. Etzold happen to discuss her hiring an attorney to represent her in this matter?"

"Objection."

"Overruled."

"We might have."

"Ever watch that commercial of Mr. Autrey's on TV, Mr. Mower?"

"Objection, Your Honor! This is inadmissible."

"Counsel," the judge addressed Stefan, "I am going to sustain Mr. Autrey's objection if you cannot demonstrate to this court the purpose of this line of inquiry, immediately."

"Your Honor, thank you, I intend to do that with another question or two."

"Very well. Objection overruled."

"Your Honor," objected Autrey, "this is completely inappropriate."

"I just overruled your objection, Mr. Autrey."

"Ever watch that commercial, Mr. Mower," Stefan continued, "where Mr. Autrey says, if you've been harassed, he'll get you back in the saddle again, and win big bucks for you? Ever watch that commercial?"

"Your Honor, objection," Autrey said.

"Your objection, counsel, is overruled," the judge admonished Autrey.

"Ever watch that commercial?" Stefan resumed.

"I might have, I don't recall," Mower said.

"Be just about impossible to watch TV all day long and miss it, Mr. Mower."

"I don't remember."

"Fact is, Mr. Mower, you didn't just talk about hiring Mr. Autrey with Ms. Etzold, did you, Mr. Mower? You called him, isn't that correct?"

"Objection."

"Sustained."

"Were you at Ms. Etzold's residence the day she came home from the office, the day of the alleged harassment?"

"I don't know what day that was."

"I think you do, Mr. Mower." Here Stefan again consulted the transcript of Susan Etzold's testimony, and found the date, along with Susan's allegation she had come home severely traumatized, and told Rolfie what had happened, and moreover, they had discussed it all evening long. Stefan read this to the court.

"It was your idea, wasn't it, Mr. Mower, to call Mr. Autrey?"

"I don't remember."

"It was you, Mr. Mower, who started thinking in terms of those big bucks Susan could win, wasn't it, Mr. Mower?"

"She was harassed, she deserves justice."

"It was you, wasn't it, Mr. Mower, who talked her into embellishing her account of what had happened at the office?"

"Objection. Counsel is answering for the witness."

"Sustained."

"No further questions of this witness, Your Honor," Stefan said.

The trial consumed four days. On the last day, psychiatrists for each side provided expert testimony. Expert testimony was an open joke; it was really advocacy. Under direct examination from Edmund Autrey, plaintiff's physician spoke of the "betrayal" that underscored the case.

"Doctor," the attorney inquired, "would you kindly tell the court what in particular sets Ms. Etzold's case apart?"

"Ms. Etzold was betrayed by someone she trusted."

"Her superior, Gregory Hesse?"

"Precisely."

"And with what might you compare this?"

"A child being abused by a parent. They are very similar."

"Objection!" Stefan said. "This is prejudicial. We are not discussing child abuse."

"Overruled."

"Ms. Etzold," the doctor went on, "had no reason to distrust her superior. She trusted him completely. She respected him."

"And then he comes along and puts his hand where it most decidedly does not belong and proposes this ugly affair?" said Edmund Autrey.

"Precisely."

"And this is the kind of thing that can have such a devastating impact on the victim?"

"Precisely. You don't even really need a doctor's opinion on that. It's self-evident."

"By self-evident, what exactly do you mean, doctor?"

"We never understand betrayal, we never adapt to it, it's always a shocking surprise, whenever it happens, all our lives."

"With devastating consequences that can last for years, if not a lifetime?"

"Precisely."

"Thank you, doctor." It was Stefan's turn.

"Now doctor," he began, "you have testified that betrayal is one of the harshest things we must deal with in life, correct?"

"Correct."

"Something that happens, unfortunately, to all of us, sooner or later?"

"Precisely."

"Doctor, would it surprise you if a single person in this courtroom disagreed with your conclusions about betrayal?"

"It would."

"Now doctor, may I ask you, are you familiar with the saying, 'When did you stop beating your wife?'"

"I've heard it."

"You understand its meaning?"

"I believe so."

"Would you be good enough to explain to the court the meaning of this commonly used phrase?"

"Objection. Relevance."

"Overruled."

"Well I may have spoken too soon. I don't believe I can explain it."

440

"The idea, doctor, is to create a false issue, isn't it? Ask a man when he quit beating his wife, when he never beat her in the first place."

"I see, yes," the doctor said.

"Divert attention from the real issue?"

"Objection."

"Overruled."

"Divert attention from the real issue?"

"If you say so."

"I do say so, doctor. Now you have told the court, doctor, Ms. Etzold was betrayed, correct?"

"Correct."

"Which made all the worse what happened to her, correct?"

"Very much worse."

"Very much worse, as you have so aptly testified, doctor. But like that man falsely accused of beating his wife, if Ms. Etzold wasn't fondled in the first place, then she cannot have been betrayed, can she, doctor?"

"Objection."

"Sustained."

"She can't have been betrayed, wouldn't you agree, doctor, if she's made the whole thing up?"

"Objection."

"Sustained."

"No further questions of this witness, Your Honor," Stefan said, smiling at the physician.

The jury regarded the testimony they were instructed to disregard and returned a verdict for Gregory Hesse in two hours. Stefan, uncharacteristically, was not in a celebratory humor. An ill-formed idea in his head was nagging him. He could neither shake it, nor understand its lingering power. A voice in him said speak with Alan, but how likely was this to be fruitful? Alan probably would not even remember talking about divorce and employment, and, anyway, what was Stefan going to ask him? He had actually called once, spoken with Jeanne, who said Alan was better, but still at the hospital. She said the doctors were struggling with Alan's medications, trying to find the right combination, the right balance. She said Alan spoke animatedly of his visit to St. Louis.

"You're his best friend, Stefan," she had remarked. Stefan shook his head. This he was not.

Weeks went by. Stefan's behavior was altered, his mind often seemed elsewhere. His wife noticed. His partners noticed. When his clients started noticing, something had to be done. As if sensing this himself, one day Stefan sat down with Art Feinberg. There was nobody he trusted more. Feinberg sat quietly in a chair in Stefan's office and heard him out, Stefan having said he needed the floor for ten minutes.

"Well, Stefan, interesting stuff," Art said when he had finished, "although the way you compare the three concepts, adultery, desertion and cruelty, with refusal to work, disloyalty and incompetence, if I am remembering your terms correctly, sounds like apples and oranges to me."

"Manifest incompetence, Art, is what I said. It would have to be that."

"Right, manifest incompetence. It's still apples and oranges. I don't agree with you these concepts are related. They just aren't. And you can't really say a divorced wife is bereft, either. She gets maintenance. Support too, if there are kids. Many husbands would say they're the ones hung out to dry."

"Not that many."

"What if the wife's the one who wants out?"

"If she has grounds, sure. Otherwise, no. This cuts both ways."

"And the guy who wants to quit making widgets and do something more with himself, he's stuck making widgets?"

"He's stuck making widgets." Stefan sounded unsure of himself. "Art, I'm still working on this, okay? Maybe it's all foolishness, but I'm not ready to let it go."

"Well, look, you're not a kid with a wild notion in his head."

"No, I'm a middle-aged litigator and partner in Pasadena's most prestigious law firm with a wild notion in his head."

"Point well taken, but that's what I'm saying. Keep your perspective."

"I appreciate that."

"Frankly, Stefan, this all sounds to me like the kind of polemic to which you might devote an hour in law school. You know, those on left side of room argue at-will employment and no-fault divorce are one and the same, those on the right argue they are not."

"I like to think there might be more to it than that." Stefan had not said this entirely good-humoredly. His colleague's remark stung; Stefan thought it was a put-down.

"Moreover," Feinberg continued, "even if you could make the analogy, so what?" Yes, so what?

442

"I haven't gotten that far."

"Who is the Alan Young fellow, anyway? You said you went to college together. I'm pretty sure I've never heard you mention his name."

"I probably haven't. We haven't really kept up. Talk occasionally, letter or two."

"Is he a lawyer?"

"No, gosh no." Stefan refrained from adding his friend occupied a bed in an asylum.

"I didn't really get that business about the seesaw, either," Art said. It wasn't complicated, but Art's attention had drifted. "What were you getting at there?"

"I was making an analogy, Art, about the parties not being similarly situated. Like being on a seesaw. You can't seesaw with somebody not approximately your size. Wouldn't you agree?"

"Haven't been on a seesaw lately, Stefan." Stefan did not much like this comment, either. Why had he bothered to bring the matter up? Perfectly useless. Art seemed to be thinking along similar lines. "What say we grab a drink?" he said. "Talk about something else?"

"Yes, and yes." And they did, they did grab a drink, and they did talk about something else, but it was not enough. Stefan couldn't shake whatever it was clouding his thinking.

It was decided he should take some time off. Stefan was due a vacation. Overdue. Maybe he was more fatigued than anybody realized. A month was agreed upon. This was unusually long, in fact, it was unprecedented. Nobody got a month off. Would the firm suffer? Likely not, but it was going to take some juggling of responsibilities. But clients would understand. Nobody could work all the time, as Stefan very nearly did. Yes, they would understand. Besides, wherever his leave might take him, he could be reached, in a pinch.

"A pinch it had better be," Stefan said the day he left. He had an empty feeling in the pit of his stomach, because while he did not doubt some time off was advisable, he had no plan. Stefan Kopinski, whose life was a plan, who never uttered an unrehearsed word, had no plan.

He elected to go to St. Louis first. This implied something came second, and at the moment, nothing did, but start somewhere he must. Alan Young, for whom he had harbored little but contempt for a quarter of a century, saw ... Alan saw ... the connection in things. That was the closest Stefan could get to articulating it to himself.

This venture to St. Louis was different. Stefan wasn't exactly eager to make the trip, but there was no reluctance this time.

Sharon drove her husband to the airport. Goodbyes were affectionate. Sharon was completely befuddled by her husband's strange behavior. His attempts to explain had not gotten far, because he couldn't explain it himself. She decided perhaps it was a "midlife crisis," but wouldn't he be flying off to some remote island for rejuvenation? Palm trees and bare-breasted women? Why would he be going to St. Louis, Missouri to see somebody named Alan Young? Alan Young was a total non-entity for Sharon. She had never met him, and since her husband had never spoken of him, who was he?

"We went to college together," Stefan said. "Up in Santa Barbara. We were good friends. This was long ago. Late sixties."

"You have never talked about this man," Sharon said in bewilderment. "Even when you got back from that overnight trip you made to St. Louis. You've never said a word about that trip. I didn't ask. Now, you're going back. Who is Alan? Who is his wife? What does he do? You said he's sick. Are you his doctor? What are you going to do, Stefan, sit by his bed and hold his hand? This makes no sense."

"All right, it doesn't make sense. What if it doesn't? I'm at a loss myself, truthfully. I've made nothing but sense for thirty years, I'm entitled to do something nonsensible."

"Darling, I'm not going to let you go if you are not going to be sensible." How she was going to prevent him wasn't clear.

"Oh for goodness sake, you know I'm not going to do anything hasty. I just need to talk with Alan. Jeanne says I help him. He's an old friend. He's in the hospital. I'd think you'd say it's right to go."

"I might say that, if even once over the years you had spoken of this man." There was no reply from Stefan. She had said this already. But he knew she wasn't exaggerating. It was entirely possible he had never mentioned Alan Young to his second wife. Or his first either, for that matter.

Stefan entered the airport. Found his flight. It wasn't long before they began boarding. He found his seat. He had an aisle seat. Put his seat belt on. The flight was nearly full. It was the usual mess, getting people onto an airplane, followed by the bigger mess of getting them off.

"Cabin crew prepare for departure," came over the intercom. A stewardess reviewed safety procedures, including painstakingly going over what to do in the event of ditching. What water would that be? The Mississippi? St. Louis was on the left side, wasn't it?

The jet taxied. They were sixth in line. The roar of the jets taking off came and went. Their turn came. Stefan rested his head against the back of his seat. In another moment, they were airborne. He was going back to St. Louis, only months since his first and sole visit, and he did not remember he had sworn to himself, as the city had receded from view, nothing could ever compel him to return. He knew only that something was confounding him. Some question, some riddle. Stefan could not articulate it to himself, which perhaps was just as well: How do you find what you don't know you're looking for?

Jeanne wasn't waiting for him at the airport, as before, and for a very good reason. He hadn't told her precisely when he was coming. The flight had been a bumpy one, and Stefan wasn't in a particularly good humor. Back on Missouri soil, he was overwhelmed with the doubts dogging him unmercifully night and day. Nothing worked, nothing addressed a condition so alien to his nature, and he had no clue how to proceed. Perhaps getting back to St. Louis would somehow clear the fog.

Walking through the airport in search of the baggage claim was not encouraging. It seemed a remarkably small airport for such a considerable city. With Jeanne at his side on his previous trip, he hadn't noticed. Maybe St. Louis was served by more than one airport? Maybe St. Louis was not such a considerable city? Growing up in Minnesota, he had never visited St. Louis or any other city in the Midwest, Chicago excepted. The city about which Alan was fanatical was entirely unknown to him. Indeed, the only two things Stefan could remember having ever heard about St. Louis, Missouri were its zoo and its baseball team. St. Louis had a famous zoo, and a famous baseball team. Must be more to it than that.

The wait for his suitcase consumed twenty minutes, even though not a single one of the other baggage carousels was in use. Stefan did a fair amount of flying these days. Flying was less and less fun. It wasn't just the ever-expanding security measures at airports; it was people. Stefan remembered a business trip to Chicago some months past. He flew first class. Stefan's life was first class. He stayed in the most expensive suites in hotels, "Executive Level." Access required a special key, and the riffraff didn't have one. He was greeted the moment he walked into his bank and ushered to whomever he wished to see, bypassing any waiting in a line. "Preferred Customer." He had a notion people in the first class seats on a plane were a better species of humanity. In the seat next to him was a brawny, young man in need of a shave and a shirt; the one he was wearing was hardly more than an undershirt, without sleeves. His bushy underarms were exposed. Stefan wore a suit. Stefan always wore a suit. Lawyers wore suits.

The carousel finally delivered on its promise of a suitcase, and Stefan made his way to the rental car desk. A middle-aged couple, who might or might not themselves be acquiring a car, were not allowing the fact they were in a public place to inhibit their bickering. Turned out she was upset he had selected a certain company, rather than another she happened to like. She didn't say why she liked the other company better, she just did. She was loud.

"Fine," her husband interjected sharply. "Next time, you plan our trip."

"I'll do that!" she exclaimed. "I'm going to find a place to sit down. You get the car." She looked around for seats and spotted some nearby. "I'm going over there," she said, pointing at the seats. Off she went. Her husband stared at Stefan, whom he knew had heard everything.

Stefan got his car and a map of the city. He had booked a room at the old depot, which, with the disappearance of passenger trains, had been converted into a hotel. Might be fun, he had told himself, and it was right downtown. That meant he'd have a chance to see the Arch! That should please Alan. Stefan was staying a week this time, and that could be extended. There would be plenty of time for the Gateway Arch.

The hotel was somewhat distant from the airport, but he found it without difficulty. St. Louis Union Station was, in a word, cavernous. Stefan had made a reservation for seven nights. The desk clerk, a handsome, young black woman, welcomed him with an engaging smile and handed him his room key.

"Elevators to your right," she said, pointing. "Do you require assistance with your luggage?"

"I can manage, thank you," he replied.

Stefan reached his room. It was a suite, with an ample sitting area, king-sized bed, two televisions, well-stocked refrigerator, lotions and soaps galore in the bathroom, and a view of another hotel. It was mid-afternoon. Stefan began unpacking his suitcase. His mind was racing. What was he doing here? He was annoyed with himself, for this was the question he kept asking himself, rather than settling upon an answer, any answer, and moving forward. It was not his way to allow anything to nag him. The fact was, Stefan really didn't know what he was doing in St. Louis. He knew he had come to have a conversation with Alan, a conversation aimed at realizing some arcane purpose of his own. He meant to stay until this was accomplished. Perhaps, in the process, he could help Alan, too. Help him with his malaise, his mental games.

Stefan had virtually no grasp of the role he played in Alan's life. It was all too ridiculous. Stefan didn't give a fig about his college pal. He had almost no memory of those faraway days. He didn't respect Alan, he thought he was an idler, he disliked him, when you came right down to it. He had ignored him for a quarter of a century. What, given these circumstances, was he doing here? On the bedside table was a booklet about St. Louis Union Station. Stefan leafed through it. The station opened Sept. 1, 1894. At its peak in the 1940's, the train shed spanned 32 tracks. One hundred thousand people passed through the station daily. How could that be? The architect had modelled the station after the medieval walled city of Carcassonne in France. Stefan had been to Carcassonne, by golly! How was the station like Carcassonne? Seemed farfetched. He'd go exploring the place in a little while, have a drink in the cocktail lounge, dinner in the restaurant. He could call Jeanne at his leisure. He could even delay a day and poke around the city. Go find the blasted Arch and surprise Alan when the inevitable question arose. No reason at all for haste. Indeed, although he intended only a week in Missouri, he had a month; his time was very much his own.

He recalled speaking with Sharon, how she had cautioned him to be sensible, how he had answered he had been only sensible all his life, what if he did one nonsensible thing now? Yes, what if he did? Of course, he had no idea what that nonsensible thing might be. His response had made her uncomfortable. She was so perplexed by his recent behavior, it was so out of character, nearly everything he said made her uncomfortable. Stefan himself was tantalized by the notion of being nonsensible. Could it be the key to understanding whatever it was he sought to understand?

Stefan explored the old station. A section, titled "Memories," contained nostalgic reminiscences by former patrons of the facility. Stefan read several. A man identified as "R. Boises" had moved to St. Louis from Houston, Texas, in 1938. Arrived on the Texas Eagle on May 11, 1938. St. Louis!

447

His worldly goods were in a bag. He had stayed at a hotel directly across the street from the station. What he remembered about the hotel was the shower arrangement. It was a communal shower, and it was in back, in a semi-enclosed building not even attached to the hotel proper. You showered with other guests, all men. No women at the hotel. He had had breakfast in the morning somewhere, then "set out to make my fortune." He had a letter of introduction in his pocket, signed by the principal of Travis Technical School in Houston, attesting to his industry and determination, and, moreover, ability to read and write. "St. Louis was good to me," R. Boises inscribed. "I, a young man, in my 22nd year, without prospects, other than ambition and hope, and a lively city in which to begin." There was no indication how R. Boises had made his fortune. Stefan meandered on, and found the old concourse. It was impressive, or had been. It was deserted. Several large photographs on a wall depicted the concourse in its heyday. Crammed with people. Beneath the train shed, where the 32 tracks had been, he came upon an artificial pond, upon which one paddleboat was being propelled by two boys. The waterpark was forlorn. He was ready for a cocktail.

The cocktail lounge was in the Grand Hall. It was a breathtaking space. A confection of fresco and gold leaf, mosaic and stained glass, on an enormous scale. The eye knew not where to look first. Here, truly, was a gem. Stefan could not remember having ever been in an American train station, not while growing up in St. Paul, not in his present home, Los Angeles. He had been in his share of European stations.

He took a seat in the lounge. It was far from crowded. Stefan ordered a martini. It was a good one, and went a long way toward making him feel better about his trip. Didn't it say something about him, something to his credit? Hadn't it required initiative, to cut through the miasma of daily life, overcome inertia and complacency, and resistance to a change in routine? He had done it! Here he was, in St. Louis, sure enough! Returned to see Alan again, and Jeanne, and … and what? Accomplish something or other. Stefan congratulated himself. Yes, this had taken resolve. Of which he possessed an abundance!

He mulled a second martini, decided against it. Stefan liked a cocktail after a long day, but one was where he generally stopped. Maybe he'd have a glass of wine with dinner.

The restaurant was nearly empty, yet he waited a full minute for the maître d' to appear.

"Would you prefer a table or a booth, sir?"

"Table," Stefan said. He was ushered into the restaurant, where he discovered the booths were arranged in a semi-circle, seating six. He would have looked foolish in one of them. Eating alone was no fun. Stefan had little practice. His life was a busy one. His professional and social circles were large. There was seldom excuse to have a meal alone. Stefan had worked hard, and he had built a good life for himself. Law, for him, was inexhaustible. A friend had asked him once why he liked it so much, and he had replied, "Because the stakes are always high." His friend had suggested this would be a deterrent for him. But Stefan knew he was right. All jobs were hard, why not have one that mattered? And paid well?

A waiter came over and handed Stefan a menu.

"Our special this evening is trout almandine with corn on the cob and hearts of artichoke."

"Suppose I could get a baked potato, if I wanted one?"

"Certainly, sir."

"Well let me think about it for a minute."

"Certainly, sir. May I bring you something from the bar?"

"I don't believe so, thank you." He didn't want the trout, he was going to have a filet mignon. He decided against a glass of wine. There were chocolates in the room, if he wanted something sweet. Stefan usually skipped dessert.

The dinner was good. Another customer came in and was seated at a nearby table. Another man dining alone. As Stefan was signing the check, putting the meal on his room tab, a commotion came from the front desk. It was a bevy of exuberant 15-year-old girls, who turned out to be a soccer team in town for a tournament. The girls were in their jerseys, and efforts by their coaches to settle them down were meeting with no success. Stefan grinned. This would lighten things up. He hadn't realized how melancholy the quietness of the hotel was. As he walked past the chattering group, he couldn't help remembering his own girls. Stefan shook his head. He had never been able to understand how Linda had gone to pieces right under his nose, not to mention her mother's. It just couldn't be explained. Linda owed her life to her stepmother. That was the truth, pure and simple.

Back in his room, Stefan turned on the news. Tourist mugged downtown. He was downtown, wasn't he? It got worse. Two shootings on the north side, not believed related, one fatality. Body found in a car in south St. Louis, near Lafayette Park. Car had no license plates and had been reported by neighbors. Crime. When had it become a way of life in the country? Stefan turned in for the night. Everything would be clearer in the morning.

Everything wasn't clearer in the morning. Stefan had breakfast. He returned to his room and put on his walking shoes. Time to find the Arch. He inquired at the front desk and was told to step outside and look to his right.

"Can't miss it." If ever those words applied, it was now. There, indeed, loomed the Gateway Arch, down the road a half mile or so, not really distant, yet a bit of a hike. He decided to drive. He'd walk when he got there, and wasn't he planning on the famous zoo in the afternoon, where he surely would walk his feet off?

Stefan headed east on Market Street. Had he ever troubled to read Alan's letters, he'd have been informed about the structures he was passing. This was a distinguished stretch of pavement. On his right was a curious structure. It was City Hall, architecturally inspired by the Hotel de Ville in Paris and the Chateau de Chambord. Boasting ornamental dormers, called "belvederes," on all four sides. Flower trays in the windows. There was a clock, which looked to Stefan as if it had been pasted onto the front of the building. It wasn't working. Sand-blasting construction on the edifice began in 1890, and the cornerstone was laid the next year. Farther down the street was the Old Courthouse, with its impressive dome, on land donated to St. Louis for the building, 1816. First courthouse was completed 1828 with its upper dome, wrought and cast iron; exterior, Italian Renaissance style; interior, murals, called "lunettes," depicting events in city's history. Stefan would have taken a particular interest in the courthouse, since he'd have known it was the site of the first two Dred Scott trials, in 1847 and 1850. Dred Scott had sued for freedom and won in slave-holding Missouri, only to have the Supreme Court in Washington reverse. He wasn't a free man after all, only a chattel, to be bought and sold like any piece of property. Stefan would have known the small church beneath the Arch was the Basilica of St. Louis. The city's founders, Pierre Laclede and Auguste Chouteau, had deeded the tract of land upon which the church stood to St. Louis in 1764. A one-room log building was erected and housed the church until 1834,

450

when it was replaced by the current structure. Church records were kept in French until the late 1830's. This was the city's Mother Church.

Stefan was ignorant of all this. He was making for the Arch. It was big all right. The river was adjacent, but the Arch was separated from the business district by a highway. Stefan found a parking spot and headed for the base of the Arch. He looked up. Now this was undeniably majestic! The thing was immense. In its simplicity, it was a supremely graceful structure; in its uniqueness, it was as surely the city's symbol as the Statue of Liberty was New York's. It was a staggering triumph of engineering. Stefan occupied himself for half an hour in the museum, where the city's role in the nation's westward expansion was described. Manifest Destiny! Who wasn't stirred by those words? Stefan decided he knew Lewis and Clark had embarked from St. Louis, and he rather thought he had known the year, too, 1804. The two men made for a fascinating contrast. William Clark was steady and even-tempered and would go on to further triumphs during the course of a long and productive life. Meriwether Lewis was mercurial and unpredictable and would come to a bad end in Tennessee within a few years of the expedition. Paired up, they had been a force to be reckoned with. The Arch itself was 630 feet high, another 630 feet from the base of one leg to the other. It was completed on Oct. 28, 1965. Designed by Eero Saarinen. Made of stainless steel. You could take a tram to the top, but Stefan passed on this.

He headed back to the parking lot, then changed his mind and opted for a brief stroll around the commercial district. He walked north on Fourth, west on Locust, south on Eighth, and east on Pine. It was mid-morning, people were at work, presumably, and perhaps this accounted for how quiet the streets were. Stefan counted fifteen other pedestrians on his stroll. Vehicular traffic was light. The streets seemed unusually narrow. He walked past three buildings closed and boarded up, big buildings, completely vacant. Three others were adorned with large signs identifying space for lease and the phone number to call. He wandered into one that appeared to be in use and found four office spaces on the ground floor. One was a tourism business, the other three were available for occupancy, just call that phone number on the sign! He returned to the sidewalk and walked past a six-story parking ramp. Was it vacant, too? He kept walking. He didn't come across a single grocery store or restaurant. You were out of luck, apparently, if you wanted something to eat, downtown. Then, in the last block of his walk, he found a coffee shop, one of the "chain" establishments dotting the landscape from New York to California. It was busy! He got to counting, again, and the number was eighteen. Where had everyone come from? Must be a secret tunnel into the place. Stefan got coffee and occupied himself for a half hour. Then, it was back to the quiet streets.

It was just as well Stefan was ignorant of the city. Nothing was sadder than the contrast between St. Louis' grand past and its grim present. No city in America had declined more precipitously.

Stefan decided it was time to call Jeanne. He had come, he was here, he was going to do something with his week. Just get on with it, there was no use trying to plan it any further, there was no plan.

Back at the hotel, Stefan encountered the girls' soccer team. They were piling into a bus. It was pandemonium.

"Good luck," he said to a 30-ish man, wearing a jersey that read "Hoover." The jerseys were white with blue stripes. This fellow, Stefan gathered correctly, was the coach.

"Thank you, sir," the man said. He was muscular. "We will win." Stefan thought he detected an accent, but wasn't certain. He took the elevator, and on arriving at his room, promptly dialed Jeanne.

"Are you here? Where are you?" she inquired. There was no excitement in her voice. Months earlier, meeting Stefan, a total stranger, at the airport, chauffeuring him, she had been tentative and uncertain. Not now. She was completely herself, now, more than able to hold her own. She disliked Stefan Kopinski, whoever he was, and she did not believe he had returned to St. Louis for purely unselfish reasons. Whatever it was that had brought him back, there was something in it for him.

"Union Station," he said in reply to her question. "Not too far from you, I hope."

"No, as a matter of fact, it isn't that far. I'm in south St. Louis. Shall I come and get you?"

"No, Jeanne, I've rented a car. Just give me directions." Left on Market, left on Grand, over the tracks and past the medical school. It wasn't complicated. Unlike Los Angeles, the city of St. Louis was small, geographically.

"Then come on over. I'll fix us lunch. I have to work later today, but you can stay here as long as you like, or go over to the hospital, whatever works for you."

"Thank you, Jeanne. I'll make my way over in a little bit." Their conversation concluded without his asking about Alan, or her volunteering information. He had detected in her tone the absence of any real interest in his having returned. Jeanne couldn't care less that Stefan was in St. Louis. She was going about her life. He could do as he wished.

He found the apartment without difficulty. They exchanged a reasonably warm greeting. Stefan rather liked the apartment. It was small. It was a first home. Jeanne had furnished it artfully, and she kept it spotless. It was an old-fashioned, inner city apartment, well-suited to Alan, with his love for the old city. Ironically, he had had no role in securing the apartment; Jeanne had shouldered the responsibility. It could not be otherwise. Alan had been in prison.

Stefan could not help thinking of his and Debra's first residence. This was a bittersweet memory. Those had been such halcyon years, and they were gone forever.

Over lunch, the pair discussed raising daughters, Stefan refraining from any specificity about Linda's horrific adolescence. Both were polite without being warm. Stefan had not hurried in getting to the apartment, obliging Jeanne to cut it short, so she could get to work on time. Or so she said. Presently, she was a cashier at a suburban "big box store." The job was all right, despite her vulnerability to abrupt changes in her shifts. She was working the late shift at the moment, and didn't get home until after 10:00. She stopped by the hospital around midday, on her way to work. She had been going every other day, but her visits were becoming less frequent. Jeanne had not admitted this to herself, but a certain resignation had definitely affected her thinking and behavior. Alan was Alan, he was not improving and wasn't going to improve, and sitting there with him in his room, searching for conversation, was futile. There was little joy in these visits. She wasn't even sad any longer, when she left. Drained, to be sure, but not sad. Her husband had become an item on the list of a day's chores, wedged between the grocery store and the bank.

"What has brought you back, Stefan?" Jeanne asked him at one point.

"Previous visit was too short," he replied. Jeanne smiled. It was short because he had made it short. "I'm looking forward to a real visit, this time. I want to look into ways of bringing Alan home."

"He's a suicide risk, Stefan," Jeanne said impatiently. "He can't leave the hospital. I thought this was explained when you were here before."

"You're right, it was," Stefan said, with an edge in his voice. "Maybe you could explain to me how it makes more sense for Alan to be sick in bed for the next fifteen years, against the risk, assuming there really is one, of his harming himself if you brought him home?"

"We've had this conversation, I believe," she replied.

"I'm only trying to help, Jeanne," he said in a placating manner. "I'm at a loss, too."

"Well say hello to him for me," she said. "Tomorrow, I am meeting with his doctor at 11:00." This was a statement on her part. She had a meeting with the physician, and he wasn't invited. She was caring for Alan, he was in town … why? Not to take care of Alan. They agreed to talk again in the morning. Jeanne left for work, assuming Stefan was headed for the hospital. He wasn't. He was going to the zoo, the famous zoo. He hadn't been to a zoo in ages; it would be fun. Lions and tigers and bears. He could swing by the hospital afterwards.

Where was the zoo? Forest Park. Where was Forest Park?

"You really can't miss it, sir, it's smack in the middle of the city," the saleswoman said. Stefan had stopped at a store to ask directions.

"What street is this?" he inquired, pointing out the window.

"Grand Avenue. Just go north to the highway and then go west and you'll come right to the park."

"West is left, or right?"

"Left. It's really not far."

"Thank you."

Stefan followed directions and found Forest Park within minutes. Signs pointed to museums, golf courses, something called the Jewel Box, and the zoo. Stefan parked and headed for the entrance. He caught himself and laughed out loud. He pictured himself at his desk in Pasadena on this, a weekday. The usual stir of the office. Where was he, instead? At the front gate of the Saint Louis Zoo.

"How much for a ticket?" he inquired.

"The zoo is free, sir," the attendant said. Stefan went in.

It was surpassingly strange, and fun, at the same time. Stefan resisted a "sno cone." Shouldn't that be "snow," he asked himself. (The zoo had it right.) The zoo didn't strike him as noteworthy, aside from being a big one. But a bear was a bear, in St. Louis or the Klondike. That was the thing about animals, wasn't it? They were always what they were, and not another thing. A home tabby and the fiercest tiger were cats and therefore behaved like cats and did what cats do. Stefan remembered having read somewhere a chimpanzee had been taught sign language. He didn't believe it.

He came upon something called the World's Fair Flight Cage. It was an aviary. On closer inspection, Stefan found a plaque. The aviary dated to 1904, when St. Louis hosted a world's fair. The Louisiana Purchase Exposition! The fair, it turned out, gave birth to the zoo. Stefan remembered the forlorn streets downtown he had walked that morning. How could this city have been the venue for a world's fair? Stefan was entirely ignorant of the city's history. Accordingly, he was unaware that 1904 not only saw St. Louis host a world's fair, but the Olympic Games, as well. Now there was a boast, all right! Alas, it had been St. Louis' last hurrah. The contest with Chicago was lost, conclusively. When the lights at the Fair went out, and the last medal was awarded at the Games, St. Louis tucked itself into bed and fell soundly asleep. Nearly a century later, the city was still asleep.

Stefan made a point of occupying himself at the zoo long enough he could make an excuse it was too late when he left to run by the hospital. He didn't want to run by the hospital. He'd call and leave a message. He'd stop by in the morning. As he watched the playful seals in their pool, he had a thought. "Something bigger than me has brought me here." Nothing else could explain how he could have removed himself from his normal life and placed himself in front of a half dozen frolicking seals. The question, of course, was: What? What was that bigger thing? Stefan was puzzled, but not unpleasantly so. He certainly deserved some time off, and if this somehow translated to watching seals swim, so be it. They were so graceful in the water, so clumsy on the concrete!

A young boy holding his mother's hand stumbled as they walked past Stefan, and a generous portion of the boy's sno cone landed on Stefan's right shoe.

"So sorry," the woman said. "Watch where you're going, Timmy," she remonstrated. Timmy was plenty upset over the loss of the better part of his sno cone.

"Can I have another one, mommy?" He was starting to cry.

"Maybe he could just spill what's left on my other shoe, and I'll buy him another," Stefan said to the boy's mother. Where had that come from? Stefan astonished himself. The boy's mother looked at him incredulously. She wasn't amused.

"Come on, Timmy," she said, pulling her son by the arm. They disappeared down the path. Stefan put his hand over his mouth, and laughed. What an inexplicable remark he had made!

The zoo wasn't crowded. Maybe on the weekend, Stefan considered. This was a school day. Why wasn't that brat Timmy in school?

The afternoon waned. Stefan decided to skip the zoo train. He had enjoyed himself, but it was time to return to the hotel and, yes, call the hospital. He didn't feel the least bit bad about having spent his day as he had, rather than go straight to Alan's bedside. After all, Alan wasn't going anywhere, now was he?

At the hotel, Stefan had a message from Alan. This was embarrassing. He called the hospital, specifically requesting that a message be delivered to Mr. Young, that he did not want his call put through. The message was, he wasn't presently available, but would call again in the morning. His room phone rang nonetheless. Stefan let it ring. He did not want to speak with Alan just yet. Their conversation was not going to be a jolly one, and he was having himself a jolly day.

He returned to the lounge in the Grand Hall. Time for a highball. Stefan decided tonight to sit at the bar rather than in the lounge. He had no sooner sat down than a middle-aged woman took the barstool next to him. They exchanged "hellos." Shortly, they were talking. Dorothy Percer of Chicago was with a large property management concern. The firm had only one client in St. Louis, but it was a lucrative one. Mrs. Percer customarily made the trip to St. Louis six times a year.

"Isn't this Hall wonderful?" she said to Stefan. "I stay here every time I'm in town."

"Truly," Stefan said. "The city can take pride in this."

"It was once one of the nation's greatest railroad stations," Dorothy Percer said. "They have an exhibit down that way"—she pointed—"telling all about the station's history."

"I saw it yesterday," Stefan said.

"The station had the distinction of being an end-of-the-line station. No train ever paused in St. Louis, in other words. You got off here."

"Might be a bit inconvenient," Stefan said.

"I suppose so. I think it was meant as bragging rights." Dorothy Percer took a drink. She was having a glass of wine. "What brings you here, if you don't mind my asking?" She clearly was interested in conversation. In her experience, if Stefan had inquired, she'd have said, "Most folks want to talk." Stefan, on the other hand, wasn't keen on conversation with this stranger. She looked to be about his age, perhaps slightly older. She was graying, but her face remained youthful, as was her manner.

"A dear, old friend who is seriously ill," Stefan said. Not precisely the truth, the whole truth, and nothing but the truth, but it would serve.

"I'm so sorry," Dorothy said.

"And you?" Stefan said quickly. He wasn't saying anything more about Alan.

"I represent a commercial property management company in Chicago. We have an important client here. My account, needless to say, so I make the trip."

"I was downtown this morning," Stefan said, thinking about the commercial properties he had seen. "One building after another was boarded up."

"Oh, I agree. It's a little unnerving. A recent trip here, I parked in a ramp. The place was half-empty. Cars, I mean. I did not see another soul. Walked to the elevators. Waited and waited. I think there were two. Neither ever came. I took the stairs. Nobody around. I was getting uncomfortable. I take a cab, now."

"At least downtown still has your client."

"Yes, that's encouraging, isn't it? Most of the action is in Clayton, however."

"Where is Clayton?"

"It's a suburb. The new business hub. There's a cluster of high-rise buildings. Not very appealing. Sad, really, what has happened here."

"I travel," Stefan said, "and find myself in your town from time to time. Chicago looks pretty good, best I can judge."

"Oh, Chicago's doing fine." Dorothy Percer paused. "What was it I heard someone say, once?" She mulled it. "Oh yes, I remember now. Chicago puts up a building and then worries about filling it, St. Louis worries about filling it and never puts up the building. That was it."

"Nifty," Stefan said, laughing.

"Not true, of course," Dorothy said. "You don't put up a forty-story building without a solid roster of tenants lined up. Still, I think there's something in the anecdote. Chicago just seems more vigorous."

Thus they spoke on, for thirty minutes. Dorothy had three children, all grown. One boy had been a professional athlete, in Indiana, but his body had taken such a beating, he had given it up after a few years. Her husband was "in manufacturing." Stefan said he was married and had two daughters, "also grown." A perfunctory conversation, enjoyed at the moment, and forgotten the next. Neither suggested dinner.

"I hope your friend gets better," Dorothy said as she rose to leave.

"Thank you," Stefan said. "It was a pleasure meeting you."

After breakfast the next morning, Stefan called Jeanne. Initially, they decided to meet at the hospital's reception area at 10:00, but Stefan expressed an interest in also meeting Alan's doctor.

"If you have no objection," he said. Jeanne had an objection. She had gone through months of anguish, he hadn't. She felt he hadn't earned the right to meet Abraham Holdermann. Yet she consented.

Abe Holdermann was not what Stefan expected. He thought he would be an older man. Your doctor was supposed to stay older than you, wasn't he? A sequential thing. Abe Holdermann could not be over thirty-five. He wore his white doctor's smock and greeted Stefan warmly when Jeanne introduced them.

"Alan's oldest friend?" Holdermann said. "I may be picking your brain before we're done." Stefan squirmed in his chair. It sounded awfully good to call himself Alan's oldest friend, provided his listener was content with that. He could say nothing, really, of their friendship since college, since it had existed only in Alan's mind. For that matter, he could say little of their college days. Holdermann turned to Jeanne.

"We believe we have your husband stabilized," he said. "It has been a challenge, as you know." The physician was speaking specifically about Alan's medications. He was taking seven prescription medicines, five in the morning and two at night.

"Such a relief," Jeanne said. She was annoyed by how long the doctors had juggled Alan's prescriptions, changing them, revising, changing again.

"With that achieved," Stefan spoke up, "I wonder, doctor, how you feel about getting Alan back home sometime in the not-too-distant future?"

"That, I'm afraid, remains unfeasible at this time," Holdermann said pointedly. He had not liked the manner of Stefan's inquiry. He was not on the witness stand.

"The thing is," Stefan said, "and you're the doctor, not me, but I just don't see how Alan can improve as long as he's in that bed. Isn't it just common sense, really? His negative thoughts about himself, this is the problem isn't it? What can he do but dwell on them, lying in bed all day?"

"You are right up to a point," Abe Holdermann said. "It will require much more than stabilization to address your friend's suicidal frame of mind."

"I can't say that I detected a suicidal frame of mind in Alan when I saw him several months ago," Stefan said. He was becoming more argumentative, not less. "Obviously, he could be concealing it. I realize he's depressed."

"You weren't with him two hours, Stefan," Jeanne observed, with a hint of derision in her tone.

"Well now I didn't have to come at all, did I, Jeanne?" Stefan said sharply. "And it was more than two hours."

"That's true, you didn't," she said. Her gaze, and Stefan's, reverted to the doctor. If they were going to have it out, this wasn't the place.

"Alan's condition extends well beyond depression, Mr. Kopinski," the doctor said. "Your friend wants to die. This is the issue."

"Over that stupid coincidence?" Stefan said. "He wants to die over that stupid coincidence?"

"You can call it a coincidence, and I can, and this is what it is, but not to Alan. To him, it is his destiny. Have you heard him use that word?"

"Yes, I have. To die is his destiny? Is that what you're saying?"

"To die is everyone's destiny, Mr. Kopinski," Abe Holdermann said in a measured way, although he didn't care if Stefan found it patronizing. He didn't care for Stefan's interrogation one bit. He was accommodating him by meeting with him at all. "To have died, is Alan's. Your friend, you see, believes he should be dead. He believes he should have gone to Vietnam, when he was drafted, and been killed. This was his destiny. He believes if he had done this, Lt. Blassie would be alive. This is why he can't stand himself. Death would not right the wrong he believes he has committed, but it would free him from his agony. From the unspeakable wretchedness every moment of consciousness has become."

Stefan's jaw dropped. He looked at Abe Holdermann, dumbfounded. What had made no sense, made perfect sense. The doctor was right. Stefan knew at that moment Alan was doomed. He could never recover, he could only suffer and die. Jeanne was crying. She had heard this before, of course, but the tears came copiously every time.

"It's perfectly hopeless, isn't it?" Stefan managed to say.

"Mr. Kopinski, you ..."

"Stefan, please. Call me Stefan."

"Very well. Stefan, you have a very special place in Alan's life. He speaks of you, and a note of contentment, which I do not hear the rest of the time, enters his voice. He always refers to you as 'Stef, my oldest friend.' It's your college years together he always remembers. You're very special to him, a tonic, really."

"We went to school together," Stefan said, "in Santa Barbara, California. It was so long ago. Alan is a year older than me, so he was a sophomore when I started. We were in the same dormitory, that's where we met. We were friends, good friends, but we had other friends, too, it wasn't just Alan and me. When college ended, we went our separate ways, as usually happens. Alan ended up here, I stayed in California. I went to law school in San Francisco. Alan and I have hardly seen each other all these years. Quite frankly, we don't really know each other."

"Not as far as Alan is concerned," Abe Holdermann said. Jeanne had quit sobbing, but the tears were steady. She really couldn't stand to hear it. She knew it was so. Her husband cared more for this worthless friend than for her.

"It's in his head," Stefan said. "Our friendship is in his head."

"Regardless, it means a great deal to him, Mr. Kopinski. Stefan." Stefan said nothing. What was he supposed to say? What was Abe Holdermann getting at? "I wonder, Stefan," the doctor said, "if you would mind if Jeanne and I had a word?"

"No, of course not," Stefan said. He rose quickly. "You've certainly given me a better idea of what we're dealing with, here. Thank you."

"I'm glad if I've helped," Abe Holdermann said.

"I'll wait for you back in the reception area," Stefan said to Jeanne, and departed. She wasn't long. When she re-appeared, the tears had stopped.

"Shall we go see my husband?" she asked him.

"Yes, let's."

"How long did you say you'll be here?"

"Until Sunday."

"He's going to be so pleased you're here." They entered Alan's room. Stefan's incipient plan to get Alan out of the hospital was in shreds. Abe Holdermann's diagnosis had left him persuaded Alan was irretrievably mentally ill.

"Stef!" Alan exclaimed. Just as before. "You really are here! I was starting to think Jeanne made it all up."

"Hi, Alan," Stefan said with as much cheer as he could muster. He went over to the bed and embraced Alan, awkwardly. "How are you?"

"A whole heckuva lot better than one minute ago," Alan said, beaming. Jeanne was the silent observer. There he was, her husband of thirty-odd years, instantly animated by Stefan's appearance. She ... really ... couldn't ... stand ... it. "When did you get here, Stef?" Alan continued.

"Let's see," Stefan said. "Late afternoon, Sunday."

"Stef! It's Tuesday! We've lost two days."

"No, Alan, nothing's lost. I'll be here all week. This is just the first of many visits."

"Wish you had come yesterday. What'd you do? Go to the Arch, Stef? Tell me you went to the Arch."

"I went to the Arch."

"All right!" Alan exclaimed.

"Excuse me, boys," Jeanne said briskly. "I can see I'm in the way. I'm going to the store." Jeanne put her cheek against Alan's, followed by a gentle kiss and a caress of inexpressible tenderness. Stefan looked on enviously. Jeanne left.

"I have a great wife, don't I, Stef?" Alan said.

"The best," Stefan found himself saying.

"So tell me about your visit to the Arch. Has a way of growing on you, hasn't it. Closer you get."

"It is truly magnificent," Stefan said.

"Check out the museum?"

"Yep."

"Go to the top?"

"Nope. Next time."

"Tell you the truth, I think it's a bit overrated. The viewing room is very small. East St. Louis isn't the most inspiring sight. The ride is what's interesting. Like being on a Ferris Wheel."

"In what way?"

"You get into this little capsule. Seats five, I believe. Then, like on a Ferris Wheel, you go up in stages."

"Sounds unsettling. What happens if there's a malfunction?"

"Don't know, but I'm sure they have arrangements in place."

461

"Well, as I said, next time."

"What else did you do? Arch can't occupy you all day."

"Went to the famous zoo."

"You went to the zoo, Stef!" Alan said. He found this amusing. Alan was seldom amused. Truly, a visit from Stefan was salubrious. "Who goes to the zoo his first day in a new city?"

"Guess I do," Stefan said. "The only two things I have ever heard about St. Louis are the zoo and the baseball team. Had to do at least one of them."

"It's one of the best zoos in the country," Alan said. "Been a while since I've been there."

"Pretty big. I don't think I saw all of it."

"It dates to 1904, Stef. The year of the world's fair."

"I actually saw something about that. It was at the aviary. A plaque mounted on a wall."

"World's Fair Flight Cage, Stef! Got to get that right. Plenty of zoos have your run-of-the-mill aviaries."

"World's Fair Flight Cage," Stefan repeated, remembering. "I hope the birds appreciate how special their environment is."

"I'm sure they do," Alan said, actually laughing. Not a belly laugh, precisely, but a laugh. "What else did you do?"

"Kid dropped his sno cone on my shoe."

"I meant the exhibits."

Stefan embarked upon a description of his afternoon at the zoo. The subject was unexpectedly a good one. It occupied them. Responding to Stefan's eventual question, Alan said he was doing better, now that the doctors had his pills right. Stefan carefully avoided mentioning the word "destiny." There was no use going there. He stayed about an hour and a half. He promised he'd be back the next day.

His spirits were sagging when he arrived back at his hotel. The sumptuous lounge in the Grand Hall beckoned. Stefan figured a highball would brighten his mood, but tonight, it didn't help much. He was discouraged. He could see no point whatever in his trip. Abe Holdermann's diagnosis was right on the mark. Alan was beyond reach. Moreover, he and Jeanne were permanently at odds. He missed his own wife, or did he? Stefan wondered what Sharon might be doing. He was lonely, or was he? He half-wished the woman he had spoken with would show up. They could have dinner.

Stefan chided himself. There was Alan, whose life was effectively over, and he was sitting here, in this elegant space, feeling sorry for himself.

The next day was Wednesday. Stefan called Jeanne. She's obviously not going to call me, he told himself ruefully. She had not planned to stop by the hospital today.

"Jeanne," he said, "what the doctor said yesterday, you knew that already, I'm surmising?"

"Yes."

"It was a revelation to me. I mean, I had not realized how … how deep this goes. I have been reflecting upon what the doctor said. It makes sense, really, I'm afraid. How do you feel about it?"

"Considering everything Dr. Holdermann said has come straight from Alan's own mouth, I can't say that I find it all that insightful."

"I see," Stefan said. He wondered what to say next. "I'll go over there later today. Sometime in the afternoon."

"Alan will be happy to see you, Stefan," Jeanne said solemnly.

"Have a good day, Jeanne," Stefan said kindly. He felt like they should meet again. "Maybe we could plan on talking tomorrow? Lunch, or something?"

"That would be fine. Let's talk again in the morning."

Stefan stroked his chin. Jeanne Young would rather have lunch with Jack the Ripper than with him. He decided to use the morning to go anywhere but the hospital. Had he read Alan's letters, he'd have encountered effusive praise for every institution dotting the St. Louis landscape. He hadn't, and he was ignorant. He did remember Alan's having mentioned the Botanical Garden, terming it a "must." Where was the Botanical Garden? Hadn't Jeanne said it was near their apartment?

Stefan got directions again from the concierge. He followed them, now recognizing the freeway and Grand Avenue. He turned on the wrong street, however, and found himself at Tower Grove Park.

The park was an enchantment. It was studded with trees, aglow in the morning sun. The park formed a rectangle, with an avenue right down the middle. Stefan encountered roundabouts and statues: Shakespeare, Columbus, Von Humboldt. Colorful pavilions with intriguing names: Lily Pond, Old Playground, Sons of Rest. There was a structure called the Piper Plant House. Stefan drove the length of the park, turned around, and drove back. The park was a beauty. Could be in Europe. With one, very big difference. European parks contained people. Tower Grove was notably unpopulated. It was Wednesday morning, maybe that explained it. More people on weekends, probably. Picnics, ball games. Those grand, numberless old trees. Must be hundreds of them. The park dated to 1868, Stefan learned. The Botanical Garden was actually adjacent, and was itself nine years older.

Stefan elected to skip the Garden. He didn't see how it could top Tower Grove Park. He decided to get on over to the hospital. Alan would have plenty of ideas where he should spend his afternoon. They'd have a nice little chat today, and a nice little chat Thursday, and a nice little chat Friday, and Stefan would return to California, having cut short his month off by three weeks. Purposes realized, missions accomplished. That would be his version of events, in any case.

He found St. Louis State Hospital without difficulty. If you knew where to look, its distinctive dome could be spotted from some distance.

"How are you today, sir?" the woman at the reception desk said when he came inside. It was Norma.

"Very good, thank you. How are you?"

"I'm very fine, sir. You're here to see Mr. Young, I believe?"

"Yes, that's right."

"I'm afraid he's not available right now. He's in 'Yoga Exercises and Repose.' Will be for another hour." Stefan was annoyed with himself for not calling first. Nothing to do but wait. He took a seat. The hour dragged interminably, but at last Norma advised him Alan was back in his room.

When Stefan entered Alan's room, the same jubilant welcome awaited him. Now, however, it wasn't just the two of them. Another patient had been moved into the vacant bed and was sitting up with a tray on his lap. He was having a bowl of soup.

"Stef, this is Phillip," Alan said. Phillip grinned. He was a young man, mid-twenties, and he had been diagnosed with dementia. It was decades before this malady usually struck.

"Hallo!" said Phillip, loudly. Phillip always said this in greeting. He liked to go into the restroom and sit in one of the basins and shout "Hallo" at whomever came in. He took his clothes off first. Stefan merely nodded Phillip's way.

Phillip put his hand into his soup, palm down, fingers spread wide, removed it, and slapped it against his chest. On the tray, in addition to the soup, he had a liberally buttered roll, a plastic glass half-filled with orange juice, and a cookie. Phillip picked up the roll and took a generous bite.

"You want a bite of my roll?" he asked Stefan.

"No, thank you, Phillip."

"I thought you did," Phillip said. "Are you the doctor?"

"No I'm not."

"The doctor would like a bite of my roll." Alan and Stefan looked at each other. Alan struck Stefan as infinitely saner than this young man. Abe Holdermann would explain he was infinitely saner. Alan wasn't demented.

Phillip spoke matter-of-factly, yet there was a manic quality in his voice, and maybe just a hint of malice. Stefan had the impression Phillip was holding back, and that everything could fly apart at any moment. "Where is the doctor?" he demanded. He was getting upset.

"I'm sure he'll turn up in a minute," Alan said.

"Who are you?" Phillip asked Alan loudly.

"I'm your roommate, Phillip. You remember when we were introduced a little while ago? Your mother was with you." Where had she gone, anyway?

"I thought you were the doctor," Phillip said. "Have a bite of my roll." He extended it toward Alan, then deliberately dropped it. It landed on the floor between their beds. Phillip stared at it mournfully but made no effort to retrieve it. He looked at the other items on his tray. He picked up the cookie and examined it carefully, top and bottom, then put it back on the tray, going to elaborate lengths to place it exactly as it had been.

"Who are you?" he said to Stefan, loudly. Stefan looked at Alan. A woman walked into the room.

"Hello," she said to Stefan.

"Hello," Stefan said.

"I see they brought you some lunch," the woman said to her son. The imprint of his hand on his gown, left by soupy fingers, was plain to see. She said nothing. She was fifty-ish. Her hair could use a comb and a scrubbing, too. She wore a plain, print dress. The dress looked inexpensive. She went over to her son, took the napkin from the tray and wiped the soup off his gown as best she could. Then she took the vacant chair, next to Stefan, ignoring him completely. She opened a bag she had with her and withdrew a magazine.

"So what were you saying, Stef?" Alan said. "Where were you, again?"

"Tower Grove."

465

"That's right. You like it? Nothing not to like."

"I liked it, yes," Stefan said. "A gracious park."

"Did you check out ol' Willie Shakespeare? He's on one of those columns you drive around."

"I saw him," Stefan said. He wasn't confident of their conversation. Phillip, he thought, might leap into it any moment. Phillip seemed, however, to be occupied with watching his mother read.

"You get out and walk around?" Alan said.

"No, I just drove around, but I got a good look at everything."

"Stef, you have to walk around Tower Grove."

"Saving it for next time. We'll do it together."

"Aw, Stef. We could talk old times together." Alan's voice cracked.

"Get up, let's go," Stefan said abruptly. "You don't belong in here."

"No can do, Stef," Alan said sadly.

"Yes can do," Stefan said. "Must do. You can't just stay here, Alan." At this point, Stefan became irritated they no longer had the room to themselves. Phillip and his mother were listening. How could they not, in the small room?

"Where else did you go, Stef?" Alan said. "Shaw's Garden? It's right next to Tower Grove."

"No, I just went to Tower Grove."

"Aw, Stef. Shaw's Garden is the botanical garden. We St. Louisans call it Shaw's Garden after the English chap who founded it. It's not just a place with pretty flowers, it's one of the world's greatest research gardens. In the same league with Kew in London and the New York Botanical Garden. How's that for company?"

"Very impressive," Stefan said.

"This was in 1859, when Shaw started the Garden. Henry Shaw, I think that was his name. In 1859! Two years before the Civil War." Alan paused. "St. Louis is full of grand old institutions that pre-date the Civil War. Try to find one in L.A. Not a chance."

"Anything new in this town?" Stefan said.

"The Arch. 1965. That's really new for St. Louis."

"Johnny-come-lately," Stefan said. He thought they were having such an inane conversation, probably even Phillip had tuned out.

"The Arch isn't that old, I believe," Phillip's mother said. "I've lived here all my life."

"Pretty sure I'm right," Alan said. (He was.)

"I think it was later," the woman said.

"I know St. Louis pretty well," Alan said. "I love it. It betrayed me. I still love it, though."

"Now Alan," Stefan interrupted sharply. He couldn't have explained it to himself, but he didn't want his friend exposing his malady to these strangers. "I could use a cup of coffee." Stefan did not want coffee, but that wasn't the point. "Want to go with me to the coffee station?"

"All right," Alan said. They made their way down the hall. Suddenly, Stefan remembered something. It seemed to come out of the blue, but was in fact one of those memories one has but doesn't know one has, until something unexpectedly brings it forth.

"Alan!" he said. They arrived at the coffee station. Neither wanted any, but they sat, tacitly agreeing it beat returning to Phillip and his mother. "Alan, it's ironic you mentioned the Civil War, because it reminded me of something. Something I once read. Can't imagine that I remember it, but I do. Do you know what a dispensation is, Alan?"

"Special privilege of some kind?" Alan said.

"Yes! Exactly right. Well, what I read is, at the start of the Civil War, you could purchase a dispensation. You had to be wealthy, naturally. This was a way of avoiding conscription. I remember this very distinctly, Alan, although I have no idea where I read it. Definitely called a 'dispensation,' definitely the Civil War."

"So?"

"So!"

"Height of dishonesty, wouldn't you say?" Alan said.

"Yes it's the height of dishonesty," Stefan said. He had gotten the reaction from Alan he supposed he would, and that he wanted. "Now just consider, Alan," he resumed, "the contrast in this, and in what you did. You did the supremely ethical, honest thing. You didn't lie or cheat. You went to prison. Hardly anybody did that, Alan, but you, my friend, did. Yet you insist upon castigating yourself, when you were ethical. You must quit doing this, Alan. You must see yourself differently." Stefan was as earnest as he could be. He abruptly grabbed Alan by the upper arms and shook him slightly, staring straight into his eyes.

"I did not do my duty," Alan said. "Everything else is rot." Stefan was crestfallen. He shook his head in dismay. The dispensation argument was as useless as them all. It was exasperating. It was futile. He wanted to go. He was not going to spend more time here, not right now. He couldn't bear it.

"I'm going, Alan," he said. "I'll see you tomorrow." Stefan was not successful in hiding the hurt in his voice, but Alan didn't detect it.

"Going?" he exclaimed. "You just got here, Stef." They reached his room.

"Hallo," Phillip said loudly to Alan. "Hallo," he repeated loudly to Stefan.

"Phillip, dear, please lower your voice," his mother said, looking up from her magazine.

"Are you the doctor?" Phillip asked Alan, as he climbed back into his bed.

Stefan was truly disheartened. Back in his hotel room, he took his shoes off and lay down. What arrangements had he made with Jeanne? He couldn't recall. Were they having dinner tonight? That didn't sound right. Was he supposed to call her? Most likely. He stared at the ceiling, closed his eyes briefly, and snoozed. At "milking time," as Sharon termed it, he headed for his nightly highball. The lounge was about as busy as every night, which is to say, it wasn't busy. Two men watching a game on the television behind the bar were too boisterous. The bartender quieted them down, but only temporarily. They clearly had no regard for how their cheering and "high-fives" might bother others. Stefan wished the bartender would turn off the television. There was no escaping TV. In a bar, in an airport, even on a plane, there it was. Somehow, the eye was drawn to the little screen; you couldn't help but watch. It had a magnetic power. Stefan mused on how television had changed. So much of it now was … what was the word? Unwholesome. It had begun wholesome, now it wasn't.

He enjoyed his drink and then bought a sandwich to take back to his room. Definitely did not want to sit by himself in the restaurant for an hour. In the morning, he'd get down to business, whatever that was. No more sightseeing. Call Alan, go see him. Call Jeanne, have dinner. The day was set.

When he called the hospital in the morning, he was told, "Mr. Young is indisposed." Indisposed? For how long? Until he wasn't. What's "indisposed?" Indisposed is indisposed. He called Jeanne, who had already been in touch with the hospital. She reassured Stefan. Alan was sometimes indisposed. He'd be better later.

"Should I plan on getting over there later?" Stefan asked her.

"Not sure I'd plan on today," Jeanne said. "Call first, for sure." She was all business.

Now what? He had to do something with his day. How about a museum? Must be a good one somewhere. He inquired at the concierge.

"You might try the history museum," the young woman said. "They have the Spirit of St. Louis." Lindbergh's plane! Now there was a man with a wild notion, and he had pulled it off, by golly!

"Excellent recommendation," Stefan said. "Where is the museum?"

"Forest Park. Not far. Let me give you directions." She produced a small map.

"Actually, I was there," Stefan said. "That's where the … um … zoo is, right?" He felt a bit foolish admitting he had gone to the zoo.

"Right. Forest Park. You might even have driven past the museum. The park is pretty big, but you'll find it all right."

He found it all right, but was disappointed to learn the plane was a replica. The Smithsonian Institution in Washington had the original. That didn't seem right. He had lunch in the cafe and gazed out at the park. A fair number of people were about, a welcome change. Stefan again contemplated the remainder of his visit. One more trip, for sure, to the hospital. A conversation with Jeanne.

He left and drove through the park. It was indeed extensive. He came across the "World's Fair Pavilion." Another nod to that world's fair! I'd be schizophrenic if I lived here, Stefan said to himself. Comparing what was, with what is.

He got back to his hotel and decided to try to reach Sharon. Los Angeles was two hours earlier than St. Louis, so it would be mid-morning. She wouldn't be home. She wasn't.

Stefan frittered away the better part of the afternoon at the hotel. Around four he called the hospital. "Mr. Young is indisposed." It seemed alarming to him, yet Jeanne had said not to worry. In any event, he clearly was not going to the hospital today.

It finally got late enough for a cocktail. The lounge tonight was the setting for a birthday party. Balloons and more balloons. Balloons were festive. There were no un-festive balloons. They helped sell cars, too, balloons did. Car lots always had plenty of balloons blowing in the breeze. Must be thousands on any given day, in L.A.

The party was loud. Around a dozen people. Stefan couldn't make out whose birthday it was. Sooner or later they'd sing, then he'd know. He ordered his martini. He opted again for a sandwich, although he had had one for lunch. He would eat it right there in the bar. Still no singing, but plenty of laughter and horseplay. He tried Sharon again when he returned to his room, and reached her this time. There was no news. Well, he'd been gone five days.

"How is your friend doing, darling?" she inquired.

"Not so good," Stefan said. "I couldn't even stop by today to see him. They said he was indisposed."

"I'm sorry to hear that."

"Alan, when I'm with him, doesn't seem too bad, though. It's just that he has these negative thoughts, always lurking and ready to spring."

"We all have negative thoughts."

"I trust my dear wife is not having one while speaking with her faithful husband?" Stefan joked.

"Well you never know," Sharon said, and they both laughed. "Are you still coming home Sunday?"

"Yes. If anything, I might move it up. No, it's not worth the trouble. I'll be there Sunday."

Then what? What came after Sunday? He had three more weeks before he was to return to the office. He had had no plan coming to Missouri; he had no plan returning to California. Stefan was at sea.

He perused the newspaper over breakfast. Mushrooming cost overruns on major bridge work. Billikens lose soccer game. (Billikens?) Cars in downtown hotel parking lot vandalized overnight. Stuart "Stu" Schwartz dies. Owner of popular suburban restaurant more than 30 years. "Best corned beef sandwiches in town." Pillar of the community. Son uncertain whether family will continue with restaurant. Symphony's rendition of Tchaikovsky's Fifth Symphony brings standing ovation. Long-time law professor at Washington University announces retirement, after thirty-six years. Woman seriously injured in one-car accident. Eyewitness says car just suddenly jumped curb and struck street lamp.

Back in his room, he had a message from Jeanne. Alan had had a bad night. He was disoriented. Not an emergency. She was at the hospital. Please call. Stefan called her right away.

"He's settling down," she said. "They've sedated him. He gets this way. He's extremely anxious. He starts shaking violently."

"He has seemed reasonably well to me," Stefan said uncomprehendingly.

"Stefan," Jeanne said, "you ... I don't know how to say it, even, let alone explain it. You have a special place in Alan's life. I know I've said this before, but it's true. He's different when you're around."

"It is strange," Stefan said. "I can't explain it either."

"If Alan would get better, if you were to stay ... I know you can't, of course, totally ridiculous."

"Yes I'm afraid that's impossible." Of course, he could stay three more weeks. She didn't know this, and he didn't offer.

"When did you say you're leaving, Stefan?" she asked.

"Sunday." It was now Friday. "I'm not leaving without seeing Alan again, though. Does later today look possible, at this point?"

"He's under sedation, as I said. I don't think today is good. You could try calling later."

"I'll do that. I'm sorry, Jeanne." He detected she was crying softly.

Stefan was down in the dumps. He really might not see Alan again. This oddly troubled him. Yet he didn't want to go to the hospital, he didn't want to go to another museum, he didn't want to go anywhere. He didn't particularly want to go home Sunday. He was at a standstill. But he couldn't stare at the four walls in his room all day. He consulted the front desk. The clerk suggested the New Cathedral. Stefan asked if that was the little church beneath the Arch. Nope, that's the Old Cathedral. You want the New Cathedral. St. Louis has an Old Cathedral and a New Cathedral and an Old Courthouse and a New Courthouse and an Old Post Office and a New Post Office. Next question. How do you get to the New Cathedral? Central West End. Good place to knock off several hours. Lots of stores and restaurants. "Slice of New York in St. Louis." Sounded promising.

Stefan found the Central West End, which was called "CWE." There were at least three hospitals. Some high-rise buildings, looked like apartments. Stefan parked. The clerk hadn't been able to remember what street the cathedral was on, and the map they had consulted didn't indicate it, either.

"You'll find it all right," the clerk had said. "It's an amazing building. You won't be disappointed."

The CWE was perfect for walking. Stefan found himself on Euclid Street and walked a number of blocks up one side and down the other. He poked into shops. A bookstore occupied him a while. He had not been much of a reader in many years. He browsed the shelves but didn't buy a book. There was a movie theater, which turned out to be closed. Numerous individuals were in the garb of medical professionals. Stefan hadn't seen it, but the Washington University School of Medicine was part of a very extensive medical center. A woman with a camera was taking photographs randomly. She pointed at Stefan, who raised his arm over his face. She grinned. Stefan found a shady spot and got off his feet for an interval. The CWE had a nice ambiance. It was reasonably lively. Shops were open, not boarded up. Some people were dressed as if they cared how they looked. Time ticked by. Stefan remembered the cathedral. Where was it? He decided to skip it. He'd been to Durham and Chartres and Cologne, he didn't need to see a church in St. Louis, Missouri. He was liking just sitting on the bench beneath the trees, people-watching. Stefan had been in many cities, in the United States and abroad. He knew his way around London and Paris. You could sit at a sidewalk table at a Parisian café and watch the world go by. The waiter would not be stopping by after twenty minutes with his ultimatum: Buy something else, or scram.

The morning slipped away pleasantly. Stefan had lunch, then called the hospital. Alan was unavailable. Was Mrs. Young there? Yes. Might he speak with her? Jeanne came on the line. Alan was asleep. He remained sedated. He would "come to" later, but be groggy and confused. She said he had been hysterical much of the night.

"Jeanne," Stefan said, "look, I came from California to be with Alan. What if he is asleep? What if he is groggy? Any reason I couldn't come by and sit there?"

"If you wish, Stefan," Jeanne said. "You're in for a long afternoon."

"I'll be there in a bit," Stefan said. He tried to convince himself she had not sounded put out, but she had. When he reached the hospital, he found she had left for work. This irked him. She might have told him on the phone she would be leaving. Norma, at the front desk, was cordial.

"You may go to Mr. Young's room, if you like. Mrs. Young told us you would be coming, and she had no objection. Mr. Young is resting, so you must be quiet."

"Of course, thank you, Norma," Stefan said. He went down the hall to Alan's room.

"Hallo," Phillip said loudly. Stefan put his finger to his lips to shush him. Phillip put his finger to his own lips. Alan, indeed, was asleep. A nurse came in. "Hallo." She was carrying a tray upon which was a glass of water and a small, plastic container. It contained four, black capsules.

"Time for your pills, Phillip," she said. Phillip still had his finger to his lips. "Please remove your finger so you can take them." Phillip shook his head back and forth. "Phillip," the nurse said. He would not remove his finger. "Now Phillip," she said, "please don't be uncooperative." Phillip was looking Stefan's way, and since Stefan was watching the little scenario, he caught Phillip's eye.

"Take your pills, Phillip," Stefan found himself saying. Phillip nodded his head back and forth, finger pressed to his lips. The nurse reached gently for Phillip's finger and tried to pry it from his lips. This wasn't going to work, anybody could have told her that. Phillip turned quickly away from her.

"Very well, Phillip, have it your way," she said. She left, taking the capsules and water with her. Phillip kept facing the wall. Alan dozed peacefully. Stefan had grabbed a magazine in the lobby and now opened it. Phillip peeked around at him, finger still at his lips. He peeked a little more, then turned all the way back around to face Stefan. He removed his finger.

"Are you the doctor?" he asked Stefan. Stefan ignored him. He wanted to tell him to go to hell. He put the magazine down, went over to Alan's bedside, and touched him lightly on the shoulder. "He's dead," Phillip said. Stefan stayed an hour. Alan never woke up.

When he reached his car, Stefan suddenly felt he was going to vomit. He fought it back. He gathered his wits and climbed into the car. On the drive back to his hotel, he encountered a roadblock. Accident. Both lanes in the direction he was going were blocked. Police were directing motorists down a side street. Stefan turned and drove several blocks through a residential neighborhood before finding another street that looked to be a thoroughfare, going the way he wanted to go. It was a commercial street. Space for lease. Could you go anywhere in town and not see that? Hamburger place, chicken place, pawn shop, hamburger place, two-story, abandoned brick building, VFW Post No. 186, Dental Office of Theodore Swanson DDS, fish place, vacant parking lot with grass emerging from beneath asphalt, another two-story brick building with a ladies' shop of some sort on the ground floor, a bowling alley that looked closed but wasn't, Rudy's Barber Shop with non-functioning barber's pole in front, Mexican restaurant, an abandoned edifice that had once been a filling station. Stefan wasn't too dismayed. Every city had a street like this. How come American cities were so ugly? Stefan had visited Switzerland. Not an ugly city in the whole country. Of course, all those lakes and mountains helped. Still, the cities themselves were beautiful. Besides, weren't there lakes and mountains in America?

Message from Jeanne when he reached his hotel. Call her at work. Were they having supper tonight? Was that right? What day was it, anyway? Friday. My, weren't they going to have fun! Stefan had reached the nadir of his trip. Its pointlessness was complete. There was no conversation left to have, no place to go, no one to see. He was just marking time and spending money needlessly. He called Jeanne.

"Was this our night for supper?" he asked. Not that they had really planned anything specific.

"I thought it was," she said.

"But you're at work?"

"I have a thirty-minute break. There's a café next door. Pretty good fried fish, actually. We could meet there." This was supper together?

"Thirty minutes isn't much," Stefan said. "I don't even know where you are."

"Did you go by the hospital?" she asked.

"I did. Alan was asleep."

"Thank goodness," she said. "Do you have a pen and paper? I'll give you directions. Can you be here at seven?" It was 4:30. He had no idea how far she was. Presumably two and a half hours would be adequate. She began giving him directions. He wrote them down. It was complicated. Abruptly, he cancelled. All that way, probably getting lost, for thirty minutes. Probably just about how long it would take to eat the good fried fish. Stefan didn't know what they were going to discuss, anyway. It just seemed right for the two of them to talk, at some point. Jeanne wasn't keen on it, herself. She had nothing to say.

"Maybe we could shoot for lunch tomorrow, then," she said.

Stefan skipped his highball, ordered room service, and amused himself with television. In the morning, he had breakfast again in the hotel's coffee shop. It was Saturday, his last day. He was hugely relieved. He had a newspaper. Gunfire exchanged yesterday between occupants of two vehicles. One dead. Gang-related, according to police. Stefan put the paper down. He finished his breakfast and called the hospital. Last chance to see Alan. He was awake, alert. Had 'Group Therapy' that afternoon, so the only chance for a visit was this morning. Stefan made for the hospital. He hadn't bothered checking with Jeanne. Maybe he would. Maybe they'd have lunch. Didn't matter one bit, either way. Stefan was already thinking in terms of his trip home the next day.

"I told Mr. Young you would be here," Norma greeted him. Stefan found Alan lying on his back. He was awake. No sign of Phillip. Stefan went up to the bed.

"Stef! You're here. Hey buddy!" Alan sprang up to a sitting position. He was lively, alert. Enthusiastic. It was too weird. He had been too sick for 48 hours to have a visitor. Now, he was the same as before. Sort of like Dr. Jekyll and Mr. Hyde, though not really.

"Hi Alan, hello," Stefan said. "How are you doing today?" They embraced, clumsily. It was hard to hug somebody who was sitting in bed.

"Good, very good, now you're here. You come by yesterday? Must have been asleep?"

"You were. I wasn't here long."

"You should have woken me up, Stef."

"No, Alan." Stefan took a seat.

"Where have you been today, Stef? Well, it's still early. You come here first?"

"That's right. You're priority number one."

"Where'd you go yesterday?"

"Let's see. Central West End. That was it. Very nice area."

"Great little deli there called Benny's. Lunch. Great pastries. Did you go there?"

"No, but I did have lunch somewhere. Don't remember the name. It was fine."

"They call the Central West End the CWE. Big old hotel there, but I think it's closed."

"So what's on your agenda today, Alan? I think they told me you have Group Therapy. What's that all about?"

"Bunch of us sit in a semi-circle and talk. Man named Kent is the moderator. That's not the right word. The therapist. Psychotherapist. I like him. There are eight of us at the moment, but the number varies. We talk mostly about what we've been doing since the last session." Stefan wondered what that could be.

"Your roommate in the group?" Stefan really had no idea why he had asked that.

"Who? Oh, you mean Phillip?"

"Yes, Phillip."

"He isn't, but I suppose he might be. People come and go."

"He was giving the nurse fits yesterday, while you were asleep."

"Did he ask you if you're the doctor?"

"I believe he did." They fell silent momentarily. Stefan spoke up. "Do you think Group Therapy is helping you?"

"I think so. This probably is going to come out wrong, but there's some comfort in knowing you're not the only one who wants to kill himself."

"Would you quit saying that, Alan? You don't want to kill yourself."

"All right, there's comfort in knowing you're not the only person who is mentally ill."

"You're not that either, Alan," Stefan said strongly. He was going home the next day. He would not see Alan again. Not ever, most likely. "I'm not a physician, but I do sincerely believe you are not mentally ill. Aren't we having a perfectly normal conversation? Aren't you fully rational? You are, Alan. You have taken a chance occurrence that is absolutely meaningless and you are letting it bother you. To put it mildly. This is something we all do, sometimes. Allow something inconsequential to bother us. But we shake it off. That's what you must do. Just do it, Alan! Just shake it off and get out of here and back to your life." Alan was silent. The two stared at each other. Stefan knew he had said all this before. There was nothing new to say.

"What you don't understand, Stef, is what's meaningless to one person isn't necessarily to another person."

"No, I understand that."

"Nobody's destiny is meaningless," Alan said.

"That's right," Stefan said. "Nobody's destiny is meaningless." Alan was talking rubbish.

Stefan stayed an hour. Alan became less talkative. Stefan thought he was becoming withdrawn. His presence seemed to matter less and less to Alan. Their conversation was perfunctory. When he rose to go, Alan barely responded. Stefan uttered a heartfelt goodbye but did not get the same in return. Alan didn't even ask him when he would be returning.

That's that, Stefan said to himself as he left the building. He could do nothing for Alan. Time to get back to Pasadena and the routine. The office would be surprised to see him back so soon. He'd been determined, hadn't he, to have his four weeks? Stefan vaguely remembered he had intended to

476

bring up with Alan his remark about divorce and how it was like unemployment. So much for that.

Driving to the hotel, he came upon the same road block as the day before. The police had it cordoned off with yellow tape. Something was afoot. It was, in fact, a crime scene. There had been an exchange of gunfire, between two vehicles. He had seen the article in the newspaper that morning, while he was having breakfast. Stefan was again obliged to take the detour he had taken yesterday. Down the same drab commercial strip. Space for lease. Hamburger place, chicken place, pawn shop, hamburger place, two-story, abandoned brick building, VFW Post 186 with "Tonight: Ribs-St. Louis style, salad bar, mashed potatoes, hot biscuits, $6.95" posted on the marquee, Dental Office of Theodore Swanson DDS, fish place, vacant parking lot with grass emerging from beneath asphalt, another two-story building with a ladies' shop of some sort on the ground floor, a bowling alley that looked closed but wasn't, Rudy's Barber Shop with a non-functioning barber's pole in front, Mexican restaurant, an abandoned edifice that had once been a filling station.

Stefan drove on. One block. He pulled over, stopped. He looked back. VFW Post 186. Veterans of Foreign Wars. Alan wasn't a veteran. But what if … Stefan's mind raced … what if he could work … volunteer work, naturally … no pay … what if he could work at the VFW Post … must be something he could do … plenty, probably … VFW Posts undoubtedly operated on a shoestring … Stefan turned at the light, went around the block, came out again in front of the Post … oh this is crazy … he drove ahead, but found himself turning again at the light … around the block again … in front of the Post again … now, he pulled into the lot and parked … turned off the engine. He wasn't a veteran either, for that matter. Did you have to be one to go inside? Stefan had no idea, but he was about to find out. He got out of the car and walked purposefully to the door.

The door was open. Stefan went inside without hesitation. The place wasn't occupied, aside from one man who was setting up tables and chairs. There was a beery smell. In back, Stefan saw a bar with a Budweiser sign that was turned on.

"Can I help you?" the man asked Stefan. He was middle-aged. He had a sturdy build, strong, hirsute arms, a crewcut, clean shaven. He wasn't wearing a uniform.

"Yes, well, I wonder if I might speak with, um, the manager, for a moment?" Stefan didn't think the manager would be arranging tables and chairs for dinner.

"That's George," the man said. "He's not here yet."

"Well I can come back later, I guess," Stefan said tentatively.

"Maybe I could help you?" The man extended his hand, and they shook. "Name's Norquist. Jonathan Norquist. United States Marines."

"Stefan Kopinski. I'm a lawyer. Not here on legal business. Just like to speak with the manager, with George. Unrelated matter."

"Like I said, George isn't here yet. Usually pretty quiet here, this time of day. Come back later, plenty of people."

"I'll do that," Stefan said.

"Or you can wait. George should be here pretty soon, actually." No shortage of places to sit, that was for sure.

"Thank you, but I believe I will come back." Stefan extended his hand, and they shook again. "Pleased to meet you." Stefan turned toward the door and was met by a man with whom he nearly collided. This was George Willoughby, Major Willoughby, United States Army. Retired.

"This is George," Norquist said to Stefan's back.

"Morning, John," Major Willoughby said.

"This gentleman would like to speak with you," Norquist said. Stefan promptly introduced himself and shook hands with Major Willoughby. The major was a black man, 55, graying on top, handsome, deep-voiced.

"What can I do for you?" he asked Stefan.

"I thought we might speak …" Stefan hesitated. He really wanted to sit down with the major in his office, if he had one. "I thought we might speak briefly."

"Come into my office." Major Willoughby said. "Give me a minute, if you will. John here will take care of you. Want some coffee?"

"Should have asked before," Norquist said.

"Love a cup, thanks," Stefan said. He was aware the two soldiers were taking him in with some curiosity. Norquist got Stefan a cup of coffee, and shortly thereafter he found himself seated in Major Willoughby's office. It was small. Windowless. His desk was obviously second-hand. There was an American flag, and another, with "VFW Post 186" and an insignia. A picture of General Eisenhower, in uniform and speaking earnestly to several soldiers, hung on the wall behind the major's desk.

Stefan began immediately. He had a friend, he said. An old friend. In fact, his oldest friend. He was recovering from an illness. Much better. Needed to do something with himself. Had reached middle-age, done some teaching, worked at … Stefan momentarily couldn't come up with it … worked at the YMCA … that was it! … many years, many years, a good good man, but needed to be busier. Stefan now began really to "wing it." His friend had very strong feelings about how veterans are treated. The short shrift they get. He wants to help. Was there something, perhaps, he could do at the Post? Help with upkeep? General maintenance? Volunteer work, obviously. Would this be possible?

"What's your friend's name?" the major inquired.

"Alan Young," Stefan said.

"Well, Mr. Kopinski, did you say, we contract out our work, so we don't really need help with cleaning and maintenance."

"I see," Stefan said.

"Your friend's a vet, presumably?"

"No, actually he isn't."

"I don't quite get it," the major said. Just who this stranger was, and what he was doing here, crossed his mind. "You a vet?" he asked Stefan. "What's this all about?" The major was curious, if not suspicious.

"My friend, Major Willoughby, needs to help veterans. This would help him on his road to recovery. That's all there is to my errand. I thought there might be something here for him."

"Sorry." Major Willoughby stood up and extended his hand. "I hope your friend gets better." They shook hands. It was definitely time for Stefan to go. "You might try the VA Hospital," the major added. "Could be an opportunity for your friend there." Willoughby, in truth, was beginning to wonder if Stefan's friend even existed. The whole thing was bizarre.

"That's certainly a thought," Stefan said. Why hadn't he thought of that?

Stefan headed back down the dreary street. It was dreary no more. It was beautiful. He had a song in his heart. His trip to St. Louis was vindicated! Work at the VA! It was the answer for Alan. His friend sought redemption, didn't he? A way to forgive himself? This was it! Helping veterans. The country was in another war, in the Middle East. The hospitals must be taking in new patients all the time. Plus, the hospitals were notoriously underfunded to begin with. Alan would have no trouble finding volunteer work. He might even get a salaried job. This was it, by gosh! Salvation!

Stefan got his hands on a phone book. Veterans Administration Hospital was on Sycamore Street. But he couldn't just drive over there and demand to speak with someone. This would require an appointment. He was leaving the next day. Or was he? He could stay. He was so thrilled with his idea, he called Jeanne. Dinner tonight! They'd talk. He had a topic, all right. Surely she would share his belief this was the answer for Alan.

Jeanne prepared chicken, rice, and a big salad. They each had a glass of wine. Nothing was particularly savory. Chicken was chicken. Vanilla ice cream for dessert. Stefan passed on it.

"What have you done with yourself all week?" she inquired.

"In terms of sightseeing, you mean?"

"Well, everything." Stefan recited where he had gone. He was holding back on the VA Hospital idea. His ardor had cooled a little, but he continued to feel strongly about it, and was very determined to bring it up.

"I'm sorry you missed the cathedral when you were in the CWE. It's exceptional. Millions of mosaics. I can't imagine how long it will have taken to build that church."

"Mosaics? In a church?"

"Millions. Really, there's no describing it. You just have to see it yourself."

"Next time," Stefan said.

"St. Louis is okay," Jeanne said. "It's not a dynamic city, but there are some nice places. Alan, as we've discussed before, is, or was, wild about the place. He could find no fault in it, and believe me, there's plenty of fault. Now, I don't know. It's all wrapped up with his destiny. As we've also discussed previously."

"Jeanne," Stefan began. His excitement was returning, but he spoke in a controlled manner. "This afternoon, I was driving from the hospital back to the hotel, and I happened to drive by a VFW Post. You know what those are, right?"

"Veterans of Foreign Wars."

"Right. Well, I had a thought. I pulled over. Why couldn't Alan work at the Post? This went through my head. It would be volunteer work, unpaid that is, he's not exactly being paid to lie in that bed, is he, and it would give him the opportunity to help veterans. You see, a kind of penance. Alan needs to forgive himself. This is obvious to all of us, you don't need a doctor to tell you that. This could be the way for him. Well, I parked and went inside and spoke with a couple of gentlemen. Nothing at the Post for him,

480

but as I was leaving, one of them suggested I try at the VA Hospital. You know what that is, too, right?" Jeanne nodded she did. "Well, this would be perfect. Perfect. Alan would be helping sick and wounded vets. Who knows what they might have him doing, it doesn't matter. He'd be paying his debt, in a manner of speaking. Working off his guilt. I'm confident they would find something for him to do. Government hospitals are all under-funded and short-staffed. What do you think? You think this might work?"

Jeanne stared at Stefan, incredulously. He had spoken sincerely, and she didn't want to deflate him. But it was all nonsense.

"Stefan," she said, "Alan will kill himself if he leaves the hospital. He's not going to work at the VA. He's not going to work. I don't see how you can believe he's able to leave the hospital."

"When I'm with him, as I believe you yourself observed, Alan does not seem all that incapacitated. Yes, he drops hints about doing himself in, he gets anxious, but that's a far cry from actually doing it. Are you telling me his doctor, what's his name, Holdermann, really believes if Alan steps outside the front door of that institution, he'll commit suicide?"

"Yes, Stefan, he does. So do I. So working at the VA is not possible."

"When is Alan like that? Describe it to me. Is he berserk? Is he hyster-ical? Do they have to restrain him?"

"All those things. He screams he wants to die. They sedate him. Chronic sedation, I think is the term." Jeanne was at the point of tears.

"Please don't cry, Jeanne," Stefan said. He reached across the table and placed his hand on hers.

"I'll cry if I want to."

"Jeanne," Stefan said after a silent interval, "I guess I'm defeated, but I will say one thing more, which, like much of this conversation, has been said before, but I do feel strongly about it." Jeanne dabbed at the last of her tears. "We have three choices. Alan stays where he is and dies a little bit more each day, he leaves and does himself in, he leaves and works at the VA. Three choices. I'm willing to concede he might do himself in, but is this worse than dying in that bed? That's the worst of the three."

"You're not his wife. You haven't spent a lifetime with him. You haven't had his baby. You haven't faced challenges together, like money problems and seeing Mary to maturity. You haven't sat alone at this table while he was out …" Jeanne halted. She knew Alan had affairs. "While he was out doing one thing or another. Stefan, you haven't even been his friend. I'm mean,

481

I'm sorry to be so blunt, but it's true. He's been your friend. You presume now to know what's best. It isn't your decision. If Alan jumps into the river, who will have to deal with it? Who reads the story in the newspaper about the body found in the Mississippi? Who identifies the body?" Jeanne was definitely going to cry again. "You wouldn't even be here."

There was really no disputing this. Stefan was done. The VA idea was out the window. His trip couldn't end soon enough. He couldn't watch her cry. She had removed her hand from beneath his, but now he took it very deliberately.

"I'm leaving tomorrow," he said. "I'm glad I came. I hope you feel this way, too."

"Yes, Stefan, I do," she said magnanimously. Her husband really was better when Stefan was around. No explaining it. No explaining anything. They parted on good terms.

He was out the door by 8:00 the next morning. It was Sunday, traffic was light. He reached the airport and turned in his rental car. An expensive sedan, more "car" than he needed, but it had been a pleasure to drive. Stefan liked nice things.

So did Sharon. She met his plane. She gave him an erotic embrace and whispered in his ear they should climb into the back seat of the car and "see what happens." They didn't. She was a good wife, he had a good life with her. It was good to be home.

Stefan had called his office from St. Louis to advise them he'd be back Monday, so there was no surprise when he got there. Miguel Ordoñez was the first to stop by.

"The world traveler has returned, I see," he said jokingly. He did not know where Stefan had gone; Stefan had shared this only with Art Feinberg. "Welcome, welcome."

"Hey, Miguel, thanks," Stefan said. "It is good to be back." He was behind his desk, and he rapped on it a couple of times. "You're probably surprised I'm already back, since I had a month."

"Yes, well, you did seem pretty intent about having the month. Trip go okay?"

"Fine, yes, it was just time to return." Actually, it was little awkward, since the firm had gone to some pains to let key parties know Stefan Kopinski would be away four weeks. It certainly wasn't a major problem, just awkward.

"Are you going to tell me where you went?" Miguel said. "I'm guessing Mongolia." Stefan laughed.

"I went to St. Louis, Miguel. To see an old friend who's pretty sick."

"I'm sorry to hear that."

"Thank you. It's difficult. I met his doctor. Nice young fellow. He's encouraged, sort of."

"Well you're looking fit," Miguel said. "I suppose the Crombie case is the most pressing matter, since you left. The associate's over at the library. Robert Woodruff, I put him on it. We should discuss status, when you have a minute."

"Sure thing, Miguel. That's the 'kitchen sink' case, right?"

"Yes."

The kitchen sink wasn't the kitchen sink. The term was loosely used to describe a plaintiff who was throwing every possible claim into a suit. In this case, the plaintiff, Arista Crombie, had been fired and was claiming age discrimination, sex discrimination, race discrimination, national origin discrimination, and retaliation. This scattershot approach wasn't necessarily a bad idea. You never knew what the Equal Employment Opportunity Commission, the "EEOC," might do. Indeed, preposterous claims did not uncommonly survive initial review at the EEOC. Some defense counsel believed the federal agency was biased toward plaintiffs. Stefan didn't believe this, though you could make a case for it. The EEOC was actually empowered to take a plaintiff's case, and occasionally did, if it was an especially egregious claim or one of "first impression." Then, too, Stefan had heard his share of presentations at conferences where EEOC counsel made no bones about where the agency's sympathies lay. Nonetheless, in his experience, Stefan had found the EEOC consistently impartial and professional. His biggest complaint was how slow the agency was, but, of course, this was a federal agency. What else could one expect?

Stefan sorted through his "in-basket" the better part of the day. He met with Miguel. He met, near day's end, with Art Feinberg. Art knew where Stefan had gone. He knew he had a sick friend in St. Louis. He knew Stefan wished to speak with that friend about … what was it? That's all Art remembered.

"How's your friend doing?" he inquired.

"Good days, bad days," Stefan said.

"Feel like your visit was beneficial?"

"Oh, I suppose so. Alan is in a better frame of mind, everyone tells me, when I'm with him." Stefan had said nothing, even to Art, about what precisely ailed Alan. Art, however, had guessed, and Stefan was confirming his hunch now. "He's having some tough emotional issues, at the moment."

"So sorry," Art said. I hope he gets better."

"Thanks, Art."

"And what about you?" Art went on. "Find what you were looking for?"

"Would you believe, I was so occupied with my pal, I forgot about it?"

"Even better."

"I didn't find it, Art. Truthfully, I've not thought about it. Going to try to keep it that way." It occurred to Stefan, as he said this, this was just what he was lecturing Alan to do. To quit his habitual, bad thinking. Time to take my own advice, Stefan said to himself.

Chapter 23

THE DAYS BECAME WEEKS; THE WEEKS, MONTHS. IN ST. LOUIS, ALAN was much the same. An inevitable resignation had taken root. The status quo couldn't be changed, might as well accept it. This was Jeanne's thinking, it was Abe Holdermann's thinking, it was the thinking of the rest of the medical staff, it was the thinking of two or three friends who stopped by occasionally. Even Mary, Alan and Jeanne's daughter, was resigned now.

In Pasadena, Stefan had returned to his professional life. His "meltdown," as he called it, was forgotten, although not quite completely. Stefan surprised himself by discovering he cared about Alan as he had not. He could not shake the conviction Alan could be jolted back to life if his grand scheme to stick him in a VA Hospital were realized. There just wasn't any way to accomplish it. He had no control over Alan. The initiative had to come from Jeanne, and she was never going to accept that the risk was worth taking. Alan was 53. He could live twenty more years. In a bed? Stefan, when his mind reverted to Alan, sometimes thought of a woman he had known, years ago, who was obsessed with "health food." She read nutritional studies, she attended seminars, she spent hours at the grocery market, studying labels. She was going to live to be a hundred! The food she ate didn't taste good, but the plan was sound otherwise. How did Alan's circumstances differ?

From time to time, he and Alan spoke. It was Stefan, now, who picked up the phone. The calls were unsatisfactory. Alan was listless. Gone from his voice was the enthusiasm he exhibited when Stefan entered his room at the hospital. Stefan also called Jeanne, and he mentioned this. He was concerned; she wasn't. The one subject Stefan did not bring up in his calls to Alan was his VA Hospital idea. Jeanne had pleaded with him not to do this, had said she would mention it, when the right time came. Stefan had respected her wish. He harbored a notion she was afraid it might work, and it would have been his idea. The topic disappeared from their conversations.

Then, one day, unexpectedly, Jeanne mentioned it, when they spoke.

"I brought it up with him," she said.

"You did! Wonderful! What did he say?" Stefan was surprised and delighted.

"His exact words?" she said with a touch of sarcasm.

"Well, doesn't have to be that." Her tone had not escaped notice.

"He said he would be around guys who did their duty. Which he didn't do. How is that going to make me feel better about myself? That's what he said, Stefan."

Silence. Stefan said not a word. Half a minute went by. A full minute.

"Are you there, Stefan?" Jeanne said.

"I'm here, Jeanne," he said. More silence. Then he spoke up. "I wish you had let me, Jeanne." She could hear the disparagement in his voice. "I ... I might have worded ... might have approached it ..." He stopped. It was done, there was no use discussing it. Stefan, as a litigator, keenly appreciated that an argument had to be presented in a certain way. You seldom got a second chance. He laughed bitterly at himself. Imagine his having thought for an instant she was going to say Alan had embraced his thinking!

"Stefan," she said, "it just won't work." Her tone contained a note of triumph, but she refrained from adding, "I told you so."

More, many more, months elapsed. Stefan and Sharon took a long-deferred trip to Italy. Something Stefan ate in Florence disagreed with him, and he ate nothing at all for the next two days. Sharon was a good wife and duplicated his feat after a meal in Rome.

"Thoughtful of you, sweetheart," he said.

Indigestion aside, their trip was a great success. Sharon loved Naples and the Amalfi Coast. Villages perched impossibly on cliffs, somehow not tumbling wholesale into the azure Mediterranean. The sunlight had a special quality. In Florence, too. Stefan was enchanted by Florence. Everywhere they went, they ran into Michelangelo, and they went everywhere. They didn't miss a museum. Everything was wonderful. In Rome, it was churches and fountains and the Forum and the Colosseum and epic strolls. They visited the Sistine Chapel and the Vatican Library. There was Michelangelo's incomparable depiction of God and Adam, their fingers an inch apart. Stefan felt a pang, for his first wife, Debra, would have been swept off her feet by the painting. Doubtful she'd ever make it to Rome, now. There was Titian, and Canaletto, and Raphael. *The School at Athens* by Raphael: Plato, old and white-haired, pointing heavenward, proclaiming by his gesture ours isn't the real world, the real world is the ideal one we can imagine. Aristotle, his pupil, recalcitrant, his arm extended forward rather than pointing upward, the world we inhabit is the real one, and we must accept it, with all its shortcomings. At Milan, they went to La Scala and heard *Lucia di Lammermoor.* (Sharon loved grand opera.) It was exquisite. This was the world's premier opera house for good reason. Their hotel room door would not close completely. Stefan was displeased. This hotel had a Five-Star rating, the very best. He complained to the front desk, demanded another room. The hotel obliged, and the air conditioning in the replacement room was on the blink.

They walked everywhere, not only in Rome. They encountered other people walking. They encountered bicyclists, in considerable number. Yes, there were cars, but it wasn't only cars. In America, you could almost live in your car, now. What fast food restaurant holding out any hope of success didn't have a drive-through? Banks, libraries, the dry cleaners, the pharmacy, even liquor stores (in the more advanced states) had drive-up windows. All that remained was that clever entrepreneur who would find a way to install a toilet in the back seat of a vehicle.

Back home, Stefan lost a case on appeal. Only the second time in his long career this had happened. Certiorari was denied, which meant the Supreme Court in Sacramento wouldn't hear it. These things happen … he was disconsolate nevertheless.

One day, Stefan was handed an envelope. It was from the Gordon-Jessup Company. The envelope contained a letter. Affixed to it was a familiar, terse cover note: "Please Advise Immediately." Stefan grinned. This was the demand of his "Nervous Nellie" of a client. There was seldom any need for speed and sometimes not advice, either, but when you're paying your lawyer $625 an hour, you expect immediacy. Stefan read the letter:

> To Whom It May Concern:
>
> My name is Charlotte Huxtable. My husband, Mike, was employed by Gordon-Jessup Company for nine years. Nine years have gone by since his work for your firm suddenly ended. I have waited, and now I am waiting no longer.

Mike and I have been married since 1974. He is a decent, honest man, a wonderful husband and dad to our two sons. Mike is a strong man, spiritually. A good thing, too, since he barely survived the massive blow you dealt him, even with his strengths. He got fired from your company, after nine years of dedicated service.

Nine years have gone by, and I still don't know why this happened. Mike may have told me at the time, but I think I'd remember. I don't think he told me, because he doesn't know, either. He also does not know I am writing you this letter, by the way.

Mike's job loss devastated our family. I hardly know where to begin. My husband, despite every effort, remained out of work for four years. Every door he knocked on was closed. Our lives were turned upside-down. We lost our friends. Our boys had to be enrolled in another school, so they also lost their friends. They basically had to start over, just like their parents. It was very, very hard on them. Mike's reputation was destroyed. He had to resign from his club. It was a big part of his life. He couldn't find another job in insurance. He could not find anything. Do you understand me? He could not find any job at all. He lay on the sofa all day long, a defeated man.

Do you think maybe our boys noticed this? Let me tell you something. Our older son went to pieces. He became unmanageable. He had always been a responsible, obedient child. It would be an understatement to say he became disobedient. His last two years in high school, Mike and I sent him to military school. There were fights in our home, and much anger and shouting matches. Our son used words I had never heard him say. I am not going to write down those words, but I'm sure that's unnecessary in any event. He called his father a failure, he said he was ashamed of him. This was worse, I think, than even the profanity. He said he couldn't face his schoolmates. He couldn't hold up his head with them. I don't know if they were actually unkind, maybe not, but they seemed to know Mike was not working, that I was the family prop. Can you imagine what this was like for a 12-year-old boy? He is a grown man now, and he lives in Seattle, and is doing fine, he has a good job, but when he comes home, there is still, after all these years, a difference in his relationship with his dad, a kind of tension that nothing can make go away. This might just be the very worst consequence of what you did to Mike.

I have wondered, over the years, exactly what happened. How do you fire someone who has been in your dedicated service almost a decade? Mike must have been doing something right, to stay at your company that long. So what happened? Did he say the wrong thing to somebody more important than him? Did he do something unacceptable? No way, no way Mike would ever have done that. What, then? What did he do, to have this horrible disaster happen to him? You must have it written down somewhere, haven't you?

Mike has always said he got a new boss who didn't like him. I have not been inclined to accept this, since it's just too stupid to believe a man could be ruined this way. But you know what? That is why he got fired, isn't it? His boss didn't like him. If he ever told me this man's name, I have forced it out of my memory. But I'd like to ask you, are you proud of this? Does this bring credit on the company? Maybe it's part of your sales talk? We fire people we don't like. Or how about this: We fire people you don't like. Did one of your customers tell you to fire Mike Huxtable, or they would take their business somewhere else? No, I don't think even you could stoop that low.

My husband did finally find another job, although not in his field of expertise. Why did it take him so long? I can't answer that. Perhaps he did give up, at some point. Who wouldn't? He has performed his job, his second career if you could call it that, with the same dedication he brought to his job with you. That's Mike's way. His work is valued, he is appreciated. His pay is far below what he was making with you, he'll never catch up, but we have managed. Mike does not have the same level of duties he had with you, either. He is not eligible for any more promotions at his present position. So those are things gone for good.

For the longest time, I despised your company. I remember seeing an article in the newspaper, years ago, about your big new office in L.A. Maybe you used Mike's salary to help finance opening it? I tore the article into small pieces. But as the years have gone by, I have found my thinking has changed. I don't really believe you are to blame for what happened to Mike. Oh, you did it all right, you fired him, nothing's ever changing that. But you're not the ultimate culprit, are you? I don't think so. You're weak. Men are weak. Because men are weak, they do bad things. Good men, I'm talking about good men, do bad things, because they are weak. Unless, that is, there is a law that tells them they can't.

It was the law of this state that let you do what you did. It was the law that let one man cut another man's lifeline, and his family's lifeline, just because he felt like it one day.

Men need to be strong, not weak. Laws need to be wise. Our lawmakers in Sacramento need to be wise. They need to be intelligent and sensible men and women. They need to have good judgment. They need to be mature individuals. Wouldn't you agree?

For your information, I am sending a copy of this letter to Rep. Marion Yates and Sen. Joel Whittington. I don't expect anything to come of it, but I'm sending it, and I am going to call them a few days later, to talk about it. I am just one woman, and I can do no more, but I can do this.

I hope you will take what I have said to heart, especially the next time you decide to throw a man out of work for no reason. I have written from my own heart. If you wish to reply, or even speak with me, that would be fine.

Yours truly,
Charlotte Huxtable

Stefan picked up the phone. Might as well call Roderick Jessup while it was fresh in his mind. He was pretty certain what he would get from Roderick. It was time for one of his hand-holding sessions.

"How are you, Stefan?" Roderick said.

"Good, Roderick, good. You?"

"Fine, thanks."

"And business?"

"Good. No complaints. Well, except that letter. That's what you're calling about, presumably?"

"Got it right here in front of me, Roderick."

"What do you think?"

"What do you want me to think?"

"I believe the woman means it when she says she's going to follow-up with Yates and Whittington."

"You never know. I'm not so sure. Anyway, it doesn't matter."

"It matters to me. She's besmirching our reputation. You want that letter circulating around the legislature?"

"Roderick, that won't happen. They'll take one look at it and toss it. Assuming it gets past their secretaries in the first place. Good grief, you have any idea how many crank letters these guys get every day?"

"I suppose you're right," Roderick said, "although I don't know that I'd construe it that way."

"Well I would. Woman's getting something off her chest. We all need to do that, now and then. Means nothing."

"It still bothers me. How about I give Yates and Whittington a ring and talk with them about it?"

"God no, don't do that, you'd only call attention to it. As I said, they may never even see it. Sit tight and forget about it. If one of them calls you, then call me, and we'll take care of it."

"Could we sue this dame for besmirching Gordon-Jessup, if push comes to shove?"

"No," Stefan said conclusively.

"Okay, then. Sit tight. Appreciate your thinking, Stefan."

"I'm always here, Roderick."

CHAPTER 24

NEITHER SHARON NOR DEBRA COULD BELIEVE IT. STEFAN WAS TAKING a full week off for elder daughter's wedding. It had just seemed to Stefan the thing to do. Perhaps he had not been as involved in his two daughters' lives as he should have been. The elder, Linda, in particular, had gone down a perilous path. If a father was not going to be present at the most important event in his daughter's life, then when? Accordingly, Stefan was to be out of the office seven days. He meant to make the most of them.

First, he was flying to San Francisco. The errand was to get daughter number two, Lisa, and drive back to Pasadena together. Lisa was a chemist. She had a job, a good job, with the University of California. Her position was at the campus in Davis, northeast of San Francisco. Stefan felt Lisa may have been somewhat overlooked during the critical years when her sister had descended into alcoholism and near-annihilation. Now, that sister was marrying. Attention would be overwhelmingly directed toward Linda again. Thus, dad was going to get younger daughter and drive the better part of the length of the state with her. He hoped Lisa would be pleased. He hoped Linda would not be displeased.

The sisters had never looked much alike, nor thought much alike. Nevertheless, they were sisters, and they were close. Linda was a beautician and, as such, given to toying with her looks constantly. At present, her hair had a platinum coloration, and she wore it short. Her fiancé loved it. Linda was pretty, with high cheekbones, maybe too high, and flawless skin. She was given to using oddly-colored lipstick and claimed her stepmother was her inspiration, which wasn't entirely untrue. Linda was on the thin side. She had lost weight during her years of dissipation, and never completely regained it. Her stepmother detected a hint of fatigue in Linda's countenance, which found expression primarily in her eyes. There was a dullness to them that defied the wiles of the beautician's art. Sharon knew not if others shared this perception but was not, in any case, about to bring it up.

Linda took care of herself. She groomed herself skillfully. She had risen to third in seniority at one of the largest beauty salons in Pasadena. She was good at what she did, she earned a decent living, and the pride she took in what she had achieved had every justification.

Lisa, three years her sister's junior, was unflappable. Her sister's disintegration, according to her therapist, had frightened Lisa nearly out of her wits. This was little exaggeration. Neither Stefan nor Debra was entirely persuaded. Both felt the girls had been starkly unalike temperamentally from an early age, and that Lisa's phlegmatic, take-things-as-they-come nature had had much to do with keeping her on a steady course while her sister fell apart.

Lisa was the more scholarly. She had graduated with top honors from UCLA with a Bachelor of Science, having majored in Biochemistry. She had landed her current position at the Davis campus even before graduating. Lisa was a capable young woman, a dedicated scientist, and she loved her family. She was a brunette, not as tall as her sister, not as striking. She was notably not as thin, either; indeed, Lisa must pay more attention to her diet. She hadn't let herself go, but it was a danger. There was something of a contradiction in this, considering how knowledgeable she was, as a chemist, about the components of good health. Despite having an older sister who wasn't shy about lecturing her on her looks, Lisa paid little attention. A laboratory, unlike a salon, was not the place for a fashion show, she'd say by way of retort, and the sisters would have a good laugh.

Lisa had an on-again, off-again boyfriend. His name was Danny Capisteo. Danny claimed his great-great-great-grandfather, or maybe there were four "greats," Lisa wasn't sure, had come to San Francisco from rural, impoverished southern Italy, arriving in 1868. As such he was, according to Danny, one of the earliest members of what became a flourishing Italian community in the city, which was still there and still modestly influential. Danny was in the Navy and was based in Oakland. He had met Lisa in Berkeley, at an outdoor concert Lisa was attending with a friend; the two had driven down from Davis. Lisa and Danny had had a few dates. Although the distance between them, Oakland and Davis, wasn't great, it was just enough to act as a disincentive. More fundamentally, the simple fact was, Danny was more serious about Lisa Kopinski than Lisa was about Danny Capisteo.

They ate, father and daughter did, at what purportedly was the best steakhouse in northern California. Stefan's filet mignon was overcooked. They shared a slice of tiramisu for dessert, Lisa having advised portions were on the generous side. Stefan had a couple of bites, and his girl, who had a sweet tooth, polished off the rest. Stefan was enjoying himself. He chuckled when he remembered those times he and Lisa had seen a movie and then gone for pizza or hamburgers, and he had struggled to find something to say to his little girl, barely turned a teenager. No more! Lisa was a scientist, by gum, and a good one, and she was ambitious, like her dad. She was like him, too, and not like her mother, when it came to religion. Lisa was far from certain she believed in any deity. Where had that loving Lord been when her sister was falling apart? Lisa could only imagine how many futile prayers her mother had uttered.

Lisa, however, would not escape a church wedding, albeit as maid of honor. While her sister had no intention of going anywhere near First United Methodist Church of Alhambra, since her husband-to-be was a Catholic, they were marrying at Holy Angels.

Lisa had her suitcase packed when her father knocked on her hotel room the next morning. They were getting an early start. From Davis to Pasadena would be a very full day's drive.

Weeks before the wedding, Debra had gotten a phone call from Sharon. The latter wanted to be involved, wanted it very much, but she recognized, too, she was the "odd woman out," and she had made up her mind to defer to Debra completely. When she offered to stay away altogether, "if this is best," Debra reacted strongly.

"Sharon," she almost scolded, "I can't imagine you would suppose I would want anything of the sort. Your last name is Kopinski, isn't it? We're a family. Don't you dare not participate to the fullest extent you wish. My goodness, I'm counting on having you at my side, considering the decisions that have to be made." Debra was firm and uncompromising. She did not, however, additionally mention she believed it was Sharon's leadership, at the most critical of times, that had probably saved Linda's life. She had said this plenty of times before.

"Thank you so much, Debra," Sharon said. "I want to be useful. But you're in charge." Sharon was, perhaps, disingenuous. She had not believed for a moment Debra would respond in any manner except as she had. Sharon had just wanted to hear it.

There was a decided irony in Sharon's having asked about her role at the wedding. Debra, improbably, had met a man, with whom a measure of affection was being mutually shared. His name was Howard May. Howard was a Presbyterian pastor, now retired. He was a decade older than Debra. He was a native of Los Angeles and had lived there all his life. His wife had died, but he had a grown son and four grandchildren. What was his role?

Howard and Debra had been seeing each other for some months. They were not intimate. This was out of the question, unmarried. They were affectionate, they enjoyed one another's company, they had dinner together now and then. They were grateful they had met.

Maybe there was just a small amount of revenge in Debra's decision to ask Howard to be present at the wedding? Stefan and Sharon would be a couple, Troy's parents would be a couple, why should she be alone? People could speculate to their heart's content, as far as she was concerned.

Three bridesmaids, all colleagues of Linda's at the salon, complemented Troy's three groomsmen. Troy's brother, Thomas, was best man. Troy was Troy Brummer. He was employed by the City of Pasadena, in the Wastewater Division of the Utilities Department. Stefan wasn't sure what this job was, precisely. Everything had become so euphemistic. Was a wastewater expert a glorified plumber? Troy, in any event, was a likeable sort, happy-go-lucky, perfect for Linda.

Despite himself, Stefan became choked up at the wedding, when it came time to hand his daughter over to another man. What kind of dad have I really been, coursed through his head. Linda was positively beaming. Had she attained genuine happiness? It had once seemed so out of reach.

At the reception, Stefan, as father of the bride, gave the speech. It was a short, good talk. Troy's father also spoke briefly. Toasts were raised, again and again. As things began to wind down, Stefan found himself seated alone at a table beneath the big tent erected for the occasion. Sharon had abandoned him for superior amusement elsewhere. His first wife spotted him and, separating herself momentarily from Howard, wandered over.

"May I join you, or do you prefer to be left alone with your thoughts, dear Stefan? You're looking pensive."

"For God's sake, Debra, you don't have to ask me if it's all right to sit down." She sat.

"Beautiful wedding, wouldn't you say?" she said. "Everything came off without a glitch."

"Considering you and Sharon and Linda planned it down to the last minute," Stefan said, "it could not have been otherwise." Debra laughed.

"Luckily for us, somebody else was paying the bills." This brought a rueful laugh from Stefan. The wedding had come to $8,000. Stefan didn't regret a cent of it.

"One down, one to go," he said.

"Do you think Lisa is very serious about the boy she's seeing? From what you said, I gather she isn't."

"Right. I don't think their relationship will last long. She'll meet somebody, eventually. Lisa's very focused on her work, right now. It's definitely her first priority. She loves it."

"I foolishly asked her to explain what she's doing," Debra said. "I know less than I did before she told me." Stefan laughed.

"It is so gratifying to see Linda beaming with joy, isn't it?" he said.

"Oh my goodness …" Debra gasped emotionally. "I'm so very grateful she's still alive, let alone finding joy." Debra was abruptly so overcome, she was unable to go on.

"Lisa told me Linda told her Troy has a big rifle collection."

"So he's a hunter?"

"Hunts deer."

"Linda must not let that matter," Debra said. "I'm sure she won't."

"I hadn't finished," Stefan said. "He's teaching her how to shoot."

"I can't imagine Linda shooting an animal," Debra said. "Well, on the other hand, if it's important to her husband, then, yes."

"Lisa says Linda is enjoying learning to shoot."

"Well that's good."

"So there's probably some venison in our future."

"Did we ever eat venison?" Debra said.

"Not that I recall. I've heard it's kind of gamy."

"Stands to reason."

"If Linda puts it on the plate before us, we're going to like it," Stefan said. They both laughed. Debra wondered just when she and Stefan would be eating together with their daughter and her new husband.

"We'll clean our plates and ask for seconds," she said.

"What's become of Howard?" Stefan inquired. "I don't see him anywhere."

"Oh, he's around," Debra said. "I hope you like him, dear."

"I hardly know him."

"He's an old-fashioned gentleman, Stefan. He was born in 1938. His dad was in the war, of course. In Italy. Howard has two sisters, one older, one younger. Both going strong."

"I'm so glad you two met, Debra," Stefan said sincerely.

"Thank you, Stefan. I don't know what lies in store for us. Howard is so much older. He might not have many more years …" Her voice trailed off.

"Make the most of them," Stefan said. They fell silent. Then Debra spoke up.

"I want to say something to you, Stefan," she said firmly. She looked him squarely in the eye.

"Okay," he said.

"Do you remember Madeleine Ullstater?"

"That marriage counselor you dragged me to see that time?" he said.

"Yes." Debra was mildly surprised he remembered Madeleine, which was not the same thing as remembering what she had said, which indeed had not remained in Stefan's head as long as it had taken them to reach their car, when the session was over. "I happened to think of Madeleine the other day," Debra continued, "when the girls and I were out shopping. My, we had fun."

"I did, too," Stefan joked. "I wasn't with the three of you."

"I got to thinking," Debra continued, "about something Madeleine said. I kept seeing her, for about a year. On one occasion, she said something that shocked me. Until I understood it, that is."

"What was that?"

"She said, Stefan, a husband and wife should put their love for their children second. This floored me. I was astounded. But she went on to say, their love for each other should come first, and by doing this, husband and wife create a very powerful example for their children. Because kids see everything. Watching the devotion their father and mother give each other, they do this, too, when they grow up and marry. They also feel absolutely safe and absolutely loved. What Madeleine was saying is, you love your children to the greatest extent possible by loving your spouse to the greatest extent possible. So, you are not really putting them second, after all."

"Guess we get an 'F' in that department," Stefan said uneasily. He was not comfortable with Debra's odd introduction of a lost conversation with a therapist he had met once. Debra was implicitly criticizing him, wasn't she?

"Stefan," she said, "for years I blamed you for destroying our family. This is hardly a revelation. Our divorce, I believe, was the biggest factor in Linda's unravelling. I can't prove this, but I just know it, the way you know something. Linda hated me. You should have heard some of the things she said to me, some of the words she used." Debra winced thinking about it. "Stuff you can't take back, not that she ever offered to. She was young, she was sick. I understand that, and I've let it all go."

"Debra, the court would have granted you a change in placement. You refused to consider it, if you will recall, and that even trumped Linda's wish to get out of the house."

"She belonged with her mother and her sister, not with you and another woman," Debra said uncompromisingly. "Why would you even bring this up now, Stefan?"

"I thought you brought it up." Stefan elected to leave it at that.

"I suppose I did," Debra said. "Let's not get sidetracked. I was saying, I blamed you for years. I prayed to Jesus our Lord, every day, every day. It was wrong of me not to forgive you, I knew it at the time, but I couldn't help myself. Well, nothing changed overnight, but I believe Jesus did enter my heart. In just the last few months, I have come to understand it wasn't you I should be blaming. You were led into temptation. By the change in the law. We are weak, we human beings, aren't we? The law allowed you to do something very wrong, and you weren't strong enough to resist it. If you are to blame for anything, it's human weakness. I'm weak, too."

"So you blame the law? What do you mean? The legislature?"

"Yes. They make our laws, don't they?"

"You can't stop progress, Debra. It's no use blaming the legislature."

"It's not progress, first, and second, I can, too, blame the legislature, and I most definitely do. I voted for them, you voted for them, the entire state voted for them, we put our trust in them, to serve our interests, and look what they do."

"Well thank you for not blaming me anymore," Stefan said.

"Stefan, don't you see, this is what Madeleine Ullstater was getting at. The importance to children of a rock-solid, unbreakable bond between parents. Divorce once required grounds, this was vitally important, before progress, as you put it, came along. We have to go back. We were wiser, before. We were more grown-up, as a society. I do believe this."

"I can see that you do," Stefan said. He wondered what role Howard May might have played in all this. (It was none.)

"I know I have had a tendency to talk too much about faith," Debra said. Stefan rolled his eyes. "You should hear the discussions Howard and I have. He's been almost overcome by a crisis of faith many times, standing right there at the altar, during Communion, or when he was in the pulpit. 'Why doesn't Jesus return, why doesn't Jesus return?'" He's told me he'd grab his wrist and squeeze until the crisis passed. At first, I found this strange, a man of the cloth, so dedicated to the faith, crumbling in God's House. But it is understandable, isn't it? That it would happen there?"

"I suppose," Stefan said. The conversation had about run its course, he felt. As if on cue, Howard turned up.

"You seem to be in a rather intense discussion," he observed, placing his hand on Debra's shoulder. Howard stood perfectly erect. His voice was deep, he had a low forehead and uneven teeth. If an aging Presbyterian clergyman's countenance should be patrician, he didn't fit the bill. "Am I intruding?"

"No, no," Stefan and Debra said simultaneously. Debra got up and looped her arm in his, affectionately.

"We were just comparing notes on the church," she said, giving Howard a gentle kiss on the cheek. "I shared with Stefan the difficulty you've told me about, that you had in the middle of a service, occasionally, when doubt came over you." Howard laughed.

"Those were tough moments all right," he said. "I got so I could tell when they were coming. About ten seconds' warning. Not much help."

"What did help?" Stefan asked idly.

"A belief," Howard said after a pause, "in life itself. Our lives are miracles, aren't they? If the birth of a baby isn't a miracle, what is?" Howard paused again. He took a seat. Debra sat down, too. The preacher in him was emerging; it was never far below the surface. "We're given three score and ten. Maybe death is extinction, I don't believe that, but let's say it is. Where does that leave us?" Howard fell silent. Stefan realized he was expected to reply.

"Have no idea where it leaves us," he said. "You tell me."

"Let me tell you a little story. Years ago, I was at a meeting one day. In Los Angeles. I don't remember what it was, exactly. It's been a good while. But I do remember a program given by a doctor. A surgeon. He had a slide show. Must have been about two dozen slides. Pictures of boys and girls, all school-aged. Eight, nine, ten years old. Each child suffered from the same condition, cleft palate. I'm sure you've seen pictures of persons with this condition. It's a grotesque disfigurement. The doctor had a before-and-after picture of each child. The first slide showed the child before surgery, and the second, after. The difference was staggering. It would not be possible to overstate how improved these children's lives were. This was in Lima, Peru. I think the doctor, who was an American, had gone down there on some sort of stipend." Howard stopped there, although he obviously wasn't finished. The preacher had emerged, and along with it, his sense of drama and timing. Stefan, bemused, waited patiently.

"When I've had these crises of faith," he resumed, "in church or else-where, I remember this doctor, and what he achieved. The combination of circumstances that took him from America to faraway Peru, where another combination of circumstances had brought these parents with their terribly deformed children to meet this doctor and allow him to operate. I expect you understand what I'm getting at. This doctor made a choice, didn't he? He was going to accomplish something strongly affirmative with his life. He learned a skill. He employed it to maximum advantage. A lot of people believe nothing much matters in life. Try telling those Peruvian children that. They wouldn't accept it in a thousand years."

"So it is this doctor you remembered, when these doubts came over you?" Stefan said.

"Yes," Howard said. "That doctor can meet our Lord on even terms. Some might call this irreverent, but it's what I believe. He isn't responsible for the horror of the world, but he didn't flinch before it, did he, no, he responded magnificently."

"Well," Stefan said good-humoredly, resisting an impulse to ask the former pastor who is responsible for the world's horror, "I haven't sat in a church in some time, not counting today, so looks like the church came to me." Howard May laughed.

"Like looking for something you just can't find," he said. "It finds you." Howard rose. Everyone did. Debra looped her arm through Howard's again.

'You'll like my next sermon, too," Howard joked.

"How do you know I liked this one?" Stefan said.

At his office Monday, Stefan had a mid-morning meeting scheduled with Fred Shaw to discuss a settlement offer. Otherwise, his day was clear. Around four, he asked his secretary to bring him the Gordon-Jessup file. It was a thick one, but he knew what he was looking for, and he found it readily. It was the letter Roderick Jessup had sent him, from the disgruntled wife of a former employee of the insurance firm. Roderick had been worried she was going to send it to her state senator and representative. Nothing had come of that, assuming she had made good on her threat.

Stefan re-read the letter. Charlotte Huxtable, that was the woman's name. All about her husband, about his job loss and its consequences for their family, about her contempt for the firm where he had worked so loyally, only to be booted out, causelessly, one day, about how she had harbored these feelings for years, yet gradually come around to understanding the real culprit was the law, about how men are weak. Gracious! Mrs. Huxtable's words and Debra's were nearly identical! Only the context differed. Debra had said practically the same thing. It was as though they were reading the same script! It was a striking coincidence.

Stefan put the letter down. He was spooked. He was shaky. He found himself taking several deep breaths. His heart was palpitating. He felt he might faint. He needed to grasp something. He held his hands tightly together. Calm returned, gradually, but he remained at his desk, immobilized.

Chapter 25

I T HAS BEEN SAID THERE IS NO ZEALOT LIKE A CONVERT. IF THIS WERE true, Stefan Kopinski would promptly have given all his worldly goods to charity, donned a sackcloth, and embarked upon a life of mendicancy. This would never be Stefan's way. Moreover, he wasn't a convert, which was not, however, to say he couldn't become one.

Stefan's friend, Alan, was past his second year in his bed at St. Louis State Hospital. He was wasting away. His self-hatred filled his conscious hours. He was waiting to die.

Alan and Jeanne's daughter, Mary, was in St. Louis for one of her periodic visits. They were becoming less frequent. Mary, too, was helpless in the face of her father's determination to persecute himself. She lived in Columbia, where she had gone to school. She was married. She was 29 years old.

Her visit with her father this Saturday had been like them all. Mary began glancing at the clock. It was time for her father's physical therapy. An attendant came into the room, with a wheelchair. Mary gave her father a hug and said she'd be back tomorrow, on her way back to Columbia. Alan was wheeled out of the room. Mary gathered her things. The phone rang, and she answered. It was Stefan Kopinski, in California. Who?

"Stefan Kopinski, in California. Your dad's old friend." He was coming to St. Louis. "Third time's the charm," he said. He was going to get her father out of that hospital bed, since it was literally a matter of life or death and nobody else could do it. Mary hadn't the faintest clue what to say.

"I'll tell dad you called," she said.

"Thank you, Mary," Stefan said. "Please let your mother know, as well."

"Yes, I will," Mary said.

"Just say Stefan Kopinski, in Pasadena. They know me."

"Got it," Mary said.

"Actually," Stefan said, "I'll try again to reach your dad, but do tell him I called, in the meantime." Mary said she would. Mary had heard Stefan's name countless times from her father. It was always high praise. She had never met him. She had never spoken with him, until this phone call. She knew what he looked like, except that the photograph was more than thirty years old. She knew nothing of the current state of his bond with her father, nor, for that matter, of the former state, or the one before that. It was just as well she didn't inquire. Stefan could not have given her an informed answer. He did not even remember exactly how Alan had come to be in St. Louis in the first place. Who moved to St. Louis, Missouri?

Mary could have answered that question, had Stefan asked. A lass moved to St. Louis, Missouri. A spunky lass. A spunky lass from Quebec. A spunky lass from Quebec with an infant daughter to care for, and a husband in prison. Moved to St. Louis, Missouri.

Stefan and his partners met in the board room at the firm Wednesday afternoon. Miguel Ordoñez, Art Feinberg, and Fred Shaw. All three knew something was coming. They didn't know what.

"Gentlemen," Stefan began, "I am leaving Fulton & Shaw. It's been a good run, but it's time. I have been given two, new goals in life, and I'm going to give my remaining years to them. You've heard me speak of an old friend I have, who lives in St. Louis. His name is Alan Young. We went to college together, up in Santa Barbara, but haven't had a lot of contact since. Long story short, Alan is sick and he needs help desperately. As matter of fact, he's lying in a hospital bed as I speak. St. Louis State Hospital. Yep, it's what it sounds like, the state asylum. Alan's allowed a ridiculous matter to destroy him. He figured out something, you see, when he was 20, that I'm still working on. How to stop the Vietnam War. Ironically, he's renounced his great insight, and I've embraced it. We've switched places, you might say. So when I saw him in St. Louis before, he happened to mention at-will divorce. That's what he called it. I corrected him. We must have been talking about family and employment law, I don't really remember, and he confused the two. I got to thinking, though, kind of intriguing, maybe they are related. Art, I know I shared this with you one day. Well, to get to my point, I think they are definitely related. So, I'm going back to St. Louis because I owe Alan, he's my promise, and I'm going to get him out of that bed. I know how to do this and I will do it. Funny how things come full circle, isn't it? My dear wife made a similar intervention, she's my model.

"Then, I'm coming back to Pasadena and getting started on goal number two. I'm going to sit down with Joel Whittington. Going to tell him I'll write the legislation he's going to introduce on the Senate floor. We're restoring cause for divorce and establishing it in the employment at-will context. He isn't going to do this, hardly needs saying, so I'm going to run against him. Hate to do that, I like Joel. I'll win, too. I'm going to draw huge crowds when I campaign. This is an idea whose time has come. I'm going to get a ton of votes. I hope I can count on you fellows to help, when the time comes. I'm certainly going to miss you, and as I said, it's been a good run, a very good one. I'll never forget my years here." Stefan paused momentarily. "I would imagine you're going to want to send out a short note about my departure. 'Dear friends, we regret to announce our long-time colleague, Stefan Kopinski, is leaving the firm to pursue other goals. We wish him well.' That oughta do it." This met with the silence of the tomb.

"Or," Miguel Ordoñez finally said, "we could just say you're insane."

"C'mon, Miguel," Art said. "That was uncalled for."

"You took me wrong," Miguel said. "Everything Stefan just said is crazy, okay?"

"No, Miguel," Stefan said, "you're mistaken. I'll tell you what's crazy. The law, that's what's crazy. Letting a man walk away from his marriage. Or a guy ruin another guy's life because he happens to sit behind a bigger desk. Now you're talking crazy." Stefan was a little worked up. "Did you know," he continued, "one state, Montana, has enacted a statute establishing good cause in the employment context? Yep. Had it for years, and somehow Montana has survived. If Montana can do it, so can California."

"Have you talked this over with your wife, Stefan?" Fred asked calmly.

"Haven't spoken with her yet," Stefan said. "Thought you fellows should come first."

"Very considerate," Fred said. "We're the guinea pigs."

"Sharon will understand," Stefan said. "Heck, she can go with me to St. Louis, if she wants." Sharon wasn't about to do this, as Stefan knew perfectly well, but he didn't really feel bad about leaving her. She had run off to Portland. He could run off to St. Louis.

"I don't pretend to understand half of what you've said, Stefan," Fred said after an extended silence. "I'm sure that goes for Miguel and Art, too, but it's apparent this is something you've got to do. Frankly, I don't see very much point in talking about it further. We've heard what you had to say, you're going to act upon it, well and good. We'll take care of the letter to clients, and work out the amount of your pay-out. You get on that plane and on over to St. Louis, and keep your promise to your friend. Do what you must do. Help your friend. We'll still be here when you get back. Won't we, Miguel?" Miguel nodded, uncertainly. "Won't we, Art?" Art nodded, more uncertainly. Fred was the senior partner, and his take-charge manner now made clear to all he would not allow this to turn into a lengthy, possibly contentious, ultimately futile discussion.

"I didn't promise Alan, Fred," Stefan said. "He is my promise."

"I don't know what that means, Stefan."

"Well, it's taken me close to a lifetime to figure it out, might take that long to explain it."

"Then don't," Fred said, not unkindly.

"I hope I didn't speak out of line, there," Miguel said contritely to Stefan.

"Of course not, Miguel," Stefan said.

"How did your friend stop the Vietnam War?" Art asked. He got a frown from Fred.

"He went to jail. He went to Canada, but that was a mistake. So he came back and went to jail."

"Glad I asked," Art mumbled.

"Art, you mustn't be dismissive," Stefan said. There was no remonstrance in his voice. "I realize you know nothing about Alan. He was drafted after college. Let's see, this would have been … 1968. I still had one more year at UCSB. Alan went to Canada. Some guys did this, remember? It wasn't the right decision. I really don't know what he did there, not much of anything, except he got married. Alan can't bear to talk about his time in Canada, and it's hardly real to me, but he did it. He finally figured out he'd made a mistake. I think he was in Canada only about a year, maybe a little longer. He figured out the right way to protest the war was to submit to the law. So he did. He goes to Leavenworth. I think he's there about three years. He returns to California when he gets out, no, that can't be right. Jeanne's in St. Louis by then. Jeanne's his wife. Look, I'm not certain of dates, but the point is, Alan ended up doing the right thing. He figured it out. When he was 20. He thought about it, punished himself over it God knows how often, but he figured it out. This is a great thing. Sadly, he doesn't believe in himself any longer, but you know something, I believe in him. That's it, in a nutshell."

"Well thank you for that explanation, Stefan," Art said.

"Yes, thank you," Fred said indifferently. The men looked at each other. What remained to be said? Nothing. They all rose from around the table and shook hands with Stefan. He was wished good luck once, twice, three times. The foursome had together guided the firm's fortunes for many years, with conspicuous success. Now, they were breaking up. It was inevitable, yet sad, too, and vexing, because Stefan's decision was incomprehensible.

Stefan reached the door, and turned.

"Gentlemen, you should envy me. I can only fail by not trying." He was out the door.

"I hope he finds what he's looking for," Fred said with a long sigh.

"I think he's having a nervous breakdown," Miguel said.

"I don't think so," Art said. "I think he's got religion. Going to fix what's wrong with the world."

"How is that different from a nervous breakdown?" Miguel asked.

"I don't know what a nervous breakdown is, Miguel," Art said.

"Actually, you raise a good point, Art," Fred said. "If he comes back to Pasadena to fix the world and runs for the legislature with that rant, we may have to distance ourselves from him. Stefan knows his way around Sacramento." Indeed, Stefan was the firm's representative on the Trial Lawyers' Association of Southern California, a lobby. He was on a first-name basis with many members of both House and Senate.

"Let's hope we don't have to cross that bridge," Art said. He was genuinely upset. Stefan wasn't just a colleague, he was a friend. They discussed everything. "I wouldn't underestimate him," Art added.

"Agree completely," Fred said. "I'll have Cora draft a clients' letter. It won't be yours, Miguel."

"Should never have opened my big mouth," Miguel said.

If there had ever been hesitation in Stefan Kopinski's step, and there hadn't, there was none now. Up the steps of the St. Louis State Hospital he went, suitcase gripped firmly in his left hand, and through the familiar, front door. Would Norma be at her post? Stefan thought this might be an advantage, since she knew him and had no reason to distrust him. Norma wasn't there.

"Stefan Kopinski to see Alan Young," he announced to one of the two receptionists. "He's expecting me. I've been here many times before. We're old friends."

"Sign here, sir," one of the women said, indicating the place on a log the hospital kept. Signing in and out was mandatory. Stefan signed the register, deliberately leaving space for a second name. "Mr. Young is in … in Room 105. It's down the corridor and …"

"Thank you," Stefan interrupted. "I know where he is. As I said, I've been here before."

"Yes sir," the woman said. She was a comely black woman, in her early thirties. Her hair was elaborately braided, and she wore bright pink earrings in the shape of large hoops. She did not have a name tag, which was unusual.

Stefan headed for Alan's room. The hospital was busy, as he had anticipated. It was visiting hours. He entered Alan's room, ready for anything. It was empty. Both beds were unmade, which meant Alan had a roommate. Could this be a problem? Everything could be a problem. It didn't matter. Stefan put down the suitcase and took a seat. Within a few minutes, an elderly gentleman was wheeled into the room by an orderly. Stefan recognized the orderly. They exchanged "hellos." The old man had a considerable beard. It was completely white, as was the hair on his scalp. His facial skin was sagging wherever it could, and it had a definite pallor. He was wheeled around to the far side of his bed, where the orderly helped him into it.

"You waiting on Mr. Young?" the orderly asked Stefan, knowing he was.

"I am," Stefan replied. "Shouldn't he be here?"

"Should be, but I think he might still be in E&W. Want me to check for you?"

"No, thanks, that's not necessary," Stefan said, wondering what E&W was. "I'm sure he'll be here shortly. No problem waiting." The orderly left. Stefan looked over at the old man, who had closed his eyes.

It was another twenty minutes before Alan appeared. He, too, was wheeled in. It was a different orderly, an ungainly woman in her middle years.

"Hi Alan!" Stefan said. Alan looked at him. For an awful moment, there was no recognition. Stefan was expecting the exuberance he had been repeatedly told Alan reserved for him.

"Stef!" Alan said. "Where'd you come from? Golly!" Alan wasn't exuberant, but it was better than nothing.

"I'm in town again, obviously. This is my first destination."

"Well that's great," Alan said. This, too, was well short of exuberance. Stefan, who felt he was prepared for anything, was unprepared for Alan's nonchalance. It was plain something had gone out of Alan since his last visit. Something was missing ... some ... vitality. Alan struck Stefan as altogether too placid, as if in a drugged state. Which he was. Stefan recovered quickly from his dismay, and his resolve was reinforced. He was right. Alan was slowly dying in this place. All the more reason to do what he had come to do. Right now!

Alan climbed into bed, unassisted. He had lost weight. The unbecoming mustache was gone. The orderly left. The old man in the other bed was dozing. It was the bewitching hour.

"Alan!" Stefan said sharply. He rose and placed the suitcase in the chair he had occupied. He snapped it open. "Get out of bed. Get out of bed, Alan. I'm not fooling around." Stefan gave Alan a look of frightening determination.

"Why?"

"Because I said to." Stefan grabbed Alan's arm and tugged. "I'm pulling you out of that damn bed if you don't get up." Alan got to his feet, uncooperatively. Stefan withdrew a dressy, long-sleeved, white shirt from the suitcase. "Get out of those pajamas, Alan. Put on this shirt."

"What are you talking about, Stef?" Stefan reached back into the suitcase and withdrew a pair of trousers.

"Put these on, too. Pull them up over your pajama pants. I didn't bring underwear."

"Stef?" Alan got no further. Stefan began unbuttoning Alan's pajamas. "Stop that, Stef," Alan said. "I can take off my own pajamas."

"Then do it," Stefan said with command. "Do it, Alan."

"Are we going somewhere?" Alan said. He was out of his pajama top. Stefan thrust the shirt at him.

"Hurry up, Alan." Alan buttoned the shirt clumsily. Stefan handed him the trousers. The waist was much too big. Stefan had not counted on Alan's having lost so much weight. There was no belt. Alan would have to hold onto the trousers, or they would fall off. Back to the suitcase for the shoes. They were too big, too, but Alan would manage. Stefan grabbed the suitcase and put it on Alan's bed.

"Now listen to me, Alan," Stefan said, staring him in the eye. "For the next ninety seconds, you're Dr. Persakamum, understand?"

"Who?"

"Dr. Persakamum."

"How do you spell that?"

"Never mind how you spell it. We are walking down the hall into the lobby. We stop for no one. At the desk, I'll sign us out. You keep going straight for the door and through it and down the front steps and wait for me there. Do you understand? Just keep going, no matter what." Stefan grasped Alan's upper arm, and they went into the corridor. Stefan was moving as quickly as possible, in view of Alan's need to hold up his pants. The corridor seemed incredibly long, to Stefan, but fortune was with them; they didn't meet a soul. Into the lobby they went. It was busy. Stefan released his grasp and shoved Alan toward the door. He then swung around and pushed past two people to reach the front desk. He signed out, smiling ingratiatingly at the receptionist, who was too occupied even to acknowledge him. Perfect! Stefan was out the door. Lord, that had gone too well! Alan, who would not have had time to disappear had the thought occurred to him, was waiting dutifully at the foot of the steps, pants held up in his right hand.

"Where are we going, Stef?" Alan said, struggling to understand. Was he really outside?

"No time for talk." Stefan had Alan's arm again. He had found a parking space in the front row of the lot, so the distance wasn't great. In no time, he had Alan inside the car. He scurried around to the other side and jumped in. "We did it!" he said to his friend. "You're out of there. Glory be." Stefan started the car, and away they went. "Say goodbye to that place, Alan," he said. "You're never coming back. You should never have been inside there in the first place."

"Where are we going, Stef? What about Jeanne?" Alan was dumbfounded.

"I've got a place. We'll call Jeanne when we get there." Alan said nothing more for a minute. Then, he spoke up again.

"I think you just committed a crime, Stef." Alan stared at him. Stefan stared back.

"Probably," he said. "Hell with it."

"Jeanne? What about Jeanne, Stef? She'll be out of her mind with worry."

"We'll call her in a minute, Alan. I just told you. Listen, I left some paperwork in that suitcase. It explains everything. You're in good hands. Old Stefan's thought of everything."

"What does the paperwork say?"

"It's a waiver. Hospital is cleared of any liability. It's all on me." Stefan half-laughed. The hospital was unconditionally released, and if something happened to Alan, Jeanne could come after him.

"I think you've kidnapped me, Stef."

"Sounds about right." Stefan stopped at a red light and turned to look at Alan. "Quit worrying, Alan. It's all you have done for two years. All your life, actually. No more worrying. I forbid it." The light turned green. "Purpose, contentment. The rest of the way, old friend."

"I can't imagine what you're talking about, Stef." It was time for his pills. Skipping them was hazardous.

"Alan, think of this as an adventure. My wife, second wife, her name's Sharon, probably saved my older daughter's life. Linda's her name. Her mother is Debra, first wife. Long story short, Linda had become an alcoholic when she was still in her teens. She was a wreck. Rehab wasn't working. Sharon, one day, decides she's going to act. Cut through the excuses, cut through the inertia. Act. Know what? She didn't even consult me first. She consulted with Debra, and they weren't great buddies, obviously. She finds this detox place in Portland, Oregon. It's another residential facility. Linda's been in these places. Sharon announces one day, Linda is going to this place in Portland. And she takes her! She gets her on a plane, and they fly to Portland. It's a done deal before I can raise an objection. And it works! Against all odds, Linda gets better. Alan, she's a married lady now, got a good husband, she goes to her AA meetings, faithfully I think, she has two moms who love her. Only one dad. Sharon did it. She pulled it off. I don't even know how she thought it up, but she succeeded. Well, I'm sure you've followed my drift. I've gotten you out of that hospital, and Jeanne and I are going to see you to complete recovery, Alan."

"So Jeanne's in on this?" Alan said disbelievingly. The enduring friction between his wife and his oldest friend was not lost on Alan.

"Hmmm ..." Stefan said, grinning at Alan. "I haven't told her yet."

"You must be completely out of your mind, Stef."

"I hope so," Stefan said merrily. "Sanity never was much use."

"Jeanne's going to be frantic. We've got to call her immediately."

"I agree. We'll call her as soon as we reach my place."

"What about my pills, Stef? Do you have them?"

"No more pills, Alan. Done with that, too."

"I can't just stop taking them," Alan exclaimed.

"Oh, I know that, Alan. Don't take me so literally. We will absolutely get them tomorrow."

"How, if I'm not going back to the hospital?"

"Leave it to me." Stefan turned into the parking lot at a modern condominium.

"This is Clayton, Stef. I disapprove of Clayton."

"Why?"

"It's the county. I don't like St. Louis County."

"Too bad."

Stefan parked, and they went inside. The condominium was well-appointed, though not truly luxurious. He was on the ground floor. Parlor, dining room, kitchen, den, two baths, two bedrooms. Patio in back. Decent yard.

"I'm calling Jeanne, Stef."

"Please do." Alan dialed, not certain he'd find Jeanne at home. He did.

"Hello," she said.

"Jeanne, it's me, Alan."

"Alan! What's happened? Are you all right? Darling, what's happened?"

"I'm okay, I'm fine, sweetheart. I'm fine."

"Why are you calling? Tell me what's happened."

"Actually, I'm with Stef. He told me he told you he was coming to St. Louis. He's here."

"So he's there with you?"

"No, I'm with him. We're at his condo in Clayton."

"What? You're where? What condo? You're not at the hospital?"

"No, I'm not at the hospital. Stef is standing right here next to me. Stef, say hello." Alan handed Stefan the phone.

"Hi, Jeanne," he said. The merriment was still in his voice. "Alan and I are right here, awaiting your arrival. Then we'll pop open the champagne. Life's good."

"Champagne? Where are you? This is crazy." Disbelief was rapidly becoming anger. Stefan was unfazed.

"Jeanne, calm down and hear me out. Please. Everything is all right. I promise."

"I'm listening," she said.

"Get a pen. I'm going to give you my address. Can you come on over, or do you have to be at work?" Stefan figured she would be at work, if she had to be. He was right. She was working the early shift; her workday was over.

"Do I have a pen? Stefan, I want an explanation. How did they let Alan leave the hospital without consulting with me, first? What's going on here?"

"We just walked out," Stefan said. "Sort of."

"What! You walked out? Without telling anyone?" Jeanne was screaming. "They don't know you left? This is totally crazy."

"Jeanne, I left a note. They know Alan is with me." Stefan said. "Got that pen?"

Jeanne was out the door in minutes. She missed the phone call that came minutes later. It was the St. Louis State Hospital.

Stefan figured he had about half an hour before Jeanne showed up. With or without the police.

"How'd you find this place, Stef?" Alan asked. "You find it in L.A., or have you been in town a while and not told anybody?"

"From L.A., Alan. It wasn't a problem." The old friends looked at each other. "Jeanne will be here soon, Alan, and I have a little something special planned, but in the meantime, can I get you anything?" Alan nodded "No."

"Actually, I could go for a great big steak," Alan said. Stefan laughed. "After two years of that hospital chow, anything will taste good." Stefan laughed again. "It wasn't that bad, really," Alan added.

"Two years. Defies belief you were in there that long, Alan."

"Saved my life," Alan said. Had it? Stefan wondered. He could see with his own eyes, and hear with his own ears, how Alan had slipped. "Can't believe I made you laugh, Stef. I haven't made anybody laugh in a long time, let me tell you. I can make people cry, though. I couldn't count how many times I've made Jeanne cry."

"No more talk like that, Alan. I really mean it. Your illness is over and done."

"I've made Mary cry a few times, too," Alan said. This brought a disapproving look from Stefan, but he refrained from another admonition. "Mary's the sweetest daughter," Alan continued. "I love her dearly. Why don't you tell me about your girls, Stef. Two, right?"

"Right. Older one got married not long ago. Husband works for the City of Pasadena. I think they're very happy."

"What's his name?"

"Troy."

"I'm glad they're happy. Are you expecting a bunch of kids, gramps?"

"I'll say." Stefan meant it. He figured he'd been a flop as a dad, maybe he'd get a chance to redeem himself as a grandfather.

"What about your other daughter?"

"She's still single. Lisa's a chemist. Got a good job with the University of California at Davis. She's a highly motivated young woman, and she loves her work. Hard to argue with that."

"Not even a boyfriend?"

"She dates, I think. Not serious about anyone, to the best of my knowledge."

"Science was never my strong suit," Alan said. "I remember chemistry lab in high school. I never knew what I was doing."

"Ditto."

"Mary lives over in Columbia. Married, two kids. She comes to see me. Doesn't bring the children. They're too young."

"I spoke with her on the phone not that long ago."

"I don't believe she comes as often as she used to, though. Responsibilities of a wife and mother, I suppose, or maybe she's just given up on her old man."

"Don't say that, Alan!" Stefan warned. "I won't listen to it. You have put yourself down for the last time. You have plenty of good years before you, and that's what they're going to be. Or do you prefer for me to berate you constantly? Because I will, Alan." Alan managed a brave smile.

"Now listen," Stefan resumed. "When Jeanne gets here, you answer the door." More orders!

"She must be worried out of her mind. I hope she's driving safely."

"I hope she's not bringing the police," Stefan said. He laughed at himself. She might do this, yes, but he was betting she would not. He'd deal with it, regardless. Stefan was coolly confident.

His hunch was right. The police were not with Jeanne. They were at the St. Louis State Hospital. Four squad cars. It was an exciting time at the old hospital.

Jeanne drove up with a screech and began honking the horn repeatedly. She was making a huge racket. She jumped from her car, and Stefan, peering through the window, saw it was she, and she was alone.

"Here she is, Alan. You get the door." Stefan stepped aside.

"Alan!" she screamed as he opened the door. She embraced him fiercely. She cupped his cheeks in her hands. She was crying. "Are you all right, darling? Oh my goodness, I was so afraid." Again she pulled him tightly to her.

"I'm all right, you can see I am," Alan said. He had released his trousers for their hug, and now had to catch them as they slipped from his waist. In spite of herself, Jeanne giggled at this.

"Where did you get those pants?" she exclaimed. "Where ... how ..."

"Stef got them for me. Why don't you say hello?" Stefan had remained unobtrusively behind them. Jeanne turned to confront him.

"You maniac," she screamed. "Are you completely out of your mind? How could you do this? You must be insane."

"Getting tiresome how many people are saying that to me," Stefan observed.

"Listen, I started to call the cops. You've committed a crime, Stefan. You could be arrested."

"Go ahead, if that's your wish." Stefan calmly pointed at the telephone. "There's the phone."

"How did you get out of the hospital? How did you do this? Didn't anybody stop you?" Jeanne's harangue was not letting up. Alan stepped in.

"We just walked right out," he said. "Nobody stopped us. I don't think anybody noticed, did they, Stef?"

"I can't imagine how you could do that," Jeanne said. She could see Alan was all right, and she began calming down. Stefan took charge.

"Jeanne," he said, "I want to ask you and Alan to take a seat, please. There are a few things I have to say." Stefan indicated the sofa. Jeanne and Alan sat down. "First things first, however. I arranged for some refreshments." Stefan disappeared into the kitchen. When he returned, he was carrying a large, white box. It looked like what it was, a box you'd get at a bakery. He placed it on the coffee table and opened it. It contained three dozen extravagant pastries. Jeanne's and Alan's jaws dropped. "Help yourselves," Stefan said. He returned to the kitchen for plates and napkins, and three champagne glasses. Once more into the kitchen, where he popped a cork, and returned to the living room. "Who's for champagne?" He didn't wait for answers, just began filling the glasses. "There's lots more where this came from," he said with a grin. He handed Jeanne a glass, then Alan.

"You aren't supposed to have alcohol," Jeanne said to her husband.

"Here's to the two of you," Stefan said, raising his glass by way of a toast. "Alan, you're the best friend I ever had, and Jeanne, you're the best wife any man ever had." The toast didn't come off, as the other two were too astonished to take part.

"You have truly lost your mind, Stefan," Jeanne said. She said this quietly, without censure. Alan raised his glass to his lips. "Darling, no!" Jeanne said. "No alcohol."

"One swallow in two years?" Alan protested.

"No! What about your meds? You know you can't drink liquor with them." Jeanne was becoming frantic again. "Your pills, did you bring them? What about them? You can't miss one, Alan."

"Not bad, not bad at all," Alan responded, upon taking a generous swallow of champagne.

"Dig in," Stefan said, indicating the pastries. "I didn't buy those for us to look at them." Stefan wasn't a big dessert eater, but he took a cream puff and bit liberally into it, leaving pastry around his mouth. He looked up at the other two; neither could prevent a smile. "Oops," Stefan said, wiping his mouth. "Can't eat one of these things daintily." He promptly took another bite. Alan and Jeanne followed suit. Jeanne made no further comment on Alan's drinking champagne. The glass wasn't large.

"May I have your undivided attention, please?" Stefan said. Jeanne sat back on the sofa, and crossed her legs. Alan survived another generous swallow of champagne. "The two of you are, in my humble opinion, in the throes of terror. You're paralyzed with fright. This has been going on for two years, or is it more? Neither of you has any perspective on the situation. And do you know what you're afraid of? Living. You are both scared to live.

"Now that probably sounds pretty dramatic. I don't intend that. I save that for the courtroom. I am simply stating what I believe to be true. Jeanne, you're afraid for Alan every waking hour, and Alan, well ... I am not a trained therapist, obviously, so I am not going to attempt a diagnosis, other than to say, you have clearly decided you'd rather lie in that hospital bed than be out of it. Trouble is, you're dying, if you will forgive my bluntness, in that bed. You don't need to be a doctor to figure that out." Jeanne took

Alan's hand and squeezed it, but said nothing. She'd hear Stefan out. She knew he was right her husband was dying.

"Now you would be mistaken if you think I'm going to devote much more time to what has transpired. The very opposite. I have already told Alan, Jeanne, so I'll tell you, we are not looking back. Do you understand? Not looking back, not once. I mean it." Stefan was speaking in the strongest possible terms. "Looking back is poisonous. We're looking forward. There is so much ahead.

"I have left a General Release and Waiver at the hospital. It's in a suitcase I had, Jeanne, in which I had the clothes Alan's wearing. It's a boilerplate. I don't suppose I spent twenty minutes on it. The hospital's counsel will find it satisfactory, I'm sure. Indeed, they're in a cold panic right now to get it signed. It releases the hospital and everybody in any way affiliated with it unconditionally for any adverse consequences stemming from my having spirited Alan out of that place. Of course, Jeanne, it doesn't absolve me, so if Alan jumps into the river, which he won't, you can sue me and take every dime I have." Jeanne stared at Stefan, who poured another round of champagne for everyone, without objection. Time for another pastry, too.

"Tomorrow," Stefan continued, "we'll call the hospital. I've given them a time, so they'll be ready. They'll have their lawyers and the CEO. Who knows, maybe they'll include the governor." Stefan grinned. "We're going to talk it through. I'll take the lead, but Jeanne, you may be called upon to say something. Don't worry, it's going to go just fine.

"I left two copies of the waiver. They sign both, send both to us, Jeanne, you sign both, send one back. How easy is that?"

"What if they refuse, Stef? What if they come for us? Could they force me to go back to the hospital? Couldn't you be arrested?"

"There you go worrying about everything, Alan. I forbid it! No, they can't take you back to the hospital against your will. As for me, I'll take my chances. Believe me, what that hospital wants is for all this to go away as quickly as possible."

"This is so crazy, Stefan," Jeanne said. "I can't believe you've done this. When did you get the idea? How long have you been planning it? When did you come back to St. Louis?"

"That's a lot of questions, Jeanne," Stefan said cheerfully. "Which one shall I answer first?"

"Boy, they must be running their tails off over there," Alan said, "trying to figure out how I escaped."

"After the call tomorrow, Jeanne," Stefan said, "we'll go to your place and get Alan back into his own clothes. Alan, you and I have an appointment at two tomorrow afternoon. About which more in a minute.

"Now, this condo has a separate bedroom and bath. It's for the two of you, anytime you want it. Frankly, I am so determined Alan will sever his ties with the past, I'd prefer you move out of that apartment. But it's your home, I understand that. It's up to you. There's a place for you here, if you want it." Alan and Jeanne couldn't believe their ears. It was all so fantastic. The champagne was starting to brighten things up, as well.

"Now, about your medications, Alan. We'll make suitable arrangements when we talk with the hospital tomorrow. Your doctor can phone them in to the pharmacy you use. Holdermann, that's his name, right? It's even all right with me if you keep seeing him, provided it's not at the hospital. You are never returning to that place for any reason, Alan. Over my dead body.

"Finally, about that appointment tomorrow." Here Stefan faltered slightly, in spite of himself. He had saved this for last. Saved it until everyone had had some champagne. It was here he felt he might meet angry resistance, which even his iron resolve might not overcome. "At two, Alan, you and I are meeting with Otto Zollmeyer. Captain Otto Zollmeyer, I should say. He runs the VA Hospital. He's arranged for you to do some volunteer work there. You start immediately." Stefan hesitated. "This is going to be good, you must both believe me. Really good." Stefan gave both a stare and then went quickly into the kitchen. Pop! Stefan returned to the living room and poured champagne.

"Would each of you kindly sink your teeth into one of those custard tarts?" Stefan said. Alan reached for one. Stefan sat back down uneasily. Jeanne's silence was a concern. He looked her again straight in the eye. "The two of us," he addressed her, "are working in concert, every step of the way, aren't we, Jeanne, to restore your husband to solid health. Aren't we, Jeanne?"

"So are you staying in St. Louis, Stef?" Alan said. "For how long?"

"Long as it takes." Stefan kept his gaze on Jeanne. "We're going to be at Alan's side, one if not both of us, all the time. Day and night, until Alan is well again. This won't work if you and I aren't a team, Jeanne. So if you're not on board, now's the time to get on board." Stefan halted there. He had said enough.

"What about your job back in California, Stefan?" she inquired. "What about your wife?" Jeanne was not argumentative in the least. The staggering improbability of what Stefan had done, combined with an evolving appreciation for it, and the realization Alan was home, left her beyond astonishment.

"Sharon's fine with this, in fact, she approves. As for my practice, I quit. Going to do something else, when I get back to California."

"You quit your job, Stef?" Alan exclaimed.

"Yep. Didn't just walk out, of course. Had a nice chat with my partners." Stefan didn't like how that sounded. "They're great guys, I don't mean to suggest anything to the contrary, we worked together a long time, and I think the world of all of them. But it was time."

"Time?" Alan said. "For what?"

"Oh, let's not get into that right now." Stefan poured more champagne. Jeanne giggled.

"Much more of that and no way I can drive home."

"Excellent," said Stefan. "Your private quarters await you." Jeanne again took her husband's hand.

"You really are out of that place," she said quietly, almost reverently. She gazed lovingly at him and gave him a tender kiss. "I'd given up all hope." Only now did Jeanne realize how completely she had. She was mellow in a way Stefan had never witnessed. A third cork was popped. The laughter and nonsense increased commensurately. Stefan had never seen Jeanne laugh that way. He decided he'd never heard her laugh at all. Finally, he rose to his feet, a trifle unsteadily. This was funny, too! When had he had too much to drink? Back in college?

"Let's wrap this up," he said. He reached into his pocket, withdrew a key and handed it to Jeanne. "You'll need this, and, um, take some more goodies and … hmmm … um … um … forgot what I was going to say." Stefan laughed royally at himself. "Conversation with the hospital is at eleven. You two be at my door at 10:30, or I'm coming for you."

"Stefan," Jeanne said quietly. "I can hardly …"

"Bedtime, no more talk," Stefan interrupted. "By the way, you will find towels, soap, toothbrushes, toothpaste. That's what I was going to say!"

"No pajamas?" Jeanne said, trying to give Stefan a sly look, but it was closer to bleary.

"I thought they might get in the way," Stefan replied.

Husband and wife were not intimate that night, but they snuggled inseparably. The warmth of each other's bodies was heaven. How long had it been? Well, 26 months, to be precise. Jeanne found herself wondering if she was dreaming. Could this be? Could they be together this way? How had it come about? Stefan. How had he done it? Jeanne snuggled closer to her husband, if that was possible.

The pair were at Stefan's door punctually at 10:30 the next morning. Jeanne was apprehensive. Alan was so anxious, he was visibly shaking.

"Got to get Alan's medications, Stefan," Jeanne said urgently.

"We will, we will. Very soon. I've made some coffee, it's instant coffee, but it's really not that bad. Want a cup?"

"Coffee's fine, thanks," Jeanne said.

"Sleep okay?"

"Like a log," Jeanne said.

"Listen, Jeanne," Stefan said meaningfully, "we've been antagonists, sometimes." He extended his hand for a shake. "No more, ever, agreed?" Jeanne took his hand.

"Stefan, you've pulled off something close to miraculous. I know you're right about Alan. He had to get out of that hospital." She had to pause and compose herself. "I don't know what lies ahead, but it has to be better than what lies behind. You have my support." She hugged Stefan, and the tears came. They would disagree again, to be sure, but never as before.

Stefan quickly reviewed what they could anticipate from the forthcoming phone call. At eleven, he dialed the hospital. He knew the hospital's counsel would be on the other end. He was.

"Mr. Kopinski? I'm Larry Exeter, General Counsel. With me are Douglas Shumaker, Chief Executive Officer, Abraham Holdermann, M.D. and Sgt. Lewis Smithson, St. Louis Police Department. I am putting everyone on speaker phone."

"Good morning, Mr. Exeter," Stefan said. "I will put us on speaker phone, as well. With me are Alan and Jeanne Young."

"Could we have 'hello' from each of them?" Exeter said.

"Of course," Stefan said. "Please say hello," he said to Alan and Jeanne. They did so.

"Mr. Kopinski," Shumaker said, "I am sure you realize what you have done is outrageous and unlawful. You have placed Mr. Young's well-being in acute jeopardy. You have caused a disruption here at the hospital I cannot exaggerate. Last night was havoc. The police were here, the newspapers were here, nobody knew what was going on, there was fear and perplexity among patients and staff, people were very, very afraid. You should be arrested and prosecuted, Mr. Kopinski. It is a miracle nobody got hurt."

"Mr. Shumaker," Stefan said, his voice measured. "I regret any momentary confusion, but I feel sure it did not reach the proportions you have described."

"It most certainly did, sir," Shumaker said. "Why would I exaggerate? It was pandemonium."

"Mr. Kopinski," Sgt. Smithson said. "Mr. Shumaker has not exaggerated in the slightest. You caused an emergency that lasted for hours. An all-out search of the hospital and grounds had everyone on edge. You can understand that, can't you, Mr. Kopinski?" The police officer's voice was uncompromising.

"Well this is very hard to understand," Stefan said. He was confused. "My note and waiver will have told you where Mr. Young was, and that he was in good hands. So how could you spend hours looking for him? This is very strange."

"We didn't find the note right away, did we, Mr. Kopinski?" Exeter said. "Since you put it inside a suitcase under the bed."

"Under the bed!" Stefan exclaimed. "I didn't put it under the bed. I left it on the bed."

"That isn't where it was found, Mr. Kopinski," Exeter said matter-of-factly. Stefan needed a moment to take it in. Obviously they weren't making it up. Someone had put the suitcase under the bed.

"I left the suitcase on the bed," Stefan said. "I have no explanation how it got under the bed."

"That's where it was," Exeter said. "If you didn't put it there, who did?"

"I have no idea," Stefan said impatiently. "I'm not disbelieving you when you say it was under the bed. You are not to disbelieve me when I say I left it on the bed. Why would I put it under the bed? Completely absurd."

"Not as absurd as what you have done, Mr. Kopinski," Shumaker said. The conversation was veering toward acrimony.

"Seems like somebody might have looked under the bed immediately, since Alan could have been hiding there," Stefan observed.

"For your information, the beds are too low for a person to get under them, Mr. Kopinski," said Shumaker.

"You said nobody got hurt," Stefan said. "That's the important thing. Let's drop where the suitcase was." Stefan had long ago learned no amount of planning could anticipate every contingency, but he was dismayed at himself now, because he had not foreseen that someone, for some reason, might put the suitcase under the bed. Who did this? The old man in the other bed? It had to be him. But he was asleep at the time, wasn't he? Nor could he get out of bed, unaided. And, he was witless.

"Mr. Kopinski, it is not quite so simple as that. Have you read the newspaper this morning? Have you turned on the television? You have made news, Mr. Kopinski." This from Shumaker. "You are the news, and while, Mr. Kopinski, we certainly shall not release Mr. Young's identity, I frankly have no compunction about identifying you."

"As you please," Stefan said amicably. "Are you still present, Mr. Exeter? I think we should get down to business."

"I am still present," Exeter said curtly.

"Excellent," said Stefan. "Presumably you have had time to read the General Release and Waiver, Mr. Exeter?"

"I have read it, yes."

"May we then look forward to the hospital's signing the document without delay?"

"Mr. Kopinski, have you been retained by Mrs. Young?" Exeter inquired.

"I have," Stefan said, which wasn't so.

"Are you licensed in the State of Missouri, Mr. Kopinski?" Exeter asked.

"Are you licensed in the State of California, Mr. Exeter?"

"What is that supposed to mean?" Exeter said with annoyance.

"Mr. Exeter, does your client find the waiver satisfactory, or not? There is no issue but this one."

"It's adequate," Exeter responded.

"Excellent. Mr. Shumaker, if you would be so good as to sign it and mail it to us, we can be done with this business very shortly. You don't want the newspapers sniffing around, well, they won't if there's nothing to sniff."

"Is it your wish, Mrs. Young, to sign this document?" Shumaker asked Jeanne.

"It is," Jeanne said, upon realizing she had been asked the question.

"Does your client fully understand the implications of signing, Mr. Kopinski?" Exeter asked.

"Of course she does," Stefan said.

"Very well."

"May we then be confident of Mr. Shumaker's signature, Mr. Exeter?"

"You may," Exeter said after a pause.

"Thank you. I have no doubt executing this agreement is in everybody's best interests."

"Alan?" This came from a voice not heard before. It was Abe Holdermann's. "It's Dr. Holdermann."

"Yes," Alan said. Like Jeanne, it took him a moment to realize he had been addressed.

"It is imperative, Alan, that you maintain your medication schedule scrupulously. You do understand this?"

"I do."

"He does, Dr. Holdermann," Jeanne said simultaneously.

"Will you then be coming by the hospital to meet with me?"

"He will not be doing that, doctor," Stefan said. "You are to call the prescriptions in to the pharmacy Jeanne and Alan use. I have the phone number for you." Jeanne handed a slip of paper to Stefan, who promptly read off the number to the physician.

"Mr. Kopinski," Holdermann said, "I trust you understand swinging by a drugstore and picking up some pills is far short of what Alan requires. He has been on a comprehensive treatment program for many, many months. It most assuredly was not conceived overnight. It has amounted to a great deal more than swallowing pills. Alan cannot abruptly stop. This is foolish."

"If you say so, Dr. Holdermann, but I am not persuaded Alan was improving at the hospital, which leaves me wondering if the treatment program was as effective as you claim." Stefan did not say it, but his implication Alan not only wasn't improving, but was declining, was lost on no one.

"What is your pleasure, Mr. Kopinski?" Holdermann said peevishly. "I gather you do not wish that Alan continue with me as his physician. This is not your decision, Mr. Kopinski."

"I never said it was, doctor," Stefan replied. "Alan can speak for himself."

"I haven't given it any thought," Alan said haltingly.

"Doctor," Stefan said, "I don't believe Alan or Jeanne has any complaint with your care, nor, I should add, have I, to the extent we've been acquainted. However, Alan is not returning to the hospital. He can continue seeing you, provided it's elsewhere. If that's not possible, we will count on you for a referral."

"My only office is here at the hospital," Holdermann said, barely containing his ire over Stefan's condescension. "However, I could make arrangements for Alan to meet with me elsewhere."

"We don't have to decide this immediately," Stefan said, getting a nod of agreement from Alan and Jeanne.

"Mr. Kopinski," said Sgt. Smithson, "you could be placed under arrest. As an attorney, I'm sure you understand this."

"I have no intention, sergeant, of resisting arrest, but I can't see what it would accomplish. Jeanne … Mrs. Young, that is, has no wish to press charges." Stefan pulled out his trump card. "She might find it harder to sign that waiver, if the police want to make an issue of this." This made Exeter furious.

"That negligence claim isn't the slam dunk you think it is, Mr. Kopinski," he said. Stefan knew he was right. The hospital could claim what Stefan had done was unforeseeable, which, if established, would allow them to prevail. Stefan, of course, was not about to concede this.

"Want to try your luck, Mr. Exeter?" he said sarcastically.

"I have no wish to press charges," Jeanne spoke up forthrightly. "Everybody's okay. What would you arrest him for, kidnapping?"

"Grown-up napping," Stefan said mirthfully. Nobody was amused. "Guess I'll stay away from stand-up," he said.

"Gentlemen," Shumaker said with authority. "Gentlemen and lady, I should say. I believe we've reached an accord." Shumaker turned to Exeter. "Would you agree, Larry?"

"I do agree," the lawyer said.

"Excellent," Stefan said. "May we then anticipate receiving the signed waiver in the mail within the next day or two?"

"You may," Shumaker said begrudgingly. With this, the conversation concluded.

"If she's retained that shyster, I'll eat my hat," Exeter said to Shumaker, Holdermann and Sgt. Smithson. "Somebody needs to bring him before the State Board."

At Stefan's end, it was Jeanne who spoke first.

"My goodness, darling," she said to Alan, almost gasping, "you are through with that hospital forever." She clutched Alan and began to cry. She held him tightly for fully half a minute, then released her hold and turned to Stefan, making no attempt to hide her tears. She couldn't speak, but her immense gratitude was unmistakable.

"Let's go!" Stefan said. "We've got things to do." What the morrow might bring nobody knew, but this day already belonged to him.

Jeanne drove, Stefan followed in his car. She wept quietly all the way to the apartment. Alan stared out the window at the city he had so loved. He had not gazed upon it in two years. It was peculiar. Everything was familiar, yet not familiar. Jeanne whisked past the Science Center, with its Planetarium. Its shape was distinctive, not the usual domed structure. More like a saucer. It glowed different colors at night. Alan had gone there less often after Mary became an adult, since it was primarily a family destination; he nonetheless went. He went everywhere in St. Louis, all the time.

"I can't believe you're with me, darling," Jeanne said. "I'm so used to being alone in this car."

If observing St. Louis from the car window had been a little unsettling for Alan, stepping into his apartment was more so. Again, there was that ambiguous familiarity. The coffee table? Was it the same one? Looked bigger. Drapes? They had never had drapes, had they? The floor lamp? Had they had a floor lamp? It must be new. The adjacent apartment building? Who had moved it so much closer?

"Home sweet home!" Jeanne exclaimed. "That phrase never meant more than right now." She squeezed Alan's hand, without getting a squeeze in return. Alan was genuinely uneasy. She detected it. "Darling, you may need a few minutes to get adjusted, but this is our home." She kissed him tenderly. Alan had not had his morning medications, not to mention last night's. Holdermann had promised to phone the pharmacy immediately, so they should be ready shortly, if not already. Alan wandered throughout the apartment. Where had two years gone? What had happened to him? He was shaken.

Stefan arrived. He had the box of pastries and three more bottles of champagne.

"I thought you were right behind me," Jeanne said.

"No, I had to go back for these supplies. We're just hours from party time!"

"I have to go to work," Jeanne protested unsuccessfully. "Not sure I'm good for another bottle of champagne."

"Nonsense," Stefan said.

"Now that you're here, Stefan," she said, "I'm going to the drugstore for Alan's prescriptions." She wished she had worded this differently, since it was apparent she was afraid to leave Alan alone. How were they going to watch him all the time? How? It was impossible. She was suddenly gripped with fear Alan would kill himself at first opportunity.

"I'm going to have the longest, best, hot shower in history," Alan announced.

"I'll make myself at home," Stefan said. He got a look from Jeanne that plainly said, "Watch my husband!" He nodded discreetly.

Halfway to the pharmacy, Jeanne had to pull over and stop. She was trembling with fear. The shower was in the tub. Alan would fill the tub and drown himself! She pictured him doing this.

"I'll be too late," she told herself. "Got to turn around." She checked for traffic, failed to see one vehicle, and barely avoided a collision. This, ironically, helped settle her nerves. She parked along the curb and sat there, taking deep breaths, until she felt she could proceed. She went on to the pharmacy, where the prescriptions were indeed ready. The pharmacist informed her Dr. Holdermann had been very specific in saying he wanted her to call him.

"He must have said this at least three times," the druggist said.

"I will call him as soon as I get home," Jeanne said. "Thank you."

Jeanne made sandwiches for lunch. At one, Stefan told Alan he must substitute a suit for the casual wear he had on.

"We going to meet the mayor, Stef?"

"The captain, Alan. Otto Zollmeyer is a captain. He likes to be addressed that way, understandably."

"Otto who?"

"Otto Zollmeyer."

"Who's he?"

"He runs the VA Hospital, Alan. I told you yesterday."

"I have to be at work," Jeanne said. "Stefan, what is this all about, exactly?"

"Jeanne, and Alan, I have met with Otto Zollmeyer three times in the last, let's see, five days. We have gotten well-acquainted. He's a delightful fellow. I'm sure you are going to like him, Alan. We're going to meet with him and then with your supervisor, who is going to show us around the facility and explain what you will be doing, Alan. Volunteer work. Helping wounded vets. It's a great opportunity."

Both Jeanne and Alan were silent. Alan had no memory of Stefan's having ever suggested he could work at the veterans' hospital, and accordingly did not remember how he had opposed the idea. This was a tremendous piece of luck. Jeanne, on the other hand, had not forgotten, but her initial hostility was leavened by Stefan's actions of the past day.

"Well boys, you better get going," she said. Fact was, she wanted to reach Abe Holdermann before she went to work, but was intent upon having a private conversation. Somehow, she thought he intended that, as well. She was correct.

"What am I going to do at the VA, Stef?" Alan inquired when they reached Stefan's car.

"Volunteer work, Alan. I'm not sure what, myself. We'll learn more when we get there." Alan had to settle for that answer.

Meanwhile, Jeanne dialed Abe Holdermann.

"Jeanne," he said, "I want you to keep something at the forefront of your consciousness at all times. This is very, very important. Mr. Kopinski is not a doctor. He is a lawyer. He is not a doctor. I am a doctor, not a lawyer. I would not presume to give you legal advice, and you must not accept medical advice from Mr. Kopinski. You must not allow him to make medical choices for your husband. Right now, Mr. Kopinski seems to be in charge, and I would not for a moment put it past him to start making medical decisions. I think he means well, but he is not competent to do this. Please be prepared to resist, if he does this, and remind him he's not the doctor. Remind him you will be consulting with me on every medical question. This really is very important, Jeanne."

"I understand, Dr. Holdermann," Jeanne said, "and I agree, of course. Stefan can be overbearing all right, but I don't think he plans to play doctor. All the same, I'll be on the lookout, and I do appreciate your warning." She hesitated. "I appreciate the care you have taken of Alan," she added.

"Thank you for that, Jeanne. I'm not finished, though. Alan has been under 24-hour care for two years. Suddenly, this has been yanked away.

527

Twenty-four hours of top-notch professional care have vanished. A drastic change like this is imprudent. It's dangerous. Indeed, it illustrates Mr. Kopinski's lack of any medical judgment at all, since if he possessed it, he would never have attempted this … this risky step. You've picked up Alan's prescriptions, right?"

"Yes."

"Dosage must be rigidly monitored, Jeanne. At no time, in the hospital, has Alan had the opportunity to take more pills than those ordered. He had no access to them. Now, he has free access. This cannot be allowed. What are you going to do to insure he does not abuse his prescriptions? You see, Jeanne, an overdose could be lethal. Have you any place, by chance, where you could keep them under lock and key?"

"No," Jeanne said. She was frightened. Abruptly, she remembered one of the drawers to Alan's desk had a lock. "Wait," she said. "There's a drawer I can lock."

"Use it, Jeanne," Holdermann enjoined. "Absolutely use it. Share with Mr. Kopinski this concern. Your husband has a high regard for him. He'll listen to him, I think." This was a none-too-subtle hint Alan didn't listen to her, but the doctor didn't care. He had a point to make.

"I will mention this to Stefan. I agree with you Alan listens to him."

"You must decide if you want to continue with me, or see someone else. I do have a referral for you, if you want it. Remember, though, this is up to you. Mr. Kopinski says Alan is not going to return to the hospital. This isn't up to him. It's up to you. If at any time you want to bring Alan back, Mr. Kopinski cannot prevent you. You can call me, you can call the police, if necessary. As it is, Mr. Kopinski has dodged arrest by the narrowest of margins."

"You are scaring me, Dr. Holdermann."

"I'm sorry, Jeanne, but maybe that's not a bad thing. I am just seeking to impress upon you the extreme unorthodoxy of what Mr. Kopinski has done, and the possible, adverse consequences." Jeanne again hesitated. Was he telling her she should bring Alan back to the hospital? She wasn't sure. She gave it voice.

"Are you telling me to bring Alan back right now, Dr. Holdermann?"

"That would be advisable," he said. Jeanne had a very bad moment. She was in an agony of indecision. What should she do?

"I think, Dr. Holdermann ... I think ..." She couldn't think. How could she decide? What was best? The knowledge Alan's life was ebbing away at the hospital came to her, and it decided her. She started weeping.

"Please don't cry, Jeanne."

"Dr. Holdermann," she said through the tears, "I am deeply grateful for the care Alan has received. I guess I have to agree with Stefan, though, that Alan wasn't getting better, so let's give this a try."

"Very well," Holdermann said. "Remember you can call me any hour. I'll be here."

"Thank you, Dr. Holdermann," she said, "thank you. I'll go find the key to that lock, and lock up the pills, right now."

"Yes, do that, and why don't I plan on calling you in a day or two, just to see how things are coming along?" the physician said.

"Please do."

At the VA, Stefan found a parking spot. Alan gazed at the edifice. It was a monolithic, four-story structure that looked exactly like what it was, a government hospital. The sign was unnecessary. It was brick, with windows that looked undersized to Alan. There was an attractively landscaped, semi-circular drive to the front door.

"This is the only time we'll be using the visitors' lot," Stefan said. "You're on staff, my dear old friend." Alan gave Stefan a look of misgiving.

"I don't get this, Stef. Not at all. Sounds like you got me a job? Why would I want to work here?"

"Alan, this is going to be just great. Trust me, Alan. You always have, haven't you?" Stefan reflected Alan had trusted him, when that trust was wasted, for thirty years.

They entered the facility. This being Stefan's fourth visit in a week, he was familiar with procedures. It was five minutes to two o'clock. In short order, they found themselves seated in Otto Zollmeyer's office. Zollmeyer was a contemporary of Alan's and Stefan's, mid-fifties. He wore a uniform and had a crewcut. Alan always thought a crewcut was odd on a grown man. Zollmeyer was a big man, though not tall. He had thick arms and an ample neck. He had played football in school. He was freckled. His look of strength was deceptive, unfortunately. He suffered from numbness on his right side which, while not debilitating, was much more than an inconvenience. He was a veteran of the Vietnam War and had been wounded, though not seriously. He and several others had been blown out of a trench, but he had not suffered shrapnel wounds, nor been shot; his injuries were burns, primarily. His skin on the right side of his face and chest betrayed those burns, and always would. The numbness, however, could not be tied to the war wounds. It seemed more likely to be the result of a stroke, but Zollmeyer had undergone extensive tests, and there was no evidence of a stroke. Thus, the numbness lacked explanation. Because the trouble was on the right side, where he had been wounded, Zollmeyer always suspected a connection. It was a moot point, in any case. He suffered from the numbness, and nothing could be done about it.

The upshot was, he walked only with considerable difficulty. He did use a cane. He categorically refused a wheelchair, and whenever somebody suggested a walker, his reply was, "I'd rather fall."

"Hello, Mr. Kopinski," Zollmeyer said, shaking hands with Stefan. "How are you?"

"Good, captain, thank you. And you?"

"Fit as a fiddle." Zollmeyer extended his hand toward Alan, and they shook. "This must be Mr. Young?"

"Right," Stefan said.

"Please be seated, gentlemen," Zollmeyer said.

Their meeting consumed thirty minutes. It was immediately apparent to Alan, Stefan and Zollmeyer had spoken already, and arrangements, whatever those were, had been made. He was not long in finding out. Alan would be helping the custodial staff keep the facility clean. His hours were largely up to him, up to a maximum of fifteen per week. This was the cap on volunteer work. He could start as soon as tomorrow. His work at the hospital was provisional until a "criminal background check" was completed. Almost the first thing Stefan had told Zollmeyer was that Alan had voluntarily gone to prison rather than submit to conscription to fight in a war he conscientiously opposed.

Keith Johnson was the head of the custodial staff. Keith was 36. He hailed from a military family and was himself in the Army Reserve. He had never finished college but was now enrolled at the University of Missouri's St. Louis campus, where he was taking his coursework none too seriously. Keith Johnson, Alan would discover, was taking nothing at all seriously.

It all began with a mop. This would be Alan's task, to mop every square inch of the St. Louis Veterans' Administration Hospital. He would wear the uniform of the custodial staff. He could eat in "the mess" at half-price. He started at eleven the next morning.

That evening, Jeanne fixed a chicken and rice dish that was one of Alan's favorites. Stefan was present. Nobody, somehow, was completely at ease. The champagne stayed uncorked, and the pastries untouched.

"They won't stay fresh," Jeanne observed. "Why did you buy so many?"

"Didn't want to run out," Stefan said. "Alan and I will take them with us to the VA tomorrow. I'll bet they disappear in a hurry."

The next day, Stefan parked in the staff parking lot at the VA, rather than drop Alan at the door.

"Are you coming in, too, Stef?" Alan asked. His heart was sinking.

"Yep. I'll occupy myself in the lounge until you're done. If you need some help, come get me."

"This is so unreal, Stef. What am I, a middle-aged candy-striper?"

"You sure are an ugly one," Stefan joked, and Alan could not help laugh. Laughter was good. Laughter was something to make sure to do in life, wasn't it? He had not laughed in so long, he'd almost forgotten how. How do you forget how to laugh? Alan shook his head. This stunt of Stefan's was nuts, no doubt about that, but if he was laughing again, that was good, wasn't it?

"As such as one were glad to know the brine salt on his lips, and the large air again," Alan said, gazing skyward and drawing a deep breath. It was a bright, sunny morning.

"Poem?" Stefan asked, without a trace of his customary impatience with Alan's penchant for introducing rhyme into conversation.

"Sonnet by a fellow named Lang. Wrote it long ago."

"Well let's have the rest."

"That's all I memorized."

"Very disappointing, Alan, very disappointing," Stefan said in mock dismay.

They proceeded to the front door, and Stefan held it open for Alan. They knew where Alan was to report, and Keith Johnson was waiting for him there.

"Hey, Keith," Stefan said.

"Morning, gentlemen," Keith said.

"Morning," Alan said.

"Ready to get going?" Keith said to Alan, rubbing his hands together.

"I suppose," Alan said tentatively.

"Follow me," Keith said.

"I'll be in the lounge, Alan," Stefan said. He then lowered his voice so Keith wouldn't hear. "One day at a time, old buddy."

'One Day At A Time' it became. This was Alan's motto. Many, many adjustments lay ahead, but Alan had Jeanne dependably at his side (as he always had), and now Stefan as well, who made a terrific nuisance of himself, which delighted Jeanne rather than annoy her, and gradually, but surely, Alan improved. Alan had Abraham Holdermann, too, with whom he met regularly at a suburban clinic. He became a participant in a new support group he actually liked better than the previous one, and he had the work at the VA, which amounted to mopping and very little else, but the benefit to Alan, upon which Stefan had gambled everything, began to emerge.

Friends, too, began to trickle back in. Most knew Alan had had "mental issues" and was living at a facility. Jeanne had said only this, except to a few very close friends, whom she wanted to visit Alan. They had, at first.

Alan's passion for the city defied resurrection. He saw St. Louis now much more realistically, and he could not disagree with Stefan's observations, which were frequently negative.

"Where is everybody, Alan? Streets are empty, parks are empty, where is everybody? It's spooky."

"Stef, you've said that before. I don't disagree. It's not just St. Louis."

"Really? I've been around the country. Most places aren't deserted, like St. Louis. Detroit, maybe." Stefan had not been to Detroit, only read about it.

"My hometown, too, I imagine." Alan shook his head. He had not been home in many years.

"L.A. isn't shrinking, Alan, it's growing. It's immense. Second only to New York. Lots of money in L.A., let me tell you. You can almost smell it in the air."

"What does money buy, Stef?" Alan said.

"I wouldn't scorn money, Alan. It can come in very handy."

"My grandfather used to tell me to save my money. I never could figure out why. Wasn't money for buying things? He'd say it was for a rainy day, and you couldn't escape those no matter how hard you tried. His mistake was not telling me what a rainy day meant. I was just a boy. I thought it meant rain."

Alan's changed feelings for his adopted city did not mean they didn't go places. There were hours to be filled, somehow. When Stefan admitted he had not set foot in the New Cathedral, Alan was aghast. They walked up the steps, and Alan instructed Stefan to close his eyes while he opened the door.

"Open now," Alan said as they stepped inside. "Don't try to count the mosaics. There's millions." It looked to Stefan their number was well beyond any means of counting.

"This place is as jaw-dropping as the great Gothic cathedrals in Europe," he said. He regretted the remark a little, since Alan, as a convicted felon, could never get a passport, and thus was barred from travel outside the United States, except to Canada. But the New Cathedral had indeed matched Alan's description.

They went to the Botanical Garden. Alan showed Stefan where he usually had sat in the café, grading the tests he gave his tutorial pupils. The Garden was lovely, Stefan agreed, but certainly not any better than the Huntington in Pasadena. Having grown up in Los Angeles, Alan had been to the Huntington himself.

"The difference, Stef, is, St. Louis' dates to 1859. It ranks as one of the foremost research gardens in the world."

"Flowers are flowers," Stefan said amiably.

One day, Stefan actually suggested a baseball game. He reminded Alan the baseball team, along with the zoo, were St. Louis' two claims to fame. He'd seen the zoo.

"I think I've been to two games," Alan said, which was two more than Stefan would have guessed. Neither Alan nor Stefan had ever been particularly devoted to sports, and neither had a shred of athletic ability. Stefan, however, had learned quickly that sports counted for a great deal in his professional and social circles. Ignoring them was out of the question, and he hadn't.

To the ballpark they went, where they found the cognoscenti wore red. They had neglected to wear red. The Cardinals' opponent was the San Francisco Giants, who won, 6-1.

One day, at Tower Grove Park, the two encountered a man with his dog. He was throwing a stick, which the dog tirelessly retrieved.

"You remember Rosie, Stef?"

"No, who's she?"

"A dog, Stef. A Dalmatian. Don't you remember, we'd go over to that park in Santa Barbara with Rosie, and we'd toss a Frisbee back and forth while she ran around. We got her at the rent-a-dog place."

"Rent-a-dog place? What's that?"

"It's where you rent dogs. There was this place in Santa Barbara. You don't remember at all?"

"Sorry."

Their recollections of their college days were not very satisfactory. Alan remembered better than Stefan. The supreme irony, however, was that the one thing Stefan remembered, as though it were yesterday, the lines at the cafeteria in the Union, Alan couldn't recall.

"You don't remember they had two lines, Alan, one for *a la carte* meals, and the other was the *plat du jour*? It was cheaper, naturally. Remember?"

"I don't, Stef. Tell you the truth, I don't even remember the cafeteria."

"We ate there together every day, my old friend, for three years," Stefan said.

"Aw, Stef, we must have missed a few."

"I don't think so."

"Well, okay. Does it matter?" Stefan smiled. Yes, it matters, he said, but only to himself.

His precious memory was secure. Of course, there remained that indefinable … elusive … something … he could not pin down. He had given up on it. The core memory, that was what mattered, and it belonged to him, and him alone.

The work at the VA Hospital was not without its issues. Alan was the man with the mop. He never saw another soul doing this. It was a big hospital, four floors. He couldn't do this alone, but clearly this was the expectation. He began to resent he was unpaid. (This would not remain the case.) He was denied any meaningful contact with patients, which, however, seemed to matter more to Stefan than himself. Alan had no idea what he might say. He was not fond of Keith Johnson, who paid no attention to him. They had managed one day to have a brief, uncomfortable exchange.

"You went to Vietnam, I imagine," Keith had said, "seeing as how you're about the right age."

"No, Keith, I served a term in jail, in protest." Alan skipped mention of his eighteen months in Canada. Nothing was less real to him than that time, and he could no more explain what had prompted him to take that step than he could take wing and fly.

"What protest?"

"The war, Keith, I was protesting the war. Many people opposed it, as I'm sure you know." Keith, at 36, had not been born, when the Vietnam War began.

"Hospital's full of guys who served," Keith noted.

"I'm well aware of that."

"So how long were you in jail?"

"Three-and-a-half years, Keith, or to be exact, 41 months."

"What did that accomplish?"

"I felt I was doing the right thing."

"Pretty weird choice, if you ask me," Keith said.

"I didn't ask you, did I?" Alan replied tersely. This ended their conversation, and it wasn't resumed. Nor did Alan say a word about it to Stefan. It deserved to be forgotten, and he intended to forget it.

Alan did introduce that he was finding some aspects of his work dissatisfying.

"Alan, every day you are doing your part to help make the lives of our wounded vets better," Stefan responded. "Look at it that way."

"I do look at it that way, Stef. It's still a bit discouraging, mopping floors day after day." Stefan winced when Alan used the term "discouraging." Alan was coming along wonderfully on his road to recovery. No discouragement could be allowed.

"What would you think of becoming a rehab therapist?" Stefan said on one occasion. "I don't know what all it would involve. You'd have to go back to school. So what? You could do that. Then you would have contact with the vets, and you'd be helping them more directly."

"I'm 54, Stef. I'm too old to go back to school."

"Really? Why? Why would you say that, really? I don't understand."

"I'd first have to get into school somewhere. Who knows if that would happen? How long would it take? Two years, minimum, for sure. How much would it cost? What happens when I finish? You think there'd be a job waiting for me at the VA? You've said yourself they're strapped, and you're right. More likely to be cutting jobs than adding them."

"Quite a line-up, Alan. You can always find an excuse. Don't look for ways not to succeed. You can do what you make up your mind to do." This begged the question, since what Alan could not do was make up his mind.

The months went by. Alan had his bad days, to be sure. The acute anxiety that had dogged him so long would return, without warning.

"I don't think, Jeanne," Abe Holdermann declared, "it is realistic to believe Alan will ever be completely free of his anxiety. This has been in him long before the crisis. It would be good if he could come around to accepting this about himself. It would alert him to certain triggers."

"Is he ever going to stop taking all those pills, Dr. Holdermann?"

"Those medications are crucial to keeping his anxiety in check. Maybe we can look at a reduced dosage eventually, but it's far too soon." Jeanne shuddered at the recollection of Alan's breakdowns at the hospital, when he begged to die. His self-hate was terrifying. She'd get into his bed and put his head in her lap, and run her fingers through his hair, until he was quiet, no matter how long it took.

One evening, Alan and Jeanne asked friends over. This was the first time, since he had come home. Alan had kept up with a Spanish teacher he had known way back when he was on the faculty at Saint Louis University High. His name was Jorge Mendoza. His wife was Guadalupe. Jorge brought along a friend, whom Alan didn't know, named Eric Woodrow, who also taught Spanish at the high school. The six of them sat on the floor around the coffee table, munching on cheese and crackers, and sipping wine. The three Spanish speakers were not inhibited about using Spanish from time to time; nobody minded. Stefan reflected on his crowd in Pasadena. Had he ever heard a word of Spanish, or any other foreign language, spoken at a social occasion? He could not think of one instance. Not even Miguel Ordoñez spoke Spanish. Stefan never could get that to add up. He had spent thirty years in the rarified air of influence and wealth, posturing and self-importance, without having once sat on the floor of a cramped, little apartment, taking nothing seriously, beginning with himself.

Stefan shook his head. Deep down, he knew this wasn't fair. You had to keep striving, in his world. You couldn't stay in that little apartment, you had to move into that big house. You had to live in that certain neighborhood. You had to sit on those committees and boards, you had to belong to that club. Why, there was even a certain church you were "encouraged" to join, the Episcopal Church, but not just any Episcopal Church, no, St. Joseph's

Episcopal Church. It was all part of the narrative, which must be followed to the letter. It wasn't that this world was inherently phony or dishonest. It wasn't. The people Stefan ran around with weren't bad people. Yet something was exacted, something very fundamental. What was it? An acquaintance came to mind. Chap from San Francisco who had relocated to Pasadena. Stock broker, wasn't he? Something like that. Bruce somebody-or-other. Stefan couldn't remember. What he did remember was Bruce's having told a decidedly off-color joke in mixed company. No one had laughed. There was only an excruciatingly uncomfortable silence. Not a word was ever said about it, and Bruce never did it again.

Eric Woodrow was talking about "String Theory." This was the latest explanation for the universe. Itsy-bitsy strings, Eric said, were the substance of everything. "Including us."

"Like Angel Hair pasta?" Guadalupe said.

"*Lo mismo,*" Eric responded.

"I'm sticking with the Big Bang," Jeanne said.

"Me, too," Alan said. "You have to wonder, though. I mean, it was Einstein, wasn't it, who said for every action there's an equal and opposite reaction? So if the universe began in a micro-second, won't it end that way, too?"

"So poof, we're all gone?" Stefan said.

"Poof, we're all gone."

"*Este pensamiento no me permite dormir,*" said Jorge.

"*Tome mas vino,*" Eric said.

"*Me da dolor de cabeza,*" said Jorge.

"*Con dolor hay vida,*" said Guadalupe.

One Friday, shortly before Stefan returned to California, Alan and Stefan acted upon Jeanne's urging that they have a "boys' outing," and embarked upon a weekend trip to Ste. Genevieve, a small town south of St. Louis, said to be the oldest European settlement in the state. Alan warned Stefan it was a tourist trap, but Stefan didn't care. In any case, he wouldn't need to visit the historic sites to learn about them, since Alan already knew everything and spoke of little else.

They had a satisfactory visit, and Sunday morning, leaving for St. Louis, they stopped at a coffee shop for breakfast.

"Good thing St. Louis outgrew Ste. Genevieve," Stefan said. "Nobody would ever have spelled it right." Alan laughed. Their waitress brought them menus.

"Interesting that we say St. Louis, but Louisville, Kentucky, is pronounced differently," Alan said.

When the waitress returned, Alan asked for an omelet, and Stefan ordered French toast.

"Sorry, we're out of French toast," she said.

"Just my luck," Stefan said. "Guess I'll have the omelet, too, thanks." The girl departed.

"Pretty hilarious, wouldn't you say, Stef?" Alan remarked.

"What?"

"Being out of French toast. How do you run out of French toast?"

"Yeah, it's just bread and milk and eggs, isn't it?" Stefan said sheepishly. Other patrons were enjoying all three items. How had he missed something that plain? When their waitress returned with their orders, Stefan asked her if the restaurant ran out of French toast often.

"I wouldn't say that," she said. "Sometimes, though."

"Chef know about it?"

"Well I would think so!" the girl said curtly.

Stefan stayed his six months in St. Louis. It wasn't less than necessary; it was more. He was joyful. Alan was incontestably on the mend. Abe Holdermann was not a little astonished, and idly wondered from time to time how he was going to incorporate "Smuggled from hospital" into Alan's medical record. At the airport, Jeanne wept as she hugged Stefan and told him, by no means for the first time, he had saved Alan's life. Abruptly, she kissed him on the mouth. She had not done that with another man, since marrying Alan, and she surprised herself, not to mention Alan, who was standing adjacent, and Stefan, who nearly fell over. There was, however, a complete understanding she had needed something above and beyond a mere expression of gratitude, to convey her feelings. The kiss had served admirably.

Sharon met Stefan at the Los Angeles airport. Since he had returned once a month since going to St. Louis, and they had spoken often by phone, this wasn't really such a special occasion. Still, he got an enthusiastic reception. Sharon had continued with her life without missing a beat. Her husband had inexplicably left his position, and she knew something was in store, but she refused to worry about it. Stefan would land on his feet, whatever he did. He had told her only that he was opening his own law office. He had said nothing about his plan to run for the legislature, since he felt he owed Joel Whittington the "right of first refusal." His former partners knew, but they had agreed to keep it confidential.

"Darling, I asked Brian and Judy McFarland to dinner tonight," Sharon said when they reached home. Sharon was the ultimate entertainer, Brian and Judy were especially close friends, and she felt Stefan would be delighted.

"Tonight?" he said, not very delightedly, but it was all right. This was Sharon. The McFarlands were indeed dear friends. When they arrived, Stefan found himself instantly back in his milieu, just as if the past six months had never occurred.

Stefan sorted through his mail at his leisure the next morning. He could not help but reflect he should be sitting at his desk. He pictured his office, his spacious desk, his swivel chair, his lamp, his bookshelf, the lush carpet, the painting depicting Big Ben from across the Thames, on the south wall, the west wall, behind his desk, plastered with the degrees and licensures and encomiums he had received over the years. There were more than two dozen of them, and plenty more in a closet. He was done with it! In the months with Alan, he had given relatively little thought to his new life in Pasadena. The time had come to get serious.

His third day back, he rang Joel Whittington. Lunch at the club? Absolutely. Stefan got there first and was warmly greeted, but hardly anybody asked him where he had been. It wasn't very flattering not to have been missed. Whittington arrived.

"So good to see you, Stefan," he said. "Somebody said you've been out of town."

"I have, Joel. Been over in St. Louis. I have an old friend there, who's been pretty sick. He's much better, though."

"Glad to hear that."

They ordered lunch. Stefan looked around the club. This was easily the most exclusive address in town, where the decisions that mattered in the community were made. The place itself was not in the least meretricious, rather, it had about it an understated elegance that effectively imparted power. Stefan loved it, he coveted his membership and meant to keep it, despite the radical change in his professional life. Of course, he could be booted, potentially.

"What's on your mind, Stefan? Whittington asked. "I can see you're preoccupied."

"You're right, Joel. You know I've left Fulton & Shaw?"

"Now that you mention it, yes. Seems to me I got a letter. Been months, hasn't it?"

"It has. About six months."

"Pretty drastic move. Are you all right? Health, I mean."

'I'm fine, Joel, but thanks for asking."

"So what's on your mind, counselor?" Whittington said.

"Joel, I'm going to need the floor for five minutes, or so."

"Of course, Stefan. I'm all ears."

Stefan needed much more than five minutes. Whittington would have had trouble speaking, in any event. He was flabbergasted. Nobody was more level-headed than Stefan Kopinski, Esq., and here he was, saying nothing level-headed.

"Well Stefan," the senator said when Stefan reached his conclusion, "I certainly appreciate your having extended me the courtesy of speaking with me first. Thank you. I confess I am so amazed at all you have said, I've even been wondering if this is some kind of April Fool's joke, even though it isn't April Fool's. I realize, however, you are very serious." The senator paused. "Stefan, I'm sure you know I am not going to introduce your bill. Forgive me, but it's lunacy. It would be political suicide. Moreover, I don't agree with your conclusions, and hardly anybody else will, either. You can't go back. Divorce laws were changed with the times. Nobody, man or woman, is going to be in favor of this. Women especially, I think. They're not going to be obedient little housewives, again. As for employment at-will, you're the lawyer so you know, but I know, too, it has always been the law of the land, and it's a pretty darn sacred cow. You said you're going to Montana, where the law's changed, you're going up there to study the legislative history and meet folks, well, good luck. California isn't Montana. California isn't going to follow suit, no way. Do you realize who you'll be up against? Unions and employers. Both camps. That might be a first."

"Don't forget all the women whose bread and butter is divorce law," Stefan said. "Don't forget all the cottage industries that have evolved, like a marriage counselor on every corner."

"Yes, well, do you want to make enemies, Stefan? It almost sounds like it. Not to mention your reputation. I don't even want to think about how this will damage it. You'll never get it back." Whittington paused momentarily. "Good grief, Stefan," he resumed. "Take a very long cruise until you've got your head screwed on straight again." Stefan laughed at this, which didn't please the senator. "I'm not kidding," he said.

"I'm not either, Joel. I have to do this. I appreciate your remarks. I respect your opinion. That goes without saying. But I have to do this."

"No, you don't," Whittington said strongly. "That's just it. You don't have to do it. Nobody's holding a gun to your head."

"Maybe I am," Stefan said, though he immediately thought this was a curious thing to have said.

"Then remove it. You're in control."

"Joel, I have to do this. If you won't sponsor the bill, I'm going to run against you."

"You said that already."

"So I did," Stefan said.

"You're going to be the Harold Stassen of California, Stefan. You're going to be a laughingstock. You're going to be put out to pasture. Nobody's going to listen to a word you say."

"Anything else?" Stefan said amiably.

"I think that about covers it," Whittington said.

"You know, Joel, we can do amazing things if we make up our mind we're going to do them. This old friend who's ill, he did something amazing when he was a young man. I did something amazing when I was with him recently. May I tell you what? I took him by the arm, and we walked out of the hospital he was in." Stefan chuckled at the recollection. "No reflection on the hospital, I think he got excellent care, his doctor is dedicated to his welfare and he's a smart guy. Alan just wasn't getting better, due to his own issues. He couldn't stay there any longer."

"You've lost me, Stefan. What's your point?"

"Just what I said. Make up your mind, you can do anything. Take a pair of bad laws and stand them on their head. It can be done."

"I see," Whittington said. Their conversation flagged.

"I hope we stay friends, Joel," Stefan said, with obvious sincerity.

"Hope so, too," Whittington said. He wasn't smiling. "You never know." Stefan did not much care for this remark, but he let it go. He wasn't ignorant about politics. If there were votes in attacking him, Stefan knew Whittington would not hesitate, their long friendship notwithstanding.

It wasn't long before Stefan opened his law office. The shingle went up, and business cards were printed. The sign in the window was succinct: Practice limited to Divorce and Employment Law. Soon thereafter, he found himself in the lounge at Los Angeles International Airport, waiting to board his plane for Helena, Montana. A journey lay before him, and he relished it. A journey lay behind him, and he reflected upon it. What was that thing he had tried a thousand times to pin down and just could not, something someone some time had said about the *plat du jour* and how it was similar to ... what? Similar, same as ... what? Same as what? He was 54, and this had dogged him since he had been half his present age. For Stefan was 27 when, on an autumn day in 1975, his clerkship with the Hon. Dan Bryant had concluded, and he had started out upon his career.

CHAPTER 26

IT WAS AN AUTUMN DAY IN 1975, STEFAN'S FINAL DAY CLERKING FOR JUDGE Bryant. They had had lunch at Julio's, and now were back at the judge's office, for a final farewell. Stefan's replacement, Edward Rowles, would be arriving shortly. The judge had asked Stefan, in keeping with his custom, to stick around until Edward arrived, and show him around the courthouse, introduce him to everyone, and so forth. Meanwhile, however, they had several minutes to kill. Conversation suddenly was hard to come by, until, luckily, none other than Judge Robert Young stuck his head in the door.

"I hear goodbyes are in order," he addressed Stefan.

"Yes, judge," Stefan replied, jumping to his feet. He was immensely flattered the judge had come to say farewell, instead of the other way around. "I'm heading out shortly."

"Off into the big world?"

"Something like that."

"Mr. Kopinski has accepted an offer with Martin & Yates, Bob," Dan Bryant said.

"Not familiar with them. What kind of work will you be doing?"

"Probably a fair amount of PI, some divorce, some immigration work, and I don't really know what else. Those were the things mentioned when I interviewed."

"Well, your time here with Dan will stand you in good stead, you may count on that. Very best of luck to you, I know you'll be a credit to the firm." Judge Young extended a hand, and Stefan took it. Despite having been in the same courthouse, their paths had seldom crossed during Stefan's tenure as Dan Bryant's clerk, but he had hardly forgotten it was Judge Young who had had a big part in his getting the job.

"Thank you, judge," Stefan said. "Thank you." Robert Young took his leave, and Stefan remarked to Dan Bryant that he and Judge Young's son Alan had been best friends, back in college in Santa Barbara.

"Yes, you've mentioned Alan before," Dan Bryant replied, clearly implying he had heard Stefan speak of Alan on a number of occasions. To be sure, Robert Young spoke of his son with his colleague, too, but really not that frequently. Dan Bryant wasn't sure, but rather suspected Robert Young was deeply disappointed and saddened by his son's behavior, and that it was a source of pain to talk about him at all. Nonetheless, he had heard the whole story, of his son's having been drafted, the flight to Canada, and the "fit of conscience," as Robert Young termed it, return to America and imprisonment.

"You know, judge, it's a funny thing," Stefan said. "Alan's gone his way, I've gone mine, we haven't spoken or exchanged letters in a long time, we may never be close again. He lives in St. Louis. Just a college friendship, I suppose. But I think of Alan, and when I do, the first thing I always think of isn't his tremendous ordeal, going to Canada and all that happened to him there, and then coming back and going to jail, it's our eating supper together at the Union at UC-Santa Barbara." Stefan shook his head. "We ate supper together practically every night. For three years. He'd always take the *plat du jour*, judge. That's what I remember. They had two lines, one for the *plat du jour*, the other if you wanted *a la carte*. The *a la carte* meal was more expensive, naturally, because it was nicer. I couldn't afford it, so I always took the *plat du jour*. Alan could have afforded it, but he always took the *plat du jour*, too." Stefan paused. "It's strange, how this sticks in my mind. It's such a small thing."

"Maybe not so strange," Dan Bryant said, after a pause. "They're the same, you realize."

"What are?'

"Your friend's taking the *plat du jour*, and going to prison." The judge smiled patiently.

"How could those be the same?" Stefan asked, not in the least understanding.

"What was he doing when he opted for the *plat du jour*, instead of the nicer meal? Putting your feelings before his own preferences, wasn't he? We'd all rather have roast beef and chocolate cream pie than meat loaf and Jello. When Alan went to Canada, he was going *a la carte*, putting his own

544

interests first, rather than the country's. When he went to prison, he was taking the *plat du jour.*" The judge hesitated, for his law clerk clearly wasn't getting it. "Let me say it another way. Taking the *plat du jour* instead of the *a la carte* meal was a small thing, but friendship isn't a small thing, wouldn't you agree? One man's submitting to the law's punishment to protest his country's wrongdoing is a small thing, but citizenship isn't a small thing. What if not unselfishness is the virtue your friend is exhibiting, in each instance? You can't get it out of your head, Mr. Kopinski, for the very good reason it's not a small thing at all."

"Well, judge," Stefan said uncertainly, not knowing what to make of this gibberish about chocolate pie and going to Canada, "I must say ..." Stefan was sharply interrupted by the buzzer on the judge's phone. It was Rhonda; the new clerk had arrived.

"Send him in, Ms. Ludgate," Dan Bryant said eagerly. He turned to Stefan. "I'd hold on to that friend, if possible. There is no rarer trait than unselfishness, and, I'm afraid, it's becoming increasingly rare in our fair republic." Ed Rowles came in. He was big, and wore a tie against a striped shirt that didn't match very well, and exhibited an air of aplomb. Introductions were accomplished and, after a short interval, Stefan assumed his role as guide. His first impression of Rowles wasn't entirely favorable, he found him a bit too sold on himself, but, he chuckled, Judge Bryant would take care of that. Twenty minutes later, they were back in the judge's chambers, where a final goodbye needed to be accomplished quickly.

"I want you to know you've been an outstanding clerk, in case I've failed to say that before, and I wish you well," Dan Bryant said, knowing he had said it before. Stefan gushed his gratitude, they shook hands one last time, and that was that. In the outer office, Stefan bade Rhonda adieu.

"What's your impression of Mr. Rowles, Stefan?" she asked mischievously.

"He's huge. We must have looked like Mutt and Jeff around the courthouse."

"Not really. Anything else?"

"Bit cocky."

"My impression, too."

"That won't last," Stefan said. "As we both know." They both laughed. They had been friends, exchanged friendly banter on a daily basis, and this was farewell. His apprenticeship was over. Their paths would probably never cross again. Stefan was out the door, and the judge's remarks, as they had waited for Ed Rowles, were already out of his consciousness, indeed, forgotten. Stefan walked to the parking lot, took a last, fond look at the courthouse, climbed into his car and, within a couple of minutes had become merely another motorist in the endless convoy of cars streaming down the Santa Monica Freeway. Stefan did not know it, but what the judge had said remained in his mind, filed by his memory, there for future reference, and one distant day, would alter the course of his life.

(fin)

9-3-19